D0309601

A Song in the Morning
At Close Quarters
Home Run

_____

Gerald Seymour

Diamond Books
An Imprint of HarperCollins*Publishers*,
77–85 Fulham Palace Road
Hammersmith, London W6 8JB

This Diamond Books Omnibus edition first published 1993
9 8 7 6 5 4 3 2 1

A Song in the Morning © B.V. Holland Copyright Corporation 1986
At Close Quarters © B.V. Holland Copyright Corporation 1987
Home Run © B.V. Holland Copyright Corporation 1989

ISBN 1 85813 214 2 (UK)
ISBN Diamond Books 0261 661582 (international edition)

Phototypeset in Ehrhardt by Intype, London

Printed in France by Maury-Eurolivres

The Author asserts the moral right to be identified as the author of this work

All rights reserved. No part of this publication may be reproduced, stored in a retrieval
system, or transmitted, in any form or by any means, electronic, mechanical,
photocopying, recording or otherwise, without the prior permission of the publishers.

Contents

A Song in the Morning

For all that this novel seeks accurately to portray the events
described in it in present day South Africa, all the characters
in the book are fictitious. The author acknowledges with gratitude the help
that many people have given him, not a few at risk to themselves,
in the writing of this book.

to Gillian, Nicholas and James

1

They were four.

They walked abreast, dodging the lunchtime crowd. They were unremarkable to the point of anonymity. When their line broke it was to let a White through because even for these four that was ingrained instinct. They all wore jogging shoes and loose shapeless trousers and long overcoats and their woollen caps were tight down on their skulls. The Whites passing between them, ignoring them, were still clothed for the remnants of the drought summer, girls in light frocks and cotton skirts and blouses and the men in shirtsleeves. But these four had started out on their journey to the city long before the Whites had stirred in their suburban beds. They had moved out of the township before the sun had glimmered onto the electricity pylons and over the horizon of galvanised tin roofs. When they had caught their first bus the frost was still on the ground, crystal lights on the dry dun veld.

They didn't speak.

A security policeman or an interrogator might have noticed the tightness at their mouths, or the brightness in their eyes, or a certain stiffness in their walk, but the secretaries and the salesmen and the shop girls and the clerks saw nothing. For each of them it was the first time that they had been given a mission into the very centre of the city.

A security policeman or an interrogator, any man who was accustomed to the scent of fear, might have noticed the way that one of the four held in two hands the strings of a duffel bag that was heavy and bulky. He might have seen that two others each had a hand thrust deep into the side pocket of the overcoat as if to guard or hide something of importance.

But the city was at peace and at its lunch hour, and the four young men aroused no attention as they made their way along Pritchard, going west.

For the Whites who shared the pavement with these four young Blacks the sun was high, and the violence of the townships was beyond sight, out of mind. A relaxed and safe and comfortable warmth shimmered on the fast traffic flow and the rough pavement on Pritchard. There were queues at the sandwich bars. There were men with their heads in the afternoon newspapers, not searching for the statistics of the previous night's unrest but for the selections of the local rugby teams. There were women eyeing the big plate glass windows of the department stores and the clothes that came by sea from London and Paris and Rome.

Together, at the same moment, the young Blacks saw the cream and grey Combi van that was parked against the kerb on the junction of Pritchard and Delvers. And they looked at each other and saw that they had all found the van.

A White man lounged behind the Combi's wheel.

The White couldn't have missed the four Blacks as they hesitated on the pavement, their faces split with nervous smiles, and stared at him. He couldn't have missed them but he gave no sign of having noticed them. He looked ahead and sucked the wet filter of a cigarette. The engine of the van was idling. The four Blacks went on, and one turned and saw that the rear doors were marginally open. It was all as they had been told it would be.

They waited for the green pedestrian light and crossed Van Wielligh.

Each of the four would have wanted to run now, to charge on the target, but the discipline held and so they waited for the light and then walked across the wide street and past four rows of cars. Past the Methodist Church offices and the bookshop. The one with the duffel bag stole a glance at the books in the window because he had been educated to Grade 3 at a church school, and the books in the window were something familiar to him where nothing else was familiar. The ones with their hands in their pockets and the one with nothing to carry in his tight, clenched fists were of the townships round the city. The one with the duffel bag was a country boy and a member of this cadre only because of his especial training.

The pavement narrowed, its width cut by high wooden boards, filled with advertising, that masked a building site. They were jostled by Whites and Blacks alike hurrying against their flow.

The one with his hands clenched went first, a ram against the tide. He was followed by the one who held in his overcoat pocket a Makharov automatic pistol. Next was the one whose fingers were coiled round the smooth metal of an R.G.–42 fragmentation grenade. Last was the one with the duffel bag. They were past the building site, and the pavement opened out and in front of them were the tended lawns and the mock Gothic mass of the Rand Supreme Court.

They had all stopped. One thing to walk past the court when they were clean, carried nothing. Different now because three of them were the escort and the fourth carried a duffel bag that held a 5-litre can of petrol that was strapped with adhesive tape to nine sticks of explosive each weighing 250 grammes, and taped to the can and wired to the explosive was a battery for the electrical timing device manufactured to provide a 30 second fuse. They all waited on one of the others to take a step forward.

The courthouse was an attractive building, wide steps and a dominating portico, entered through double doors. The front part of the building housed the court rooms. Behind and towering was the eight storey administration block, the work place for the clerks and their records. Two years earlier comrades of these four young Blacks had smuggled a limpet mine into the administration. It had been defused before it exploded, but it remained something of a symbol. Not enough of a symbol for the men who had sent this cadre back for a second attack. Inside the courthouse the sentences were handed down on the comrades, on the captured cadres, on the broken cells. One year's imprisonment for playing an audio tape distributed by the African

National Congress. One year and six months for engraving a tea break mug with the words MANDELA – THE PEOPLE'S LEADER. Six years for singing at the university a song in praise of Mandela who was in gaol and Aggett and Biko who had died in police custody. Eight years for membership of the banned underground African National Congress and being found in possession of T-shirts with the logo VIVA MANDELA. Ten years for collecting political information for the African National Congress. Fifteen years for possession of firearms and explosives. Twenty years for sabotage. The sentence of death for the man who in the name of the African National Congress executed a policeman. On their way to the gaols the comrades had come in their tens and in their hundreds to the Rand Supreme Court on Pritchard Street.

It was a good target.

They were beside the sweeping entrance road that went down the side of the court building and then turned sharply into the tunnel that burrowed under the tower. It was the way the prisoners went, and the informers who gave evidence against them, the most secret of the state's witnesses. A White stood at the mouth of the entrance road, blocking it, short cut hair, pressed slacks, a club tie neatly knotted, and his arms crossed and cradling a personal radio. They had seen this policeman each time that they had come to look at the court, they would have to run back past him after the bomb. They had been told that everyone would be dazed after the bomb, that the Boer too would be confused, and they had the Makharov and the R.G.–42 fragmentation grenade.

The bustle and swim of the city eddied around them. The sun shone down on them. The noises of the city drifted between them. The one who carried the duffel bag closed his eyes, seemed to look upwards and his lips moved in silence as if he repeated a single word again and again. He was the country boy who was fearful of everything that was beyond the farm where he had been raised. He was the country boy who had stifled that fear and travelled by aircraft two years before from Tanzania to the great city of Moscow, who had gone to the camp outside Kiev and who had flown back with his knowledge of explosives and his expertise in detonators and fuses. The others huddled close to the country boy and they heard the whispered hiss on his lips, the one word.

The word was *Amandla*, meaning Freedom.

Muscles strained under the overcoats, veins swelling from under the woollen caps. They were together, they were as one.

The country boy took a great gulp of air into his lungs and his hand loosened the mouth of the duffel bag and slid down inside it.

They walked along the pavement, beside the low wall that bordered the court's lawns. They saw the Blacks who lay on the grass on their backs, servants of the court and outside because it was the lunchtime recess They saw a barrister trotting towards the doorway with his gown folded like a raincoat over his arm. They saw the Japanese cars parked at the kerb immediately in front of the doors and their high radio aerials which showed they were driven

11

by the security police and the crime squad detectives. They saw a White youngster kiss his White girl. They saw a Black man wobble and swerve on his bicycle when he was cut up by a shining Mercedes. They saw the dark open doorway of the court.

The country boy wondered if the White in the Combi would really wait for them after the blast and the fire

The country boy led.

On the skin strip between the collar of his overcoat and the wool of his cap he could feel the separate breath of the one with the Makharov and the one with the R.G.–42. He knew what the bomb would do. At the training camp he had seen the scattering flame of the bomb. He liked what he had seen. What he did not like was the order that the timing of the attack should be for the lunch hour. There had been a fierce argument between those who would carry the bomb and those who gave the order for its use. Those who gave the order had said they wanted only damage to the buildings, not casualties. Those who carried the bomb had insisted on damage to the buildings and also to the Whites who were the apparatus of the state and the Blacks who were the accomplices of the state. The compromise had been the lunch hour . . . He led up the path between the lawns. His right forefinger rested on the switch inside the duffel bag, when he pressed the switch they had half a minute. The two doors were open. The lunch hour, so they said, was the likeliest chance that the lobby of the court would be empty. The country boy thought it was a wrong decision. A heavy wooden bench was placed across the doorway leaving only a small entrance through which the court's visitors could be filtered by the police when the adjournment was over, when the friends and relations of the accused would be admitted.

On the first floor judges were clustered round the table in the chamber of the most senior of them, talking not of law but of bloodstock form. In the Whites' canteen, waitress service, barristers briefed by the state sat with their poorer *Pro Deo* colleagues who would make the defence case, seldom successfully, for their Black clients, and chewed over disinvestment and the slide of the rand and the collapse of residential property prices. In the basement cells a White businessman charged with fraudulent conversion ate the fried chicken sent in by his mistress, and in their separate cells there were Blacks who squatted against the cold concrete walls and bowed their heads over bowls of porridge.

The country boy was on the bottom step. The doorway yawned in front of him. His finger was rigid on the switch. They were panting behind him. He pressed the switch. Again the draught of air sank in his throat.

"It's closed."

The Boer's voice. The enemy's voice. His hand snaked back out of the bag. The arm that was to hurl the bag into the lobby of the court was frozen useless.

"You can't go in there for another eighteen minutes."

He spun his head. He saw the one with the Makharov and the one with the R.G.–42 and the one who had nothing at all gawping back down onto the path. The uniformed warrant officer stood in the centre of the pathway, his arms were clasped behind his back on a short leather-coated swagger stick. An immaculate police tunic, knife-edge trousers, shoes that a servant had polished.

"Seventeen minutes actually." The warrant officer grinned cheerfully. "For now, get yourselves away."

The country boy flexed his arm, turned and threw the bag into and inside the doorway.

He ran.

He cannoned into the one with the Makharov, felt the bite of the barrel into his thigh, and he ran. Across the grass. Jumping the wall. All of them charging together. None of them hearing the shout of the warrant officer. None of them seeing him stagger from the shoulder charge of the one who had nothing, and then go as if from instinctive duty through the doorway, none of them seeing him grope for the duffel bag under a table deep in the lobby and take it in his arms and twist again for the bright sunlight of the doorway. All of them sprinting. None of them seeing the fast sweep of understanding chisel the face of the plain clothes policeman with the personal radio.

They were past the building site. They were running, swerving, sidestepping, jumping into the traffic on Van Wielligh, going chicken with a bus driver and having him brake when the bomb exploded.

A bomb detonated in the centre of a safe city, in the middle of a safe lunch hour.

A bomb that spewed fire, showered glass, ripped at plaster and concrete and brick work.

All four would dearly have loved to have seen the explosion. Only the country boy had an exact idea of the scale of the flame blown outwards in a blazing spray. They would dearly have loved to have seen the warrant officer disintegrate when he was a yard from the door, when he was at the moment of throwing the bomb away from him and onto the grass. In the few seconds that the warrant officer had screamed of the danger of the bomb he had attracted enough attention for there to be seven civilians and two policemen in the court lobby. They would dearly have loved to see those nine persons bowled over by the blast and the smoke cloud and the fire draught. They saw nothing of the devastation, and nothing of the policeman chasing after them, the radio in one hand and a revolver in the other.

They reached the Combi van.

They flung open the door and scrambled inside in a confusion of knees and elbows and shouts, and the van was accelerating into the wide spaces of Pritchard before they'd managed to close the doors. The last thing the country boy saw before the doors were shut was the policeman on the pavement, panting, heaving, yelling into his radio.

Jeez drove like he hadn't a tomorrow.

And he didn't reckon he had, a tomorrow.

Shit, and he'd heard the explosion. Couldn't have missed it. Half choked on his cigarette, and the windows around him had rattled fit to break and he'd seen the heads on the pavement spinning to stare up the street. He'd been facing away from the explosion, he'd had only the shock wave, none of the sights . . . left into End, up past the Kerk junction, left onto Jeppe . . . Jeez going hard, and with the frown slashed on the old weather-stained skin of his forehead. He was going hard because he'd heard the bang and a bang like that at mid-day in central Jo'burg meant a bloody big show.

Nobody had said anything other than that he was to be parked in a Combi van on the corner of Pritchard and Delvers, north side, looking east, back doors unfastened. Done as he was told, because that's what they all did in the Movement, Blacks and Whites. Shit, nobody had said it was a bloody headline grabber they'd be running from . . . Right off Jeppe and into Rissik. He was burning the tyres, hitting the turns. Way ahead, up Rissik, was the railway station, that's where he'd been told he had to get. Four kids to catch a train, that's all. He had been told that if there was a police block then a White in a commercial van would sail through.

But this was an arsehole.

Because of his initials James Carew had always been Jeez. He rather fancied it. He used that name on the telephone, used it to anyone who knew him marginally. He'd had the name since the time he left school, since he was in the army. The name was his possession, his style, like kids who had a ring in their ear, or a tattoo. He was Jeez, had been for more than 35 years.

He heard the siren.

Shit . . . Jeez saw the traffic in front of him swerving for the slow lane, and that told him that the bells and the whining were behind, and his ears told him the bastards were closing.

Nobody had told him who he would be driving. Hadn't said it was a getaway. Just that four kids who were a bit hot needed picking up on the corner of Pritchard and Delvers and needed dropping off at the station. When he'd seen them earlier, he'd thought: bright lads, these, not piling into the van straight off. They'd have been checking for a tail. Well, now they had a tail all right.

He'd been on the road of bells and sirens before, more than twenty years before, but the memory was still sharp, not the sort of sound that any bugger ever forgets. What was sharpest was the same dingy old thought, that when he heard the sirens and saw the uniforms then there wasn't a hell of a lot of point in beating your guts out and running faster.

A bloody shambles the clowns had dropped him in. Shit up to his nose.

In the back was a babble of screaming for more speed. He looked into the side mirror. The unmarked car had the bell going, and the yellow police wagon had the blue light going and the siren . . . right up to his bloody nose and down his bloody nostrils. When he looked again through his front windscreen he saw the police jeep that was slewed across the road a bit over a hundred yards ahead. There were no side turnings between him and the police jeep. Back to the mirror. The car and the wagon weren't trying to get past him, didn't have to, were sitting on his arse, shepherding him.

The poor bastards were frantic in the back, spittle on his neck the way they were shouting through the close mesh grille.

You win some and most often you lose, that's what Jeez reckoned.

He eased his foot onto the brake pedal. He changed down. He could see that there were pistols aimed at him from behind the cover of the police jeep. Down again to second, and his foot harder onto the brake and stamping.

"Sorry, boys," Jeez said softly.

If they hadn't been making such a hell of a rumpus they might have heard the genuine sadness in his voice. He brought the Combi to a halt. He took the keys out of the ignition and tossed them out of the window, onto the roadway. He looked into the side mirror. The policemen were spilling out of the unmarked car and out of the wagon, crouching and kneeling and all aiming their hand guns at the Combi. Nobody had told Jeez what the hell he was into.

Silence in the van.

"Let's have a bit of dignity, boys." An English accent. "Let's not give the bastards the pleasure of our fear."

Jeez opened his door. He stepped down onto the street. He clasped his hands over the top of his head.

In front of him and behind him the policemen began to run warily forward.

Johannesburg is a hard city. It is a city where the Whites carry guns and the Blacks carry knives. Not a city where the pedestrians and shoppers cower on their faces because the police have drawn revolvers and have blocked off a Combi and are handcuffing four kaffirs and a kaffir lover. A crowd had gathered inside the minute that it took the police to hustle their five prisoners towards the wagon and to kick them up and slam the doors on them. There was something to see. The White guy was the something to see. Must have been more than forty, could have been more than fifty, and wearing decent slacks and a decent shirt. The crowd wondered what the White guy was doing with those Black bastards, what the hell he was at.

Four long blocks away a cloud of slow moving smoke was settling above Pritchard Street.

Mr Justice Andries van Zyl had passed the sentence of the supreme penalty on 186 men, of whom his clerk had told him recently 142 had been executed. It would have been beyond him to believe that an innocent man had ever been convicted in a court over which he had presided. He attended church every Sunday morning and sometimes went back in the evening. When he retired in two years' time he would devote his energies to a charitable society supporting children afflicted by the spina bifida disease. Privately, in his room, after passing the death sentence, he would say a prayer for the condemned man; not a prayer that the man should be reprieved, but that he might go to his Maker with true repentance in his heart.

On that late afternoon in the Palace of Justice on the north side of Pretoria's Church Square he dealt first with the four Blacks deemed guilty by himself and his two lay assessors of murder. There was no theatricality. The black cap had long before been dispensed with in the Republic's courts, and his sentencing voice was a racing monotone, that of a bowls club secretary getting through the minutes of a previous meeting.

As Happy and Charlie and Percy and Tom stared back at him from the dock, expressionless, exhausted of hope, he shuffled his papers, then pressed his metal-rimmed half moon spectacles tight onto the bridge of his nose. He allowed the murmurs to subside in the public gallery.

He looked up at Jeez Carew.

Mr Justice van Zyl saw a man only a few years younger than himself, and well dressed in a dark grey suit and a white shirt and a silk tie. He saw a face which seemed to say that there was nothing new to be learned. He saw the way that the shoulders were pulled back, and the way that the man's arms were held straight down to his sides. He saw that the prisoner's bearing was more militarily correct than that of the prison service guards at attention behind him. Mr Justice van Zyl had watched this White accused through seventeen days of court room business. He thought he had detected an arrogance. He disliked arrogance. The previous day he had decided that when he passed sentence on the White he would make a fuller statement than was usual for him. He would break that arrogance

"James Carew, you have been found guilty of murder without extenuating circumstances. There is only one sentence that I may pass upon you. It was your own decision that during your time in custody you refused to co-operate with the officers who have diligently investigated a quite appalling criminal act. You chose to remain silent. You have also rebuffed the efforts of a very able and conscientious counsel to present a defence on your behalf. I understand that you chose not to brief him, and also that you refused the opportunity offered you of going into the witness stand to give the court your own version of events on that horrific day in Johannesburg. By these actions I am forced to the conclusion that in your case extenuating circumstances do not exist which would mitigate your guilt.

"I have heard in police evidence that you came from the United Kingdom to the Republic of South Africa twelve years ago. In the time you have resided here perhaps you have acquired the belief that different standards of justice obtain for our varied ethnic groups. You may have believed that the colour of your skin offers you some protection from the consequences of your actions. You would have deluded yourself, Mr Carew, if you believed that.

"The crime of which you have been found guilty involved a quite dastardly act. You acted together with terrorists of the outlawed African National Congress, one of whom had been trained in sabotage and murder in a communist

16

state, to set off a bomb inside the Rand Supreme Court in Johannesburg. The bomb consisted of explosives and petrol to which had been added a quantity of household liquid detergent, the effect of the latter being that the flaming petrol would fasten itself to any clothes or flesh it came into contact with. The casualties would have been even more severe but for the devotion to duty and the personal sacrifice of warrant officer Prinsloo. In taking much of the blast of the bomb the warrant officer without doubt saved many others from the savagery that you intended. As the driver of the getaway vehicle your guilt is equal to that of the man who made the bomb and the men who delivered it. You were an essential member of a murderous conspiracy.

"We live in a time when it is more than ever important that in our beloved country God-fearing men and women should support the legitimate forces of law and of order. No benefit to any person in the Republic, whatever his colour, can come from an outrage such as you helped to perpetrate. I truly hope that the sentence that I am about to pass on you will deter other foreigners from coming to our country, taking our hospitality, and repaying us with murder.

"I believe, Mr Carew, in the efficacy of the deterrent. A few years ago a distinguished colleague of mine said, 'The death penalty is like a warning, just like a lighthouse throwing its beams out to sea. We hear about shipwrecks, but we do not hear about the ships the lighthouse guides safely on its way. We do not have proof of the number of ships it saves, but we do not tear the lighthouse down.' Mr Carew, we will not permit our country to be used as a playground of mayhem by foreigners who conspire with such hate-consumed organisations as the African National Congress.

"James Carew, the sentence of the court is that you be taken from here to a lawful place of execution and that you there be hanged by the neck until you are dead."

There was no entreaty for the Lord to have mercy on James Carew's soul.

Had Jeez slumped or even dropped his eyes from the Judge's face, then there would have been. Mr Justice van Zyl was vexed by the prisoner's composure. He thrust his papers together, propelled himself from his chair.

"All rise," the clerk intoned.

Mr Justice van Zyl stamped out of his court room, his assessors after him.

A guard tapped Jeez on the shoulder. Jeez turned smartly and marched down the steps from the dock to the court room cells, followed by Happy and Charlie and Percy and Tom.

In prison lore they were the "condemns". While they were driven under heavy escort to that part of Pretoria Central prison a mile and a half away that was reserved for these men who were condemned, a police major sat in the emptied courtroom filling in with a ball point pen the specific details of the printed form that was the death warrant. The form would go later to the sheriff of the capital city for his signature and in due course to the hangman as authority for his work.

An age later Jeez sat on the end of his bed and stared down at the sheet of writing paper, blank as yet, that lay on the table that was fastened into the cell wall.

An endless time later. Countless days, more than a year. Long enough for the Rand Supreme Court and the ride up Rissik Street to be just a hated memory, a smell that was everywhere in the mind but couldn't be located.

It was the first time that he had asked for writing paper and a pen.

What to write? What to say? . . . He could hear the singing. Many, many voices in a slow dirge. Couldn't escape from the bastard singing. Shit, when it was his turn, who'd be singing for bloody Jeez?

On the top right hand corner of the sheet of paper he wrote the date.

2

He let himself in through the front door and the atmosphere hit him.

Before Jack had his key out of the lock and the door closed behind him, he could sense catastrophe.

The vacuum cleaner was in the middle of the hall rug. His mother always did the carpets straight after Sam and Jack had gone to work and little Will to school. There were dirty clothes at the foot of the stairs. She would have put the yesterday shirts and socks and pants into the machine straight after she'd done the carpets. Down the hall the door into the kitchen was open. The saucepans and the frying pan from last night's dinner and the morning's breakfast were in the sink.

Had to be a catastrophe.

Sam gone bankrupt? Will hurt? . . . But Will was sitting glumly at the top of the stairs, still in his school blazer, and he too had his routine and always changed out of his blazer, chucked it on the bedroom floor, as soon as he came in, and that would have been two hours back . . . Sam couldn't have gone bankrupt. What recession? Business never brighter, Sam was forever saying.

The boy on the stairs shrugged dramatically, like no one had bothered to tell him what was biting his Mum and his Dad.

Jack heard Sam's voice through the closed living room door.

"Get it into your head, it's nothing to do with you."

He heard his mother crying. Not loud weeping, not crying for sympathy. Real crying, real misery.

"Whatever the bastard's done, Hilda, whatever he's going to get, that's not your concern."

He turned to close the front door. Behind him was wretched, normal Churchill Close. Nothing ever happened in the dead end road where the cherry trees were in blossom and the pavements were swept and the mowers had been out once or twice already on the front lawns and the rose beds were weeded. Tudor homes set back from the road, where nothing ever went bad and sour. You could get a funeral moving out of neo–Elizabethan Churchill Close with half the residents not knowing there'd been a death. Jack closed the door behind him.

"He's gone out of your life." He heard the anger in Sam's voice.

Jack knocked and went into the living room.

His mother sat on the sofa beside the fireplace. Yesterday's ashes. She had a crumpled handkerchief tight in her fist and her eyes were red and swollen. She still wore the housecoat that was her early morning gear. Sam Perry was at the window. Jack didn't think that they could have been rowing between themselves, they hardly ever did, and never when Will could hear them.

Jack was 26 years old. His quiet love for his mother was the same as it had been from the time he could first remember, when there had only been the two of them.

"What's happened, Mum?"

Sam replied for her. "There's been a letter."

"Who from?"

"There's been a letter come from a gaol in South Africa."

"Will you, please, tell me who has written us a letter from South Africa."

"A letter to your mother from a condemned cell in Pretoria Central prison."

"Damn it, Sam, who wrote it?"

"Your father."

Sam turned to stare out of the window. His wife, Jack's mother, pointed wordlessly up to the mantelpiece, fresh tears on her cheeks. Amongst the delicate china pieces, next to the flower vase, was a small brown paper envelope.

His mother's voice was muffled through the squeezed handkerchief.

"You should read it, Jack. They're going to hang your father."

He went slowly across the room. He stepped over the brimming ashtray in the middle of the carpet. She had been there all day with her cigarettes and her letter. It was an envelope of flimsy paper with a blue airmail sticker and a 25 cent stamp which showed the bulged bloom of a protea plant. Tight, joined handwriting had addressed the letter to Mrs Hilda Perry, 45 Green Walk, Coulsdon, Surrey, Great Britain. A different hand had crossed out that address and replaced it with Foxhaven, Churchill Close, Leatherhead, Surrey. No one had seen a fox in Churchill Close for six years. On the reverse side of the envelope was overstamped "If Undelivered Return to Commissioner of Prisons, Pretoria", and there was a post box number. The envelope was feather-light, for a moment he looked again at the mantelpiece.

"It's inside, Jack," his mother said. "They don't seem to give them much in the way of paper."

Sam said tersely, "You don't have to read it. Not after what he did to your mother and you."

"If it's my father I'll read it," Jack said quietly. It wasn't a put down. Jack knew that Sam Perry had done his damndest to be a good proxy father to his wife's son.

He drew the single sheet out of the envelope. Across the top of the sheet was written in capital letters JAMES CAREW – C2 3/86.

"My father's James Curwen."

"It's the name he's using there," his mother said.

Jack turned the sheet over. The letter was signed "Jeez".

His mother anticipated him. "It's what he always called himself. He was always Jeez to me and to everyone."

To himself almost, but aloud, he read: "Dear Hilda, This comes a bit out of the blue I'm afraid, and I have to hope that it doesn't upset you. God knows that once I did enough to upset you and I've no right to repeat the dose. I suppose that it's because of my present situation, because I am sentenced to hang, that I thought it would be good to tie down some of the loose strings of my life, that's why I'm writing. About going out of your life, well, I'm not saying anything about that. What happened is gone. No excuses, no whining, it just happened."

"And, Christ, did it happen," Sam snapped. "Walked out on a fine lady and a two year-old child."

Jack ignored him.

". . . A lot of years later I came back to the U.K. and I found out that you were well and married, that Jack was well, that you had a new baby. I didn't see the need to drag up the past. You were in good shape. I was OK. I reckoned you were best left alone . . ."

"And why couldn't he leave her alone now?" Sam couldn't let go of it. "Suddenly, twenty-four years after he's dumped your mother, it's a sob story."

". . . So, I'm in a bit of a mess now, things aren't looking too good. As I used to say, you win some but most you lose. If you read in the papers that I'm going for the early walk then please just think of me that morning, and remember the better times. As I will. If nothing comes up at the last minute, this has to be goodbye to you and the lad. I watched him at sports once over the fence. I thought he was OK. Things aren't always what they seem. When I'm gone, ask the old man. He'll tell you. Yours affectionately, Jeez . . .

"Got all that's bloody coming to him."

Jack put the letter back into the envelope. He was very pale. His hand trembled as he gave it to his mother.

"Why should he have written to you, Mum?"

"Perhaps there's no one else he could have written to." She stood up. Jack knew she wanted to be out of the room. She didn't want her husband and her son to see any more of her tears. She laughed in a silly, brittle way. "There's jobs. Will's tea. Our dinner. Have to be getting on."

She was going to the door.

"Do you want a hand, Mum?"

"You talk with your father – with Sam."

She went out. She couldn't help herself, she was sobbing before she'd closed the door.

"Sponged for sympathy, that's what the bastard's done. Old man, indeed. I'd give him bloody old man."

"Steady, Sam. He's my father."

"I've put it together, what he did, what it said in the papers. He was involved with communist terrorists and murder."

"You're talking about my father."

"He treated your mother like dirt."

"He's still my father."

"He's not worth a single one of your mother's tears."

"Do you bloody well want to hang him yourself?"

"Don't swear at me, son, not when you're under my bloody roof."

"Isn't it enough for you that they're going to throw him in a pit with a rope round his neck?"

"He made his bed. He'd no call to bring his problems into my house, into your mother's life."

"He's still my father," Jack said.

Sam dropped his head. The hardness was gone from him.

"I'm sorry, Jack, truly sorry that you ever had to read the letter."

They had a drink together, large Scotch and small soda, and another, and there was time for one more before Hilda Perry called them to dinner. They talked loudly of business, Sam's garage and showroom and Jack's work. They sat at the dining room's mahogany table with candles lit. The man who was in a cell fifty-five hundred miles away was thought of but not spoken about. When they were having their coffee Will came in and sat on Hilda's knee and talked about the school soccer team and there were bellows of laughter.

Jack pushed his chair back and stood up. His father was going to hang. He thanked his mother for dinner. He said he had some work that had to be sorted by the morning. In a gaol on the other side of the world, dear God. He said he'd go to his room and put his head into his papers. Was so alone that the one he wrote to was the one he had most hurt. He told Will that he should learn to kick with his left foot if he ever wanted to be any good. He had no sense of his father's face. He rested his hand on Sam's shoulder, and Sam patted it. The man he didn't know was his father, and his father was going to hang.

He went up the flower-carpeted staircase to his room.

It was a little under four miles to work, across on the London side of the town. Jack Curwen was employed by Richard Villiers and his son, Nicholas. The office was an unlikely place for D & C Ltd (Demolition and Clearance). There was no yard for JCB diggers and bulldozers and heavy earth-transporting lorries; there weren't any cranes; there weren't any workmen. Villiers was a shrewd man, which made him a good employer, and he'd long before decided that the way to the maximum profit and minimum outlay was to be in the art game of sub-contracting out. He hunted out the business and then pulled in the freelance operators that he needed. A few local calls could bring in a million pound's worth of plant and transport whose maintenance and upkeep was some other bugger's headache. D & C Ltd liked to boast that nothing was too small, nothing too large. They could clear the foundations of a 5000 square yard warehouse in dockland. They could take out the stump of an oak tree. Villiers came into the office in the morning to ferret into the balance sheets and retired with a huge handicap to the golf course for the afternoon. Nicholas Villiers looked after the sub-contracting side of the business, and Jack was there to sniff out new contracts. There was a business manager who kept the books, two secretaries and a receptionist. Nice and lean, was how Richard Villiers described D & C Ltd, no waste, no fat. He liked young Jack because he didn't have to pay the lad that much, and because the lad kept the cheques rolling. When he retired there might be a directorship for the lad.

D & C Ltd were housed in the ground floor of a Victorian building. They shared with a solicitor, an accountancy practice, a chiropodist and two architects.

Jack would have preferred to have just slipped in that morning, shut himself away. No chance. Villiers had an office where he could keep his clubs and his wet weather anoraks and leggings. The business manager had his own territory. Nicholas Villiers and Jack and the two secretaries shared what had once been the ground floor drawing room.

The girls and Nicholas Villiers stared at him, like he looked awful.

"Been on the piss, have we?" Villiers asked loudly. Janice giggled, Lucille dropped her head.

"Didn't have a very good night," Jack muttered. He'd had a tossing, night-marish, sweating night. He'd nicked his right side nostril with his razor. He'd missed breakfast.

"You look pretty rough."

"Didn't sleep much."

"Not got the 'flu?"

Hadn't been on the piss, hadn't got the 'flu, only problem was that his father was going to hang. Nothing else was wrong.

"I'm fine, thanks, just didn't sleep much last night."

Only problem was that his father was going to kick it on the end of a rope with a load of crap-arse foreigners around him, with no one of his own around him.

The girls were all eyes on him. He was a good dresser, took care of himself. Wasn't every day that Jack Curwen looked as though he'd slept in a hedge. He thought they both fancied him, but they were too close to base. No future in a typists' pool relationship. Best keeping the ladies separate from work. And he was on the rebound anyway. Last girl had been with him for four months, good kid and good looker and occasionally good in the back seat of his motor, till she'd upped and offed with a doctor to Canada. She had looked him hard in the eye and said he was sweet and said her new fellow had more of a future with a medical degree than he had working at a nothing place like D & C Ltd. It was a comfort to think that Janice and Lucille fancied him, but he wasn't doing anything about it.

"Please yourself . . . The pillbox on the Downs, they can't do that today. The blaster isn't free before tomorrow. Too expensive keeping the plant hang-ing about. Going to go tomorrow afternoon. Does that mess you?"

"Not particularly. I've other places I can be." It wasn't a lie. "There's a line of elm stumps I'm chasing near Dorking. A bit of chasing'll fix it."

"And afterwards try sleeping it off, eh?"

Jack smiled weakly. He was on his way back to the door.

Nicholas Villiers said, "Anything I can do to help, Jack?"

"No."

Janice watched through the window as Jack walked to his car. She typed two lines and looked up again. She saw the car turn in the road and drive away.

"He's not gone to Dorking," she announced, proud of her keen observation. "He's taken the London road."

He had the wipers on, shovelling the rain off the windscreen, for the drive into the city.

By luck he found a parking space near the street market behind Waterloo station.

He walked over the bridge with the rain lashing his face, soaking his trousers and his shoes, and he hadn't cared.

His father had never been mentioned since his mother's second marriage. What he knew of his father was what he had been told when he was a child. A bastard of a man had walked out of his mother's life, told her that he would be away for a few days and had never come back. Jack had been two years old. He had had it drilled into him that his father was a callous man who had opted out and left a young mother with a child that was little more than a baby. There was nothing accidental about it because money had come to his mother all the time that she had been bringing up the child, and had kept on coming right up to the week of her registry office marriage to Sam Perry. Jack knew that. Never a word from his father, only the cruel mockery of a monthly stipend. He had never asked about how the money was paid or where it had come from. But it had arrived, sufficient for the household bills, food and electricity and heating oil and a caravan holiday each August, right up to the time of the wedding. It was as if his father had watched their lives from a safe distance, and stopped the money when he'd known it was no longer needed. Jack had kept his father's name and it would have been hell's complicated to change it to Jack Perry. He had been Jack Curwen at grammar school, and Jack Curwen at college. But of Jeez Curwen there was never a word in Sam Perry's household.

He turned left onto the Strand. He knew where he was going. He knew that he had first to go to Trafalgar Square.

He knew nothing of this man who was condemned to die in South Africa but his name and his age, and that he was his father. He didn't know his face, nor his habits. He didn't know whether he drank, or swore or whored. He didn't know whether he laughed, whether he cried, whether he prayed. He hadn't the least idea what he did for a living.

He had to fend off the spike of an umbrella tent, and the woman who was

24

powering out of Simpson's didn't notice him, so didn't apologise. He came into the square. Weather too awful and season too early for the tourists. The column and the lions and the statues were granite grey in the rain.

Sam Perry had been good to them. Good to his mother by marrying her, kind to her son who had no blood with him but whom he had treated as his own. Sam had worked hard to make himself into Jack's father. Jack could remember the days at the infant and primary schools before Sam had showed up. Other kids' dads helping with school projects, shouting at the sports afternoons, dropping them at school, picking them up. It didn't make sense to Jack that a man who cared so little for his wife and kid that he could walk out on them should keep a watch to satisfy himself that their survival was assured. Jack didn't know a single detail about the man who was his father.

He crossed the Strand. The rain ran on his forehead, dribbled into his eyes and his nose and his mouth.

There were six demonstrators outside the South African embassy and eight policemen standing on the steps of the building.

It was obvious enough that he should come here. He knew the embassy. Everybody who travelled through central London knew that the embassy was in Trafalgar Square, huge and powerful in its cleaned colonial yellow stone. He had seen the demonstrators on television the week before, when they started their vigil. The embassy building's solidity mocked the critics of South Africa, the orange and white and blue flag sodden but defiant on the high pole. The policemen, gathered close to the main double doors were able to take some protection from the rain. The demonstrators had no shelter. Two were coloured, four were white. They were drenched. The rain had run the paint of the slogans on their placards which they held against their knees.

FREEDOM FOR THE PRITCHARD FIVE.

NO RACIST HANGINGS IN SA.

THE ROPE FOR APARTHEID, NOT FOR FREEDOM FIGHTERS.

Before last night Jack would not have given a second glance to men and women who stood in the rain outside the embassy of the Republic of South Africa. Any more than the diplomats inside, in the dry and the warm, gave a shit for them, or their slogans.

He saw the distaste on the police sergeant's face as he walked to speak to the demonstrators. The man he picked out was middle forties, Jack guessed, because the hair that was lank on the back of his neck was streaked grey. The man was shivering in a poplin sports top that was keeping out none of the rain. He wore plastic badges for Anti-Apartheid and the African National Congress and the South West African People's Organisation. His jogging shoes were holed and worn, but he stood motionless in the streams of water on the pavement. His placard was

FREEDOM FOR THE PRITCHARD FIVE.

All six looked at him coldly, mirroring the stares of the policemen.

"Good morning. Can you tell me about your protest?"

"Pretty obvious, isn't it? You can read."

"I thought you'd want to tell me," Jack said.

"We don't need your kind of interest."

"What the hell does that mean?"

"Just go up the steps and join the other fascists."

Jack read the man's supercilious stare. He had his hair cut short, he wore a businessman's rain coat, a charcoal suit, he wore a tie.

He looked hard into the man's eyes.

"Listen, I am not a policeman. I am not a snooper. I am a private citizen, and I want to know something about the Pritchard Five."

There must have been something in Jack's gaze, and the lash of his voice. The man shrugged.

"You can sign the petition."

"How many signatures?"

"One hundred and fourteen."

"That all?"

"This is a racist society." The man rolled his words, as if they gave him a satisfaction. "There's not many who care that four heroic freedom fighters will go to their deaths."

"Who are they?" Jack asked.

"Happy Zikala, Charlie Schoba, Percy Ngoye and Tom Mweshtu. They took the battle into the middle of Johannesburg in broad daylight. It will be a crime against humanity if they hang."

"Your placard calls them the Pritchard Five."

"He only drove the car."

"And he's *white*," Jack yelled. "So he doesn't get to be a hero."

Jack wanted to get the hell away, but the man was tugging at his sleeve.

"The issue is whether the White minority government and the White minority courts will dare to hang four Black freedom fighters. That's what it's about."

Jack wrenched himself clear.

He walked the length of the Strand and on until he came to Fleet Street. Sam and Hilda Perry always took the *Daily Telegraph* at home. The *Daily Telegraph* was as routine as shaving and brushing his teeth in the morning. He asked at the Reception if he could see someone from the library. When the woman came he didn't spin a story, just asked directly if he could see a file. Nine times out of ten he would have been told that visitors were not permitted access to files without prior arrangement, but she looked at the rain-swept young man, and said:

"What file is it you want?"

"Everything on the Pritchard Five."

"The ones who are condemned to hang in South Africa?"

"Everything you have, please."

"I can tell you now there's not much. The unrest and the economic crisis and the sanctions issue, that's what has taken up the space."

But she took him to the library. She sat him at a table and brought him the file of newspaper clippings. She shrugged, she said that it was pretty thin, that there would probably be a long story on the day before the execution. She left him to read the file.

There was a clipping from the day of the bombing that just mentioned the arrest of an unidentified White. Nothing then until the trial, and most of that detailed the prosecution's evidence against Tom Mweshtu, that he'd been trained by the Soviets and had spent time in Kiev. James Carew was described as a white South African taxi driver, aged 53. Two paragraphs on the sentencing, what they were accused of, what their names were, that they showed no emotion when they were told they would hang. Months of a hole in the story and then the dismissal of the appeal, four paragraphs. Jack learned that the five had been in the maximum security compound of Pretoria Central gaol for thirteen months, that the Pope had urged the State President to exercise clemency, that three EEC Foreign Ministers had sent telegrams urging reprieves. Everything that he read had been in the paper pushed through the letter box every day at home – and he hadn't bothered, just as he hadn't stirred himself to take an interest in the shootings in the townships or in the detentions or the bombings.

And then, there it was, the photograph.

In last Tuesday's paper. It was probably still in the cupboard under the stairs. Might be lining a dustbin, or it might have been crumpled up by his mother for cleaning the front room windows. His mother always read the paper, front to back. Jack didn't know how she could not have recognised the photograph of her first husband He had never before seen a photograph of his father.

It was a mug shot, might have been a police picture, might have been for a passport. He peered down at the column-wide photograph, at the man who only managed two paragraphs with four others, who didn't rate as a hero, who was a white South African taxi driver, 53. He saw a gaunt face, staring, ungiving eyes, shadowed hollow cheeks, sparse short hair. The photograph was misting, blurring. Jack's fists were white knuckled, tight. He felt the choking in his chest. He saw the tears fall on the newsprint and be absorbed.

When the woman came back from her desk to look into the corner where the young man had been sitting she found the file neatly piled, but open. She saw the damp on the photograph and wondered what the silly man had managed to spill on it, could have been the rain from his hair. She noticed when she gathered up the file that the final clipping reported that within the next few days the State President would make his decision as to whether the sentences of death should be carried out.

Jack drove to Dorking and made sure of the contract for the removal of the thirty-two elm stumps. He rang his mother and said he'd be late home; then he set off to get himself drunk.

3

The drink hadn't hurt, had been something of a blessing because his stupor sleep didn't let him nightmare.

First thing when he came down the stairs he hunted for the newspaper and his father's photograph. It was one from the top of the pile, next to the fire lighters. He tore out the picture and folded it into his wallet.

Breakfast in the kitchen and not a word of his lurching up the stairs a little after midnight. His mother didn't ask him why he had been out so late. Big boy, wasn't he? Twenty-six years old, a grown man. Nothing had ever been said about his moving out, not that Sam would have complained if Jack had announced one Monday morning that he was off to look for a flat. He couldn't have faulted Sam for the way he had taken this other man's son into his household, but kindness and patience couldn't have turned them into father and son. Sometimes they were friends, sometimes he was a generously tolerated lodger. Jack could recognise there was more fault in him than in the attitudes of his step-father. He was close to himself, rarely gave of his affections, took his pleasures away from home; pubs and squash club friends and the girls who were casually hooked into that scene. He was aware of his own cold streak of independence. Natural enough, for a boy who had never known the companionship of a true father.

And no mention made at the breakfast table of James Carew. Didn't have to be talked about, because he was there with them. Sam too loud, his mother too quiet, and Jack behaving as if he had buried the whole matter, and all of them hurrying through the bacon and the scrambled egg the sooner to escape to their work and the privacy of their thoughts.

Jack didn't even call the office.

He drove into London and parked off the Vauxhall Bridge Road, behind the cathedral and walked through the park to Whitehall. Yesterday had been wasted, and now there was no more time to waste because time was short for James Carew.

He stood in the courtyard outside the Foreign and Commonwealth Office. He made some rapid calculations and decided to advise Richard Villiers not to accept the contract. It was just too damn four-square big. Almost intimidating.

He watched the civil servants arriving with their uniform E II R briefcases, most of them looking as though they had nothing but a morning paper in them; and the leggy secretaries, and the chauffeurs and the messengers. He went up the steps and into the dark reception area.

There was a commissionaire, blue uniform and medal ribbons, an old regular army man. There was a security man a yard or two back in the shadows. There was a woman with grey hair drawn into a tight knot. She wore a white blouse over what didn't look like regulation underwear. He wasn't asked what his business was. They waited on him to speak. He was an ordinary citizen who was calling by because his father was going to be hanged in South Africa. He wondered how often the ordinary citizen came to announce themselves in the reception area. They were all looking at him, like it was an attempt to make him grovel. Probably not worth pointing out that he and a few other ordinary chaps off the street paid their salaries.

"My name is Curwen. I'd like to see someone, please, who deals with South Africa."

There was a very slight smile at the commissionaire's mouth. The security man looked as though he hadn't heard.

The woman said, "Do you have an appointment?"

"If I had an appointment, I'd have said so."

"You have to have an appointment."

"I don't have an appointment, but I do insist on seeing someone who deals with South Africa, on a matter of urgency."

Jack wondered what the word urgency might mean under this roof. He'd used it forcefully enough for her to hesitate.

"What's it in connection with?"

"Are you an expert on South Africa?"

"No."

"Then it won't help you to know what it's about."

A flush spilled through the make-up on her cheeks. She turned her back on him and spoke into a telephone, then told him to take a seat.

He sat on a hard chair away from the desk. He reckoned he'd spoiled her day. He was more than half an hour on the chair, and she began to look herself again. He wondered what they would be doing upstairs that meant he had to sit for more than thirty minutes waiting for them. Getting the coffee machine working? Sharing out the sandwiches? Filling in the South African Department's football pool coupon?

"Good morning, Mr Curwen, would you come this way, please."

The man might have been in his late forties, could have been the early fifties. His suit didn't look good enough for him to be important, but he had a kindly face that seemed worn thin with tiredness. They went down a long and silent corridor, then the man opened a door and waved Jack inside. It was an interview room, four chairs and a table and an ashtray that hadn't been emptied. Of course they weren't going to invite him into the working part of the building. They were in the quarantine area.

"I'm Sandham. I'm on the South Africa desk."

The man apologised for keeping him waiting. Then he listened as Jack told him about the letter from Pretoria, and of the little that he knew about his father.

"And you want to know what we're doing for him?"

"Yes."

Sandham asked him please to wait, smiled ruefully, as if Jack knew all about waiting. He was gone five minutes. He came back with a buff file under his arm, and a younger man.

"Mr Sandham explained to me your business with us, Mr Curwen. I decided to come and see you myself. My name's Furneaux, Assistant Secretary. I read everything that goes across the South Africa desk."

Furneaux took a chair, Sandham stood.

A short, abrupt, unlikeable little man, not yet out of middle age, with a maroon silk handkerchief flopping from his breast pocket. Furneaux reached for Sandham's file.

"This conversation is not for newspaper consumption," Furneaux said.

"Of course."

"I understand that your father left your mother when you were two years old. That makes it easier for me to talk frankly to you. I am assuming you have no emotional attachment to your father because you have no memory of him. But you want to know what we are doing to save your father's life? Publicly we are doing nothing, because it is our belief that by going public we would diminish what influence we have on the government of South Africa. Privately we have done everything possible to urge clemency for the terrorists . . ."

"Terrorists or freedom fighters?" Jack held Furneaux's eye until the Assistant Secretary dropped his face to the file.

"Terrorists, Mr Curwen. Your government does not support the throwing of bombs in central Johannesburg. You've heard the Prime Minister on the subject, I expect. Bombs in Johannesburg are no different to bombs in Belfast or in the West End of London. It is not an area we can be selective over . . . Privately we have requested clemency because we do not feel the execution of these men will ease the present tension in South Africa."

"What sort of reply have you had?"

"What we'd have expected. Officially and unofficially our request has been ignored. I might add, Mr Curwen, that your father is only a British subject in technical terms. For the last dozen or so years he has chosen to make his home in the Republic."

"So you've washed your hands of him?"

Furneaux said evenly, "There's something you should understand. They execute a minimum of a hundred criminals a year there. There's no capital punishment debate in the Republic. From our viewpoint, your father received a fair trial although he declined to co-operate in any way with his defence advisors. The Supreme Court heard his appeal, at length."

"I'm not interested in what he did, I only care about saving his life."

"Your father was found guilty of murder. My view is that nothing more can be done to save his life."

"That's washing your hands."

"Wrong, that's accepting the reality that in South Africa people convicted of murder are hanged."

30

"He's my father," Jack said.

"His solicitors don't believe he has a chance of a reprieve. I am sorry to have to tell you this."

"How soon?"

Furneaux scanned the papers in the file, flipped them over. He fastened on a single sheet, read it, then closed the file.

"It may have been discussed by the executive council last night, but it might be next week – they're more preoccupied with the unrest – three weeks, a month maximum."

Jack stood. He looked at the table, he looked at his hands.

"So what am I supposed to do?"

Furneaux looked to the window. "Baldly put, Mr Curwen, there's nothing you can do."

"So you're just going to stand back while they hang my father?" Jack spat the question. He saw his spittle on Furneaux's tie, and on his chin.

Furneaux looped his handkerchief from his pocket, wiped himself. "Mr Curwen, your father travelled quite voluntarily to South Africa. He chose to involve himself with a terrorist gang, and it is, and from the very beginning was, more or less inevitable that he will pay a high price for his actions."

The file was gathered against Furneaux's chest.

"I'm sorry for wasting your valuable time . . ." Jack said.

"Mr Sandham, would you show Mr Curwen to the front hall."

Jack heard Furneaux's heavy tread clatter away down the corridor.

He said, "I don't understand. My father is a British citizen living in South Africa for years, suddenly turns up in a murder trial, but your man has a pretty ancient looking file on him an inch thick. How's that?"

"Don't know." Sandham bounced his eyebrows.

Sandham took Jack to the front hall, asked him for a card so that he could contact him if there were developments.

He saw the young fellow walk away, threading between the official cars. He noted the athleticism that couldn't be hidden by the disappointed droop of his shoulders. He went back up the three floors to the South Africa desk. Smoking too damned much, and his chest was heaving when he made it to the open plan area where he worked.

He thought he knew the answer to the question that Curwen didn't understand. He was old enough, and passed over often enough not to care too much what he said and to whom he said it. He knocked at Furneaux's door, put his head round the corner.

"That chap they're going to hang, Mr Furneaux, is he a bit complicated?"

"Too deep water for you, Jimmy."

"I really don't want to talk about him."

"I have to know about him, Mum, everything about him."

"You should be at work, Jack."

"He was your husband, he's my father."

"Sam's right. It's nothing to do with us."

"Mum, it's killing us, just thinking about him. Talking about him can't hurt worse."

Hilda Perry couldn't remember the last time that Jack had come home in the middle of a working day. He hadn't told her of his visit to the Foreign Office, nor about the embassy, nor about the visit to the newspaper's library. They were in the kitchen with mugs of instant.

"Mum, he's in a death cell. Can you think of anywhere more alone than that. He's sitting out the last days of his life in a gaol where he's going to hang."

She said distantly, "I've hated him for more than twenty years, and since I had his letter I can only think of the good times."

"There were good times?"

"Don't make me cry, Jack."

"Tell me."

He brought her a drink. Two fingers of gin, three cubes of ice, four fingers of tonic. She normally had her first of the day when Sam came back from the office.

She drank deep.

"Your grandfather was stationed in Paderborn, that's in West Germany. He was a sergeant major. I was seventeen, just finished school. I used to nanny for the officers' wives. Jeez was on national service. He was a cut above the rest, not classy, not like an officer, but Jeez was always correct. Treated me like a lady. He always stood in a cinema for the national anthem, stood properly. We didn't go out much, a lot of evenings I was tied with the officers' kids and Jeez was a sort of batman and driver to the colonel. He was well in with the colonel. After we were married we used to get a card from the colonel each Christmas, not after Jeez went. Jeez went back to the UK, demobbed, we used to write a bit, and then Mum and Dad were killed in the car accident, it was in the papers. Jeez wrote by express, gave his address. I was staying with an aunt and he used to come and see me. I suppose I loved him, anyway we were married. There was a cottage right down in the country that Jeez got his hands on, near Alton in Hampshire. It was only a couple of bedrooms, pretty primitive, that's where we lived. He once said the colonel had helped him find it . . . Fill me up again, Jack."

He took her glass to the drinks cabinet in the living room. Three cubes of ice, six fingers of tonic. She wouldn't notice.

"He was born in 1933 and we married in '57, and I was nineteen. It was lovely down there, cress beds, trout streams, nice pubs, walks. Jeez didn't see much of it. He was up in London when he wasn't away."

She stopped. Her hands fondled the cut glass tumbler.

"He was very close, didn't talk about his work, only said that he was a clerk up in Whitehall. He called it a souped-up secretary's job."

32

She had never before talked calmly to her son about his father.

"Jeez used to take a train up to London, most of the year before it was light and come home in the evenings most of the year when it was dark. I didn't ask him where he went, he didn't tell me. He just said that what he did was pretty boring. He'd be away about half a dozen times a year, most often for about a week, sometimes as long as a month. I never knew where he went because he never brought me anything back from where he'd been, just flowers from Alton on his way home. Lovely flowers. Sometimes he looked as though he'd been in the sun, and it was winter at home. It's hard to explain now, Jack, but Jeez wasn't the sort of man you asked questions of, and I had my own life. I had the village, friends, I had my garden. There wasn't much money, but then nobody else round about had money. Then I had you . . ."

"What did he think about me?"

"Same as with everything else, you never really knew with Jeez. He used to do his turns with you at weekends. He'd change you, feed you, walk your pram. I honestly don't know what he felt."

"And when I was two years old?"

"You're interrogating me, Jack."

"In your own time."

"It's twenty-four years ago this month. He packed, always took the same small suitcase, always took five shirts, five pairs of socks, five sets of underwear, a second pair of trousers and a second jacket, and his washing bag. He went off on a Monday morning, said he'd be gone two weeks. Two weeks was three, three weeks was four. I was busy with you so until it was four weeks I was reasonably happy. Jeez wasn't the sort of man you chased up on. I can't explain that, but it's the way it was. Then at the end of four weeks there was money lodged in our account, the same amount as he always gave me, and I knew he'd walked out on me, on us. I went through the whole house looking for something about his work, there was nothing. Can you believe that? Not one single thing, not one scrap of paper with so much as a London phone number on it. No address book, no diary, not even a national insurance card. It was so horrible to realise I knew nothing about him. I rang the bank. I asked them where the money had come from. It had come from Liechtenstein, would you believe it? I had them send me the name of the bank. I wrote and I had a two line letter back. Regret not in a position to divulge. Divulge, dear God," she said and the tears were bright in her eyes. After a time she went on: "I went to a solicitor, he wrote and had the same answer. Jeez had gone from me . . . The money was the only way I knew he was still alive. Each January the sums he sent would go up as if Jeez was keeping abreast with the prices index. The month I married Sam they stopped. But by then I was long past caring. The only man I knew who knew Jeez at all was his old colonel. I wrote to him through his regiment, and he wrote back to say he was sorry, but he knew nothing of Jeez. There was just a wall, everywhere I turned."

"So you gave up?"

"You've no right to say that to me."

"No, I'm sorry."

"I did not give up. I carried on, trying to be a mother to you, trying to get the shame out of my system. Has it ever crossed your mind what it's like to live in a small community, a village, when you're marked down as the woman whose husband walked out. I did not give up, I was building our new life. I managed to shut Jeez out for two years, close him down. Two years, and then I couldn't stand the ignorance any longer. The solicitor had gone cold on me. I did it myself. One weekend I left you with a neighbour and I took the train to Chippenham, then a taxi to the address that had been on the colonel's letter. It was my last throw . . ." She stared once more into her glass.

"Was he there?"

"Entertaining, for lunch, guests on the patio, smart cars in the drive, uniformed drivers. They all looked at me very puzzled till the colonel came and took me inside to his study where the dogs were. He was obviously embarrassed. I suppose it wasn't easy for him . . . He said that your father had been some sort of clerk up in London in a government office, that his trips away had been couriering documents or working on low-level audits. He said Jeez was a deep, close man, without friends, but the opinion was that he'd just become restless, things too quiet for him, that he'd just upped and away. His advice was that I should try to put your father out of my mind and start again. He asked after you, and I can still see his sad smile when I showed him your photograph. I think he was trying to be kind to me . . . His wife brought me some sandwiches for the journey home. When the colonel brought me out of the house all his guests stopped eating, they were all staring at me. The colonel told one of the drivers to take me to the station. The next week I went to the solicitor and filed for divorce, desertion. That's when I gave up."

"Did he love you?"

"I thought so," she said simply.

"Can you believe he'd go along with murder and bombing, or be associated with black South African terrorists?"

"No."

Jack reached into his pocket, took out his wallet. He laid the newspaper photograph in front of his mother.

"Who's that?"

"That's Jeez today," he said. "That's my father."

Jack was annoyed, stamping about the field, time wasted. And this after he had broken off milking his mother's memories to get there punctually.

A small crowd waited on the blaster. There was the farmer who was selling the field, there were three from the development company which was buying the field. There were the JCB drivers, and the oxyacetaline cutting team, and the lorry men. There was a deputation from the housing estate three hundred yards from the pillbox rabbiting on to anyone who would listen about how all their windows would be broken.

The blaster was working quietly with his spade, filling sandbags.

Jack knew the blaster was slow. He knew also that the blaster was good, and he knew there was no use at all in offering to get anyone to help him. It was the blaster's way that he did his own work, himself, because as he'd often told Jack that way there wasn't any other bugger to get things wrong.

D & C used George Hawkins as often as he was available. He was their regular. They put up with the wizened little man's cussedness because the job was always done as it should have been, but every time they had him they cursed the old sod and asked themselves why they went on using him and always had the same answer. George would retire the day after they found another blaster who could do the job better.

A young man from the development company walked brusquely to them. His shoes were caked in mud. He had ripped his raincoat on barbed wire. He had come for an argument. Didn't they know they were running late? George Hawkins ignored him and Jack tried to shut him up with a sharp glance. Time was money, you know. George Hawkins spat to the ground and went on with his work.

"In fact your running late is causing us considerable inconvenience."

Jack said, "And unless you get out of this gentleman's way and let him get on with the job that he's damn good at then you'll be running even later."

The young man's moustache trembled on his lip. Jack thought it was shaved so thin that it might be touched up with eyeshadow.

"What I meant was . . ."

"Just make yourself scarce, and quickly."

The young man backed away. He'd seen the bloody-minded crack on Jack's face. He decided this wasn't a man to fight with.

The pillbox was part of a line that had been built along the Surrey uplands during the summer of 1940. If the Germans had landed on any of the beaches around the resort towns of Eastbourne or Brighton and if they had broken out of the beachhead then the high ground thirty miles to the north would have been the last defensive barrier before the southern outskirts of London. They might have been chaotic times, but they had known how to build pillboxes. It was squat, hexagonal, walls two feet thick with three machine-gun slits giving a wide view down towards the Surrey and Sussex county border. No one wanted the pillbox as a memento of the war. The farmer was selling his field, the developers were buying it for twelve houses to the acre, and anyway it was a hangout for the local teenagers and their plastic bags and solvent sniffing.

The last sandbag was filled, the top knotted.

"Do I have to carry 'em all myself?"

There was a titter of laughter. He had them all lifting his sandbags, right down to the developers in their shined footwear and styled raincoats.

Jack carried a sandbag beside George who carried two.

"You're running bloody late."

"It's been there close on fifty years, another fifteen minutes won't hurt."

They reached the pillbox. George stopped his helpers a dozen yards short.

"What are you going to use?"

"Got time for a lesson, have we?"

"Only asking."

"Get that shower back and I'll talk you through."

Jack waved the drivers and the farmer and the developers away.

He watched George work. All the time he worked he talked. A thin nasal voice describing the skills that he loved.

"I've drilled shot holes right through to the reinforcing net of wire, got me? Reinforced concrete, right, so there's wire in the middle. Each wall, I've got six shot holes a foot apart, and I've six more in the roof drilled vertically. For each hole there's three cartridges of P.A.G., that's Polar Ammon Gelignite to you. All in it's close to 20 pounds that's going to blow. Don't ever force the cartridges, see, don't mistreat the little fellows, just slide them in, like it's a bloody good woman you're with . . ."

Jack enjoyed working with the old man. For more than two years he'd been with George once a week, once every two weeks, and he was always made to feel it was his first time out. There hadn't been anything of a friendship between them until George had one day cried off a job, and Jack had been in his area and called by. He had found him alone with a twisted ankle and an empty larder and gone down the local shops and stocked the cupboard, and ignored all the moaning about not accepting charity. He'd called in a few more times till the old man was mended, but though they marked the binding of an unlikely friendship his visits were never referred to again.

"Bastard stuff this reinforced concrete. Takes double what you need to knock over brickwork . . ."

Jack knew that. He'd known that from the first time he'd worked with the old man. He just nodded, like he'd been given a jewel of new information.

The detonators went in on the end of white Cordtex, linked with safety fuse. Detonator ends crimped to the Cordtex, safety fuse tied to the Cordtex. Every shot hole had its own detonator, and in minutes the pillbox was covered with a web of wire.

"Always run the Cordtex and the safety fuse out carefully. Bastard if you get a kink in the stuff. You get a bloody misfire. What does a misfire mean? Means it's bloody dangerous when you get to dismantling the whole shooting match and starting all over. And another thing, Jack boy. You look a right prick if you've a shower of shit like that lot watching you."

He was wiring his cables into the charger box. George and Jack were more than a hundred yards back, down in a dip in the field's contours.

"Get that lot under cover, and get your hat on. One minute."

Jack bellowed back to the watchers and heard a police sergeant repeat the instruction by megaphone.

"You're a bloody vandal, Mr Hawkins."

"Get your nose up, so's you see. Twenty seconds."

Jack had a hard hat rammed down on the top of his head. He peered across the open ground to the pillbox.

"You all right, Jack? You're quiet today. Ten seconds."

"Fine."

He thought that if it had been put to the test the pillbox could have held up an infantry battalion for half a day. Graceless, strong and seemingly indestructible.

"Here we go."

Jack saw the flashes, then the debris moving upwards and outwards, then the smoke. He heard the echoing rumble of the detonations. He felt the blast of air on his face. He ducked his head.

"Bloody good," George growled.

Jack looked up. George was hunched beside him. The fortification was a rubble of concrete loosely held together by twisted wire.

There was a long thirty minutes before the blaster would allow the men forward who would cut through the wire with their torches.

When they stood at the edge of the rubble Jack marvelled at what Hawkins had achieved.

"That was pretty professional, Mr Hawkins."

"Explosives'll get you through anything, Jack boy, if you know how to use them."

4

On Tuesday and Thursday mornings Frikkie de Kok dressed in the bungalow's living room.

His alarm warbled quietly at three on those mornings. He dressed in the living room so as not to disturb Hermione. On those Tuesday and Thursday mornings he liked to dress well, to be at his best.

His wife knew why Frikkie rose early on those mornings, his sons did not. In a fashion she pretended that she did not know. Where he went and what he did as the dawn was rising on Pretoria, sometimes once a week, sometimes once a month, was never talked about between them. She knew, and in her own way she supported him. There were only small ways that she could help him at those times. She never troubled him with family difficulties or nagged at him to pay bills when she knew he had set the alarm for his early rising. He was sure that the boys, aged seventeen and fifteen, knew nothing of their father's work. The boys were the apples of Frikkie de Kok's eyes, especially Dawie, the elder.

He dressed in a white shirt, a tie that was the darkest blue, shoulder holster, a grey, almost charcoal suit and black shoes. He brushed his teeth brutally to try to erase the taste of yesterday's cigarettes. He took a glass of orange juice from the fridge. His wife wanted a new fridge and he could see from the packed shelves that the present one was inadequately small. Hermione had last mentioned the need for the new fridge on Sunday, she had not mentioned it on Monday. She'd be back again, he thought, tomorrow.

From behind the sofa he picked up his small case. He went to the front window, drew back the curtain and looked out. There were two cars waiting.

He left his home in the Waterkloof suburb of Pretoria at 3.40 on those Tuesday and Thursday mornings. He let the cars wait for two more minutes, then emerged from his porch at 3.39. The cars would be moving off at 3.40. His was an exact science, and he had nurtured exactness in most aspects of his life.

At the front door he paused. He could hear the faint sounds of his sons, asleep. They shouldn't have had to share a room, but all government salaries were falling behind the private sector. Costs were steepling and taxes too, and there was no chance of a larger bungalow so that the boys could each have a room of their own. Great boys, doing well at school, and they'd do well when they went into the army. The boys would be a credit to their father and mother because their parents had scrimped to give them an education that had not been possible for the young Frikkie de Kok. The boys thought that he worked as an instructor in the carpentry shops. Time enough to tell them what he did when they had finished their schooling and perhaps not even then. He closed the door gently behind him. There was no tightness in his legs, no nervousness as he walked. If Frikkie de Kok showed either emotion or hesitation then the effect on the men around him would be catastrophic

He saw the glow of two cigarettes in the second car. On those mornings he always had an escort of two plain clothes policemen. His work was classified as secret. When he went to the prison before dawn he always had the armed men in support and he carried his own hand gun in the shoulder holster.

The first car was driven by his assistant. A fine young man, heavily built, bull-necked, hands that could pick up a blown football, one in the right and one in the left. The assistant had been a policeman and had served in the *Koevoet* unit in the Owambo area of South West Africa. The "Crowbar" men were an elite inside the South African police confronting the S.W.A.P.O. insurgency campaign. The assistant was equally at home with the F.N. rifle, the M79 grenade launcher, 60mm mortars, and .50 cal machine guns. There was nothing squeamish about the assistant's attitude to his civilian work. Frikkie de Kok thought him the best of young South Africans. If Frikkie had had a daughter then he'd have been pleased for her to become his assistant's wife.

He climbed in beside his assistant and closed the door noiselessly.

The cars pulled away. Waterkloof was a fine suburb for Hermione to live in. They weren't in one of the better avenues, but it was a good district. They lived alongside good clean-living people. Just hellish expensive for a man who worked with his hands for the government.

The capital city of the Republic slept.

They came fast down Koningen Wilhelminoweg and past the bird sanctuary.

Frikkie loved birds, all of them from the big predators to the little songsters. When he retired he hoped to buy a small farm in the north east of the Transvaal, not that he would do much farming but he would be able to study the birds. All dependent on bastard politics. Farms were already selling cheap if they were up in the north east of the Transvaal because the farmers were quitting, and those that were staying were buying rifles and German Shepherds and spending their thin profits on high wire fences. Just like Rhodesia. But if he bought a farm he'd take some shifting. Take a big, big fire to burn out Frikkie de Kok if he'd put his life savings into a farm house and some acres and some stock.

In the centre of the city they came on the first of the corporation's street cleaners. No other sign of life. The city slept, and it didn't know and didn't care that in the state's name Frikkie de Kok and his assistant were going to work.

They drove through the empty streets, past the great buildings of commerce and government power. He had lived 35 years in the capital, he was proud to be a part of it. No way that the communists and the terrorists and the agitators were going to undermine the authority of Pretoria. Over Frikkie de Kok's dead body . . . They turned onto Potgieterstraat. Nearly there. He noticed that the breath came faster from his assistant. He'd learn. Frikkie de Kok had been like that, panting, tightening when he was the assistant to his uncle, and he'd conquered it.

They went under the railway bridge.

The floodlights of Pretoria Central were in front of them.

The assistant was changing down, slipping his clutch, shaking the car before the right turn in front of Local. Frikkie de Kok never criticised his assistant. On from Local and past the high walls of the White politicals gaol. They came to the checkpoint. From his hut the armed prisons man stepped into the middle of the road. The lowered bar was behind him. The assistant dipped his lights. The prisons man cradled an F.N. More than a hundred times a year this car and Frikkie de Kok and his assistant came up this side road, Soetdoringstraat, to the road block. They held their ID cards up against the windscreen. The prisons man had seen their faces, good enough for him. The car slid under the raised bar, was inside the perimeter of the prison complex.

Left now, past the prison service store on Wimbledon Road, past the prison service swimming pool, past the prison service tennis courts, past the rows of prison service houses and flats, past the old gaol where he had worked his apprenticeship with his uncle.

A long lit wall rose in front of them. They were high on the wooded hillside above the scattered lights of Pretoria.

They were at Beverly Hills. And in Frikkie de Kok's opinion that was a hell of a silly name to be given to a section of a gaol. But maximum security had always been Beverly Hills to both the prison staff who came in and out on their shift pattern and to the inmates on their one way visit. Beverly Hills, Frikkie had heard, was a flash hotel down in Durban. Frikkie disliked Durban. Too many English down there, too many liberals, not his place for a holiday. But the new gaol, opened eighteen years before, the most modern in the country, and the most secure, was Beverly Hills to all who talked of it. The most modern and the most secure.

The detectives parked the escort car. They would wait outside for Frikkie and his assistant until their work was done.

The assistant drove to the gates. The lights beamed down on them. A television camera jutting from the wall followed them. By a hidden hand the gates glided open. The car drove inside. The gates closed behind. More gates in front. An airlock. Close walls. An iron grille for a roof.

Through a glass panel a warrant officer looked down into the car from his control centre.

The assistant wound down his window, showed their two cards perfunctorily, then passed their hand guns up to the waiting hand. It was two minutes to four o'clock. The gates ahead of them opened and they drove on.

The hangman and the hangman's assistant had reached their place of work. All of the "condemns" who had been sentenced to death in courts throughout the Republic were brought to Beverly Hills to while away the months before their appeal, before the State President deliberated on the matter of clemency. All of the condemns whose appeal failed, whose plea for clemency was rejected, died on the Republic's single gallows beam in Beverly Hills.

They were in a small parkland. Their headlights caught a startled antelope and a warthog in the white light. Frikkie thought it a good thing that a hanging gaol should harbour a small nature park between the perimeter walls and the cell blocks. He liked to see the animals. If he had been asked he would have said that he thought it unfortunate that the cells of the condemns did not have windows that looked out onto the animals. The windows were set too high for the condemns to see out. But Frikkie was never asked what he thought, and he would not have ventured an opinion of any matter that was not his business.

As soon as he was inside the administration with its cathedral steps he heard the singing. The singing used to upset him when he first came to the old Pretoria Central with his uncle. He had learned through his uncle's indifference to accept it. The whole of A section and B section singing, all of the Black condemns. Not a sound from C section, the White condemns hardly ever sang. Frikkie de Kok was a regular churchgoer, he knew his hymns. He'd never heard singing the like of that in Beverly Hills on the mornings that he worked. Wonderful hymns that the Blacks had learned in the mission schools and their own fine natural rhythm. When the Black condemns sang about Jesus, then they sang with feeling and with love. Best thing. He had many times told his assistant, the singing helped their work.

They were escorted to the duty officer's room. They were given coffee.

The singing helped because it calmed the condemns who were to be handled that morning. The singing gave them strength, seemed to drug them, meant they didn't give any trouble.

Creamy coffee and sugar. Only half a cup. As Frikkie had told his assistant, he didn't want his bladder under strain when he was working.

There hadn't been any trouble for years, but the trouble then had been so bad that Frikkie de Kok would never forget it, so if the singing helped to quieten the boys then that was fine by him. His last assistant had packed it in after that piece of trouble. Four condemns had barricaded themselves in a cell and they couldn't be forced out when the execution detail came for them. They'd sent for the riot gas canisters and the whole block had been screaming, and they'd kept Frikkie de Kok waiting. Once they'd opened the doors the execution detail had moved so fast that they hadn't stopped to get their masks off before they reached the gallows building.

The duty officer passed a remark about the weather. He didn't think it would rain, not from the forecast given the previous evening on the S.A.B.C. It hadn't rained for three and a half months in Pretoria so it was a fair bet that it wouldn't rain. Frikkie just acknowledged him. The assistant didn't speak.

Most of them went well. Most of them had a lot of guts. The Whites always went well, especially after the Blacks were gassed to the gallows. The sort of

White that he hanged was the sort of guy who wanted to show that he had more guts than a Black.

At three minutes to five Frikkie de Kok levered himself up from the easy chair. He nodded his thanks to the duty officer for the coffee.

They crossed the prison. There was the slither of their shoes, and the crack of the boots of their escort. There were voices that warned of their approach so that doors could be opened ahead of them. The singing was rising to its pitch.

They climbed the steps.

Frikkie de Kok pushed open the heavy double doors. This was his preserve, where his orders were not questioned. He was in the preparation room. A high room, brilliantly lit by a fluorescent strip. There were a dozen men waiting there, all in the uniform of the prison service. He recognised three of them, they were three who were always there. It was a job of work for Frikkie de Kok, but he always marvelled that some made it their business to be present each and every time. The other nine were youngsters, five Black and four White. It was the law of Beverly Hills that every man who served there must attend a hanging. None of these execution virgins caught his eye.

He opened the interior door. He switched on the lights. No official from the prison service would have presumed to go ahead of him. The gallows room was a blaze of light. Along the far wall, where the railed steps went below, lay the shadows of the long beam and four nooses. The four ropes above the nooses were coiled and fastened with cotton thread. It was as he had left it the previous day when he had made his arrangements, tested the lever and the trap, measured each rope for the drop, made his calculations based on height and weight.

The district surgeon came to him. There was the first sheen of dawn in the skylight. The district surgeon told him that the four men were in good shape and none of them had asked for sedation. The district surgeon, a pale-faced gangling young man, was the only person that Frikkie de Kok would speak to at this time. That was privileged and valuable information.

He stood on the trap. Firm.

He wrapped his fist on the lever. Shining and oiled.

He looked at the cotton holding up the nooses to chest height. Correct.

He glanced at his watch. Three minutes before half past five.

He nodded to the duty officer waiting at the door of the preparation room. The duty officer raised his personal radio to his mouth.

Frikkie de Kok knew of the crimes for which the four had been convicted. One had stabbed to death a White housewife after they had disagreed on what he should be paid for sweeping her drive. One had raped a six-year-old girl, White, and strangled her. One had shot to death a petrol station attendant during an armed robbery in East London. One had been sentenced to death for ritual witchcraft murder, the killing of two men and the cutting out of their organs for *muti*. To Frikkie de Kok's mind execution by hanging was the correct penalty for such crimes.

42

He had stipulated in which order the four should be brought down the corridor and into the preparation room. He had heard once of a mistake, many years ago, before his uncle's time. Two men, one heavy and tall, one slim and small, brought in the wrong order. The small fellow had had the short rope and they'd had to pull on his legs under the trap. The big fellow had been on the long drop and nearly lost his head with his life.

Frikkie de Kok had never made a mistake.

The singing approached him. A tumult of harmony. He liked it when they were brave because that made it easy for him, and if it were easy for him then he could do better by them.

He waved the spectators into the gallows room and over to the far wall. He saw that the governor had arrived in the preparation room. They acknowledged each other. Frikkie straightened his tie.

A good hymn. Not four weeks before that hymn had been sung in his church in Waterkloof. Sung in Afrikaans, of course. Good theme, good words. He had the four freshly laundered white cotton hoods in his hand.

They came fast into the preparation room. The first man had a prison officer supporting one arm and the chaplain the other, the three that followed had a prison officer on each side of them.

They were wide-eyed, they were shivering. In the preparation room the words of the hymn died in their throats and the chaplain sang on alone, lustily. All the reading of the warrants, all the formalities, had been completed back in the cell block . . . time now just to get the work finished. Frikkie de Kok remembered each face from the view he had had of them in the exercise yard the previous afternoon. They were in the right order. He nodded his head. No man spoke in the hanging shed, only the chaplain sang. The four whimpered and seemed to fight to find their voices. They were moved inside. Moved onto the trap. If it were one man, or even two, then the assistant would have pinioned the legs, but with four it was necessary for the hangman to take two and his assistant to take two. They moved quickly and quietly behind the men, fastening the leather thongs. The chaplain was in front of them. The chaplain knew he was at God's will, otherwise how could he have looked them in the face.

Hoods on.

Two of them were singing. Muffled, indistinct, quavering.

Nooses round the necks. Frikkie did this himself. Tightened the knot under each of the left side jaw bones. He saw the feet in line of the trap. He flicked his hand. The prison officers stepped back, releasing their hold on the condemns.

With both hands he gripped the lever.

The explosion of the trap.

Jeez lay rigid on his bunk.

His breath came in great pants.

The silence.

He had heard the feet stamping and shuffling on their way to the gallows. He had heard the swell of the singing, seeking out new heights of sympathy. Then the crash of the trap.

An awful sorrowing silence. The singing was to support four men, and the men were gone from where singing could boost them. The singing had ceased with the fall of the trap, cut in mid phrase.

The God awful silence around Jeez, like he was alone, like he was the only man in the bloody place.

He always heard the trap go.

He heard it the day before when the hangman was practising his drops with the earth-filled sacks, he heard it go on the morning of a hanging. As the crow flies or the worm crawls, Jeez lay on his bed just 29 yards from the gallows beam. He heard everything in the hanging room, and everything in the workshop and the washhouse underneath. They'd be suspended now, they let them hang for twenty minutes. Then there would be the water running in the washhouse as they cleared up the mess after the district surgeon had completed his postmortem. Then there would be the hammering in the workshop as the trusties nailed down the coffin lids. Last there would be the sounds of the revving of an engine and the sounds of the van pulling away, running down the hill.

Beverly Hills wasn't a place for seeing what happened. Christ, it was a place for hearing.

Listen to a multiple execution.

Singing, trap, silence, water, silence, hammering, van engine.

Those were the sounds of four men getting to be stiffs. God Almighty, Jeez . . . It was the route they had in mind for Jeez. While he had been at Beverly Hills he had heard the sounds of one hundred and twenty-one guys getting stretched. And now one hundred and twenty-five. Jeez had heard the trap go under each last one of the mothers.

He shouldn't have written the letter all the same.

The letter was weakness. Shouldn't have involved her. But he had heard the trap go so many times. Shit, and he had to call for *someone* . . . he felt so alone.

This was a civilised gaol, not like the one a long time back. There were no beatings here, no malnutrition, no rats, no disease, no forced labour. Here, his cell door wouldn't be thrown open without warning for a kicking and a truncheon whipping. No risk that he would be frog marched into a yard and kicked down and shot in the nape of the neck. This was five star. So bloody civilised that Jeez had sat in a cell for more than a year, a cell that measured six foot by nine foot, while the lawyers debated his life. Three meals a day here, a good medic here, because they wanted him healthy on the day. He had written his letter because he was losing hope.

What were the bastards doing? Why hadn't the bastards got him out?

He hated himself for believing they'd forgotten him. They'd got him out the last time. Took the bastards long enough, but they'd got him out. They couldn't let a man, one of their own, couldn't let him . . . never finished. Couldn't let him . . . Course they couldn't. He hated himself when the hope went, because that wasn't the Jeez way.

He was one of a team, a bloody good team, a team that didn't forget the men out in the field.

He was fine on the days when he didn't hear the trap fall. It was only on those sodding days that the doubts bit.

He'd done them well. He'd kept his mouth shut through interrogation, bloody weeks of it. He'd kept his mouth shut through the trial. He'd kept his mouth shut when the security police from Johannesburg and the intelligence men from Pretoria had come to talk to him in his cell. He hadn't let the team down.

Jeez heard the spurting of the water hose in the washhouse.

On the high ceiling of the cell the bulb brightened.

Another day. God Almighty, it just wasn't possible that the team had forgotten about Jeez.

In an hour, and after he had eaten his breakfast, he would hear the hammering start.

It was difficult ground for the Minister. Any by-election would be in these days, but the Orange Free State was the heartland of the Afrikaner world. A dozen years before, in Petrusburg and Jacobsdal and Koffiefontein, he'd been cheered to the echo by the White farmers when he talked of the inviolability of the policy of separate development. Today he would have to speak to the same White farmers with the currency collapsed, with further foreign sanctions in the air, with unrest in the townships, with taxes up, with markets disappearing. No easy matter up here to sell the ending of the homelands policy, to uphold the repeal of the Immorality Act, to defend their record in the collapse of law and order. One thing for the State President and his ministers to talk in Pretoria about dismantling separate development, quite another out in the constituencies to explain to the faithful the reasons for the retreat. They had a big enough majority in Parliament, the National Party, but by-elections counted. The most recent by-elections had shown the subsidence of the Party's vote and the increase of the pulling power of the Conservative right. The State President was enjoying the greasepaint and the television lights and his broadcasts via satellite to the American networks where he spoke earnestly of reform. The ministers, the donkeys, they were the ones who legged it down to the grass roots to explain that everything that was traditional and taught from the mother's knee was now subject to revision.

The Minister of Justice had a long day in front of him. Public meetings at breakfast, midday and late afternoon. The by-election was to be held in twenty-seven days' time. The Minister of Justice had been preceded by Water Affairs, Forestry and Environment Conservation, and by Community Development and State Auxiliary Services. In this constituency alone he would be followed before polling day by State Administration and Statistics, by Transport Affairs, and by Minerals and Energy.

The minister had slept in the back of the car for most of the drive from Bloemfontein to Petrusburg. He woke when they were three miles short of the town. His secretary passed him a battery shaver. The secretary sat in the front beside the police driver. In the back of the Mercedes with the minister was the local area Chairman of the Party, a fellow Broederbonder.

"What'll they be like?"

"Cool."

"Which means iced." The minister strained his chin upwards to get the razor's teeth against the skin of his jowl.

"We all want to know what the future holds."

"Change."

"You won't find this audience applauding talk about change. They like the old ways. They want reassurance that *we're* running our country, not American bankers."

"I'll get them laughing . . ."

"You'd have to get your trousers off to get a laugh."

"What do they want?"

"To know that our government is not abdicating its responsibilities in the face of overseas pressure, and Black pressure. Persuade them and we might just win."

"It's rubbish to talk of abdication."

The Party man shrugged. "Fine when you say that to me. Tell your audience that and they'll shout you out of the hall, I promise you."

"What'll satisfy them?"

"You know the name of Prinsloo?"

"Should I?"

"Gerhardt Prinsloo."

"Don't know"

"His parents live in Petrusburg."

"Don't give me riddles, man," the minister snapped.

They were coming into the town. One street on a main road, low buildings, a small shopping arcade, a decent church.

"His father runs a hardware store. His mother teaches in the nursery school. You should go to Gerhardt Prinsloo's grave."

"If I knew who he was."

"Everyone in Petrusburg knows the name of Gerhardt Prinsloo. He's the nearest thing they have to a genuine South African hero."

"Tell me, man."

"If the people here thought that you didn't know who Gerhardt Prinsloo was and what he did, then I assure you our vote would be halved."

"What did he do?"

"Warrant officer Gerhardt Prinsloo gave his life to save others. He smothered the terrorist bomb in the Rand Supreme Court . . ."

46

The minister bit his lip in anger. "You caught me cold, early in the morning."

"I've heard it said in this town that our government of today is so preoccupied with foreign opinion, with the shouting of the liberals, with appeasement, that the men who murdered Gerhardt Prinsloo might receive the State President's clemency."

The minister leaned forward, tapped his secretary's shoulder. "Give me my speech and your pen."

Resting the speech on his knee he made a long addition to the back of the first page.

The car came to a stop. There was desultory applause from a small group of the faithful out to greet the minister.

"Straight after my speech I will visit the grave. I will lay some flowers there, and I want a photographer."

A tiny cramped cell, Jeez's home for thirteen months.

In the top half of the heavy door was an aperture covered by close mesh, too close to get the fingers through. Beside the door, and looking out onto the corridor of C section 2 was a window of reinforced glass. Against the far wall to the door was the flush toilet, and beside that, set in a cavity, was a drinking water fountain. If he sat on his bed, at the far end of the pillow, then his legs fitted comfortably underneath the work surface area that jutted out from the wall. He had brought no personal mementos with him to Beverly Hills, there were no decorations on the walls, no mementoes of any previous condemns. Eight feet above the floor a heavy metal grille made a false ceiling. The cell was sixteen feet high. On the corridor wall, above the grille, were slatted windows, and the guard who patrolled the catwalk above the corridor had a clear view down through these windows into the cell. In the ceiling the light burned, bright by day, dimmed by night, always burning. No daylight could reach the cell. Natural light came from windows above the catwalk, and then by proxy into the windows above Jeez. From his cell he could see no blue sky, could never see the stars. The windows onto the catwalk and into the cell were always open, so the temper of the seasons reached him. Stinking hot in high summer, frosty cold in winter. Now the cool of the autumn was coming. He doubted that he would shiver again in the winter cold.

He had eaten his breakfast, he had shaved under supervision, he had swept out his cell. He waited for his turn in the exercise yard. Other than his turn in the exercise yard, this day would go by without him leaving his cell.

He was the celebrity, the first White political to face death by hanging since John Harris and that was more than twenty years before. No one who worked in Beverly Hills had ever before handled a White political who was condemned. Many times in each day he would look up from his bed to the corridor window and see the flash of a pale face, the face of a watcher. They might have had a camera on Jeez for all the time they watched him. They watched him while he slept and while he ate and while he read and while he sat on the lavatory.

He knew why they watched him, and why his shoes were slip-ons and without laces, and why he had no belt, and why there were adhesive tabs on his prison tunic in place of buttons.

When he had first arrived at Beverly Hills he had been told why they would watch him. One guy, a White, had once stood on his bed and nose-dived onto the concrete floor to try to cheat them out of his appointment. No chance that they would provide Jeez with an opportunity not to show for his appointment.

Because Jeez was a political he was allowed no association with the other two White condemns in C section 2. They were new boys. One had moved in three weeks before, and one had been there for four months, and three had gone because their sentences had been commuted to imprisonment. The other White condemns were permitted to exercise together in the yard leading off C section 2, but Jeez was only taken out when they were back and locked in. Jeez's cell was at the far end of the section corridor. The cells of the other two condemns were opposite each other and beside the door that led to the main C section corridor; there were empty cells separating the White criminals from the White political. He had never seen their faces. He had heard their voices in the corridor. He knew they called him the "bleddy commie" or the "bleddy ter". These two bastards wouldn't be singing for him, not if it came to him keeping his appointment.

Sergeant Oosthuizen was the prison officer who had responsibility most days for Jeez. Most days Sergeant Oosthuizen escorted Jeez to the exercise yard.

Each time he heard the slam of the door that separated the main C section corridor from the C section 2 corridor, and each time he heard the key slot into his cell door he hoped, a short soaring hope, that the governor was coming with the message that would tell Jeez that the team had not abandoned him.

They always slammed the door between the main corridor and C section 2.

The team had been his life. The team was names and faces, clear as photographs, no blurring with time. The captain of the team was Colonel Basil, big and bluff and with thin blue veins surfacing on apple red cheeks. The men in the team were Lennie who had a patter of whip crack jokes, and Adrian who flirted with the fresh new recruits, and Henry who on a Friday evening at the end of the working office week played the piano in the saloon bar of the pub that the Century men used. Colonel Basil and Lennie and Adrian and Henry were his team and his life.

He hadn't let them down, neither a long time ago nor in Johannesburg. Of course they'd be working for him, moving bloody mountains for him. Probably old Colonel Basil would have set up a special task force desk to supervise the prising of Jeez out of the hole he was in.

Sergeant Oosthuizen was smiling at him from the opened cell door. They were cutting it rather fine. Hell of a good time he'd had on the team, the real friendships, home and away. Being on the team mattered, because membership of the team was the guarantee. Shit, the guarantee was important to a leg man. It said that the team would never stop working their balls off for a leg man who was in trouble. And Christ, was he in trouble. Jeez Carew, member of the team, was going to hang. And his faith in the team was slipping.

"Nice morning for a walk. Come on, Carew."

The solicitor had driven that morning from Johannesburg because it was useless to telephone for information, and worse than useless to write letters to the Justice Ministry.

He was not shown in to the civil servant's office until after the lunch hour.

It was a brittle meeting. The elderly Afrikaner South African and the young English heritage South African. The man on government pay and the man on private practice.

The solicitor's questions were blunt enough.

Had the decision been taken by the State President on whether James Carew would hang?

The civil servant had parried. "The decision has been taken, but the decision is not yet public."

Could the solicitor's client know of the decision of the State President?

"He'll know when he needs to know."

Surely, if he was going to get clemency then he should be told immediately?

"If he's not going to get clemency then he's better not knowing."

Couldn't the solicitor be given an indication of the State President's thinking?

"Look, I'm not going to tell you what is the State President's opinion. The way we do it is this, the deputy sheriff will go to the gaol not more than four or five days before an execution and he will then inform a prisoner that the appeal to the State President has been turned down. I'm not saying for certain that the sentence will stand in the case of your client, but I can tell you that if it does stand you will know at the same time that Carew knows."

It had been spelled out to him. The young solicitor softened.

"Not for Carew, but for me to know."

"You're asking me to read the mind of the State President."

"A bit of guidance."

"The minister was in Petrusburg this morning. He made an addition to his prepared speech. He said . . . 'There are people who say that your government is soft on the matter of law and order. We are not. There are people who say that our legal processes can be influenced by the threats of foreign governments. They can not. There are people who say that terrorists will get away with murder in our fine country. They will not. I warn people who seek to bring down our society that they will face the harshest penalties under our law, whether they be White or Black, whether they be our citizens or jackals from outside.' . . . It's not me that's answering your questions, it is my minister."

"How long?"

"Not long, not a month."

"It's cut and dried?"

"Listen. At the moment we have a police strength of around 45,000. In ten years we will have a force of more than 80,000. Right now we have to fight this unrest with an under strength force. If any South African police line cracks then there is nothing to save us from anarchy. We have to sustain the morale of the police or we go under, and supporting the morale is not best served by reprieving police murderers."

"I appreciate that you've spoken to me in confidence. What can save my client?"

The civil servant examined the file in front of him. He was a long time turning the pages. He looked up, he gazed steadily at the solicitor.

"If at this late stage your client were to give to the security police every detail of his knowledge of the African National Congress, then there might be grounds for clemency in his case alone."

"The others would go?"

"We could handle one reprieve, not more. We have never understood why your client ever involved himself in terrorism, and he hasn't helped us. If we had names, safe houses, arms caches, everything he knew, then we could talk about clemency."

"Guaranteed?"

Fractionally the eyebrows of the civil servant lifted.

"You should tell him to talk to the security police, that's all that can save him."

Sergeant Oosthuizen stood by the locked door of the exercise yard and talked. He talked of his daughter who was big in wind-surfing down on the Cape, and of his son who owned a liquor store in Louis Trichardt.

Sergeant Oosthuizen had been 38 years in the prison service, the last eleven of them in Beverly Hills. He was to retire in the next month, and then he'd be able to spend time with his daughter and his son. Sergeant Oosthuizen didn't require Jeez to have a conversation with him. He just talked, that was what he was happiest at.

It was more of a garden than an exercise yard. Against the walls was concrete paving. Each wall was nine paces long. Thirty-six paces for a circuit. Forty-nine circuits was a mile's walk. The centre of the yard was Jeez's garden. The soil was twelve inches deep, then concrete. It was Jeez's garden because none of the other condemns showed any interest in it. The garden had not been looked after since a child killer had gone to the rope the month before Jeez arrived at Beverly Hills. Last spring Oosthuizen had brought Jeez seed. The geraniums had done well, the marigolds had threatened to take over, the chrysanthemums had failed. Jeez crouched on his haunches and picked discoloured leaves and old blooms off the geraniums. The sunlight was latticed over the bed and the concrete by the shadow of the grid above him. The garden was a cell. The song birds could manage it through the grid and out again, but nothing as large as a pigeon could have squeezed down to feed from the grubs that he turned up when he weeded his flowers.

In the exercise yard Jeez could see the sky and he could feel a trapped slow breath of wind, but he could see no trees, and no buildings, and no men other than Sergeant Oosthuizen and sometimes the guard at his catwalk window. He could see the wall of C section 2, and the outer wall, and the wall of C section 3, and the wall of the C section corridor. If he stood with his back to the wall of C section 2 and raised himself onto tip-toe he could look over the roof of C section 3 onto the upper brickwork of the hanging room.

He wondered if Sergeant Oosthuizen would have retired before it was his turn, Jeez's turn, to take the early walk. He wondered if the sergeant would walk with him.

That was stupid thinking, because there was no way the team would let it happen. Burning the candle they'd be. Couldn't for the life of him think how the team would pull him out. Thought about it often enough, but couldn't work it out. Colonel Basil wasn't the one for ideas, nor Lennie. Adrian was good with ideas, better than Henry. Have to be Adrian who was going to crack it, and then the team would all thrash it round. Wouldn't see their feet for dust once they'd settled on an idea. Clear memories, faces clear in his mind, Colonel Basil, and Lennie who had the limp from the ambush in Cyprus, and Adrian who'd bloody near lost his career in the gentlemen's toilet at Piccadilly underground, and Henry . . . Shit, and wouldn't Henry have been up for retirement, gone to breed the bloody pigeons he always talked of. What if they'd all gone? Couldn't have done . . . All bloody older than Jeez. Colonel Basil was, certain, Henry was. Bloody Lennie *looked* older. Couldn't tell Adrian's age, not with the hair rinse. What if they weren't there at Century . . . ? Stupid thinking. No way the team would let him hang.

"Carew, I'm speaking to you."

Jeez started up. "Sorry, Sergeant."

"You weren't listening to me."

"Sorry, Sergeant, I was far away."

"You don't want to brood, you know. It's where we're all going. You don't want to think too much."

"No, Sergeant."

"Why I was talking to you was that I'd just seen your fingers, first and second on your right hand. How long is it since I've been with you?"

"It's thirteen months, Sergeant."

"And I've never noticed your fingers before."

"Just fingers, Sergeant."

"I've never noticed them before, and my wife says I'm the noticing kind."

"What didn't you notice, Sergeant?"

"No nails on the first and second fingers of your right hand."

Jeez looked down. Pink skin had grown over the old scars. "Someone took them out, Sergeant."

"Ingrowing, were they? I once had an ingrowing big toe nail, when I was serving at the old Johannesburg Fort gaol. That's closed now. They thought they might have to take it off, but they cut it back and it grew again, but not in. Hell's painful."

"Someone took them out for fun, Sergeant. Can we go inside now, please, Sergeant."

"Who took them out for fun . . . That's a very serious allegation."

"Long ago, Sergeant, long before South Africa."

He could remember the pliers grasping at the nails of the first and second fingers of his right hand. Pain rivers in his whole body. He could remember the smile of the bastard as he jerked the nails off. He hadn't talked to the bastard who had ripped his nails off, just as he hadn't talked to the security police in Johannesburg.

"And you get yourself washed up for the medic."

They went inside. Jeez going first and Sergeant Oosthuizen following and locking the door to the exercise yard. The doctor saw Jeez once a week, and weighed him. Jeez knew why he was weighed each week.

Sergeant Oosthuizen stood by the door of Jeez's cell.

"That must have hurt when they took them out."

"A long time ago, Sergeant."

5

Hilda Perry liked to see her family on its way in the morning.

Sam had taken Will to school, and ten minutes later she was back at the front door holding Jack's raincoat ready for him. He came hurrying down the stairs. If he ever managed to get himself married or get a flat of his own, she'd truly miss him. She always thought it was because of the time they had been together, the abandoned wife and the fatherless son, that they had a special bond . . . He wasn't sleeping properly, she could see the eye bags. She reckoned she looked the same.

Today she hugged her boy. She knew they were both thinking of the man half way round the world from them in a cell, thinking of the man she wouldn't have recognised, her Jack couldn't have remembered. He told her he would be home early, he would have seen her gratitude. They'd keep a sort of vigil in the house, the two of them, for however many days and weeks it took, until Jeez was . . . Just the two of them. Sam didn't know, but she'd started to take Librium three days earlier, just one tablet each night when she was getting into bed, so that she wouldn't dream. She shrugged him into his raincoat. He managed a smile for her, and was away down the front path to his car. The telephone rang behind her. She wanted to see Jack go before answering the telephone, but he had taken a chammy out of his car and was cleaning the windscreen. She went back into the hall and lifted the telephone.

"Could I speak to Mr Curwen, please?"

She could see Jack at the rear window, finishing off.

"Who is it?"

"Name's Jimmy Sandham. He'd want to speak to me."

She ran awkwardly in her slippers down the path. The engine was starting, coughing. She caught him just in time.

She saw the frown. She heard him say, "I'll be right with you."

He put the telephone down.

"Only work, Mum."

She knew when he lied. She had always known. He was away, running down the path. She thought she was losing him. Could no longer reach him in the way she had before. He had changed when he had broken with that nice Miriam. She knew what had happened from Miriam's mother when a rain squall had driven them off the course into the lounge of the golf club. Something methodical and cheerless about his life. Two nights a week, after work, at the squash courts, working himself out until he was near sick from exhaustion . . . and the same with his studies again, picking up the lost degree course, working late into the nights. She preferred him the way he had been before, when he was with Miriam. She could never understand how he had lost the degree chance, thrown it up four months from his finals, seemed ridiculous to her, and so trivial.

She watched him drive away.

He had been so matter of fact that evening. He had come home from college and told her that his university days were finished. He'd told her the circumstances, like they didn't matter. A single student who was a paid-up member of a Fascist party being heckled by a group of Trotskyites between chemical engineering and applied mathematics. A point of principle, he'd said flatly, didn't like bullies. He'd told the Trots to leave it, they hadn't and they'd jostled the lad and were spitting in his face. Remembered Jack remarking that he'd thrown a punch, broken a boy's jaw. So matter of fact. Jack spelling it out that he had been up before the disciplinary court of the senate that morning, and the provost had asked him for an apology, and his reply that he would do it again, because it was bullying, and being told that he must give the assurance, and refusing, and being told that he'd have to leave, and leaving. Telling it like it wasn't important, telling it just like Jeez would have. And here he was, back at his books.

She closed the door. She was alone with herself. The Librium didn't last into the morning. She worked at speed with the hoover and the dusters and the brush and pan, upstairs round the beds and downstairs through the kitchen.

The front door bell rang.

It was a cosy and predictable household. It was her home that was being damaged by nightmares and sedation pills and lies. The doorbell rang again. She didn't want to answer it, she didn't even want to go to the door and peer through the spy hole. Another long ringing. The milkman had already been, the post was on the sideboard in the hall beside the telephone, the newspaper was on the kitchen table. She looked through the fish eye spy hole. It was a tall man, still short of middle age she thought, and he wore a light grey suit and his face was tanned and his moustache was clipped short into a crescent over his upper lip. She tightened the belt on her housecoat. The door chain was hanging loose, unfastened.

She opened the door.

The man was smiling.

"Mrs Perry? Mrs Hilda Perry?" A soft casual voice.

"Yes."

"Did you used to live, Mrs Perry, at 45 Green Walk, Coulsdon, in Surrey?" Another smile. She couldn't place the accent. There was a lilt in his speech that wasn't English.

"Yes."

"Could I come inside, please, Mrs Perry?"

"I don't buy anything at the front door."

"It's about a letter you had, Mrs Perry."

"What letter?"

"You had a letter from a Mr James Carew in Pretoria Central prison. My name's Swart, it would be easier to talk inside."

She recognised the accent as South African. "What if I did have such a letter?"

"I'm from the embassy, consular section. The letter Mr Carew wrote to you is the only letter he's written to anyone inside or outside our country. We're trying to help Mr Carew. Sometimes a man's background, his personal history, can help a prisoner in his situation. It would be better if I was inside."

Because Jack had lied to her that morning she was fine tuned to a lie. She knew this man lied. The man was taller than her even though he stood on the step below the front door.

"If you could help us with Mr Carew's background, his friends and his work and so on, then there might be something you told us that could make a difference to his situation."

Whatever he said he smiled. She wondered if he had been on a course to learn how to smile. She knew Jeez's letter word by word. Each guarded sentence was in her mind. Jeez didn't want them to know that Hilda Perry was his wife, that Jack was his son.

"I've nothing to say to you."

"I don't think you understand me, Mrs Perry. James Carew is going to hang. What I'm trying to do is to find out something that might lead to a reprieve."

His foot was in the doorway. Jeez wouldn't have wanted him in her house, she was sure of that.

"I just want you to go away."

The smile oiled across his face, and then he was inside the hall.

"Why don't we just sit down and talk, Mrs Perry, with a cup of tea."

She thought of the good years with Jeez, and the misery without him. She thought of the way she had willed herself to hate him after he had gone. She would have sworn that the man who had pushed himself into her home was Jeez's enemy.

She picked up the telephone. She dialled fast.

"Who are you ringing?"

"Police, please," she said into the telephone.

"That's a hell of a stupid thing to be doing."

"Mrs Hilda Perry, I've an intruder in my house – 45 Churchill Close."

"Are you trying to put a rope round his neck?"

"Please come straight away."

She put the telephone down. She turned to face him.

"They're very good round here, very quick. Why don't you come into the kitchen and sit down, and then you can explain to the officer who you are and what you want."

Cold anger, no smile. "He'll hang, Mrs Perry."

He was gone through the door. She saw him trotting down the path. When he was outside the garden he started to run.

Years of placid and sedate domestic life were disintegrating. For a long, long time she had loathed Jeez. For the last few short days she could remember only the times that she had loved him.

By the time the police car turned into Churchill Close, Major Hannes Swart was two miles away, going fast and fuming.

It had taken him long enough to track Hilda Perry from the address used by the prisoner, Carew. Some good, honest footslogging had translated Green Walk into Churchill Close, and for nothing. Swart had been in the South African police for seventeen years, but he hadn't done footslogging for more than a dozen. Security police officers were too precious to have their time wasted on door-to-door and scene-of-crime.

For some of his work he was a businessman promoting in the United Kingdom the sale of Stellenbosch wines. At other times he was an accredited journalist at the Foreign Press Association specialising in financial affairs. Most often he was a lowly member of the visa section of the embassy's consular staff. He worked to a police brigadier from the fifth floor of the embassy. He was one of the bright stars amongst the detail of security police officers assigned abroad. He had blown what ought to have been a simple task. A dowdy housewife had seen him off.

By the time a bemused police officer was leaving Churchill Close, having been told only that a South African male had tried to force entry into the house, no explanations of why, the temper of Major Swart had matured to controlled fury. They should have jazzed the swine, used the helicopter on him, and the electrics when they had him in John Vorster Square. Too damn correct they had been with him in the interrogation cells.

And a hell of a damn good thing that he had taken the precaution of parking his car out of Churchill Close. At least the cow didn't have the number plate to add to whatever bloody story she hatched to the local force.

Sandham had said that this was an, ah, irregular meeting, if you follow.

He sat with Jack in a tea bar off Victoria Street, some way from the Foreign Office.

"It's irregular because I haven't cleared it with my superiors and because I'm giving you the gist of F.O. thinking that may turn out to be incorrect. Your father's going to be hanged, and neither the private nor the public shouting of our crowd is going to change that. Your father's solicitor has told our people in South Africa that they'll spare him if he turns state evidence. Up to now he's told them nothing. He doesn't sound to me like a man about to splash through a sea change. That's one pointer, there's another. A few days ago their Justice Minister made a speech that effectively shut out all prospect of clemency. They want to show they're strong. They want blood."

"What would happen if I went out to see him?"

"You wouldn't get a contact visit. You wouldn't be able to touch him, hold his hand. You'd have a glass plate between you. You'd speak down a voice tube. My opinion, it would be pretty distressing for you and for him."

What would they talk about? Jack shuddered. The man would be a stranger. God, and small comfort he'd be to his father.

"What's your interest in his case, Mr Sandham?"

Sandham shrugged. "Something stinks."

"Meaning what?"

"I'll tell you when I've found out."

"When my father's dead and buried?"

"I can't say."

"What stinks?"

"Sorry, Mr Curwen . . . but you'll hear from me when I know, I promise you that."

"I don't know where to go except to you," Jack said simply. "That's the hell of it, and time's running out."

Jack drove back to D & C.

Janice looked at him curiously, then gave him the message that his mother had rung. He telephoned her. He cradled the telephone on his shoulder, his elbows were on his desk top, his hands in front of his mouth. Janice noted his attempt at privacy.

He heard about the visitor and the questions. He told her that he had been to the Foreign Office, that there wasn't any good news. He rang off abruptly. He was sagging over his desk.

"Why don't you go home?"

He looked up. He saw young Villiers staring down at him.

"Why should I go home?"

"Because you look knackered."

"I'm fine."

"You're not, and you should go home."

Jack was shouting. "If I say I'm fine, then I'm bloody fine. And I don't want any one bloody tip–toeing round me."

"Just concerned, old boy."

"Well, don't be fucking concerned."

Janice and Lucille studied their typewriters. Villiers flushed, flexed his fingers. His father had told him everything that he needed to know about Jack Curwen, that he had been two years and one term at university and left on a disciplinary matter, that a drop–out added up to a cheap work horse for D & C Ltd, that Jack Curwen was lucky to have his job however dedicated and able he might be.

"Nice to know that nothing's wrong," he said evenly.

Because he had a good nose, Jimmy Sandham's diplomatic career had long ago been stunted. He said what he felt it right to say and then managed a quaint look of hurt when his superiors rewarded him with lack of advancement.

As a young man, in Teheran, at a time when British factories were on overtime and weekend shifts to turn out Chieftain tanks for the Shah's army, Sandham had briefed a visiting journalist on the help with direct interrogation methods that British Intelligence were giving to Savak. In Amman he had filed a formal report to the ambassador stating that the representatives of British construction companies were buying their contract to build a hydro plant with back handers; two of the representatives were at that time putting up at the ambassador's residence.

He couldn't be fired, but he could be disliked, and he could watch his promotion prospects going down the plug hole.

It was eight years since the industrious Jimmy Sandham had last been posted abroad. He never complained, never sought explanations as younger men leap-frogged him. But the word was out. If there was a bad smell in a section then keep Sandham's nose at arm's length.

The Carew case was a thoroughly nasty smell to Jimmy Sandham, and the error of Peter Furneaux, assistant secretary, had been to let him within a mile of it.

The friend Sandham had telephoned had been his best man at the English church in Bangkok. The friend thought the day spiced with pleasure because the ambassador had been the guest of honour eleven days after receiving the query from the crown auditors concerning his wife's frequent and private use of the Rolls. Jimmy Sandham's bride had been his friend's secretary.

That had been a long time ago, but they had stayed as close as two men can who meet each other for a couple of meals a year and exchange cards at Christmas. The friend worked from a nondescript tower block on the south side of the Thames, home base of the Secret Intelligence Service. The friend loved Sandham for his pig-headed obstinacy, and made certain they were never seen together.

They sat on a bench in Battersea Park, shielded by a towering shrub from the nearest path. The fun fair hadn't opened for the summer season, the kids were at school, it was too short of pickings for the tramps, too draughty for the lovers.

"Furneaux's a total arsehole," the friend said.

"I get this garbage from Furneaux about 'deep water', and we have a file with Carew's real name on it. Furneaux didn't put the file back into records, it's locked in his own safe."

"To keep your prying eyes off it."

"What would I have seen?"

"Enough to whet your appetite."

Sandham grinned. "What about your file?"

"Enough for you to choke on."

Sandham stared into his friend's face. "Is James Carew one of ours?"

"Fighting talk, Jimmy. You should know, there's a D–notice."

"What else?"

"I reckon there'd be Official Secrets Act, Section I. Closed court. Ten years minimum, could be fifteen . . . You want cream on your raspberries? There's a fair bit of bad blood in the Service over Carew. Desk men say it's entirely his own fault, leg men say that once a man's on the team then it's marriage vows, for ever. Trouble is that the Service has changed since Carew started out. Desk men count, leg men are dinosaurs. Evaluation and interpretation is the name of the game, and you need an Oxbridge degree for that. Running around on the ground's out of fashion."

"And the desk men'll let him hang?"

"He had a fairy godmother, but that's over. They got him out the last time, second time's one too many. The leg men say that Carew wasn't asked to do what he did."

"So you bastards are going to write him off."

"Come off it, Jimmy . . . Are we going to go to Pretoria and tell them that a staffer, a wallah on the pension scheme, is driving the scoot car from a daylight bombing. He was there to infiltrate, provide the raw intelligence for assessments. He wasn't there to lead the bloody charge down the Johannesburg High Street. I tell you what we think happened. We think he had infiltrated the A.N.C., just inserted himself under the skin. We think the A.N.C. learned to trust him and one day, bad luck for Carew, they trusted him enough to do a little job for them. We think the poor creep probably didn't know what he was into."

Sandham said bitterly, "I thought it was holy writ that you lot looked after your own."

The friend laughed out loud. "That's gone with the ark."

"What sort of chap is Carew?"

"Brilliant. You want to know what he said when he was lifted. 'Let's have a bit of dignity, boys.' That's what he said to the four guys with him, and they'd just knocked half Jo'burg over. He'll keep his secret. Our secret." The friend looked at Sandham keenly. "You won't forget the ten years minimum and the D–notice, Jimmy?"

"It's the nastiest story I've ever heard."

"It's *realpolitik*."

"The politicians have backed this, leaving him to hang?"

"Who needs to tell them about the big bad world?"

"When he left his wife . . ."

"We got him back, without ten years of his life, four stones, two fingernails, and he never told them anything. But he had the old godmother working for him then. Right now, he's no-one rooting for him."

"Why not?"

"March of time, Jimmy, comes to us all. The godmother got retired, a bit before Jeez was lifted. There was Lennie Abrams, he's posted to Djakarta for expenses trouble. There was Adrian Mountjoy, fairy, he's in an open prison in the Midlands, groped a vice-squadder in a gay club, once too often. There was Henry Willcox, took an early out and skipped with one of the library girls. Jeez's problem is that no one's shouting in his corner."

Sandham shook his head, as if the smell was suffocating him.

"Where was he, the first time, those ten years?"

"Try a happy little holiday home called Spac. A stint of Albanian hospitality."

"It's disgraceful."

"Keep in touch, Jimmy."

"For what?"

"So's I know whether I'm going to have to traipse down to Parkhurst for the next ten years of visit days."

A West Indian woman pushed a pram past him and gave him a long sneering look, like she'd spied out a flasher or an addict. His friend was gone, vanished into the trees and shrubs. For more than a quarter of an hour Sandham sat bowed on the bench. Finally he stood, and tried to pull the creases out of his raincoat. On his way back to the Foreign Office he found a telephone kiosk, rang Jack, and fixed to meet him the following day.

He was a man heavy with anxiety.

Jack knew from Sandham's voice that he was to be told something that was worse than he had been told before.

They met in a pub south of Westminster Bridge. Sandham found them a corner where neither could be seen from the door, where he could not be seen from the bar.

Jack told Sandham that a South African had been to see his mother. Sandham said that the man would be either from security police or intelligence. He'd check it. Sandham said that they had to have been working on tracing Hilda Perry ever since Jeez's letter had given them her previous address.

Sandham said there was a civil war being fought in South Africa.

". . . And they'll play dirty if they have to."

"How dirty?"

"Four Blacks from Port Elizabeth, big guys in the opposition United Democratic Front, get a telephone call from what calls itself the British Embassy asking for a meeting. They set off, and they disappear on the road. When they're found they've been burned and hacked to death. We never made the call. That was last year. I'll give you another one. Victoria Mxenge, a Black lawyer representing some of the accused in the treason trial. She was coming home after dark to her township outside Durban. Shot dead on her doorstep. No arrests."

"This isn't bloody South Africa," Jack said.

"They have a keen idea of national security. They're a serious *volk*, and they couldn't be caring too much about international frontiers."

"These people in South Africa, the government murdered them?"

"I didn't say that. I said they were opponents of government, and they're dead. There *might* be a difference. Do you know what a D-notice is?"

Jack shrugged. "It's when the government tells the newspapers they shouldn't print something."

"Do you know about the Official Secrets Act, Section I?"

"The charge that's brought against foreign spies and our traitors."

"What I'm going to tell you is covered by a D-notice and the Official Secrets Act, Section I."

"We're going in up to our necks, aren't we?"

Sandham told Jack what he knew.

He knew that James "Jeez" Carew was on the payroll of the Secret Intelligence Service, had been for a quarter of a century. He knew that Jeez had been in South Africa for the last dozen years with the job of infiltrating the military wing of the African National Congress. He speculated that Jeez had overstepped his brief and become involved in a guerrilla attack. He knew that Her Majesty's Government were not prepared to go to Pretoria and cough up that a White under sentence of death was in fact a leg man in deep cover for S.I.S. and therefore should be spared the rope.

A gasp from Jack. "I can't believe it."

"You're on the horizon of a tough, rough old world."

"They always get their people back, that's what you always read."

"It might have been true once, but isn't true any more, and your father wasn't acting under orders and that's government's let out. There's more to it. Technically South Africa is a major trading partner. We've billions invested there. We may have as many as a quarter of a million jobs dependent on South African purchasing power and South African mineral resources. Government's dislike of apartheid comes a poor second to economics. I'm just telling you what I know."

Jack flared. "I'm going to blow this off the rooftops."

"Don't even try it. The papers won't print it and telly won't broadcast it. That's the D-notice. You'd be charged under the Official Secrets Act, and when you get to court it'll be long after your father's been executed. And then it'll be *in camera*, the court'll be cleared, the doors locked, the Press out."

"So who's lifting a finger for him?"

Sandham picked up their glasses, went to the bar. Jack sat slumped on the upholstered seat. He was drained. He could not absorb that this was happening to Hilda Perry and Jack Curwen. Worse than a nightmare. Sandham put two large Scotches on the table and sat down.

Jack asked, "If I blew it would you go to prison with me?"

"Worse than that. Breach of official trust."

"You've taken a chance on me."

"It was the only decent course to take."

Jack gripped Sandham's hand, held it tight. His face was screwed into lines, as if he agonised over the question.

"Is Jeez Carew worth crying over?"

"You know the answer."

"You have to tell me."

Gently Sandham released Jack's hand. "You're his son, you don't have a choice. And from what I've discovered I'd say that your father is a man you should be very, very proud of."

Sandham said he had set up a meeting at the Foreign Office for the following morning that was to discuss Jeez. He didn't elaborate. He left Jack, grim and drawn.

He walked back to his car.

Waves of outrage lapped over him, outrage against the forces that had intruded into his life, his mother's life. His tongue twisted round obscenities, sometimes silent in the spring evening wind, sometimes out loud. Terrorism, prisons, and the sentence that a man should hang by the neck until he was dead had never before owned a corner of Jack Curwen's mind. Many targets for his hatred. He hated White South Africa. He hated the security policemen who had arrested Jeez. He hated their prisons and their gallows. He hated the Secret Intelligence Service of his own country. He hated the men who had washed their hands of responsibility for Jeez's life.

A long, bitter walk, a mile beyond his car.

When his mind was made, when a certainty had slashed through the rage and bafflement, he retraced his steps.

South Africa was a place on a map. He had no thoughts on the future of that country, it was of no interest to him. He had no Black friends. In a year he could have counted on his fingers the times he had spoken to Black men and Black women.

Jack knew nothing of Black Britain or Black South Africa. He knew nothing of the Black dream of freedom, and he cared less.

But his mind was made.

He went in search of Duggie Arkwright.

Duggie Arkwright was the best start Jack could think of. Each new year, Jack transferred from his old diary to his new one the addresses and telephone numbers that he had consolidated over the years. The previous New Year, when he had determined on retaking his degree as an external student, he had searched out Duggie to beg and borrow the library books from college that he knew Duggie had squirreled away. He had an address that was a squat off Camden High Street. He thought they were all Marxists, or they might have been Stalinists, and there was a Revolutionary Socialist Workers Party poster sellotaped to the wallpaper in the hall. He was given a second address.

Duggie had nearly been a friend in the little more than two years they had shared at London University. They had known each other first when they had adjoining rooms in the hall of residence, when they shared coffee, or were short of sugar, or needed to borrow a book. Duggie was an idealist. In his first term he had joined DebSoc, LabSoc, AASoc, and DramSoc. Jack hadn't joined the Debating Society nor the Labour Society nor the Anti-Apartheid Society nor the Dramatic Society. He had joined the rugby club. Jack would have been satisfied to end up with a 2nd (Lower) in Modern History; he knew Duggie had kicked himself for ending up with that grade. Jack had dogged application, Duggie had brains. He'd gone to Duggie for the books because he was damned if he was going to go back to college and request library facilities.

He went gingerly down the dark basement steps in Paddington. When he rang, a woman shouted at him from a window above. She gave him a third address. She said she'd been chasing the bastard herself for his unpaid rent. She may have been misled by Jack's suit to supposing him another creditor, because she wished him well.

They had drifted apart during the second year. But it would not have been possible for Jack to lose sight of Duggie. Duggie Arkwright was the darling of the Left's societies, the regular lambaster of government and institutions. He wrote in the student paper under a photograph and a by-line. He made principal speeches at debates. He had twice been arrested in Trafalgar Square, once on the Anti-Apartheid ticket and once on a C.N.D. demonstration.

He ended up in Dalston, quite a long way east over the tracks from tarted-up Islington. It was the doorway beside a newsagent. The newsagent was open. He went inside and asked if next door was right for Duggie Arkwright. He got a cold nod from the young Pakistani at the cash till.

Last year Jack had seen Duggie's photograph, second row in a demonstration in Liverpool. He couldn't think of anywhere else to start.

Jack had rung the bell and a girl had opened the street door and led him upstairs. It wasn't really a flat. It was a room with a table and some chairs, a baby asleep in one of them, and a line of washing and a paraffin stove and a collapsible cot and an electric cooker. For a bed there was a mattress on the floor with rumpled sheets and blankets. Posters on the wall, and Jack fancied they hid the damp.

They looked at each other and Duggie beamed.

"Bloody hell, it's priggy Curwen, the refugee from Modern History. What in God's name . . ."

"Nice to see you, Duggie."

"I suppose you want my notes now, and my essays."

"No."

"Ditched it all, have you? Come to tell me you've chucked it?"

"I'll take my degree the year after next, and pass."

"God, what a crass prig. Do I have to wait till then for my books back?"

"When I've finished with your books I'll be sending them back to the library."

Duggie was laughing out loud, Jack was grinning. The student that Jack had hit had been standing in front of Duggie Arkwright. Duggie had said at the time that it didn't matter, the student having his jaw broken, because he was unsound, a revisionist.

"Come on in, sit yourself down."

But there wasn't anywhere to sit down. The baby was in the one comfortable chair, and of the two chairs at the table one was deep in washing bags and the other was a book store.

"Bloody good to see you, Jack bloody Curwen. Jack, this is Anthea."

The girl stared coldly at Jack. He could measure her dislike. His suit and his raincoat, wasn't it? His hair that was cut every fortnight. She turned away from him, as if she was a bank manager's daughter, as if she detested a reminder of where she had once been.

"That's Joshua Lenin Arkwright, sleeping thank God . . . Don't just stand there, get your bloody coat off. You look like a bloody bailiff."

Jack grinned. "Your last landlady spoke well of you."

"Remember that cow, Anthea? Should have had the rent tribunal on her, and the Health and Sanitary . . . You're bloody welcome, if you're not after a loan."

"I do need some help," Jack said simply.

Duggie's laughter pealed through the room. His smile was huge and his teeth were awful.

"You must be in desperate shit if you need my help."

Anthea snapped that he'd wake the baby.

Duggie pulled a face. "Come on, if you've the price of two pints."

They went down the stairs, and were in the street before Jack realised that neither of them had said goodbye to the girl. "One glorious night behind a hedge when we'd gone up to help the miners picket some hideous power station. Her daddy said he'd cut her out of his will if we didn't marry. High price to pay for coal, if you ask me, but he's seventy-one next birthday."

Jack plunged. "Are you still involved in South Africa?"

"You don't just lose interest because you've left college."

"It's important to you?"

"Course it is. Most days I'm at Anti-Apartheid."

"Do you know people at the A.N.C.?"

"Conscience hasn't stricken priggy Curwen, has it? You going to make a donation?"

"It's not a joke, Duggie."

"I have dealings with the A.N.C., I've been on liaison committees. I know people there."

"They have a military wing, right?"

"They've Umkonto we Sizwe – Spear of the Nation – that's the military wing."

Jack stopped him outside the pub.

"I want an introduction."

"You're not a bloody spook are you? I mean, you wanting that, it's ridiculous . . ." He tailed away. He saw the seriousness on Jack's face.

"You have to trust me, Duggie. Trust me when I tell you that I intend nothing that will harm that organisation. I have to have an introduction to this Spear of the Nation. I have to know the man I am meeting is able to get things done."

"They'd kill you if they found you were bent."

"That's not what they'll find."

"You didn't tell me what work you were in."

Jack cracked a thin smile. His mind was made. He was on his road.

"I'm to do with explosives."

Duggie pulled an old envelope out of his pocket. On it Jack wrote his home number and his office number.

In the pub they had three pints each, paid for by Jack, and they talked about college days and laughed too much. They laughed too loud because Jack had said he worked with explosives and Duggie had heard him.

6

"I see the world's looking up on you."

Nicholas Villiers noted the change in Jack.

"Sorry about the snap. I was a bit under the weather. The problem's sorted out."

"Glad to hear it."

Janice and Lucille heard the satisfaction in Villiers' voice. The girls liked Jack for his apology.

Jack told Villiers that he was going straight out to do his elms, that he'd be back in after lunch. He asked Lucille to mind his telephone. He said that a Mr Arkwright might phone him, and to be sure to get the message exactly.

He drove down to Dorking, then came off the main road and took a winding tree-lined route to Ockley. He reached a remote farm, far up a lane, with post and rail fencing for the hunters. Hell of a backwoods place for thirty miles from London. The owner had looked as though he'd had a death in the family when he'd first had Jack down, when the elms were toppled on their sides, felled but waiting to be cut up and carted away. Taking out the stumps was small business to Jack, but he'd had to work for the contract because the owner seemed hesitant to uproot his final memories of the elm avenue.

For once George had beaten Jack to the site. Just the two of them. The JCBs and the lorries would come in the owner's own time. Jack had asked that the horses be kept well clear and there was no sign of them. Some beef bullocks watched them. They'd take plenty to be frightened.

George had already dug neat holes at the side of each of the stumps.

By his small unmarked van was the wooden crate that held the nitroglycerine, ammonium nitrate based dynamite, and also the metal box in which he carried his no. 6 detonators, and also a drum of Cordtex and a drum of safety fuse.

"Are you going to sit on your arse, or are you going to help?"

"I'd like to help, Mr Hawkins."

They worked together. Jack at George's shoulder as the old blaster stowed the 4 oz cartridges of explosive down under the arches of the roots. Jack didn't speak, didn't interrupt. He watched as George slid the aluminium tubed detonators into the cartridges. He saw him crimp the Cordtex to the open ends of the detonators. He was learning. He was watching a master at work.

"Set 'em off all together," George muttered. "Cordtex and safety fuse are cheaper than my time."

Jack had many times witnessed the routine. He had seen the laying of the explosive, the insertion of the detonators, the crimping in of the Cordtex, the linking of the Cordtex to the safety fuse, the unwinding of the safety fuse back to the van and the charger box.

"You're bloody quiet this morning, Jack boy."

Jack didn't answer, just watched. A long job with thirty-two stumps to be taken out.

If Sandham was nervous then he was good at hiding it.

A secretary had come up to the South Africa desk to collect him.

Furneaux had been in the open plan area, he had seen Sandham summoned, and known who the secretary worked for, and wondered what in hell's name was going on. Sandham, Grade 2, having an audience without it going through the Assistant Secretary running his desk.

Sandham came into the hush of the outer office, where the girls' fingers whispered over the electric typewriters. He thought a funeral parlour might have been more cheerful. The Permanent Under Secretary was waiting in front of the closed inner door, ill at ease. Sandham understood. When a Grade 2 man requests a personal meeting with the Foreign Secretary on a matter concerning national security then the fat cats would be wetting themselves, one and all. There had been some exquisite moments in Jimmy Sandham's life. He reckoned this would knock spots off *les affaires* Bangkok, Teheran and Amman.

The P.U.S. opened the inner door, waved Sandham inside.

It was the first time that he had been inside the Foreign Secretary's office. He was too far down the ladder to take part in the South Africa policy meetings, where strategy was hammered over. He thought the Foreign Secretary's wife must have had a hand in the decor. It was seven years since his own wife had left him, shouting from the pile of suitcases at the front door that she couldn't endure one more day with a man so pompous and self-opinionated. And nor had she. But he still recognised a woman's hand. The Foreign Secretary, tepid and small, wouldn't have had the wit to choose the colours and the fabrics and the gentle hidden lighting.

The Foreign Secretary had his nose into a paper-covered desk.

There was a second man in the room. He sat in a low chair with his back to the door, the bald crown of his head just visible over the chair's back.

The P.U.S. announced Sandham. He pointed to a plain, upright chair and Sandham went to it, and sat. Sandham wondered if they had any inkling of what was about to drop into their laps.

The Foreign Secretary raised his head. He had pale skin and owl spectacles.

"Ah, Sandham. Thank you for coming. You wanted to alert us to a matter of national security, I think. I have asked the Director General to sit in. You know P.U.S., of course, who will make any notes that may be required . . . The floor is yours."

The Foreign Secretary had his elbows on his papers, his chin in his hands. The P.U.S. lounged back on a short settee, a pad on his knee. The Director General gazed with frank hostility into Sandham's face because he had read the wretch's file. J. Sandham, Grade 2 man, given the moment could be mischievous or impertinent, but he needed a deep breath. He had expected that the P.U.S. would sit in with the Foreign Secretary. He had not expected that the Director General would have been summoned across the Thames from his Century tower. The Director General as the man in place in the Secret Intelligence Service had responsibility for Jack's father. The Director General was the employer of Jeez Carew, alias James Curwen. A hell of a deep breath before launching into his accusation.

"Thank you for seeing me, sir. I thought there was a matter that you should be aware of. It is a question of life and death and that is why I have requested this personal meeting with you."

The P.U.S.'s propelling pencil was poised.

"In South Africa, in about three weeks time, a man called James Curwen, but who goes under the name of James Carew in that country, is going to hang . . ."

Sandham saw the muscles tighten under the pug dog chin of the Director General.

"I'll call him Carew because that's the only name that the South Africans have for him. Carew was convicted of driving the getaway car used by African National Congress guerrillas in their escape from the Supreme Court bombing in Johannesburg fourteen months ago. At the time that Carew drove the vehicle he was a full-time operative of the Secret Intelligence Service . . ."

He saw the eyebrows of the P.U.S. flicker upwards, he saw him begin to write.

"A situation has arisen where a man working for his country is going to hang because the British Government has not chosen to exercise its influence, first to secure clemency and second to win Mr Carew's release."

There was a cloud of surprise on the Foreign Secretary's face. Sandham wondered what had surprised him. The allegation, or the fact that a Grade 2 man knew the history.

"If you'll forgive me, sir, I think it's unacceptable that a man doing his job should be abandoned"

The P.U.S. closed his notepad, pocketed his gold pencil.

"What's your source?" The Director General beaded Sandham with his eyes.

"I saw a file that I was not entitled by rank to see, sir."

"Have you passed on this allegation to any other person?" The Foreign Secretary spoke through closed teeth.

"No, sir." It was Sandham's second instinctive lie. With it clear of his tongue he thought of the earnest, sincere, concerned face of young Jack Curwen.

"And that's all that you wanted to tell the Foreign Secretary?" The P.U.S. seemed to make a trifle of Sandham's statement.

"Yes, sir."

The P.U.S. shone Sandham an affectionate smile. "We're very grateful to you for drawing this matter to our attention. If it's not inconvenient for you, would you mind waiting a few minutes in my office?"

The Foreign Secretary had twisted in his chair to look down from his window and into the park. The Director General stared at the tapestry screen that masked the open fireplace. The P.U.S. ushered Sandham towards the door. They wanted him out. They wanted to thrash it round. It had been bloody good entertainment. He would have liked to dance a bit, and shout.

"No problem, sir," Sandham said easily.

"I'll get someone to take you down to my room. You won't be kept long."

They watched him leave. They waited for the door to close behind him.

The Foreign Secretary spoke with a squeaking, nervous voice. "You knew about this, Director General."

"I did not."

"Your department, your man."

"I'll be making it my business to find out, Foreign Secretary."

"If this Sandham is to be believed . . ."

The P.U.S. swirled his hand above his knee, cut the Foreign Secretary short. "He's to be believed. Our Mr Sandham is always to be believed. More important, he's a difficult man, that's his history."

"What's to be done with him?"

The Director General looked up. "He should go home, Foreign Secretary, that's best. He should be at home where he can commit no damage. I'll have a man take him home."

"If this allegation were to become public property . . ."

"It won't," the Director General said quietly.

"You can guarantee that?"

"Foreign Secretary, leave if in my hands. You give me that authority?"

"Whatever authority you want."

"Thank you, Foreign Secretary, just the authority to isolate him."

They had the hard hats on, and they were crouched one hundred and fifty yards from the nearest stump, and they were sheltered by the van. George always crouched, didn't matter what protection he had. They'd done the checks together.

Jack had watched each step. He reckoned he could have gone through all the procedures himself.

"Well, don't hang about all day, lad."

Jack thought he'd die old waiting for a bit of politeness from George.

"What's so bloody funny?"

"Nothing's funny, Mr Hawkins."

"Get on with it."

Jack rested the palm of his hand over the bar of the plunger.

"Don't stab it, ease it."

He closed his fist on the bar. He looked at George, warts and wrinkles and thinned out hair protruding from under the garish orange rim of his helmet. George winked. Jack pressed the charger bar slowly, steadily down.

There was the clap thunder of the detonations. There was the rich loam soil spurting up, the shuddering climb of the tree stumps, the thumping patter of earth and roots landing, the furious croaking of rooks.

Jack gazed fascinated at what they had achieved. Away beyond the line of uprooted stumps the bullocks were in flight.

George studied the scene. His face was closed. Jack looked into George's face. One thing to know a man and work with him, another thing to trust him. He thought he could trust George Hawkins, but what he thought didn't really matter because he had to trust the man.

"Get on with it, Jack," George said tersely.

"Was it that obvious?"

"Say what you've got to say."

He told George that his father had disappeared from his life when he was two years old, before he could remember. He told him that he had been brought up to believe that his father was cruelty incarnate. He told him that there was not even a photograph of his father that had been kept by his mother when she had cleared out her husband's possessions. He told George of the letter, how the missing James Curwen had been resurrected as James Carew, under sentence of death. He told him that his father had been working for the government, an agent in place, that his life was not going to be pleaded for.

"That's the history, Mr Hawkins."

George's was a low gravel voice. "You could have spoken to your M.P., a journalist, one of those lads on television. Why didn't you cry on their shoulders? Why do you talk to me, a blaster?"

"Had to be you."

"You didn't have to come today and watch me lift a few bloody tree stumps."

"Right."

"You want some know-how?"

Jack nodded.

George said softly, "Where are the targets?"

"Not here, waste of time in London. I know where the target is, I don't know what it'll take."

"Explosives?"

"Has to be."

George was striding fast to his van.

"Hope you're not asking me for explosives. Every last cartridge of mine has to be accounted for. You're going to South Africa? Even if you could get them here you can't just put them in your bloody suitcase and fly out of London. Don't think the x-rays and the sniffers would miss it. You wouldn't get as far as the 'plane."

"I'll get the explosives there."

"You got the right friends?"

"I'm finding them." There was the obstinate thrust to Jack's chin.

God, he was racing ahead. He hadn't the targets, he hadn't the explosives, he hadn't the friends. So bloody innocent, and talking as though he could just snap his fingers and achieve them.

George cuffed him. "Come back to me when you've some answers."

Major Swart resented having any more of his time taken up with the Carew affair. The file was hardly worth the effort of couriering it from Pretoria on the overnight 747 of South African Airways. Carew was a home desk problem, and following up stray ends was unrewarding work for a major of security police. The woman had seen him off. He'd have thought she'd have spilled her heart out given the chance to save a man from the rope. A week earlier he thought he had placed her in the game. All by leg work and tracking back in the files of Somerset House. Before her divorce Mrs Hilda Perry had been Mrs Hilda Curwen. She had been married to a James Curwen. James Curwen was his man, until he had driven down to the Hampshire village which was listed as the woman's address at the time of her marriage. He'd had a photograph from Pretoria, taken in the gaol but especially so as not to look like a police shot. He had found three men who remembered James Curwen in a pub by the cress beds. A retired postman, the man who kept the village grocery store, and the vicar. He had said he was the London representative of a South African based legal firm. He had said he was trying to trace this James Curwen because there was money left to him. He showed them all the photograph, and he had seen each one of them shake his head and heard each one of them say the photograph was not that of James Curwen. Wrong face, wrong physique.

So, he hadn't linked Hilda Perry to James Carew, and it didn't have a high priority from Pretoria, and there was a limit on his time.

A higher priority was the man who had come in from Lusaka.

If there was a matter that could make Major Swart emotionally ill, it was that the United Kingdom, on top of all its cant about the suppression of terrorism, could allow African National Congress murderers free rein to visit their chummies in the London office.

He thought he might get to see the bastard from Lusaka that evening, not certain, but a good chance.

In the late afternoon Jack came into the office.

Janice was making up her face over the typewriter, her mirror propped against the ribbon. She waved to indicate the paper she had left on his desk, too busy to speak. Nicholas Villiers had gone home, so had Lucille.

He recognised most of the names and numbers that he was to call back. The people with the chimney in Streatham, a good one for George and he'd get his photo in the local rag. The brewery who were pulling down the Bunch of Grapes in Addington, a ball and chain job. The clearance of a small council house development at Earlsfield where the precast concrete units were disintegrating and it was cheaper for the local authority to demolish than to repair . . . Duggie Arkwright and a number were half way down the list, and again at the bottom of the list.

It was Duggie's girl who picked up the phone, Anthea. She sounded high. She dropped the telephone, and he heard Duggie Arkwright curse her. Jack introduced himself.

"You meant what you said?"

"Yes, I want to . . ."

"Open phone, priggy."

Jack swallowed hard. And this was London. He felt juvenile, naked.

"Same place as we had a drink, same time – we'll go on."

Jack wanted to ask who they would meet, where they would be going, but the line was dead.

He rang his mother. He wouldn't be in for supper. He'd be back late. The habit was catching, no explanations.

Next he called Sandham's number at the Foreign Office. He wanted to hear about Sandham's meeting, what the new information was.

He was told Mr Sandham had gone home.

There was no reply at the home number.

"I'm dying for a drink," Janice told him. "They're open now."

Jack said, "It's the nice thing about pubs these days, that a girl can go in and have a drink on her own."

He settled back to his list, the people with the spare chimney and the brewery and the local authority. The chimney people had gone home, so had the local authority, but he had a good talk with the brewery.

The Prime Minister was obsessive about "banana skins", and over the years the Secret Intelligence Service and the Security Service had had more than their share of disasters. It had been only too often the Prime Minister's misfortune to get to the despatch box in a gloating House of Commons and wriggle in the mess. With this Director General the Prime Minister felt secure. The confidence was reciprocated with an all-consuming loyalty.

The Director General was "clean" in the matter of James Carew. He had been transferred from a diplomatic career the previous year. He had come in after Carew's arrest and trial.

The file on Carew revealed ample evidence of an approach to intelligence gathering that was provenly dangerous.

The man's career was a joke, a pathetic confidence trick.

Colonel Fordham should have been put up against a wall and shot for what he had done for Carew. At the very least Carew should have been wound in the morning after Fordham's retirement. The file was horrifying reading.

Colonel Fordham had transferred from the regular army to the Service. He had recruited his batman for leg work, a man without higher education. In due course a small operation had been run into Albania. Albania was the most irrelevant corner of mountains on the European continent. Colonel Fordham had sent this devoted but second-rate individual into Albania on a mission based on rotten information. The Soviet Union scowling at Yugoslavia *might* do a Hungary or a Czechoslovakia, and then N.A.T.O. *might* deploy troops and armour in North West Greece, and if N.A.T.O. were up on the Greek Albanian border then they just *might* need to know what was on the far side of this most closed and guarded frontier. Colonel Fordham had sent this man into Albania for a bit of map reading and reconnaissance, and to see which bridges would carry 55-ton tanks. As if he had never heard of satellite photography.

In the file were the minutes of the meeting where the mission was agreed. It wouldn't have happened in the Director General's day. There was a brief paper on the aims of the mission. There was a telex, decoded, from the mission's forward headquarters in Corfu reporting that radio contact had been lost. And the poor bugger sat in prison there for ten years.

No record of a minute to Downing Street. Alec Douglas Home, Wilson, Heath, none of them ever heard a whisper of it. And of course the Albanians had never known who they had, right to the end, because Curwen had never confessed anything in ten years. It had ended shabbily with the payment of £100,000 from the service contingency fund, into a Venezuelan bank account.

Colonel Basil had brought his man home, and about bloody time.

The Director General came to four sheets of lined paper that might have been extracted from the centre of a school exercise book. The writing was close, joined up, in ball point. At the top, in capitals and underlined, was SPAC LABOUR CAMP 303. In the ruled margin, written with a different pen but in the same handwriting, he read "Col Fordham, I thought this might be important to you in case anyone else of our team ends up in the place, Respectfully, Jeez".

It was a factual account of life in the Spac labour camp. It was compiled without a trace of self pity. It described the work of the camp – the mining of pyrites from which copper is taken – eight hours a day and six days a week, and a seventh day if the week's target had not been reached. He read of 10 foot high barbed-wire fences and guards with searchlights and attack dogs. Unheated concrete barrack blocks where more than three hundred inmates would sleep on straw mattresses on three tier bunks. Of a diet that hardly ever included protein, fresh vegetables or fruit. Of the beatings and the punishment cells. Of finger nails ripped off with plumbing pliers. He read of strikes, riots, reprisal executions.

And every day of the ten years this poor bastard had nurtured the assumption that the Secret Intelligence Service was working for his release. It was a disgrace. He tidied the faded sheets of paper.

Anon, the leg man had been brought home, privately fêted as a hero.

But he'd lost his wife, lost his son, lost the best ten years of his life, so the agent had been given a warm berth in South Africa. Controlled from London, working for Colonel Fordham.

The telephone rang.

73

He thought the man who had done ten years of his life in Spac was indeed second rate. He thought also that the man must have a near limitless well of courage.

He picked up the telephone. He said to send them in. He put the Curwen/Carew file to the side of his desk.

Perhaps Duggie believed him. Extraordinary that priggy Curwen should have sought him out to set up a meeting with the African National Congress, not just any old Joe there but the military wing, and should have said he worked in the explosives racket. Explosives weren't a joke. Explosives and detonators and time delay fuses were serious business.

They left the pub. Then went in Jack's car, north up the Essex Road. It was dark and raining.

"You scared?"

"No," Jack said. "Not now."

"Perhaps you should be."

"This isn't South Africa yet."

"It's a war. We're fighting to destroy them and they're fighting to survive. Point is, we're winning, but that doesn't mean they'll stop fighting. What's at stake is whether South Africa is governed by the representatives of nearly thirty million people, or whether it's run by nearly five million who happen by accident of birth and breeding to have a different pigmentation of skin . . . Jack, if you're getting into South African resistance politics, if you're into explosives then, my opinion, you ought to be a bit scared."

Jack said curtly, "I've my own reasons for getting involved, they're good enough for me."

"Learn first that you don't talk on open phones. Learn fast that they can get a hell of a lot rougher than phone taps. There's bombs in London and Paris and Zimbabwe and Botswana and Swazi and Maputo. Big bombs down to letter bombs. They've got infiltrators. They pay burglars to turn over resistance offices right here in safe old London."

"Got it." Even as his father had. He had known what was for real.

"These people you're going to meet don't piss about, not the sort of man you're going to meet. Fighting repression in South Africa is their whole lives."

"They'll trust me."

Duggie noticed the assurance. He gave the instructions. Right turn, then a left, then straight on over the lights, another right.

They walked across the poorly-lit playground of a junior school.

There were posters up on the playground fences to advertise the meeting. Big deal . . . It wasn't the Albert Hall, nor the Royal Festival Hall. It was a junior school in Stoke Newington.

There was music beating out through the open doors of the gymnasium. Through the door Jack could see the lines of chairs. They stopped at the door. Duggie turned, hand out, and Jack gave him two pound coins. It bought them admission and a photocopied sheet detailing the evening's programme.

"I'll start you off, then you're on your own."

Jack looked around him. There were posters and flags fastened to the wall bars. There were pictures of Mandela and Tambo. There were the slogans of the Anti-Apartheid campaign. There were a hundred people. He thought he must stand out, a fly in a tea cup. There were eyes watching him. The uniform was jeans and sweaters and shawls and long skirts.

"You said it," Duggie chuckled. "You said you knew what you were getting into. Now you find out."

The apple of Major Swart's attention was Jacob Thiroko.

The Black lounged at the back of the hall away from the low stage and out of sight of the door. He leaned against the gymnasium's vaulting horse. His eyes drooped, as if he was still exhausted from the long flight out of Lusaka. Of course he would be cold after the Central African heat. Around him were a clutch of his European-based comrades.

Swart wore patched denim trousers. He had not shaved that day, his cheeks were rough below the tinted glasses. His hair was brushed up. Before coming he had rubbed his hands in the earth of his office pot plants, getting the stains into his palm and under his fingernails. He sat in the last-but-one row, unremarkable and unobserved.

There was a young man at the doorway, in a suit, staring round him. He saw the man who was with him. He recognised him. Douglas William Arkwright, 27 years old, unemployed, unpaid worker at Anti-Apartheid, verbose and useless. He saw Arkwright speak in the young man's ear and then lead him the length of the hall to stand respectfully on the fringe of the group surrounding Thiroko.

Swart was interested. He couldn't hear what was said, but he saw the young man in the suit shake hands with Jacob Thiroko.

It was for Jack to start. There was casual amusement in Thiroko's expression. Jack saw a handsome man, soft chocolate skinned, mahogany eyed. He couldn't tell the age, anything between middle thirties and late forties.

He was Jack Curwen and he lived in Churchill Close, and he paid into a private medical scheme, and he voted to maintain the status quo. He was Jack Curwen standing in a run down school, shaking hands with a member of a revolutionary movement committed to the overthrow of a government half the world away. Preposterous enough to make him laugh, but his father had three weeks to live.

"I was brought here to meet someone from the African National Congress."

"There are many of us here, Comrade." A soft, swaying voice.

"I wanted to meet someone from the military wing of the A.N.C."

"Then you should be in South Africa where they are fighting the freedom war."

"I was told that if I came here I would meet someone from the Umkonto we Sizwe wing of the A.N.C."

"There is no war in London. The war is in our homeland."

Jack moved close to Thiroko.

"My name is Jack Curwen. I am an expert in explosives. I have to meet, and urgently, someone from the military wing."

"Perhaps in a month such a person."

"I don't have until next month. I've two days at most to meet someone from the military wing."

"What sort of person?" Thiroko's face was a mask.

"Someone who can make decisions and see them through."

"I doubt I am that person. There is no one from the military wing at a meeting such as this."

"I have to talk to you."

"You said that you wanted the military . . ."

Jack cut in. "I told you I don't have time to be pissed about. I can tell you how you are different from these creeps round you. Different face, different eyes, different hands."

"How different?"

"Different because they are a soldier's."

"Perhaps you are mistaken."

From behind Jack there was a burst of applause. He turned to see the stage filling.

"In this room you are the only man who is a soldier."

"Who are you, Mr Jack Curwen?"

"My father is going to hang in South Africa in three weeks. My father is an activist of the A.N.C."

The mask fell. Astonishment flooded Thiroko's face.

"Jeez Carew is my father."

The applause grew. The audience stamped their feet as they stood and clapped the principal speakers of the evening as they climbed onto the stage. Major Swart could no longer look behind him. He had seen the young man and Thiroko deep in talk. He had to stand with the rest and beat his palms together. He heard the chairwoman of the meeting coo her gratitude that their meeting was honoured by the presence of a distinguished guest from the A.N.C. headquarters whose name for security reasons could not be given out. He saw Thiroko going forward. The bastard didn't look a fit man. When the audience settled down, Swart looked behind him.

There was no sign of the young stranger.

His eyes darted to the door. He saw the back of Douglas Arkwright's duffel coat disappearing.

He sat with his mother in the living room. Sam was upstairs, in bed before

Jack had returned. He held cupped in his two hands the mug of coffee she had made for him. His hands were rock still.

"My mind's made up. I'm going to South Africa."

"To see your Dad?"

"Yes."

"I've told you, Sam'll help you with the airfare."

"Not his business, it's mine."

"What does he mean to you?"

"As much as if I'd known him all my life."

His mother held a square of lace, dabbed it into her eyes. "Will you have the strength when you go to see him, when you have to say goodbye to him?"

"It's not just to see him, Mum. I'm going there to bring my father home."

7

Janice and Lucille stared at the open office door.

Jack was on the phone. He had spun his chair round so that he could rummage into his filing cabinet as he talked. He didn't see Duggie Arkwright. He was a disaster, wearing his oldest patched jeans and a scarlet t-shirt under a skimpy denim top. He saw Jack, and whistled. Jack spun, saw who it was, and with a brisk apology finished his phone call.

Jack stood and muttered something to the girls about being out for most of the day. He took his coat. He felt their questions on his back and ignored them.

They went out of the office and into the mild morning air.

When Jack looked back from the pavement at the office window he saw that Nicholas Villiers and the girls had their noses pressed to the panes.

"You said you were going to ring," Jack said.

"The kiddie was crying in the night. I got up, I was holding the kiddie near the window and I saw this guy on the far side of the road, covering our place. The kiddie had a bad night. I was up again a couple of hours later, he was still there. I didn't go back to bed, I just stayed in a chair. Each time I went to the window he was there."

"Have you ever been under surveillance before?"

"Not that I've known . . ." Duggie had a brittle, nervy laugh. "I went on the tube this morning, travelled a few stops. There was another guy in the carriage, he got up when I got up. I came right across London, did two changes, he was always in the same carriage. I fixed him with the old 'on-off'. Stay on till the doors are closing, then you squeeze off. He went on down the line, he looked pretty pissed off. He must have been a South African . . ."

Jack was sombre, chewing at his thumb nail. "Why not our police?"

"They don't have an underground railway in Johannesburg. 'On-off' is the oldest one in the book, any London copper would know that one. Have to be a Boer not to know that one."

Jack felt sick. "Why follow you?"

"Perhaps they were there last night, saw us with the big fellow. Perhaps they're wondering who you are, perhaps they want a line into Thiroko. I don't know."

They were still watched from the window. Jack would have loved to have turned on his heel, walked back into the offices of D & C. He would have loved to have remarked easily to Nicholas Villiers that the distractions of the last days were a thing of the past.

The sneer came to Duggie's mouth. "Don't bloody whine. You were the one whispering about explosives, you were the one wanting to meet the military wing of the A.N.C."

"Sorry."

"I couldn't ring you. I couldn't be sure you weren't tapped here."

"Thanks."

Duggie looked exhausted. "Let's go meet the big boy." They drove into London.

Thiroko had come early. He was not a frequent visitor to London, but he was familiar enough with the British capital to be able to select his own rendezvous. He had chosen Lincoln's Inn Fields, a square of lawns and shrubs and tennis courts and flower beds and net ball courts. He liked open air meeting places where there were exits at all corners.

He was intrigued by the young man he had met the previous evening. And the young man was a distraction for his mind from the physician's message. He was sufficiently interested in the young man's brief explanation to him to have agreed to the meeting. And he knew, of course, of James Carew. He knew of the taxi driver who carried messages between dead letter drops, transported weapons between arms caches, could take photographs and draw maps. A White had access to many target areas where it was not safe for a Black to go. He knew of the usefulness of the quiet-tongued taxi man.

Thiroko was forty-eight years old.

He had been out of South Africa since the military wing was formed, since the banned African National Congress had gone underground. He had never been back. His homes had been in Moscow and Dar in Tanzania and Luanda and Maputo and Gaberone and now Lusaka. Some months he dreamed of a triumphant return with the war won and the apartheid regime humbled and beaten. Most years he doggedly refused himself horizons of hope and struggled on, organising the infiltration of men and munitions into his former country.

Thiroko straddled two generations of the Movement. He was neither a part of the old political hierarchy who wanted the military wing to attack only hard targets where the gesture mattered more than the mayhem, nor was he among the ranks of the young hawks who demanded the right to hit the soft targets of the White supermarkets and railway carriages and resort hotels. To his colleagues he was dedicated, humourless and reliable. To the South African police he was a murderous enemy, one they would dearly love to have trapped when the Recce Commando went into Maputo and Maseru in Lesotho and Gaberone. He had been out of Maseru less than twenty-four hours when the Recce Commando stormed the A.N.C. base houses. He hated the White war machine. He knew of no sacrifice too great if the regime could be brought down.

He saw Jack come into the square. He watched him pass the office girls playing net ball in their morning break. He saw him look around and pass the gardener laying out the first trays of the year's bedding plants. He knew of the boy's father. The Movement was peopled with men and women who could not keep their mouths tight shut. Carew had never been suspected of leaking information. A dozen years was a long, long time to have survived the resistance war in Johannesburg.

It had been Thiroko, from his office in Lusaka, who had suggested that Carew should drive the getaway.

He owed it to Carew that he should meet his son.

He watched Arkwright settle onto a bench close to the net ball pitch. He disliked the foreign Whites who lionised the Movement from the comfort of their European cities.

He watched to satisfy himself that there was no tail on the young man. The young man saw him, and Thiroko recognised the relief on Jack's face. The relief told him of the strain. The strain told him of the genuineness of Carew's boy. He presumed he was to be offered explosives, that he would have to explain gently that the Movement had all the explosives it could handle. He would do it in a kindly fashion.

"I am sympathetic to you, as I am sympathetic to the families of Happy Zikala and Charlie Schoba and Percy Ngoye and Tom Mweshtu. To all of the families goes the very sincere sympathy of the Movement."

"And what should those families do about it?" A harshness in Jack's voice.

"They will pray, they will attend protest meetings, in South Africa they are going to make video cassettes that will be sent to every head of state represented at the General Assembly of the United Nations."

"Prayers and protests and petitions, Mr Thiroko, are a great waste of time."

"Tell me what is not a waste of time."

"I am going to go to South Africa. To the gaol where my father is held. I am going to blow a hole in the wall, and I am going to take my father out."

"Should I laugh because you are so stupid, should I cry because you are so sincere?"

"It's not a joke to me."

Thiroko was hissing back at him. "You know what the gaol is, boy? The gaol is the peak of a security system. From every other gaol in the country men are escaping, and no man has escaped from that gaol for ten years. They are desperate men, they are going to hang, they are sitting in their cells for more than a year, most of them. They are *thinking* of escape, and for more than ten years none of them has managed it."

Jack on the offensive. He had the man arguing, not laughing. That was good.

"Anywhere that's maximum security is vulnerable. Maximum security breeds complacency."

"The gaol isn't up against the street. The gaol is in the middle of a complex. You would be shot hundreds of yards short of the walls. If you are shot dead, how does that help your father?"

"How does it help him if I sit on my arse, and pray and shout outside their embassy and ask politicians to watch a video? That's doing fuck all to help him."

"You would be killed."

"He's my father," Jack said flatly. "So be it."

Thiroko leaned back against the arm of the bench. He was trying to read Jack.

"You are a good boy. You work here, you have a family. You have to exist through the next weeks, then you have to resume your life. After it has happened you have to forget your father."

"I'm going to South Africa."

"Do you listen to anybody?"

Jack couldn't help himself, a snap grin. "Hardly ever."

"It is not my intention to help you to kill yourself."

"I'm going to bring my father home."

"Impossible, you understand that word?"

"Give me the chance."

"Your failure would hurt us, and it is *impossible* that you could succeed."

"Not if you helped me."

Thiroko shook his head, as if he did not believe what he learned in the slate grey eyes of Jack Curwen.

"I can't do it."

Jack's hand covered Thiroko's fist, a hard unyielding grip. "Where were you when the Court bomb went off? Where will you be when five men hang? Sitting on your arse and comfortable?"

"You take a chance with me, young man." The anger was brilliant on Thiroko's face.

"Lying in your pit and snoring?"

"I care about my men," Thiroko spat the answer.

"Your Movement took a chance with the lives of five men. You owe it to them to help me."

"No one tells me my duty."

"Your duty is to help them, not to sit on your bloody hands."

Thiroko softened. He had never been in combat in South Africa. He had never fired a Kalashnikov assault rifle at the Boer police or the Boer troops. He had never carried a bomb to a target and known the fear sweat in the fold of his stomach. He thought of what the physician had told him.

"What do you want?"

Jack felt the glow of success. "I can't take explosives with me, I can't get them through the airport. I want access to explosives in South Africa – and I want a team."

"Why should I trust you with a team?"

"When I get to Johannesburg, give me explosives, that's all. Sit on your hands, on your arse, and wait, and listen to the radio. You'll hear what your explosives have done, the radio'll tell you, what I've done on my own, and when you're satisfied then you'll give me a team."

"What is it you want exactly?"

"When I arrive I want a minimum of twenty pounds of explosive. I want detonators and Cordtex and safety fuse. I will hit the target of my choice. Then you'll know I'm worth the team."

"All for your father."

"To bring him back."

Thiroko took a notepad from his pocket. He wrote out an address. He showed the address to Jack, told him to memorise it, let his eyes linger on it, then folded the paper and tore it into a hundred pieces that he threw to float away and disperse over the grass. He told Jack to meet him at the address the following morning.

"You're going to help me?"

"I am going to think about helping you."

"Time's very short."

"I too learned to count. I know how many days are available."

Thiroko walked away from the bench. He was soon gone from sight. Jack was trembling. God, the assurance and the bombast had fled him. God, and was he frightened.

He was an age finding a phone box that worked.

He rang Jimmy Sandham at work. He wanted to meet with him, had to talk to someone.

A brisk voice answering, stating that he was through to the Foreign Office. Jack gave the extension number. Sandham had started him on his road. Jack wanted to meet him for a drink, to listen to his quiet control.

"Could I speak to Mr Sandham, please – a personal call."

A woman's voice, "Not here I'm afraid."

"Will I get him later, this afternoon?"

"He's taken a few days' leave."

"Since when?"

"He left yesterday."

"How long is he away?"

"Who is it asking for him, please?"

Jack put the phone down. He tried the home number. No reply.

He rang George Hawkins and invited himself over. He rang D & C and said he wouldn't be back that day.

It hit him. He had forgotten Duggie Arkwright. After leaving Lincoln's Inn Fields, he had walked into the West End, and then he had spent another ten minutes looking for a phone that wasn't broken or occupied. Duggie had sat down at the entrance to the square when Jack had gone forward to meet Thiroko. He hadn't been there when Jack had left. Duggie had done the introduction and had himself a tail, and Jack had put him out of his mind. He'd ring him when he could. He'd ring him when he came back.

He looked into a shop window. There were three layers of television sets:

cash, sale, and credit. They all carried the same picture. Of high armoured personnel carriers driving through a South African township of tin roofs and brick walls, and of gas plumes, and of the blue uniforms blasting with their shot guns, of running crowds, of police chasing with the long whips held back to strike in anger. The caption said they were old pictures, had to be because the camera crews were banned from the riot areas.

He wasn't going there to take a side in a civil war. He was going there to bring his father home. And it wasn't real. It was only old pictures on a bank of television screens. He knew what was bloody real. It was that his father was going to hang in three weeks, that Duggie had a tail that morning, that a woman had said Sandham had gone on leave.

He went to find his car, then to George's to talk about explosives.

He was the moth, the file was the lamp.

The Director General had read, word by word, every page in the Curwen/Carew file. He had started to imagine that he knew the man.

There was a photograph in uniform, early twenties from its date. There was a portrait shot before the fiasco in Albania. There was another shot taken during the debrief and after the hospital check-up. There was a blow-up of a Johannesburg newspaper photograph of Carew being brought out of court. The change was Albania. The flesh had been stripped off the man. But he couldn't mistake the defiance in the features, especially in those taken after the decade in Spac.

He had read Carew's South African reports. They were poorly written, but they were dense with names and gossip. There was no analysis, no interpretation, all as raw as sewage in a down flow. It crossed his mind to wonder whether the security police in Pretoria often had access to such quality information.

In the Alexandra township, three doors down Fifteenth Avenue from the north side junction with Hofmeyer there were stored under the back room floor boards, two R.P.G.–7 anti-tank rocket launchers, and eight missiles for the launchers were in waste ground beside the church wall on Second Avenue.

A 49-year-old street cleaner, who lived on Key in the Jabulani district of Soweto, had for two years been Umkonto we Sizwe commander of the whole township.

Seven Kalashnikov rifles were buried in protective grease wrapping in Dobsonville in the park that was bordered by Mahlangati and Matomela.

At a house, number given, on Mhlaba in the Chiawelo district, military planning meetings were held, when security conditions allowed movement in the night of the first Tuesday of each month. The fall back rendezvous was on Pilane in the Molapo district.

There was the house number in the Mamelodi township of Pretoria where a press printed A.N.C. literature. There was the name of the school from which that literature was dispersed, the identity of the schoolmaster who wrote the broadsheets.

Lists of officials in South African Laundry, Dry Cleaning and Dyeing Workers Union, and in Textile Workers Union (Transvaal), and in South African Chemical Workers Union, who were either politically or militarily active in A.N.C.

The names of couriers, African names, who carried low-level messages around the townships. One White named. J. van Niekerk, aged 19, disabled, student. And a White girl, named. Both addresses.

Careful maps showing infiltration routes into South Africa from Botswana.

The numbers of bank accounts, and the addresses of those banks. Accounts and banks where the A.N.C.'s money was lodged.

The Director General read through lists of intended targets. Police stations, power lines, railway track, a sewage filtration plant, a military recruiting office. A long list . . . There was a sketch plan of the approach route to be used for the rocket attack on the Sasolburg fuel storage tanks. There were the operational orders for the strike on the Voortrekkerhoogte army base. There were verbatim arguments between cadre cells on the priorities of attacks. Damned hard material to come by, no mistake.

The reports from years back had been worked over, he could see the pencil and ink ticks and underlinings that showed him that once these reports had been valued. Not the reports of the year before Carew's arrest. They were unmarked, and he thought they had gone unread into the file.

He was fitting together his picture of his man. He read that the S.I.S. officer attached to the British embassy in Pretoria used to come once a month to Johannesburg and go to a certain taxi rank at the South African Airways terminal and take a certain licensed taxi and pay for his fare and receive the latest Carew report with his change. All as amateurish as if his service had been playing boy scout pranks.

Carew had never come home. An addendum note stated "Gone native". A note in Fordham's handwriting to the effect that Curwen wouldn't trust himself too close to his former wife and his grown-up son should he ever return to London.

All the time the poor devil was being paid. Last Friday of every month a pay cheque rolling into a bank account in Liechtenstein. Signatories to the account: James Curwen, Col. B. Fordham. Statements from accounts at Century concerning the amounts deducted from his salary to make allowance for monies earned from his taxi driving.

He had misjudged his man, but he still believed he was past saving. He rose from his desk.

Silently he paced his carpet.

Past saving?

He pondered the options.

He extended the forefinger of his right hand. They could come clean to the South African government and make an apology and plead for clemency.

Second finger. They could scuffle around for sufficient leverage to ensure that Pretoria would respond to negotiation and spare his man and hold silence. Third finger. They could break the leg man out from the hanging gaol.

He snapped his fist shut. Absolutely not on. Inconceivable in the time, and fantasy.

Past saving.

He had a meeting scheduled with the Permanent Under Secretary for the late afternoon. The P.U.S. outranked the Director General for all that the Director General was in a position to control the flow of information available to the P.U.S. In the matter of James Sandham, the flow would be dammed at once. He had set aside 45 minutes directly after lunch, for himself and his principal officials to discuss the Carew case. It was a gesture, the setting aside of senior men's time, and unless someone came up with something right out of the ordinary it was the last gesture the Service would and could make.

Major Swart had fretted through the morning. He had sat in his office at the end of a corridor behind an automatic locking steel-barred door, willing the telephone to shout for him.

The two warrant officers who did most of the footwork in his small empire had called earlier to report that they had lost Arkwright, been tricked by him on the underground. Their second call had told Swart that they had picked him up again when he returned to his flat. Swart wanted badly to know the identity of the young man in the well-cut suit who had been huddled at the meeting with Thiroko. That young man was probably worth opening up, and Arkwright should have been the way to him.

There was a third call. Arkwright had just drawn the curtains to his room. From his state of undress it was to be assumed he was taking his slut to bed.

They sat in the kitchen. The sink and the stove needed three hours' work from a strong-willed woman. Jack doubted there had ever been a woman in George Hawkins' life, certainly no kids. The blaster never talked about a woman, talked mostly about his three cats. Big, confident brutes they seemed to Jack, sleeping on the kitchen table or striding over the stove or licking at used plates in the sink bowl. Jack sat on an old explosive box, upturned and covered by a grimed cushion. George was scooping cat food from a tin. Jack thought the cats ate better than the old blaster.

"Was it just kiddie's bullshit?"

Jack said, "I've found the right man, probably."

"For trusting?"

"I have to."

"Genuine guy?"

"He's on the military side."

The cats were chewing fiercely. George put a page of newspaper over the tin, left it on the window ledge above the sink.

"The targets are in South Africa?"

"Yes."

"Do you have a bloody conscience?"

"I don't."

"It's explosives, lad. It's not just a firework show where everyone has a good laugh and hears a big bang. Explosives get to hurt people."

"I don't want to hurt people. I just want to get my father out of that place."

"That's a piss poor answer."

"I don't know where yet, the first target will be in Johannesburg."

"Good and big, where the whole city sees it. I'll rot in hell, certain. You're talking about an act of war. It's bloody Harrods, lad; it's the Grand Hotel, it's the bandstand in Regent's Park, it's the Household effing Cavalry you're talking about. Have you got the guts for that?"

"I have to, or he's going to hang."

"There was a bomb in Northern Ireland, the La Mon House hotel . . ."

George went to a drawer. He excavated among cartridge boxes and pamphlets and books and old newspapers and older bills. He took out a nearly clean sheet of blank paper. He flicked his fingers for Jack to pass him a pen. He started to draw the diagram.

Firm and bold strokes of the pen.

"If they ever knew George Hawkins drew this for you then I'd be bloody lucky, Jack boy, if they just shot me."

"My father hasn't told them anything, I'm not intending to start."

"You take that away with you, and you learn it by heart, and you flush it away. Don't take that on your bloody aeroplane . . . What's the gaol?"

The marmalade cat had eaten too fast. It vomited on the linoleum. George seemed not to notice. Jack told him that Pretoria Central was a complex of five gaols. In the centre was the hanging gaol. He didn't know the layout, didn't know where his father's cell was, didn't know the guard patterns. He didn't know any bloody thing.

"If I told you it was just daft."

"I'd say you should mind your own business, Mr Hawkins."

"By helping you, am I just getting you killed?"

"Without you, I'd help myself."

George turned over the sheet of paper.

"Is it an old gaol or a new one?"

"I think it's newish."

"It'll have a wall round it. If it were old it would be brick or stone. If it's less than twenty years then it'll be reinforced concrete . . . You'd be better off just getting pissed every night 'til they hang him . . ."

"How do I knock a hole in reinforced concrete?"

"We're not even talking about how you're going to get into a security area, up against the bloody wall . . . You're not going to be able to drill holes and use cartridges. You're not going to be able to use lay-on charges, because you'd need a dumper load of earth to cover them or you'd have to shift a ton of sandbags."

"Don't tell me what I can't do."

"Easy, lad . . . Professor Charles Monroe, Columbia University, way back before we were born. It's what's called the Monroe Effect. It's the principle of armour piercing, what they use against tanks. Shaped or hollow charge, it's what it's called. Jack, they'll shoot you dead . . ."

"Draw me the shaped charge."

It was dusk when Jack left. He was in his car, the window wound down. George was bent to talk to him.

"I'll miss you, lad."

Jack grinned. "I won't be gone more than three weeks."

"I'm a bloody fool to have talked to you."

"Could it work, Mr Hawkins?"

"'Course it can work. If you remember everything I've told you, and if you remember everything you've seen over the last two years, and if you do everything like you've seen me do it, then it'll work. Forget one thing, a little small thing, and you're gone."

"I'll come on down and tell you how it worked."

George snorted. He turned away quickly, so Jack shouldn't see his face. He went back through his front door. He didn't look over his shoulder as Jack drove away.

When he was clear of the lane, out of sight of the bungalow, he stabbed the engine into life. The excitement gripped him. The same excitement as when his final school exam results had come through, and his university admission, and his first girl, and his winning of the job at D & C Ltd. Brilliant flowing excitement, like the first time George had let him do a blast. If he remembered every last little thing, then he could do it. He could take his father out.

"We're to meet tomorrow with the Prime Minister to talk damage limitation."

"I don't think there'll be damage," the Director General said. "I have learnt many things from our man's records. One of them is his tried and tested loyalty to the Service. He won't talk."

"Then he'll hang with his secrets." The P.U.S. rocked his glass slowly, willing the juice from the slice of lemon into further circulation.

"*Our* secrets."

"The Prime Minister would look unkindly on the least embarrassment."

"It won't come to that. I'd bet money on Carew's silence." He paused. "The fact is, I should like very much to save this man. I quite accept that it is politically unacceptable to go cap in hand and ask for his freedom, tell them who he is. We have looked at the odds against a team of men lifting him out of this gaol, and they are high."

"Too high, I don't doubt, and the Prime Minister wouldn't countenance the risk of failure. For heaven's sake don't let's have any old-fashioned stunts. The saving of Mr Carew's life just doesn't warrant the risking of anyone else's, not when you add the political risk."

Neither in London nor Lusaka did Jacob Thiroko have to consult with colleagues.

That night, alone, he would take the decision on whether the military wing of the African National Congress would back the venture proposed by Jack Curwen.

Amongst the senior officers of the Umkonto we Sizwe there were some who saw Whites, even if they were prepared to make the same sacrifices, as having no place in the Movement. Those Blacks of the military wing treated all Whites associating themselves with the A.N.C. with suspicion. They believed all of those Whites were communists first, true to the South African Communist Party, and loyal to the African National Congress, second.

Thiroko was not a communist. He had been to Moscow. He believed the Soviets, for all their aid in weapons and money, to be more racist than the Italians or the English or the Dutch or the Swedes.

If he were to have admitted to those senior officers of the military wing that a White had come to him with a plan of action and that he had supported him without consulting them then there would be questions circulated about his fitness to lead. Nevertheless, it would be his decision alone.

He sat in his room in the "safe house" in a quiet road in North Finchley. He drank coffee.

Better to have tried and failed than never to have tried at all.

Sentimental rubbish.

Revolutionary warfare was about victory. He was no advocate of glorious failure martyrdom. If a cadre of the Umkonto we Sizwe were to attack the maximum security section of Pretoria Central then they must succeed, they must free their condemned comrades. The agony of the decision lay in a particular area. It was the area that had stuck with him, caused him to drink his fourth and fifth and sixth cups of coffee, stayed with him through half a packet of cigarettes. The physician had told him to smoke as much as pleased him. The pain was more frequent. Was the Movement better served by saving Happy Zikala and Charlie Schoba and Percy Ngoye and Tom Mweshtu and James Carew from the gallows? Did the Movement gain more from the martyrdom of the Pritchard Five?

Which?

Better for the Movement to have at freedom five men who had bungled an attack, or better to have five heroes buried while the world screamed anger at Pretoria?

Which?

8

"Have you made your decision?"

Jack had come early to the "safe house". When the door had been opened to his ring he had smelled the aroma of sweet spices from the kitchen. She had been a tall woman with the dark skin of the Bengali and had two children clinging to her sari. She had shown no surprise, only taken him to the foot of the stairs and pointed upwards to the closed door.

"So direct. Should you not give me time to offer you coffee, to ask you to sit?"

He thought Jacob Thiroko had slept less than he had. The coffee mug stood amongst stain rings on the table. Beside it was an ashtray and the empty matchbox that had been used when the ashtray had spilled over. Thiroko sat at the table. The haze of smoke filled a strata of the room, morning mist over a damp meadow. Thiroko sat at the table. There was no other chair, only the unmade bed for Jack.

"I just need your decision. I want explosives, I want to prove myself to you, then I want help."

Jack saw the sadness on Thiroko's face. He knew it was the sadness of a military commander who sent young men onto the dirty battleground of revolutionary warfare.

"I'm going, Mr Thiroko, with your help or without it. With your help I'll make a better job of it."

Thiroko stood and pulled out his shirt from his trousers. He lifted the back shirt tail, and then his vest up to his shoulders. Jack saw the thin welt of the scar, pink on the dark skin, running diagonally across the length of his back.

"*Sjambok*, rhino hide whip. It is the way the police break up demonstrations. They use the *sjambok* when they do not think it necessary to shoot. I was a politician before they whipped me, I was a soldier afterwards"

Jack had his answer, his elation shone.

"I take a gamble on you, a small gamble. A few pounds of explosive. Nothing more until you have proved yourself."

They clasped hands.

Jack said he would fly within two days. Thiroko told him where he should stay, to wait for a contact, and thereafter, since he would be travelling in his own name, to keep on the move.

"Where will you be, Mr Thiroko?"

"I will be in Lusaka."

"You won't have long to wait." Jack was smiling.

Thiroko's face clouded with anger. "You are all children. You think it is a game. Last night l shamed myself with my thoughts. I thought whether it was better for our Movement if those five should hang. I considered whether five men dead was of more advantage to us than those five men free. I know the answer and I prayed for forgiveness on my knees . . . What will be your target for your explosives?"

Jack could smell the sweat on the sheets. "I don't know."

Thiroko laughed with amusement. "You are clever to be cautious."

"I don't know what the target will be, honestly."

Thiroko seemed not to have heard him. "We say that we trust each other, and we are strangers. There are men and women whom I have worked with for many years, and I do not know whether I can trust them. It was sensible of you not to have gone to our offices."

"I trust you, Mr Thiroko."

"It is a small building. Always full of people hurrying, busy, greeting each other, telling each other of their commitment to the Movement. But there are worms there rotting our cause. They may have been purchased by the Boers, they may have been compromised by threats against their family still in South Africa. No way of knowing. But you have my word that only those who *must* know will know of your journey."

"Thank you."

"You will be foolish if you underestimate the forces you are up against. If you are caught, you will wish that you could die to escape the pain the Boers will inflict on you. They will put electric shocks on you, keep you from sleeping, they will spin the chambers of a service revolver beside your head, they will starve you, they will hang you upside down from the ceiling with a broomstick under your knees and spin you, they will parade you naked in front of the men and women who work in the security police offices in John Vorster Square. It is where your father was, John Vorster Square . . . Trust nobody, trust only yourself."

"Do you know my father?"

"I know of him. He would know of me."

"I'll tell him about you."

Thiroko asked quietly, "If it were not your father."

"I wouldn't have known who the Pritchard Five were."

"I like honesty, Mr Curwen, but honesty will not help you in South Africa. Be the cheat. Cheat the Boers out of the satisfaction of five hangings."

Jack saw a fast grimace of pain on Thiroko's face, momentary, then wiped away. "Perhaps we won't ever meet again, but I'll tell Jeez that you're a good man."

Jack was lucky to have caught Dickie Villiers in the afternoon, a miracle that he wasn't hacking his way down the fairways. Villiers was at his desk. A quizzical look upwards from his boss. Nicholas would have briefed him, that in a bit over a week Jack was a changed man. Out of the office without explanation, effing and blinding in front of the girls, hangovers, an extraordinary creature coming in to collect him. Villiers had been steeling himself to call the lad in.

"I gather there are some problems, Jack." Villiers fondled his polka dot bow tie, chaffing at the awkwardness. He thought Jack Curwen was one of the best, one worth keeping.

"I have to go away, Mr Villiers," Jack said.

"You're not leaving us . . . ?" The blurted question. "I'm sure we could find more money."

"No, it's for three weeks only. I'm going tomorrow."

"That's damned short notice." Dickie Villiers leaned forward, his avuncular manner. "Are you in some kind of trouble?"

"I've a problem, I've three weeks to beat it."

"It's often better to talk something through."

"I am afraid I can't do that."

"Where are you going?"

"Sorry."

Villiers' patience was failing. "That's just impertinence."

"I hope my job stays open to me, Mr Villiers, and I hope to be back in three weeks."

"Are you involved in anything criminal?"

Jack smiled at him, shook his head.

"Let's not beat around, you're very fortunate to have this job." Villiers recovered quickly. "There're enough graduates looking for work, not to count those who never made it through. We gave you a real break. I made it my business to find out why you were sent down from university, and I've never held it against you. This is no way to be repaying my kindness."

"I've worked hard for you, Mr Villiers, but I'm not begging any favours. I'm going to be away because I've no choice. If you've given my job to someone else when I get back, I'll just have to find another one. Goodbye, Mr Villiers."

And before the older man could answer him, he was gone. Jack went to his desk and picked up the contracts pending file and took it to Nicholas Villiers' desk, dumped it. He put on his coat. He waved a kiss to Janice and winked at Lucille. He went out of the door. He walked out of the building.

He had turned his back on the world he knew.

Jack heard it on the car radio. He was driving across Leatherhead towards Churchill Close. He had just bought his ticket, open return, to Johannesburg, for the following evening.

". . . The soldier who has not yet been named was a member of a foot patrol in the strongly Republican Creggan district of Londonderry."

"A junior diplomat has been found dead below the summit of Carnedd Llewelyn in the Snowdonia range. It is believed that he fell more than 400 feet onto a ledge where his body was found by a mountain rescue team. He has been named as James Sandham. Mr Sandham, aged 52, was on a walking holiday in North Wales. It is thought that he lost his way last night and fell to his death while trying in darkness to make his way down from the 3,400 foot summit of the mountain which is described by local experts as treacherous for the inexperienced."

"The Chancellor of the Exchequer said this morning at a news conference before leaving for . . ."

Numbly he switched off the radio.

He was living in Britain. He was living in the oldest democracy and he was frightened. He was living where the government's agencies existed through the will of the people. Crap . . . Jimmy Sandham didn't look like a man who would have climbed two flights of stairs if there was a lift. He had taken Jack into his confidence, into the area of the Official Secrets Act, Section I, and into the area of the D-notice. Jimmy Sandham hadn't died on a walking holiday, for Christ's sake, he had died because he thought he'd found something rotten at the core of his country's government and had had the guts to say so.

In deep, controlled anger, Jack drove home.

Since Peter Furneaux had made the announcement of Sandham's death to the staff of South Africa desk, that office had been a sombre, lack-lustre place. The staff had packed up, gone home, on the stroke of half-past four, turning their backs on the empty table beside the radiator and the window.

Only Peter Furneaux stayed. He knew Sandham could be a cursed nuisance. He had seen him called to a meeting by the secretary of the P.U.S.; he had no idea what the meeting was about and he hadn't seen him again. He had received a memorandum from personnel informing him that the Grade 2 officer was going on immediate and indefinite leave. Sandham hated physical exercise, despised joggers, sneered at the lunchtime keep fit fanatics. With a straight face, with a stolid voice, he had told his colleagues that Jimmy Sandham had died in an accident while walking in Snowdonia.

Furneaux remembered the meeting when he and Sandham had faced the son of a man who was to hang in South Africa. He knew a little of the history of James "Jeez" Carew, enough to realise the sensitivity surrounding the man. He deliberated and he decided. He would make no mention to his superiors of the meeting with Jack Curwen. He would not report it. He had not put a minute of the encounter on the file and he wouldn't do so now. To have reported the meeting would have been to involve himself, to have put a spotlight on . . . Well, the odds were that the meeting with the P.U.S. had nothing to do with Carew. Furneaux's decision ensured that the operatives of the Secret Intelligence Service, the men of Century, had no line on James Curwen's son during the twenty-five hours that remained before the departure of his flight to South Africa.

He had come by the back route into 10 Downing Street. The Director

General always came through the Cabinet Office entrance in Whitehall, and the underground tunnel to the Prime Minister's office. The P.U.S. had taken the same route.

The Prime Minister said, "Director General, you were appointed to suppress the type of clandestine nonsense you are now telling me about."

The P.U.S. said, "In fairness to the Director General, Prime Minister, Carew was sent to South Africa long before his time."

The Prime Minister said, "I want to know exactly what was Carew's brief."

The P.U.S. nodded to the Director General. For him to answer.

"Carew was sent to South Africa with the job of fastening himself to protest and terrorist organisations operating in that country. The job was created by a Colonel Basil Fordham for whom Carew had previously worked. It was the assumption of the Service that in the years ahead it would be important to know the planning and capabilities of the revolutionary factions." The Director General paused, relit his pipe. He had the Prime Minister's attention. He fancied the P.U.S. thought him a windbag. "Some statistics, Prime Minister. South Africa is our twelfth biggest export market. We are the principal exporter into South Africa. We have the largest capital investment there. We have the most to lose if the place goes down in anarchy. We have 70,000 jobs directly linked to South Africa, another 180,000 indirectly dependent in that they are supplied by raw materials mined in South Africa. Should the present regime collapse, then we have to be sufficiently well-informed to ensure that any administration born out of revolution would be friendly to our interests."

"All of that seems to fall within the scope of conventional diplomatic observation."

The Director General puffed his disagreement.

"With respect, Prime Minister. In recent years South Africa has attempted to shield itself from guerrilla incursions by agreements with Mozambique, Angola, Botswana and Zimbabwe. This has led to the formation of cells, cadres, of A.N.C. activists inside the country. They act autonomously. General orders are given from outside, specific actions are usually initiated from inside. Conventional diplomacy can monitor outside, Lusaka headquarters of the A.N.C. Carew's brief was to infiltrate and report on the men inside . . ."

"To report . . ." the P.U.S. mouthed softly.

"Not to take part." The Prime Minister was hunched forward.

"Indeed not." The Director General stabbed his pipe stem for emphasis.

"Without being instructed to do so he engaged in terrorism?"

"So far as we know, Prime Minister, Carew's role was strictly on the periphery."

"An act of quite shocking violence?"

"I don't think we can assume that Carew, who was only the driver of a getaway vehicle, knew of the intended violence."

"But in which a courthouse was bombed and a policeman was killed?"

"Correct, Prime Minister."

The Prime Minister leaned back. "Then, periphery or no, he deserves the gallows."

"What if he talks?" the P.U.S. asked mildly.

"He won't." A rasp in the Director General's voice.

"Should he make a confession from the death cell then our position will be that this was a freelancer who supplied occasional and trivial information . . ." The Prime Minister shrugged. "A private individual, whose terrorist actions we totally and unreservedly condemn . . . I have to be back in the House."

They were in the corridor outside. It was an afterthought from the Prime Minister.

"This fellow, what sort of man is he?"

"A very brave man and intensely loyal to our country . . ."

The Director General saw the Prime Minister turn towards him, puzzled.

". . . who will die the victim of one horrendous mistake."

A spark of annoyance, and then the Prime Minister no longer listened. The meeting had run a little late. The black car was waiting for the drive to the House of Commons.

The Director General and the P.U.S. were left in the corridor, abandoned, because the circus was on the move.

"Why didn't you say that during the meeting?" the P.U.S. asked.

"No point, Carew's beyond our reach."

The P.U.S. touched the Director General's arm. There was a rare uncertainty in his eyes.

"That fellow we met, Sandham?"

"Happens to people who climb without the proper equipment. A very silly man."

Sam Perry stood by the window. He looked out over his tended garden. His wife sat in her usual chair, where she would have done her sewing or her knitting, where she would have watched television.

Jack paced. He couldn't have been still. He owed it to his mother, to talk to her. Couldn't have avoided the talk.

She stared all the time at the airline ticket that was on the arm of her chair. She said that she had thought it was just stupid talk when he had told her he was going to South Africa to bring his father home. She said that she had thought that he was just being emotional.

Sam hadn't spoken. Jack couldn't remember a time when Sam Perry had had nothing to say.

"You can't bring him home, can you?"

No reason to tell his mother about the man who was a military commander of the Umkonto we Sizwe wing of the African National Congress, nor about the man who was expert in his knowledge of shaped and hollow charges, nor about the man who had fallen to his death down a mountain in Snowdonia.

"It's just silliness, tell me it is."

And no reason to tell her about the man who lived in a cramped bedsit in

North London, who had a tail on him, and who had to play the "on-off" game on the underground to throw the tail.

"I'll see him."

"You'll give Jeez my love?"

Sam strode to the dark wood cabinet. He poured Hilda's sherry into a whisky tumbler. He poured Jack a beer.

"It'll be all right, Mum, I promise you that," Jack said.

He doubted she believed him. She had no reason to. She liked to say that her Jack was a bad liar. She muttered about Sam's and Jack's dinner. They watched her go towards the kitchen, nursing her drink.

"Is there a chance?"

"I've no choice but to try," Jack said.

"It'll break your mother's heart if anything happens to you."

"I can't leave him there for them to hang."

The proxy father gazed at him. In many ways he regarded Jack as his own achievement. He thought his influence had given the young man his work ethic, his straightness, and his honesty. He thought he had the right to be proud of the way his step-son had grown. But the quiet authority and the bloody-minded determination, they weren't Sam's. Since he had met Hilda, when she was a bitter, introverted young woman, he had thought of Jeez Curwen as a right bastard. The authority and the determination weren't Sam's and they weren't Hilda's. They could only be Jeez Curwen's hand down to his son. The man could not be a right bastard, not if this was his boy. He understood that he and Hilda could douse the boy with affection, love, he understood that Jack must go to find his true father. He was ashamed, because he felt envy.

"Come home safe," Sam said hoarsely.

They'd picked up the scum when he left the flat to go for his drink.

Piet used the pay telephone in the lounge bar, Erik stayed in the public bar to watch. They wouldn't be thrown again. The business in the underground still smarted with Erik, and the yelling he'd had from the major. No chances taken when the scum had gone to the pub, Erik walking behind the scum and Piet on the far side of the road in case the subject spotted the tail and dived into the traffic for a quick jump on a bus.

The scum had been two hours in the pub, sitting on his own, nursing his drinks to make them last. Near to closing time when Piet had gone to the telephone. The warrant officers did as their major told them. Independent action was not their right.

Erik watched Duggie Arkwright. Scum was a good word for the subject. What did the scum know of South Africa? What did he know of the melting pot of the ethnic minorities that made up the Republic's population? Scum, Arkwright, would think of all non-Whites as being the same. The scum wouldn't consider that there were Asian Muslims and Asian Hindus, and

Coloureds, and then the groupings of Africans – Tswana and Xhosa and Tsonga and Swazi and Zulu, all the others. Chuck power at these groupings and there would be anarchy. If the Zulu had power over the Xhosa, or the Swazi over the Tswana . . . the State President knew what he was at when he kept the brakes on, which was more than the morons knew who shouted in London about oppression.

Erik was at the bar, leaning back, naturally, overlooking the scum. He could never read Piet's face, had to wait to be told what were the major's instructions.

"Shake the creature a bit. Says he has to know who the creature took to meet Thiroko."

Erik looked down at Arkwright. All skin and bone and wind. Erik had played open side flanker for Transvaal B. The scum would have no muscle and no balls. If they shook the scum he'd rattle.

Arkwright walked home.

He had drunk four pints of Worthington, it was social security day. He was feeling low, feeling used. He'd put his bloody best bloody foot forward for priggy Curwen, and priggy Curwen had gone off into the wind. No thanks, no call. No bloody decency from priggy Curwen. And Anthea was pregnant again. First vomiting that morning. He was thinking of priggy Curwen and of Anthea heaving in the john, and with the beer inside him it was hard thinking. He never looked behind.

They took him fifty yards from his door. One from the front, one from behind. He thought he was being mugged, which was a laugh, last bloody penny for the last bloody pint . . . Down an alley. No lights. He smelled day old aftershave and day old body lotion, and he knew he wasn't being mugged. A punch in the solar plexus to double him, an uppercut to straighten him. He went down.

For a moment he saw them. He knew they were South Africans. Knew they were Boer pigs. Something of the width of the shoulders, the breadth of the hips. The hands were coming down out of the blackness to pull him up. He saw the pale blur of the faces, grinning. They reckoned he was insufficiently shaken. He was never asked to say who was the young man that he had introduced to Thiroko. It was Piet's hand that groped for Duggie's beard, to pull him up, to hit him again. The fingers found the beard. Duggie bit him. Closed his jaw on the hand and bit and shook his head as a terrier will with a rat. Bit and chewed at the hand, and heard the Boer pig scream, and felt the fingers loose his beard, and clung on while his teeth were half wrenched from his head. Piet heaved backwards and blocked Erik's chance to get his boot into the scum's rib cage.

Duggie staggered and ran.

He ran towards the lights and safety of the main road. He thought only of flight. He heard the pounding feet behind him. He ran up the alley, across the pavement, and into the path of a 38 London Transport double decker bus.

At the end of the alley Erik gripped Piet's arm, stopped him from going forward. He held him back in the shadow. Erik could see the white-shock face of the conductor of the bus as he knelt beside his front wheel. He could hear the screams of a woman who had bent to look under the bus.

"You should get some medication for that hand, the scum might have rabies," Erik said.

Jack's flight was delayed for fifty minutes.

Because of the late departure, sitting in the lounge, he read the evening paper front to back. He read of the death of Douglas Arkwright. It was said that Douglas Arkwright, 27, married and one child, had been drinking, that he had walked under a bus. The story made the paper because the traffic jam that followed the fatal accident had held up a royal princess on her way to open an art exhibition in Hertfordshire.

When the flight was called, Jack dropped the newspaper into a rubbish bin and walked briskly towards the boarding gate and his aircraft.

9

Jeez sat on the end of his bed.

He had eaten his porridge breakfast and given back his bowl and kept his mug. He was allowed to keep his mug and use it for drinking water during the day. He had washed and shaved under supervision. He had swept out his cell, not that there was much to sweep away because he had swept the cell floor every morning for the thirteen months that he had been in Beverly Hills. After he had swept the floor he had scrubbed it with a stiff brush and the bar of rock solid green soap that was for the floor and for his body. Sweeping the floor and scrubbing it were the only workloads demanded of him. No other work was compulsory for the condemns.

There was no singing that morning.

He sat on his bed because it was the only place he could sit when the floor was damp. Later in the day he sometimes sat on the floor and leaned his back against the wall that faced the cell door, beside the lavatory pedestal, but only for variety. Most of the day he sat or lay on his bed. He read sporadically, books from the library. He had never been a big reader. At Spac he had learned to be without books. If he was not reading then there was nothing but the time for thinking to disturb the events of his day which were his meals and his exercise session.

The thinking was hell.

Difficult ever to stop thinking. Thinking when his eyes were open and when they were closed, and when he was washing, and when he was eating, and thinking through dreams when he was asleep.

He hadn't had much of an education, but there was no stupidity in him, not until he'd been hooked into driving the getaway out of Pritchard. Jeez knew the days were sliding. He knew the legal processes had been exhausted. He knew his life rested on the State President's decision. He knew that the State President refused commutation of the death penalty to the cadres convicted of murder. He knew that in these days of unrest the State President would hardly waive the penalty just because Jeez was White ... Here we go, alto–bloody–together we go ... Jeez didn't have to have a university degree to know.

He wondered how much notice they would give him. He wondered whether it would be the governor who would tell him.

He wondered how he'd be.

Some thoughts took charge in the night, some in the day. The overwhelming thought was the fear of fear. The fear of buckling knees, the fear of his bowels and his bladder emptying, the fear of screaming or crying.

His thoughts of the team were increasingly rare. When he had first come to Beverly Hills he had thought every day of the team he had been a part of. Then there had been the favourite thought, an indulgent memory. He had been flown back from Greece after the exchange, with two guards down the steps of one military aircraft, marched across eighty paces, head back, elbows stiff, outpaced the guards, somebody signing something, the rest lost in a blur, up the steps into the RAF transport, mugs of hot tea laced with something by Lennie and then what seemed like two days' sleep before he had been met at Northolt by Colonel Basil. He'd had his hand pumped and he'd been whisked into the big black car. He'd expected that he would be booked straight into a medical examination. Hadn't reckoned with bloody good old Colonel Basil. Directly into London. Over the bridge, down the ramp to the underground car park. Up the lift. Onto the 7th floor of Century. Into East European (Balkan). All of the team there, all of them sliding up from their chairs, and then Henry clapping his hands over his head, getting Adrian going, and Lennie following. And all of them giving Jeez the big hand, and Adrian kissing him on both cheeks and then on the lips, and the back slapping so hard that they half blew him away. And Colonel Basil smirking by the door and saying in his Brigade of Guards whisper, "The team never forgets a man in the field. The team always gets its men back." One of the girls scurrying off for beakers, and the champagne corks rocketing into the ceiling, and Jeez grinning like a Cheshire cat. And much later the car to a private clinic . . . His favourite thought. The good thoughts had faded with the months. The thought of how the team would be working for him came only infrequently now, usually when he was dreaming, and when he woke and felt the cold dawn air then the thoughts of the team were bloody smashed. It wasn't that he doubted that the team was working for him, he doubted now that the team had the power to take him out from Pretoria Central.

He yearned for quiet outside his cell. But the C section corridor, and the small corridor through C section 2 were never quiet in the daylight hours. There were always the voices of the prison officers as they told stories, laughed, talked about the papers and the television. There was always the shout of a duty officer approaching a locked door, and the door clattering open, and the smack of it closing. Those were the noises that were on top of the singing. No singing that morning, and that meant no hammer of the trap being tested in the afternoon. Each time he heard the shout for the doors to be opened, and then the clatter, and then the smack, he stiffened, and the sweat sprang to his forehead and his armpits and his groin. There would be a shout and a clatter and a smack when they came to tell Jeez that it was commutation, or when they came to tell Jeez which day it would be, which dawn for the short walk.

He often thought of the others.

He hadn't seen the others for thirteen months, not since the passing of the sentence and the drive in the meshed police wagon across Pretoria and up the hill to the gaol. He hadn't seen them since the apartheid of the reception area at Beverly Hills. They had gone right to B section, he had gone left to

C section. That was "separate development" for you. Four for B section because they were Black, Jeez for C section because he was White. They'd been laughing that day thirteen months before, walking loosely, easily in their leg irons and hand-cuffs. He wondered how they'd be now, waiting to learn if they'd all go. A bastard, that, if one or two of them were reprieved, and the others were taken to the hanging room . . . Wouldn't be a bastard, they'd all five go, because it had been a policeman. He'd meet them again in the preparation room. There they'd be together, apartheid waived, "separate development" non-operable.

There was a shout. There was the clatter of a door opening. There was the smack of a door closing.

Still and upright on his bed, Jeez waited.

He knew all the distances that sound carried through the unseen parts of the gaol. He had heard the door that was the entrance to the C section corridor. There was a murmur of voices. Another door opening. The door into C section 2. The unchanging ritual. He wondered why they always shouted their approach to a locked door, why the door was invariably slammed behind them.

He felt the wetness on his skin. He saw the flash of a face at the grille.

He stood at attention. He stood every time a prison officer entered his cell. A key turned in the oiled lock.

Sergeant Oosthuizen, smiling benignly.

"Morning, Carew. You slept well, did you, man? Your room's a picture. Wish my lady kept our house like you keep your room. You're going to have your exercise early, straight after your lunch . . ."

Jeez closed his eyes. All the shouting, all the clattering of the doors, all the slamming, to tell him that he was to be exercised an hour earlier than was routine.

"Yes, Sergeant."

"There's a nice afternoon for you, you've a visit."

He was very slight. With his crash helmet on, Jan van Niekerk seemed almost misshapen. There was something grotesque about such small shoulders capped by the gleaming bulge of the helmet.

The Suzuki 50cc was his pride and joy. For insurance purposes it was a moped, but in Jan's mind it was a fully-powered scrambler/road machine. He passed only cyclists and joggers, he was forever being buffeted in the slipstream of overtaking lorries and cars, but the Suzuki was his freedom.

In term time he came each morning from his parents home in Rosebank down the long straight Oxford, onto Victoria and Empire, and then along Jan Smuts to the University of Witwatersrand.

He loved the moped, whatever its lack of speed, because the under-powered Suzuki provided him with the first real independence of his 21 year old life. His club foot, his right foot, was a deformity from birth. He had endured a childhood of splints and physiotherapy. He had had to be ferried in his mother's car to and from school, he had never played rugby or cricket. The wedge that was built into the raised heel of his leather ankle boot gave him a rolling limp and prevented him from walking any great distance. Before the moped he had been dependent on others. Along with the moped came a black leather two-piece riding suit. The combination of his stunted physique and his taste for biker's gear made Jan a student apart. In the huge university he was virtually friendless, and that bothered him not at all.

His friends were far divorced from the Wits campus. His own comrades. He had his own contact codes. He enjoyed a secret area of life that was undreamed of by his colleagues on the Social Sciences course. In this society, dominated by muscle power and sports skills where he could play no part, his Suzuki and his comrades gave him the purpose he craved.

His parents marvelled at the difference in their son's attitude since they had bought him the moped. They thought of him as a good serious boy, and one who showed no inclination towards the radicalism that they detested and that seemed so rife on the campus. At home, Jan gave no sign of interest in politics. They knew from their circle of friends who had kids at Wits that their Jan had no links with the students, mostly Jewish, who led the university demonstrations and protests, who were whipped by the police, savaged by the security staff dogs. Jan had described those activists to his parents as ridiculous middle class kids with a guilt complex. They knew Jan had left the campus early on the day that Dr Piet Koornhof, Minister of Cooperation and Development, had been pelted and heckled. On another day he had walked away from the burning of the Republic's flag and the waving of that rag of the African National Congress. His parents thought the making of Jan had been his moped and his studies.

There was a White girl doing ten years in the women's prison at Pretoria Central. She had been active in radical politics before devoting herself to the collecting of information for the A.N.C. Impossible to make the switch from overt to covert work. Jan had always been covert. Anyone who knew him, his parents, his sister, his lecturers, the students he sat with in lectures, would have been thunderstruck to have discovered that Jan van Niekerk was a courier for the Umkonto we Sizwe.

A harmless little figure on his bumblebee of a moped, Jan pulled into the campus, parked behind the Senate House.

He limped past the portico and columns at the front of the building, across the wide paved walkway and down over the lawns. He preferred to walk on grass, easier and less jarring on his right foot. He walked around the amphitheatre, ignored the swimming pool and slogged his way up the steps to the modern concrete of the Students' Union. He saw the posters advertising the evening meeting to protest against police brutality on the Eastern Cape, went right past them. His greatest contempt was for the students who shouted against the government from the safety of the campus. He believed that when those students had graduated they would turn their backs on decency and honour, that they would buy their homes in the White suburbs and live out their lives with privilege stowed in their hip pockets.

Crippled and forever awkward, Jan van Niekerk would be there on the day of reckoning. He believed that absolutely. A day of reckoning, a day of fire. His struggle with his disability had tempered his steel strength of purpose. That purpose was the cause of Umkonto we Sizwe.

On the first floor of the Students' Union he had a metal locker, opened by his personal key. He had depressed the top of the door at the centre, where it was weakest, a full quarter of an inch. The locker was where he kept his biking leathers and it was his dead letter drop. Four other men only in the sprawling mass of the city of Johannesburg knew of Jan van Niekerk's locker. In these days of the state of emergency, of the regulations justifying widened police power, to be cautious was to stay free, to be exceedingly careful was to avoid the interrogation cells of John Vorster Square.

He stripped off his leathers. He unlocked the door.

The note was a tiny, folded, scrap of paper. The corridor holding the bank of lockers was always crowded, a concourse for students and lecturers and administration personnel and cleaning staff. Good and secure for a dead letter drop. Hidden by the open door he read the note as he packed his leathers into the locker.

About once every two weeks he was contacted.

A small link in a long chain, there was much that Jan van Niekerk was unaware of. A message from Thiroko had been telephoned from London in numbered code to Lusaka. Part of that message had been relayed on from Lusaka to Gaberone in Botswana. A smaller part of the message had been handcarried towards the international frontier and on by bus to Lichtenberg. From Lichtenberg that smaller part had been telephoned to Johannesburg.

He read the message. He had the paper in the palm of his hand as he closed the locker's door. He went to a lavatory and flushed the message away.

He had to hurry. He was late for the morning's first lecture.

The aircraft lurched, the engine pitch changed. The captain announced the start of the descent.

Around Jack the South African nationals were crowding to the windows to look down, excited. God's own country was unfolding below them. Jack's mind was a blank. Too tired to think. The stewardess was collecting the blankets and the headsets. He felt as a small boy does, sent alone for the first time on a train journey. The fear of the unknown. The stewardess took his earphones that he hadn't used, and his blanket that he hadn't unfolded.

He drew his seatbelt tighter round his waist. The fear was new to him. He did not know how it should be conquered.

Frikkie de Kok had slept in.

He'd hardly heard Hermione leave her bed when she'd gone to get the boys up and dressed and fed for school. He was allowed his peace. She was in a fine mood, fine enough for her to have allowed Frikkie, in the night, out of his own bed and into hers. Fine enough for her to bring him his breakfast once he had grunted, coughed a bit, cleared his throat. He thought she was in so fine a mood that she wouldn't bother him if he smeared his marmalade on his sheets. Well, he had capitulated to her, he had promised that she would have her new refrigerator. Imported, of course. And since the rand had gone down and the foreign bankers had sold the South African currency short, the refrigerator would cost him a small fortune, not so small because his mind was working better, because he was waking, counting the cost and the tax. But she was a good woman, and she needed the new refrigerator.

With his breakfast of juice and coffee and thick-sliced toast, there was his mail. Frikkie de Kok always opened all the family post himself. A postcard from his sister, and a bill from the electricity, and there was a familiar brown envelope carrying the official stamp of the Ministry of Justice, and there was a letter bearing the crest of the boys' school. He read the postcard, snarled at the bill. He opened the school's envelope.

Brilliant . . . The principal writing to say that Dawie's progress was excellent, he was working hard, and could well be university material . . . Hell, there had never been a graduate in Frikkie's family.

Calculations in his mind. Could he afford the weights that Dawie hankered for? If he could afford the weights as well as the refrigerator then he would be helping Dawie towards a place on the fifteen, and a boy on the school fifteen with good marks would be more likely for a scholarship when the university time came. But if he bought Dawie the weights, if he could afford them, would that make young Erasmus jealous? No, no problem, because Erasmus could share the weights.

He would have to work harder. Work harder, that was good.

He opened the letter from the Ministry of Justice. The Ministry always posted first and then telephoned two days later to confirm the notification of another early rising.

The judder as the undercarriage was lowered.

Jack could see the ground below as the Boeing banked for final approach. Row upon row of small squares reflecting back the sun. The tower blocks of Johannesburg were on the horizon. He realised the squares were the tin roofs of tiny homes. Endless straight lines of light flashes, and then the patch of yellow dried-out veld between the townships and the city. The chief steward was hurrying along the aisle, steadying himself against the seatbacks, checking that the seatbelts had been fastened and the cigarettes extinguished. Jack read through his answers on the blue foolscap sheet for immigration. Questions in English on one side, Afrikaans on the reverse. OCCUPATION – Manager. PURPOSE OF VISIT – Holiday. LENGTH OF STAY – 3 weeks.

If he hadn't managed it in three weeks then he might as well have stayed at home.

They liked her in the office. They thought Ros van Niekerk was one of the most conscientious girls that they employed. They thought her sensible, level-headed, and able to take the limited responsibility that could be pushed her way in the Insurance high rise tower on Commissioner.

She was twenty-four years old. She was plain because she didn't care to be otherwise. She worked in the property insurance department. On most household policies there was reassessment as the policy became renewable at the end of a year's cover. Ros van Niekerk could have told the Minister of Finance where the economics of South Africa were going. It was in front of her from 8.30 in the morning to 4.30 in the afternoon five days a week. Three years earlier when she had gone into the property department, a good bungalow in the better Johannesburg suburbs would have fetched 350,000 rand and been insured for that value. The market had gone from bad to worse. A year ago that same property might have changed hands for 200,000 rand and now it might fetch 120,000 rand, it was that great a change. The home owner wasn't going to renew a 350,000 rand policy if his home would only fetch 120,000 rand. But the rates of insurance were going up. The political uncertainty, the unrest, the quagmire of Black and White relations guaranteed that insurance rates would rise. For very nearly every policy that Ros renewed there was a correspondence. She was busy. She rarely took more than twenty minutes of her lunch hour. She alone knew her way through the hillocks of files that covered her desk-top.

She used no lipstick, no eye shadow. She washed her auburn hair herself, combed and brushed it from a central parting. She dressed functionally and without ambition. The men in the office, the married and the unmarried, had long ago lost interest in her. She was not taken out. She had been asked, when she was a new girl, and she had invariably declined, and the invitations were no longer offered. The salesmen and the junior managers were polite to her but distant. If her social isolation in the company disturbed her then she was successful at disguising the disappointment. To those who worked alongside her she seemed happily self-sufficient. They knew she came from a good home, that her father was a professional man. They knew she had a younger brother at Wits. They knew very little else about her. In truth, there was very little else they might have known. At the end of each day she went directly home in her Beetle VW, she had her dinner with her mother and father, and her brother if he was back from the campus, she listened to music and she read. They might have thought of her as a boring girl who was on the road to end up an old maid. The young men in the office had decided she wasn't worth the trouble, there was easier game.

Her telephone warbled. A pay box call. A frown of irritation at the interruption.

Her brother on the telephone. The irritation was gone. Her young kid, her Jan, her crippled brother. Always so close, brother and sister. Since he was little more than a baby she had loved the young kid. Perhaps a reaction to a time long ago when she had seen the poorly-disguised dismay of her father that his only son was handicapped.

Could Ros tell her mother that Jan would not be home for dinner. Jan couldn't call his mother direct, of course, their mother was out at whist.

To Ros, her brother was a more precious part of her life than anything she thought she would find in the hands of the young men in the office.

A radio news bulletin on the hour. The correct English diction of the South African Broadcasting Corporation.

"One person was killed in unrest at a Black township on the Western Cape. A spokesman at the Police Directorate in Pretoria said the Black teenager was shot dead when a policeman's relative fired into a crowd that was trying to set light to a policeman's home."

"A total of 107 Blacks were arrested during unrest in the East Rand following incidents during which administration board vehicles and municipal buses were stoned."

"In another incident of unrest in the East Rand a White woman driving an administration board car fired in self-defence on a mob that had stoned her. No injuries were reported."

A pretty quiet night.

But since the state of emergency had been declared by the State President, and since the curbs had been slapped on Press reporting, fewer details of attacks and incidents and deaths were furnished by the Police Directorate.

A quiet night, and the unrest was far down the order of the bulletin. The unrest came after a speech by the Foreign Minister, ahead of the results of the Springbok men's gymnastic team on tour in Europe.

The message of the bulletin to its White audience was polished clear. Difficulties, of course there were difficulties. Crisis, of course there was no crisis. Inside the laager of the old wagons the Republic was holding firm. Holding firm, and holding tight.

That was the message of the S.A.B.C. as the Boeing from far away Europe taxied on the long Jan Smuts runway.

Jack came down the steep open steps onto the tarmac.

Around him the passengers blinked in the crisp sunlight. Jack was tired, nervy. Had to be nervous because he was going to walk up to immigration and make the pretence that he was a tourist with his head full of sea and sunshine and safaris. He was part of a shuffling crocodile that moved past four Black policemen, immaculate and starched, and into the terminal.

A young White policeman was seated by the doorway. He was lounging back on a tilted straight chair. He wore short drill trousers, long socks to the knee, shoes to see his face in, a tunic and a Sam Browne belt onto which was hooked a shined brown leather revolver holster. Jack caught his eye, looked away. He thought there was an arrogance about the bastard, a contempt for these unshaven, crumpled flotsam spilling in from Europe.

He took his place in the FOREIGNERS line.

It was brief and it was correct.

All that anxiety had been for nothing. Passport examined, immigration form looked over, the belt of the stamp on the slip of paper that was stapled into his passport, his passport returned.

They had given him six weeks.

He had to grin.

He would be out in three weeks or he would be dead, or he would be staying as a guest for twenty years.

He collected his bag, was waved through customs, and took a taxi. He was driven away on a sweeping multi-lane highway. He flopped in the back seat. The tiredness was aching in his shoulders and legs. The driver was middle-aged, White, overweight. Beside his speedometer there was sellotaped a photograph of his family, an obese woman and two plump children.

"You're from England, eh? What brings you to South Africa, eh?"

The driver ignored Jack's silence.

"Don't get me wrong, man, I've nothing against you, but that's where our problem is, foreigners, specially English foreigners. People telling us what to do. People who don't live here, don't know a thing about South Africa, and all they can think of is telling us how to get on with our lives. The English tell us . . . That's rich, that's a real joke. The English tell us how to treat our Blacks, and they've riots in Birmingham and London . . . What more do I have to say?"

On either side of the road Jack could see the effects of the months of drought, high dried out grass. Then modern industrial estates, sprinkled with the For Sale and To Let signs.

"Eh, man, we know our Blacks a sight better than they do. We've had years of them. You know that? What a Black man respects is strength. If you pussyfoot to the Black man then he'll cut your throat. If you're firm with him, then he behaves himself. You have to be firm with the Black man and you have to remember not to trust him, not an inch. What I say about the Black man is this – if he can't steal it or screw it, then he'll break it. My sister, she's on a farm up in the North East Transvaal. She's got a neighbour who's come from Rhodesia, started again, started from nothing, building up a new farm. You know what her neighbour told her, as God's my witness? He said, 'Winnie, if there's trouble, just a hint of trouble, first thing to do is to slot the nanny.' Good advice, because you can't trust the Blacks."

The road was lined now with small concrete bungalows. White homes. Perhaps the homes of taxi drivers. Higher up on the hill, on sites that were scraped from the ochre-red soil were the speculators' town houses.

"What they don't understand, those people in England, preaching to us, is that the violence isn't about Blacks and Whites, it's Black against Black. You didn't know that, I'll bet. You should see what they do to each other. They're savages, they chop each other, burn each other. And people in England say we should give them the vote. Most of them can't read . . . They don't want the vote. Most of them just want to live quietly, have their beer, work on a farm. They don't want politics and they don't want violence. The blame's with the agitators and the commies, winding them up. All the encouragement they're getting from liberal places, England, America, it's doing nothing for the Blacks. I've a nephew in the police, great young man, in the anti-terrorist unit, uniformed, he tells me it's all the fault of agitators and commies. They're too soft on those A.N.C. people, that's my criticism of the State President. They should hang the lot of them. Shouldn't just hang those they get for murder, like those swine that did the court, they should hang any of them they find with guns and bombs."

"Are they going to hang them?" Jack asked.

"You know about them, do you? In your newspapers, was it? It was on the radio last night. No clemency, not for any of them. All the liberals in England will be shouting when we hang them, but we're a long way from England and we don't hear the shouting . . . You a rugby man, eh? That's the Ellis Stadium . . ."

Jack saw the huge terraces of concrete, the rows of red seating.

"My idea of heaven. Up in the West Stand with a few beers and the Boks in their green jerseys, and even that those radicals have managed to spoil. I had tickets for the All Blacks last year, I thought they had more guts in New Zealand, I didn't think they'd cancel on us. Here you are, man, your hotel."

Jack slid out of the taxi. He was bathed in sweat. He paid the driver, gave him a tip before he realised how much he loathed the man.

"Thank you, very kind. I've really enjoyed our conversation. You have a good holiday, sir. And you take my advice, get yourself to the Ellis Park when the Transvaal are playing."

There were grinning faces around him, smiling faces of the Black doorman and the suitcase boy. He was led across the ornate hotel lobby, past the jewellery and curio shops, to the front desk. He wondered what they would have to say about the supreme penalty and the Pritchard Five. He filled in the registration form. He reckoned that he was thirty miles from Pretoria Central prison.

As soon as he walked into the room Jeez recognised the colonel.

Sergeant Oosthuizen had brought Jeez from his cell to the visit. He had known there was something extraordinary when they had walked on past the line of doors for C section's visit rooms, and on into the administration block. He had not been back in that block since his first day at Beverly Hills.

Jeez stared from the door into the colonel's face.

Jeez had been through the Spac labour camp and before that through the investigation centre in Tirana. Only the thought of being hanged frightened him. The sight of the colonel did not make him afraid.

The colonel's empire was the interrogation floor of John Vorster Square police station in Johannesburg.

On the tenth floor where he ruled, the gaze of the colonel was reckoned to buckle a man's knees, a Black man's or a White man's, to make water of his bowels. The colonel never hit a prisoner, he was always out of the room by the time that a prisoner was stripped, was gasping, was screaming. The colonel ordered what happened to the prisoners. The servants of his empire were the captains and the lieutenants and the warrant officers of the security police.

Jeez knew the colonel. An old acquaintance. Jeez had never given him anything. Each time that the colonel had come back into the interrogation rooms of John Vorster Square after the beating, when the torturers were panting from their work, Jeez had stayed silent.

"I hate you, all you White bastard commies. I want to kill you White filth. I want to shoot you with my own gun." Jeez could remember the straining red blotched face as the colonel had shouted at him, early in the days of John Vorster Square. The colonel, with his retinue of phone-tappers, searchers, tailers, letter openers, frighteners, had screamed at him through the spittle. Jeez reckoned he'd given up early. Jeez reckoned the colonel had given up on this one prisoner when he had realised he was fighting a losing battle, and he hated to be close to failure.

The colonel was Jeez's "visit".

The colonel and his warrant officer. Jeez knew the W.O. He had done time on Jeez at John Vorster Square, hand slaps and punches, and twice the boot. He had started in on Jeez as soon as the colonel had gone back to his office. Jeez had heard in the basement cells of the Pretoria court house, when he was locked in with Happy and Charlie and Percy and Tom, that it was the W.O. who had got Percy talking first, and Tom second, and then Charlie and Happy. They had all been softened by the W.O. and then made their voluntary statements to the colonel.

They were in a senior officer's room. There was a glass-topped desk and comfortable chairs and vase of flowers on a shelf over the radiator and a photograph of the State President on the wall and curtains. Jeez hadn't known that such a room existed inside Beverly Hills. The door closed behind him. Jeez looked round. Oosthuizen had gone. He was alone with the colonel in his slacks and his blazer, and the W.O. in his lightweight suit. Both sitting, relaxed, as if they'd enjoyed a good lunch.

"I am a convicted prisoner, sir," Jeez said firmly. "I do not have to submit to further police interrogation."

The colonel smiled, bending the line of his snipped brush moustache. "Who said anything about interrogation, Carew?"

"Sir, I would like to go back to my cell."

"You're jumping the gun, man. I'm not here to ask questions."

He would have seemed a slight, frail figure to them. Jeez thought that the W.O. would have dearly liked him to raise a fist to the colonel, would have enjoyed beating the hell out of him.

"We wanted to have a talk with you, Carew. We wanted to see if we could be of help to you."

An old trick that Jeez had taught himself in Spac, with the real bastards among the interrogators. Take away the uniform, strip off the shirt and vest and socks and boots. See them only in their underpants. See a menacing man in his underwear, see his hanging white belly and his spindly legs, see him without the uniform that makes for fear, creates authority. His mind gave him the picture of the colonel in his underpants. He stared back at the colonel.

Eyes meeting, neither man turning away.

"Has the governor seen you today, Carew?"

"No, sir."

"You haven't been told of the State President's decision regarding clemency for you?"

"No, sir."

The colonel turned slowly to his warrant officer. "You'd have thought Carew would have been told, with it on the radio and all that."

"Too right, Colonel."

They were winding him up, Jeez knew that, turning the screw. He stood his ground. He listened to the silence in the room. There would have been a conspiracy between the colonel and the governor, news to be kept from Carew in order that the condemned man might prove more pliable to the colonel of security police.

"I'm very surprised that you haven't been told, Carew."

He bit on his lip.

"When a man's been here thirteen months, waiting to know whether he's going to hang, you'd have thought he'd be told which way it's going for him."

"You'd have thought that, Colonel." The echo from the warrant officer.

Jeez imagined the hot sweating hair on the gut of the colonel, and the pig-bladder bulge of his belly, the milk white matchstick legs.

"You want to know what the State President has decided, Carew?"

There was an ache of pain in Jeez's lips. He thought the skin must be near to breaking. The colonel's voice hardened.

"You are an impertinent little swine, Carew, and not for much longer. You are going to hang, Carew. That's the State President's decision."

Jeez felt the skin open. There was the warmth of the trickle of blood heading for the point of his chin.

"You're going to hang, Carew, hang by the neck until you are dead. You are going to hang through the due process of law. You can be impertinent for two more weeks, and then you hang. "

He tried to see the men at Century, the men on his team. He tried to find the image in his mind of when he had come back from the clinic and they had taken him down to the pub behind Victoria railway station and made him pie-eyed, and made him talk about the conditions in Spac. They couldn't have acted the way they hung on his words, Lennie, and Adrian and Henry, the way the eyes of the youngsters they'd brought along shone with admiration. What was the length of Century's bloody arm? Couldn't be true, that the team couldn't reach him.

"You have been an enigma to me, Carew. I'll admit to you that we know very little about you, but look at the way you're standing, man. You're standing like a soldier. I don't know which army, I don't know when, but you've been a soldier and served your country. Look at you today, man, you stand your ground because you've got guts. But where is having guts taking you? To the rope, and an unmarked grave."

"Carew, there is nothing about you, that I know of, that gives me an idea of why you should be associated with Black terrorism, but it is that association that is going to hang you. Do you think those Blacks of the A.N.C. care about you? They care shit all for you. They used you and they dropped you right in it. You know, Carew, there have been some protests in Europe about these death sentences, pretty pitiful protests, and your name's not mentioned. You know that? All the talk is of Zikala and Schoba and Ngoye and Mweshtu. You'll hang and nobody'll care."

"Can I go back to my cell, sir?"

Whatever the torment, misery, always address the interrogators with courtesy. Courtesy brought a small victory over the bastards. The bigger victory was never to plead. He wanted the loneliness of his cell, he wanted the anguish to be private. He wanted to cry alone within the walls of his cell for help from his team.

"I don't want to see you hang, Carew. It would give me no pleasure to have you hanged by the neck until you are dead. I come here today with the offer that can save you from the executioner. Are you listening, Carew? Don't play the 'Mister' with me, man."

The blood rolled from his chin onto his buttonless tunic.

"On your behalf, Carew, I had a meeting with the Minister of Justice this morning. I have made a bargain with him."

It was the colonel's moment. He took a sheet of headed paper from his pocket. He unfolded it, he waved it at Jeez. He laid it on his knee.

"If, even at this late stage, you agree to co-operate fully with me, to make a detailed and verifiable statement concerning every dealing you have had with the A.N.C., then the minister will go to the State President and get an order of clemency for you . . ."

He heard the singing, and then the trap, and then the spurt of water, and then the hammering, and then the cough of the van engine.

"A detailed statement, Carew. Personalities, safe houses, arms caches. Give us those and you get clemency, that is the bargain, here in writing."

Jeez was rocking on the balls of his feet. Swaying as a sapling in light wind.

110

Moisture bursting all over his body. Tickling fear at the nape of his neck.

"Make it easy for yourself, Carew, help us to help you. There's a good chap. The A.N.C. doesn't give a damn for you. It's martyrs they want, photographs of martyrs to drape round Europe and America. You owe them nothing, man. You owe it to yourself to co-operate with me. Are you going to be a good chap?"

He was burdened with his secret. He had never reneged on that secret, not during the years in Spac, nor during the weeks in John Vorster Square, nor during the months in Pretoria Central. To renege on the secret was to believe that the team had abandoned him. Better to hang than to believe Century had ditched him. Still the small kernel of hope, whittled down, the kernel said the team at Century would never believe that Jeez Carew would betray his secret.

He turned on his heel. It was a parade ground swivel. He was facing the door.

"You're putting the rope round your neck, Carew," the colonel snarled.

The warrant officer shouted for Oosthuizen.

Still in his clothes, his shoes kicked off onto the carpet, Jack slept. Beside him on the wide bed was a copy of *Star*, open at the page that reported the decision of the State President that five convicted terrorists should hang.

10

From his eighth floor window in the Landdrost Hotel Jack Curwen stared out over the city and beyond to the open ground. He looked past the office towers and away across the pale yellow pyramids of goldmine waste. He saw a modern city where less than a century before there had been only flat veld. He had read the books in his hotel room, and had to smile. An Australian, one George Harrison, had come here in search of gold, and stumbled on the main seam, and been given his discoverer's certificate – and sold it for ten pounds. It was all down to George Harrison from Oz, all the towers, all the wealth, all the unrest And poor George Harrison had disappeared with his ten pounds into the Eastern Transvaal, never to be heard of again. All that Jack saw was built upon the discovery of George Harrison, poor sod, loser. Waste heaps stretching to the south into the early morning haze mist, the towers to the east and north, the concrete streets to the west. Wherever he was, George Harrison, he must be crying in his box.

He took the lift down to the lobby. He had wondered if he would be contacted on his first afternoon, first evening, in the hotel. He had lain on his bed, sometimes reading, sometimes asleep, and waited. He hadn't taken breakfast, couldn't face a meal.

Time to find the target on which he would prove himself. He was crossing the lobby. He heard his name called. The Indian day porter was coming from behind his counter.

"You want a taxi, Mr Curwen?"

"No, thank you."

He saw the frown pucker the Indian's plump forehead.

"I'm going to walk," Jack said.

"Be careful where you walk, Mr Curwen. Some very bad things happen to tourists. Definitely, no walking after four o'clock, Mr Curwen. Please not, sir."

"I'm just going to walk around the main streets."

"Anywhere, sir, it is better by taxi."

He had seen the printed slip on the desk in his room. "You are warned pickpockets have been known to assault tourists in Central Johannesburg." He walked outside into a bright sunshine.

Once he had turned the corner from the front of the hotel he lost the sun. Buildings too tall for the width of their streets. Into shadow. Into the grey of concrete buildings and cracked litter-strewn pavings where the grass sprouted. A dirty city. He passed two paint-peeling, dowdy-fronted escort agencies, then on to Bree Street. Clothes shops and dismal coffee shops. The few Whites went on their way and hesitated not at all, and the Blacks leaned in the doorways, tilted themselves against the lamp posts. A beggar pleaded to him, Black, squatting over a crippled left leg, and Jack flushed and hurried on. The Blacks seemed to watch him, size him, weigh him.

Back into the sunlight.

He had come off Jeppe and onto Van Brandis. A square opened in front of him. He felt the warmth of the sunlight. Safety from the loiterers. He came past a high tower that gave way to a mock Gothic front, to a building of tall rectangular windows, and entrance steps leading to a wide portico. He saw the street sign ahead of him. Pritchard. He looked back across open lawns to the doorway and saw the spider web of scaffolding obscuring the black scorched stone work.

He gazed at the Rand Supreme Court.

He thought there must be a terrorist trial at the court. Too many police, too many yellow police wagons parked on Pritchard. He looked at the policemen, White and Black, some in denim blue overalls and forage caps, some in trousers and tunics and caps. He saw the way their holsters were slung from their webbing belts, slapping their thighs. There were high fire stains around the doorway. He wondered where his father had sat in the van. He wondered from which direction the four had approached with their bomb. He saw some flowers lying at the side of the steps leading up to the court. He wondered who in South Africa would want to put out flowers all those months later for his father, if he hanged . . .

Bullshit. Bullshit, because Jeez Curwen wasn't going to hang.

. . . He was standing on the pavement beside the path to the front entrance. A Mercedes pulled up beside him. A policeman saluted. The chauffeur sprang out to open the passenger's door. Jack watched the small and unremarkable man go slowly up the path between the lawns. Shrunken by age, his suit now a size too large for him, a judge going to work. A judge like another judge. A judge like the judge who had sentenced his father.

Not enough of a target.

He heard a faraway siren. He saw the police stiffen to alert, then move to cordon the pavement, to shepherd the drifting Blacks back from the kerb. A policeman standing in the junction of Van Brandis and Pritchard, beside his motorcycle, had his arm raised to halt the oncoming vehicles, leaving the road clear for the siren. Two cars, coming fast, and sandwiched between them a yellow van with tight mesh over the side window. Jack saw the blur of a Black face. He thought he saw the momentary image of a clenched fist, couldn't be sure.

A Black, a dozen yards from Jack, roared out loud the one word.

"*Amandla.*"

Jack thought he heard an answer shout from the speeding van. The convoy turned along the front of the court, down the far side of the building. A policeman, Black, truncheon drawn, stalked the man who had shouted.

He walked away. He had said that maximum security was the breeding place for complacency, but there was no complacency at the Rand Supreme Court. Strong enough for a target, but not Jack's because he would fail.

He looked at his map. He cut across Pritchard and President and Market. He had gone from the sunlight. He had returned to the gaudy world of fashion clothes and patent shoes. A Black man at a bus stop eyed him, head to toe, then turned his head and spat into the rubbish filled gutter.

He walked onto Commissioner.

He stopped to stare into a gun shop window. In the window were targets. Not rabbits, nor squirrels, nor pheasants, nor duck. The silhouettes were of men. The size of men. Black men. White background. Jack could buy himself a life-size target of a Black man to pump away at, and it would cost him 50 cents. There was a poster on the outside of the shop door. Omar or Yousuf or Moosa Latib offered the Dunduff Shooting Range along with the slogan "Defence with an unknown Firearm is Meaningless". Nothing about game. Learn how to shoot a Black man. He went inside. He had no reason to explore this shop, but it fascinated him. He had never used a firearm, not even an air pistol on an empty tin. He went down into the basement. The customers were two deep and stretched the length of a long counter. Men and women, all Whites, were handling pistols and revolvers in the front rank, while those behind waited for them to make their choice, pay their money, get the hell out of the way. There were two young men behind the counter. No big deal for them that men and women, all Whites, were crowded in their shop to buy pistols and revolvers for personal protection, to blow away Blacks. Such difficult choices to make, between Smith & Wesson and Browning and Beretta and Colt and Heckler & Koch and Steyr and Walther. The men wanted to know about range, and the women wanted to see whether it would slip in their handbag. The men argued about cost, because up to 1,000 rand was a hell of a sum to pay for stopping a Black man. The women wanted to be shown mother of pearl in the weapon's handle. The counter men said the supplies were short, that they didn't know when they'd be topping up on stock, that was what they had. Jack saw they wore waist holsters, filled, strapped in their trousers belts. He saw that no customer wanted more time to think about a purchase. Everyone ended up producing a firearms licence and writing a cheque.

Jack spoke to the man standing in front of him, queuing.

"Is it easy to get a licence?"

"Not the year before last. Pretty simple last year. Dead easy this year." He was a soft spoken man, could have been a schoolmaster. "Just a formality now. You a visitor here? If you've got a good property, if you're a city centre trader, if you're living on your own, if you have to put your takings in a bank night safe, if you have to go home regularly after dark – that's just about everyone. You're English?"

"Yes."

"I came out eleven years ago, from Weston-super-Mare. You know that place? I'm getting a gun for my wife, she's nervous on her own. We've a Doberman, but my wife says it's too easy on Blacks . . ."

"Perhaps you should have stayed in Weston-super-Mare," Jack said mildly.

"I pay my taxes, every last rand of them, I pay for the police, but the police are all out in the townships."

He was still talking as Jack turned away.

He went out of the shop. He pocketed his map. He went west down Commissioner.

He saw the building ahead of him. It seemed to block his path, far ahead. He was going towards John Vorster Square.

He had read in the first clipping in the newspaper office library that his father had been taken to John Vorster Square. Thiroko had told him about John Vorster Square.

Not really a square, a wedge of ground between Commissioner and Main, curtailed at the far end by the raised De Villiers Graaf motor link.

John Vorster Square was nothing more than a police station. Jack grinned to himself. The toughest, most feared police station in the country named after a Prime Minister and State President.

John Vorster Square was their power. Where the guns were, where the uniforms were, where the interrogation rooms were, where the cells were, where Jeez had been held.

He couldn't know what had been done to his father in John Vorster Square. He could remember what Thiroko had told him. Rivers of pain. The helicopter. The screams. If his father had been there why should it have been different for him?

John Vorster Square was the place for the proving target. It was out of sight of the offices of the multinational corporations. It was far from the tourist routes. He thought it was where the real business of the State was done.

There was a central block of brilliant sky blue panels topped by layers of plate-glass windows. There were three wings. He walked past the door that led into the charge office, and then past the security check and the heavy metal turnstile. He saw the armed police guard, languid, bored. He walked round the back of the buildings where there were tended gardens and the wide sweep of a driveway for staff cars. He saw the ten foot high railing fence, and at the Commissioner Street end a long brick wall set with small barred windows. He retraced his steps, went around the building again, seeming to have lost his way. He would come back in the afternoon. When he came back in the afternoon he would wear different clothes.

Jan van Niekerk carried out his instructions to the letter.

It was his way. It was why he was useful to the Umkonto we Sizwe. He had been given those instructions the previous evening.

He disliked being given jobs for the daytime. Daytime jobs broke the routine of his studies and he believed that his routine at Wits was his best defence against suspicion. In common with most White comrades he found it hard to consider the possibility of arrest. Arrest was what happened to Black comrades. The Whites, graduates, were too bright to be caught out by the Boer security police.

He rode his Suzuki towards the Alexandra township, but before reaching it he turned north into the industrial estates of Wynberg. He found the rubbish heap where he had been told it would be, close to the corner of 6th Street and 2nd Avenue. There was a dirty plastic bag on the edge of the rubbish heap. No-one was in sight. He picked it up, twenty pounds, more. It was an effort for Jan van Niekerk. He carried it to his moped. He put his face close to look into the bag and sneezed. The irritation welled in his nostrils, the sneezing convulsed him. He knew then that he carried explosives. Pepper was always strewn over explosives and between the wrappings of foil and plastic to throw the police dogs. He put the package into two new shopping bags from the Checkers store group, first one, tied it with string, and then into the second. He strapped it to the back seat of his moped.

He rode carefully, avoiding the pot holes. He knew nothing of the volatility of explosives, and he presumed that if there were explosives then there would also be detonators.

He came back into Johannesburg, making for the Landdrost Hotel.

Jack lay on his bed.

It was the smartest hotel he'd ever booked into. Overnighting for D & C would never be the same.

A soft knock at his door. He sat up.

"Come in." He thought it might be the maid to turn down his bed.

There was a second knock. He padded across the room in his socks. He recognised the bellboy.

"Your shopping, sir. Very heavy, sir."

He had it on his tongue to say there was no shopping to be delivered. The heavy parcel was bending the kid's shoulder. He bit off the denial. He gave the bellboy a tip. He closed the door. He carried the Checkers bag to his bed, laid it down. He lifted out the second bag that was inside, that stank. He carried a chair to the door and lodged it under the doorknob. He opened the window wider.

He opened the second bag.

He sneezed.

His head rocked back, couldn't help himself. He lifted the shopping bag into the bathroom and spread out yesterday's *Star* on the floor, and gently opened the black plastic. He stripped off a cooking foil wrap.

The explosive was in three piles, layer upon layer of half inch thick quarter pound slabs. He could tell it was fresh, the grease-paper on each slab was firm. He thought it would be plaster gelatine, couldn't tell from the print on the wraps. The writing was in Cyrillic.

He had liked Thiroko, but he hadn't known how much he trusted him. I love you, Jacob Thiroko. Listen to your radio. Wherever you are, keep your finger on the tuner button, keep following the news bulletins. Keep your ear to the seat, Mr Thiroko.

116

... There was a small jiffy bag, cut off and the top stapled down to half size. Gently, he pulled it open. He found four small pinched bundles of cottonwool with Sellotape binding. He prised one open. He extracted the gleaming detonator. There were lengths of wire. One roll would be the Russian-made equivalent of Cordtex, and the other their own safety fuse. From the thickness he thought he could tell which.

He could smell the explosive. The sickly scent of almond sweets. Like the marzipan under the icing on his mother's Christmas cake, and on the cakes she made for his birthdays, when there was just the two of them, when she had been without a husband and he without a father. He replaced each layer of wrapping as neatly as he could, then brought out his underarm deodorant canister. He sprayed over the package, then opened the bathroom windows to let in the sounds of the traffic below, to let out the scent of his spray and the scent of almonds. He put the package into his suitcase, locked it, returned it to the bottom of the hanging cupboard.

Jack sat on his bed and drew up a shopping list.

A grip bag, a ten-litre can, a roll of heavy adhesive tape, a pair of washing-up gloves, a packet of 1.5 volt torch batteries, electrical flex, a watch, a litre of two stroke oil, nine litres of petrol.

He had tidied his room. He had sprayed again with his deodorant.

He had made up his mind. He was on the road, far on the road.

Jack Curwen went shopping on a sunny Johannesburg afternoon.

An everyday afternoon at John Vorster Square.

The army of prisoners whiled away the hours in the half basement cells of the east wing, some under investigation, some in detention, some criminal and some political.

The hard everyday afternoons were reserved for the politicals. The criminals were just *tsotsis*, the hooligans, the thieves of the townships. The criminals made only a slight impact on the smooth running of the state's apparatus. The politicals needed breaking, putting in court, locking away. The politicals threatened the state's apparatus.

Bars dominated the east wing cell blocks. Bars across the windows, bars across the corridors, bars across the light wells. A filthy place where the prisoner is dehumanised, where he cannot believe that anyone cares about his fate. A place where the grime of years coats the cell floors and walls. Where the graffiti is of despair. Since the state of emergency on the East Rand the prisoners had been brought in their hundreds to John Vorster Square. Many Blacks and a few Whites. The elderly and the schoolchildren, the community workers and the trade unionists, the revolutionaries and those registered by computer error or an informer's malice on the police records. Better to be a robber of banks than to have publicly denounced as "mere tinkering with apartheid" the State President's package of reforms. Better to have mugged the migrant workers in the shadows outside their township hostels when they

117

have wages and are drunk, than to have protested on the streets the right to vote.

The politicals were the targets of the security police working on the upper floors of the south wing of John Vorster Square. Pleasant offices, airy and light behind the plate glass windows, but in their interrogation rooms the air and the light could be cut with the dropping of blinds.

The security police at John Vorster Square were good at their work. A White Methodist priest once held in John Vorster Square had written afterwards of the "decrepit docility of despair" that cowed the Blacks in the townships. The policemen exploited that despair in the interrogation rooms, they found little resilience in those they questioned. Even the comrades of the Umkonto we Sizwe condemned themselves in their statements given on the 10th floor. Happy Zikala and Charlie Schoba and Percy Ngoye and Tom Mweshtu had made their statements here, gathered the noose closer to their necks here. All the Whites, those who talked and those who stayed silent, those with the privilege of third level education, those who were active in the cadres, would speak of the expertise of the security police on the 10th floor. Most cracked.

Jeez hadn't. He was a rare exception.

And Jeez was now little more than a faded statistic in the hand-written ledgers of John Vorster Square, remembered only by a very few.

The colonel was principal amongst the few.

The instruments of his power were the Terrorism Act, No. 83 (1967) with a minimum sentence of five years and a maximum of death – the General Law Amendment Act, No. 76 (1962) Section 21, also five years to death – the Internal Security Act, No. 79 (1976) giving the power of preventive detention and banning orders. There were not many prisoners, politicals, who did not feel the sliding bowel weakness and the tickle of terror when they stood in the presence of the colonel.

He would have described himself as a patriot. He would have said that every action he undertook in John Vorster Square was for the benefit of his beloved South Africa. He would have said that he stood in the front line of the battle against the contagion of communism and the drift to anarchy.

On that everyday afternoon, the colonel watched with grudging satisfaction as a full time clerk of F.O.S.A.T.U. made a voluntary statement. Small beer, a Coloured, an insignificant creature, admitting to handing out leaflets demanding the release of political prisoners. With the vermin's own guilt tied down, the work might begin of extracting information from him on more senior members of the Federation of South African Trade Unions. He would be charged under the Terrorism Act. They could do for the clerk under "activities likely to endanger the maintenance of law and order", or they could do for him under "activities likely to cause embarrassment to the administration of the affairs of state". They had him by the throat, they had his confession, and now they could bargain the length of his sentence against the incrimination of the leaders of F.O.S.A.T.U. It was the leaders that the colonel wanted, not this rodent.

The clerk sat at the table and dictated a stuttering statement to a White corporal. He was watched by the colonel who stood in the doorway.

The journey to Pretoria was a sore in the colonel's mind. He did not comprehend how a White preferred to hang rather than to come clean about the Blacks with whom he had collaborated. The visit to Beverly Hills had been a failure. He would happily have hanged James Carew himself to have expurgated that failure. He was no fool, he could rationalise his failure. He supposed that he had failed with Carew because he was unaccustomed to interrogating White politicals. One or two a year came into his domain on the top floors of John Vorster Square. Some he categorised as dedicated communists, some were gripped with the martyr wish, some he regarded as mentally deranged, some were all three. All of them he thought stupid. To suffer in the cause of Black freedom was idiotic. Carew was outside his categories, a mystery. He thought he hated the man which was why in this same room he had lost his temper, shouted.

There was no further reason for the colonel to stay and watch the clerk. He went back to his own office.

The sun was dipping between the mine waste mountains to the west. Far below him were the gaudy street lights and the ribbons of the headlamps of the homegoing traffic.

There was a sheaf of telex messages on his desk. There was a photocopy of a report from Major Swart in London.

The colonel thought that Pretoria overrated Swart.

Darkness was falling on the city.

He gutted Swart's telex. More failure. Buck passing and excuses. Failure to make the connection between Mrs Hilda Perry and James Carew. Failure to link one Douglas Arkwright, deceased, on a contact between a White male, unidentified, and Jacob Thiroko. Failure to maintain a tail on Jacob Thiroko.

Categorised totally incompetent, that Swart. The one and only link to Carew's earlier life and Swart had failed to make anything of it. The report was soon pushed aside, categorised not useful, back in the tray beneath less intractable problems.

The piece of paper that had failed, that he had reckoned a guarantee of success, the piece of paper that carried the minister's signature, lay in the colonel's personal safe. He would shred it on the morning of the execution. That failure would die with Carew.

But failure it was. At the heart of the failure was the void that was Carew's past, exacerbated by the man's refusal to talk. The bachelor apartment in Hillbrow had been searched and searched again and revealed not a clue to the past. The drivers on the taxi ranks had been quizzed, interrogated even, and found to know nothing significant about the man at all. The bombing team had all said in their statements that they had never seen the man before he drove them away from Pritchard. The void spirited up the colonel's suspicions. No man could so effectively hide his past, unless he had deliberately hidden it, had a very good reason for hiding it.

He consumed the paperwork on his desk. He had promised his wife that he would not be late home.

He had waited until the bus load of tourists filled the hotel lobby with their stacks of suitcases.

He had taken the lift down twice before, holding the grip bag sagging close against his knee, and each time the lobby had been almost empty and he would have been noticed by the night porter and the bellboy and the luggage boys and the doorman. Twice he had gone back to his room to while away the minutes before trying again. Very tense, close in his thoughts. All his concentration was on the hulk that was John Vorster Square, and the fence around it, and the lights, and the armed police sentries, and on his father and on suppressing his fear. The plan called for him to expose himself to challenge and gunfire. He knew of no other way.

He stepped into the lobby. The lift doors shut behind him. The bellboys and the luggage boys were marshalling a huge pile of suitcases, the doorman was loudly supervising their distribution. The reception was lost in a half moon of argument because there was a double booking problem. The night porter was doling out keys to those who had been checked in and who had allocated rooms. They were Americans, fresh from safari.

Jack crossed the lobby unnoticed. Unseen, he went out through the swing doors. Behind him rose a tumult of angry voices.

Dark streets. Streets given up by the Whites. The Whites were powering home to the suburbs in their BMWs and Jaguars. Jack walked with a brisk purpose. He stayed far out on the pavement, close to the kerb and the cars' lights, avoiding the shadowed shop entrances from which spurted the flash of a match, the glow of a drawn cigarette. There was no reason that he should have attracted attention. He was a young White who was late, hurrying with a bag that might contain his sports kit, whose weight he struggled to disguise.

He took the route that he knew, down Van Brandis, right onto Commissioner. Above him the lights were flickering out in the towers, the last workers leaving. The security guards with their polished staves patrolled the wide entrances.

Jack saw the lights in John Vorster Square, an oasis of work as the rest of the city shut down for the night. He took from the bag a rough stone, picked from a street building site on Commissioner. The stone gripped in his left hand, the size of a cricket ball. At school, in the team, they'd played him for his fielding. He could certainly throw. The stone was now his weapon and his protection.

There was a constable guarding the back gate.

A presentable young man, straight-backed, clean-shaven, and he wore his uniform and his Sam Browne well. He was often given the 6 pm to 10 pm shift on the rear entrance because his sergeant thought him the right sort of constable to open and close the gates on the comings and goings of the top brass. The constable sat in his box. His service revolver was holstered, the flap buttoned down because that was tidier. In the box was a loaded F.N. rifle, safety on, a gas mask, a telephone link to the operations room inside, and his personal radio.

He saw the car approach. He saw the lights flash and the indicator wink to him. He saw the uniform of the driver, and the uniforms of the passengers.

Behind him he heard the revving of an engine outside the gates, and he heard the shout for the gates to be opened.

The constable had a car to let in and a car to let out.

He went forward. He slipped the bolt that was accessible only from the inside. He swung the near gate back towards him, pushed away the further gate. He had to step back smartly to avoid the car coming from the outside, from Main Street.

There was a moment when he was back at the edge of the driveway, readying himself to salute, and the gates were fully opened, and the cars were jockeying to pass through.

There was a moment when he did not think to study the shadows across the road.

He only saw the blur of a man running. He saw the figure coming fast across the road. He saw the low-slung bag trailing from the figure's arm. He stepped forward, picking at the flap of his holster. He hesitated. He turned back for his rifle. Whichever way he looked he was dazzled by the headlights. The figure ran past him on the far side of the incoming car. The constable was rooted to the concrete floor of his sentry box. The figure charged to the main doorway, pushed it, swung the bag inside. The constable saw the bag sailing into the rectangle of light, and lost sight of it.

He was spinning, trying to get the lights from his eyes. He saw the figure for a moment more, seeming to fill the doorway into the hallway area. He reached again for his holster, then for his rifle, then for his radio, then for his telephone link. The constable had never before confronted an emergency, and nothing had ever happened at the back gates of John Vorster Square. And the bastards in the car hadn't reacted.

He saw the shadowy shape of the figure turn and run back from the doorway. He hadn't the flap off his holster, nor the rifle in his hand, nor was he reaching for his radio, nor had he lifted his telephone.

Everything too fast for the constable. The figure running to get by the car that was coming out. The driver of the car that was entering seeing a figure, no longer in shadow, bright in the headlights, swung the wheel to block the figure, run the figure down. The figure stumbling to a stop, backing away, into the courtyard, trapped. An anorak hood over the figure's upper head and a handkerchief knotted over the figure's lower face, and a dark slash where the eyes would be. So fast, too fast. The arm of the figure swinging back, whipping forward. The crack of the windscreen, like a bullet snap. The constable saw the windscreen freeze, shatter to opaque. The incoming car swerving. The outgoing car turning away from collision.

He yelled, not into his radio, not into his telephone, out into the night air.

"BOMB!"

The presentable young constable ran from his box. The outgoing car careered from a side-on collision towards him. He was blinded by the lights. He ran for his life, and behind him his sentry box was taken down by the impact of the outgoing car's radiator and engine weight, squashed away through the shrubs, flattened against the low wall and the high railings.

There was the thud of running feet. He saw the figure come down the driveway, skip past the incoming car.

He had the flap off his holster now. He had the pistol butt in his hand, lifting. The figure gone, out into the street. The pistol was in his hand, his thumb had taken across the safety. He had the running figure, seen between the railings, over the end of his barrel. Steady, squeeze . . .

The constable was bowled over by the blast that erupted from behind the plate glass of the hallway area. And with the driven wind came the glass shards, and then the crimson and orange billowing of the flames. Before he lost consciousness he was aware of the glass splinters fragmenting around him, and of the heat of the spreading fire.

Jack ran two hundred yards. He had pulled the handkerchief off his face, tugged the anorak hood down from his head. Up Main, cars overtaking him, up Market, into the narrow side street off Becker, no-one in sight, off with the anorak, dump it, a distant siren, along the lanes off Diagonal, two men sitting, their backs against the wall, neither moved, past the closed Stock Exchange, onto Bree. He was walking when he reached Bree. He controlled his speed, harder to control his breathing. He tried to window shop, to appear to be strolling away the evening.

Two police trucks racing, sirens wailing, and the whine in the streets around him of approaching fire engines.

From the far side of Bree he looked back towards John Vorster Square . . . a bloody lunatic plan . . . He saw the orange glow reaching for the night sky. He saw the dark climbing column of smoke. Can you see that, Mr Thiroko?

He walked along Bree towards the Landdrost Hotel. He straightened his tie in a window, he casually wiped the sweat off his forehead. He knelt to wipe the earth from the gardens of John Vorster Square off his shoes. The last hundred yards, forcing himself not to look back. He steadied himself, and went inside. He stood in the lift with his back to a cluster of tourists. He went down his corridor, into his room. He went first to the cupboard. He saw that the packaged pile of explosives was undisturbed. Of the three slabs that had been delivered in the Checkers bags, two were still inside his suitcase. He might have failed. But now he thought he had enough dynamite still to blow his way into the hanging gaol.

122

Jack dived onto his bed. His face was buried in his pillow, his legs shook without control.

God, what had he done? For his father, what had he done?

11

Just before eight o'clock, Jack joined the office workers and the labourers and the vagrants at the junction of Market and Main and Commissioner to see the damage. Police with dogs and soldiers in full combat kit kept the watchers far back from the fire darkened building. There was little to see, but that was no discouragement to the crowd.

Jack had already seen his morning *Citizen* with the special colour front page. The main photograph showed the orange flame ball alive inside the ground and first floor, billowing up the stairwell. He had read of the "miraculous escape" of the policeman on desk duty inside the door, how the heavy steel-panelled furniture had protected him from the immediate force of the fire and explosive blast. He had read that the offices above the hallway had been unoccupied, that had they not been the officers who worked there would have been killed when the floor above the hallway caved in. He had read that the steel and concrete construction of the block had prevented the spread of the fire, and that within 48 minutes the fire service had brought the blaze under control. He had read that a single man was believed responsible, that there were reports that the man was a White, that the police were "keeping an open mind". The smell of a water-soaked fire is unlike any other. It was a familiar odour for Jack to sniff at as he stood with the crowd, and he thought of George Hawkins, pictured him beside him, remembered the demolition of a fire wrecked office in Guildford, and seemed to hear George's growl of approval. The newspaper said it had been the most dramatic attack against the country's security system since the car bombing of the Air Force headquarters in Pretoria and the rocket firing at the Voortrekkerhoogte base of the South African Defence Forces. All down to you, Mr Hawkins.

He listened to the talk around him, mostly in English, a little in the Afrikaans language that he could not understand, all of it angry.

He took a last look at his work, and at the fire engines far up the street, and the police wagons. It was the controlled anger on the policemen's faces that would stay with him.

"You know what I heard?" A man with a loud voice and a florid face and a butcher's apron. "I heard that last night the *bandiete* in the cells over there were shouting and singing, all the bastard politicals, cheering they were. Pity the scum didn't roast."

John Vorster Square still stood, foursquare. But he had shown them, he had singed its beard.

He walked down Commissioner to the junction of Harrison. Another thought as he walked. There had been Blacks among the sightseers, and he had not heard them speak above a whisper. He had heard the vengeful fury of the Whites, but he knew nothing of the Blacks, whether they cheered his attack, whether they feared the reprisals that would follow the violence he had directed against the principal police station in the city. He thought that in the world of Jack Curwen the Black man's opinion was irrelevant. Their fight was not his fight. His fight was family.

He took a taxi to the railway station.

The colonel sat in on the conference. He was not himself responsible for the direct gathering of intelligence. Many times Intelligence knew of an impending attack. Not the exact location, nor the timing, but Intelligence generally knew of a major infiltration, of the movement of explosives, of an order from Gaberone or Lusaka. Intelligence had many sources. There were covert watchers, small teams of Recce Commando operating deep inside Angola, observing the Umkonto we Sizwe camps, listening to their radios, hooked into remote telephone lines that served those camps. There were deep sleepers in the overseas offices of the African National Congress. There were traitors, arrested in great secrecy, interrogated, frightened, turned, released. There were men and women inside South Africa who were under constant surveillance, their names having been first revealed to Intelligence by the S.A.D.F. capture of documents from A.N.C. offices in Gaberone. A treasure chest.

Intelligence had this time had no word.

The conference was boring the colonel.

For a while he endured in silence, then intervened.

"Was it a White or was it not a White?"

He could not be given an answer. The vehicle drivers had said they had seen the shape of a man, momentarily in the lights, nothing else. The gate sentry had been the only continuous eyewitness to the attack. The gate sentry had been concussed, was still sedated. The colonel was told that the gate sentry had rambled a description between reviving from concussion and being given sedation. A hood, a mask, eyes in shadow, always moving too fast.

"I think he was a White," the colonel said. "If he had been Black then there would have been a fire support team. I think it was a White working alone. He ran away. There is no report of a pick-up vehicle. If this had been A.N.C. then there would most certainly have been a pick-up. This one man, one White man, is at best no more than on the fringe of the A.N.C. It is now more than thirteen hours since the explosion, and Lusaka has said nothing. How many times do they wait thirteen hours? By the news agencies they would have known of the explosion within thirteen minutes, and they have still said nothing. I believe they have made no claim because they do not know who is responsible. I suggest this is the work of an individual, not of a cadre of Umkonto we Sizwe. Gentlemen, we have a White, we have a male. He ran forward fast, he threw a bag or sack weighing perhaps five kilos, he threw a fist-sized stone accurately through a windscreen. In my submission, we have a White male who is athletic, reasonable to assume that he is aged between 18 years and 30 years. We should meet again when we have the forensics."

The fire service had moved back from the hallway of the building.

Detectives and scientists moved amongst the sodden debris searching and picking. What they had collected in this initial examination was placed in metal bins to be sifted and then carried to the laboratories. A slow process, one that no detective experienced in this work, nor any scientist, would rush.

Jack went to the Whites Only ticket office.

He bought a day return ticket to Pretoria.

He went down the Whites Only entrance to the Whites Only section of the platform, alongside which would stop the Whites Only carriages.

Once the train had cleared the industrial and mining areas of Germiston and Edenvale and Kempton Park, it should have been a pleasant and picturesque journey. Past the factories and the gold waste mountains the train ran by the dry farm lands of the Witwatersrand. But Jack Curwen was not a tourist. He was an unidentified terrorist. He was on a journey to the city where his father was held, condemned to die. He thought it better to travel by train. No driving licence to be produced, no forms to be filled in at Avis or Hertz. In a train he was a lone microbe swimming in the vein of the state. He was in the heart kingdom of the Afrikaner regime. He was passing through the pretty satellite towns of Irene and Doornkloof and Verwoerdburg, rolling by the Johannesburg highway and the Fountain Valley Nature Reserve and the massive modern University of South Africa. He was coming to Pretoria, he was coming to his father.

A moment of confusion when he stepped down from the train. Which way to go? Streams of men and women, White and Black, crossing the platform around him. Confusion until he realised that the Blacks went left, the Whites went straight ahead. "Separate development" for leaving a railway station. He went through the Whites Only exit, and out into the Whites Only hallway of the station. His ticket had been clipped by a White official. He knew the cause of his confusion. His was a fear of going through the wrong exit, sitting on the wrong seat, urinating in the wrong lavatory, and being shouted at, called back, by a man in uniform.

There were uniforms all around him in the hallway. Soldiers with the berets of the Parabats, and of Armour, and of Artillery, and of the Medics. Scrubbed clean conscripts who were serving out their army time in administration in the capital city. Haggard young men changing trains on their way home for leave from the operational areas of South West Africa and the fearsome close quarters of guerrilla war. The airforce technicians of the Mirage squadron at Hoedspruit. The bearded and confident elite of the Recce Commando.

Jack eased his way through them. He was so very close to his destination. He went into the station magazine and sweet shop. He bought a map of Pretoria.

His finger nail searched for and found Potgieterstraat. He memorised the turns, the roads he would follow. He folded the map, stowed it away in his hip pocket. He would not be seen on Potgieterstraat studying a map.

He went out of the station. Pretoria was higher on the veld than Johannesburg, cooler, and the first frosts were not long away. He ignored the taxis. He would walk. He could see more by walking. He went past the booths where Blacks could buy their railway tickets, then out of the station yard. He went past the Combi vans that ferried Blacks between the station and the townships of Mamelodi or Atteridgeville, by the small street market where fruit and milk was sold, and vegetables. He could sense the difference to Johannesburg. He felt a little at ease walking here, because there seemed no threat, no scowling eyes gazing at him. He walked past the big dairy, and there the pavement ended, as if Whites' territory was bounded by pavements. He crossed coarse open ground. Potgieterstraat was ahead of him.

So very close to the road he had taken when his mind was made.

Under the old railway bridge of darkened steel and cut stone.

Potgieterstraat stretched away up the hill.

Far in front of him, across the road, was a high slag yellow brick wall. He was within sight of Pretoria Central, of the Local gaol of the Pretoria Central complex.

Hell, and his gut was tight, and his legs were jellied.

He was the insect brought to a night light.

The wall was the colour of the mine mountains in Johannesburg. Pristine, dirty yellow and new. He walked up the hill. He was again on a pavement. Sometimes he looked to his left where there was nothing for him to see, sometimes he looked straight ahead at the tilt of Potgieterstraat. He pleaded with himself for naturalness. He was on foot, alone, and approaching one of the most security conscious square miles of the State. If he were to be challenged he had no story. Jack Curwen had sneered at Jacob Thiroko, he had told his mother that he was going to bring his father home, and he had planned bomb making with George Hawkins, and because of his hot headed nature and his arrogance Sandham was dead and Duggie Arkwright was dead. Lunacy and arrogance had carried him on the wing to Potgieterstraat. And thank God that Sandham and Duggie couldn't see him with jelly legs and his tight gut as he flickered his eyes forward to the high yellow brick walls of Local.

He looked right. He had seen on the map that he would pass what was labelled as D.H.Q. . . .

Couldn't believe it . . . D.H.Q. He was walking past the Defence Headquarters of the Republic. The bastards had built Pretoria Central up the hill, same side of the road, spitting distance, rifle range distance, from the Defence Headquarters of South Africa. Throwback to the days of Empire, stone pillars

127

holding the portico, weathered red brick, barred windows, creeper-draped railings topped with coils of barbed wire.

Eyes moving. From the nothingness of scrub and railway sidings to his left, on to Potgieterstraat and the walls that grew in height as he came closer, on back to the formal gardens of Defence Headquarters where the sentries patrolled with magazines fitted to their assault rifles. Duggie and Sandham were dead, and Jack hadn't even known that D.H.Q. was right alongside his target. All the sentries, and all the back-up that would be out of sight but there in support of Defence Headquarters.

The excitement seeped from him.

The building next to Defence Headquarters, sandwiched between D.H.Q. and Local, was that of the South African Airforce. More wire, more sentries.

Thiroko had said it was impossible.

Across the road from him was Local. He stopped, and bent down to flick his shoe lace undone. It took him several seconds to retie the lace. He looked down the side street that ran under the wall of Local, he stared down Soetdoringstraat while his fingers fumbled to make the knot. Immediately across Potgieterstraat, at the top of the angle of the Local walls, was a jutting fire position. There were dark slits, Jack couldn't know whether he was observed. The main gatehouse of Local was down Soetdoringstraat, covered by another fire position. At the end of the Local wall on Soetdoringstraat he saw the lowered barrier of a check point. The walls of Local were thirty feet high. Local was covered by enfilading gun positions, and Local was only the gaol for the short-term Black criminals. Further down Soetdoringstraat, past the checkpoint, was the gaol for White politicals, and away and hidden from the road were the old Pretoria Central and the women's gaol, and further away and further hidden was Pretoria Maximum Security. At that moment Jack Curwen would have believed Jacob Thiroko.

He stood. He tried to resume a casual walk, and the walk was dragged and slow.

He went on up Potgieterstraat.

Over the height of the Local wall he could see the top floor cell windows of five blocks. There were clothes hanging from some of the windows, underpants and socks and shirts, and once he saw the face of a Black who gazed out into the bright morning light. A terrible quiet about the place. Difficult for him to realise that hundreds of men were held behind that wall, that they made no sound. At the end of the Local wall the brickwork gave way to a mesh wire fence that stood between the road and tropical gardens, and then the wildness of high trees climbing over a steep hillside. He knew from his map that the hill was Magasyn Kopje. He knew that Beverly Hills was set back on the slopes of Magazine Hill.

Behind the trees, out of sight, were the walls of Beverly Hills.

A daft fantasy in Jack's mind. If he yelled his father would hear him. He reckoned he must be within eight hundred yards of the cell blocks of Beverly

Hills. And he had seen high walls and gun positions and sentries with assault rifles. The fantasy slumped. He was eight hundred yards from his father, but he might as well have been in Churchill Close and five and a half thousand miles away. Despair, hurrying after the fantasy. He thought there was nothing more for him to see on Potgieterstraat. Despair, because he thought the bomb in John Vorster Square was for nothing.

Jack retraced his steps. He came briskly down the hill. He snatched one glance down Soetdoringstraat. He saw the checkpoint barrier rising, and a car coming out, leaving the cocoon of wire and walls and fields of fire. He looked away. On down the hill, back towards the ordinariness of Pretoria. The car that had come through the checkpoint sped past him. He went back towards the railway bridge. He felt he had turned his back on his father because he had been intimidated by the walls of Local that he had seen, and the walls of Beverly Hills that the trees obscured.

He took the first train back to Johannesburg.

Jacob Thiroko had heard the news of the John Vorster Square bomb on the radio in the morning.

He was astounded. He had thought in terms of an unguarded civil administration building, a noisy gesture simply.

John Vorster Square was something else . . . He had heard on the radio that the attacker had picked his moment to charge through an opened gate, hurl his bomb, and then escape under the nose of an armed sentry. An attack with the spontaneity of passion, nothing that was cold and predetermined. Thiroko recognised the extent of the danger. The most feared soldier was the man who was prepared to make the ultimate sacrifice.

Thiroko thought that he had gambled hugely on Carew's son, and the boy had repaid him by throwing a bomb into the most hated institution on the whole of the East Transvaal. The radio had said that long into the night there had been crowds on the streets of Soweto cheering the success of the attack, jeering at the police in their Casspirs who had come to disperse them with gas and bird shot.

The Indian owner of the safe house had long since gone about his business of selling motor car accessories when Thiroko came down stairs. In the kitchen he ate a slice of toast and drank strong coffee prepared for him by the Indian's wife. He ate increasingly little. Easier not to eat. His suitcase was packed, his room ready for another guest. He said his goodbyes to the Indian's wife, and left her home, and walked slowly with his suitcase to the Finchley Central underground station.

For the first time since he had arrived in London he journeyed to the offices of the African National Congress.

A terraced house in a side street off the Pentonville Road. A heavy green door beside windows covered with close mesh that was proof against fire bombs.

He endured the back slapping greeting of the London comrades – Blacks and Indians and Whites. He elbowed his way with little grace through the earnest congratulations of those who fought the regime from trenches that were separated from the battlefield by thirteen hours' flying. A small few he trusted. A great many he regarded with contempt. Thiroko was a military man. These were the pamphleteers and the speakers at fringe meetings, and the dreamers who said that the total revolution was at hand and that power was at the corner to be grasped. Thiroko was at home in the training camps of northern Angola, or with the young people of the Solomon Mahlangu school in Tanzania, or with the fighters when they retired across the Botswana border to rest up in Black Africa. He thought they were all communists in the London office. They were the men and women with whom he hardly cared to pass the day. There was one man in the terraced house with whom he would have entrusted his life. A man who was old, a skinny tent pole with a pebble rolling accent of Hungary, a man they all called Magyar and who had spent fourteen years in the regime's gaols, and served his time to the last day without an hour of his sentence remitted before travelling to London and exile. A pale, pinch-faced man with a whispered voice who had never been heard to boast of his commitment to the Movement, a man who had made his sacrifice and expected no praise for himself. This one man he would trust.

Thiroko handed his plane ticket to Lusaka to a young White who he thought was at heart a Boer because he wore jogging shoes and a tracksuit and cut his hair as if he were a conscript in the S.A.D.F. He asked to be booked on the evening's flight home.

He took Magyar to a small room, and when they had sat down amongst the cardboard cartons of A.N.C. literature that were expensively printed but not distributed, he turned up the volume of a cassette radio. Thiroko took few chances. He had no right to take chances, not with the safety of a young man who was prepared to run inside the John Vorster Square perimeter with a homemade bomb.

Magyar wouldn't ask him, so Thiroko gave the information.

The Hungarian had been in the Movement from the early days of the dive underground at the time of the banning of the African National Congress. He had stood in the same dock six years after it had held Nelson Mandela and Sisulu and Mbeki and Mhlaba and Motsoaledi and Kathrada and Denis Goldberg and Mlangeni. And now, in his 67th year, he was hardly listened to by the members of the London office. He pushed paper and he drafted press releases that would be rewritten. He was the one for Thiroko to talk with.

Thiroko told Magyar that the attack on John Vorster Square was the work of a single committed individual supplied by the agencies of Umkonto we Sizwe. He saw the quiet pleasure on the wrinkled face. Thiroko knew what the security police had inflicted on the old man.

Their voices were low against the barrage of the music.

"You were in the maximum security section of Pretoria Central?"

"What we called Beverly Hills, the hanging gaol. Yes."

"For how long were you there?"

"There was a group of us, White politicals, we were there for two years and eight months. From 1980 to 1983 we were there. It was after Jenkin and Lee and Moumbaris escaped from the White political section that all of the rest of us were taken up the hill while they rebuilt our former place."

"Such an escape is only possible once?"

"Of course. From the new gaol for politicals it would not be possible."

"From Beverly Hills?"

Magyar smiled sadly. His mind was taken far back.

"Nothing is possible from Beverly Hills. Before our time, a White condemn, Franz von Staden, escaped. He was at exercise and the wall of the exercise yard was not as high as it is now, and in those days it had no grille. He saw his chance, took it, and then he went to the station and a policeman who was not on duty saw him and remembered his face. They took him back and they hanged him. Now nothing is possible from Beverly Hills."

"From the outside?"

Magyar shrugged. "What is on the outside, Comrade Jacob? What do I know of the outside? I was brought to the gaol in a closed van with slit windows. I saw some trees, I saw some houses for the prison staff, I saw their self-service store, but I have no detail. It is the same inside. I lived in the gaol for 32 months, I was in C section 1. I can tell you about each inch of the floor of C section 1, not of C section 2, not of C section 3. I would have to imagine that C section 2 and C section 3 are the same as our section. I can tell you nothing of B section, nor of A section, where the Blacks are. There are gardens inside the outer wall that come up to the sections. I saw those gardens when I went inside and when I left. You are there a long time and you know very little. It was the same for all of us who were there . . . It is not a place that I care to remember."

Thiroko was hunched towards him.

"For me, I want you to try to remember."

For more than an hour the radio played light music, and a disc jockey doodled away his time in a London studio. The old man covered a dozen sheets of foolscap paper with his drawings. At the moment of his arrest he had been an architect's draughtsman in Cape Town.

He drew a plan, as best he knew it, of the square mile to the west of Potgieterstraat, a square mile that encompassed Defence Headquarters to Pretoria Central to Magazine Hill. He drew a plan of the whole of Beverly Hills, cursing the gaps in his knowledge.

He drew C section. He drew C section 1. He drew an individual cell. He drew a cell in relation to the catwalk above the linking corridor. He drew the corridor of C section 1 and the catwalk. He drew the exercise yard of C section 1, and after that he drew a top view plan to show the positioning of the metal grid over the yard and of the supporting beams. He drew the visit rooms. He drew the gallows shed as it had been described to him. Last he drew the airlock entry through the outer wall.

He said drily, "Under the Prisons Act, I could get ten years for drawing you such plans . . . should I be returning to South Africa."

Thiroko accepted no time for banter.

"Firearms?"

"There is an armoury in the administration block where they keep hand guns, machine guns, grenade launchers. There are guns available at all times in the gatehouse and at the reception at the entrance to administration. There are guns on the watch tower that is set onto the highest wall on the hillside where the sentry can overlook the whole of the compound. The men on the catwalks have F.N.s or Lee Enfields, they are issued with six rounds for a duty. No one carries a gun if they are in contact with prisoners."

"What is the closest guard to the condemns?"

"I cannot tell you about B section and A section. Over C section there is the armed guard on the catwalk. Through the windows he can look down into each cell. In addition there is one guard, not armed, who is locked for the night into the individual corridors of C section 1, and 2 and 3. Each of those men has a telephone line to the Control in the gatehouse."

Magyar looked up to see the fighting concentration in Thiroko's eyes.

"Comrade, I do not think you can go to any of the others of us who were there and find more. One man's experience is the same as every man's. I have forgotten nothing that I knew. You cannot break out. You *cannot* break in."

Thiroko said, "Last night a man broke into John Vorster Square."

Again the sad smile, as if it was a disappointment to the old man that he played the bearer of bad news.

"John Vorster Square has public roads on all sides. Go east from Beverly Hills, you have half a mile before you get to Potgieterstraat, all a control area. Go south, and you are climbing Magazine Hill which is within the prison complex. Go west, you have a rifle range for the military, and then you have the police training college, and then you have the police dog centre. Go north, you are into Defence Headquarters and the Air Force command bunker. There is not just a high railing. You cannot break in nor out of Beverly Hills . . . Is it because five comrades will hang?"

A defiance in Thiroko, an echo in his words from a park bench. "It is not right that we should do nothing."

"Sentiment from you, Comrade Jacob? There was one amongst the White politicals serving with me, serving longer than I. He used to say, 'Why don't they hurry up with their bloody revolution, get us out of here?' I tell you, every man in Beverly Hills, political or criminal, yearns by the candle of hope for freedom, that is what I know. Comrade, there are five of our men in there who are going to hang and they have no hope."

Thiroko put the drawings into his briefcase.

"If you hold the candle of hope for them then that is wonderful," the old man said.

Their farewells were curtly made. Thiroko switched off the radio. He went out of the room. He was given his ticket. It had been taken to the Zambian airlines office in Piccadilly, and endorsed for that night's flight.

He was photographed when he left the green painted front door, as he had been when he had entered. The cameraman freelanced for the Special Branch and operated from the Metropolitan Police offices on the opposite side of the street. Thiroko would have expected to be photographed. He didn't care. He had curtailed his visit to London. He was going home with the pain in his stomach. And when he got there he was going to provide the support that an extraordinary young man had asked of him.

Jeez knew of the bomb.

The sentries changing duty on the catwalk would have been disciplined, up before the governor, if it had been known that they had let slip such a nugget of information.

Jeez had heard them talking.

It seemed a small matter. What seemed a big matter was that Sergeant Oosthuizen had informed him that his solicitor was driving from Johannesburg the next day to see him.

He thought the days were sliding fast, each day shorter. He thought his time was bloody racing.

George Hawkins was driving to inspect a chimney when he heard the one o'clock news.

He was preoccupied with the chimney because he was certain it would be difficult. The chimney was 112 feet high, and to bring it down he required an additional 28 feet of clearance on the fall line. It was a built-up area of Hackney, and the oaf who had telephoned him hadn't known whether there was 140 feet clear. He was going to see for himself and he was going to charge them for his time whether or not he agreed to do the demolition.

Johannesburg's central police station? Stone the bleeding crows.

He knew it was his boy. The fire told him that the blue print for the bomb had been his own diagram of the La Mon Hotel device.

Christ, and he hadn't told the kid much. Hadn't told him much because he hadn't thought the kid was getting far beyond having his arse shot off. He'd given the boy nothing but the barest and the briefest. The boy must have followed to the letter what he had been told, must have memorised every bloody word. And what he'd told him for the hotel job was sweet bugger all of what he'd need to know to blow a hollow charge job against a prison wall.

Hadn't even told him of the safety procedures to go through in the loading of a hollow charge job with Polar Ammon.

He thought that if Jack Curwen died that he, George Hawkins, would never forgive his bloody old miserable self for allowing the boy to stuff such nonsense in his head.

Hard for the student to concentrate on his afternoon lecture.

The subject matter was The Role of the State in Support of the Single Parent Family. Hard for Jan van Niekerk to concentrate on anything. All the talk in the cafeteria, and over the whole campus was of the bomb in John Vorster Square.

He had read that there was a theory that the bomber was White. Jan van Niekerk had carried a package to the Landdrost Hotel. A few Blacks got to stay at the Landdrost, token Blacks, but he thought that the Mr Curwen to whom the package had been carried on by the bellboy must be White, a White name. He was involved, certain of that. He was guilty under the terms of the Sabotage Act, 5 years to death. Always, since he had begun, they could have manufactured a case against him. There would be no need to manufacture anything when he had carried explosives, when those explosives had been used in something so super fucking fantastic as the bomb *inside* John Vorster Square.

After the lecture, managing almost a bounce in his crippled stride, he made for his locker. There was no message for him.

Frikkie de Kok liked a drink, and he liked to talk. There were few men he could drink with because his working life was his secret, a matter that put him apart from other men. His assistant was his natural drinking partner, on Wednesdays in the late afternoon and early evening, if they did not have to be out of their beds while it was still dark on the following morning. Frikkie de Kok liked the Harlequin Club for his drinking and the chance to watch a rugby match from the old dark wood long bar. He had a small circle of acquaintances amongst the solicitors and barristers and government servants and accountants who patronised the bar on their way home from work.

His place was a corner table against the wall and the window, where he could talk to the man who would succeed him on his retirement. Where, also, he could watch the match.

He gave all he knew to his assistant.

He thought that was the least he could do for this young man who was so keen to learn. He had decided when the time would be, very soon, that he would allow his assistant to take over the full role of judging the length of the rope to be used, of fitting the pinions and the hood, of handling the lever. He reckoned that an assistant had to be given a chance to learn for himself. Not for a multiple of course, but for a single execution, and as long as they had no reason to think that the man would not go quietly . . . probably be best if it were a Coloured, that's what he thought, because in Frikkie de Kok's experience, the Coloureds were usually no trouble . . .

Frikkie de Kok checked his watch. The players should have been out of the dressing room by now.

He carried on talking.

"You see, there's a great irony about the method of execution, hanging. We now support the method of hanging over firing squad or gas chamber or electrocution because we say it is the most effective and the most humane. It didn't start like that. Look where it started, hanging. They wanted the most degrading way of death, and they wanted it to be slow and painful because that was good deterrent. What they were looking for was something that shocked and terrified the people who came to watch a public execution. The slower the better, because that way the spectators were most frightened. That's the irony. We have taken the most inefficient method and changed it into the most efficient. I like to think that in Pretoria we have the very most efficient and the very most humane system. You can go anywhere in the world, you won't find anything that is better organised than our situation. It's something that we in South Africa can feel genuinely proud of . . . I think they're stupid not coming out earlier, that's the way you get to pull a hamstring, when you're not properly loosened."

There was a ripple of applause from the touchline, and shouts from members in the bar. The players ran onto the pitch.

"There was one thing that concerned me the first time I was an assistant, that was the heart of the man. The heart kept beating for a full twenty minutes after he'd dropped. I'd been told all the things that I told you when you first started. Fracture dislocation of the cervical vertebrae with crushing of the spinal cord. Immediate unconsciousness, no possibility of recovering consciousness because there is no chance of breathing. But that heart was still going. I put my ear against his chest, while he was hanging, and I could hear the heart. It took me several minutes to get accustomed to that heart keeping going . . . They want to watch the new boy at out half. Fine boy, off last year's high school side. He could go all the way. I'd like to think my boy could get to play for Harlequins."

"He's on the school team, Mr de Kok."

"But the school's filling his head with university, not with rugby. He's in his books, that's why he's not on the line watching."

There was the question that the assistant had waited two years to ask, the question that fascinated him. For two years he had waited for the opportunity to appear. He thought it was the moment.

"Does he know?"

"Know what?"

There was the roar as the Harlequins kicked off.

"Know what his father does."

He wished he hadn't asked. He saw Frikkie de Kok hesitate.

135

"I've never told them, not Dawie, not Erasmus. You could say it's like telling them about the sexual functions. There's never a right time, and anyway they'll learn it all at school. There's never been a right time to tell Dawie what I do, and if I tell him then do I tell Erasmus, and he's two years younger. I suppose I'll wait until they're adults. They might not understand, funny things are young boys' minds. He thinks I run the carpentry courses at Central."

"If my Poppa had done such work, I'd have been proud of him."

"Who knows what they might think . . ."

The assistant was hunched forward. "Mr de Kok, what would happen to us if the political situation were to change?"

"Change how?" Frikkie de Kok was entranced by the game, nose close to the glass.

"If the present government were to fall."

Frikkie de Kok chuckled. "No chance. And we'll survive, our job isn't political. Every government needs us . . . Let me tell you an anecdote from history. There was an executioner down in the Cape, and he hanged and he quartered and he severed limbs, and he was paid by each item, then the British came. We're nearly two hundred years back. The British said that he should just do hanging. The poor man saw his livelihood going, so what did he do? He went and hanged himself."

They were both laughing.

". . . A little bit of change never hurts anyone. I won't be hanging myself, not even if they abolish maximum security. Too damned fast I'll be off to buy a farm. You won't see me for dust . . . That man, he's offside."

"Me too, Mr de Kok, I would have said he was offside."

Frikkie de Kok said from the side of his mouth, casual, "Next Thursday, tomorrow week, that's the Pritchard Five."

"All together?"

"They killed together, they were convicted together. Look at that."

"That referee's a disgrace, Mr de Kok."

Jack, still dressed, slept on his bed. Exhausted. Harrowed by the high walls he had seen.

He had turned his back on Magazine Hill, he had walked away from the green tree slopes where his father was held.

12

The minibus driver kept the stops short. Just enough time for the tourists to take their photographs, and for the guide to give her spiel to a German couple, four Americans, and Jack.

The guide was an attractive girl, might have been thirty years old but she wore her hair young in the blonde Diana style. She had sensible shoes, and perhaps that was the giveaway that the girl who had the job of introducing tourists to Soweto was not a child. She talked well. She had to talk well because the material for her to talk about was pathetic in the uniform dreariness of the streets and the homes.

They had come through the Orlando area of the township city. They were on high ground and looking down over the corrugated roofing and the straight roads and across the railway yards and away over further hills that were blistered with roofs.

The guide said, "We don't really know what the population of Soweto is. It's very difficult to get these people to fill in a census form, and they have their relations come to stay with them. They aren't the sort of people who are good with forms. So, it could be anything between one and two million people, we really don't know."

The first reason for Jack to come to Soweto was that he must behave as a tourist. Yesterday he had gone to Pretoria. Today he was waiting for his contact. And he needed desperately to be out of the hotel, was fearful of every footfall in the corridor, dreaded having to go back, wondering whether his room would be staked out, the explosives discovered.

The day porter had made the telephone call, placed the booking. The Rand Development Board tour was back on schedule, he said, because Soweto had been quiet for a week.

"You can see with your own eyes that this is a community into which a great deal of government money has been placed, millions of rand have been spent on making the living conditions of our Black people more acceptable. Most of Soweto now has electricity, most of it has running water. All of the main roads now have tarmac, and later you will see that we have started to build shops, the supermarket type of shops. The amount of money that we are spending is a very great drain on the country's resources, but we are spending it . . ."

The second reason for Jack to have made the journey into Soweto was vaguer. He felt that he had joined a war, that he had become a part of the armed struggle of the people who lived in this and other vagabond townships. He wondered how many of the one or two millions who eked out an existence in Soweto acknowledged the legitimacy of the tactic of bombs and bullets to change the conditions of their existence, how many of them knew the name of Jacob Thiroko. Not one of them would have heard of Duggie Arkwright. He thought of his journey into Soweto in part as a tribute to Duggie. He had thought that he might learn something of the people in whose cause Duggie had laboured. Driving past the stunning repetition of the homes of one million, or two million, people gave him not an iota of an idea of what their notion of a political future might be.

"Why are there high lights in the middle of open ground, illuminating nothing?"

The German man waved airily in the direction of hugely tall arc light stands that were dispersed over an open area of rubbish and building debris and raw earth. The German woman looked at her husband sheepishly as if she thought it impolite to ask a question.

The ready answer. "They are there to make it safer for the residents. Unfortunately, Soweto is a very lawless place. On average, every weekend, there are thirty murders in the township boundaries. The gangsters prey on the wage earners, rob them and kill them when they are coming back from the beer halls. We call the gangsters *tsotsis*, they are just hoodlums, sometimes they are ordinary criminals, sometimes they are agitators trying to intimidate the peace loving people . . ."

"I was told," the German said, "that they put the electricity in so that the Africans would buy televisions and radios and all the electrical appliances that are sold in the White owned shops. I was told it was just to expand the market that they put the electricity in."

"Whoever told you that was lying." The guide withered the German.

She had a fixed smile when she was talking to the tourists. But in the front seat beside the driver her smile dropped. When the tourists were muttering amongst themselves or trying to photograph from the moving bus, then Jack saw the reality of her face. He saw the frowns on her neat forehead as she talked with the driver, discussed where it was safe to go. The driver would pause at each cross roads, and the White guide and the Black driver would stare and hesitate. Jack couldn't help but see the reasons for the hesitation. Slogans aerosol-ed on walls.

KILL ALL WHITES. Be Kind to Animals, Adopt a Policeman. Death to Traitors and Informers and Collaborators. Children of the African Heroes Do Not be Afraid of Whites.

Jack thought it was lunatic to be running a scenic drive round friendly Soweto. The Germans and the Americans didn't seem concerned. The Germans were preoccupied with their focal lengths. The Americans were so busy in a denunciation of their own media, and Edward Kennedy and all the liberal East Coasters who gave them the picture of South Africa in flames, that Jack wondered if they had even seen the armoured personnel carriers parked at the side of the petrol station, and the second group that were parked close to the big school complex. He wondered if the Black police were local, what it was like for them to be on law enforcement in their own community. He kept his peace. Jack thought the rows of small brick homes, match boxes, and the pitted streets and the piled rubbish and the pitifully few shops were pathetic. He couldn't understand how the authorities could put a bus on, with a pretty girl as guide to boast about how much had been achieved, and drive tourists round so that they could see with their own eyes how bloody awful the place was.

"The impression you get back home, back in the State of Washington, is that the whole place is aflame. Looks pretty peaceful to me."

"What I reckon is that all these folks want is work and to be left in peace."

The bus jerked to the right. Jack saw the guide pointing to a group of young Blacks standing on waste ground a hundred yards ahead. The driver had turned down a holed track. They went fast past a fire-blackened house. He saw the driver's face when he turned to the guide for instructions. There was a sweat sheen on the driver's skin. Jack wondered how it would be to go back to the township each night when your job was driving White tourists round your backyard by day. They came back onto a main road. There was no commentary from the guide. He could sense the mood between the driver and the guide, that they had been around too long. There were school children streaming along the sides of the road.

An American woman said that the kids looked cute in their white shirts and black trousers or skirts. The German woman was complaining that the minibus was going too fast for her to take photographs through the window. They went along two streets where the houses were larger. Black middle class homes. The guide started to talk about the owner of a taxi fleet, and the owner of a Black football team. Jack thought the houses belonged to White clones, because there were leaping German Shepherds in the front gardens. There was smoke rising ahead.

The German man was tapping the guide's back, then pointing to a bungalow that was larger than the others, once the queen of the street. A smoke charred bungalow, with fire scorched beams littering a front lawn.

"What happened there?"

The guide turned to speak to the German, wasn't looking ahead, hadn't seen the smoke rising from tyres in the road.

"That was the home of the Mayor of Soweto. That is the work of the agitators. His home was burned down. It was an attempt by the agitators to intimidate those who are trying to better the life of the Blacks in Soweto . . ."

The driver was slowing, but he was Black. He couldn't tell the guide to shut her mouth and concentrate on what was going on in front of them and tell him what the hell to do. Over the guide's shoulder, Jack saw the school-children, cute, running forward from the tyre barricade towards the bus.

"It would be quite wrong to think that the majority of Blacks are hostile to the reforms that we are making, only a very few try to sabotage the sincere efforts that the State President is making to involve Blacks in local government . . ."

Cut off in her speech the guide looked irritably at the driver. The bus was stopped. He was wrenching through his gears, looking for reverse and panicking, spinning his wheel. She was about to snap her impatience at the driver, when she saw the sprinting children.

Jack saw the fury on their faces.

The faces were blurred in the dust-dirty windows of the bus, but the rage was unmistakable. Ecstatic loathing. Arms raised, stones held up. Boys and girls running together, shouting together.

The bus was across the road, the engine racing.

The guide was shouting high-pitched at the driver, and covering her face with her arm. She shouldn't have screamed at him, she should have let him get on with taking them clear.

He stalled the engine.

Stones rained on the minibus. The windscreen cascaded into the driver's face, across the guide's lap was a shower of diamond glass. Jack was rigid in fear, couldn't move, didn't know how to help himself. Everyone inside the bus shouting, and one of the Americans starting a prayer, and the German pulling his wife back from the side window and replacing her head with his wide-angle lens.

Black faces against the window. A hand with a knife, fists with stones. Muscles to rock the bus. Almost a darkness inside, because the window light was blocked by the Black faces, Black bodies, Black fists.

It was over very suddenly.

Jack hadn't heard the crack of the gas grenade guns, nor the patter of the shotguns, nor the roaring power of the Casspir A.P.C.

When he was aware of the silence he lifted his head. The screaming had stopped. There was a whimpering from one of the American women, the one whose husband had said that the Blacks just wanted work and to be left in peace. The guide was shivering, but upright, and was painstakingly starting to pick the windscreen fragments from her sweater. The Casspir had gone past them. The schoolchildren had scattered.

The Casspir bumped on the body of a kid who had been shot in the legs and was writhing, and who was still when he emerged to view again from under the wide heavy tread of the tyres.

A police jeep pulled up alongside the minibus.

Jack saw the savage expression on the officer's face as he climbed out. He couldn't follow the detail of the language as the officer tongue-lashed the guide in Afrikaans. The message was clear enough, they were bloody fools to have been there, they should get the hell out.

Subdued, they drove back to Johannesburg.

The German had damaged his wide-angled lens but by God he'd have a picture or two. The American, from Washington state, announced that he'd be making a donation to the South African police. The guide looked straight ahead, hugging herself against the wind through the jagged edges of the windscreen. Jack had learned something of the war. He had seen twenty kids who would have stoned him to death because he was White. He had seen a kid, minutes out of the classroom, become a statistic in death because he was Black.

At the Carlton Hotel where the bus dropped them off there were no goodbyes, no tips for the driver. The guide had nothing to say to them, not even about communists and agitators.

He went back towards the Landdrost. He approached it as calmly as he could from three angles. No sign of a police presence. And eventually just a friendly greeting from the day porter. Infinite regrets that sir had not had the best impression from his tour.

There was no message.

The solicitor looked again at his watch. In four and a half minutes it was the third time he had looked at the gold face on his wrist.

The prison officer stood behind him, ignoring him.

He sat on the hard wooden chair and looked through the plate glass at the mirror of the room that was opposite him. The room he looked into was the same in each detail to the one in which he sat. There were no decorations in the visit rooms. A room divided by a wall and a window of plate glass. An identically placed door in each section. Identical tables below the plate glass. A single chair on each side of the glass, and a voice pipe that was like an inverted elephant's trunk for speaking into and for listening through.

He hated this little room, had hated it each time that he had come to visit his client. His one aim was to get his work done, to get back to his car, to drive with his escort to the airlock gate in the outer wall, to get himself through the identity check point on Soetdoringstraat, to get himself out onto Potgieterstraat, as soon as it was marginally decent for him to do so. They had treated him like dirt when he had come in through the checks and searches and delays. They seemed to despise him as they had walked him across the lawn to the visit room. No small talk, as if the presence of a solicitor, a man trying to cheat them from their work, was an irrelevance to their way of work. He had the job because he had once represented James Carew in a case involving a minor traffic accident. In John Vorster Square Carew had given the name of the young solicitor, and a damned black day that had been. He wished to God he had never been involved.

Because he was frightened being so close to the hanging shed, and to the man who was to walk into that shed, he felt resentment against Carew.

He had been telephoned by the colonel of the security police. He had endured a lecture from the Boer policeman.

He knew what had happened. He was a lawyer and he was a citizen of the Republic of South Africa. He had done his damned best to represent Carew at committal, at trial, and since sentence. He had not considered it possible that his client would reject the colonel's deal, not when the rope was the irrevocable alternative. He had done his best for his client, and he had hoped to God that his client would do the best thing for himself and talk to the security police about the A.N.C. The solicitor's parents lived in Durban; that city had been the target of a bomb at Christmas of all times; the A.N.C. were foul murderers. From all he had seen of his client he could not place him in the same category. But then Carew, for all the sessions they had had together, remained an enigma to the young solicitor. The man had a past, he was certain. The nature of the past, his ignorance of it, burned as resentment.

He had done as much as he could for Carew and Carew had done nothing for him, nothing for himself.

He was quite justified in his resentment.

He heard the approach of footsteps down the corridor, sounds distorted through the tube that was the link between his outside world and Carew's inside world in the hanging place.

He had prepared what he would say to Carew. He would tell Carew that he had done all that was possible to save his life. He would tell his client that rejecting the colonel's offer had been an act of egregious folly. He was going to tell his client that it would be a waste of time to attempt another clemency petition. That in his view it was so damned unnecessary.

The door was opened.

Jeez was led in.

Through the glass the solicitor stared at Jeez. He thought his man was frailer than when he had last seen him, as if he had lost weight, as if the skin on his cheeks had been peeled back and the flesh underneath scalpelled away and then the skin rolled back again to sag over the hollowness.

Jeez sat down opposite him.

God, how to be sharp with a man who was going to walk to the gallows.

There was a small smile on Jeez's face. The solicitor understood. The bastard knew. The obstinate bastard had known what he had done when he had walked out on the colonel. The solicitor could not consider how a man voluntarily turned his back on life, not when the choice was his.

"Good of you to call round, young man. Did you have a pleasant drive over?"

The solicitor swallowed hard. The resentment died in him. In a torrential flow he told Jeez that the legal options were exhausted.

It was all because of a series of coincidences.

Because an assessor had been called back into the army for reserve service, and another assessor had been at home with his wife and newly-born baby, and her supervisor had thought it would be good experience for her to be out of the office, Ros van Niekerk had gone to a fire damaged home in Sandton. The cook/maid had left the electric chip frier on all night. The chip frier had finally caught fire in the small hours, gutting an expensive kitchen. She had gone to work that morning in a pure white skirt, and that skirt had been dirtied as she had moved about the kitchen assessing the damage and agreeing the size of the claim. Ros went home to change after the call.

Because her father was at work and her mother was at morning bridge, she let herself into the house that she expected to be deserted except for their maid. The maid had been a young nanny once, but with Ros and Jan grown up the nanny's role was gone. She could hear the maid in the back washhouse. Ros didn't announce herself, went up the stairs to her room.

Because the radio was playing in Jan's room she went to the slightly opened door. It surprised her to hear the radio. She thought her brother must have left it on when he had gone to Wits – always late. She eased the door open. The room was empty. The bed was made. The radio was playing. There was a sprawl of papers on the small teak wood desk where he did his studying.

Because Ros sometimes wished that she had gone to university and not straight to work when she had left school, because she always took an interest in what Jan read and what he wrote in his essays, she glanced down at the papers on the table.

Because of that short series of coincidences Ros van Niekerk found herself staring down at the drawn plans made by the old Hungarian for Jacob Thiroko.

She was no fool. She understood immediately the content of the map drawn on the uppermost sheet of paper. The broad strokes of the roads were marked. Potgieterstraat, Soetdoringstraat, Wimbledonstraat. There were rectangular blocks drawn beside the roads. Local, White Political, Pretoria (Old) Central, New Women's, Beverly Hills. She knew what she looked at.

Mechanically, as if she sleepwalked, she lifted the piece of paper. The second sheet was drawn to a larger scale. A rectangular block enclosing another block, and a part of the inner block was drawn in detail. She read. Gate house and radio control, wooden gates, steps, light, watchtower. She read measurements. The longest of the outer lines was marked as 200 metres, what she took to be an inner wall was marked at 100 metres.

She heard the toilet flush down the landing. Her eyes didn't leave the detail. She read. Corridor, C section 1, exercise yard, visit room . . . She heard Jan's trailing footstep shuffle towards his room . . . She read. Workshop, washhouse, preparation room. She read the one word . . . She heard him stumbling from the door towards her . . . She read. Gallows . . . Jan's hand caught at her, spun her away from the papers.

"What the hell are you doing?"

She faced up to him. He was the boy but he was no taller than her. She could look straight into his eyes.

"You bloody ask yourself what you're doing."

She had never before seen such violence on Jan's face.

She said, "This is bloody treason."

He shouldered past her, he was snatching at the papers. She caught his arm.

She said, "You can't undo what I've seen. I've read the word. Gallows. That map's treason."

He shook her hand off him. There was a high livid flush on his face. He was vulnerable, in her eyes always had been.

"You shouldn't have come snooping in here."

"I come in here, I find a map of Pretoria prison. I find a map of the place where they hang people. You have to do better than tell me I'm snooping."

He thrust the papers into his desk drawer. He locked the drawer with the key on his waist chain. He turned to her, defiant, cornered.

"So what are you going to do?"

"What the hell does that mean?"

"Are you going to inform on me?"

"I'm your sister, Jan. Your bloody sister. Where did you learn that sort of bloody talk? Sister, got it."

"Are you going to Father, are you going to the security police?"

"For God's sake, I'm your sister. I love you, you're my brother."

They clung to each other.

Ros said softly, "How long have you been living a lie, Jan?"

"I swore an oath of secrecy."

"I'm your sister, I'm not your enemy."

"It was an oath, Ros."

"We never had secrets."

"You wouldn't understand."

"That my brother is involved in treason, perhaps I wouldn't understand that."

"Treason is their word. It isn't mine."

"Jan, I love you, but you are involved in something that is *against* the law."

"That's important?" He shouted at her. "It's only important because it's against the law? Don't play the bourgeois cretin, Ros. The evil in this country is ending, its time's up. We're on the march, going forward. It's over for the Boers and the racists."

"The Boers make the laws." Her voice raised against his. "If you go against the law then you go to prison."

"I swore the oath, Ros."

"For what?" A snap of contempt.

"To be able to look in the eye the men and women of our country. To have my pride. You have to fight something that is wrong. Not like those bastard businessmen fight it, mealy statements about 'concern', plane trips to Lusaka to plead with the Freedom Movement not to give all their shares and their stocks to the people when the revolution comes. Not like those crappy Liberals at Wits, all piss, all wind. I fight the evil with the language the system understands."

She snorted at him. "What do you do?"

"I do my part."

She couldn't help herself, there was the sneer of the elder sister. "What's your part? Running messages on your little moped?"

"My part."

"How can little Jan van Niekerk *hurry* the revolution?"

"I do my part."

"The Blacks wouldn't trust you."

"They trust me."

"How do they trust you?"

He turned away from her. He went to his bed, flopped down. His head was in his hands.

"I swore an oath of secrecy."

"How do they trust you?"

She knew he would tell her. She had always had the power to take anything from him, even the things that were most precious. He was always weak in her hands.

"Is it the terrorists of the African National Congress? How do they trust you?"

He spoke through his fingers. She had to lean forward to hear him.

"The bomb in John Vorster Square. I delivered it to the man who placed it."

"What?" Incredulity widening her mouth.

"They trust me that much. I moved that bomb."

"You could go to prison for the rest of your life."

"That's a God-awful reason for backing off the fight against evil."

"Rubbish."

He looked up at her, clear faced. "You go to the police, Ros."

She hissed, "Say that again."

"Just go to the police, Ros, turn me in."

She took the step towards him. She raised her hand. He didn't flinch. She slapped his face. His head rocked. She saw the smile that was beaming up at her.

"What are you going to do?"

She stared out of the window. She saw the maid hanging the washing on the rope line. She saw her father's good quality shirts, and her mother's good quality underwear, and she saw Jan's T-shirts and her blouses. She saw neat gardens ablaze with shrubs and flowers. She saw a Black man collecting grass cuttings. She saw their world that was comfortable and familiar, and now threatened.

"I'm going to fight to keep you out of prison."

"What does that mean?"

"It means that on your own you'll rot the rest of your life in prison."

The words were music to Jan van Niekerk.

Quietly he told her that he was under instruction to go to a certain place and deliver a message for a man to make a rendezvous. He knew the name of the man. He said it was the man who had taken the bomb into John Vorster Square police station. He told her that he had to meet the man and give him the plans of the Pretoria Central prison complex.

"Left to yourself, little brother, you'll rot for the rest of your life," Ros said.

The man was White.

He had been born in Latvia. He was a colonel in the K.G.B. He was marked for assassination by the security police and National Intelligence Service in Pretoria. He was the chief planner of Umkonto we Sizwe operations inside South Africa. More than a year before he had authorised the fire bomb attack on the Rand Supreme Court. That attack was one of a long list of projects that had crossed his desk. He had approved the bombing of the Air Force headquarters in Pretoria, and the attacks on the Sasol synthetic petrol refinery and on the Koeburg nuclear power plant and on the Voortrekkerhoogte military base. More recently he had sanctioned the laying of mines in the far north east of the Transvaal on roads that would be used by civilians, and the detonating of a shrapnel bomb in a Durban shopping mall crowded with Christmas custom. The long retaliatory arm of the security police and N.I.S. had swiped close to him. His former wife had died, mutilated by a letter bomb in her office at the Centre for African Studies in the Mozambique capital.

The meeting was in a small air-conditioned office at the back of the A.N.C. compound on the outskirts of Lusaka.

Jacob Thiroko was not interrupted.

He stated his plan. Five men, Kalashnikovs, grenades, one hundred kilos of explosives, four cars for the run to the Botswana frontier, the skill of the White explosives expert now loose in South Africa. Thiroko had spoken of John Vorster Square, he had sung of the pedigree of the expert. He had been heard out. He kept his high card for the end.

"I will lead the cadre."

Nothing astonished this White man. His eyebrows flickered a trace of surprise. He stayed silent.

"I will go back myself into South Africa, into my motherland. I have not been there since I was a young man. Perhaps it is a hallucination. Perhaps it is my duty to the men who otherwise will hang. I have a responsibility for them, five times of responsibility. You gave the authorisation, I prepared the plan. I cannot escape my responsibility . . . The young man in Johannesburg is the son of James Carew, the driver. The son taught me about sacrifice, when I thought I had nothing to learn. For his father he is prepared to sacrifice his life. I should be prepared to make the same sacrifice. They are sons to me, Happy, Charlie, Percy and Tom. What did we do when Benjamin Moloise walked to the gallows? We issued statements . . . I don't want to issue a statement this time!"

"Tell me about London, Comrade."

"In London I went to see a physician."

"What were you told, Comrade Jacob?"

"To live each day of my life to the full, to enjoy each minute of each day."

"Is there pain?"

"The pain will be nothing to the joy if I can give life to my children."

"Is it possible, to bring them out?"

"I would have said it was impossible for a stranger to carry a bomb into John Vorster Square. I no longer know what is impossible."

146

The pain was deep in the lower bowel of Thiroko's stomach. He winced as he stood, as he shook hands with the man from Riga. He had chosen the four men who would go with him, who would return with him to South Africa.

The physician had not been specific, he had spoken only of the few months that remained.

Jack came back into his room, closed the door behind him, slipped on the security chain, checked the suitcase.

In the afternoon, after the experience in Soweto, he had had to force himself to go out into the city, to walk on the streets amongst Blacks, be a tourist. Be a tourist and also make some enquiries.

He had gone to a small engineering firm in the back streets down from Marshall. He had asked about the availability of a short length of 8″ iron piping.

When he crossed the room he saw, lying on his dressing table, left there by the bellboy, a sealed envelope.

He saw the bold handwriting. He thought the envelope had been addressed by a girl.

When the colonel left the meeting he brought back to his office a copy of the initial forensic report.

Embedded in the walls of the hallway of John Vorster Square had been found the synthetic fibres of a cheap bag. Blown clear through the doorway and into a flower-bed had been a piece of a metal can. This first examination stated that the fibres came from a little-used bag, and the fifty cent sized piece of metal from a clean painted can without corrosion or rust.

The colonel had given it as his opinion that both items had been bought specifically for the bombing, for the making up of the explosive device, for carrying it.

"I'm truly sorry, Carew."

"Thank you, sir."

"There's not a decent man I know who can get pleasure out of this moment."

"I'm sure there isn't, sir."

"For what we do in life . . . we have to take the consequences of our actions."

"Just so, sir."

"I take no delight in seeing a man go to his punishment, whatever he's done."

"I appreciate that, sir."

The governor stood ramrod straight in the doorway of the cell. Behind him, his message read, the deputy sheriff of Pretoria waited, his arms hanging, his hands clasped in front of his trouser flies. Jeez had the centre of the floor space, he was at attention, his thumbs on the seams of his trousers. He thought the sympathy was genuine. He thought the governor was an honest man. The governor didn't frighten Jeez, not so that he had to imagine him out of his tailored uniform, shorn of his medal ribbons, stripped to his underpants. The governor was nothing like the bastard who had run Spac, who had been Jeez's gaoler way back for so many long years.

"I like a man to go proudly. I like a man to behave like a man. I can tell you this, Carew, go like a man and it will be easier for you. A prisoner who makes difficulties hurts himself, not us."

"Thank you, sir."

"I'd bet money on you, Carew, that you'll go like a man who is proud."

"Yes, sir."

"I always tell a man at this time that he should think through his life, think about his affairs, and stay with the good times. We don't want any melancholy."

"No, sir."

"Carew, you wrote a letter a few weeks ago, I checked with Records and you've had no letter back. I'm sorry. Of course, you are permitted to write as many letters as you wish."

"There won't be any more letters, sir."

"Is there anyone we should contact, anyone you would like to be offered facilities for a visit?"

"No, sir. There's no one who should visit."

"I tell you frankly, I've never met a man who has been here, White, who has been as private as you. Nor of your bearing, if I may say so."

"Yes, sir."

"There's a point I would like to make to you, Carew. The State President has refused you clemency, he has named the date of your execution. There have come from abroad several representations to the State President urging him to think again. From His Holiness the Pope, the Secretary-General of the United Nations, many others. Carew, you should know that in these matters the State President will not alter his decision. I tell you that, man to man, because it is better that you prepare yourself without the distraction of false hope."

"Yes, sir."

"The decision that you hang next Thursday is irreversible."

"I know that, sir."

"The colonel from the security police, he will come back and see you, Carew, if you care to reconsider his proposal."

"I have nothing to say to the colonel, sir."

13

He took a taxi from the hotel to the zoo gardens.

Jack had memorised his instructions and flushed the sheet of paper away down the lavatory.

The driver hissed against the wooden toothpick that was clamped in his teeth through each detail of the bland police statement of unrest overnight in the Cape and the East Rand on the early morning news. Two shot dead by the police in the Cape, and a Black woman burned to death in an East Rand township.

"Seems to be getting worse," Jack said.

The taxi driver looked over his shoulder. "You'd need to be smiling from your cheeks to your backside to think it's getting better."

"What has to happen for it to get better?"

The taxi driver settled comfortably in his seat, like the question was a box of chocolates, to be enjoyed.

"My opinion, take a tougher line with the Blacks. That's not what we're doing at the moment. Right, the State President's put the military and the police into the townships. Wrong, each time he makes a speech he's talking about reform. Result, they think they're winning, they reckon if they keep up the murder and the arson that they're on their way to government. On the one hand the State President is trying to intimidate the Blacks into ending the violence, on the other hand he's trying to buy them off with promises. The two don't sleep in the same bed . . ."

Jack slid out of reach of the driver's eyes in the rear-view mirror, took a fast, deep breath, and asked: "Did you know the taxi man, the one they're going to hang?"

"Carew, that bastard?"

"Did you know him?"

"I didn't myself. I've a friend who did."

"What sort of fellow was he?"

"Mystery man, that's what my friend says. When the name was in the papers he just didn't believe it, says he was a very private fellow."

A recklessness in Jack. "Where did he live?"

"He had a flat, behind Berea, furnished, that's what my friend says. When he was arrested he gave instructions to his lawyer man that everything in the flat should be sold, went to a children's home charity. My friend says there wasn't much, bits and pieces and his clothes, but they've all gone, like he knew he was never coming out. My friend says that he used to talk quite a bit with this Carew, but he never knew anything about him. I mean, they didn't talk about family, just used to talk about the motor, that sort of thing. Long time ago, he wrote to ask whether Carew would like a visit, and the letter came back from the authorities that Carew didn't want any visit . . . . What's your interest?"

Jack said, "I read about it in the English papers."

He was dropped at the main entrance.

He must have been one of the first customers that morning because the wide sloping grounds with the autumn in the trees were near-deserted. He walked over the dun yellow parched lawns. He did exactly as he had been instructed. He went to the cafeteria where they were still putting out the tables, and he ordered a cup of coffee. When he had drunk it he walked away past the big wingspan vulture in a tall cage, and past the compound where a young gorilla gambolled, and past the green water pool of the sea lions. He understood why the instructions had demanded that he followed a set route. He was being watched and checked to see that he had no tail. He climbed the hill and strolled slowly past the big cat enclosures. Well before the heat of the day and the leopards and the jaguar and the lions were pacing. He sat on a bench in front of the Bengali tigers. He didn't look around, he made no attempt to identify the people he assumed to be watching him. Up again and past the stink of the elephant and the rhino, past a bee swarm of tiny Black children out with their teacher, past a party of shambling mencaps with their nurses. He followed the instructions.

He went up the long hill towards a huge memorial, to British victory in the Boer War of nearly a century ago. He drifted into the military museum. More schoolchildren, but middle teens and White, and with a pretty young teacher who had a strident voice as she quizzed her pupils on Bren gun carriers, Churchill tanks, 25 pounders, an 88 mm recoilless anti-tank. They'd be needing that knowledge, the little sods. Their country was going into automatic rifles and armoured personnel carriers and White conscripts in the townships, and by the time these kids were fattened up then it might have come down to tanks and artillery. It was a bad image for Jack. His thoughts ran fast to Potgieterstraat and Defence Headquarters and the guns of the sentries and the fire slits on the walls of Local. A bad awful bloody express train of thought because he had never believed that Beverly Hills could be so well protected.

If he had known it would be *that* well protected then Jimmy Sandham would be alive, and Duggie would be alive, and Jack Curwen would be in his office, at his desk, on the north side of Leatherhead.

Bit bloody late, Jack.

He sat on a bench. He waited.

Jan and Ros had argued half the night away. They had argued in the car on the way to the zoo. The argument had continued as they tracked the Englishman.

"Violence doesn't change anything."

"The Boers listen to violence, they don't listen to debate."

"Blowing people up, killing and maiming people, won't change the government."

"Change will only come when control of the townships is lost."

"The state is committed to real change, all that's needed is a breathing space for the moderates on all sides to come forward and negotiate."

"The *moderates?* What do they want to talk about? About opening up Whites beaches for non-segregated bathing? Do you think they care in the townships, where they're queuing up for charity food parcels, about a nice little swim on a Whites Only beach? The moderates aren't relevant, might have been twenty years ago, not now. It's about power, not about which beach you're allowed to swim on. Anyone who has power will never hand it over voluntarily. The Boers'll have to be burned out of power."

"Your way, Jan, only slows the pace of change."

"They're *playing* with reform, Ros. They want to get the Americans off their backs, so they can go back to living the way they've always lived, the White boot on the Black throat."

"Are you ashamed of being White?"

"I've no shame, because I'm fighting against a White evil. I didn't ask you to spy in my room. You can get out of my life."

"I'm stuck with your bloody life. I'm your sister. On your own you're dead or you're locked up. I won't turn away from you. I wish I could, and I can't."

For half an hour they watched the Englishman move through the zoo's gardens. At the sea lions and the compound for the big cats they had split and gone in opposite ways so that each of them could be sure they were free of a tail. Jan thought that his sister learned fast. If there had been a tail he believed they would have seen it.

For Jan there was the fascination of seeing the clean shouldered back of the man who had achieved the remarkable, and carried a bomb into John Vorster Square. For Ros there was the fascination of seeing the man who had come as an activist to their country, who was capable of murder. For what he had achieved, Jan thought the stranger was a hero. For involving her brother, Ros thought him an enemy.

They came into the military museum.

Through the heads and shoulders of the schoolchildren, between the snub barrels of the artillery pieces, they saw him. They were a boy and a girl out walking, there was nothing about them to excite suspicion. They looked at the man who sat hunched on the bench.

Ros said, "Once you've spoken to him then you're more deeply involved than ever before. You could turn round, you could go home. Father would get you a ticket, you could fly out of the country tonight. You could be safe."

Jan said, "I don't run away."

"You don't run away because you can't run . . ." She hated herself.

"They don't listen to reason. Last year when they hanged Ben Moloise they had petitions from all over the world. They didn't give a shit. They strung him up because what the rest of the world says doesn't count."

"He was convicted of killing a policeman."

"Now they're going to hang five men, and again the rest of the world's pleading for mercy. They don't give a shit. This man knows it, fight force with force. Fight the force of John Vorster Square with the force of a fire bomb."

"And Pretoria Central?"

"I don't know," Jan said.

He had the diagrams of the gaol in the inner pocket of his windcheater jacket.

"You're getting to be a real creep, Jan."

They went forward, Jan limping and ahead, and Ros trailing him.

He turned when he heard the voice. The voice spoke his name.

Jack saw the boy. He saw the shallow body and the thin face. He saw the way the shoulder drooped. He saw that the boy was crippled. The boy was behind the bench, trying to smile a greeting.

He looked the other way. The girl was standing back two more paces than the boy. A nice looking girl, and older than the boy, and she wore a summer skirt and a blouse buttoned to the throat. He could see the lines at her mouth, tension lines.

"I'm Jack Curwen."

"I was ordered to contact you. You followed the instructions, thank you."

They stared at each other. As if neither had quite believed the ordinariness of the other.

Jack smiled, the boy grinned. Jack wondered why the girl didn't smile.

"I'm Jan, this is my sister. You don't need any more names."

Strangely formal. Jack shook hands with them.

A shyness in Jan's voice. "What you did at John Vorster Square was incredible."

Again the silence. None of them knowing what to say. Out of earshot the schoolchildren were spidering over the hulk of the museum's largest tank.

Jan drew the envelope from his pocket. He passed it to Jack. Jack ripped open the fold. He saw the diagrams. He leafed quickly through the sheets of paper, the frown settling sharp cut on his forehead. He knew the girl's eyes never left his. The school teacher's voice carried gently to him. She had raised her voice because she was describing to her class the cyclic rate of fire of a heavy machine gun from the Great War. He saw that the diagrams were detail of Pretoria Central. He saw the positioning of Beverly Hills, he understood why he had not seen the walls when he had walked on Potgieterstraat.

"What happens now?"

Jan said, "I have to take you into the north of the Transvaal. There is a rendezvous there for you, close to a town called Warmbaths. It is a spa town about a hundred kilometres from Pretoria. You should go back to your hotel, and you should check out of your hotel, then we drive to Warmbaths."

"Do you know why I have come to South Africa?"

"No."

Ros snapped, "And he doesn't need to know."

Jack saw the anger on the boy's face.

Jan said, "I'm just a courier. I am ordered to deliver you to a rendezvous. I do what I am told, just as I brought you the envelope today, just as I brought you the package of explosives."

"You don't know why we are hitting the gaol?"

"As he said, he's just a courier."

Ros twisted away, swirled her skirt. Jack stood up and walked behind her and Jan hobbled after them. Jack caught up with her.

"You're not a part of it," she said bitterly.

Her eyes were on her sandals, striding out.

Jack bored on. "I'm not a part of it, it's true. In England, my home, I'm not an activist, I'm not political. I don't give a damn for this war. I have to be here, probably like you have to be here."

She tossed her head back, rippled her hair, gestured at her brother behind her. She said, "It's lunatic for him to be involved."

"Lunatic for all of us."

"So why did you honour us with your presence?"

"A week today they're going to hang my father."

She looked away. He saw her close her eyes, squeeze them tight shut. They stood together and waited for Jan to catch them.

There were eighteen detectives from the plain clothes branch of the security police who had taken the desks and tables in the large room set aside for the investigation. The detectives worked with their telephones and notebooks eight floors above the back hall of John Vorster Square.

Ten of the detectives worked on tracing the grip bag. Eight worked on finding the source of the petrol can.

In front of each man was a commercial telephone directory of the greater Johannesburg area. By the middle of the morning it was believed that a manufacturer had been identified for the bag, a factory employing similar synthetic fibres to those retrieved by forensic. The detectives then took sections of the directories to ring each and every number where the bag could have been sold. The information given to the detectives pointed towards a White attacker. It was therefore probable that the bag and the petrol can, if bought in Johannesburg, had been bought either in the city centre or in a White suburb. The outlets through which the bag might have been sold were fewer than the outlets for petrol cans. It was thought that the bag, rather than the can, would prove decisive.

Twice that morning the colonel had come down the two flights of stairs to the incident room.

He was not directly involved, not yet. His involvement was two stages away in the process of the investigation. First the source of the sales must be identified, second the purchaser must be described.

Jacob Thiroko and his group travelled apart, but on the same aircraft.

He carried a Tanzanian passport. He had never used that passport before. It described him as an engineer. He carried letters of introduction from the Botswana Enterprises Development Unit, and also from the Botswana Meat Corporation for whom, he could tell immigration, he was designing a new abattoir. The younger men were on a variety of Black African passports, and each was equipped with the cover to talk his way through immigration at the international airport at Gaberone.

With more time for planning and for taking advice, he might have attempted to travel overland from Angola, or overland from Mozambique, both difficult but both possible. The fast way to South Africa was through Gaberone, not the safe way.

It was eighteen months since the Recce Commando squads had been heli-coptered into Gaberone at night to kill twelve of Thiroko's comrades, to blow up their offices, to bring home what was described as a treasure trove of intelligence material. Since the raid, the Botswana government had ceded areas of their sovereign independence to permit covert members of the National Intelligence Service to operate in various guises from their territory.

Thiroko walked from the aircraft across the tarmac towards the single storey building housing lounges and offices. He walked almost in the shadow of the squat, square built, air traffic control tower. He was concerned with the immigration officers. He should have been concerned with a White air traffic control supervisor. His photograph was taken. It would not be a good likeness, but it would serve as confirmation of this supervisor's opinion, made instantly, that he had sighted Jacob Thiroko.

By the time that Thiroko and his four men had collected their baggage, queued for immigration, gathered together to be met by their contact driver, there were two vehicles waiting to follow them out of the airport car park. There was a land rover with the markings of a locally based safari holiday company driven by a White with a Black passenger, and there was a Peugeot 504 estate carrying three Blacks.

Inside the car, when it was speeding on the Palapye road, Thiroko told his companions that they would cross the border that night in the wide area between Martin's Drift and Oranjefontein, that they would be moved south by lorry, that they would meet with a sixth man at a place where weapons and explosives were stored. He saw they were cool to what he said. Not excited. They were all in their middle twenties. They had all left South Africa as children, they were coming home as men.

The Peugeot 504 was eight hundred metres behind. It did not have to be closer. If the car ahead turned off the metalled road it would have to give up tarmac for dirt. A billowing grit storm would telegraph a detour from the Palaype road.

Jack paid cash for the two lengths of steel tube.

Hell's expensive for just a metre in length apiece, but the steel was as thick as the width of nail on his little finger, and the diameter was nine inches. It was what he wanted.

A White in the front hall of the engineering works tried to strike up a conversation with Jack while a Black was sent to the rear yard to bring out the tubing. Jack didn't respond, gave no explanation for buying the tubing.

He refused the White's offer that the Black carry the tubing to his car. If he had been a South African, if he'd stopped to think, he would have allowed the Black to take it to the car. But he didn't want any one to be able to link him to Jan who sat in the back seat of the Beetle, nor to Ros who was behind the wheel.

Two blocks away, down on Anderson, Jack again paid cash for a set of heavy wire cutters.

The tubing was on the back seat of the car. Jack's case was in the boot.

They took the Pretoria road. They would bypass the capital on their way to Warmbaths.

The chaplain could have sat on the lavatory seat, or on the bed beside Jeez, or on the table that might have come away from the wall under his sixteen stones. He said he spent too much time sitting, and he stood.

Jeez sat on the bed. The chaplain wore uniform, identical to the other officers' but for the purple shoulder flashes. A big man with a big gut and mane of white hair, and a voice that barked even when he tried to be kind.

"Are you a child of Christ, Carew?"

Jeez hardly knew the chaplain. He didn't go to the chaplain's Sunday services. Religion was not compulsory at Beverly Hills. When you were a condemn you could take God or you could leave Him. Religion, like work and exercise, was voluntary. Jeez took only exercise.

"I'm not a praying man, sir."

Many times the chaplain brought his chess set or his draughts board into a condemn's cell, and talked and whiled away afternoon hours. He had never played chess or draughts with Jeez. Duty had brought him that day to C section 2, and the prodding of the governor.

"You don't help yourself, Carew."

"My problem, sir."

"You should place yourself before God in a state of humble repentance."

In daylight hours there were fifteen prison officers administering the White condemns, all bored out of their skulls and reading picture magazines and polishing their kit, and kicking footballs in the exercise yard, and laughing too loud and joking too much. Jeez wondered if, for variety, they'd come on their toes to the door of his cell to listen to the chaplain.

"You know, Carew, many of the Blacks that go, they thank me just before. They thank me because they say they have found repentance, they say they are at peace with God. They say I have guided them to God . . ."

Jeez said, "I reckon you *enjoy* working here."

"You're a hard man, Carew, without contrition."

"My life's going to end the hard way, sir."

The chaplain smiled, avuncular. "I'll be with you when you go."

"Wouldn't miss it, would you, sir?"

"To offer you comfort."

"Do you go and have your breakfast afterwards?"

"I don't get provoked that easily, Carew."

"We've not much to talk about, sir."

Jeez thought the chaplain loathed him. In the eyes of the man there was a watery gleam, as though the chaplain thought this man would crack at the last, cry for help. He thought the chaplain wanted nothing more in life than to walk the corridors of Beverly Hills with young Blacks on their way to their Maker with mission hymns in their throats.

"Do you want me to ask the surgeon to give you a sedative?"

"What for?"

"We sometimes give a White a sedative."

"I want nothing from you, sir."

"Others, they ask for a drink, a big whisky or a brandy."

"I want nothing, sir."

"Carew, the Blacks sing for each other, you know that. When you go then you will have the men with you, those that were arrested with you, and they will be singing the penny rhymes of the African National Congress. I cannot believe you want that. I could get in a church choir to sing for you. It has been done before."

"Why should I want that?"

"Damn you, to give you comfort, man."

Jeez thought the man might have been organising a confirmation service. And did he want some flowers, and did he want his hair cut, and did he want a clean shirt? And if he said that he wanted a choir then they could settle down for a cosy chat to decide what the choir should sing, and then whether the choice would be suitable for bass voices as they might be a bit short on contralto and soprano.

"I'm not dragging anyone else in here. I'm not dirtying anyone else's day."

The chaplain sighed.

"You can always send for me. I am always available."

The Chaplain rapped on the closed door of the cell.

"Thank you, sir."

The door clattered shut on the chaplain's back. Jeez lay on his bed. He was dry eyed. For ten years in Spac he had believed, known, that the team was working for him. And after ten years in Spac there had been the fêting and the restaurant meals and the debriefs for the Balkan desk and the weekends down at Colonel Basil's home. He had to believe in the team, or his cheeks would have been wetted.

Facing another shortening day.

Jack talked softly.

Ros drove well. She kept her attention on the road, but she listened.

In the back, curled round the metal tubes, Jan was quiet.

". . . Right through the time when I was a kid my father was held up to me as being just about the most rotten man that ever lived. Had to be rotten because he walked out on his wife and son, left them for dead with an impersonal financial arrangement to make sure they didn't starve. But I found out why he'd gone missing, and who was responsible for him, and how he'd been ditched, but that was only confirmation material for me. I'd have come here anyway, whatever he'd done when he left my mother. I have to see him and talk to him and bring him through, nothing else seems important. He's the fall guy, he's the expendable leg man . . . You know what I want to do? More than anything else I just want to walk him through Whitehall, that's where all our government sits on its backsides, and I want to walk him into the fat cats' rooms, and I want to say that I did what none of them had the guts to do. And after that I'm not going to give a shit about their security and their Official Secrets Act. I'm going to blow it all open. I don't care who the bloody casualties are, and I don't care if I'm one of them. There are people in London who are going to pay a bloody great price for what's happened. They'll have to kill me to keep me quiet.

"You know, since I started out on this I've never even thought that it might not work. Right, there are times when I don't know what the next stage is, how we're going to crack the next barricade, but it's going to happen. When I went up to Pretoria, then it looked impossible, like everyone had told me it would be. After I'd seen Local and Defence H.Q. I could have packed it in, gone off for the airport. I sorted myself out. Doesn't matter how difficult it is, it has to be done. I mean, there isn't any way out of it, not for me. My father's going to hang, that's the beginning and the middle and the end of it, and something has to be done."

"Even if it is, actually, impossible?" Her gaze was straight ahead.

"Has to be tried, because he's my father."

Jan shouted. "Roadblock."

Jack hadn't seen it, nor Ros.

They were on the N1, a little past the turn off for Randjiesfontein.

There were two police vans, primrose yellow, drawn across the road. There was a short queue of cars. Ros was going down through her gears. Jack winced.

Only he knew of the explosives in his suitcase. Hadn't told Jan, nor his sister, that he had squirrelled away fifteen pounds of explosives. And the prison plans . . . The pain was immediate, and then gone. None of the cars was being searched. They were the seventh car in the line. A police sergeant came towards them, stopping by each driver. He wondered how Ros would be, couldn't tell. No-one spoke in the car as the sergeant approached. Beyond the vans was parked a high armoured personnel carrier, off the road. Jack saw policemen standing and sitting in the open top, displaying automatic shot guns and F.N. rifles.

"We're running escorted convoys down the next ten kilometres, Miss."

"What's happened?" Ros asked, small voice.

"A gang of Blacks stoned a car, a kilometre down. White woman, elderly. Car went off the road. The bastards got to her, dragged her out. They had rocks and knives, Miss. They set light to her, she was an old lady. We've a big search op in there, but it's a wilderness. Supposed to be a helicopter coming. She wouldn't have had a chance."

Jack saw the pallor on Ros's face.

There was a Klaxon blast from the A.P.C. and exhaust fumes fanned from its tail. More cars were behind them, the sergeant had moved on. The A.P.C. set off down the road, they followed in a twenty mile an hour crawl.

Ros didn't speak. Jack didn't have to scratch his mind to remember the crowd coming down the shabby street in Soweto, and the din of the stones on the coachwork and the rocking of the vehicle and the screaming of the woman from Washington state. Not hard to imagine the last moments in an elderly woman's life as the stones started to fly and the windows were caving in, and the mob was materialising out of the long grass that flanked the road. Not hard to see the fingers ripping at the doors of a crashed car, and the fists raised and the clawing nails and the knives and the sharp edged rocks. He shuddered. He prayed that she had been unconscious when they had poured the petrol on her, thrown the match. They passed the burned car. There were skid marks on the tarmac, then the wheel tracks through the grass and then the blackened surround where the earth had been scorched near the car and under the body of the woman.

Ros retched. Jack looked away. Jan was breathing hard.

She snarled, "Great bloody day for the freedom fighters."

Jan rose to her. "Of course they're brutalised. What else could they be given the regime they live under?"

"That's the work of the people you're so bloody fond of."

"I don't condone that, and the A.N.C. doesn't condone that, but when you treat people like filth then they'll behave like filth."

"Pathetic excuses."

"It's the price the Whites are going to have to pay for half a century of naked racism."

"Childish slogans."

"Think of all the Black children that have been shot by the police."

She let him have the last word. Ros drove on towards Pretoria. All her life she had let her brother have the last word. It was why she was driving her car north, it was why she had entered a state of madness. The tie of family had captured her. She understood the young man sitting bowed in the front seat beside her. She believed herself to be as captured by her brother as he was by his father.

The White from the safari land rover watched as the Blacks kicked the resistance out of the driver of the pick up car.

They had tracked the pick up car after it had turned off the Palapye road, when it had headed south towards the border hamlets of Sherwood Ranch and Selika. Through field glasses they had watched Jacob Thiroko and the four other men get out and unload their bags. When the car had come back up the road it had been blocked.

The driver was a loyal member of the Movement, but the beating and the kicking were ferocious. The driver told his captors that the older man in his car had been addressed as Comrade Jacob. He told them that this Comrade Jacob had spoken of striking a great blow for the Movement. He told them that the old man had spoken of Warmbaths.

When he had nothing more that he could tell them, the driver was kicked to death. Boots in the stomach and the head killed him. The kicking was without mercy. When he was dead he was dragged to his own car and thrown inside. It was intended that he should be found.

It surprised the White that the Blacks under his command kicked the victim of their own colour with such enthusiasm. The White worked to trail out fifty feet of radio aerial from the short wave transmitter in the land rover to a branch high in a thorn tree.

His coded broadcast was picked up in the offices of the security police at Potgietersrus 160 kilometres away.

Jacob Thiroko and his cadre were to hike across country to a road junction outside Monte Christo, ten kilometres. At midnight they were to be met at the road junction and driven by lorry to a rendezvous north of Warmbaths. He believed they could cover that distance before the breaking of the morning light. At the rendezvous they would find a cache of weapons and explosives, buried there more than two years before.

They moved by compass bearing.

It was difficult for Thiroko to keep his attention on the animal track in front of him, and on the dried grass that cracked under foot, and on the wind scattered branches that snapped under his tread. He had come home, he was back in his own place. The scent of the scrub as familiar to him as his mother's body had been when he was a child. The smells of home, and the whirr of the insects, and the fear of snakes, and the bright light of a clear sun shining on his homeland. Nowhere else in Africa had he tasted the same smells, sounds, shining sun as he found on the hike towards Monte Christo, going back inside his country, his fighting ground.

Inside the operations room at the Hoedspruit base, home of 31 Squadron (helicopters), they followed a familiar routine. The Puma was tasked to take off in the late afternoon, and to reach the point of the border incursion before dusk. The quarry was to be given time to move away from the frontier and so to be unaware of the military movement behind them. The Puma was a good old workhorse, with improvised replacement parts it had flown for eighteen years in South Africa's colours.

In the thrash of the rotors it took off into the low slanted sun. Behind the two pilots were eight White soldiers of the Recce Commando, a dog handler with his golden labrador, and a skeletal Bushman. The Bushman wore only shorts, his shock of black hair was ringed by a green tennis sweat band. He spoke his own language only, that of the Kavango region of South West Africa.

The officer commanding the hunting team had been given an exact reference for the border incursion.

As they were coming in to land, as they looked ahead into Botswana, the pilots could see a car parked on a dirt track, and pulling away from it were a land rover and an estate car.

It took the Bushman only a few minutes to be sure of his starting point. When it became too dark for him the dog would take over the tracking.

It was not a difficult trail to follow.

Ros drove into the poorly lit one street of Warmbaths.

They checked into a hotel. They took single rooms.

At the reception desk, as they wrote false names and false addresses in the book, Ros remarked to the owner that they were breaking the journey north west to the Ebenezer Dam where her brother and his friend would be fishing.

160

14

"If they knew what Jan was into, my Mom and my Dad, they'd die."

"I told my mother that I was coming here to bring my father home – it must have sounded so daft that she didn't bother to argue with me."

"Being daft isn't being a traitor."

"You have to live your own life, for yourself, you can't live your life for your parents."

"Try telling them . . ." Ros laughed.

Jan was at the hotel.

Jack and Ros walked along the pavement of the street that sliced through Warmbaths. A desultory conversation, and blotted out when the big lorries and their trailers passed. The road through Warmbaths was the principal route from Johannesburg and Pretoria to Potgietersrus and Pietersburg and Louis Trichardt and on to the Zimbabwe border. The road rumbled under the lorries. Jack liked this small town, it was an escape from the threat of the cities. Agricultural country.

He had met the farmers the previous evening.

With Jan and Ros he had eaten a quiet meal in the hotel's dining room. He'd gone for a stringy t-bone and shared what he couldn't eat with the hotel cat. It had been a quiet meal because the brother and sister had been arguing in her room, and they hadn't anything to say to each other in front of Jack. He thought she might have been crying before she'd come down to dinner. Her eyes had been reddened and her upper cheeks puffed out. It could have just been the strain of the drive, but he thought she'd been crying. He'd left them after the meal and gone into the bar. One of those God awful entrances. The talking had stopped. A warble of noise when he had opened the door, silence when he had come forward to be served, as he was looked at and stripped for information. They would have known he was English from the moment he opened his mouth to ask for a Castle. He'd been lucky because the old soak who propped himself in the corner of the bar had a grandson in England, at an agricultural college in the West. Jack had listened and laughed aloud at the alcoholic's jokes, and he'd been included in a round, and stood his own for half the bar. They were huge lads, the young farmers. He knew they thought he was all right because each one of them through the long evening had come to him to try out their English. There wasn't much politics talked, a bit towards the end. Jack had thought they were all as confused as hell. What the hell was their government doing? What was all this crap talk about reform? Was the State President in the business of giving the country over to the *kaffirs?* Funny for Jack, because back home the State President

161

was seen as the high priest of conservatism. In the bar at Brown's, the State President was the missionary of liberalism. He quite liked the young farmers, and it was a good evening, and it cost him three visits to the lavatory along the open veranda from his room.

Jack and Ros turned off the main road.

Ros pointed out to him the weather worn red stones of trekkers' nineteenth century graves. They walked into a network of straight avenues bounded by bungalows and glorious gardens. Flowering shrubs, cut lawns, beds in bloom, and the drone of mowers and the hiss of stand pipes.

"Jan's right," Jack said. "He's taken sides and he's right, because it can't last."

"What's he right about?"

"That it can't last, that it's going to collapse. It's beautiful and it's doomed because nobody outside White South Africa cares a damn for you. Not the Europeans, not the Americans, not the Australians. Nobody's going to lift a finger for you when it all goes wrong."

She looked at him. She had a small and pretty mouth. A strand of hair was across her face.

"I don't want a lecture, Jack, and I know what I want from my country. But my way of getting there doesn't include old ladies being pulled out of their cars and being knifed and being burned."

He thought she walked beautifully. He thought there was a sweet loose swing in her hips. She had her arms folded across her chest, her breasts were lifted to push hard against the crumpled cotton of her blouse. She wore the same clothes as the day before.

"Do people care about hanging here?" Jack asked.

He saw a frown puckering and her eyebrows rising. They were a couple walking in a flower filled suburb, with a blue mountain ridge in distant sight, and he had asked her to talk about a court sentence that a man should hang by the neck until he was dead.

"It's not an issue. It's accepted that the penalty for murder is death by hanging. You've seen what they're like, our Blacks. Hanging protects us, the Whites. There's overwhelming support for hanging."

"If it wasn't my father."

"And if it wasn't my brother."

". . . then I'd probably think the same."

"If it wasn't my brother that's involved then I wouldn't cross the road for you, not if you were bleeding in the gutter."

He ducked his head. He walked faster. As surely as he had involved her brother, he had involved her. Just as he had involved Sandham and Duggie.

"What would you do for your brother, Ros?"

"I'd do for him what you're doing for your father."

"And after today?"

"We drop you this afternoon, we turn round, we drive like hell back to Johannesburg. I give Jan my ultimatum, big word for a big speech, I tell him that he quits or I inform on him. I don't have to go to the security police, I tell my father. He'll do as my father tells him, or my father will turn him in. That's what's happening today and after today. I'm not going to spend the next weeks and months wondering how close some pig-eyed policeman is inching to Jan, and I'm damned if I'm going to spend the next few years traipsing to White Political at Pretoria Central."

They turned back. He couldn't think of anything to say to her. He ought to have been able to talk to her because she wasn't an activist, neither was he. They were near to the hotel when she stopped, dead, swung to face him. They were in the glare of the sun, on a wide pavement, they were dusted by the lorries passing on the road.

"Please, if you're trapped then get yourself killed."

Jack squinted at her. "Great."

"If you're held they'll make you talk. If you talk, Jan's implicated."

"And you're implicated, if I talk."

"So just get yourself killed." She was angry because he laughed. "I'm in deadly earnest. The decent thing for you to do if you're trapped is to get yourself killed."

Jack straightened. There was a mock solemnity in his voice. "Goodbye, Miss van Niekerk, it has been a most pleasurable acquaintance."

"You're pretty ordinary, you know that?"

"Meaning what?"

"So ordinary that you're quite interesting . . . If you were a mercenary or if you had some political hang-up about fighting racism, God you'd be boring. You're an ordinary person, ordinary attitudes, ordinary life. As I read you, there's nothing that ever happened in your life that wasn't just ordinary. Then you took a plane, then you burned the back off a police station, then you planned to explode your way into a hanging gaol. But that doesn't change you, doesn't stop you being just ordinary."

He took her hand. She didn't try to pull away. "Thank you for what you have done for me."

"God damn you if you get yourself captured."

They went into the hotel. They went upstairs to pack their bags. Later they would pay the bill, check out, and drive together to the rendezvous that Jan had been given. Jack could picture it. The car would stop. He would get out. The car would drive away. He would be met at the rendezvous. He would never see the car again, nor the boy with the crippled foot, nor the pretty girl who couldn't be bothered to make herself beautiful. In his room, before throwing yesterday's socks and yesterday's shirt into his case, he looked over the plans of Pretoria Central. By the time they met, later that day, he would have the germ of a strategy to put to Thiroko.

The Bushman and the dog had led the troops to the road junction outside Monte Christo.

Through night binoculars they had observed the five men who waited for their pick up. They had seen them eat and urinate. They had heard the murmur of their voices. They had called in by radio for the necessary support. It had been a fine moonlit night. An ideal night for the operation. They had seen the collection of Thiroko and his comrades. Over the radio link had been passed a description of the vehicle and its registration plate.

A motorcycle, travelling without lights, had picked up the vehicle at Ellisrus, south of Monte Christo. It was the only route the vehicle could have taken. Moving behind the motorcycle was an unmarked saloon car carrying four more members of Recce Commando. The vehicle had been trailed through the night as it came south through the Waterberge mountains towards Warmbaths.

The Puma had come again and made a night landing in the play area of the school at Monte Christo, and roused the village as it picked up the troops. By a relayed radio link the pilot was able to keep in contact with the car that followed the motorcycle that followed Thiroko's vehicle. The Puma, with its range of 570 kilometres, had had no difficulty in holding the contact before the last message was passed to the cockpit from some four kilometres north of Warmbaths.

A morning of rare excitement for the colonel.

The fire bomb investigation in the hallway ten floors below was no longer priority. His plan personally to interrogate the Methodist priest, White and elderly and stitched for subversion, was shelved. Set aside, too, was the case file that would convict two and possibly three of the F.O.S.A.T.U. leadership.

One file on the colonel's desk. The heavily stencilled title was JACOB THIROKO. At the top of the file was a wire print of the photograph taken at Gaberone airport. The picture showed a slight, insignificant man walking on the tarmac, and there was something in his expression that told the colonel of pain, as if the wind were caught in his bowels.

The file was three quarters of an inch thick. Intelligence material collected over the years from Gaberone, Maputo, Luanda, Lusaka and London, and for embellishment there were the statements of the men from the "suicide squads" who had allowed themselves to be captured . . . It always amused the colonel that the A.N.C. cadres liked to call themselves "suicide squads" and then chuck away their weapons and emerge from their bolt holes with their hands held high . . . He knew Jacob Thiroko well, as well as he knew an old friend. He thought he had evidence enough to put him away for twenty-five years. He was less certain that he would be able to stick upon Thiroko a charge of murder without extenuating circumstances.

It would be good to hang the man, it would be a disappointment only to lock him away. Whether Thiroko hanged, or whether he was imprisoned, would depend on what information the bastard gave his interrogators. If he talked he would hang. Clear cut. The colonel would be responsible for the interrogation, responsible for making him talk. The photograph pleased the colonel. If Thiroko was in pain, if he had pain in his gut, then that would make easier the job of lifting the bastard onto the gallows trap.

The latest report was that Thiroko and four other Black males had crossed the border and were now resting up, that his resting place was surrounded by the Recce Commando. The soldiers were ordered to hold off until it was clear whether a further rendezvous was to take place. He had been told that the military would move in by mid-afternoon, that directly after his arrest Thiroko would be flown by helicopter to Johannesburg.

The colonel was wondering at the risk of it, why a man of Thiroko's prominence in Umkonto we Sizwe would dare to travel back inside South Africa, when his telephone rang.

It was the direct line, with the unlisted number. He reached for it. He heard his wife's voice.

Had he read the morning paper? About Aunt Annie?

No, my dear, he had not.

So he did not know that yesterday afternoon Aunt Annie, his brother-in-law's sister, had been killed by a Black mob on the Pretoria road?

To his wife and himself she was always Aunt Annie, though only a few years older than they were. A dour old lady, and she had given them, as a wedding present, a silver tea pot which they always used in the afternoons when he was at home.

He consoled his sobbing wife. He said he would not be able to come home before the small hours, persuaded her to go at once and spend the day with her brother, probably best to stay overnight too. He rang off.

Land mines, bombs, murders, riots, and the hacking and burning of Aunt Annie. And the statistics of revolt spiralling. As if a roof had sprung leaks, and as fast as a leak was blocked there were more water springs soaking through. It was the bastards like Thiroko who pick-axed the roof, made the leaks, slaughtered old Aunt Annie who came to tea on each of their wedding anniversaries, and who poured from the silver pot.

Thiroko lay on his back. His bed was loose straw, wrenched from a string tied bale. He was the only one awake. The boys were sleeping, snoring at the roof of the cow shed.

They had arrived in the dark, and stumbled from the road across rough ground to the cow shed. The place stank of the animals. The shed was used by the farmer for storage and for when he had a difficult calving and the cow needed attention. They had dug against the back wall of the shed to uncover the weapons cache. Each of the A.K. 47 assault rifles was well sealed in plastic bags, each was dry and oiled. They had taken five of the rifles stored in the shed. They had taken also 50 kilos of plastic explosive, and detonators and firing wire. What they had not needed they had buried again under the soil and manure.

When it was first light he had crawled to a place where the overlapping metal walls of the shed had been prised apart by the winter storms. The cow shed was on rising ground. He could see where the road ran close by, where they had been dropped after the drive down from Monte Christo, and he could see in the far distance the grain silos of Warmbaths.

He had tried to sleep. The pain ate inside him. It might have been the long flight from London, and then the flight from Lusaka to Gaberone that had welled the pain. It might have been the bone-shaking drive from Monte Christo. It might have been the twenty-four hours without food. It might have been fear. The pain was sharp in his stomach.

Travelling with the boys, he had learned much. Each of them had looked good enough in the training camps, and the instructors from the German Democratic Republic had said they were as good as any, and Thiroko had thought they were good until he had walked with them. Now he thought they were crap, because they had talked rubbish to him of a welcoming uprising. No inkling of the danger of coming as a stranger into their own land. They were going to have to shape up and learn fast and much between here and the gaol.

He lay on his back, in his pain, and he thought of the Englishman. An anxiety simmered in him, of business not yet talked through. Happy and Charlie and Percy and Tom were held in cells on the opposite side of Beverly Hills to Jeez Carew, and they would have to be reached before the assault on C section . . . He thought Jack Curwen would understand that four men must come before one.

Thiroko pushed himself awkwardly to his feet. The motion hurt him. He went out through the open door. He breathed in the cool clean air of his mother country. Down from this height was the sprawled town and beyond it the hazed flat veld. It was right that he should have come back, that before he died he should smell the air of his home.

He squatted beside a bush. His bowels were water, and he had no paper to wipe himself. When he stood and pulled up his trousers he saw that there was blood mucous in his mess.

He saw no movement except the birds skimming the long grass, he heard no sounds except their shrill calling.

The soldiers who watched the cow shed were the elite of the South African Defence Force. They were used to sterner tasks than this. In total and motionless silence they lay up in cover, at the nearest point a hundred metres from the rusted metal building, watching the four walls from behind machine guns and automatic rifles. They had seen Thiroko come out of the shed. It had been noted that he had no paper.

Six hundred metres away, where the road curved, hidden by a coppice of eucalyptus and scrub, was parked the car that had travelled after Thiroko from Ellisrus. The four men who sat in the car, or squatted outside it, wore civilian clothes, slacks and sweaters. Their hair was not cut short in the style of the military, two were bearded. They were unremarkable.

Crouched down in the coppice were the dog handler, his labrador, and the Bushman.

All watching until mid-afternoon to see if there would be a contact.

Ros drove away from the hotel. It was just past one o'clock, but they hadn't bothered to eat. They were not hungry, and Jan cracked a thin joke about Jack wanting to wait till he could have maize porridge with his friends.

Jack said that Brown's was like something from the cowboy pictures. The open veranda, the swing slat doors from the street into the bar, posters for Saturday night live music and dancing, the carving in the dining room that was an F.N. rifle in relief. Jack said that as long as he lived he'd remember the springs in his bed. Ros didn't speak. They went right down the main road, then turned off towards the mountains. Past the huge modern angles of the roof of the Dutch Reformed Church, up along the straight tarmac strips that bisected the bungalow land, past the White school where the small boys were having rugby coaching and the girls were playing hockey. Jack thought Warmbaths was an oasis. Abruptly they were out of the town's limits, lawns and residences giving way to grazing lands. There was another three kilometres to go before the pale dust road ahead began to climb for the foothills and then the mountains. The high ground was grey hazed, cool and with-out threat.

Jan spoke to Ros in Afrikaans. She nodded. Jack sensed they were close to the drop point.

Jan switched to English.

"We're hardly stopping for you. You can see the place from the road, that's what my message said. It's a place where they can keep cattle if the weather's bad. You'll have to carry it all yourself, your bag and the tube things."

"That's fine."

The sun was high. The light bathed them through the car windows. Ros wound her window down, Jack followed her. There was the rush of air on his face, her hair streamed across her cheeks and nose and mouth.

"There it is."

Jan was leaning forward between their shoulders. He pointed ahead, through the windscreen, under the central mirror. For a moment the sun had caught the roof of a building that was set back from the road. Beyond the place was a clump of tall trees. For only a moment the light hit at that particular angle and reflected from the tin roof.

"We'll put you down by those trees. Wait until we are gone ten minutes before you move."

"Goodbye, and again, thank you," Jack said softly.

"Good luck, Jack. I hope you pull it off," a fierceness from Jan.

"I'll put you down in those trees," Ros said.

Jack grinned. "Not a chance that we won't."

The last of the big boasts. They had lost sight of the shed. The big boasts were all right for his mother and fine for George Hawkins, great for Duggie, brilliant for these kids. Ros was braking. The big boasts would stop when he joined Thiroko's men. Jack thought they were familiar trees, peeled bark trunks, but he couldn't put a name to them.

There was a car parked off the road and in the shade of the trees.

Jack saw two in the front and two in the back of the saloon car.

"I can't put you down next to them," Ros said.

They were passing the car.

As a flash, Jack saw the front seat passenger hunched forward, something in his hand, and his hand close to his ear. As a flash, Jack heard the distorted snatch of a radio transmission. Just a flash . . .

He had heard a radio transmission.

He swung to Ros.

His voice was a whisper. "Just keep going."

She turned to him, mouth sagging open.

"No sudden movements. Don't slow, don't accelerate."

Her face was washed with questions.

"Just drive as if it's normal, like nothing's important to us here."

Jack could hear her breath spurting.

"Don't turn round, don't look back."

God, and he wanted to look back. He wanted to look back and into the parked green saloon car and see whether the attention of the men inside was on the Beetle that had sidled past.

"Just drive on, as if it's natural."

Past the trees, he saw a cattle track leading from an iron gate away across a crudely fenced field, uphill towards a cow shed. He could see no movement at the shed. Above the engine were the crisp calls of the birds. He felt Jan's fingers on his shoulder.

"Don't stop, drive on," Jack snapped at Ros.

Christ, the girl was good, didn't argue, didn't talk back.

"Keep driving," a rasp in Jack's voice.

They went on up the slow incline. Jack pulled the map from the glove compartment. He unfolded it over his knees. His finger was searching for Warmbaths.

The girl was great, the girl was driving with her eyes on the road like it was a Sunday outing.

"When we went past the parked car, as we passed it, did you hear anything?"

"I hardly saw the car."

"It was taking a radio message."

"So what?" Jan spoke before he had thought.

"There's not going to be a taxi out here. It was taking a radio message which means it's a police car. Cop on, kid."

"Christ."

"Which means that the drop is under observation."

"Shit . . ."

Ros was expressionless. Jan sagged back into his narrow space alongside the metal tubes. Jack went back to the map. He was a long time poring over it. He traced a route on to Mabula, and then a secondary road to Rooiberg, and then on until the turn off to Rankin's Pass through the mountains, and a crossing of the Mogol river and back to Nylstroom that was twenty miles north of Warmbaths. Without measuring the distance with his finger, he thought that the whole journey was more than a hundred and fifty kilometres, and that was the most direct route to Warmbaths without going again down the road past the cow shed and past the parked green saloon car.

"If they're there, in the shed, and the police move in on them, what would they do with them?" Jack asked.

A dulled response from Jan. "They'd take them to the police station at Warmbaths. From there they'd probably helicopter them out to Pretoria or Johannesburg."

"I have to know, what happens to them."

Jan flared. "It wasn't us that was followed."

"Pretty bloody irrelevant right now."

"I have to see what happens."

He gave Ros the route that he wanted her to take. She nodded, she was impassive.

"Is that all right?" Jack asked.

"I'm just your chauffeur," Ros said.

"You know what's there, Carew, and you know it's something that I never thought you'd let me see, too right."

"What's there, Sergeant Oosthuizen?"

"Can't you see what's there for yourself, Carew?"

Sergeant Oosthuizen liked a little game. He liked a child's riddle. Mostly Jeez humoured him. Most times in the last thirteen months Jeez had played along with him. Buggered if he wanted a joke that afternoon.

"I can't see that anything's there, Sergeant."

Jeez was pacing the concrete of the exercise yard. Sometimes the yard seemed large enough for him to stroll in. That afternoon he was constricted within the walls, caged by the roof grill shadows on the ground. Oosthuizen stood beside the locked door that led into the corridor and Jeez's cell. His arms were folded. The great jowls of his chin were spread with his smile.

"Now, come on, Carew. You're not trying for me."

Jeez thought Oosthuizen so thick-skinned, and yet so innately kind, that he could rarely be sharp with the man. Truthfully, Jeez thought it would be cheap to squash Oosthuizen. Nothing to do with the disciplinary measures that queued up behind Oosthuizen, not many privileges they could take away from a man when they were scheduled to take away his life within a week. He would hate himself if he put down Sergeant Oosthuizen. But buggered if that day he wanted to play a game, and buggered if he knew how to tell the old fool to shut his mouth.

Perhaps Oosthuizen knew of Jeez's wish for quiet. Perhaps he was determined to deny it.

"You've got to try for me, Carew, like a good man."

Jeez surrendered, as he usually did. "Where am I supposed to be looking, Sergeant?"

"I'm giving you a good hint, you're supposed to be looking at the flower bed, Carew."

Jeez stared down at the flower bed. Most of the geranium blooms were over, should have been pinched off. The lobelia was straggling, should have been pulled.

"I'm looking at the flower bed, Sergeant."

"And there's something in the flower bed that I never thought you'd let me see."

"I don't know what it is, Sergeant."

"You're not trying for me, Carew."

"Please, Sergeant, what is it that's in the flower bed?"

Oosthuizen tugged at his moustache. He stood at his full height and dragged in his belly so that his belt buckle sagged. He was hugely satisfied.

"There's a *weed*."

"A fucking *what?*"

"Watch your language, Carew . . . You've allowed a dandelion to grow in your flower bed."

Jeez saw the dandelion. It had no flower. It was half concealed by a geranium plant.

"Yes, you can see it now, but you hadn't noticed it before. I'd never have thought you would let me find a weed in your garden, Carew."

Jeez wondered what would happen if he smashed Oosthuizen with his fist. He thought the man might burst.

Jeez knelt on the concrete.

The concrete was not warmed by the sun, the grilled shadows kept the heat off the concrete. He hadn't noticed the weed because he hadn't watered his garden for two days. He could see that the geranium leaves were dropping and that the lobelia was parched. He pushed his fingers into the earth, he tugged at the dandelion root. He felt the root snap under the earth. The weed would grow again. He smoothed the earth over. The weed would grow again, but not surface before the following Thursday morning. He carried the dandelion to the plastic bag in the corner of the yard, where the dirt sweepings were left for a trustie to take away.

"Doesn't do to let it get the better of you, Carew," Oosthuizen said quietly.

"No, Sergeant."

"Believe me, man, you have to keep your standards up from the first day you come here, right up to the last day."

"Thank you, Sergeant."

"That's solid advice. You have to find something to think about. Whatever's

170

going to happen to you, you have to keep going, keep those standards . . .
Have you got no visits coming?"

"No."

"All those other fellows you were with, they've all got their families coming."

"No one's coming."

"I never saw a man who was so really alone, Carew."

"No one."

Oosthuizen looked once, almost furtively, over his shoulder and up to the empty catwalk window. He dropped his voice. "I'm only supposed to make little talk with you. I'm out of order, but there's something I should like you to know, Carew. I'm retiring next week. Wednesday's my birthday. I should have retired on the coming Tuesday evening. They have a party all lined for me."

"Will they give you a gold watch?"

"I don't think so, I think it'll be a decanter and some crystal glasses . . . But I've said to the governor that I don't want the party on Tuesday, nor on Wednesday. Our governor's a real gentleman, he said that I could have the party on Thursday. You understand me, Carew?"

"You're going to be here on Thursday morning. Thank you, Sergeant."

Jeez looked up. He followed the flight of a grey wagtail to the catwalk window.

Oosthuizen said simply, "It's because you don't have any visits, Carew."

He saw the wagtail start away from the narrow ledge below the window.

There was a face at the window, a pale face against the darkness behind. He saw the collar of a suit jacket and the brilliance of a white shirt. He knew who he had seen. He knew who would wish to look over him while he was at exercise.

Their nerves were raw because the rendezvous had not been kept.

It was two hours past the time of the rendezvous.

Thiroko had started to ponder what he should do if Jack Curwen had not arrived within an hour, when the next transport was due to pick them up. He could think of many reasons why Jack should be delayed, but as the minutes slipped to hours each reason had grown less credible. He knew the boys were on edge, strained, because they talked more, because it was harder for him each time to quiet them.

"JACOB THIROKO, YOU ARE SURROUNDED BY UNITS OF THE SOUTH AFRICAN DEFENCE FORCE . . ."

It came as an amplified bellow. The noise of the magnified voice swept through the half opened door of the shed and coursed round the four walls. They were all frozen. They were all rigid. They were held in their postures of sitting, lying, squatting, crouching, standing.

"YOU SHOULD SURRENDER IMMEDIATELY. YOU SHOULD

THROW YOUR WEAPONS OUT THROUGH THE DOOR, THEN YOU SHOULD COME OUT WITH YOUR HANDS ON YOUR HEADS."

Movements now. Each man's hand moving stutteringly towards the stock of his Kalashnikov. Frightened little movements, as if the voice that overwhelmed them had an eye to see them.

". . . YOU HAVE ONE MINUTE TO COME OUT. IF YOU COME OUT WITHIN THE ONE MINUTE THEN YOU WILL NOT BE HARMED IN ANY WAY . . ."

The four boys looking at him, broken hope in their faces. He saw the accusation of betrayal. He could have cried. They all looked to him. He was their commander. He had told them of a great strike against the Boer regime, and they were in a cow shed and amongst cow dirt and they were surrounded by their enemy.

". . . WE ARE STARTING THE ONE MINUTE, FROM NOW . . ."

Thiroko crawled to the doorway. He hugged the shadow. He looked out. He could hear the drone of insects and the cry of birds and the whispering of the afternoon wind in the dry loose grass. He could not see his enemy.

"Are we the heroes of our revolution, or are we the frightened children that the Boers think us?"

None of the boys had voices in their throats. They nodded dumbly to Thiroko.

"Their promise of no harm is twenty years in their gaols."

One boy cocked his rifle. The chain was started. The rattling of the weapons being armed rung inside the shed.

"I have to win time, time for a young friend who is braver than I."

He saw the chins jut, and the eyes blaze, and the hands were steady on the rifles. He saw the trembling pass.

". . . THIRTY SECONDS. YOU THROW YOUR WEAPONS OUT. YOU COME OUT WITH YOUR HANDS ON YOUR HEADS. YOU HAVE A GUARANTEE OF SAFETY . . ."

They shouted together, the four boy's and Jacob Thiroko. The word in their shout was *Amandla*, the word ballooned inside the tin walls.

He waved them to the sides of the shed, each to a firing position. He stripped from his rucksack a khaki pouch. He tore a wad of papers from the pouch and ripped at them and made a cairn of them. He lit the heap of papers. His boys began to shoot. The smoke eddied through the shed, and with the smell of the burning paper was the stench of the cordite. Incoming fire, punching, ricocheting, into the shed. He lay on the straw and the manure and he drew the air down into his lungs and breathed so that he could fan the small flames licking into the papers. He saw his notes curling. He saw names blackening, the coded plans flaking.

So little time, and the boy against the back wall was whimpering, hit in the buttocks and the stomach. He blew again on the papers and prayed in anger for the fire to be fiercer. The boy close to the front door was coughing mouthfuls of blood onto his chest. He shouted for the two boys at the side walls to keep firing. No reply. He could see the clumsy postures in which they had died. The boy at the back wall no longer whimpered. The boy at the door toppled suddenly out of the door frame into the sunlight, and was hit and hit before he fell into the dry hard dirt.

Jacob Thiroko summoned a prayer for the comrades around him and reached for his rifle.

They stood in the crowd outside the police station in Warmbaths.

The men of the Recce Commando had come and gone. They had come by police truck, and then run to a helicopter with their arms held over their faces to save their features from snapping cameras. The crowd could hardly have seen them but had cheered their every stride. It was an all White crowd outside the single storey brick police station, a crowd grimly satisfied.

Ros never showed her emotions. Jack didn't know what she felt.

They stood and they watched as the bodies were lifted from a van and laid out in the forecourt, between two low sand-bagged emplacements, for the police photographer.

There were four young Blacks. They were laid on the dirt, their clothing and the bodies torn, shredded. Last to come was the corpse of Jacob Thiroko. His face was intact, recognisable to Jack. He blinked, felt a sickness in his gut. The back of Thiroko's head was gone, a mushy wet crater. He thought Thiroko must have put the barrel of his weapon into his mouth. His talk had brought Thiroko back to South Africa, and killed him. They dropped the body, like it was a meat carcase.

Jan was cold faced. Jack short punched him in the kidneys. Jan had tried to look as though he enjoyed what he saw, and made a piss poor job of it.

The green saloon car drove to the police station steps. Jack half remembered the front passenger of the car, who had worn a red shirt when he was parked off the road against the trees. A man in a red shirt carried from the car five A.K. 47 rifles, each sealed in a separate cellophane bag.

He watched a detective wash his stained hands in a fire bucket. He saw the driver of the green saloon car walk to the doorway, tight in his fist was a clear plastic sack. Jack saw that it was filled with charred paper. He felt the weakness sinking through his knees, into his legs.

The light was going over Johannesburg.

The colonel hadn't lowered his blinds, hadn't switched on his strip light. He had sat unmoving, nursing his frustration, since the news had been relayed to him from Warmbaths.

His aides had abandoned him. Now, in the outer office, they warned the detective of his mood. The detective had shrugged, knocked and gone in.

"I thought you should know, sir, of the developments in connection with the bomb investigation. A youngish man, English accent, purchased a similar bag and a similar can of petrol in the city centre on the day of the bomb. The description given by the two sales points is pretty much the same. We're working on a photo–fit likeness, sir. I'll have a copy of the full statements for you first thing."

15

Ros took charge.

Someone had to. Her brother couldn't speak, was utterly drained. Jack was black in his mood, brooding. While her brother and Jack floundered, Ros assumed the decision taking. Into the car. Away down the long road and back towards Pretoria and Johannesburg. She wondered whether they were already compromised, all three of them. She anticipated that the security police would be waiting for the van Niekerk kids when they reached their home city, the Beetle having been traced. She didn't air her fears.

She asked clipped questions of Jack. She ignored her brother.

"Do you want to fly out tonight?"

"No."

"There's a British Airways every night after the S.A.A. flight, there's Lufthansa and Alitalia. What's the point in staying?"

"I'm not flying."

"You don't have a group, you're one person. Do you have any other contacts to get help?"

"I don't."

"It's idiocy to think of anything but getting yourself out. Don't you see that?"

"I've no choice."

"Then you've got a death wish."

He told her about Sandham. He told her about Duggie. "I've debts that have to be paid off. They helped me and they were both killed. They were murdered because I involved them. Do you think, because it's getting hot, I can just pack up and go home? 'Sorry you got chopped, chaps, but it's getting too difficult for me, I'm not going to risk *my* skin . . .' Ros, it can't be done."

"Suicide."

"I'll tell you about suicide. The old one amongst the bodies was called Jacob Thiroko. I don't know what was in his mind about coming here, but he hadn't been in South Africa for more than twenty years. And inside his own country the last thing he did was to blow his own brains away. That was suicide. That was so he couldn't be made to talk. And before he blew his mind out he burned his papers. He stayed alive long enough to burn his papers and then he killed himself. He can't tell them my name, or any name, or what was the target. That's a hell of a debt to be paid off. I can't walk away, not from them, and not from my father."

"On your own you won't even get to see the gaol."

"Then in Beverly Hills they'll all hear the gunfire. The plans told me that they'll hear it. They have high windows into the catwalks, and up in the catwalk space there are more windows that look down into the cells. Those windows are always open. My father will hear the gunfire. Everyone in that bastard place will know that someone came, someone tried."

She couldn't look at him. She didn't dare to see his face.

"It's madness."

"If I walked away I'd have to live with next Thursday morning. I could be back in London. I could be sitting and filling my gut with booze, and I could take all the tablets that get you to sleep. Wouldn't matter. I'd be in that cell, wondering whether he was scared, what he was thinking. I'd hear them come for him. I'd see them walk him along the corridors. What do you want me to bloody well do, Ros, go to sleep, set the alarm for five in the morning, wake up to know that my father's being pitched off a trap? What do I do then? Turn over and go back to sleep?"

Jan had leaned forward. Pushing his head between the high seat backs.

"It's to break out one person?"

Jack said, "Yes."

"It is to save *one* of them?"

"Yes."

"There are five that are going to hang."

"The one is my father."

"And you don't give a shit for the other four?"

Jack dropped his head. "Jan, believe me, I'm not interested in five, I'm going to break out one."

"He's like every other White," Jan shouted. "He's a racist."

Ros snapped, "Grow up, for Christ's sake, he doesn't give a fuck for your grubby little Movement."

"To leave four Blacks to hang, and to try to save one White, that's racism."

"They're killers, those four murdering swine."

"You're a racist, too, Ros."

They were both yelling. Jack's hands went up, palms open, on either side of his head.

"I'm not proud of what I've decided but it's my decision, alone."

"It's all horseshit about you being alone," Jan said.

"If you were alone you wouldn't be in my bloody car," Ros said.

Jack leaned across and kissed her on the cheek, and she didn't pull away. He took Jan's hand and shook it fervently.

Christ, what a bloody awful army.

Ros said she was going to Hillbrow. She said there was a studio flat there that belonged to a friend from school. Her friend always gave her the keys when she took her small son back to Durban and her parents. Ros said that there wasn't a husband, nor a live-in man. Ros said that her friend liked to know that someone came to keep an eye on the flat when she was away. Ros said that Hillbrow was the home of the drifters in Johannesburg, where Blacks and Asians and Coloureds and Whites lived alongside each other in tower blocks without being constantly harrassed by the police for violating the residential codes. Ros said he wouldn't be noticed in Hillbrow.

It was dark when they reached Johannesburg.

And he needed to think, because the days were slipping away, Thursday was rushing to him.

The studio flat, fifth floor, was an untidy mess.

They'd come in the back way. The car parked at the rear, so that they could all climb the five flights of the concrete steps of the fire escape. Heavy going for Jan, and Ros and Jack had their hands full. Ros had the key, took a bit of finding in her handbag.

Just one dismal room for living. All there. Bed, cooker, shelves, cupboards, prints on the wall of views of the English Lakes.

He went to the one window. He reckoned he was less than a mile from the Landdrost, but this was a different world. A crowded pavement below him. He could see Blacks and Whites strolling, and there was a café opposite with chairs and tables in the open where he could see the colour mix. Music from radio stations and records merged, deafening, from the street, from alongside, from above. A prefabricated block, and he thought he heard the bed springs going upstairs and he didn't like to look at Ros. A fight below, same side of the street as the block, and he had to crane to see two guys, White, kicking hell out of a third guy, White, and a girl watching, Black or Coloured or some mix. People walking round them, letting them get on with it.

Jan told him that they had to go home, Ros nodding. Jack understood the risks they took. He had the airport, they had nowhere to run for. Ros had her mouth clenched as Jan said that he would ring at eight and at ten and at midnight. Jack should let the phone ring, but not pick it up. If there were a trace on their home telephone then it would only operate when the phone was lifted at the receiver's end. The ringing phone would tell Jack that all was well with Jan and Ros . . . Jack didn't ask what he should do if the phone didn't ring. It was for Jack Curwen to make decisions, not to ask what he should do. His responsibility, all on his shoulders. Jan said he would come back to the flat in the morning. Ros didn't say when she might see him again. He thought he was alone because he could not imagine how a crippled student and an insurance office desk worker could help him work the break out from the maximum security cells of Beverly Hills. Hard put to see how he could help himself.

He hadn't eaten since breakfast.

He looked in the fridge. There was yoghurt, and some cream cheese, and the remains of a bowl of salad, and some salami slices. He reckoned the girl who lived in the studio flat must be a virtual skeleton. He cleaned out the fridge. He quartered the large room. It was a compulsion, to see how the single parent lived, what she read, what she wore. He couldn't have answered for this violation of her privacy other than by saying it was a symptom of his aloneness.

He found the building bricks.

They were the same as he had had when he was a kid. They were the same as Will had back at Churchill Close. Lego bricks, product of Denmark, there was a bread bin of them.

Jack sat on the floor and laid out his plans of Beverly Hills, and built the gaol in plastic bricks of blue and red and yellow and white. He built technicolor perimeter walls.

He made C section from red bricks, and administration in yellow, and A and B sections in white. He made the exercise yard of C section 2 in blue. He made a watchtower behind the gallows block, and he built towers where the flood light stanchions were set.

He was a child at play.

There were no roofs for his buildings. He could look down into each cubicle he made, into the cells, into the corridors, into the exercise yards. He put a door between C section's corridor and C section 2's corridor. He put a door on a cell. He could count the number of the doors, he could count the number of the walls.

With the bricks that remained he located Pretoria Local and Pretoria Central and the White Politicals and the Women's. He scattered the prison staff homes, and the self service store, and the recreation and swimming areas, all on the north slope below Beverly Hills. Level with the gaol, on the west side, he put the Commissioner of Prison's residence. He laid out a sheet of paper for the rifle range on the east side. He made a broken line with the last of the bricks to make the outer ring of wire fences on Magazine Hill to the south.

He sat cross-legged, his back against the bed, and gazed down at the gaol. A long time he sat, unmoving, searching for the plan, worrying for the route. He sat in the half light, only the light beside the bed on. Searching and worrying.

Jack stood. He went to the kitchenette area of the room and rifled the drawers and cupboards until he found a set of cooking scales. From his suitcase he lifted out the package of explosives. He didn't think the wrapping would weigh much, not enough to confuse his calculations. He weighed the explosives.

He had fifteen pounds and four ounces of plaster gelignite.

He replaced the gelignite in the suitcase, laid it beside the wrapped detonators and the firing wire.

There was a telephone beside the bed.

It was an impulse, born of aloneness. It was eight minutes to three in the morning, Sunday morning.

Below the flat, Hillbrow slept. The streets had at last quietened.

He wondered if his father slept.

Jack knew that if he did not make the call then he might just as well take a taxi to the airport in a dozen hours' time and book a flight and fly out.

178

He found a book with the code and dialled. He had made up his mind.

The ringing of the telephone scattered the cats.

The bell drove them from the newspaper covering the kitchen table, and from the cushioned chair beside the stove, sent them scurrying to the dark corners.

George Hawkins blundered into the kitchen, groping for the light switch, reaching for the telephone. He heard the distant voice. No rambling small talk, no crap about the weather, nor about the time in the morning.

The wall was twenty feet high, it was eighteen inches thick. What was the minimum explosive required with a conical shaped charge of nine inches in diameter to knock a man-sized hole at ground level?

"Bugger . . ."

George needed paper and pencil. Couldn't find them. Didn't know where he'd last put them. Had to do the calculation in his head. And he was half asleep.

"Shit . . ."

And the boy was talking about minimums. If he was on about minimums, then the boy was in trouble, deep bloody trouble.

"Twelve pounds is absolute bloody minimum. Problem with the minimum is that the concrete on the far side of the reinforcing mesh may not be broken clear. Ideal would be fifteen to eighteen."

The minimum?

"That's twelve pounds."

How could the reverse end of the firing tube be blocked?

"Concrete mix."

Could the conical shaping be lightweight, aluminium?

"Not important that it's heavy. It's good if it's lightweight."

How much stand off should there be from the firing end of the metal tubing to the wall?

"For a man-sized hole you should have six to nine inches . . . Twelve pounds of explosive, that's the absolute bloody bottom line . . ."

The telephone purred in his ear.

For a full minute George Hawkins held the receiver against his face, shivered in his pyjamas. He put the telephone down and went and sat in his chair and he called for the cats and rubbed the warmth into his bare skinny feet. George Hawkins shook his head, slowly, sadly. He had been asked for the minimum. He had answered the question. Twelve pounds was the bloody border line. The boy was in trouble.

He sat for an hour with his cats on his lap before he eased them off and went back to his cold bed.

As the city slept late on Sunday the colonel worked at his desk.

He had excused himself from taking tea with Aunt Annie's relations after church. He had told his wife to offer his apologies to the minister.

He read the reports that had come in late the previous evening. He couldn't have waited for them the previous evening, because the loss of Thiroko had been too great a blow. It should never have been left in the hands of Recce Commando, that he was certain of. He had been sure of it all through the late hours at home as he had listened to his wife, sniffling and talking of Aunt Annie.

Another day, another opportunity.

He gutted the reports.

A White male. Age between middle twenties and thirty years. Grey trousers and a green sports shirt and a mauve sweater. Common to both sales.

An English accent.

The reports were specific. Not an English accent that was South African. Not the accent of a long term English immigrant . . . and they were pigs who should never have been let into the country, hanging on to their British passports, shovelling money out of the country, sending their kids away to avoid army service, sneering at the Afrikaners who had made the country . . . The accent of an *English* Englishman.

The purchases had been made within one hour of each other on the day the bomb exploded.

Under the reports he had two photo-fit portraits. They had been built as mosaics from the descriptions of the two shopkeepers. The hair style, the deep set eyes, the strong nose, the jutting chin.

It was the colonel's belief that he stared at the two faces of one man. They were the faces of the man who had destroyed the back hallway of John Vorster Square. And his mind could wander. If he had been consulted he would have argued strongly against the use of Recce Commando in the tracking and failed capture of Jacob Thiroko. He had not been consulted and as a result he had been denied the chance of extracting information from one of the best sources he'd ever been close to. He had scarcely slept for rage.

He went down the stairs to the incident room. He let it be known, that in his opinion, from the weight of his experience, the bomb was not the work of Umkonto we Sizwe.

"I believe it was thrown by an individual who arrived recently from England, otherwise more care would have been taken in the purchase of the materials. It should be assumed that he came to South Africa very shortly before the attack. The airports should be checked. You should look for a flight from Europe because the shop men have given him a pale complexion, he hasn't been in the sun. You should also check every one of the city's hotels. That is my suggestion."

He knew his suggestion would be taken as an order.

"You slept on it?" Jan asked.

"My decision, yes."

"No flight?"

"No," Jack said.

A pointless question. Jan could see beside the unmade bed the toy building that was Pretoria Central.

"I don't want to . . ."

Jack cut in. "You don't want to get shot."

"I don't want to start something that is impossible."

"It's an over-used word."

"You don't have explosives and you don't have weapons."

Jack waved him quiet. He told Jan about the fifteen pounds of gelignite, saved from the John Vorster Square bomb. He told him about the detonators and the firing fuse. He saw the surprise growing on the boy's face.

"Didn't you trust us?"

"Nor myself."

"Each one of us, the activists of Umkonto we Sizwe, each of us has an implicit trust in our Movement."

"It was sensible to be careful, it's nothing to do with trust. Jan, I have to have more explosives or grenades, and I have to have firearms. I have to have them."

"I'm just a courier," the boy said, and the nerves showed.

"I have to have them, Jan."

"By when?"

"Tonight."

"That's impossible."

"Over-used word, Jan."

Jack started to make the bed. Jan paced the floor, there was the rhythm of the shuffle and the thud of his feet. Jack smoothed down the coverlet. He thought he would never understand this boy. He could understand a man such as Thiroko, and the young men who had died with Thiroko. Blacks fighting for what Blacks thought was theirs. Couldn't place this crippled boy in the game, a White fighting for what Blacks thought was theirs. He thought it was all to do with the foot. He thought the misshapen foot had alienated the boy from the White society around him. He thought the boy must find a satisfaction from his hidden betrayal of his own people.

The boy stopped, turned. He faced Jack squarely.

"I'll be back in an hour for you."

After Jan had gone, Jack sat again on the floor beside the model. He was drawn to an approach to Beverly Hills from the south side, over Magazine Hill. He knew why that approach appealed to him. Defence H.Q. was to the north. The east approach was through Pretoria Local and Pretoria Central. From the west he would have to cross beside the police dog training school, and the secure mental hospital. He did not know what was on Magazine Hill, and ignorance was a comfort, his only ally.

"You're not usually here on a Sunday morning, Sergeant."

"Overtime, Carew. I get time and a half on a Sunday morning. I need the money, what with retirement coming. You can always get overtime on a Sunday. The young fellows don't want it. They want to be with their families, get outside the city, get away from here."

Jeez had eaten his breakfast. His breakfast on a Sunday morning was the same as on any other morning. Jeez had eaten porridge made from maize, with milk. And two slices of brown bread, with thinly smeared margarine and jam. The same as on every morning that he had been in Beverly Hills. He had three more breakfasts to eat. He would be gone before breakfast was served on Thursday. He had drunk his mug of coffee. He knew that he would get one meal that was different to all the other meals inside Beverly Hills. On Wednesday afternoon he would have a whole chicken for his dinner, cooked by the chef in the staff canteen. For the last meals there was always a whole chicken for the condemns who were White. He couldn't remember where he had heard that, whether it had been from way back when he was on remand, or whether he had read it in the newspapers before his arrest. It was a part of the lore of the condemns that they were given a whole chicken the dinner before they were hanged, just as it was part of the lore that the Blacks only had half a chicken. Jeez couldn't believe that, that the pigmentation of the skin made the difference between two legs and two wings and two breasts, and one leg and one wing and one chicken breast. And he wouldn't get to know, because he was buggered if he was going to beg an answer from Sergeant Oosthuizen.

Jeez wasn't sharp that Sunday morning.

So dull that he didn't even question Oosthuizen's claim that he was only at work to get time and a half for his nest egg. There was a weakness in Jeez's legs and in his belly. It was with him more frequently, as if he had a cold coming on, and the microbe was fear. Couldn't rid himself of the fear, not when he was locked in his cell, not when he was alone, particularly not when the high ceiling light about the wire grille was dimmed, when he was alone with his thoughts of Thursday morning and the rambling night sounds of the gaol.

The sounds carried into the upper areas of the cells and through the open windows to the catwalks, and from the catwalks they eddied to the next window and floated down from there to the next cell, and the cell beyond that.

The young White, the one who hadn't been there for more than a few weeks, always cried on a Sunday morning, in the small hours. Oosthuizen had told Jeez that he had been an altar boy, was a Roman Catholic, and cried because when he had been a teenager he was out of bed early on a Sunday morning and away to his local church for first Mass. Oosthuizen had confided that the young White was getting to be a pain with his crying. The old White, charged with killing his wife for the insurance, he coughed and spat each morning to clear the nicotine mucus from his throat. Oosthuizen said that the old White smoked sixty cigarettes a day. Oosthuizen had once said, in his innocence, that the old White would kill himself by so much smoking.

There was the crying and the coughing and the slither tread of the guard on the catwalk, and there was the sound of a lavatory flushing. There was laughter from out in the corridor, where the prison officers played cards to pass away the day.

Faintly he heard the singing.

Just a murmur at first.

The edges and clarity were knocked off the singing by the many windows and the yards of the catwalk that it passed through. The singing was from right across the far side of Beverly Hills, from A section or B section. Jeez saw Oosthuizen fidget.

"Who's it for?"

"I'm not allowed to tell you that."

"Sergeant . . ." Jeez held Oosthuizen with his eyes.

Oosthuizen pulled at his moustache, then shrugged, and dropped his voice. "For the boy who's going on Tuesday."

"Who is he, Sergeant?"

"Just a Coloured."

The whole place was mad. There was a worry that a man smoked too much and might harm his health before it was time for him to have his neck stretched, which might just do his health a bit more harm. There was worry that a prison officer who was retiring on Thursday might get into trouble for a quiet conversation on his last Sunday morning.

"What's he like, the fellow who does it?"

"You trying to get me on a charge sheet, Carew?"

"What's he like?"

The voice was a whisper. "He's damned good . . . Doesn't help you to think about it, forget what I told you . . . He's as good as anywhere in the whole world. He's fast and he's kind, a real professional."

He won't hurt you, Jeez. So get a grip on it, Jeez, because old Sergeant Oosthuizen says the executioner's a hell of a good operator. Great news, Jeez . . .

"I'll walk with you on Thursday morning, Carew. I'll hold your arm."

Jeez nodded. He couldn't speak. He didn't think Oosthuizen had attended a hanging in years. He thought that Oosthuizen had made him a bloody great gesture of love.

"I'm going to do the rosters so's I get Monday in here for the day shift, and then I'll have Tuesday off, and then I'll come on again for Tuesday night, and then I'll have Wednesday off and I'll be back on again for Wednesday night, and I'll stay on through . . ."

"Why, Sergeant?"

The words came in a flood flow. "Because you aren't the same as the others. Because you're here by some sort of accident, I don't know what the accident is. Because you're covering for something, I don't know what it is. Because you shouldn't be here. Because you're not a terrorist, whatever you've done. Because you had the way to save yourself, I don't know why you didn't take it . . . It's not my place to say that, but it's what I think."

Jeez smiled. "Not your place, Sergeant."

He watched the cell door close on Oosthuizen.

A hell of a week to look forward to. Clean clothes on Monday, and fresh sheets. Library on Wednesday. Early call on Thursday.

Jan had been home, spoken to her, and gone.

Ros waited for her father to leave for his Sunday morning round of golf.

He played every Sunday morning, then came home for his cold lunch. In the afternoon he would do the household bills and write letters. Her father didn't take a drink on Sundays, not even at the golf club. She waited for her father to leave the house, then went to their bedroom.

Her father always brought her mother breakfast before he left to play golf. The maid had all of Sunday off. The family fended for itself without her for one day a week. Every Saturday night and every Sunday night the maid took the long train journey to and from Mabopane in Bophutatswana where her husband was out of work and where her mother looked after her five children. The maid was her family's breadwinner. And when she was away the van Niekerks let the dust accumulate and filled the sink with dishes and were content in the knowledge that it would all be taken care of on the Monday morning.

Ros told her mother a little of the truth, a fraction.

Ros said that she and her brother had met a pleasant young Englishman. She said that she was sorry that she had stayed out for a whole night the previous week, and offered no explanation. She said that she was owed time from work, and she was going away with the Englishman and her brother for Monday and Monday night and all of Tuesday. She'd laughed, and said she'd be chaperoned by Jan.

When she was her daughter's age, her mother had used to drive with her father through the night to Cape Town, for the weekend, more than 1400 kilometres each way, and sleep together in a fleapit, before they were even engaged.

She wondered why her daughter bothered to tell her what she was doing, and couldn't for the life of her fathom why the girl was taking that awkward, intense brother with her.

She thought it would do her daughter the world of good to be bedded by a strong young man. Half the daughters of her friends were married at Ros's age, and some of them already divorced. She thought there was something peculiar about her own girl's plain dressing and shunning of make up.

She slipped out of bed. She slung a cotton dressing gown across her shoulders.

She took Ros to her dressing table and sat her on the stool. She did what she had not been allowed to do for ten years. She took the girl in charge. She changed Ros's hair, lifted it, swept it back and gathered it into a red ribbon. She put on for Ros her own eye make-up and cheek highlight and a gentle pink lipstick. She didn't dare to stop. She could hardly believe she was permitted to make the transformation. She let Ros gaze at herself in the mirror above the dressing table.

She said, "This young man, he's an immigrant?"

"Just a visitor. He's hoping to go back to England on Wednesday or Thursday."

Ros saw the flush of her mother's disappointment.

Later, when her mother had gone back to bed, Ros went to her father's desk and took from the bottom drawer the key to the gun cabinet that was bolted to the wall of the spare bedroom. Gingerly she took out a pump action shot gun, a box of cartridges, and her father's two revolvers along with a second box of .38 ammunition. She returned the key before hiding the weapons and ammunition in her bed.

The road was straight and the ground on either side of it was barren waste.

Jan talked, too bloody much. He turned his head and shouted through the visor of his crash helmet, and Jack had to lean towards him to hear anything through the thickness of his own helmet. For Jack it was little short of a miracle that the Suzuki moped was able to carry the two of them. He felt a complete, conspicuous idiot perched on the pillion, squashed into Jan's spare helmet, towering above the kid as they dribbled along at thirty five miles an hour.

They were heading for Duduza, some fifty kilometres southeast of Johannesburg.

Staccato bursts of explanation from Jan.

Past mine workings, through small industrial towns, past a row of empty bungalows deserted because the White staff had left when the mine was exhausted and the homes had been left to the weather and to disintegrate alongside a shanty town for Blacks.

They were on a straight stretch. High grass beside the road. Jan leaned back to shout.

"A White woman was driving past here, couple of years back, before the state of emergency, she was pulled out of her car, killed. It was kids from Duduza did it. Just about here . . . ?"

Jack remembered what he had seen on the Pretoria road. The picture was clear in his mind.

"At that time the Whites had killed hundreds of Blacks, and Blacks had killed two Whites, but the fascist law and order lobby went to work. It was vicious what the army and police did in Duduza. Most of the mothers tried to get their boys out, in girl's clothes, get them away and over the border. Just like the class of '76 in Soweto, there is a class of '85 out of Duduza. Those kids, now, they're in A.N.C. schools in Zambia or Tanzania. They'll come back when they're trained. There's no escape for the Boers."

"I don't want a bloody debate," Jack yelled.

"You'll be in a debate when we get to Duduza."

"Then it'll keep until we get there."

Why should anyone help Jack Curwen? Why should anyone in Duduza lift a finger for Jack Curwen? He didn't give a damn for any of their slogans. His only commitment was to his father.

"You know that racism is endemic among Whites?"

"Not my business, Jan."

Warm air blowing past Jan's helmet, dust skimming from the tinted screen of Jack's visor.

"Take the courts. Take the difference between what they do for A.N.C. fighters, and what they do for the right wing scum of the Kappiecommando or the Afrikaner Weerstand Beweging, that's A.W.B., pigs. Are you listening, Jack?"

"Jan, shut up, for Christ's sake."

Jack heard Jan laugh out loud, like he was high.

"Jack, listen . . . If a Black throws a petrol bomb it's terrorism, if it's the White backlash then it's arson. A Black explosion is treason, a White explosion is a damage to property charge. A Black arms cache is plotting to overthrow the state, but if he's White he's done for possession of unlicensed weapons . . . Isn't that racism?"

"I'm not listening to you, Jan."

"You better make the right noises when we get to Duduza, if you don't want a necklace."

Jack wondered what the hell the kid was shouting of. He didn't ask. Right now he thought the kid was a pain. He thought that if he hadn't needed the kid he would happily have jumped, walked away from him . . . But he *had* involved Jan van Niekerk, and he *had* involved Ros van Niekerk. He was leading the crippled boy and the office worker girl towards the walls and the guns of Pretoria Central.

"I'm sorry, Jan. You have to forgive me."

Jan turned his head. Jack saw the wide grin behind the visor screen, and the moped swerved and they nearly went off the road.

"Nothing to forgive. You're giving me the best damned time of my life. You're kicking the Boers in their nuts, and that's nothing to forgive . . ."

The shouting died.

Over Jan's shoulder Jack saw the dark line of the edge of the township. Red and black brick walls behind a fence of rusting cattle wire. Low smudges of dull colour, nothing for the sun to brighten.

Jan had told Jack, before they had started out, that Duduza was the only place where they had the smallest chance of raising his munitions. He was too junior in the Movement to be able to contact senior men at short notice. Part of the protective cover screen, in place to maintain the command chain's security, meant that a junior, a Jan van Niekerk, only responded to anonymous orders in his dead letter drop. Jan had said there was a Black he had once met, at a meeting in Kwa Thema township, a lively happy faced young man with a soft chocolate au lait complexion who had said his name and said where he lived, and been too relaxed and too confident to stay with the ritual of numbered code indentifications. Jan had said that the young Black's name was Henry Kenge.

They saw the block on the road into the township.

Four hundred metres ahead of them. Two Casspirs and a yellow police van.

Jan had been very definite, that he hadn't any way of promising that he would find Henry Kenge. Couldn't say whether he was one of the thousand detainees, whether he had fled the country, whether he was dead. Jan had said that trying to trace the man was the only chance he knew of getting weapons by that evening. He had told Jack that it would be many days until he was contacted through the dead letter drop. The Movement would wait with extreme caution to see whether the death of Jacob Thiroko had compromised that part of the Johannesburg structure that had known of the incursion towards Warmbaths. Jan had said that every person who had known of the incursion would be isolated for their own safety, for the safety of those who dealt with them. And they would all sit very tight for a while anyway until it was discovered how Thiroko was betrayed. Jan said he would have to be under suspicion himself, having known of the rendezvous.

The moped slowed. Not for Jack to give advice. For the boy to make his own mind. Jack's frustration that he was a stranger, without experience, unable to contribute.

The jerk off the tarmac. Jan revved all the power he could drag from the engine. They surged and bumped away across the dirt, away from the road and the police block.

Jack clung to Jan's waist.

The boy shouted, "Carry yourself well, and for God's sake don't look scared. Scared is guilt to these people. If you see me move, follow me. If we have to get out it'll happen fast. The mood changes, like bloody lightning . . . and this is a hell of a scary place we're going into."

Jack punched the boy in the ribs.

Away to the right there was the bellow of a loudspeaker from the police block. Jack couldn't hear the words. He thought they were beyond rifle range as they slipped the cordon.

There were holes in the fence. Jan searched for one that was wide enough for the Suzuki and jolted through it.

Jan cut the engine.

A terrible quiet around them, and then a dog barking. No people. Jan pushed his moped. Jack was close behind him. They went forward down a wide street of beaten dirt. Jack thought that Soweto was chic in comparison. He saw overturned and burned cars. He saw a fire-gutted house. He saw the dog, tied by string to a doorpost, angry and straining to get at them.

"Straight roads make it easier for the police and military to dominate. They haven't electricity here, the water's off street taps, but they've good straight roads for the Casspirs."

Jack hissed, as if frightened of his own voice, "Where the hell is everybody?"

187

"A funeral's the only thing that gets everyone out. They've had enough funerals here in the last eighteen months. It's a tough place, it's hot. There's not a Black policeman can live here any more, and the Black quisling councillors are gone. Shit . . ."

Jan pointed. It was a small thing and without having it pointed to him Jack wouldn't have noticed. Jan was pointing to a galvanised bucket, filled with water, in front of a house. Jack thought of it as a house but it was more of a brick and tin shack. He saw the bucket. When he looked up the street he saw there were buckets filled with water in front of each house, each shack, in the wide street.

"Means bad trouble. The water is for the kids to wash the gas out of their faces. If there's going to be trouble everybody leaves water on the street."

"If you don't put the water out?" Jack asked.

"Then they would be thought of as collaborators and they get the necklace. Hands tied behind their backs, a tyre hung on their shoulders, that's the necklace. They set light to the tyre."

"Bloody nice revolution you've started."

"It's hard for these people to touch the police, they haven't a cat in hell's chance of hurting the state. What are they left with, just the chance to hurt the Black servants of the state."

"So what do we do? Scratch our backsides, then what?"

"We just have to wait."

It was a huge funeral.

The gathering was illegal. Under the amendment regulations following the state of emergency it was prohibited that mourners should march in formation to open air funeral services. It would have required a battalion of infantry to have prevented the column reaching the grave that had been prepared for the body of a thirteen-year-old girl, knocked over ten days before by a speeding Casspir.

Sometimes the regulations were enforced, sometimes not. Enforcement depended on the will of the senior police officer for the area, and the size of the forces available to him.

On this Sunday the military were not present. The police seemed to have stayed back and watched from a distance as the migrant ant mass of men and women and children took the small white wood coffin to the cemetery.

An orderly march to the grave. Hating faces, but controlled. The young men who had charge let the priest have his say, and they allowed the bereaved family to get clear in an old Morris car, and they gave time for the old men and the women and the small children to start back towards the township.

There was organisation of a sort in what happened afterwards.

A single police jeep was out in front of the main force, there to overlook and photograph. A shambling charge at the jeep, and the driver had lost his gears, and lost time, and the men who guarded the photographer and his long lens had fired volleys of bird shot and gas to keep the running, stoning crowd at a distance.

The driver of the jeep never found his gears. The crowd surged on, vengeance within reach. The police ditched the jeep, left it with the engine howling, ran for their lives. Good and fit, the policemen, and running hard because they knew the alternative to running fast, knew what happened to policemen who were caught by a funeral mob. The photographer didn't run fast, not as fast as he had to run. The lens bouncing awkwardly from his stomach, and the camera bag on his shoulder, and none of the policemen with guns taking the time to cover him.

The officers commanding the police were still shouting their orders when the fleetest of the mob caught up with the photographer. The photographer was White and a year and a half short of his fiftieth birthday. A growl in the mob, the breath intake of a mad dog.

The hacking crack of rifle fire, aimed at random into the crowd at four hundred metres. The crowd of youths not caring because the photographer was caught.

The Casspirs came forward, and the kids fled before them, back towards the township.

The photographer was naked but for one shoe and his socks and the camera with the long lens that lay on his belly. His clothes had been taken from him as vultures take meat from bones. He was dead. An autopsy would in due course state how many knife wounds he had received, how many stone bruises.

The start of a routine township battle. An hour of unrest.

Shotguns and rifles and tear gas grenades from behind the armour plate of the high built Casspirs. Petrol bombs and rocks from the kids. Pretty unremarkable happenings for the East Rand.

The police saw the kids back into the warren streets of Duduza and left them to their destruction. Eighteen months after the start of the petrol bombing and the rock throwing against the Black policemen's homes and councillor's homes there was little left for the crowd that was worth burning.

Two shops were destroyed by fire. The days were long since gone when the elderly would try to prevent the kids burning a shop out. To have tried to have saved a shop from the fire was to have invited the accusation of collaborator. Two shops burned.

Four kids died. Eighteen kids were treated for buck shot injuries in Duduza's unregistered clinic. No chance of them going to hospital.

A thirteen-year-old girl had been successfully buried.

Sunday afternoon in Duduza, and time to bring the buckets indoors.

His eyes were red rimmed.

He sat on a wooden chair in a small room.

Faces peered at him through the cracked glass of the window. Jack looked straight ahead, looked all the time at the man who had been introduced as Henry Kenge, and at Jan.

He dabbed his eyes with his water-soaked handkerchief, and each time he did it he heard the pitter patter of laughter from all around him.

He had made his speech. He had asked for help. He had been heard out. He had been vague and unspecific until Jan had waved him quiet, taken over and whispered urgently a statement of intent in the ear of the one identified as Kenge.

He was filthy from the ditch he had lain in as the Casspirs had rumbled down the main street. With Jan in the bottom of a ditch that doubled as a street sewer.

He thought that if the youngsters he had seen that afternoon had been Black kids on the streets of London or Birmingham or Liverpool then he would have rated them as mindless and vicious hooligans. He thought the kids of Duduza were the bravest he had ever known. So what was the morality of that? Fuck the morality, Jack thought.

Kenge brought Jan a holdall. Jan passed the bag to Jack. He counted five R.G.–42 grenades.

Jack tugged at Jan's sleeve. "This shouldn't be in bloody public."

"The necklace has made ashes of informers, they're scrubbed out of Duduza. The eyes of the security police have been put out with fire, that's why they're losing. They have a song about you. They don't know who you are, but they have a song in praise of you. They made a song about the man who carried the bomb into John Vorster Square."

Jack shook his head, like he'd been slapped. "You told them about that?"

"You've been given half of this township's armoury. You grovel your thanks to them."

When they left they could see the lights of the road block vehicles. Jan kept his own headlight off and drove cross-country in a loop taking them well clear of the block. For a short time a searchlight tried to find the source of the engine sound in the darkness, and they stopped in shadow until it lit upon some other threat, and then rode on.

Jack thought he was pretty damn fortunate to have the grenades. He appreciated that after Thiroko was killed Jan would be isolated from the Movement. That's what any Movement would do. He pounded Jan's back, in gratitude, in relief to be out of Duduza.

Ros was at the flat in Hillbrow. She showed Jack what she had brought. Only after he had seen and handled the pump action shotgun and the two revolvers and the ammunition did Jack realise that she had changed herself.

He thought Ros van Niekerk was quite lovely.

He had fifteen pounds of explosives and detonators and firing fuse and five grenades and a shotgun and two revolvers. And he had a crippled student to help him, and a girl who worked in an insurance office and who was lovely.

No going back, but then there had never been a time for going back.

16

A crisp, bright, autumn morning over the flat veld, the diamond frost going with the sunlight.

Monday morning. Another week. One more used up.

Jack had dismantled the model. He had returned the pieces to the bread bin.

In a corner of the yard at the back of the block of flats he discarded one of the two metal tubes. He had explosive enough for one tube only. He had to go out the way that he went in.

Jan carried the suitcase to the car. Ros had the shotgun, broken and carried under an overcoat, and the two revolvers. Jack brought the tube.

Jack had told them he needed a stop on the way for a bag of readymix concrete. He said that he would sit in the back of the car, that he needed to think. He sat in the back of the car and concentrated on an approach from the south side over Magazine Hill, and diversions on the north side near the guarded perimeters of Defence Headquarters.

They could rent a service flat in Pretoria, Ros said. It wouldn't be difficult to find one, but it would be expensive. Jack passed her a wad of rand notes. He slipped back to his thinking.

How much could he ask of them, of Jan and Ros?

The principal hotels were tried first.

Two detectives, with the two original photo-fits and also with a third photo-fit that was an amalgam of the shopkeepers' opinions, were briefed to visit the city's four and five star hotels. Other teams were directed towards the two and three star hotels, the booking offices of South African Airways, of the European airlines, and to Jan Smuts.

Every one of them worked from John Vorster Square, had been violated by the bomb. The two with the four and five star list appreciated that the hotels worked shift systems of reception and porter staff. They knew that if they drew blanks with this visit that they must come back to interview those staff who were not on duty that Monday morning.

At the Landdrost, first visit, the detective found the Indian day porter on duty. He left his colleague with the brunette on reception, poring over the composite photo-fit. She had known the face. The detective showed the day porter the photo-fits.

The day porter recalled the features. He had quite liked the man. He'd had a good tip for arranging the visit to Soweto, and another tip when the man had checked out. He nodded his head. He understood that the detective was from the security police. And if it was the security police then it was not pilfering or the fraudulent use of a credit card, it was sedition or terrorism. Heavily, the day porter nodded. He wrote a room number on a slip of paper and pushed it across his desk to the detective. He was asked whether he knew the man's name.

"His name was Mr Curwen."

"*Was?*"

"The middle of last week he left, sir."

The day porter was in work. Not big pay but the tips were good. He'd remembered this man, for courtesy and for a warm word of thanks when the man had gone, carrying his own suitcase out, he hadn't forgotten that. It hurt the day porter to implicate the young Englishman.

The detective went to the cashier's desk. With the name and the room number it took only half a minute for him to be given a copy of the bill, and the dates of the guest's stay.

Soon afterwards a watch salesman from Port Elizabeth, sleeping in late with a Coloured call girl, was disturbed in his room. They were given two minutes to get their clothes on.

The salesman was in the corridor zipping his trousers, his 100 rand companion was beside him buttoning her blouse, as the dog was unleashed in the room. The salesman, in increasing desperation, tried without success to discover why his room was being searched. The detectives stayed in the corridor and gave him no satisfaction. Just the handler and his small black labrador dog in the room.

The dog explored the bed, and the drawers of the bedside tables, no reaction. It covered the desk beside the window, and the drawers there. It went past the television set. The cold nose flitted over the dressing table. The dog and the handler had made a slow circuit of the room when they reached the wardrobe in the corner opposite the bathroom door.

The dog snorted.

It had been trained over months to recognise the scent of minute traces of explosive. The dog had no skill at tracking a man, nor at finding hard or soft drugs in luggage. It was an explosive sniffer dog. The dog pawed at the wardrobe door, scratched at the varnish finish. The handler slid open the door. The dog sniffed hard into the bottom corner of the wardrobe, then up to the inside of the door. The dog barked, the tail going, then came out of the wardrobe and sat, and the handler gave it a biscuit.

"There were explosives in this cupboard," the handler told the detectives. "My guess would be that the suspect had traces on his hands from handling the explosives when he closed the cupboard door. The dog has found the traces inside only, but the outside would have been cleaned by the maid staff. But there's no doubt, there were explosives very recently in this room."

He had the name of Jack Curwen. He had an address in the Surrey town of Leatherhead. He had a date of arrival in South Africa.

192

The colonel dictated his telex.

He had forensic confirmation that the explosive traces found on the inside of the wardrobe door matched the types of plaster gelignite most generally issued by the Soviets to the military wing of the A.N.C.

By choice he was an overworked man. He drew to his own desk as many strands of investigation as it was possible for him to gather in.

He missed a link.

He did not marry the information he now possessed with the report sent from London by Major Swart before the John Vorster Square bomb, which had been circulated to the colonel by Pretoria.

The colonel had so much to concern himself with, it was understandable, only human, that he missed the link.

The telex had been transformed from a jumble of numbers to a demand for immediate information. The telex lay on the desk of Major Swart.

Major Swart's office was deserted. The telex was placed on the untenanted desk.

Half way through that Monday morning.

There had been a short hail shower. The forecast was for rain later.

Major Swart thought it a dismal occasion. A burial service without dignity. But then Arkwright had been a pathetic creature.

It was an hour's drive out of London for Major Swart. Piet had brought him down the M4 to the village beyond Reading.

They were dressed for the part, the major and his warrant officer.

The major was unshaven and in jeans with an old donkey coat on his shoulders. The warrant officer had chosen denims with a Campaign for Nuclear Disarmament logo on the back of his jacket. The major had thought there would be a better turn out. It was the last chance perhaps to get a tail on the young man introduced by Arkwright to Jacob Thiroko. And the bastard hadn't shown. He could have saved his time.

He recognised faces from Anti-Apartheid. No one that was special. A few kids out of the secretaries' pool, a man who made speeches at the really bum meetings when the seniors didn't want to know. He saw Arkwright's parents, country people, and they looked as embarrassed at the contingent from London as they were by the attendance of Arkwright's wife's people whose Jaguar was a flashy intrusion in the lane outside the church.

The group was around the open grave. He could hear the vicar's voice, as sonorous as the clouds. He and Piet were standing back, amongst the old head stones.

"Pleasant surprise to see you here, Major Swart."

He turned fast. He didn't know the man who had come silently over the wet grass to stand behind him. A big man, wearing a good overcoat.

"Detective Inspector Cooper, Major Swart. Didn't expect you'd be out and about to offer your condolences at the death of an Anti-Apartheid activist."

The anger was crimson on the major's cheeks.

"I'd have thought the embassy could have done better on the clothing allowance, Major Swart."

Swart saw the amusement on the detective inspector's face. "There is no regulation restricting the travel of South African diplomats inside the United Kingdom."

The detective inspector looked him over, with mocking enjoyment. "None at all, Major. Going on afterwards to the family for a drink and a sandwich, are we?"

"Go and fuck yourself," Major Swart said.

"Nice language for a cemetery, Major, very choice. I doubt you'll tell me why you're here, but I'll tell you why I'm here. Our investigations tell us that Douglas Arkwright was followed out of a public house on the night of his death. It is our belief that he was attacked as he walked home. Some of his injuries were consistent with a kicking. Stroke of luck for us, really, but when he went under the bus only his head and shoulders were hit by the tyres, that's how we can say for sure what were other injuries he had very recently sustained. It is our belief that Arkwright was running away from his assailants when he fell under the bus. Wouldn't be murder, of course, manslaughter would be the charge. You'd know about that, Major Swart, you being a policeman back home. Any ideas on who would be interested in roughing up a creep like Douglas Arkwright?"

"Any time you want advice on how to police your inner cities, just telephone me, Inspector."

"The National Theatre could give you a hand with your costume, Major. And you, Warrant Officer. It is Warrant Officer Piet Kaiser, isn't it? I thought so. Ask for the wardrobe mistress at the stage door. Very helpful folk."

The major walked away, his warrant officer close behind him. He didn't look back. He presumed the man was Special Branch.

They drove off, crashing through the gears, causing the vicar to pause in mid flow.

Major Swart and Warrant Officer Kaiser stopped at a pub on the Thames and didn't leave before closing time.

It would be late afternoon before he found the telex on his desk that required immediate attention.

The funeral of James Sandham, held by coincidence that same Monday morning, was an altogether grander affair. The Foreign and Commonwealth Office saw to the arrangements. The Personnel Department had booked a chapel of rest, and the official fleet of cars, and the crematorium, and enough flowers to make Sandham seem to have been a loved and respected colleague.

194

His former wife had married again, and successfully, and was able to afford a clinging black frock that set her off well against the men from the F.C.O. She was allocated the front row in the crematorium chapel, never whimpered, never produced a handkerchief. The P.U.S. was behind her, and sitting alongside him was Peter Furneaux, head of the late Jimmy Sandham's section.

They didn't speak, the P.U.S. and Peter Furneaux, until after the curtains had closed on the coffin, and the taped organ music had come to a stop. As the mourners scraped to their feet and followed the former Mrs Sandham to the door and into a light shower of rain, Furneaux said, "I wonder if I could have a word with you, sir."

"I've lunch out of town, I am afraid, then the Cabinet Office, so I haven't a lot of time."

"It's quite pressing, sir."

"Let's walk a bit."

There was a garden around the crematorium, trimmed lawns with staked trees and ordered borders.

"Well, Peter, let's have it."

"This fellow, Carew, sir, that's going to hang in South Africa"

"Thursday, right?"

"I know that Carew is an alias. I know that his true name is Curwen . . ."

"Classified, Peter, in the interests of national security."

"Shortly before James Sandham died, a young man came to F.C.O. His name was Jack Curwen. He said that James Carew was his father. I saw him, and Jimmy Sandham was with me . . ."

"Was he now?" the P.U.S. mouthed softly.

"Then Sandham disappeared, then he was dead. So we move on . . . I have regular reports coming in from Pretoria, the run of the mill embassy material, and I have a note on Carew. Last Friday I get a confirmation that Carew will definitely hang this Thursday. No more speculation. Finish. He's going to hang . . . This Jack Curwen, he was a stroppy fellow but he was decent. He told me to my face that I was washing my hands of his father and I wasn't pleased at being told that, but in his position I reckon I'd have said the same, so I thought he deserved a call. He'd left his numbers. On Friday evening I rang the home number . . ."

Furneaux saw a thoughtful, concerned face, he saw a gathering frown. Behind them the cars were pulling away. Another line of vehicles waited at the gates for the next cremation.

"I rang the home number. I think the phone was answered by Curwen's mother, who was first married to Carew. I told her what I knew, delicately, and then asked for her son. She put the phone down on me. I wanted to speak to the boy himself so this morning, before coming down here, I rang the office number that he'd left with us. He wasn't there. Young Curwen had taken abrupt leave. I spoke to his employer, I was told it was a very sudden departure."

"You're taking, Peter, a long time getting to the point."

"I asked the nature of young Curwen's employment. The firm he works for is called Demolition and Clearance. Curwen drums up business for the sort of work that required demolition by explosives . . ."

"The point, please, Peter."

"It's conjecture, of course . . . I would hazard that Curwen has flown to South Africa. That blast at police headquarters in Johannesburg, our people report that the rumour in security circles is that a White with an English accent planted the bomb. I would further hazard that Curwen, having launched one attack, is going to make something of a noise at around the time his father hangs . . ."

"Thank you, Peter. You're going by train, I'll drop you at the station."

They walked to the P.U.S.'s official car, the doors were opened for them by the chauffeur.

"There wasn't anything strange about Sandham's death, was there, sir?"

"What sort of strange, Peter?"

"He'd no more go mountain climbing than I would, sir."

"You never can tell, can you, with people?"

The P.U.S. asked the chauffeur to find the nearest underground station. They drove away.

"It's my duty to tell you, sir . . ." Furneaux was muttering, difficult ground. ". . . there's been a fair amount of disquiet on the desk. So far out of character that he should be mountain climbing. He spoke to no one about talking leave. It's caused quite a bit of anxiety on the desk, and I thought you should know that, sir."

"As head of department, you'll want to discourage idle speculation."

"Yes, sir."

Lighting a cigarette, the P.U.S. said, "Thank you, Peter, for your guessing game about Carew's boy. If it needs to be taken further I'll handle it. You don't have to concern yourself with the matter. By the by, Peter, you probably heard that there's going to be a gap in Nairobi. Needs a most responsible and sensitive man to fill it. Quite a posting for a youngish man, don't you think, eh, Peter?"

They shook hands, the P.U.S. smiled a watery smile. Furneaux went down into the underground and bought a ticket. He shrugged. Every man had a price. And he was not much of a mountaineer himself.

The Director General scraped with a match at the mess in the stem of his pipe, and listened.

"Let me give you a scenario. Young Curwen has gone to South Africa, unconfirmed, but possible, and you will check it at once. Through his work he is familiar with explosives, that we know. A bomb goes off in Johannesburg and is rumoured to have been planted by a White. For the sake of our scenario let us assume that James Carew is to hang on Thursday, at the moment intending to take his secret to his grave, and let us assume that young Curwen is arrested in the hours remaining before the execution. What chance *then*, if they put the screws on him, so to say, that Carew would remain silent?"

The P.U.S. had cut short his lunch and driven to Century House for the meeting. Still the Director General said nothing.

"Or the related scenario: Carew hangs and Curwen is subsequently arrested. How much does the boy know? He met Sandham; Sandham knew only so much and probably hadn't told him. Would the boy talk?"

"Probably."

"I believe it is back to Downing Street, Director-General."

"For what earthly reason?"

The Director General filled his pipe. It was a mechanical action. His eyes were never on the bowl, but none of the tobacco fibres fell to the polished surface of his desk.

"I don't intend to finish my career in an expose on the front page of Sunday's newspapers. Never forget, Director General, our job is to advise and to execute. The politicians are paid to make decisions, whatever a ham-fisted job they make of it. Keep this one in the dark and I reckon we'll get swamped by home-flying chickens. Lay it all before them and we safeguard ourselves and possibly them too. I'll fix an appointment for early evening."

"If the Prime Minister's schedule permits."

"No problem. Any Prime Minister I've worked with would meet one in a dressing gown at four in the morning if the matter under consideration involves an intelligence foul-up."

When the P.U.S. had gone, the Director General called in his personal assistant and named a man who was to be called to his office immediately.

Major Swart read the telex.

They'd had to stop once at a service station on the way back to London. Heavy stuff, English beer. He read the telex, then went back to his private lavatory, and back again to the telex.

Shit, and he was half cut. He was never at his best after he had drunk at lunchtime.

He knew the name of Curwen. Checked it out, hadn't he, days before. Checked and found that Mrs Hilda Perry had been married to a James Curwen. Thought he'd cracked the connection between James Carew and Hilda Perry. Had it all sewn up until he had taken the photograph of James Carew to the village in Hampshire and been told four times that the photograph was not that of James Curwen. From Somerset House he knew there was a son of the marriage between Hilda Perry and James Curwen, he knew from those same records that the son had been christened Jack.

Johannesburg wanted information on a Jack Curwen. They wanted background, and they wanted confirmation of a photo-fit likeness.

Major Swart could have sent off an answer straight away . . . But he wanted to piss again . . . He reckoned he could have established the link between Jack

Curwen and Hilda Perry and a letter written from Pretoria Central by James Carew.

With too much beer inside him, and a foul temper still from the encounter at the funeral, he chose a different course.

He would first stitch the matter, then he would send his message.

He would stitch it so tight that there were no call backs, no demands for follow up information.

He rang Erik. Yes, the bloody man had replaced his bloody television set. Yes, Erik would be at the embassy within forty-five minutes. He shouted down the corridor to Piet that if he had plans, life or death, for the late evening then he should bloody well forget them.

And then hastily back to his private lavatory, fumbling with his private key, to leak.

He came heavily down the staircase. A beautiful staircase, oak, probably Jacobean, he thought.

The hostility swarmed from the short, slight woman. The hostility was in the wrinkle lines at her throat, and in the flash of her eyes, and the curl of a tired mouth.

"I hope you're satisfied. I hope you understand why he couldn't come to London to see you."

Mrs Fordham had told the Director General over the telephone that the colonel was ill and could not take a train to London. He hadn't believed her.

They stood in the panelled hallway. He thought the house and its interior were magnificent. Perhaps she read him.

"It was all my money, my family's money. The colonel wasn't interested in material reward, all he cared about was the Service. The Service was his life. And how did the Service repay his dedication? There wasn't even a party for him. More than two decades of work and the Service simply discarded him. We've had just one visit from the Service since he was thrown out, and that was some grubby little man who came here to see that there weren't any classified documents in the house."

The Director General was still shaken by the sight of the shell of the man he had just seen in the large bedroom. Colonel Fordham, curled in a wheelchair near the window, unable to move and unable to speak, had kicked the fight from the Director General.

"It's a great shame, Mrs Fordham, that you didn't feel able to alert us . . ."

"I wouldn't have had your people in the house."

They moved towards the front door. No way he was going to be offered a cup of tea. Of course they had retired the crass old fool, and years too late at that. A dinosaur, really, who believed the Service was still packing off agents to suborn the Bolshevik revolution or to run around the hillsides of Afghanistan.

"I came to ask for specific information."

"Then you wasted your journey."

"There was one man who was very close to your husband."

"I'm not a part of the Service, and at this time of the afternoon I have to bath Basil."

She dared him to stay. The Director General smiled. He fell back on his rarely used reservoir of charm. Outside his chauffeur and his bodyguard would be waiting for him, enjoying the thermos and a smoke. God, and he'd be glad to be back with them.

"The man who was close to your husband was called James Curwen. I understand he went by the nickname of "Jeez". I need your help, Mrs Fordham."

He saw the same short slight woman, but hurt. He saw her fingers make a tight fist, loosen, grip again.

"That's what did it to him," her voice quavered. "It wasn't long after he'd been dismissed."

"He read of the arrest in the papers?"

"He'd read *The Times*. He didn't finish his breakfast that morning. He walked out into the garden. It was about twenty minutes later that I went looking for him. He'd just collapsed, the dogs were with him. What you've just seen, he's been like that ever since."

"You didn't tell us."

"After what you'd done to him?"

"You knew Curwen?"

She shrugged. "He lived here when he came back from Albania, before he went to South Africa. He was a sort of batman to Basil, and he did jobs in the house and he drove the car and did things outside."

The Director General had to mask his disgust. The man had done ten years in an Albanian prison camp, and had come back to be patronised as a loyal serf. Lost his marriage and lost ten years of his life, but the kindly old colonel and his lady let him drive the car and change the fuses and make a rockery in the garden.

A desperation in her face. "Why haven't you brought Jeez out?"

"I am afraid it may not be in our power to save him."

"But you're trying?"

"Certainly we're trying," the Director General said. "Tell me about him."

"He's a wonderful man. He came back here, after the awfulness of what he'd been through, and he just seemed to put it behind him. I'd known him before, when he was a well built, strong man, and when he came back he was a skeleton, unrecognisable. Never a complaint, not in any way bitter. His attitude seemed to be that since he'd been sent into Albania by the Service his mission must have been justified, that it was simply the rub of the green that he had been caught. He had a marvellous stoicism, I think that kept him going. Sometimes, not often, he would talk about the bad times in the camp, when men from his hut were taken out and shot, when his companions died of malnutrition, when the camp guards were particularly brutal, when it was cold and there was no heating. When he talked about it there was always his humour, very dry. He was honoured to be a part of the Service, just as Basil was. The Service was Jeez's life, just as it was Basil's. Is that what you want to hear?"

"How resolute would he be, in his present situation?"

"You'd want to know whether he'd betray you, to save his neck?"

"That's very bluntly put, Mrs Fordham."

"It is insulting to Jeez that you even think of asking me the question. I just pray to God and thank Him that Basil cannot know what Jeez is going through now."

"It must be a very painful time for you, Mrs Fordham."

"His wife came here . . . God, I'm going back, more than twenty years ago. We were entertaining, a weekend lunch party. The poor woman came here to try and find out something about where Jeez was, what he'd done. He said afterwards to me that it was one of the worst days of his life, having to lie to her, telling her to put her husband out of her mind. Jeez understood. When he was down here Basil was very frank with him. He had to tell him that the marriage was just a casualty of life with the Service. He told Jeez that his wife had got a divorce and remarried, that it would be wrong of him to disturb her, that he should try not to make contact with his son, however hard that was going to be. Jeez always did what Basil said. Just before he went to South Africa, Jeez went up to London and he must have gone out to where his wife and his son were living in their new home. I think he saw her bringing the boy home from school. Jeez was quite bouncy at supper that evening, as if his mind was at rest."

"The Service did all that to the man, and now you're going to let him hang. Now all you care about it is whether *he'll* talk, whether *you'll* be sacked as a consequence. You disgust me . . ."

The Director General turned to the door.

". . . I hope he talks. I hope he shouts his head off and destroys the lot of you, just as you destroyed Basil."

He let himself out.

He left her to bath her husband.

The man who had been a friend of Jimmy Sandham found a telephone kiosk in the centre of Leatherhead and rang in to Century.

Villiers had been helpful, he reported. He had posed as a policeman. He had said it often enough, that Curwen wasn't in trouble. He carried identification as a policeman; he rarely used the polaroid card but it was always with him. He had been told by the Director General that he must call in as soon as he had completed his interview. He knew on the grapevine that the big man was for Downing Street that evening.

When he had dictated his preliminary report, he mentioned to the personal assistant that he had been given the name of a fellow that Curwen often worked with, and the address. He said he'd get himself down there. He said that he'd telephone back in if anything worthwhile came up.

Major Swart drove an old Fiesta out of London. It was one of four cars available to him for clandestine work, and the least prepossessing of them in terms of the bodywork, but the engine was finely tuned. It was a slow journey, appalling traffic.

Erik sat beside the major. Piet shared the back seat with the canvas bag into which had been put the tools for the evening's work.

In the bag, along with the jemmy bar and the screwdrivers, were two balaclavas and two pairs of plastic gloves.

"I won't tell you anything," Hawkins said.

"Then you lose your licence as a blaster. Pity, that."

"Threats won't change me."

"Not a threat, Mr Hawkins, a promise, and I always keep promises. Anyway you've told me plenty."

"I've told you nothing."

He thought the place stank. He thought it was pitiful that a man should live in such conditions. Everything he saw was filthy, every surface was grimed. There was a cat mess under his chair. But he believed the old blaster. Threats wouldn't change him.

"I know he's your friend. If he wasn't your friend then you wouldn't be covering for him. I know he's in South Africa . . ."

He watched the old man closely. Hawkins looked away, picked his nose, but his eyes didn't come back. That was good enough, Curwen was in South Africa, confirmation.

"I know that you told him how to build the bomb that he carried into John Vorster Square police station. In the trade, I gather, it's called the La Mon Mark One. I don't think Curwen could have made that bomb without expert help."

"I won't tell you nothing."

"But he didn't go there just to blow a hole in a police station . . . What did he go there for, George?"

"Nothing."

"If John Vorster Square which is the most important police station in the country was just for starters, then he's aiming to follow it with something that's hells big. You following me, George?"

"Bugger off."

"I've just been cremating a friend of mine today, George. He was an awkward sod, but he was my friend. I told my friend about Jack's father, my friend told Jack . . . I'll deny I ever told you that . . . It was my friend that told Jack the truth about his father. I expect Jack told you what the truth was."

No denial.

"Let me get back to where I was before. If it's something big, then it stands to reason that it's dangerous. You with me, George?"

Hawkins was with him. The old blaster was on the edge of his chair, hanging on the words.

"He must have been pretty lucky not to have got himself killed at John Vorster Square."

Hawkins bit. "Your friend that died, what happened to him?"

"Murdered . . . But that's not what I'm here for. I have to know the boy's next target. If I'm to help him I have to know."

"How can you help him?"

"Where I work we're like the priest's confessional. We're not interested in names, we don't care where the information comes from . . . This isn't a conversation that ever happened . . . I can't tell you how we can help him. You have to believe me that it makes it easier for us to help the boy if we know what he's at."

"You're too late in the day to come bellyaching about help. You're talking shit, it's your lot that pissed on Jack's father."

"What's he going to do, George?"

"What would you do if it was your father?"

The gamble, the big throw. "Take him out."

Hawkins gazed down at the torn linoleum. Over his yellowed teeth his lips were tight closed.

"I'd try to take him out of Pretoria Central gaol, and I'd think I might know how to set about that because I'd talked to an explosives expert called George Hawkins."

"He's on the minimum. He's no chance."

"What sort of minimum, George?"

"Gelignite. He hasn't an ounce of margin."

"That's tough on the boy."

Hawkins said, "If you betray him then it'll go with you for the rest of your life. There'll be the time, the hour before your death, when you'll be bloody sorry you betrayed him. You'll cry for his forgiveness. So help me, Christ, and you won't deserve to be heard."

"That's well put, George."

"I'm thought to be a hard, mean bugger. I cried when the lad went."

"Because he's going to try to blow his way into Pretoria Central, and take his father out."

"I'd be proud to call Jack Curwen my son."

The light was gone, the room in shadow. The man left Hawkins sitting in his chair. He could no longer clearly see the old blaster's face. He understood how Curwen had won over Jimmy Sandham, just as he had won over a hard, mean bugger who was an expert in explosives.

There was a light on in the hall of Sam Perry's house. The rest of the house was darkened.

Erik and Piet listened a long time at the back door before they were certain the house was empty. The major had told them there was no dog, he was sure of that from when he'd called. No alarm box on the outside walls.

They taped adhesive paper over the glass panel of the kitchen door, broke it, were able to reach inside and turn the key. It was better going in the back, always gave one a head start if the householder returned to the front door and could be heard messing for the key. The major had said they should take their time, so long as they weren't disturbed. It was a great bonus that they hadn't had to wait until the small hours to break in, hadn't had to wait until the householders were in bed and asleep.

Erik and Piet were experienced burglars. They'd seen the real thing frequently enough when they were young policemen, before their transfers to security.

They knew what they were looking for.

Three streets away, Major Swart dozed in his car, head back, snoring.

The friend of the late Jimmy Sandham stopped his car at the barrier across the entrance to Downing Street. He showed his identification. He was waved forward to park.

Inside the hushed, well-lit hallway, he asked to see his Director General.

17

The Prime Minister was irritable. The Prime Minister had that day coped with hospital funding, the price per barrel of crude oil, diplomatic manoeuvres on Falklands sovereignty, unemployment statistics, and security at the G.C.H.Q. Far East listening post. He had had lunch with the Venezuelan Ambassador. Finally questions in the House. When the Carew meeting was over there was scheduled a key note policy speech that would be carried on the late evening news broadcasts.

"It is purely conjecture that the son of James Carew has carried out a criminal and terrorist attack on the territory of South Africa," the Prime Minister said. "And I'm not going to give you a decision based on conjecture."

"Rather more than conjecture," the P.U.S. remarked quietly. "And conjecture or no, we still have to finalise a position in view of what can be regarded as changed circumstances."

"Carew hangs on Thursday, what has changed?"

The Director General said, "Prime Minister, we believe that Carew's son is aware of his father's true position, that his father was an employee of the Service, that is what has changed. Further, we believe that if he were arrested by the South African security police he would very probably give them that information. We also believe that if Carew were to know, before his execution, that his son had been killed or arrested, then *he* might divulge what he has so far withheld. On two fronts we confront a new danger."

"Very well . . . what do you recommend I do?"

The P.U.S. ducked his shoulders. The Director General was reaching for his pipe.

"Silence all around me . . . ?"

The Prime Minister smiled, mocked them.

". . . Not normally so reticent, gentlemen. It's surely clear that we find ourselves with two choices of action, both unacceptable. I suggest we hold onto our seats, and trust that nothing happens."

"Shifting ground is a poor foundation for trust, Prime Minister," the P.U.S. said.

"This afternoon, Prime Minister, we confirmed that Jack Curwen did indeed fly to South Africa shortly before the police station bombing took place," the Director General said. "Also that in his work for a demolition company he had acquired a knowledge of explosives. In my opinion, something *will* happen."

"This young man, can he be stopped?"

"By calling in the Ambassador and putting all our cards on the table . . ." the Director General said.

"In the present state of our relations with the government of South Africa that would be intolerable."

"Then as you put it, Prime Minister, we hold onto our seats and hope that we have anticipated only the blacker prospects."

There was a light tap at the door.

The Prime Minister shifted in annoyance at the interruption.

A secretary came in, glided past the Prime Minister with a grimace of apology. The secretary spoke in the Director General's ear. He gestured his excuses and followed her from the room.

The Prime Minister reached for a worn leather case, as if to indicate that the meeting was concluded.

"If only a few small bombs are thrown at police stations, we can weather that, I believe."

"I thought you'd like to be kept fully informed, Prime Minister."

The P.U.S. pushed himself up from his chair.

The Director General stood in the doorway. There was a man behind him, a creased raincoat, hair that hadn't been combed. The Director General ushered him into the room.

"Just tell the Prime Minister what you've told me, what you understand to be Jack Curwen's objective."

The man who had been a friend to Jimmy Sandham looked around him.

It was a moment to savour.

He spoke drably, without expression, flat monotone. "It is Mr Curwen's intention, apparently, without anyone else's help, to blast his way, using a home-made device, through the walls of the hanging section of Pretoria Central prison to his father's cell. This with a view to taking his father out."

There was an aching silence in the room.

The Director General nudged his man away through the door, and closed it. The P.U.S. whistled his astonishment. The Director General was stony-faced.

The Prime Minister's head swayed, right to left, left to right, slow movement, bemused.

"God help us, Director General, let's call the meeting to a halt before you spring any more surprises on us. I'm going to camp in the air-raid shelter for the next five nights and pray. Either that he makes it out safely with his father, or that they're both killed, with their lips sealed. Given the choice, which do you think the good Lord would wish me to pray for?"

Sam Perry had thought it a good notion to take his wife to the golf club social.

She'd lost nearly a stone in weight in the days since Jack had left for South Africa. She was gaunt, and moping through the house each day. She knew most of the wives at the club and he'd thought it would be best for her to be out, not sitting in the house and knitting and unpicking what she'd knitted. He'd taken to coming home for his lunch because then they had a chance to talk it through without young Will being there. They made a show for the youngster when he came rattling in from school in the late afternoon, but the child must have known from his mother's appearance that crisis touched his family. They talked in the middle of the day, but there was nothing to talk about. Her first husband was going to hang, her son was in danger and beyond her reach, and Sam Perry could only say that they had to live with it, live in hope.

On any other evening at the golf club she would have sailed into the drinking, shouting crowd, confident, happy among friends. Not on this evening. She was by his side from the moment they went through the doors and into the bar. As if she were frightened to be more than a yard from him. While he put away four gins she sipped at two tomato juices, and every ten minutes she looked at her watch.

It hadn't worked out. He wondered if it would be better when it was over, when Jeez was dead and buried, when Jack had been . . . when Jack had come home. He thought it would be a bloody long convalescence. It was a swine of a thought for Sam Perry, that she might never recover, might never regain her fun and the gaiety that he loved in her.

He knew she had made an effort to come out with him. He realised she couldn't last long that evening. He saw the pleading in her eyes, he started to make their excuses and shake hands. As soon as was decently possible. He thought of the tittle-tattle that would follow their backs out of the room. There'd be a few of them who'd get a laugh out of speculating on the problems of Sam and Hilda Perry.

It was still too early to pick up Will from Scouts.

They'd go home first . . . He heard the strong sigh of relief from Hilda when they were in the car park and clear of the raucous celebration of the bar.

A mile to their home.

Sam Perry drove slowly. He let his left hand rest on her arm, moved it only to change gear.

He turned into Churchill Close. He could hear her crying, very faintly.

"Don't hurt yourself, love," he said. "You couldn't have stopped Jack going."

He looked at her. He was going to kiss her cheek. He saw her startled, staring eyes. She was peering through the windscreen and at their home at the end of the cul de sac. He saw what she had seen. They always drew shut their front bedroom curtains when they went out in the evening, nice curtains but not heavy curtains.

He saw the traverse of the torch beam.

Sam Perry braked. He backed away to the end of the road. He drove fast to the police station.

*

206

To the two constables the Ford Fiesta was an obvious target of interest. It was far from commonplace for an old car to be parked in the shadows between the extremities of the street lights in this sedate suburb. Via their radio link the constables had heard that two men had been arrested following a forcible entry to a property in Churchill Close. They had heard that four officers had used truncheons to subdue the intruders. They had heard that no getaway vehicle had been found in Churchill Close. They had heard that the arrested men's accents were thought to be South African. Two streets away the Fiesta and the man sleeping behind the wheel were worth a check. It was smoothly done. Door opened, keys out of the ignition before the man had tumbled awake. Major Swart was escorted to the police station.

"Twice in one day, Major Swart. Extraordinary."

Detective Inspector Cooper thought the sullen silence of the South African amply repaid the hassle of being called out from home, of having to drive from north London into Surrey.

"There's ways for foreigners to behave in our country, Major Swart, and there are ways that are outside the tramlines. Sitting in the getaway while your muckers are managing a spot of larceny is right outside the lines."

Three South Africans held while in pursuance of a crime was sufficient reason for a call to be made from Surrey Constabulary H.Q. to the Scotland Yard duty desk. The detective inspector was a member of Special Branch.

"I'm here, Major Swart, because when we searched your two muckers we found their embassy ID cards. Now, Major Swart, I'm sure you'll agree with me that the Libyans wouldn't stop short of a spot of larceny, or the Nigerians, perhaps, or the Eastern bloc chappies, but the representatives of the South African government, that's going to raise an eyebrow or two. Is it because they don't pay you much, Major Swart? Is it a bit of burglary to supplement the overseas allowance?"

He sat on the plastic-topped table in the interview room, swinging his feet casually. Swart was on a chair, rigidly straight-backed, as though he was at attention. It amused the detective inspector to think of the turmoil in the mind of the South African. Exposure. Disgrace. Expulsion.

"I have to wonder why half the diplomatic mission from Pretoria should have travelled out of London to burgle a home in this nothing town. Very puzzling, Major Swart, because next door I have laid out on a table the items that your muckers were intending to take away with them. All pretty peculiar, but not so peculiar that I can't hold you and charge you."

He saw the South African stiffen.

"Oh yes, there'll be charges. Conspiracy to rob, in your case. Your friends are in deeper trouble, of course. Theft, assaulting police officers in the execution of their duty. You might get away with eighteen months, three or four years they'll get. You'd thought of that, I expect. You knew you'd be gaoled if you were caught, surely you did? Not nice gaols like yours. You'll probably all get

Pentonville, that's where they send the short termers. Pentonville isn't segregated like those nice gaols of yours, Major Swart. You'll have a bunch of *kaffirs* on your landing for company."

He thought the young constable by the door would be having a field day listening to this heap of crap. He would tell the constable that if a word of this interview got out then the boy could kiss his promotion up his arse.

"I claim diplomatic immunity."

"Bollocks."

"I am Major Hannes Swart. I am an accredited diplomat."

"You're a burglar, and what's more you dress up in funny clothes and make a spectacle of yourself at funerals."

"I am Second Secretary in the Consular Section of the Embassy of the Republic of South Africa."

"You are a security police agent who has engaged in criminal activities."

"I demand the right to telephone my embassy . . ."

"Refused." The chief inspector grinned.

". . . in order that my embassy can verify my credentials."

"No chance."

He turned, and he walked out. He left the constable with Major Swart. He went into the adjoining interview room and collected off the table the plastic bags inside which were the items collected by the men arrested in Churchill Close.

He carried them back for the Major to see. He laid them on the table in front of him. There was a letter in an opened envelope. There was a booklet offering South African holidays. There was a pamphlet entitled *Blasting Practice – Nobel's Explosive Co. Ltd*, and another *Blasting Explosives and Accessories – Nobel's Explosive Co. Ltd*. There was a sales brochure issued by Explosives and Chemical Products Ltd of Alfreton in Derbyshire.

He saw the South African's eyes hovering over the display.

He played a hunch. He thought he had kept the best until the last. From behind his back he produced a see-through plastic bag in which was a framed photograph. It was the photograph of a young man. He held it under the South African's nose.

"Shit."

Major Hannes Swart made the two links. He linked the photograph with the photo–fit picture sent from Johannesburg. He linked the photograph with the young man who had met Jacob Thiroko.

"Shit . . ."

Jack Curwen was the bomber in Johannesburg, and Jack Curwen was the one whom he'd seen talking to Jacob Thiroko. Explanations hammering into place.

The detective inspector watched him keenly. "I demand the right to contact my embassy."

"Crash job, is it, time of the essence?"

"I have the right to telephone my embassy."

"To tell them what your muckers found?"

"It is my right to make a telephone call."

"So it can all go on the encoder and hum back home?"

"I can establish my identity. You have no right to hold me."

"Major Swart, this isn't parking a C.D. car on a double yellow outside Harrods."

Major Swart stared at the photograph of Jack Curwen. He no longer listened to the detective inspector. His eyes flickered on, up to the table, up to the opened envelope and the spider writing that addressed the envelope to Mrs Hilda Perry. He was a trained policeman, excellent on faces. He remembered the photograph of James Carew. He looked at the face of Jack Curwen, the son.

"Shit . . ."

"I *demand* the right to make a telephone call."

"They all say that, every piss-arsed, common thief, they all want to telephone their embassies . . ."

"I claim diplomatic immunity."

"I must be getting hard of hearing in my old age."

Major Swart smiled. He thought it was his winning smile. He chuckled. He beamed up at Detective Inspector Cooper. There was a fractional wink.

"Heh, man, we're all policemen together. I'm security police, you're Special Branch. Same job, same problems. Both fighting the same enemy. We're on the same side, man. We have to help each other. If you had a problem in the North of Ireland and we could help, of course we'd help. Just a telephone call, man. What do you say?"

"I'd say you are a common burglar, and I'd say you are pissing in the wind, Major Swart."

The detective inspector told the constable to take Major Swart to the cells.

Down a white tiled corridor. A locked door ahead. The echo of the feet and the clanging of the keys.

As if a calmness had come to the major now that he was freed from the sarcasm and goading of his interrogator.

The door ahead was unlocked. They went through. The door was locked behind him.

Closed in by the walls to the corridor, and by the bright ceiling lights, Major Swart understood.

The cell door was open, waiting for him. Folded blankets on the bed, and a bucket and a roll of lavatory paper on the floor beside it.

The door slammed behind him. He sagged onto the bed. He understood.

He understood why he was refused normal diplomatic facilities, why immunity was denied him, why a telephone was kept from him, why a senior Special Branch officer had been brought late at night from London to this shit pit town. He had grasped the importance of James Carew. He understood that James Carew was their man . . .

He ran the three steps to the door. He was beating with his fists at the steel facing, bruising his hands, bellowing his anger.

"I know who your bloody Carew is. Heh, got it, I know. He's your bloody undercover man. I know he is. I demand a telephone. I demand access to my embassy . . ."

His words rang around his head, beat at his ears.

He knew that no bastard heard him.

It was a bleak little room. There were posters of the smiling leader on the walls and boxes of pamphlets piled on the bare floorboards.

The Prime Minister's speech to the constituency workers had failed because, before it was delivered, the message had come through that the Director General was arriving for discussion on a matter of the utmost urgency.

"They're incommunicado at the moment?"

"Yes, Prime Minister. But Major Hannes Swart, an accredited diplomat, can, if he is released as diplomatic procedures require, furnish the security police authorities with information that in my opinion could lead them to judge that Jack Curwen will attack the Maximum Security section of Pretoria Central prison. If those authorities were to receive such information it would, in my judgement, considerably improve their chances of arresting or killing Curwen."

There was a gleam of mischief in the Prime Minister's eye.

"When would Curwen move?"

"Tonight, perhaps tomorrow night. I doubt he'd leave it until darkness on Wednesday, too fine."

"Does he stand any chance?"

"Let me sidetrack . . . Recently a man called Jacob Thiroko visited London. He was a principal officer in the military wing of the African National Congress. The Special Branch officer controlling the business at Leatherhead has given us the basis of a connection between Curwen and Thiroko, albeit a fragile one. Last week Thiroko flew back to Lusaka, and immediately set off with a small team back across the South African border. He was ambushed and killed, with all the members of his group, in the northern Transvaal. I suggest Thiroko would only have ventured into his country to lead a major operation. A major operation could be interpreted as an attack on the Maximum Security gaol where four members of an A.N.C. cadre are held and who will be hanged on Thursday with Carew. Now Thiroko's dead. Very possibly young Curwen now stands alone."

"No chance?"

"In my opinion, no. Perhaps I exaggerate . . ."

"Tell me."

"A few years ago three men broke out of the White Political prison. That's about a quarter of a mile from where Carew is due to hang. In the annals of escapology it was pretty remarkable. Every time they saw a key on a warder's chain they memorised it, and when they were in the workshops they used those memories to make a key. Their collection opened just about every door in this very secure compound. At night they used to let themselves out of

210

their cells, with their keys, so that they could try every route that was available to them, but each time they came up against high walls that were floodlit, overlooked by watch towers. They decided the only way out was through the front gate, and that's the way they went . . . If you'd asked me, knowing what they planned to do, what were their chances, I'd have said one in two million."

"If he were to succeed, if he were to bring his father home, I would face the collapse of this government's foreign policy in relation to South Africa. Our position of persuasion towards reform would become meaningless."

"Pragmatic politics demand that they fail, Prime Minister, and die silent."

"Emotion requires that they succeed, Director General . . . It is only for his father?"

The Director General said, "I doubt that a month ago he'd ever given South Africa ten minutes' thought."

The Prime Minister said, "I hope he succeeds . . . Hold them at Leatherhead, to give the boy his chance."

"And after he's had his chance we have to face the music."

"The man at Leatherhead, we'll shrug it off."

The Director General left by a back exit, picking his way between the garbage bags.

It was past midnight. Ros and Jan still not back.

Jack worked methodically.

He was on the floor of the living room of the service flat.

Ros had rented it, using Jack's money, paid over the odds in deposit and said she'd be back to sign the papers the next day.

He had the tube on the floor. From a sheet of light aluminium he had cut a triangular shape that he had bent into a cone, a squat witch's hat. With pliers he had fastened steel wire at intervals along the cone and then secured the wire with heavy adhesive tape. George Hawkins had told him that the speed of the detonation would be 6,000 metres per second. The wire and the sticky tape would hold and do their job for the mini-fraction of time before the aluminium cone fused in white heat to become the boring projectile travelling ahead of the explosive force.

He placed the cone into the metal tube, the open end leading, pushing it gently forward till his arm was lost in the tube. Cautiously he took the slabs of explosive and worked them, putty-like, down the long length of the tube, squeezing them with his finger tips first into the angle between the cone and the tube's sides, and then back to the central point of the cone . . . He knew that explosive without a firing agent was harmless, but it took some faith to believe it . . . The explosive was packed round the cone. He had used three and a half pounds. Working on with care, not hurrying, because the Hawkins method was care and never hurry. He packed a further eight and a half pounds of explosive, weighed meticulously, into the tube and behind the point of the cone. George had been very specific. The packing must be even, and firm.

Jack worked long and hard at the packing, sweat sheening his forehead.

George's lessons kept flickering into his head: three and three quarter pounds of explosive will punch 31 inches into sandstone with an entry hole a maximum of 12 inches wide. He had a tube that was nine inches in diameter. He had twelve pounds of explosive to use. Nine inches of diameter and twelve pounds of explosive were the only facts that mattered a damm to him.

And he had no primer, no priming charge.

George had talked to him of six ounces of priming charge to lie between the detonator and the Polar Ammon Gelignite for the high velocity trigger into the explosive. He didn't have a priming charge. Forget the bloody priming charge.

He had three detonators.

He taped two together. With his finger he worked a slim hole into the packed explosive in the tube. The two taped detonators into the slim hole, the beginning of the arming of the shaped charge bomb. With a sharp knife from the kitchen he cut a yard off the length of Cordtex equivalent. Very slowly, maximum care, he had eased the Cordtex equivalent into the protruding socket of one of the detonators. Making it live, powerful enough to explode him through the walls of the flat, to devastate that corner of the block. With pliers he crimped the socket of the detonator to the Cordtex equivalent. Had to be two detonators because he had no priming charge.

He made a sludge of readymix concrete. He kneaded it against the explosive and around the detonators and around the length of Cordtex equivalent. Set concrete to make the block at one end of the tube to drive the explosive force forward, undiluted, against the cone at the other end of the tube.

Later he would tie a length of safety fuse to the Cordtex, knot it and bind it.

Jack had completed the shaped charge when they came back.

When they came through the door he was assembling the last of his explosive in a three pound charge linked by his last detonator to Cordtex equivalent and safety fuse.

All clear in his mind. Where he would use the shaped charge and where the smaller explosive charge, and where the Cordtex equivalent on the grilles because George had told him that Cordtex would blow away the grille bolts, slice them.

He was on his knees on the carpet when they came back, and writing on a torn scrap of paper. He had written "rope" and "bent metal".

"We took a car," Ros said.

Jan said, "She didn't know it was so easy, to open a car up and drive it away."

The two stared down at Jack's handiwork.

A breathlessness in Ros's voice. "Is it going to do the job?"

"If it doesn't I'll be giving hell to an old guy in England when I get back." Jack grinned.

"How so?"

Jack said, "This is the first time I've ever built anything like it."

212

"The first time?"

"But you're supposed to be . . ."

"It's the first time," Jack said.

Ros turned away. She was shaking her head, broad sweeps, and the red ribbon in her hair flowing. A crack in her voice. "And you haven't even thought how you'll get away in the car, where you'll go."

"My father'll know."

"I think it's pathetic."

"I don't have the time, Ros. It's way past midnight. I've only today, I don't have the time to go running around the getaway routes. And I'm bloody tired, and I don't need lecturing. If you want to give a lecture then bugger off out through the door first . . ."

"I'll make a cup of tea," she said.

Jan levered himself down onto the floor beside Jack. They studied the plan of Pretoria Central and Magazine Hill. Jan pointed to the place where the car would be waiting, shrugged away the distance between Pretoria Central and the car. Jack led Jan through the map points where the grenades would be thrown, where the pistol shots would be fired.

". . . And then you'll get the hell out. You have to give that promise. You do what you're going to do and you get clear. You don't stay about to see the show. You go home and you get into your beds, and you go to the university in the morning, and Ros goes to work. It never happened, you were never involved."

He saw the struggle working at the face of Jan van Niekerk.

Jack said, "I have to know that you're clear. That'll be a strength to me. You have to make me that promise."

He saw the way that the crippled boy's fingers stroked the heavy arms of the wire cutter. Light, delicate fingers. He thought the boy should never have been there.

Ros stood in the doorway. She held two mugs of tea.

"To give you strength, we promise."

"Never hesitate, turn your backs on me."

"I promise," Jan said.

Ros leaned forward with the mug of tea for Jack. Her eyes were misted. He thought she was at the limit.

"When are you going to sleep, Jack?"

He smiled. "I'll catnap when the old man's driving. Bloody old taxi driver can drive all night."

The smile swiped off his face.

"Oh, Christ . . ." Furious concentrated anger spreading over him.

"I missed a window," Jack hissed. The mug rocked in his hands. "I have the outer wall. I have the wall onto the exercise yard. I have the window onto the catwalk. I have the grille down into the cell . . . I've all of that accounted for . . . I don't have the window between the catwalk and the grille over the cell . . ."

"You're going to kill yourself," Ros said.

He didn't seem to have heard. He was ripping at the adhesive wrapping he had made around the three pound charge.

"What are you going to do?"

"Just hope that a pound and a half on each will do the two windows, and one without a detonator."

They left him. They couldn't help him. They left him on the floor with the sweet almond smell of gelignite. They would sleep together on the one bed, dressed and in each other's arms. They would hold each other to shut out the certainty of their fear.

He lay on his bed. He could not sleep. He stared up at the frail light patterned by the grille wires.

The trap had been tested during the afternoon, the trap falling under a weighted sack.

There was a cool wind, and the cold came into Jeez's cell through the window between his cell and the catwalk, and the window between the catwalk and the night. He heard the shuffle of the feet of the guard on the catwalk above and the guttering cough as the man cleared his throat. He heard the snore of the prison officer who was locked into the corridor of C section 2. He heard the dribbling of the singing, muffled because the sound swam along the catwalks all the way from A section or B section. Keeping a poor bastard company, because there was a poor bastard who was going to hang in four hours' time. Jeez wondered if anyone slept when they were going to hang in four hours' time. Jeez had another fifty hours of living, and he couldn't sleep either.

Tuesday already started. Wednesday tomorrow. Wednesday was library day. He'd hear the trap going on Wednesday, and the sack under the trap would be of his weight.

He could end it all.

Of course he could. He had it in his power to make an end of it.

He could shout for the officer sleeping in the corridor. The officer would send for the duty major. The duty major would ring through to the night duty officer at John Vorster Square. The night duty officer at John Vorster Square would rouse the colonel. He had the promise of the colonel for his life if he coughed the details on the cadres and the safe houses and the arms caches . . . Just one shout. Fucking cruel . . . Typical of the pigs that they offered the Judas Kiss as the price for living.

It had just been a job for him, watching over the African National Congress. Just an assignment from old Colonel Basil. Wasn't supposed to get involved, not physically and not with the heart. Just supposed to be bumming on the fringe, just supposed to be a listener, and a writer of reports. He'd hang with Happy and Charlie and Percy and Tom. Fucking cruel, that it was better to hang with them than to make the Judas Kiss, and live a life sentence in a Boer White gaol.

Jeez reckoned to find friends where he was. Didn't go looking for them, found them when he needed them. There'd been a guy in Spac, good guy, teacher, they'd been friends for six years. Close enough to pick the lice from each other's heads. A good guy and a good friend, and he'd died in the snow with a bullet hole in his nape. His best friend in Spac and Jeez had been on the detail that pickaxed the grave out of the iron-frozen ground. He wouldn't have given that friend the Judas Kiss, not just for life.

He would make new friends.

He would be friends with Happy and Charlie and Percy and Tom in the corridor, going towards the door that was always closed. He'd be their friend in the preparation room, and when they went through the doorway and into the shed. He'd be their friend when it was the hood and when it was the noose. He'd not give them the bloody Judas Kiss.

No way he would shout for the bastard sleeping in the corridor of C section 2.

He did not understand why the arm of Century hadn't reached for him.

Hurt, hurt hard, lying on his bed, gazing at the dull light bulb through the mesh of the grille, to think that Century had dropped him off the team. He had the proof that they had dropped him, the proof was the bloody cell he was locked into, and the hours that were left to him.

Couldn't think about it, because thinking of the team was fucking agony for Jeez. Think of some other bloody thing.

Think of why Hilda hadn't written.

Think of Hilda in a nice house with a nice husband with a nice life.

Think of the boy who was his and who was Hilda's.

Think of the boy who would be twenty-seven years old next birthday.

Think of the boy Jack.

Think of anything other than the trap hammering in practice on Wednesday afternoon, after library.

He couldn't picture, now, what the boy, his son, looked like.

First thing in the morning, first thing at his desk, the colonel called London. The London embassy told him that Major Swart was not yet in his office.

The colonel said that he would not be calling unless it was of great urgency. The London embassy told him that the major's home had already been contacted, that the major's wife had not seen him since the previous day.

The colonel said that it was an outrage that they had no contact with their man. The London embassy told the colonel that as soon as they had contact with Major Swart they would pass on the message for him to call John Vorster Square, priority.

As if a door slammed in the colonel's face. His investigation had been at a gallop. A name. An address overseas. A photo-fit likeness. Because the door had slammed, he did not know how to go forward. A piece of basic, beginner's school, detective work was all that was required from London, but Major Swart had gone walkabout and the door was slammed.

He went down the stairs to the incident room.

Expressionless, he reported that London had not yet been able to furnish the material necessary for short circuiting a lengthy investigation. He knew he had lost ground. He made a lame suggestion. He suggested that all the two and three star hotels in Johannesburg should be checked again.

"Is he standing firm, sir?"

The civil servant had brought the first briefing papers of the day. The Minister of Justice smiled.

"The State President? He's in great form. I was with him yesterday, firm as they come."

"No question of clemency?"

"I'm surprised you ask."

"Because of the overnight telegrams ... Washington, the Vatican, the Speaker of the European Parliament in Strasbourg, the Security Council, the Secretary General of the Commonwealth. They all came in overnight."

"A formality. But you have missed one."

"Those are all the cables, sir."

"What about the United Kingdom? No word from Her Britannic Majesty's ratbag."

"I noted that," the civil servant said. "No message has come from the United Kingdom."

The Minister of Justice clapped his hands. "Did you see the opinion poll from the Free State. We are going to win that by-election, because I was photographed at the grave of Gerhardt Prinsloo, and because the Pritchard Five will hang."

"But curious that the United Kingdom is silent."

Jack stood with Jan below the wide climbing steps leading to the rearing stone hulk of the Vortrekker Monument.

Jan spoke savagely of this edifice to Afrikaner power and mythology.

As if it were something evil, a national monument to privilege and superiority. He showed Jack, with an angry pointing finger, the carved relief of trekker wagons that formed a laager around the monument, and the great hewn corner statues of the Boer leaders with their rifles, and the bronze of the trekker woman and her children. Jack thought the boy's intensity was unreal, just a drug to give him courage. For himself, he didn't listen. He stood with his back to the monument and looked across the valley to the south side slopes of Magazine Hill.

There was a wire fence at the floor of the valley, at the bottom of the hill. The ground on the slope was rough, half cleared, cut by a stone vehicle track. To the right side, as he looked, of Magazine Hill, was the sweep of the Johannesburg motorway, the Ben Schoeman Highway, that would come round behind the hill on which the Voortrekker Monument had been built. To the left side of Magazine Hill was a separate fenced area, which his plans told him was the army's firing range. Directly ahead, the crown of Magazine Hill was covered with tall and heavy pine trees, rich green, and he could see buildings in the shelter of the trees.

He made his estimates.

He tried to judge the distance from the floor of the valley to the crown of Magazine Hill. He tried to see where he could lie up if he were ahead of schedule, over which ground he could hurry if he was late.

He thought it could not be more than two hundred yards from the crown down the hidden tree-covered slope to the walls of Beverly Hills.

He turned his back on Magazine Hill and walked to the far side of the Voortrekker Monument to see down below where the car would be left. It was a hell of a distance to come back. More than a mile. His own thought . . . that in the chaos after the attack he and Jeez would be better on the scrub hills on foot than immediately into a car, but a hell of a way for all that.

In the line between Magazine Hill and the Ben Schoeman Highway was another stony outcrop. He saw the summit of it had been shaped.

"What's that?"

"Skanskopfort. Built to protect Pretoria, historic monument, colonial cannons and that crap."

"Lived in?"

Jan shook his head. "It's just a museum, and an army store."

Jack walked again to the steps. He stood in the morning sunlight. He gazed again on the slope of Magazine Hill, the slope that he would climb that evening.

They went to Ros's car. Jan drove back to Pretoria.

In two heaps, Jack's possessions were laid out on the floor. In one heap was his suitcase and his coat. He had told Jan to dump them from Ros's car, once they were on the way back to Johannesburg. The other heap was what he would take with him that night. There was the metal tube, and the prepared Cordtex equivalent and safety fuse lengths, and the two charges for the windows, and the shotgun and the ammunition, and the wire cutters, and the rope and the bent metal hook that was lashed to it, all to be carried up Magazine Hill.

The bedroom door opened.

Ros had taken the ribbon from her hair. She had washed the make-up from her cheeks and her eyes and from her lips.

She was ice calm, pale, matter of fact.

"Lose yourself, Jan."

Jan looked at her, blinking, not understanding.

"Just get rid of yourself. Lose yourself."

"What for?"

"Because I tell you to."

"Where to?"

"Go and check the other car, make sure it isn't being watched, walk the streets, anywhere."

Ros came to Jan and took his arm and kissed him on the cheek and led him to the door. She opened the door and pushed him out through it.

She closed the door. She came to Jack. She reached for his hand. She might have been leading a child. She led him into the bedroom. He thought she might have been crying while he had been at the Voortrekker Monument and looking over Magazine Hill. She did not look into his face. She was clumsy with her fingers as she unbuttoned his shirt, slid it away across his shoulders to let it fall from his arms. She knelt in front of him and lifted away his shoes and peeled off his socks. She reached up to unfasten his belt and to ease down the zipper. She was kneeling as she pushed her light sweater up and over her head. Jack stood in his nakedness and watched her. He knew he loved her. He loved every part of her scrubbed clean body. She stood to step out of her skirt. She drove her pants down to below her knees. Jack reached for her, he felt the loveliness of her. She stepped back from him. A slow sad smile. She took his hand, she took him to the bed.

She broke. She pushed him hard down onto the bed. She came down onto him. She was sobbing her heart to him. She tore at the skin on his back with her nails. She hurt him as she bathed him in her tears. She was stretching apart over him, reaching for him, guiding him, driving onto him.

"You cruel bastard, Jack, for coming into my life . . . for going out of it."

18

She lay beside him, and her cheek rested on the centre of his chest.

She could feel the steady rhythm of his heart in her ear. She thought he was at peace. With her fingers, with her nails, she made shapes and patterns amongst the hairs of his chest. She formed the letters of his name, she wrote amongst the hairs of her love for him. The curtains in the room had been open when she had taken him to the bed. She could see that the skies were darkening now over Pretoria, and she could sense the thickening of the traffic on the streets below the window. She hated the coming of the evening. She felt a safety with this man as they lay against each other, damp warm and loving safety. There was a safety when his arm was around her, his hand over her breast. She knew that she could not hold him in the bed, she had seen the way that a few minutes before he had shifted his hand from her stomach to look down at the face of his watch before returning his hand to the place of pleasure and comfort. She knew that when the hour hand had trickled and the minute hand had rushed that he would leave her. She acknowledged that on this evening, on this last evening, that she played the role of second best. She accepted that she was secondary to the work of the evening that would start when he leaned across her, kissed her, pushed her back onto the pillow, and left her bed. She thought that she had helped him. Her friends had told her that the first time was awful. Ros van Niekerk, happy in her moist heat, safe with a man's hand over her breast and with his fingers over the flatness of her stomach, thought it was not at all awful. He hadn't used anything, she hadn't used anything. Not an act of gratification, not an occasion when adults who knew their minds discussed the merits of pills and coils, a time for soft urgent loving between two young people who would part when the hand of a watch had run its hour. She thought she did not care about the consequences of his not having used anything, of her not having used anything.

His hand moved.

She felt the aloneness of the skin on her stomach. She felt his fingers climbing the slow length of her body, and brushing the nipple of her breast. She opened her eyes. She saw that he looked at his watch. She hated the watch.

"How long?"

"Just a few minutes."

"I can't keep you?"

"You knew you couldn't."

"To have found something precious, and to lose it."

"Something wonderful to remember, Ros."

Jack kissed her, closed her eyes with his kisses. With his tongue he ran over the nostrils and the fresh lips of his girl. So calm. As if when he left her he would go for an evening walk, a stroll that was without danger.

She clung to him. Her arms were around his neck, her breasts were forced against the jutted strength of his jaw.

"Please, no hurting yourself, Ros."

She thought that if she cried she would weaken him. She thought that to weaken him was to further endanger him. And that was absurd because there could not be more danger than where he was going. She choked on the tears, she squeezed the wetness from her eyes.

"Trying."

"Great girl."

"How long?"

"Less than a few minutes."

"Will I ever see you again . . ." She faltered.

"Remember the brilliance, Ros, of being loved, and remember the brilliance that you gave me with your love."

He looked again at his watch. She felt him start to move. And, God, she didn't want him to go. And, God, she was without the power to stop his going. She rolled away from him. She lay on her back and the bed sheet hid her knees. She laid her arm over her eyes, so that she would not see the moment of his going from her bed, from her side.

"It was only for you, Jack."

"I know that."

"Because I love my country."

"That's my guilt, that I've made you fight what you love."

"My country, Jack, that's more than a rabble of politicians."

"Ros, my country's politicians, and the bastard desk men, they ditched my father and left him to hang. But I, too, can still love my country."

"And I love my brother. And I hate his cause, because his cause is bombs and guns. His way is killing and loathing and fear. His way takes us to ruin, destroys the country that I love, and will destroy the brother that I love . . . How long?"

He kissed her. As if they both knew it would be for the last time. He snapped off the bed. He went to his clothes, he started to dress. She lay in the darkness, her eyes under her arm. She heard the movement of his body. She could not let her eyes see him. She felt his hands on her head, lifting her head. She felt the cold of the chain on her neck, on the skin above her breasts. She opened her eyes. She saw the gold chain, she lifted the crucifix of gold to see it better.

"Wear it and remember."

"I won't forget you, Jack, not ever."

She watched him go out through the door.

She heard his desultory conversation with Jan in the living room. She heard him speak aloud as he went through his check list of the items he would carry up Magazine Hill, and down Magazine Hill, to the gaol.

She was numbed. Too unhappy, now, for tears. She swung her legs off the bed.

As she dressed she heard Jack talking to Jan. They had moved on to the list of street places at which the grenades would be thrown, where the pistol shots were to be fired. Her fingers played with the crucifix. She thought she would wear it for the rest of her life, for the ever of her life. She had promised that in the morning she would be at her office desk, and Jan had promised that he would be in the lecture theatre at Wits. At home, in the top drawer of her wardrobe, there was a yellow silk scarf. She thought that when she was again in her room, that night, when she was back with her parents and everything familiar, she would leave her curtains open and she would tie the yellow scarf to the handle of the window, and she would allow the light from beside her bed to be thrown against the yellow scarf and to be seen outside her window. It was important to her that the yellow scarf should be seen, should be her beacon to save him. Her fingers were tight on the edges of the crucifix.

When she was dressed she went into the living room.

Sitting on the floor with the street map of Pretoria spread out in front of him, Jan looked up at her. He was grinning, amused. She blushed.

"Bit bourgeois, Ros, handing out home comforts to the troops before the battle."

She ignored her brother. "Can I do anything, Jack?"

"Have you a nail file, metal?"

"Yes."

"Please, would you take the serial number off the shotgun."

"Aren't you going to take it with you, to the border?"

"Just in case I get separated from it," Jack said easily.

"You'll need it all the way to the border."

"Wouldn't want it to fall into the wrong hands, come back to you."

It was insane to be thinking about the border. Jack passed her up the shotgun, and he pointed to the serial number. She took it into the bedroom where she had left her handbag. She would remember him for ever, as she had seen him in her bed, because she would never see him again.

The assistant dropped Frikkie de Kok off home.

Pretty damned stupid when he thought about it, that he should have an armed escort every time he went to Pretoria Central and an armed escort back from Pretoria Central, but nothing when he took Hermione shopping nor when he took his boys to the Loftus Versfeld for rugby.

It had gone pretty well, a pretty damned good day's work.

The assistant had done him proud. Right from the start in the morning, right from the time his assistant had picked him up, he had told him to take his time, not to get himself rushed, just to go through the procedure the way he had seen Frikkie do it. It had been fine because it was only one man. The assistant had executed his first man. Not that he had *officially* executed the man, not that it went into the paperwork that he had done it, but the arrangement had been made with the governor. The governor could not really have put the spoke in, because the governor had to accept that if a man was booked for hanging on a Tuesday or a Thursday and Frikkie de Kok happened to have the influenza or he had ricked his back in the garden, then the man still had to go. Frikkie de Kok with influenza or a bad back shouldn't be a reason for a stay of execution. And the time came when an assistant had to prove himself, show that he could manage the work himself, and pretty damn well he'd done for a first time. Frikkie had been behind him, ready to lend a hand if he was needed, and he hadn't been. All right, his assistant had been a little clumsy when they brought the fellow into preparation, but who wouldn't have been, on his first time with the responsibility. A little aggressive with the pinions, a little rough moving the fellow onto the centre of the trap, a little hard when he had hooded him, a very little bit fierce when he had ringed the fellow's neck with the noose. Little things, not grounds for complaint. Little things to be pointed out over a beer. No trouble with the drop. The assistant had made his calculations to the inch and to the pound, just right the drop had been. Frikkie de Kok had shaken his assistant's hand while the rope still shivered, while a young creep on compulsory attendance was in the corner throwing up over his uniform . . . Just Frikkie de Kok's view, and privately held, but it wasn't right to have youngsters in the hanging gaol, not the youngsters who had joined the prison service as an alternative to conscription into the army and service in the "operational area". The hanging gaol should be for professionals, not for shirkers. Just his opinion.

Afterwards he and his assistant had stayed all day in Maximum Security, because Thursday was a multiple, five on the trap. Thursday took preparation. Six was the most he could do, but that was a hell of a business even with a good assistant. Two and three and four at a time were pretty much all right, but fives and sixes were hard on everyone present. When he was busy round the trap he never looked at the spectators. Too much on his mind with the pinions and the hoods and the feet being right and the noose, but he could hear them. He could hear his audience gasping, willing him to go faster. Stood to reason that fives and sixes couldn't be as fast as hanging one man alone. Frikkie de Kok, as he always said to his assistant, would never hurry. To hurry was the fastest way to a fiasco. So, they had stayed at the gaol all day, and they had made their preparations, and because he had a combined condemns weight of 325 kilos on the trap he had gone down underneath and checked each single bolt and screw of the trap. It paid to be careful in Frikkie de Kok's job. A good day's work, and after his tea his assistant was coming back to collect him, and there would be a good evening's entertainment at the Harlequins, a floodlit Cup match. He was thinking of his shower, and of getting out of his suit, as he pushed open his front garden gate. He was thinking of the match as he came up the path, and how the second team flank forward would cope, because he was replacing the injured first choice.

He opened his front door. He could see into the living room. His two boys, singlets and shorts, red cheeks and sweat, pumping iron on his living room carpet. So they shared the weights. Beautiful to Frikkie de Kok to see his boys working on the weights. And beautiful for him to hear that his Hermione was in the kitchen making his tea. Beautiful also to be going to the Harlequins for a match.

And beautiful to know that he had a quiet day to follow before his waking before dawn on Thursday.

He thought he could smell a meat pie from the kitchen, and he thought the Harlequins would beat Defence, and he thought he would make a hell of a fine job of dropping five on Thursday morning.

The colonel listened intently.

Sometimes it was a good line from London. That evening it was a poor line. He was listening on an open line to the brigadier who headed security police operations throughout Western Europe. Major Hannes Swart enjoyed a particular autonomy in London, but nominally he reported to the brigadier.

He had forgotten the funeral, slipped it from his mind. Aunt Annie was dead, buried, gone. He had forgotten the minister's rallying words and the repetitive threat of the Afrikaners' vengeance. He had forgotten them because they were meaningless, they were rhetoric when set against the real warfare of his own battlefield.

"They would have been carrying their IDs, so it cannot be a hospital situation. If they had been in any form of accident then we would have heard from the police or from a hospital. I have checked back over the instructions that were sent to Hannes yesterday morning. I have had a man go down to this Churchill Close address. Not easy, there is a police car parked outside the house. So, I have a problem. What sort of inquiry am I to make? Delicate, eh, you understand me? This afternoon I have been to the Foreign Office and I have reported that Hannes and his two colleagues are missing. Perhaps the man I meet is lying, perhaps he is in ignorance. He tells me that he has no knowledge of the whereabouts of these three members of our staff. I cannot ask him if they are in police custody, because he will ask me why I should suppose that. I'm at a halt."

The telephone purred in the colonel's ear. He thought the brigadier didn't give a shit for the John Vorster Square bomb. The bastard was swanning in Paris and London and Amsterdam and Bonn, the bastard was freeloading in Europe.

He rang through to the library. He requested all communications over the previous month from Major Swart of the London Embassy. He was told such records were classified. He said he knew they were classified. He was told that for access to classified communications he needed the countersignature of the head of library on the docket. He shouted into the telephone that he knew access to classified communications required the counter-signature of the head of library. He was told the head of library was at supper, had left the building, would be back in 40 minutes.

What a fucking way to run a fucking intelligence gathering operation.

He telephoned his wife. He told her he would not be home until late. He said he thought the funeral had gone well. She told him that the immersion heater had broken, the thermostat had failed, that there was no hot water in the house. He asked her what she wanted. Did she want South Africa sleeping safe, or did she want her husband as a plumber, for God's sake.

They moved all of their possessions to the corridor leading to the front door, their bags and the explosives and the firearms.

Each of them held a handkerchief underneath the kitchen tap and then set to work methodically to clean the rooms of finger prints. Jack took the bedroom, Jan the living room, and Ros did the kitchen. Not for the sake of Jack's prints, but for the brother's and the sister's.

When they had finished they carried the bags and the explosives and the firearms down the back fire escape to the car park, to Ros's Beetle, and to the car she and Jan had stolen.

Jeez sat on his bed.

Sergeant Oosthuizen had moved his chair from the end of the C section 2 corridor, by the locked doorway, to outside Jeez's cell. He allowed Jeez's door to be three, four inches open.

It was in direct contradiction of regulations. At this time in the evening, with the lights dimmed, Jeez should have been locked into his cell.

He was like a terrier with a rabbit, with conversation. If Jeez didn't respond to him then Sergeant Oosthuizen asked a question that demanded an answer. As though good Sergeant Oosthuizen had determined that a man who was to hang in less than a day and a half was best served by making conversation.

Jeez didn't know his mind, didn't know whether he wanted to hear the retirement plans over again, didn't know whether he was better with the silence and the worm of his own thoughts. A new worm crawling. The worm was money. Money in the bank. Earning interest, accumulating. He had the account number and Century had the account number. Who would tell Hilda the number? The guy who used to know him in accounts, old Threlfall, bloody long time retired. Worry worming as a cash register, and trying to hold the thread against Oosthuizen's battering. He understood why Sergeant Oosthuizen talked about his retirement and about his kids. It was all Oosthuizen could talk about that did not drive coaches through the already broken regulations. He couldn't talk about the State President's plans for reform, because Jeez wouldn't be there to see them. He couldn't talk about the unrest, because Jeez to him was a part of that unrest. He couldn't talk about Jeez, about Jeez being the centre of whispering interest through the gaol, because it was Tuesday night and Jeez was to hang at dawn on Thursday. Good Sergeant

Oosthuizen ploughed on from his exhausted retirement plans into the difficulties at his son's liquor store in Louis Trichardt.

The murmur sounds of singing.

Jeez heard them.

Not the great choir of that dawn when a single man had gone to his death, when the whole company of Blacks had sung the hymn to strengthen him as he walked the corridor to the shed of execution. A fist of voices only.

Oosthuizen heard the singing, and the slam of a door that cut into the singing, and he was off his chair and straightening his tunic and heaving his chair away from Jeez's door and back to the proper place beside the exit door from the corridor of C section 2.

Firm, bold singing. More of an anthem than a hymn.

"I'm sorry, Carew, believe me. I have to lock you up."

The singing was approaching. A few voices, along with the stamp of boots, and the shouts in Afrikaans for doors ahead to be opened.

"What's happening?"

"They're bringing the others down. The other four. They're going to double them up in two cells in here."

"Why?"

Sergeant Oosthuizen snorted. "You know I cannot tell you, man."

The door closed. Oosthuizen turned the key. The corridor door opened. Oosthuizen had keys only for the cells, not for the door leading into the main corridor of C section. Of course Sergeant Oosthuizen could not tell Jeez why the Pritchard Five were to be together. Of course the prison officer couldn't chattily explain that for the final few hours it was more convenient to have all five men in one wing, one section, where the disruption to prison life would be minimised. Not an ordinary hanging because the five men were from Umkonto we Sizwe. A hanging that raised the tension pitch in the gaol. Jeez knew another reason that of course good Sergeant Oosthuizen could not explain to him. Thursday morning, dawn on Thursday, and they wouldn't want to be bringing four men from B section and one man from C section, because they might not have their watches together, and one might walk too fast, and one might have to wait in preparation, and some might have to be scrambled down the corridors to the hanging shed. Get them all cosily together, separated from A section and B section, so that the rest of the gaol was less disturbed. Made sense to Jeez.

The door into the corridor of C section 2 was unlocked.

Jeez heard the singing.

"Rest in peace, Comrade Moloise . . ."

He heard the voices of Happy Zikala and Charlie Schoba and Percy Ngoye and Tom Mweshtu.

"Long live Comrade Mandela . . ."

Brilliant voices that were without fear.

"Long live the African National Congress . . ."

He shook his head. His chin was trembling. He felt the moisture welling in his eyes. He heard them all shout, together, Happy and Charlie and Percy and Tom.

"Heh, Comrade Jeez, heh, Comrade – *Amandla* . . . Hear us Comrade Jeez, *Amandla*, Comrade Jeez . . ."

His voice was a quaver.

"Listen, you bastards. Don't you ever bloody listen to anything I bloody tell you? What did I tell you? Let's have a bit of dignity, lads, that's what I told you bastards, way back."

He heard the shrieks of their laughter. He heard the orders of the duty major. He heard the driving shut of two cell doors. He heard the duty major demanding they should settle down for the night.

He heard the closing of the door into C section's main corridor.

They were still singing. Jeez thought his friends had found him. He called for Sergeant Oosthuizen. He saw the bulk of the man at the grille aperture on his cell door. He thought of the way they had laughed when he had called for a bit of dignity.

"Doesn't it frighten you, Sergeant Oosthuizen, that they aren't afraid?"

Jack parked the stolen car a hundred yards from the turning onto the Ben Schoeman Highway.

He switched off the lights. Eyes closed, he sagged back in his seat.

It was the inevitable moment he had come for.

He felt an awful tiredness through his body. He heard Ros bring her Beetle to a stop behind him. He stepped out of his car. It was a Renault, he thought it had a decent engine and could make some speed, he had filled the tank and had checked the oil himself.

He walked to the Beetle. Jan was in the back, half buried with equipment and the bags. He settled in beside Ros. Stretching above them was the slope to the fort that Jan had said was called Skanskopfort. Ros drove away. She reversed sharply, swung and went back to the Ben Schoeman. She took them to the far side of Skanskop, to the road at the bottom of the valley between Skanskop and Magazine. She drove off the road and onto a stone chip track, and jolted them as she braked.

Jack was out fast.

Jan passed him the cumbersome shape of the metal tube that he had been cradling in his lap because the shaped charge was armed, then the bag that held the smaller charges and the lengths of Cordtex equivalent and safety fuse and the rope. He laid them on the stones, then took the shotgun that was loaded to capacity, and the opened box of cartridges that he stuffed into his anorak pocket. Last came the heavy wire cutters. Difficult in the dark, because Ros had cut the lights as soon as they had left the Ben Schoeman. He studied the luminous face of his watch. He called the time. The time was 9 o'clock and 32 minutes and 30 seconds, and he counted through to 9.32 and 45 seconds. Three watches synchronised. He had given himself one hour, less three minutes, before the decoying diversions. He slung the bag over his shoulder. He hooked the metal tube into the angle of his elbow, more than forty pounds weight of it, he pushed the wire cutters into his pocket with the shotgun ammunition. He reached his hand into the darkness of the back of the car, he felt Jan's two fists grip his hand. Next he leaned across the front passenger seat and his fingers found Ros's chin and drew it forward so that he could kiss her mouth. Brief, an instant.

"I'll wear it always."

"My mother gave it me. If she knew you she'd like you to have it."

He stepped back. He picked up the shotgun. He pushed the passenger door shut with the toe of his jogging shoe. He didn't know what was in her face, couldn't see her face.

The engine exploded to life, the wheels bit into the loose stones. The car pulled away. She did not turn on her lights until she was back at the main road.

Jack laid down the metal tube and the shotgun and took a handful of earth in his cupped hands and spat on it to make the soil moist and then smeared what was mud over the pale surfaces of his face. He looked into the distance, away to the main road. He saw a single set of headlights and then the red flash of tail lights, between trees and bushes. He lifted the metal tube and the shotgun, one under each arm, and he started to walk away from the track and towards the start of the slope up Magazine Hill.

There was a sharp wind, small clouds, a half moon.

Enough light for him to move without lumbering into the thicker scrub bushes. He had thought when he had seen the slope in daylight that the ground had been cleared a dozen years or so before, then allowed to grow again.

He made himself a pattern.

He climbed for a counted fifteen paces, then stopped to listen for ten seconds. When he stopped he could hear a radio playing music, ahead of him, where the prison service buildings were on top of Magazine. The stream of traffic on the Ben Schoeman was below him and away to the west, a ribbon of fast moving lights. As he climbed the sounds of the main road guttered, and he was alert to the new sounds of the hillside.

The radio playing music, the frantic wing clatter of a disturbed nesting bird, and a drum beat on planks. It took Jack the full ten seconds of a listening pause to identify the drum beat . . . He remembered that when he had stood with Jan at the Voortrekker Monument and looked across at the slope of Magazine that he had seen a low wooden watchtower half way up the hill, away to the east of where he climbed. The tower had not been manned in daylight. He realised he had heard the sounds of booted feet stamping on a plank platform, perhaps for warmth, perhaps out of boredom. He couldn't see the tower, not high enough for it to be silhouetted against the grey blue faint light of the night sky. He could sense the general direction of the tower and he could picture what he had seen from the Voortrekker Monument. He knew that the tower was set the far side of the wire fence that he had identified when he had stood with Jan on reconnaissance. He wondered if the bastard who stamped his feet on the plank platform would have a night sight on his rifle. Sod all use having the bastard there if he didn't have a night sight, because if he didn't have one then the bastard was as blind as Jack. Had to reckon that he had a night sight on his rifle, or infra-red binoculars, or an image intensifier spy glass. The reckoning pushed Jack down on his knees, had him crawling forward. The slope was a dark and indistinct mass above him. He could only see the trees and scrub bushes that were within three, four yards of his face, less when the clouds hid the moon.

The fence seemed to rush at him, to materialise above him when he was on the point of collision.

Very gently he laid down the metal tube and the shotgun.

He wriggled the bag on its strap over into the small of his back so that it would not impede him. His fingers groped forward. So bloody insensitive, his fingers, because they were cold and bruised from when he had crawled on his hands and knees. His fingers stretched to feel the pattern of the wire mesh. A dark mesh fence against dark ground, and his fingers must do the work for him, and he must lie still and move only the barest minimum in case the bastard on the platform had a night sight or an infra-red or an image intensifier. His fingers traced the diamonds of the wire mesh.

He found the strand that he feared.

His forefinger brushed the single strand that ran along the face of the fence a foot above the ground. He touched the first tumbler wire. If the wire were disturbed an alarm would ring. He noted it, stored it, his fingers moved on and traced the mesh above the tumbler, desperately slow. He dared not look at the luminous hands of his watch, dared not see how much of his precious time he was spending in the search for a second tumbler wire.

God, if he was late . . .

Bloody stupid, Jack. Had the time he needed. Didn't know whether he had the patience he needed. Jack bloody Curwen, second class businessman from the south of England, paid a second class wage to drum up second class work. What the hell was he at lying on Magazine Hill searching for a second tumbler wire?

He found the second tumbler wire.

The second tumbler wire was four feet above the ground, four feet above where the mesh was buried in the rough soil. With the wire cutters he made a square hole between the bottom tumbler wire and the second tumbler wire. He lifted the square mesh clear. He could feel the heave of his breath. He could hear the radio playing and the stamp of the sentry on his platform. He lifted the metal tube through the hole, and then the shotgun and then his bag. He was half way through the hole, head and shoulders and chest through, when a strand of jagged cut mesh caught at his anorak. His knees were on one side of the wire, his elbows on the other. He squirmed his trunk to reach with his fingers to free himself.

When he was through he lay on his stomach.

He was gasping.

He took his handkerchief from his pocket and looped it through the mesh immediately above the hole.

It was a risk, but everything was a risk. It was necessary to leave a marker.

Jack gathered up his metal tube and his bag and his shotgun and the wire cutters. So tired. He crawled forward. He was on his knees and using the hand that held the shotgun for leverage. He dared not let the metal tube buffet the ground. The metal tube was twelve pounds of explosive and two detonators and Cordtex equivalent, the metal tube was a primed bomb, held close against his chest. He was going forward.

He saw the light on his hands. His head started up.

The light from the gable end of a concrete building was thrown from his right, fell on him. He had crawled forward, concentration locked, nursing the shotgun and the tube, and he had not realised that he had reached the summit of the slope of Magazine Hill. He moved fast to his left, shuffling as a crab to reach shadow. He could hear the music clearly, he could hear voices and laughter. He lay on his stomach and he heard the sounds of men who had no care, no suspicion.

Shadow was his security. He stayed with the shadows as he moved away across the top plateau of the hill, towards a line of trees. He crossed paths, he ducked past buildings. He froze against a wall when a uniformed man came belching out of a doorway to urinate on the edge of a lawn.

High trees coated the skyline ahead of him, and above the trees was an umbrella of hazed white light.

The tube was an agony on the muscles of his left arm. His feet were leaden heavy, but the white light above the trees was a talisman for him, pulling him forward. He came into the trees. Going slowly, because under the conifers' canopy he could see only the white knuckles of his fingers that were tight on the stock of the shotgun.

He broke from the trees.

His path was crossed by a tarmac road. He could see darkened buildings and more trees ahead of him, and the light above the trees were fiercer. He looked right and he looked left. He stood still and he listened. He heard dogs barking. He ran across the road and sagged against the back fence of a garden. He thought, from his map, that he had reached the line of senior officers' homes that were set on the hillside above Beverly Hills. The moon helped him. He saw a narrow track leading between two garden fences, not wide enough for a vehicle. There was another road crossing the far end of the track and he could see street lights. Ahead of him was a great cascade of light, fit to blind him.

He felt the energy surging through him. He was going forward.

A voice . . . A man talking as to a child. A voice and footsteps . . . A caressing voice as if to quieten a child. Down flat, squeezing his face, side down, into the dirt of the track. He was in darkness, short of the light thrown from the road ahead. He saw a dog handler with a German Shepherd. The dog handler was cooing soft nonsense to his animal. Jack saw that the dog handler had an automatic rifle resting on the elbow of his right arm. He heard the voice drift away. He waited thirty seconds before he slowly rose to his feet and went on down the track to where the darkness merged with the light. He laid down his tube and his bag and his shotgun. He crawled forward.

He saw the high concrete wall in front of him.

He saw the sentry tower rising above the wall, and above the sentry tower was the bank of floodlights. He could see low tilted roofs beyond the high concrete wall. He was separated from the wall by a narrow paved road and by a strip of lawn.

Jack Curwen had come a hell of a long way.

He gazed at the outer wall of Beverly Hills, the outer wall of the hanging gaol. If he had shouted then, his father would have heard him. He looked down at the luminous hands of his watch. He had six minutes before the diversion. The wall was brilliantly lit in the wash of light from the close set bulbs ahead of him. The sentry in the tower had his back to him. Jack could see the hunch of his shoulders.

He went back for his metal tube and his bag and his shotgun. He crouched down. He was shaking. He had to will himself to control his fingers. He checked the safety fuse length that was knotted to the Cordtex equivalent. He checked that the Cordtex equivalent was firm where it disappeared into the readymix block in the metal tube. He opened his bag and ran his fingers, stuttering, over the charge that contained the detonator and over the charge that did not. He felt for the lengths of loose Cordtex equivalent and of safety fuse. He found the rope that was lashed to the cold bent iron. He eased the safety catch off the shotgun, he had eight cartridges in the magazine. He emptied the remaining cartridges from the carton into his pocket. He touched the smooth weight of the wire cutters.

It was all a matter of belief . . . and arrogance.

The wall that he faced was of no use to him. The wall fronted onto B section and onto the hanging shed. He had to be against the wall that fell away down the hillside to his right, down towards the glitter lights of Pretoria.

Arrogance and now courage.

He rose to his feet.

There was a softness in his knees, there was a wetness in his belly, because he must now walk in the light along the paved road, in front of the homes of the senior officers, under the watch tower, walk for a hundred yards to the corner of the wall.

Cheek, too, because he must walk as though he belonged.

He looked at his watch. He had a minute and a half. He had the metal tube under his arm, and the bag on his back. He cocked the shot gun. He must walk. No running, no stopping.

He came off the track.

He ducked his head as the light found him, so that the smear marks of

230

mud on his forehead and cheeks could not be seen from the watchtower. In the middle of the road he walked at a steady pace. He waited for the rasp of a weapon being cocked. He waited for the challenging shout. He walked towards the corner of the wall, along the road and towards the bend where it followed the side wall down the hill.

There was a yapping chorus.

There was a white bundle flying through the open gates from a large garden. There was a Pekingese dog circling his ankles. He saw the garden shielded an elegant bungalow. A large elderly woman in a housecoat and bedroom slippers was in pursuit of the dog.

Jack's heart hammered.

The woman saw a young man who carried a long circular length of metal and a bag and a firearm. She lived in the heart of the Pretoria Central complex, she was the wife of the major general who was Deputy Commissioner of Prisons (security). Her bosom lurched forward as she bent to catch the collar of the darting beast. She yanked it off the ground.

The woman spoke to Jack in Afrikaans, and he smiled and nodded and she chastised the dog and Jack nodded again and the dog yapped at him and earned itself a volley of reproach and Jack took one step away and then two and then the woman was lecturing the beast in earnest and making for her garden and Jack was away free.

The sentry in the watchtower saw the wife of the deputy commissioner talking at her front gate to a man. The sentry knew the dog. It was rumoured that ferret dog had killed the Siamese cat of the daughter of the Assistant Commissioner of Prisons (personnel). He thought the man must have had business at the Deputy Commissioner's house, come there before he had come on duty forty minutes earlier. He thought the dog must have chased the man down the drive. He thought it was a pity the old cow had come out so fast, a pity the man didn't have a chance to put his boot firmly into the ferret dog's arse.

He walked on. He felt the nakedness of his back. The wall rose beside him. The lights showed him thin, knife-edge cracks in the wall between the faced brickwork. Thiroko had told him that Beverly Hills was built on a rubbish tip. Heart hammering. He wondered if that helped him, helped his twelve pounds of explosive, the tip. Wailing siren, very faint. No. Must be singing. So bloody frightened.

There was for Jeez a sort of warmth in the singing. Listening to the singing he had put off his undressing and changing into his coarse cotton pyjamas. He knew that once they had started they would not finish. They would sing until the rope strangled the breath out of their throats. And a warmth, too, from the wheezed bronchitic breathing of old Oosthuizen. He wondered what the other two Whites in C section 2 thought about sharing their block with Black terrorist Commies, what they thought about Jeez being amongst friends.

He was at the corner. He was at the furthest point from the sentry tower, and when he was round the corner he would be at the furthest point from the remote camera on the wall above the airlock entrance . . .

Ros drove fast down from the motorway and onto Potgieterstraat. Jan had his window down, and the grenades and the pistols in his lap.

He heard the men singing, a murmur in the night as with leaves in a gentle wind . . .

The colonel swayed back in his chair. The words, telex typed, bounced at him from the page. James Carew had written to Mrs Hilda Perry. Mrs Hilda Perry lived at Churchill Close, Leatherhead, Surrey. Jack Curwen lived at Churchill Close, Leatherhead, Surrey. He swept open the drawer of his desk. He needed the telephone directory of the Department of Prisons.

He glanced at his watch. He was on the countdown. He started to mouth away the final seconds . . .

Jan ripped the lever of the first R.G.–42 high explosive grenade, tossed it through the window. The Beetle was coming slowly now past the wall of Local, at the junction with Soetdoringstraat. His finger was in the loop of the lever of the next grenade as they approached the gates of S.A.D.F. headquarters.

He could see the camera rotating patiently towards him. He was fifty yards from the corner behind him, seventy-five yards from the camera ahead.

Jack twisted, ducked towards the wall. He heard the crack thump of the first grenade.

God, I love you, little bastard kids.

. . . The tube down on the ground, a foot from the wall, paying out the Cordtex equivalent and the length of safety fuse, looking for the camera and the camera moving at steady, inexorable pace towards him, about to include him in the vision arc. The second grenade explosion, the metal box thump of

232

the grenade going. He looked again for the camera. He saw the camera swinging away from him, aiming for the main approach road that came from the direction of the grenade blasts. Struggling in his pocket for the lighter, and his fingers floundering with the car keys. The third grenade explosion . . .

Brilliant bloody kids, because you've pulled the camera off.

. . . Pistol shots in the night, soft fire crackers half a mile away. The lighter in his hand. The flame cupped. The flame held round the cut edge of the safety fuse. Jack ran back. He flung himself down onto the hard road. He pressed his face down onto the road surface. A moment of desperate stillness.

He felt the blast bludgeon over him. He felt the pain roaring in his ears. He felt the fine draught of the debris hurtling back past him.

He crawled on his knees and elbows into the grey dust cloud. He groped until he found the hole. His hands were in the hole and scraping to find the reinforcing steel cords. Coughing dust, spitting fragments. Cutters from his pocket. Finding the steel cords, fastening the cutters on them, heaving with his hands at the arms of the cutters, squeezing the arms of the cutters until there was the snap and the tension break. He was in the hole, choking, hacking. His shoulders were in the hole. If his shoulders were in then the hole was large enough. He wanted to scream, he wanted to shout that he had won. He was crawling through the hole and pulling his bag and lifting his shotgun. He wanted to shout because he thought that he had won something.

He came through. He crawled into a lit garden. Ahead of him was another wall, and the ground between him and the other wall was lit as by sunlight. He saw to his right the white flood brightness high on the stanchion poles.

He was charging forward.

It was 22 seconds after the exploding of the shaped charge. He fired six shots from the pump action to blow away the lights. Not darkness, there were the distant lights above the watch tower on the back wall, but shadows thrown by trees and shrubs and bushes that were the gardens around the hanging gaol.

A charge now. Only speed mattered. He saw ahead the pointed roofs of C section 1, and C section 2, and C section 3. The gaps between the roofs were the exercise yards, covered by the grilles.

He ran towards the gap that marked the exercise yard of C section 2, and his fingers were in his bag, reaching for the rope that was lashed to the length of bent iron.

19

He could hear nothing.

His ears were dulled by the explosion at the outer wall.

In silent ballet a deer that was no taller than his knee cavorted away from him. He saw between shadows the noiseless flight of a young warthog.

The piece of bent iron was in his hands, and the rope. It was his grappling hook and his climbing rope.

Jack came to the wall.

He arched the bent iron over the wall. He lost sight of its fall. He heard the first sound that infiltrated his senses. He heard the scrape of the bent iron on the metalwork of the grille above the exercise yard. New sounds now flooding his ears as he pulled on the rope, tested the strain. There was the sound of a siren, rising as if it were cranking itself awake. There was a shout. He heaved on the rope. He slid back as the bent iron slipped, fastened again, slipped again, held. Once more he tugged at the rope, using desperate strength. The rope and the hook were steady. The iron was lodged as a hook into the grille. He tucked the shotgun, barrel up, under the shoulder strap, weighed in by the bag hanging across his stomach and his thighs, and he started to climb. His feet stamped on the wall as he dragged himself upwards.

It was fifty-two seconds of time since the shaped charge had detonated against and through the outer wall. A life time of Jack's experience. All about speed, all about confusion, all about men staying rooted in their positions for precious seconds, all about officers who made decisions seconds after being asleep in their homes or dozing in the armchairs of their mess. Speed from Jack, confusion from the prison staff, his certain purpose, their being taken by surprise, on these his chance depended.

He tried to walk up, throw his body back from the wall. The way the marines or the paratroopers did it. But the marines and the paratroopers weren't carrying a shotgun, and the marines and the paratroopers had proper combat packs and not a grip bag on a shoulder strap. And the marines and the paratroopers wouldn't be alone. Jack climbed the wall. His ears now were filled with the howl of the sirens.

He reached the top.

He was a darkened figure that swung first an arm and then a leg and then a shoulder and then a torso over the top of the wall, nursing his weight off the shotgun. He rolled from the top of the wall to crash onto the grille above the exercise yard. There was a moment when he was dazed, when he saw below him the dull colours of flowers in a small square of earth under the grille. If he let himself stop for more than a split second he was dead. He pushed himself away from the wall, out over the grille, the shotgun free in his hands, pressing back the safety catch.

He saw the spit of flame from the window to his right, from the window that gave air onto the catwalk above the corridor of C section 2. He was rolling, swivelling his hips to turn himself, to keep the momentum from his fall. Because he was rolling, moving, the rifle shot had missed him, and the second shot missed him. Sharp, granite chips of sound against the blanket wail of the siren. He aimed the shotgun at the window. There had been a pale face visible between the slats of the window. The pale face was scarlet, peppered, gone. A scream of pain, of fear, to merge with the siren.

Jack crouched.

Left hand in his bag. The charge with the detonator in his fingers. The moment when he had to stop. The moment when he had to put down the shotgun on the grille. He had the charge in his hand and the roll of adhesive tape. Fast movements as he pulled himself onto the sloping roof above the cell block, as he reached for the window in front of him, the window that led to the catwalk. The window was a set of vertical bars, four inches apart, concrete, with louvred glass slats. He slapped the charge against the central bar. His fingers were stripping adhesive tape from the roll. He was kicking with his feet to hold a grip on the metal of the sloping roof. He had the charge in place, he had the adhesive tape back in his bag, when he saw the man who lay on the catwalk and moaned and who held his hands across his face. He dropped the length of Cordtex equivalent and safety fuse back down the slope of the roof. He let his grip go, his feet slide, came to rest on the grille. The lighter was in his hand. He guarded the flame against the safety fuse. He ducked, reached for the shotgun, plucked out of his pocket more cartridges, reloaded.

The blast sang in his head. The explosion blotted out the siren sound, and the shouting, and the first rumble of booted feet on the catwalk.

Jack scrambled up the roof. A gaping hole for him to pitch himself through, left arm first with the shotgun, left elbow through, left shoulder, and his forehead caught against a shard of glass and was slashed. No stopping. He tumbled onto the catwalk and his fall was softened by the cringing body of the guard.

He stood.

He opened his lungs.

He shouted.

"Jeez."

He heard his voice boom back at him from the confines of the catwalk, from the short corridor below him, from through the cell windows around him that were flush into the catwalk.

"Jeez. Where are you?"

It was one minute and twenty-four seconds of time since the hollow charge had detonated.

He heard a gravel voice. He heard the reply.

"I'm here."

A babble of voices springing from the personal radios, concentrating around the controller in his glass-fronted booth beside the airlock main entrance.

"It's not in B section . . ."

"A section's fine. What's with B section and C section?"

". . . over."

"I repeat, nothing in B section."

"Is this a fire practice, Johan?"

"Are we to stay or are we to move . . . ?"

"If you have nothing to report for Christ sake keep . . ."

"Who's giving orders . . . ?"

". . . several shots, rifle fire, I think, sounded like A section."

"Was that a bang on the outer wall . . . ?"

"What has happened to the lights . . . ?"

"Duty Officer, do you hear me?"

"Has the military been telephoned . . . ?" Chaos sweeping the ears of the controller.

The guard in the sentry box thought of the man he had seen with the gun and the length of circular metal, the man who had been talking with the wife of the deputy commissioner. He felt the crimson of panic, that he would be blamed, surging up from his gut.

There were five prison staff locked into the main C section corridor. None of them had a weapon, they were in contact with prisoners. They cowered on their haunches in the corridor.

Locked into C section 2's corridor, Sergeant Oosthuizen shouted into the wall telephone, but he could find no one to listen . . .

Jack blew the window out that looked down onto the cell. The charge without the detonator, gone a cream cake. Back on his feet. The cell below him was a dust box, a grey cloud haze, and the ceiling light had been smashed. He peered down, trying to probe the dust and darkness to see the man. Time running, and time that was his life and Jeez's life. He fell through the window gap. He bounced on the mesh over the cell. He had Cordtex equivalent and safety fuse in his hand. Six feet of Cordtex equivalent and twelve feet of safety fuse. He laid the length of Cordtex equivalent against the angle of the mesh and the vertical wall. It was above the bed.

"Under the bed or the table," Jack shouted.

He jumped for the smashed window. His hands ripped on cut glass and torn metal and broken concrete. He saw the uniformed man beneath him, beneath the catwalk, pleading with the telephone. Hadn't time for the bastard. He lit the safety fuse. Christ only knew what it would be like underneath.

Sirens invading the long seconds, cut off by the blast.

He saw that a length of mesh had been torn from the wall. He saw the plaster battered away from the concrete.

"Get yourself onto the mesh, Jeez. Hurry."

He saw the man. He saw a small hunched figure crawl out from under the bed. The man's face was pale grey from the plaster dust. The man was dazed. Slow motion movements. Jack was back on the catwalk, reaching for the shotgun. Booted feet hammering, running on the catwalk close to him. He knew the catwalk was the causeway that covered the whole gaol. No locked doors on the catwalk, the briefing papers said. He heard the wheeze of the man's breath, he saw the white head of short hair at the hole where the window had been. He saw the face of the man, wide-eyed, staring at him. Jack grabbed the collar of the man's tunic, he pulled him over the glass edges and the torn metal and the broken concrete.

It was one minute and fifty-eight seconds of time since the charge had detonated.

Jack had hold of the man's tunic. Not stopping to look at him. He heard the voices welling through the windows onto the catwalk.

"*Amandla*, Jeez . . ."

"Fly on the wind, Jeez . . ."

"Tell them about us, Jeez, that we were singing. . .

The man who was loose in Jack's grip stiffened. The lines cut and broke the grey dust on his face and forehead. Jack tugged at him, couldn't move him. The man broke Jack's grip.

Jack watched the man who was his father, who was Jeez.

Jeez picked up the rifle of the guard lying on the catwalk. He poked the barrel down through the grille of the catwalk.

"Oosthuizen, drop that telephone. Unlock those doors, unlock my door. You have five seconds, Oosthuizen . . ."

He fired once into the floor below him.

"Four seconds, Oosthuizen, or you're dead. You don't get to retire . . . Three . . . Don't play heroes, Oosthuizen . . . Two . . . I don't give a shit about shooting you . . . One."

Jack couldn't see. He heard the rattle of the keys. He heard a door opening, another door opening.

"Clever, Oosthuizen, that's being clever . . ." He fired once more and the telephone flew from the wall socket.

The catwalk crowded as the four Blacks came up in fast succession.

Jack saw a shadow figure materialise at the corner where the catwalk over C section 2 joined with the catwalk over the main C section corridor. He fired. He pumped the shotgun, fired, pumped again, fired again. Shrill shouts of surprise. Should have been gone, on their way, and still on the catwalk.

237

It was two minutes and thirty-five seconds of time. Jeez and four Blacks crouched by the blown window, the route to the sloping roof. Jack motioned them gone. They helped each other, and Jack last, through the narrow window. Children on a fairground slide they tumbled down the roof. Into the night air. Out into the embrace of the unforgiving, perpetual siren. As they scrambled across the grille above the exercise yard, Jack turned and aimed a shot at the window. Keep them back, keep their heads below the window.

The controller bellowed his frustration. "I don't care what colonel you are. I don't care about John Vorster Square. I have a break-out here, man, so clear the line."

He slashed down the telephone. He depressed his microphone switch. He could be heard by every prison officer with a personal radio.

"This is control. The armoury is now unlocked. All unarmed personnel are to go straight to the armoury. Armed officers on B section and A section are to remain at their posts. All further orders will come from the duty major on Alpha frequency of transmission. The point of entry is believed to be the east perimeter wall. Captain van Rooyen orders all personnel to the central hallway as soon as weapons have been drawn. I repeat, further orders will come direct from the duty major."

The controller was a senior sergeant. He looked up. The duty major was panting, red-faced and sweating. The duty major had run all the way from administration to the radio control to take charge, he weighed eighteen stones.

The controller said quietly, "C section, that's where the terrorists are."

The duty major struggled for his voice. "Have the police been informed?"

"More than one minute ago, sir."

"Get the internal phone into C section 2."

Sergeant Oosthuizen sat on his backside and his spine rested against the inside of the locked corridor door. The telephone, dead, was in his lap. In front of him, gaping, laughing at him, were the opened doors of three cells.

They went down the rope.

Jack led.

His shotgun was in his right hand. His left hand clung to the sleeve of Jeez's tunic. The Blacks ran alongside them. He led them through the gloom of the gardens. He was not aware of distance, just that the great wall was ahead. Still the siren filling the night, and then the first sporadic shots down from C section's upper windows. Searching for the bastard hole. Couldn't see it. He thought the shots were random, aimed haphazardly into the gloom light. With their impetus Jeez and the Blacks were bouncing against Jack as he slowed, as he searched for the gap. He went to his right, went fifteen strides, and they were running again with him. No bloody hole, he stopped, he cursed. Fighting for breath. Again the bodies smacked against him. He turned, he went left and back over the same fifteen strides. There was a jabber of voices in his ear. Couldn't the bastards see that he was trying to find the hole? They trampled through a bush. He tripped on the debris. He saw the hole, close to the grass.

God, had he ever made it through that hole? In hell's name, how had he ever made it through? So bloody small.

Two of the Blacks went first, eel-like, then Jack. Jack wriggled through the hole. He loosened his hold on Jeez for the first time since they had come down the sloping roof. His hand was back and into the hole to take Jeez and work him through.

There was a spatter of bullets. Jack saw the dirt kick close to his legs, close to where the two Blacks sheltered against the wall . . . The sentry in the high tower, and the lights above the sentry's platform. He wrenched Jeez clear. He heard the man cry in pain, he heard the ripping of the man's shirt where it had caught on a cut edge of steel cord. Jeez was through, Jeez and his rifle.

"Take the lights out," Jeez hissed.

Jack ran forward. He must stand if he were to see the lights. He fired three times. With the shotgun it was like knocking skittles away in an alley. First time, some out. Second time, more out. Third time, most out. Most of the light gone.

They ran in a tight group towards the corner of the wall.

They were outside the walls of Beverly Hills. Ahead of them were the street lights and the road through the senior officers' quarters. When they were on the road they would be in the clear field of fire from the sentry in the tower.

They came to the corner.

"Where are we going?"

"Across the road, up that track."

Jeez said, "The rifle'll keep his head down. They're not soldiers, won't take it when it's coming back at them. How many shots?"

"He fired twice at me, you fired once."

"Three left, they carry six." Jeez was fluently taking control. "Happy – Charlie – Percy – Tom – when I fire at the tower, run like shit."

Jeez gestured at the track opening that Jack had pointed to.

Jeez had the rifle to his shoulder. He edged round the corner of the wall. There was the crack of a shot. The Blacks ran. They ran bent low, weaving over the tarmac, sprinting for the darkness of the track. Jeez fired a second shot. Jack ran, he thought Jeez was immediately behind him. Jack was in the middle of the road going like smoke. The sledgehammer hit him. The darkness at the track's mouth was yawning for him. He felt the crow-bar smash into him. He never heard the shot. No pain. Just the staggering blow of the sledgehammer, the crow-bar.

It was three minutes and forty-nine seconds of time.

Jack felt the hard road against his face, his chest, no breath left, and a fist snatched at his arm and held him up, dragged him across the road towards the track.

"I hit one. Definitely a hit."

The message squawked into the headphones clamped down on the major's bald head.

"Identify your position."

"South sentry tower."

"How many of them?"

"Can't be sure, sir, two for certain. Armed. Shot out the tower lights before they ran for it."

"Going in what direction?"

"Going south onto Magasyn Kopje."

"Out . . ."

For the first time a glimmer of a smile. He had hard information.

He was reaching for the microphone that would link him to every personal radio inside Maximum Security when he heard the door click open behind him. He turned, he saw the governor standing in the centre of the room, his arms folded across his chest. The governor wore his dinner jacket, well cut, and above the folded arms was a line of miniature medals topped by vivid coloured ribbon. The governor gestured with his hand, a small movement, for the duty major to carry on with his broadcast.

He gave out the information. He issued his orders. A much rehearsed plan involving prison staff and police and military had slipped into place. He switched off the microphone.

The Governor pursed his lips, there was a frown of surprise cutting deep in his forehead.

"I think I heard you correctly, that one man alone came in and took five out."

The duty major nodded.

"Extraordinary, I would not have conceived it as possible."

"The blocks will be in place within a few minutes." The duty major spoke with pride.

"Perhaps in time, perhaps not . . ." The governor seemed to speak to himself, left the duty major as an eavesdropper. ". . . If they are not all back with us in time to face the penalty of the law on Thursday morning then the scandal of one man's achievement will destroy me."

The duty major swung away and snatched for the telephone that would connect him to Defence Headquarters. He did not wish to look again at his governor, to witness the fall of a fine man.

"You have to tell me what's ahead."

240

They were crowded together on the track. Jeez was bent over Jack. The sledgehammer blow was to Jack's right knee. Jeez could see the blood. Not much blood. Blood on either side of the trouser leg, as if the bullet had pierced his knee, gone straight through.

"There's just buildings ahead, then you go down the hill, and there's a fence, that's all, after that you're out under the Voortrekker Monument and the Skanskopfort."

Jeez put up his hand, cut Jack off. He turned to the others.

"You heard him, get bloody going. Move your arses."

He pushed the one who was nearest to him away. Each one crouched, slapped Jeez's shoulder, gripped his arm. An ecstatic farewell and the last one said: "God go with you, Jeez, and you too, friend. We'll fight together again." And was gone. There was the patter of their feet. They were shadows and then they were nothing.

"Go with them," Jack said.

Jeez stood and hoisted Jack up. He slung Jack's arm over his shoulder. He was on Jack's right side. They stumbled together up the track.

"I said, 'Go with them.' "

Jeez's fist was tight into Jack's anorak, under his armpit. Jack doubted he could have torn the fist free. They made the best speed that was possible for them. His leg was numb, useless.

The pain came later. Into the ripped hole, into the wrecked ligaments, into the broken cartilage, into the splintered bone. The pain was in water surges, damned and then rushing in intensity. Flash floods of pain in Jack's whole leg as they went forward, up the hillside and through the trees. Skirting the buildings and holding to the black holes where the lights did not reach. Silence around them. No cordon. No dogs. Only the sirens pulsing behind them. Together, Jeez supporting Jack, they started down the hill, down the south slope of Magazine. They couldn't crawl because Jack's wound would not have permitted him to crawl. Jeez walked, Jack, leaning on his shoulder, hopped beside him. In the pure darkness they went down Magazine.

Jeez said, "Where are the wheels?"

"Far side of Skanskopfort."

He heard the whistle of surprise.

"What I was trying for . . ."

"Save your strength."

Jack found the hole that he had cut in the fence. He found his handkerchief. They slithered through. Jack, in his life, had never known such agony as when Jeez worked him through the wire and over the lower tumbler strand. He thought they should have been going faster, he knew he was incapable of greater speed. They crossed the road at the bottom of the valley between Magazine and Skanskop, and they climbed again. They climbed over the stone hard earth and the broken rock, and through the matted thorn scrub.

Against the clean night sky were the ordered plateau lines of the old fort's ramparts.

They looked down.

Jack gazed down the south face of the Skanskop slope to the road and the place where he had parked the Renault. The triumph was bolted in his gut, the words were blocked in his throat. He could see the Renault. The Renault was illuminated by the lights of a jeep. There were many lights, many jeeps and transport lorries for moving troops. The lights of the vehicles shone on to the hillside where it fell to the road. He heard the rising drone of engines to his right, and to his left, and away behind him. His eyes squeezed shut.

The voice grated in his ear.

"You bastards took your time, and now you've blown it."

"It was the best . . ."

Jeez snapped. "Bloody awful best, and after I've been sitting there thirteen fucking months. Bastards."

"Who are the bastards?"

"Your crowd."

"What's my crowd?"

Teeth bared, "The team."

"What team?"

"Where's the back-up?"

"There's just me, me alone." Still leaning on Jeez's shoulder.

"Where's Colonel Basil?"

"Never heard of him."

"Lennie, Adrian, Henry."

"Don't know them."

"Who sent you?"

"I sent myself."

Jeez looked up at him, searched his face. Didn't understand, couldn't split the mist.

"So who are you?"

"I'm Jack."

"And who the hell's Jack, when he's at home?"

"He's your son."

Jack hung on his father's neck. Jeez buried his face in his son's shoulder. And around them, far beneath them, was the tightening circle of lights.

They had come off the motorway, they were close to their parents' home.

After Jan had thrown the grenades at Local, and the S.A.A.F. recruiting office, and the creeper-covered fence of S.A.D.F. H.Q., and after he had fired a whole magazine of pistol shots at the sentry box at the bottom of Potgieter-straat, Ros had taken a circular route to Johannesburg. Not a word was spoken. Ros's knuckles were white on the wheel all the way. Their nerves were stretched like wire. They expected every moment the flail of the siren in pursuit, the road block in their path. The number plates were mud-smeared. She did not think that the sentries would have noted her number plate, they'd have been lying in the dirt and shielding their heads from the shrapnel and the pistol bullets. She had driven fifty kilometres out of her way, across to the east before doubling back through Bapsfontein and Kempton Park and Edenvale. She hadn't been followed, there had been no road blocks. They had heard one explosion. Jan had said it was the main charge going against the wall, and then they had finished with their diversion, and he had wound up the passenger window. They had heard nothing more.

Now the radio was on in the car.

The midnight news bulletin. A bland English accent.

". . . English service of the S.A.B.C. Good evening. In the last ten minutes police headquarters in Pretoria has announced that the area to the south of the capital between Verwoerdburg and Valhalla has been declared an emergency military zone. All persons travelling through that area until further notice are subject to S.A.D.F. and police control. Residents in the area are advised to stay in their homes throughout the hours of darkness . . ."

"They made it," Jan squealed. "They're running."

". . . Late this evening it was reported that explosions and firing were heard in the area of the S.A.D.F. headquarters on Potgieterstraat in the capital, but as yet there is no official police confirmation of these reports."

"In London a demonstration by an estimated two thousand people outside the South African embassy was broken up by police after violence . . ."

Jan switched off the radio.

"It didn't say he made it," Ros said bleakly. "It just said he was being hunted."

"Wrong, not a military zone unless he's taken his father out."

She drove on. She held the wheel lightly with one hand. The fingers of her other hand played listlessly with the shape of the crucifix at her neck. She wanted only to be home. She wanted to tie the yellow scarf in the window of her bedroom.

"Did you love him, Ros?"

She turned the car into the driveway of her parents' home. She parked beside her father's BMW.

"You're best to go straight to bed, Jan, or you'll be sleeping right through your classes in the morning."

All Pretoria had heard the gunfire and the explosions. Frikkie de Kok had heard them.

Pretoria is a valley city. The gunfire and the explosions on the southern hills were cradled above the community by the northern slopes. Distant gunfire and muffled explosions, and the city was an armed camp and the sounds were insufficient to disturb the celebration between himself and his assistant. Right that they should take some beers in the Harlequins bar after the assistant had performed well at dawn. A celebration for the two of them in the corner by the window going on long after the field floodlights had been switched off, away from the talk at the bar.

When it came to be time to go home, the bar closed, the hangman did not know whether the gunfire and explosions were part of an army night exercise or the result of a terrorist attack.

At his front gate he waved his assistant goodnight. He came up the path. The porch light showed him that Hermione had been weeding in the evening after he had gone to the match. A fine woman, the rock of a fine family. He let himself inside, moved quietly into the darkened hall.

He could hear Hermione snoring softly. Down the corridor he could see the edge of light under his boys' bedroom door. He thought they would be interested to know the score of the match, and how the Springbok who played for Defence had performed. Fine boys, with a fine future. Boys such as his would survive whatever. He pushed gently at the door. The flicker of a frown played at his forehead. Erasmus was curled in his bed, asleep and facing the wall and avoiding the light that was between the beds. Dawie's bed was empty, the coverlet not pulled back. He was annoyed. Dawie had been working so hard, and there was talk of a university scholarship, and all the school exams were important, and the boy should have been in his bed. He would tell Dawie of his displeasure, perhaps he was too soft on the boy.

He went into the living room.

He saw the white sheets of paper on his desk. He went to them. He picked them up, and recognised the papers that had come that morning from the school, the entry forms for university application. The envelope was beside the papers. The boy was normally so tidy. His leg brushed against an obstruction. He glanced down and made out the black leather, wide-built attache case with which he went to work. The lock catch of the black leather case was unfastened. He cursed himself for his own carelessness in leaving the bag unlocked. He was as careless as his Dawie – heh, that was rich – father and son as careless as each other. The smile extinguished. So fast developing, the picture in his mind. His Dawie skimming through the university entrance form, and his Dawie seeing the bag that had never been opened in his presence, and his Dawie succumbing to curiosity, and his Dawie feeling for the lock and finding it unfastened, and his Dawie opening the case that carried the tools of the hangman's trade.

Chilled, Frikkie de Kok stood for a moment motionless. He lifted back the flap of the black case. The ropes were coiled neatly in see-through cellophane bags. To count them he did not have to lift them out. New ropes, drawn from the prison store that day, signed for that afternoon. He loved his boy, and he did not know how his boy would react on finding that his father was the executioner in Pretoria Central.

There were four ropes. When he had brought his case home there had been five ropes. The ropes he would use at first light on Thursday. Only, because he loved his Dawie, Frikkie de Kok had never summoned the courage to tell his boy what work he did for the state . . .

He thought that he knew where to look.

Frikkie de Kok went to the window. He stared out onto his back garden. The ceiling lights of the living room threw shadows across the lawn. The

244

lights groped as far as the old pear tree from which the autumn frosts had stripped the leaves.

Cold, shivering now, the hangman saw the slowly revolving shape.

The colonel stood beside the stolen Renault car. Above him the bleak outline of the hillside. With him was an army brigadier. Between the palms of his hand the colonel held a warming beaker of coffee. Technically the military had been called in to aid the civil power, in practice they had taken control, and the colonel was outranked and deferential, and damned tired because he'd not slept, and he had left his office at a quarter past two in the morning for the drive to Pretoria. He had no place in the cordon line. He could not have stayed away, could not have borne it in John Vorster Square with only the telephone and the telex machine to feed him the news.

The brigadier munched at a sandwich.

". . . I tell you this, we were pretty poor getting the act into place. The operations room had us under sustained attack at Defence Headquarters, so we lost critical minutes. I'll kick someone's arse for that. It's why we've only got two of them up there for definite, but those two are bottled, and anyway there's a blood trail so they're not going anywhere."

"Which ones, which two?"

"A sentry on Magasyn had an image intensifier on them when they came off the hill. Can't be sure, not through that thing, but he reckons they are both White. There was only one man came into Maximum Security and he was White"

"So the other is Carew." The colonel heaved his relief. "What'll you do?"

"It's what they're going to do. If one of them's hurt he'll need the medics. When they're cold enough and hungry enough and hurt enough, they have to come down. They've nowhere to go."

"I'd like them alive."

The brigadier smiled sardonically. "So you can put them back inside, hang them?"

"It's no help to me to have them dead."

"They have a rifle and they have an automatic shotgun, and I'm not having my men shot up by desperate men who are going to end on the rope anyway. If they shoot first, they're dead. If they don't shoot, they'll live. It's pretty simple."

"Would you allow me to broadcast that to them?"

The brigadier snapped his fingers, brought his adjutant hurrying. He asked for a loudhailer.

"You can tell them that if they don't shoot first they will not be harmed." The brigadier's voice dropped, "Then they'll be able to meet the hangman on another morning."

The colonel drank from his beaker and stared again up at the silent hillside. Around him were quiet voices, the occasional clatter of weapons being checked.

There was the low throb of turning engines. The crackle of brief radio messages. If there were only two on the hillside then he knew those two were James Carew and his son.

The loudhailer was handed to him.

The dawn was coming.

The blast of the message had slipped away, dispersed amongst the surrounding hills.

A mauve streak in the east.

They had talked through the night. They had met as strangers, and during the dark hours, in faintest starlight, they had lurched through understanding towards friendship. Jeez sat with his arms gathered round his knees as if to find warmth for himself against the cold on the Skanskop. Near to freezing on the hillside and he wore only his prison tunic and cotton trousers and his thin prison shoes. Jack lay prone beside him, sometimes twisted by the agony in his leg, sometimes able to rest in relief between the spasms of pain.

They were together, it was as if they had never been apart.

They talked of Hilda Perry and her life with Sam and the house in Churchill Close, and Jeez seemed pleased at what he heard. They talked of Jack's job and Jeez chuckled at the stories of the blaster George Hawkins. They talked of the Foreign Office and of the man called Jimmy Sandham, and Jeez spat into the dew damp earth. They talked of a girl called Ros van Niekerk and of her brother with a club foot, and Jeez heard his son through. When the pain came to Jack then Jeez held his hand. When the pain spurted then Jeez's fingers clenched over his son's fist.

They could see the lights of the vehicles around the base of the Skanskop, a mesmerising cage of lights. When they were not talking they could hear the idling engines of the trucks and jeeps.

"You won't be afraid?"

Jack shook his head. Enough light seeping onto the hilltop for Jeez to see his son's face. Through the night he had talked to his son and he had not known his son's face. Jack gazed at the face of his father. A thin pinched face, stubble on the chin, short back and sides where there was hair to cut. Jack thought he saw a love in his father's face.

"Not having been a talking man, Jack, not any of my life, it's hard for me, to say what I want to say to you . . . To say thank you, that's not enough. Just crap to say thank you. I'll tell it better if I say what you've given me . . ."

Jack watched his father's head, clearer against the sky.

"It won't be by them, that's rich to me. It'll be in our time, not at the time they'd open my cell up, the time they've decided. Because it'll be us, by ourselves, who decide the time, that's bloody fantastic to me. Free hands and free arms and free legs. No pinions on my ankles, no hood over my face, that's wonderful for me. Yesterday I couldn't have imagined how wonderful. You understand me, Jack?"

"I understand you, Jeez."

"You're the son that I made with your mother, you're the son that I bloody failed, and you came here to take me out when none of the other bastards were coming. You've given me the thing I wanted most."

Almost a shyness on Jeez's face. "Where I've been you don't get to see the morning coming, and you don't feel the wind on your face. I wanted most to see the morning coming, the sun rise, and feel the wind. And I don't have to be counting. Got that?"

"Got it."

"In that place you may be counting in months, weeks, days, I was down to counting hours. I'd got to counting meals. Day before yesterday I was counting how many socks I'd be needing. Day before yesterday they gave me a new uniform, but it wasn't new, oldest they'd got, look at it. You mess your clothes when you're hanged, Jack, so they give you an old uniform before they drop you off. You got me out of the counting. You got me to see a morning coming. You got me to feel the fresh wind on my face."

He was between the pain. He was lying back. He was aware of the light building in the sky.

Jack said, "Everyone I spoke to, they all said it was impossible."

A dry smile from Jeez. "Probably was."

"The car was wrong."

"Just as wrong as when I said we had to stop and take the boys. We had to bring them, Jack."

"You don't get a choice. You had to take the boys, just as I had to come for you."

"They *might just* make it. Us going so slow might have drawn the flak off them. You know what, if they do make it, you *might just* get to have a street named after you in some real African shit-heap up in 'saka or Dar."

"I don't blame you for anything, Jeez."

"You're not afraid?"

"It's like I'm happy."

"You screwed them proper."

"Cheated them."

"It's the best morning of my life, the cleanest air. Thank you."

"For nothing, Jeez."

"So let's get this fucking show on the road."

"They don't take us."

"No way they take us."

"It'll be what they wanted in London."

"They'll be breaking open crates in Century, swilling champagne."

Jack said, "There must be some people who know, who'll want to tell the truth."

Jeez said, "They'll promote them. Promotion and the honours list, they're good silencers."

"I wanted to walk you down Whitehall. I wanted to take you into the Foreign Office. I wanted to see those bastards' faces."

"The bastards don't get to lose that often, not there, not here."

Jeez stood. For a long time he looked away to the clipped, half rising sun. He breathed in. He dragged the morning air into his lungs. He wondered how long it would be before the dandelion weed showed again in the garden of the exercise yard of C section 2. He clapped his hands. Jeez took off his tunic shirt and started to rip strips from it. He made five strips. He came behind Jack and put his hands under Jack's armpits and lifted him up. With the strips from his tunic, Jeez bound Jack's right leg. He knotted the strips tight.

Jeez checked the shotgun. He checked the rifle.

"You heard their message, what they want of us."

"They don't take us, Jeez."

"We're close as family, boy."

They stumbled forward to the edge of the hill. The pain swam again through Jack. Behind them were the walls of the old Skanskopfort, and the light of morning, and a gathering wind. It would be a short pain, the pain would not last. They were stiff with cold. It took them a few strides to find the rhythm. He wondered whether he could live with the pain from his stiffening, ruptured leg. He looked into Jeez's face, saw the chin jutting bloody-minded defiance. He saw his father's face, the face he had grown to know in a dawn haze.

They came to the edge.

Jack clung to Jeez's shoulder, supporting himself, trying not to shake, trying to hold back the agony tremors. Jeez had the rifle to his shoulder, aimed. Jack saw a jeep far below, a bristle of aerials. He saw the pygmy figures evacuating the jeep. He could hear the faint alarum calls. One shot, one bullet left. He understood the controlled pleasure at Jeez's mouth. Hitting back, after thirteen months. Aiming on the jeep, finger squeezing over the trigger, the report of the shot, the kick in Jeez's shoulder.

Jeez whipped the rifle down, gave it to Jack as a support, as a stick. Jeez took the shotgun. They came down the slope. They were juddering forward, faster. Jack's arm tight across Jeez's shoulders. They were one, father and son.

Down the slope, and the pain gone from Jack's knee. Just the echo cracks of the shotgun and Jeez's laughter. Laughter pealing at the sun and the clean cold of the wind, and the blast of the shotgun. Jeez firing from the hip at the vehicles that seemed to soar to meet them, and all the time his laughter. No pain for Jack, only the laughter and the shotgun blasting. He didn't hear the shouted order of the brigadier. He didn't see the barrel of a Vickers machine gun waver and then lock on their path. He didn't know that the colonel of security police howled his frustration in the ear of the brigadier and was ignored.

He only knew his own happiness and his father's freedom and the hammer whip of the shotgun.

They were wrong, all those who said it was impossible.

They were wrong because Jack had come for his father, and had taken him out.

At Close Quarters

to Gillian, Nicholas and James

*The song "Wish Me Luck (As You Wave Me Goodbye)"
by Phil Park and Harry Parr-Davies is from the
Twentieth-Century Fox film "Shipyard Sally"
and is reprinted here by kind permission
of Chappell Music Ltd.*

1

He turned sharply. He disliked to be touched. He shook the sallow hand from his sleeve. Around him the reception was warming. He was, for a moment, alone. Alone except for the man whose hand had tugged at his jacket for attention.

Seconds ago he had been disposing of a small but tiresome problem with his Australian counterpart, minutes earlier he had been deep in conversation with his French colleague. He heard around him English and French and Spanish and Arabic, and European Russian. His glass was empty; the Australian had left in search of a waiter. His host, the host of all of them gathered in the gold and white, tapestry hung, chandelier lit salon, was stationed beside the high double doors for the entry of the General Secretary. The tides of many languages flooded his mind, and the hand rested once more on his sleeve.

The Australian was lost in the throng. Cossé–Brissac had insinuated his way close to the door, no doubt to be among the first to shake the General Secretary's hand. His private secretary was out of reach and engrossed with an angular blonde from the Finnish contingent. He lifted the hand from his sleeve and dropped it as if he were in the street and the hand were the wrapping of a sticky sweet that had attached itself to his jacket.

The man was short, dumpy at the waistline. He thought the man's suit certainly cost more than all of those in his own wardrobe. The man wore a vivid orange silk tie, knotted wide in contrast to his own slim knot that carried the faded emblem of the All England Lawn Tennis and Croquet Club. The man seemed scented by a cocktail of lotions, and his thick dark hair was heavily oiled.

"If I might have the privilege of a moment of Your Excellency's time . . ."

"I would be so grateful if you would kindly remove your hand," he said.

"Sir Sylvester Armitage?"

"I am."

"The Ambassador of England?"

"Of the United Kingdom," he corrected.

For a fleeting second the Foreign Minister himself caught his gaze over the shined head of this creature, but then the Foreign Minister raised his two hands, fingers and thumbs extended, indicating another ten minutes before the General Secretary arrived, then turned his back. His sleeve was tugged.

"Please don't do that again," he said.

"I have the honour to be, Excellency, the Political Counsellor of the Embassy of the Syrian Arab Republic."

"Do you indeed?" Extraordinary that the Australian had not cornered the wine waiter by now. And he'd have a sharp word for his private secretary for leaving him exposed to the Syrian.

"It is difficult at this time for there to be effective contact between our two governments. You would agree, Excellency?"

He could clearly see an airliner in flight. He could see rows of passengers. He could see the cabin crew moving along the aisles of the huge airliner.

"It is intended to be difficult, otherwise my government would not have severed diplomatic relations with the Syrian Arab Republic."

The political counsellor had edged closer. In a rhythm his hands clasped and unclasped. There were two heavy gold rings on his right hand fingers, one on his left.

"There were misunderstandings, Excellency. Through a restoration of normal relations between our two governments such misunderstandings can be erased."

He could see a young woman passenger. He could see her nervousness. It was the first time she had made a long-distance air journey. He could see the bag that had been given to her by her fiancé, nestled between her legs and close to the brightly decorated shell of the aircraft. He could see the restless movement of the digital clock face of the pocket calculator resting at the base of the bag.

"My government does not accept that there were misunderstandings," he said.

The political counsellor's voice was a whisper. "My government can see no benefit to either of our countries by continuance of a situation of misunderstanding. Please to listen carefully to me, Excellency. I have the full authority of our Head of State to say . . ."

He saw a flash of light. He saw the rupturing of the outer wall of the aircraft. He saw the disintegration of the young woman, the passenger.

"How interesting."

The Syrian looked up, surprised, but he resumed, "Our Head of State wishes it to be known to the government in London that privately it is accepted in Damascus that junior functionaries in a division of the military planned and attempted to execute an attack on an El Al jet while en route between London and Tel Aviv. I am further instructed to inform you, Excellency, that our Head of State sincerely regrets the actions of these junior functionaries who have now been severely punished."

He saw the snow topping the steep peaks of the mountains of Austria. He saw the spiralling fall of the airliner down towards the nail bed of the rock crags.

"Have they really?"

He did not notice that the Australian ambassador stood a pace behind him holding two glasses of brandy. He did not register that his private secretary was at his shoulder.

"I can tell you that these junior functionaries have been purged from the armed forces. I am instructed to tell you that my country is totally and without equivocation opposed to international terrorism, and we are thankful that the attack on the airliner was thwarted in London. Without reservation we condemn such attacks. What we seek, Excellency, is the speedy restoration of diplomatic links and the ending of this most unfortunate period of misunderstanding."

He said, "I will of course pass on your remarks to London."

"I am most grateful, Excellency."

"For nothing."

"We look forward to the quick return of your ambassador to Damascus, and ours to London."

"My opinion, personally, is that we'll want deeds, not words."

A frown formed on the forehead of the political counsellor. "What deeds?"

"Off the top of my head . . . The expulsion from Syria of all terrorist groups, Abu Nidal and all the other abattoir gangs. An end to the financing of such groups . . ."

Colour lit the cheeks of the political counsellor's face. "We are innocent of all such involvement."

Because he was angered, because he was tired, because he wished to be among his friends, his voice rose. He sought to be rid of the creature.

"And you might just use your *influence* in Lebanon to win the freedom of the foreign national hostages."

"We are innocent of hostage-taking."

He was not aware of the turned heads, of the talk congealing around him.

"So innocent that evidence of Syrian involvement in terrorism just about keeps one of our computers turning full time. My dear sir, we have found your country's finger on the trigger, on the grenade pin, too often."

The political counsellor said, "I insist on our innocence."

He was not aware of the audience gathering about them. "Bloody nonsense."

"We deplore terrorism."

"*Bloody nonsense . . .*"

"I am instructed . . ."

"*Then your instructions are bloody nonsense.*"

Half the salon was hushed, following the sport. The Australian laughed out loud.

"Innocent."

"In a brothel, sir, you would not be believed. Senior officers in your armed forces planned, and did their damnedest to achieve, the destruction in mid-flight of a fully loaded civilian aircraft. You and your clan, you disgust me."

The laughter ran. The tittering amusement spread over the end of the salon.

The political counsellor seemed to rise on his toes.

"You insult my government."

He boomed, "The man's not born who could do that."

The political counsellor swung on his heel, thrust his way through the diplomats. The laughter would have been a tide in his ears. His back vanished.

The Australian handed the British ambassador the glass. "Bit strong, Sylvester, but you gave us a good laugh."

He looked keenly at his friend. "My elder daughter, Aggie, she's doing a year's voluntary work on a kibbutz in southern Israel. If those bastards had had their way she'd have been obliterated along with 300 others. She happened to be on that flight."

After two more drinks and a full minute's conversation with the General Secretary, he left the reception, down the steps to his waiting car. He shuddered. The dark depression of autumn was settling on Moscow.

2

Just before midnight the British Airways Boeing 737 touched down at Shere-
metyevo, modern and miserable and the gateway to Moscow.

An hour later, Customs and Immigration on high quality go-slow, young
Holt met his girl.

"Pretty damn late, young man."

"They had to hold the flight so I could say goodbye to my lady."

"Pig," Jane pouted.

And she came to him and grabbed him and hugged him and kissed him.

The Second Secretary stood back and looked at his watch and coughed and
shuffled, and wondered whether the Foreign and Commonwealth Office had
got itself into the business of love-broking, for crying out loud. He had to
cough twice more, and there was a ring of petal pink smudges around young
Holt's mouth.

"Fifteen pairs, right . . . Just the same as usual. Fifteen at Extra Large, *with*
gussets . . . Just as long as you don't forget . . . and give my love to
Hermione . . . Bye, darling, keep safe."

The ambassador put down the telephone, and looked up. God, and the boy
seemed young. Not tall and not short, but with an impact because of the set
of his shoulders and the sturdiness of his hips. The sort of boy who would
have captained the Fifteen at Marlborough, an adult's body and a youngster's
face. He had been in the room through the latter part of the ambassador's call
and had stood midway between the door and the desk as if on a parade
ground and at ease, relaxed and yet formal.

"So, you're young Holt. Welcome to Moscow, Mr Holt."

"Thank you, sir."

"None of that formality. I'm not 'sir'. We're a family here. I may be the
patriarch, but not a frightening one, I hope. What's your first name, Mr
Holt?"

"It's Peter, sir, but I'm generally just Holt."

"Then we have a bargain. I'll call you Holt, and you don't call me 'sir'.
Done?"

"Thank you, Ambassador."

"You're a stickler for etiquette, young man . . ." Did he not look young?
The smile was that of a teenager, bright and open. He liked his naturalness.
He reckoned a man who could smile well was an honest man. ". . . What do
you think of the job they've given you?"

"It seemed to me that private secretary to the ambassador was about the best first posting that a Soviet specialist could expect."

"I was where you were three weeks before the Cuban missile crisis broke. I loved every day of my year here and I hope you will . . . No, I wasn't talking in code on the phone. My wife's had to go back to London, mother not well, and she may be stuck there for a couple of weeks. We have a tradition of always bringing back some presents for our staff, the Soviet staff. Money doesn't matter to them, so we try to get them merchandise that's hard to come by here. You won't have seen the ladies who clean our apartment, cook for us, but they're all former Olympic shot putters, so it's Marks & Spencer's tights that keep the cobwebs out of the corners and the pots scoured. We're a small compact unit here. We all have to pull our weight. It is as interesting and fascinating a posting for me as it is for you, but it's only by damned hard work that we stay afloat. There are no passengers in this embassy. Now I have to move on to the facts of life for you in the Soviet Union. Everything you have been told in London about the hazards of illicit contacts with the local population is true. We call it the honey trap. If the KGB can compromise you, then they will. If you don't believe me then go and talk to the Marines, the American Marines, at their embassy, they'll tell you how sticky a honey trap can be. Our security officer will brief you at much greater length, but my advice is always, always, always be on your guard."

"Understood."

The ambassador liked the reply, couldn't abide waffle.

"Miss Davenport showed you in, she's my personal assistant, but you as my private secretary will be responsible for keeping my schedule workable. You're my trouble-shooter if things need sorting out, and you'll find I have a very short fuse when the planning goes awry."

"I hope it won't come to that."

"In twelve days we're heading for the Crimea, that's something of a bonus for you, getting out of the rat cage so quickly. We're away for five days, based on Yalta. You'll find it all in the file that Miss Davenport will give you – pity there couldn't have been a hand-over from your predecessor."

"I understood he has pneumonia."

"We flew him out. Always get a man out if he's sick, standard procedure . . . I'd like you to go through the file and check each last detail of the programme. I don't want to be pitching up at a hotel where the booking isn't confirmed, and I don't want to be in a black tie when our hosts are in pullovers."

"I'll get on with it."

The ambassador's head ducked, but his eyes were still on Holt. There was a glimmer of a smile at his mouth. "I hear you're engaged to be married."

Holt couldn't help himself, blushed. "Not officially, it'll happen sometime."

"She's a lovely girl, our Miss Canning, broken all the bachelors' hearts here, a touch of romance will lift our spirits. You'll both be in demand. But I expect it to be a circumspect romance."

"Yes, Ambassador."

"Nose to the grindstone, Holt."

Holt took his cue, left the room.

The ambassador was Sir Sylvester Armitage. When he had been young he had cursed his parents for the name they had christened him with, but as he had risen through the ranks of the Diplomatic Corps, as the honours and medals had gathered in his pouch, so the given name had achieved a certain distinction. A tall, bluff man, working crouched over his desk with his suit jacket hooked to the back of his chair, and his braces bright scarlet. He had warmed to young Holt, and if young Holt had won the heart of Jane Canning then there had to be something rather exceptional to be said for him. He had a silly idea, but enough to make him laugh out loud. He loved the hill stream freshness of youth. He loved romance, which was why he spent all he could afford on scholarly works on the Elizabethan poets. He had meant it; he generally said what he meant. A youthful romance inside the embassy that looked across the river to the towers of the citadel of the Kremlin would hurry them all towards the Moscow spring, and young Holt had seemed to him the sort of man who could keep it circumspect.

He gave a belly laugh as he jotted the note on his memory pad.

He had always been young Holt.

The name had stuck to him from the time he was first sent from his Devon home near Dulverton to the south of the county and boarding school. Something about his face, his appearance, had always been younger than his age. He'd lost his first name at school, and there was always enough of his school contemporaries staying during the holidays to call him by his surname. His parents had picked the name up from the boys who came to stay. At home he was just Holt. At University College, London, three years and an upper second in Modern History, he was just Holt. Nine months in the School of East European and Slavonic Studies, language learning, he was just Holt. Two years in the Soviet department of the FCO and still just Holt. He didn't discourage it. He rather liked the name, and he thought it set him apart.

For the whole of the first morning in the outer office attached to the ambassador's, Miss Davenport watched him. Large owl eyes, and her attention distracted sufficiently for her to make more typing errors in 140 minutes than she would normally have managed in a month. Holt had looked once at her, wondered if she was in the running for a set of Lady Armitage's tights, and discarded the thought as cheap.

She brought him three cups of coffee as he unravelled the file for the visit to Yalta. If his predecessor had stayed the course then Holt would have been glad of a gentle run in to his duties. But it was a mess, had only been taken so far, had missed two necessary weeks of knocking into shape. Holt reckoned the file could have been part of the aptitude test they'd given him at FCO after the entrance exam. He attacked the problem, and wished Miss Davenport didn't smoke. Holt was a smoker and trying to kick it and the Camel fumes were rich temptation.

He wrestled the Crimea programme into shape, so that he could dominate it. First flight to Simferopol. Helicopter transfer to Yalta, check in at the hotel, hire car booked with Intourist. Lunch at the City Authority with the chairman and the deputy chairman, and then back to the hotel for an hour's break before meeting the local newspaper editors. Dinner at the hotel, the British hosting, and the guest list including the same chairman and deputy chairman and the legion of freebooters they would have in tow. That was day one . . . day two in Sevastopol, day three in Feodosija, and the ambassador had said that if he was coming all that way he was damned if he was going to be prevented from walking the length of the Light Brigade's charge – his predecessor's note on that was underlined twice.

Another note in the handwritten scrawl of his predecessor. The ambassador intended to lay a wreath at any British military cemetery that was still fit to visit. "Stormed at with shot and shell, While horse and hero fell, They that had fought so well Came thro' the jaws of Death, Back from the mouth of Hell." Good for Sir Sylvester if he was going to remember Cardigan's heroes with a poppy wreath, but there was no sign of the cemetery yet. That he would have to do himself.

Holt worked late that first day, and he didn't see Jane. Only a cryptic message on his internal phone to state that she was going straight from the office to the *Oklahoma* rehearsal, that he should get his beauty sleep.

For young Holt the first week flew. He would have sworn he had learned more from life in the capital of the Soviet Union in that one week than he had gathered together in two years shuffling paper, and calling it analysis, on the Soviet Desk at FCO.

He went with the ambassador to the Foreign Ministry and was present at a preliminary planning meeting with the Secretariat of the Deputy Foreign Minister for the arrival in Moscow the following month of the Inter-Parliamentary Union from London. He attended a reception thrown by the Foreign Trade crowd for a Scots firm working on the natural gas pipeline across Siberia. He explored the Metro. He was taken out to dinner, with Jane, by the Second Secretary Commercial and his wife. He was invited to supper, with Jane, by the First Secretary Political and his wife. He went to the disco, with Jane, at the British Club. He drove out of the city, with Jane, in the British Leyland Maestro that he had been allocated, to the embassy's dacha for a weekend picnic with her boss, the military attaché, and his wife. That he was determined to be circumspect, and that Jane had the curse, were the only drawbacks.

At the end of that first week he had the programme for Yalta beaten, also the draft of the programme for the Members of Parliament when they flew out, and he had persuaded Miss Davenport to restrict his coffee ration to two per day, and he had seen the wisdom of the ambassador.

Because of his girl, he was the centre of attraction in the confined oasis that was the embassy community. Of course he didn't touch her, not in public, not where anyone could see. But they were light in the darkness. Their laughter and their fun and their togetherness were a lift to the embassy personnel who had endured the short day, long night misery of the Moscow winter.

At his morning meeting with the ambassador, Holt presented the programme for Yalta.

"There's one problem. Lady Armitage isn't back so her aircraft seats are extra; should we cancel them?"

"Wouldn't have thought so."

"Whom would you like to take, Ambassador?"

"I'd like to have a hostess for our receptions, and I would like to take the most competent Russian linguist on my staff. To you she may, among other things, just be personal assistant to the military attaché, to me she is a very highly regarded member of the team . . ."

"Jane?" A flood of pleasure.

The ambassador's voice dropped, "Miss Davenport has hearing that puts to shame the most sophisticated state security audio systems . . . I fancy that a few days out of the clutches of our colleagues' wives would not distress you."

"That's very good of you."

"She's coming to work, and don't forget to make double sure that you've booked an extra single room for every hotel we're staying in."

"Will be done."

"Holt, it's a good programme, well presented. I learn more about the life blood of the Soviet Union from these visits than from anything else I do. And, most important, we are on show. We are the representatives of our country. You'll give Miss Canning my respects and request her to accompany us, having first checked with the military attaché that he can spare her. You will fix the hotel accommodation, you will sort out the necessary travel permission for her from the Foreign Ministry . . . Get on with it, Holt."

"Darling, nothing's what it seems . . . Ben's not an agony aunt . . ."

"He talked about us getting out of the clutches of the embassy wives."

They were in the bar of the British Club, not up on the stools where the noise was, where the newspaper men and the business community gathered, but against the far wall. She was on her second campari and soda, and there was a strain about her that was new to him. He drank only tonic water with ice and lemon because besides cutting out cigarettes he had forsworn alcohol from Monday to Friday and he was suffering.

"Don't be silly, Holt, don't think he's taking me to Yalta just so that we can have a cuddle in the corner without anyone knowing."

"Why is he taking you, then?"

"Put your thinking cap on, Holt. I'm a hell of a good linguist. At East European and Slavonic I actually had a better mark in the oral than you did.

Had you forgotten that? I'm in Moscow. I'm personal assistant to the brigadier who is the military attaché. An excuse has been found to take me down to the Crimea."

He stared at her. She was taller than he was. She had fair hair to her shoulders. She had gun-metal grey eyes that he worshipped. She wore a powder blue blouse and a severe navy blue suit.

"As I said, Ben's not thinking of you and me, Ben's thinking of the job."

"And at Sevastopol there is . . ."

"I don't want to talk about Sevastopol, nor do I want to talk about what's at Simferopol – I want to have a drink at the end of a vile day."

He was bemused. "I honestly didn't know that that was your line."

"When do you tell a bloke? First date? First time in bed? First night after you're married? Bit late then. Leave it . . . Raise your glass to Ben – curse is over tomorrow, poor darling . . ."

His elbows were on the table, his chin rested on his knuckles. He didn't know whether to be shocked or proud. He'd always thought of Jane as a souped-up secretary, and now he had lit upon the truth that there was enough to her line for her to be required in the Crimea. Bloody hell. She was probably on a higher grade than he was.

"To Ben," she said. Holt raised his glass, clinked hers. "To adjoining rooms in Yalta." Under the table she squeezed his knee.

"Why do you call the ambassador Ben?"

Her voice sunk, and he had to crane to listen, and from the bar it would have seemed like sweet nothings from the love birds.

"Remember the guy who tried to plummet the El Al, spring of '86? He was organised by Syrian Air Force Intelligence. Name of Nezar Hindawi. Nasty man, put his lady on a plane with three pounds of Czech-made explosive in the bottom of her hand baggage, timed to detonate over Austria. The Syrians didn't just burn their fingers, they were scorched right up to their armpits. Shouted like hell, but they were caught still smoking when Hindawi rattled off his confession. So we broke off diplomatic relations, big deal, told the Syrians that if they didn't behave like gentlemen then they were going to get booted out of the club. They were pretty upset, big loss of face, and they started doing their damnedest to get our ambassador back. They made their first overtures right here at a reception in the Kremlin. One of their diplomats sidled up to Sylvester and gave him the glad news that the El Al had all been a dreadful mistake, the wild fantasies of a couple of bottle washers, that Syria was dead against terrorism. What their little man didn't know was that Sylvester's beloved daughter was booked on that very same flight. He's got a big voice, right? Well, half the Kremlin heard him dismiss these fervent Syrian protestations of innocence with repeated and thunder-clap replies of 'Bloody Nonsense'. You'd have thought he was a Guards sergeant at drill. Stopped the show, he did, they heard him all over the room. 'Bloody Nonsense . . . Bloody Nonsense . . . Then your instructions are Bloody Nonsense'. Just like that."

"Spirited stuff."

"Everyone heard him. First world chaps and Second, and Third world, they all heard him. Within days he was known all over the place as Bloody Nonsense Armitage. It came down to B. N. Armitage, and from that to Ben. In this little-minded town he's Ben, half the time to his face."

"So our man in Moscow won't be taking his summer holidays in Damascus."

"You're very clever tonight, my darling."

"I wish I'd known how clever you were," Holt said.

"Cleverer even than you think. Clever enough to get Rose and Penny tickets for the ballet tomorrow. Will you by any chance be free for dinner?"

He would like to have kissed her, but circumspection ruled and he simply smiled and gazed at her lovely grey and laughing eyes, and their wretched bloody secrets.

"So you're young Holt. I was going to look you up, but you've beaten me to it. What can I do for you?"

It was his first visit to the secure section of the embassy. Next to the diplomatic section the largest in the building was that of the security officers. The former policemen and army officers were a group apart, he had already recognised that. They had staked out their own corner in the British Club, and they had the ingrained habit of closing down their conversations when anyone came within earshot.

Jane had pointed that out to him and said they were probably talking about the price their wives had paid for potatoes on the market stalls, or why the Whitbread draught had gone cloudy, but they still went silent.

The security officer's face was florid, a jungle of blood vessels, and his head was lowered as he sat at his desk so that he could see over tiny half-moon spectacles. He wore a thick wool shirt, loud checks, with twisted collars, and a tie that was stained between the shield motifs. Holt took him for a regular army half colonel on secondment to the security services in London, and on double secondment to FCO.

"I was letting you settle in for a bit. So much to learn, eh? I find if I rush in with the heavy security lecture the new chaps tend to get a bit frightened, best wait, eh? Sit down."

They were in the heart of the building. Holt thought that further down the basement corridor would be the Safe Room. He had heard about the Safe Room in London, the underground steel walled room where the most sensitive conversations could be conducted without fear of electronic eavesdropping. He was disappointed that he had not yet been invited to attend a meeting in the Safe Room.

"My wife was saying only last night that you must come round to supper, you and Miss Canning – super girl, that. My wife'll be in touch with Miss Canning, that's the way things get done here."

Holt reckoned that he had spotted the security officer, allocated him his responsibility, by the second day he had been in Moscow. It was his little game, but he was still searching through the faces for the top spook, the guy from the Secret Intelligence Service who was Jane's real boss – might be the one in Trade with the Titian beard who looked like a naval officer, could be the one in Consular who always kissed Miss Davenport's hand when he came to see the ambassador.

"I'm a busy man, youngster, so what's troubling you?"

"No crisis."

"Be a bit soon for a crisis."

"It's only that I'm going with the ambassador and Miss Canning to the Crimea on Saturday, and I wondered if there was anything I should know."

"About what?"

"Well, about security, that sort of thing . . ." He felt absurdly pompous. He should have stayed at his desk.

The security officer looked sternly at him. "Just the obvious. What you'd naturally assume. You don't discuss anything of a confidential nature in your hotels, nor in any vehicle. You don't accept invitations late at night to a Soviet household – what they'd have told you in London. Your rooms might be bugged. There will probably be a KGB operative with you as chauffeur or interpreter, a natural assumption. But His Excellency and Miss Canning know the form. Should be rather a nice trip. Good idea of H.E. to take in the battlefield, wish I was with him, if you could walk down that field with a metal detector, God, you'd make a fortune"

"There's nothing else I should know?"

"Like what?"

"Well, I just wondered . . ." Holt stopped, making a fool of himself.

"Ah, I get you." The security officer beamed, all avuncular. "You wondered about security, your own security, eh?"

"Just that."

"This is not Beirut, young man. H.E. does not have minders in Russia. This is a very peaceable country. Hurts me to say it, but H.E. can walk the streets of any city in the Soviet Union, any time of day or night, and have less prospect of getting mugged, assaulted, stuck up than in a good many cities at home. This is a highly policed country. The Moscow posting is categorised as Low Risk. I'm not a bodyguard, the personal security of the staff here is about bottom of my agenda, and that's the same with every western embassy in town. My job, young Holt, is to protect the confidentiality of this establishment, to block KGB attempts to compromise and recruit our staff, and that takes the bulk of my time. Right?"

"That's all I wanted to know."

"Good – well, as I say, my wife will be in touch with Miss Canning."

"You're very kind."

Holt left. He dreaded being summoned for the full security briefing. He thought it would be as hideous as the promise of dinner with the man and his woman.

*

"A penny for them, lover."

She lay on her side, and her clothes were on the floor, and the street lights gleamed through the thin curtain, and her fingers played with the hairs on Holt's chest.

What to tell her? To tell her that he had been rotten in bed, again, because he couldn't get it out of his reinforced concrete skull that this lovely girl of his worked with the embassy spook? To tell her that he thought spooking was a shoddy, grubby way of life? To tell her that he had thought Bloody Nonsense Armitage was doing them a favour, when in reality he had contrived an opportunity for a well-qualified operative to run a trained eye over the port facilities of the Soviet Navy at Sevastopol, and over the cap badge insignia of the troops in the garrison town of Simferopol?

He turned to face his Jane. He took his stranger in his arms. Over her shoulder he could see the travelling clock – and no bloody time, because in half an hour the other girls would be back from the Bolshoi. No time to tell her. Body to body, and his head was buried in the softness of her breasts, and he ached with his love for her. He could think it out, he could work it through but it would take him an age. He had thought he knew everything about her, every mark of her mind and her body, and he knew nothing. What he thought he owned was not his. Clinging to her, holding her for the comfort.

He fell away. Her head and the silk of her hair were on his arm.

"Just a bit tired, that's all"

She kissed him, wet and sweet and belonging.

"Stay safe, darling."

"What else?" She laughed at him, head back, hair falling.

3

By rights they should have travelled in the embassy Range Rover out to
Vnukovo airport from which the internal Aeroflot flights left. The Range
Rover was supposed to be used for all the ambassador's journeys that were
not official. But Holt had decided they would go in style, and so Valeri had
been roused early, and the Silver Cloud Rolls Royce was at its polished best.

The ambassador and Jane sat far back in the rear seat upholstery, while
Holt shared the front with Valeri. Holt reckoned that the chauffeur was about
his own age. He had expected an old retainer, had not anticipated that His
Excellency's driver would be a smartly turned out young man with the sort
of hair cut that any limousine man in Mayfair would boast. It was still dark
when they pulled away from the embassy courtyard onto the riverside across
from the Kremlin. There was no traffic. He had learned that at the best of
times cars were in high demand and short supply, even at rush hour the streets
were good for a pretty fast run, but at this time they were empty. The
pavements showed life. The dribble of a night shift heading for the Metro
tunnels, and street cleaners and the office advance guard appearing at street
level, making darting runs across the wide streets.

He had barely spoken to Jane when they had met, while they waited for
the ambassador. Mercifully the man had been punctual, striding down the
steps from the main door with that unnecessary glance at his watch to demonstrate that he was on time. He hadn't known how to communicate or what to
say. So there was a problem, last night's problem, and he didn't want to talk
about it, not in whispers.

He had known Jane for two weeks under three years. Met at the School.
Met in the way that most young men meet the girl who will one day become
their wife – one seat free at a canteen table, and a curled gammon steak that
needed disguising, and a request for the tomato ketchup, please. Two young
people, both older than the average students around them, the one shuffling
the tomato ketchup and the other pushing the salt and pepper. What a meeting
– the young man thinking that the girl was quite beautiful, and the young girl
thinking that he looked interesting. The young man able to say, quietly and
without conceit, that he had done well in the Civil Service entrance examinations, and then well in the Diplomatic Corps entrance aptitude tests. She
had said, looking straight at him, that she was just a secretary in Whitehall,
nothing specific, and that she was damn lucky to have been plucked out of
the pool and given the opportunity to learn Russian. More time together, and
he'd thought she was struggling sometimes in the tutorials, and the relationship
started when he made a habit of calling round at her Earls Court bed-sit to

give her a hand with the essay that was the fortnightly chore. Fingers touching, mouths meeting, the unhurried building of something lovely. Weeks and months of learning to share lives, work and fun. A young man who was determined to be something special at his chosen career, and a young girl who was just a secretary in Whitehall. Right, no messing, he'd been pretty shattered by the marks she had won at the end of the course – not quite at his overall level, though pretty close – but young Holt had never questioned how it was that a girl who was just a secretary won marks that were pretty damned close to his own . . .

"How do you like Moscow, Mr Holt?"

"Very well indeed, thank you, Valeri."

His thoughts drifted away from Jane, away from him being hopeless in bed with her, away from the deception. His thoughts were on the ambassador's driver. Be a chosen man, wouldn't he? Not chosen by the British, chosen by the Organ of State Security. Nice looking fellow, but he'd large ears, and they'd be well rinsed. They would hear everything said in the car. Holt wondered how it was done. Did the men from KGB call by on a Friday evening after Valeri's shift finished for a quick resumé on what he'd learned that week while piloting the Rolls? Did he write out a little report every Saturday morning before he took his small kids to dancing class or the ice rink? He was far gone, concerned now with whether Valeri had a large wife, or an extra large wife, whether he was on Lady Armitage's list for tights with gusset.

They travelled in the fast lane, where the government officials were driven. Big blasts on the power horn to keep clear the path of Her Britannic Majesty's ambassador. There were men with brushes, there were old women with bundles of sticks; the street and pavement cleaning had started.

Holt could have cried, he felt so bloody miserable.

But how could she have told him? Of course she couldn't have bloody told him.

At the airport there was already a slow-moving confusion of queues. Valeri deposited their luggage at the rear of a queue and checked with Holt when they would be back, and the time and number of the return flight. He wished them well, and said the Crimea would be beautiful after the Moscow winter. He had good cause to be pleased. With the big man away he'd have time on his hands, the chance to burnish the bonnet of the Roller with a leather. Holt carried the ambassador's briefcase, and Jane carried her own, and Holt hoped to hell that there wouldn't be a foul-up with the tickets.

There wasn't.

Nor were there special facilities for the ambassador and his party. It was the way he liked things done. Didn't want a brace of officials there to shake his hand and wish him well. That's what he'd said to Holt. On such a trip he could sense the mood of the nation, and the temperature could not be taken in a VIP lounge. They took their place in the queue. The ambassador lit his pipe and unfolded yesterday's *Times* from London. Holt craved a cigarette, the prohibition could not last. And Jane touched his arm. They had been in the queue for five minutes and not moved an inch.

"Do you know the hoary old one about queuing here? If you do you're still going to hear it again. Ivan was in a queue for two hours trying to buy a pair of winter boots, and he snorts to the people around him that he's had enough, and he's going down to the Kremlin, and he's going to shoot old Gorbachov, and that's going to be his protest about the inefficiency of the Soviet Union. Off Ivan goes, and three hours later he's back. He's asked if he's indeed shot Comrade Gorbachov. 'No,' Ivan says, 'I couldn't be bothered to wait, the queue was too long.' Like it?"

Holt managed a small smile. Jane squeezed his arm, as if to tell him to calm down, as if to say that a queue at Vnukovo wasn't his fault.

"Certainly hoary, Miss Canning," the ambassador intoned. "I have heard that anecdote told in turn of Messrs Brezhnev, Chernenko, Andropov and now Gorbachov. But I think that I am safe in stating that it was never said out loud during the revered leadership of Uncle Joe Stalin . . . Don't fret, Holt, it won't go without us."

The blockage at the head of the queue was removed. A man was shoved aside, hoarse with complaint and waving a ticket. Jane said it meant the flight was overbooked, and they were shedding the least important. A sour-faced woman behind the counter examined their tickets, looking at them as if to ascertain whether they could possibly be forgeries. They were checked once more by a bored militiaman at the gate, who then took an age studying Holt's and Jane's Foreign Ministry permission to leave the Moscow environs zone. They went on to the security barrier. Two more militiamen, an X-ray machine, and a metal detector arch to pass under. Jane had a camera, a palm-of-the-hand-sized Olympus that she took out of her handbag before it went on the belt. The ambassador's spectacle case attracted the flashing red light and earned him a cursory body patting.

They were in the departure lounge. Holt and Jane went off in search of coffee for themselves and an orange juice, diluted, for the ambassador.

"Bit heavy, wasn't it, the security?"

"They've their quota of nasties just like the rest of us." He'd noticed, since reaching Moscow, how much she enjoyed filling him in on insider detail. Couldn't have happened in London, when he was doing his initial FCO time and she was just a secretary in Whitehall. "Georgians and Jews and Estonians and Ukrainians, they've all got grievances, they all foster little cells that want to get out. Not easy. They've sent up fighters to shoot down aircraft that have been hijacked in the past. And if there's half a chance of settling the problem on the ground then they go in firing. Happened last year. They don't play about here, none of your patient negotiation. Storm and shoot is their answer. Not that they admit there's a political problem. It's always drug addicts and delinquents. I laugh like a drain each time I hear of a hijack. It's the biter bit, isn't it? That little shit Carlos was trained at the Patrice Lumumba University right here in down-town Moscow. And he's only the tip of the iceberg. They train them to do horrible things to us, and we broadcast on BBC World Service and the Voice of America what they've done, and the folks back home pretty soon get into the same act."

"Is that what you specialise in?" Holt asked.

She smiled at him, a big and open smile. She said, "God knows why Ben wants orange juice, it's quite foul here . . . There's a fancy dress party at the dacha next Saturday, what'll we go as?"

"I'll go as a boar with a ring in my nose, and you can go as a farmer and lead me round, and show everyone who's boss."

They both laughed. She thought it was funny and he thought it was sad, and the ambassador's orange juice looked as awful as their coffee tasted.

They boarded, and take off was only 25 minutes late. The ambassador was behind them, in the aisle seat, and next to a man in a dark suit with a bulging briefcase. Before the belt sign was off the ambassador was booming out his conversational Russian, angling for a rapport. A one-class aircraft, a Tupolev 134, rear engines and 72 passengers. He had hardly slept, not after she'd run him back to the embassy, and he'd been plagued with the niggling worries about getting the trip moving well – he started to doze. There was the drone of the voice behind him, and he was wondering how the ambassador managed to test the waters of Soviet opinion when he talked so much that the fellow next to him barely had the chance to get three consecutive words up his gullet. He'd sort it all out. He'd sort it all out with Jane in time, because he had to, because he loved her. Up to cruising altitude, and he was nodding, eyes opened then collapsing shut, so damned tired. He was a wild pig, and she was pulling him round, and they were all laughing, all the Second and Third Secretaries and their wives, and all the personal assistants, all laughing their heads off because his girl had him on a leash.

Flying due south. A journey of 750 miles. A route over Tula, Kursk and Charkov. Cruising at 29,000 feet, ground speed 510 miles per hour.

He felt her pull him forward, and then to her. And his eyes were closed, and he waited for the soft brush of her kiss behind his ear, where she always kissed, and he waited. He opened his eyes. She was looking down at her watch, concentrating. His head was forward, as if guarding her, hiding her breasts and her hands and her lap. Away from her watch, looking through the porthole window, the visibility was stunning and the daylight spreading, the fields sharp and the roads clear and a city laid out as a model. She took three photographs quickly, and the camera slipped back into her bag, and she grinned at him and eased him back so that he was fully into his seat. Then she kissed him, behind the ear, a fast peck.

He was a pig on a lead, and he didn't have the strength to argue.

The vapour trails of the airliner were brilliantly clear five and a half miles above the ground surface. The first airliner of the day, and a lorry driver leaned from his cab to watch the slow progress of the puffy white scars in the blue skies. The lorry driver was delivering prefabricated walls for a factory development on the east side of Charkov. The factory development was an extension of 260,000 square feet, and when in production would manufacture one-piece cast turrets for the T-72 tank.

It was the evaluation of the boffins in British and American Intelligence who concerned themselves in such studies that the T-72 main battle tank was technically superior to those of the NATO forces. The factory, when enlarged, could greatly increase its output of the low silhouette turret, so low that the crews fighting in them could be no taller than 5' 4". To have a photograph of the tank turret factory extension would not be an Intelligence coup, but it would be useful. There were few coups in that painstaking world, but much that was useful. The size of the extension would enable the analysts to calculate the increased output of new T-72s.

The vapour trails bowled on. The lorry driver reached the building site gate.

At a military airfield west of Moscow, an Antonov transporter bearing the insignia of the Air Force of the Syrian Arab Republic was in the final stages of loading. The manifest listed a cargo of MiG interceptor spares, a sizable cargo, but not enough to fill the aircraft because space had been set aside for basic seating forward in the hold. The pilot was engaged in his final checks before take off clearance and the start of a filed flight plan that listed a brief stop at Simferopol to take on personnel and then a direct onward flight to the El Masr base close to Damascus.

On that Saturday morning in the Yalta spring, a major had command of the city's militia force. His superiors were at home in their gardens, or in the shops with their wives, or in the mountains with their children. This particular militia major, 49 years old and twice passed over for promotion, sipped a poor imitation of gritty Turkish coffee and cast his eyes wearily over the backlog of reports on his desk. He was responsible for the Department for Combating Theft of Socialist Property and Speculation, for the Department of Criminal Investigation, for the Internal Passport Service, for the State Automobile Inspectorate, for the Patrol Service and the Preserving of Public Order in Public Places, and for the Department of Visas and Registration of Foreigners. His in-tray contained the overnight reports of apartment block caretakers, reports on the hunting of draft dodgers, an essay on the failure of the traffic lights on Botkin Street, a surveillance report on two Latvians who would be arrested in the following week to face charges of leading an Anti-Social and Parasitic mode of life.

The radio in the control room spluttered occasionally to life to disturb his half-hearted concentration. He had to last until six o'clock in the late afternoon, and then he could take off his uniform tunic, put on a sweater and go home to his family.

270

Deep in his in-tray was a memorandum stating that the British ambassador was arriving in Yalta in company with his private secretary and an interpreter for a semi-official visit, and would stay at the Oreanda Hotel. He was not required to furnish the delegation with a militia car escort.

It was the militia major's belief, for what little that was worth, that unless the traffic lights on Botkin Street were repaired their failure would lead to an accident, but there was nothing he could do. A waste of his time to try to dig out an engineer from Roads and Transport at a weekend.

In his briefcase was a book that would help him through the afternoon.

He was held up at the lights at the junction on Botkin. A main intersection and all the lights showing red, and the dumb fools waiting as if they had a day to kill.

Could not have happened in Moscow. Could only happen in this second-class junk yard to which he had been consigned. After eleven months in the backwater of Yalta it still burned in him that he had been dismissed from the capital and posted to oblivion.

He had been a captain in the Organ of State Security. He had had a promising future in the KGB. By hard work, by passing his exams, he had entered the favoured Guards Directorate. He had served in the personal protection squad of the Politburo member who was First Deputy Prime Minister. He had been tipped for membership of the guard assigned to the General Secretary of the Party. And he had drunk too much, been smashed out of his skull. He had been reduced to corporal and transferred.

He was no longer the high flier. He no longer possessed the plastic card that gave him access to the luxury goods at the State Security Commissariat. He no longer lived in a three-bedroomed flat with a view over the park. One bottle of vodka, after a stint of 41 hours continuous duty, had greased him down the pole. Caught drunk in uniform on the street, on his back in the gutter, and dumped with his wife and two toddler children onto a 23-hour train journey to nowhere, Yalta. Of course it still burned. From the personal protection squad of a Politburo member, with the magic card and the right to carry a Makarov PM 9mm automatic pistol, down the chute to KGB corporal. He was unarmed. He was at the wheel of a sluggish Chaika car which needed a new gear box. He was a chauffeur, and held up at the lights on Botkin Street, and his job was to drive the ambassador from Great Britain.

The KGB corporal hit the horn to clear the dumb fools out of his way.

Holt didn't wait for the lift. There was too much of a queue. He went up the two flights of stairs, and down the corridor to the ambassador's room, knocked, went in.

"The car's here, finally."

"Relax, Holt. You are in one of the most unpunctual regions of a country noted for its tardiness. If we're there on time we'll be standing around on our own, scratching our backsides – not Miss Canning, of course, but you and me certainly."

"I've checked the room for this evening, and the menu . . ."

"Don't try too hard, Holt, for heaven's sake. Foul-ups make life so much more entertaining . . . I feel a younger man already, damn nice air down here."

The ambassador slipped on his jacket, straightened his tie, knocked his pipe out into an ashtray.

"I'll go and rout Jane out."

The ambassador frowned sharply at his private secretary. "Damn it, Holt, haven't you been listening? I am not in a hurry. I want to make an entrance. I will not make much of an entrance if I am the first to arrive. You may put it down, if you wish, to old imperial grandeur. But I do mean to make an *entrance* when I visit the worthies of the Yalta municipality. Got me?"

"Got you."

"You've the Bridport stuff?"

"In my briefcase." Holt wondered how on earth Bridport on the English south coast had made the decision to twin itself with Yalta, must cost the sad ratepayers a fortune in exchange visits.

"Then best foot forward, Holt."

He snapped the door open. He went out into the corridor and rapped gently on Jane's door. The ambassador led the way down the corridor, no glance backwards, the Viceroy's procession, and Jane exploded out through her door, thrusting her small Olympus into her handbag. Down the staircase, the ambassador leading, and Jane happily in pursuit.

"Thanks be to God that we didn't forget our camera," Holt said. He was always useless at sarcasm.

"Don't be childish, Holt," she said coolly, quietly so that His Excellency would not hear.

Down the stairs, across the foyer. The ambassador smiled warmly at a group of exhausted tourists speaking German and attempting to check in, and none of them had the least idea who it was that smiled at them.

Holt reached the door first, pulled it open and stood back. He saw the driver moving to open the rear door of the vehicle. He saw a young man, dark-skinned, long hair, ambling across the road towards the hotel and holding a windcheater across his stomach. Distraction, because the ambassador had passed, playing the old-world gentleman, ushering Jane through first. Jane was out onto the steps, and hesitating, as if the light of the Crimea's lunchtime sunshine were too bright for her, as if she needed to adjust. Slow, stilted moments, and each slower than the last. Jane going forward and giving her winning grin to the driver, and the driver bobbing his head in acknowledgement, and the ambassador beaming, and Holt coming through the door. Each movement, each moment, slower. And the man who was dark skinned, with long hair, coming off the road and onto the pavement, and the windcheater falling past his knees and past his shins and past his ankles. And something black and stubbed and squat in his hands, something that he was lifting to his shoulder, something that was a protuberance from his head and mouth and nose, *something* that was a gun, for Christ's sake.

He stared at the man. He stared at the barrel of the rifle. No longer slow movement, the moment the world stopped.

Jane in front of the ambassador, Holt in the doorway, the driver with his back to them all, bent inside the car to smooth down the rug that covered the leather upholstery.

Everything frozen. No voice in Holt's throat. The warning scream locked in his mind.

Gazing into the face of the man, and then the flash, and the flash repeated, and the smoke. Then Jane spinning away, beaten and kicked and punched backwards. Jane falling against Ben, and Ben not there to hold her upright. Ben fading from his feet, sliding down. The glass shattering to his right and to his left, caving in. Holt shaking his head, because he couldn't understand . . . looking at the face that was topped by a wig that had inched over the right ear, looking at the scar on the man's left cheek, puzzling how a face came by a scar that looked like a crow's foot.

The rifle dropped to the man's side. He peered forward as if to be certain of his work.

All movement now, speed returning to the world.

The man ran.

In that moment Holt found in his ears the crash of the gunfire, and the cordite in his nostrils, and the scream from his throat.

He was on his knees. His body covered their bodies, to protect them.

So bloody late.

4

He lay across them, sheltering them, as if they were still in danger. Blood was on his hands and on the cuffs of his shirt, red on white. He had taken Jane's hand in his, an unresisting hand, as it was when she was exhausted or sleeping.

The scream in his throat had died with them.

He was aware of men and women, fearful, around him. They formed a circle at the level of the door, and on the steps, and on the pavement. The shoes of one of them crunched the glass fragments, and the shoes of another nudged the spent cartridge cases.

"Ambulance," Holt said, in English. "Get us an ambulance."

The duty day manager called that the ambulance was sent for. Holt saw his face, quivering and streaming with tears. He saw that the driver was talking urgently into a personal radio, couldn't hear the words, could see the white-faced shock of the man. The street was blocked from Holt's view, only the line of knees and skirts and trousers and shoes for him to focus on. Empty ground between the legs and the feet and where Holt lay covering the bodies of Jane and Ben, empty ground laced with blood trickles and with shards of glass. He held tightly onto Jane's hand as the misery welled in him. He had seen the face of the man. He had seen the smooth pine varnish skin, and the eyes that were burnished mahogany, and the thin chisel of the nose, and the clip of the moustache. He had seen the scar hole on the man's cheek and had followed the lines that ran from it, four lines, into the shape of a crow's foot.

There was the far away sound of a siren.

He had been behind Ben and behind Jane. He had been behind them and safe. He had seen the man with the aimed gun, and he had done nothing. Could not explain to himself how he had watched the slow ballet movements of the man raising the weapon and aiming, and done nothing. Desperate misery, and it had all been so slowly drawn out in front of his eyes. He squeezed Jane's hand, her fingers, hard enough for it to have hurt her, and she did not flinch.

The driver broke the circle. He jostled the people back, and was shouting to them to retreat, pushing a corridor clear through them. Holt could see down the corridor, down the steps, across the pavement, into the street. He could see where the man had stood and taken his time to aim. He was aware of the closing bleat of the siren.

His view of the street was cut by the white bulk of the ambulance.

The driver was tugging at his shoulders, trying to pull him upright, trying and failing to break his hold on Jane's hand. He still held her while the ambulance men swiftly heaved Ben onto a stretcher, carried him away down the corridor to the open rear doors. They came back for her, for his Jane. He saw the shrug in their shoulders. The shoulders and the faces told him that they knew this was not work for ambulancemen. They lifted her more gently than they had lifted Ben, and more awkwardly because his hand never unclasped hers.

The doors closed behind him. Ben's litter lay on one side of the ambulance's opaque interior, Jane's on the other. Holt crouched in the space between. One ambulanceman was with them, going perfunctorily through pulse checks, and bending to listen first at Ben's chest and then at Jane's breast. The ambulance was going fast, siren loud.

Her last words were clear in his memory. Scathing words.

"Don't be childish, Holt."

Young Holt had loved Jane Canning and the last time he had seen her face it had been puckered, screwed up in annoyance. He bit at his lip. He looked down at the fright that was set like wax on her face. That was the obscenity of it, that all the good times, wonderful times, were blasted out.

"Don't be childish, Holt."

He had a bowl of beetroot soup in front of him and a tub of sour cream and two slices of black bread. He had a quarter bottle of vodka in the desk drawer beside his knee. The militia major was tucking a napkin into his collar when the news broke out of the control room.

Garbled, staccato chaos. A shooting on Lenin Street. He was gulping a spoonful of soup. A killing at the Oreanda Hotel. His napkin sliding into his soup. Foreign visitors attacked with rifle fire. He was careering from his desk, the sour cream slurping over his papers. A call for all assistance . . . It was Saturday lunchtime. It was the time that Yalta closed itself down and the militia headquarters was at one-third strength. He felt sick. The tang of the beetroot and the chopped onion was choking in his throat.

Into the control room. A relay coming through on the loudspeaker from Ambulance Control. The young sergeant at the console listening at the telephone and writing urgently. The telephone slapped down.

"Major, the management at the Oreanda Hotel on Lenin Street report that the British ambassador and his interpreter were shot outside the hotel . . ."

"Dead?"

"They did not know . . . Ambulance Control report that they are carrying two cadavers and one survivor to the clinic on Naberezhnaya . . ."

A foreign diplomat, possibly dead . . . Everything he did now was going to be examined under a microscope at the investigation in a week, in a month.

"Inform the KGB Control, exactly as it comes in."

The sergeant was reaching for his telephone. To go to the clinic, to go to the Oreanda, to stay in headquarters? Which?

He picked up a telephone himself. He rang the number of Criminal Investigation two floors above, and the telephone rang and his fingers drummed on the console surface and his feet shuffled. Bastards gone to their lunch. The sergeant came off the telephone and the major told him to send all militia cars to the Oreanda.

The major ran out of the building, howled in the yard for a driver, had himself taken to the Oreanda.

The KGB had beaten him. Half a dozen of them there. Crowds gathering but back on the far side of the street. He shouldered his way forward to the knot of men all with radios, all either talking into them or listening to the return messages. In front of the broken plate glass front door he saw the blood stains. Perhaps, in the car, he had half hoped the radio at headquarters had carried an aberration . . . well, that some hysterical idiot had . . . The bloodstains and the KGB swarming over the steps of the hotel wiped that out.

They treated the militia major as dirt. They were the Organ of State Security, he was a common policeman. Brusquely he was told what had happened.

"You had a very fast call," the militia major said.

For answer there was a cursory gesture, down the steps towards a black Chaika car. A man was sitting haggard over the wheel of the car, a radio in his hand, shaking his head in response to the questions of two others. The driver, the militia major understood; a KGB driver had been assigned to the British ambassador's party.

"So you have a description, something I can broadcast?"

The man he spoke to looked away.

"If I am to seal the city, put in road blocks, I have to have a description."

"He saw nothing."

"What? A close quarters shooting, right under your own man's nose, and he saw nothing? How could he see nothing?"

"There is no description."

"There has to be," the militia major shouted.

"He did not see the killer approach. He took cover when the shooting started. He did not see the killer leave. There is no description."

"Shit," spat the militia major. "You pick your men."

The KGB officer walked away. The militia major sighed his relief. The fear of failure was shed. A KGB matter, a KGB failure. Best news he could possibly have been given.

He followed the KGB officer.

"What do you want of me?" the militia major said flatly.

"We have closed the airport, we have suspended all telephonic communication from the city, we have referred all details to Moscow. You should put blocks on all routes out of the city."

"For what are they looking?"

No response.

He sat on a long wooden bench in a corridor of white walls and polished linoleum flooring. Two old ladies had at first shared the bench with him, but they had long since been ordered away by the militiaman who stood with arms folded and watched over him. Through the flapping rubber doors on the other side of the corridor the trailing white coats of the doctors and surgeons and the white skirts of the nurses came and went. He waited. Another militiaman stood on guard by the rubber doors. He hadn't fought it, he hadn't wanted to be inside the Emergency Room. He was alert now, conscious of everything around him, aware enough to know that he did not want to see the last medical rites performed on the girl he loved and the man he admired. Each man and woman who went into the Emergency Room, or came from it, gave him a glance and then looked away when he met their eyes.

It was an older man who came to him. White haired and lean, and with his smock coat bloodstained. He spoke with his hands, his hands said that hope had gone. In Russian, Holt was told that the man was the senior surgeon on duty at the hospital. He was told that the injuries had been too severe for treatment. He shook the hand of the surgeon, and thanked him.

Holt said that he needed a telephone. Again the hands of the surgeon were in motion, it was outside his province. The surgeon backed away. Two trolleys, sheet shrouded, were wheeled through the rubber doors and down the corridor. He sat numbed, watched them go.

His attention was to his right. The man wore perfect creased slacks and a well cut wool jacket. The man flashed an identity card, didn't linger with it but it was there long enough for Holt to recognise the Komitet Gosudarstvennoy Bezopasnosti. Holt read the name of the KGB officer.

"I want a telephone," Holt said, speaking in Russian.

The KGB officer was fishing a notebook from his pocket, and a ballpoint pen.

"I said that I wanted a telephone."

"There will be a telephone, Mr Holt. But my first priority is to apprehend the despicable culprits responsible for this crime."

"Just a telephone – the street was packed solid. You don't need me to tell you."

"Mr Holt, we need to have a description from you."

He was in a police state, a state controlled by the leviathan apparatus of the Organ of State Security. A state where the KGB crushed all dissent, kept the gulags filled. He was in a country that boasted no terrorism, no law and order problem, no incidence of armed crime. He believed, as never before, that in this country nothing moved, nothing happened, without KGB authority. Now a charade about the need for a description.

"Ask someone else what the bastard looked like," Holt yelled at him.

The militiaman close to him had clenched his fist, ready to intervene, and the militiaman beside the rubber doors had his hand wavering close to the wood truncheon fastened to his belt.

The KGB officer strode away.

All so clear now to Holt. The State had butchered them. The authorities had killed them . . . He went off down the corridor, he shrugged away a feeble attempt by his militiaman minder to stop him. He went into an office that was empty because of the weekend. He picked up the telephone, he dialled a zero and then seven for long distance, he waited for the clicks, he dialled the Moscow code and the embassy number. The "unobtainable" whine sang back at him. He tried twice more. Twice more the same blank whine.

Out of the clinic. The short walk along the sea front, the two militiamen trailing him, a distance away as if he might turn on them, savage them.

He reached the Oreanda Hotel. The street and the half steps picketed off, brown paper stuck where the glass panels had been, the glisten of soap and water on the steps. In past the militia and more KGB, up to the reception desk. He wanted a telephone call to Moscow. It was regretted there was no telephonic communication with Moscow. Then he wanted a telex connection with Moscow and he wanted it now, right now. It was regretted that there was also no telex communication with Moscow. By whose authority? By the authority of State Security.

So tired, so bloody exhausted. Slowly, deliberately, "I have to speak to Moscow."

"I am so sorry, Mr Holt, but it is not possible for anyone to speak to Moscow. All the lines are closed."

"Is there a post office?"

"It is Saturday afternoon, the post office is closed, Mr Holt."

"I *have* to speak to my embassy."

"I am sure that later, Mr Holt, the lines will be restored."

The reception manager gave him his room key and then reached below the counter and shuffled to him Jane's handbag. Dropped it when she was hit. It was a small, kind gesture by the reception staff, to have retrieved the handbag, kept it for him. He offered his thanks. He went slowly up the flights of stairs to his room. He locked the door behind him. He tipped her bag out onto the coverlet of his bed. Her purse, her passport, her notepad, her pen, her embassy I/D, her lipstick, her mirror, her hairbrush, her letter from home, her photograph of Holt in Whitehall held in a small silver frame, her camera . . .

He was shipwrecked. His landfall was a room on the second floor of the Oreanda Hotel in Yalta. His sea was a closed down telephone and telex system to Moscow and a wall of silence. He had gone through shock and misery and fury, now his reserve failed. Alone, where no–one saw him, Holt knelt beside his bed and wept, and his face covered her possessions, and he said over and over again the words she had spoken to him.

"Don't be childish, Holt."

*

278

The ciphered message whispered onto a teleprinter at main headquarters in Dzerzhinsky Square. A report from KGB Yalta to KGB Moscow, giving information, requiring guidance. Saturday afternoon in the capital city. The message, still in cipher, passed to Second Directorate, domestic counter-subversion, and to Fifth Chief Directorate, suppression of dissent. Rows of weekend empty desks in Second and Fifth Chief, dust covers over the computer consoles, skeleton staffing. The minutes sliding away. Second Directorate duty officer going in search of his senior, his senior telephoning home to the man commanding the Second Department of the Directorate, the man commanding Second Department waiting for a call back from the Directorate chief out walking his dog. Fifth Chief Directorate on hold and looking for a lead from Second Directorate. Foreign Ministry Embassy Liaison stating they would take no action until briefed by Second Directorate, and until consultation with Fifth Chief Directorate. The dog was a young German Shepherd and needed a good long walk on a Saturday afternoon.

The duty officer at the British embassy whiled away his afternoon in the near deserted building, and watched the ripple of the Moskva River from his upper room.

He had run down Lenin Street. He had turned away from the shore front into a small alleyway. No more running then. He had walked as he had shrugged into his windcheater. One bad moment, when the windcheater had been on the ground and he had had to scoop it up. The gun under the shoulder of the windcheater. Another right turn, and another left turn, and the Volga car in front of him, and the man starting the engine.

The rifle – magazine detached and metal stock folded down – wrapped in sacking on the floor of the car. Going fast out of the city and towards the Alushta road.

"Did you succeed?"

He punched the air in front of his face, and turned to the wide billowing smile of his commander.

There was no obstacle to their flight. They had beaten the road blocks.

He was Abu Hamid. Abu Hamid was the name he had taken when he had joined the Popular Front for the Liberation of Palestine. He was 28 years old. His body was bone thin, spare, as if he ate little, as if he enjoyed no luxuries. The complexion on his face was smooth with the exception of the scar under his left eye. He wore no moustache and his matted dark hair was cut close to his scalp. Beyond the scar he was unrecognisable, unremarkable.

He was a chosen man.

He sucked hard, like he was panting, on his cigarette. He exploded the smoke from his mouth. He had stripped off the civilian clothes in which he had appeared on the front pavement of the Oreanda Hotel. He was now in military fatigues. They had stopped by the roadside at the city's limits and behind the cover of flourishing saplings Abu Hamid had swiftly dug a deep hole in the ditch and crammed in it the windcheater, the trousers, the shirt, the moustache, and the wig.

The city of Yalta was behind them. The high slopes of oak and beech forest that dominated the city were lost to them. In a corner of the car park of the Sechonov Climatic and Physiotherapeutic Institute, shielded by small recently planted acacia and laurel and magnolia trees, they had transferred from the Volga car to a military jeep. The car could not be linked to them. The car had been hired from Intourist. The car had been fitted with false plates. Later, the plates exchanged, the car would be returned, the bill paid. None of that was the business of Abu Hamid.

The commander knew that the journey from Yalta to Simferopol would take, given a few minutes either way, one hour and three quarters. They hammered through Gurzuf, past the signed turnings to the Defence Ministry sanatorium and the "Sputnik" Youth Camp. The commander's eyes flickered to the side mirrors of the jeep. They had no tail. Through Alushta, as if it did not exist, as if the narrowing streets in the town were merely an inconvenience on their journey. The commander pricked his ears to listen for a trailing siren. He heard nothing. The jeep straining when they climbed towards the lower reaches of the Chatir Dag that rose higher than any mountain in Lebanon, higher than the mystic Hermon of Syria, higher than any mountain of Palestine that was the homeland of Abu Hamid.

The aircraft should now be leaving Moscow. There was a schedule to be met. At the road's summit, under Chatir Dag, they did not pause to look back and down towards Yalta and the hazed seascape.

Abu Hamid leaned forward. He unwrapped the AK–47 assault rifle from the sacking on the floor space between his feet. He emptied the magazine. On semi–automatic, at a range of five or six paces, he had fired eleven bullets. He knew the weapon as he knew himself. Now he put the remaining rounds with the magazine and the rifle carefully into the mouth of the sack, wrapped it tight into a bundle and tucked it under his feet. A tradesman's tool, and he had finished with it.

Holt lay on his bed.

He had heard the whispered talk in the corridor outside his room. He had already been into Ben's room and into Jane's room and he had packed their belongings. Ben's case and Jane's were at the foot of his bed. He presumed the low voices outside were of a guard posted there. For his protection? To keep him inside the room?

Each half hour he rang reception to see if the line to Moscow was open, and each half hour he was told that it was not. Each half hour he requested a call to KGB headquarters in the city, and each time he was told that all KGB numbers were engaged.

There was no other explanation. Of course they had killed Ben and Jane.

He lay on the bed, her blood still on his hands and on his shirt.

Simferopol is in the centre of the Crimean peninsular. The city, with a population of close to 300,000, is the hub of the Crimea and from this regional capital the roads snake out to Yevpatoriya and Sevastopol and Yalta and Feodosija and Dzhankov. It is an old city, dominated now by industrial estates, its university, several research institutes. At Simferopol is also a military academy.

For the colonel commandant (foreign cadre training) that Saturday was a hell of a good day at the military academy. His best day in six months, in fact. The colonel commandant would this day wave goodbye, without a shade of regret, to the delegation of Palestinians. For the Ethiopians, the Cubans, the Angolans, even for the North Vietnamese, he could find some words of praise. Nothing good could be said for the animal Palestinians, not even as a courtesy at the farewell airport parade before the animals filed onto their aircraft. When the doors closed on the fuselage they would get the sharp index finger ... Nightly in the mess, to his brother officers, he catalogued their abuses. Three of the animals caught trying to climb over the walls after curfew hour to hitch into the city. One with the insolence to complain that a prostitute in Simferopol had stolen his wallet. One returned to the academy by the militia after being arrested when trying to sell counterfeit American dollars. One brought back to the academy by the militia dead drunk and violent. Four who would be in solitary confinement right up to the last minute for attacking a senior instructor. One accused by a fine Party man of getting pregnant his fine daughter. Not much sympathy from his colleagues in the mess, and rudeness to his face from the odious commander of the animals. One rifle lost, damage done all over the camp, and throughout the course an atmosphere of indiscipline that was insufferable to the colonel commandant. He would cheer their going, every last one of them from their ridiculously named groups. Popular Front, Sai'iqa, Democratic Front, Liberation Front, General Command, Struggle Command – idiot titles. He was a career soldier. He despised these animals.

Through the colonel commandant's office window came the blast of Western music, loud and decadent, cassette players turned to full volume. The animals taunting their instructors, because the animals were going home.

His telephone rang.

The animals were in the gymnasium with their baggage waiting for transport to the airport. A fighter from Sai'iqa had argued with a fighter from the Struggle Command, and knifed him. The fighter from Sai'iqa was in the academy military police cells, the fighter from Struggle Command was in the academy sick bay.

"Where is their commander?"

Their commander was off base.

Too much. He slammed his fist onto his desk in fury. This was too fucking much.

The teleprinters linking Moscow and Yalta murmured through the afternoon, on into the early evening. Questions and demands for more information from Moscow. Scant detail relayed from Yalta.

A crisis committee sat at Dzerzhinsky Square feeding from the teleprinter material, and going hungry. No workable description of a gunman, no getaway car identified. Cartridge cases that were from the Kalashnikov family, and there were more than two million weapons in the country that could fire such bullets. The files on dissident elements in the Crimea were being studied.

In his office, the Foreign Ministry Embassy Liaison was left to clean his nails and watch his silent telephone.

The commander drove his jeep through the main gates of the military academy at Simferopol.

He waved cheerfully to the guard. He braked to allow a squad of Soviet conscripts to march across his path. All the conscripts were marched wherever they went in the camp, a difference in attitudes, he reflected, between the training demanded by the Red Army and the training required for the fighting in Lebanon. He checked his watch. He thought they had made good time, he thought the Antonov transporter would now be approaching Simferopol airport. He stopped by the gymnasium, punched the shoulder of Abu Hamid. He was too concerned with the tightness of his schedule to take note of the three military policemen standing outside the main doors of the building.

The commander did not have to tell the young man to hold silence, to play a part of relaxed indifference when he was inside the gymnasium. His Abu Hamid would know. He drove away, drove to the office of the colonel commandant.

He breezed into the inner office. On any other day he would have waited more respectfully at the door, but it was the last day, and it was the day that was the brilliant culmination of a difficult and dangerous mission.

"Later than I thought, Colonel. Profuse apologies . . ."

He laid the jeep's keys on the desk of the colonel commandant.

". . . One last expedition for shopping in the city, an opportunity to purchase merchandise that will remind me for the rest of my days in the service of the Palestinian Revolution of the warmth shown to us by the Soviet people . . ."

He saw at once the barely controlled fury of the commandant.

". . . I trust my lateness has not inconvenienced you, Colonel. Shopping in the city is not always as fast as one would wish."

"You have been gone seven hours."

"Some shopping, a good lunch, time drifts . . ." He saw the clenched fist, the white knuckles. "There has been a problem?"

"A problem! . . ." the colonel commandant snorted. "While you took lunch and wine and shopped, your hooligans have been brawling. I have one in the sickbay, I have one locked in the guard house." The colonel commandant slapped a small double-bladed knife down onto his desk. "A knife fight while you were lunching and wining and shopping. I will tell you the military crime code for such an offence. Assault by one service person on another in the absence of any subordinate relations between them, that carries a minimum of two years confinement and a maximum of twelve years . . ."

"My abject apologies, colonel. I will deal with the offender at once . . ."

The colonel commandant stood. "You will do nothing of the sort. You will get it into your head that I have the authority to detain the entire cadre until a full investigation has been carried out."

The commander thought of Abu Hamid coming panting to the Volga car. He thought of the Kalashnikov in the sacking, hidden in the large shopping bag of the Simferopol *beryozka* souvenir store, and, hanging from his hand, the rifle listed as "lost on manoeuvres".

"But our aircraft . . ."

"Fuck the aircraft. A serious breach of discipline has taken place amongst unsupervised personnel."

"We have to take the aircraft." The bombast gone from the commander. Nervous and wheedling now. "It is of critical importance that we take the aircraft."

"A fortnight's delay, a thorough investigation, will teach these hooligans the authority of discipline."

"It cannot happen."

"Don't tell me what can or cannot happen. It should happen and it will happen."

Out of the confusion in Yalta would soon come order. The commander shivered. The trap would close.

"I make a deal with you."

"You are in no position to offer me a deal, military regulations are not subject to negotiation."

"Give me a pistol . . ."

"For what?"

"And a mop and bucket . . ."

"For what?"

"And access to the guard room."

"For what?"

"So that I can shoot your hooligan and clear up the mess and remove your problem."

The colonel commandant blanched, sat down. "You would do that?"

"With my own hand. Give me the pistol."

The knife was returned to the drawer. "Take him with you, then. Take both of them and punish them at home."

"An admirable solution. The injured man is fit to travel?" He was told that the injured man could certainly fly.

The commandant regarded the Palestinian with disgust – and with awe.

He told his duty officer to send the bus to the gymnasium.

Even in the crowded interior of the bus, 58 seats for 61 personnel, and the luggage filling the rear boot and the aisle between the seats, the commander thought that Abu Hamid was a man apart, dreaming his own dreams in his own privacy. The man from Struggle Command sat pale at the back of the bus with his left arm in a sling. The man from Sai'iqa stood in the aisle at the front, beside the commander, in handcuffs. They drove out of the gates. Only the commander and Abu Hamid and the man from the Struggle Command and the man from Sai'iqa refrained from cheering as the barrier was lowered behind them. Through the drab city where a greyness hung that even the sunlight could not lift, past the Ukraina Hotel, and over the wide bridge spanning the Salgir River, and past the museum and the terraced parkland and the railway station, through the industrial estates, out towards the airport.

Around the perimeter of the airport fence. Waved through the gates into the military section. Past the buildings and the control tower, out along the edge of the tarmac.

The sun was low in the west, and it hit the silver lower belly of the Antonov transporter. The Antonov was decorated with the green and white and black roundels of the Syrian Air Force. The commander's breath squeezed between his teeth. Military bandsmen were grouped around a rostrum. There were steps in position at the forward door. A fuelling tanker was driving away.

From his hip pocket the commander took a folded *khaffiyeh* scarf, shook it open and wound it round his head and his face, as if he were a revolutionary fighter for Palestine, not an embarking passenger at the military section of Simferopol airport in the Crimea. As he descended from the bus the commandant's transport drew up. The camp instructors, impeccably turned out, jumped down from their truck.

The 61 men were lined up in two platoon-sized squads. The anthem of the Soviet Union was played by the Red Army band, interminable, and they were a single phone-call from disaster. A phone call from Yalta to Simferopol. The band struck havoc with a fighting march of the Palestine revolution. In his ears the bell of a telephone screamed.

The colonel commandant, cold and contemptuous, scarcely pausing for the interpreter, addressed the men. If they had been seen transferring from the Volga to the jeep in the car park ... In the mind of the commander the bell of a telephone clamoured.

"Our Party supports and will continue to support peoples fighting for their freedom. We will never agree to the unacceptable American demands that the Soviet nation should cease to support its friends."

The commander stood at attention in front of his men. Only the major who was his friend, only Major Said Hazan, would have dared to launch the plan. Such daring, such brilliance. He pleaded for the speech to end.

"I wish you good fortune in your war for the regaining of your homeland. Long live Free Palestine. Long live the Soviet Union. Long live our friendship of iron . . ." The final words were drowned by the starting of the engines.

A ripple of applause from the two ranks of instructors behind the colonel commandant was lost in the aircraft's engine roar. The colonel commandant and the commander exchanged salutes, shook hands without warmth. The Palestinians gathered their luggage, and then scrambled to get aboard.

The commander came last, gesturing that Abu Hamid should be ahead of him. They threaded their way around the wooden crates that filled the centre of the hold and looked for the canvas seats, their backs to the fuselage. The light from the doorway was blotted out, a member of the aircrew turned the locking handle. A terrible tension in the commander as the Antonov inched forward and started to swivel. He seemed to hear in his mind the ring of a telephone in the colonel commandant's office, and the squawk of a radio in the control tower. His stomach was knotted – they could still be brought back. The member of aircrew was yelling at him above the drive of the engines for his belt to be fastened.

Four hours and three minutes after an incident in Yalta, the Antonov transporter lifted off the long Simferopol runway. It took a course, as it climbed, to the south west and crossed the shore line of the Crimea close to the old battlefields of Sevastopol and Balaklava, then swung south over the darkening Black Sea. The aircraft had prior permission to overfly Turkish airspace, a standard arrangement. Ahead of it was a flight of two hours and 20 minutes, cruising speed 450 miles an hour, altitude 25,000 feet. Within 18 minutes the four giant Kuznetsov NK-12MV turbo-prop engines had carried the Antonov beyond Soviet jurisdiction.

The captain made the announcement. The excited yelling rang inside the aircraft. The commander sat slumped, drained of the energy to celebrate. Beside him he saw that Abu Hamid sat back in his seat, swaying with the motion of the aircraft. The commander thought the killer was at peace, and marvelled. Moving down the aisle towards them, steadying himself against the lashed-down crates, came Major Said Hazan.

The question was in the smooth child's stomach skin around the major's eyes.

"It was successful," the commander said. "The target was destroyed."

Abu Hamid saw that the major wore smart Syrian Air Force uniform, but his face was hidden by a wrapped wool scarf and his head was hidden by his wide peaked cap. Only the eyes were for him to see. Abu Hamid leaned forward. There was pride in his voice. "There was a girl, with the ambassador, she too died."

Major Said Hazan ducked his head in acknowledgement, clasped the shoulders of the two men each in turn, with a leather-gloved hand. He made his way back to the cockpit.

The landfall would be high over the Turkish town of Samsun, the flight path would be above the central Anatolian mountains, the Syrian frontier would be overflown east of Aleppo, and then the long descent to Damascus.

The words as taught him in the camps of Damascus before the journey to Simferopol were soundless in the throat of Abu Hamid.

The thoughts echoed in his mind. The thoughts were of the Old Man of the Mountains who had built his fortress a thousand years ago in the valley of Alamut and gathered his followers, who were the Assassins. Enclosed in the valley that was paradise were palaces and pavilions, channels flowing with wine and honey, and young girls who danced and sang. Every pleasure was found here for the Assassins until the Old Man of the Mountains called one forward.

"Go from here and kill the man whose name I give you ... When you return you will enter again into paradise ... should you not return then my angels will seek you out and carry you back to our paradise."

A thousand years ago word of the skill and dedication of the Assassins of Syria, travelling from the valley of Alamut, had spread across the known world. Brilliant in disguise, unrivalled in their dedication and fanaticism, ruthless in murder, the Assassins were feared by kings and princes and military commanders and civil governors and the priests of Sunni Islam. Abu Hamid saw himself as the descendant of the old Assassins of ten centuries before.

The words, soundless in the throat of Abu Hamid, were those of the Old Man of the Mountains, handed down over a millennium.

"To kill these people is more lawful than rainwater."

There was no advance warning. The car drove unannounced into the forecourt of the embassy. Three men in the car, all pressed into service and summoned from their weekend break. A First Deputy Foreign Minister, a protocol official, a full colonel of the Second Directorate. They were shown into an ante room on the ground floor where they were watched by a security man.

The duty officer for that weekend was a Second Secretary, Trade. He was still buttoning his collar when he came into the room. Grim faces staring back at him, all three men standing. They introduced themselves, even the one from State Security. Not the moment to offer them tea, nor the moment to ask them to sit. Their seniority meant urgent business to be conducted without delay.

"I am the duty officer," he said. He produced a pencil and notepad and waited on them.

The First Deputy Foreign Minister seemed for a moment to examine the close pattern-work of the carpet, from Bokhara, then he straightened.

"It is with the utmost regret that as the representative of my government I have the sad duty to inform you that His Excellency, Sir Sylvester Armitage, and Miss Jane Canning were today the victims of a cruel and cowardly attack in the city of Yalta. As a result of this attack His Excellency and Miss Canning have died. The third member of the delegation, Mr Holt, is unhurt. I am instructed to inform you that the Soviet government has made available a military aircraft to take to Yalta any members of your staff who would wish to go. The aircraft is ready to leave at your convenience. I am able to tell you that a comprehensive criminal investigation has been launched in Yalta, and it is our earnest hope that the investigation will bear fruit soon."

The duty officer was scribbling his note, in longhand. Incredulity on his face. Lips moving, but they could not formulate the barrage of questions.

"The deaths were caused by shooting. His Excellency and Miss Canning were hit many times as they were leaving the hotel for lunch with the city authorities; they were dead on arrival at hospital. The initial indication is that the culprit was involved in an attempt to enter the hotel for the purpose of robbing the cash desk, but panicked as he was confronted by the British delegation leaving."

"Where's Holt?" The first stuttered question. "He is in the hotel. He is quite safe."

"But this happened, you say, before lunch. Why hasn't he telephoned?"

"Mr Holt is in shock."

The mind of the duty officer was racing, incoherent. "Didn't they have any protection?"

"Later there will be an opportunity for such detail."

The KGB colonel added, "There was a representative of state security at the hotel. He performed his duties with great bravery, but sadly was not able to prevent the attack."

"God Almighty . . ."

The First Deputy Foreign Minister said, "We shall be at the Foreign Ministry. We are at the disposal of the British people in this moment of anguish."

"It wasn't terrorism?"

"It was the act of a common criminal in pursuance of theft," the KGB colonel said decisively.

In darkness and amongst a sea of pimple landing navigation lights the Antonov put down at El Masr military airbase. They were checked with military thoroughness for contraband goods. They were home, in that home for these refugee strays of the Middle East was to be found in the Syrian Arab Republic. They had been together six months, now they were to disperse. Minibuses each for the Struggle Command, and for Sai'iqa, and for the Popular Front, and for the Democratic Front, and for the General Command, and for the Liberation Front. The culprit from Sai'iqa had lost his handcuffs five minutes after take off, the victim from Struggle Command embraced his attacker when they parted. The commander reflected that the Russians could never understand his children.

All went their separate ways, except that Abu Hamid with his commander travelled from the base in the Mercedes car that had been sent to collect

Major Said Hazan. Abu Hamid, unshaven and with the sweat smell on his body from his sprint away from the Oreanda Hotel, rode out of the base cushioned in the back seat between the officer of Syrian Air Force Intelligence and the officer of the Popular Front for the Liberation of Palestine.

When the car had gathered speed along the wide highway from the airport, the commander said softly to Major Said Hazan, "It was magnificent, Said. It was just as you had said it would be."

The voice was muffled through the scarf. "You played your part, friend."

Two quiet men talking casually across Abu Hamid, as if he were not there.

"But you took a great risk."

"Risk nothing, and it is not possible to achieve victory."

"When will the claim be made?"

"Claim?"

"What has happened has been a triumph for the Popular Front. The Popular Front should be, must be, credited . . ."

"There will be no claim. There will only be silence."

Abu Hamid heard the ice chill in the voice. He felt the major shift his body further into his seat.

He was in the darkness, on the bed, when he heard the light knock on his door. He thought he might have been to sleep. He felt the wet of his tears on his face when he rubbed his eyes. He heard his name called. He slid off the bed, opened the door, let in the flood of light.

The security officer said, "Thank God we've reached you, young man."

Holt blinked at him, turned away from the door.

"They gave us an executive jet . . ."

"Bloody decent of them."

"I came down with the counsellor: He's at the hospital, I've been at militia HQ."

"Super, first class."

"It's all right, Holt, you've had a bloody rough time, eh?"

Holt gazed into the security officer's face. "Rubbish. It's not bloody rough when you're *watching* a shooting . . ."

"Easy, young man."

Holt flared. "Easy . . . it's to be easy, is it? We come down here, Low bloody Risk bloody posting, we're set up for a shooting gallery. We're chopped down like Boxing Day pheasants . . ."

"I understand you were not exactly co-operative."

"Would you have been? What do they want cooperation for? They've just wiped out my boss and my girl, and they want me to help their bloody inquiry, put a gloss on their bloody lies. 'Course I didn't bloody cooperate."

A sharpness in the security officer's voice. "I have to tell you that the Soviet authorities could not have been more sympathetic and eager to help me. I have been given a very full briefing on their investigation and its conclusion . . ."

"So they soaped you up."

"A full briefing on their investigation and its conclusion."

Holt's voice dropped. "What conclusion?"

"They have told me that they identified an army deserter as the criminal responsible. It was his intention to rob the hotel at gun point. He panicked as the ambassador and Miss Canning and yourself were coming out of the hotel, and opened fire. They had good eye-witness descriptions of him, and this evening a vehicle in which he was travelling was waved down on the outskirts of the city. In attempting to evade arrest he was shot dead . . ."

"What else did they tell you about this 'deserter'?"

"That he was a 22-year-old Byelorussian."

"That's Minsk, he'd be a European."

"Did you see him, Holt, did you get a look at him?"

"At 15 feet. I saw his face."

The security officer lit a cigarette. The smoke spiralled in the quiet dark room.

"The man you saw, Holt, could he have been from Byelorussia?"

"They soaped and flannelled you."

"Give it to me straight, eh?"

"If he's from Minsk they'd had to have had a heat-wave there through this winter."

"Soaped and flannelled, as you say. I'm very sorry, very sorry about your girl."

Holt went to the window, showed his back to the security officer.

On Sunday morning a Royal Air Force VC-10 was diverted from its Cyprus to Brize Norton flight run to drop down at Simferopol.

The coffins containing the bodies of Sir Sylvester Armitage and Jane Canning were carried to the cargo doors by a bearer party of Soviet Marines. The coffins were taken past an honour guard of officer cadets from the military academy who stood sternly to attention, heads down and rifles in reverse.

The sight of the coffins, and the presence among them of young Holt and the counsellor and the security officer, was sufficient to subdue a company of paratroopers returning to the United Kingdom from a month's exercises.

5

"It was good of you to come. We appreciate it."

She was a small woman, brightly dressed, and with heavy make-up that he presumed was to hide the ravage of her bereavement. She stood in the front doorway and the rain lashed down onto the head and shoulders of young Holt. Strange, really, that in all the time he had known Jane he had never been asked to her parents home in South London. He saw the water dribbling down from the black mock-Tudor beams and down the whitewashed stucco. He hadn't a hat and so his head was soaked.

Gently he said, "Do you think I could come in, Mrs Canning?"

Her hand jerked to her mouth, and she was all movement, embarrassment.

"Whatever'll you be thinking of me? Of course come in . . . Father, it's Mr Holt here."

Jane's father took his coat off to the kitchen, and Jane's mother led him into the front room. A friendly room full of the furniture that dated back to the beginning of a marriage. Worn armrests on the sofa and the chairs, a burn mark in the carpet by the fire, plants that needed cutting back. On the mantelpiece was a photograph of his girl, a posed portrait that was all shoulder and profile. He stood with his back to the fire, with his back to the photograph of Jane, and his damp trouser legs steamed. He wondered what it was like for them to meet the man who loved their daughter and who had slept with their daughter. Around the room he counted four more photographs of her, of his girl. Jane's mother had sat down in *her* chair, the most used chair, and she had her knitting bag on her lap and was routing for needles and wool. She could see each one of the five photographs from her chair. She asked him to sit, and he said that he had been in the train a long time and that he preferred to stand. He reckoned that her clothes were a brave gesture, a Post-Office-red skirt and a white blouse and a vivid scarf knotted at her throat. He admired a woman who would dress like that for her daughter's funeral. Jane's father came into the room wiping the raincoat's damp off his hands onto a handkerchief. He wore his best suit and a starched white shirt and a tie that was either dark navy or black. Jane's father seemed exhausted, as if the strain of the past ten days had sapped him.

"Nice of you to come, young man – she never told us your proper name, you were always just called Holt by her," Jane's father said.

"That's what I am, really, what everyone calls me. Please just call me that . . . It means a lot to me that I can be with you today."

He meant it sincerely. He had been two days in London, telling his story. He had spent a long weekend at his parents' home, walking alone on the soaked wilderness of Exmoor. He wanted to be with Jane's mother and father on the day of the funeral. Jane's father asked him if he would like coffee and he said no, he was fine, and he asked him if he wanted to sit, and again he declined, and Mrs Canning knitted and Mr Canning searched for flaws on his finger nails.

"I wanted to be with you today because quite soon, I think Jane and I would have told you that we were going to become engaged to be married . . ."

She didn't look up. Her husband still explored the tips of his fingers.

"I loved her, and I like to think that she loved me."

"You've got to put it all behind you," Jane's mother said.

"When I arrived in Moscow and found her waiting for me at the airport I don't think that I've ever felt such happiness."

"Jane's gone, Mr Holt, and you're a young man and you've a life ahead of you."

"Right now I don't see it that way."

"You will, and the sooner the better. Life's for living."

Holt saw her bite at her lower lip.

Jane's father's head rose. His mouth was moving as if he were rehearsing a question, unsure of the form of words. The question when it came was little more than a whisper. "Was she hurt?"

Eight high velocity shots fired at a range of less than ten paces, that's what the post mortem had said. He could feel the lifeless hand, he could see the table tennis–ball–sized exit wounds.

"She wasn't hurt, there was no pain. What did they tell you, Foreign and Commonwealth?"

"Just that it was a grubby little business. This man was a heroin addict and an army deserter – they told us what was in the newspapers – that he had gone to the hotel to rob it. They said it was just a one in a million chance that he should have chosen that particular moment for his robbery, when our Jane and the ambassador and yourself were coming out of the hotel. They said the Soviet authorities were very sympathetic. They told us that the man was shot dead while trying to escape."

He saw the sallow face of the man with the windcheater and the rifle and the crow's foot scar on his cheek.

Holt said, "There's probably not much more that anyone can tell you."

Jane's mother stared at her knitting, her face puckered in concentration. "We were so proud, both of us, when Jane joined the Service, began to work for her country. It isn't easy for a girl to get a good position in it, and I think they thought she was outstanding. I'm not saying she told us much about it, a very discreet little soul, but we knew she was working in Intelligence. She probably told you more."

He remembered the photography over Charkov. He remembered his remark about the camera. He remembered the last words he had heard her speak. "Don't be childish, Holt."

"She was very much admired by all her colleagues."

Jane's father pushed himself up from the chair. "Like Mother said, you've your life ahead of you. It was good of you to come today, but we shan't expect to see you again."

Holt saw the black car outside. He saw Jane's mother putting her knitting and her needles back into the embroidered bag. He saw Jane's father straighten his tie.

"I loved her, Mr Canning. We were going to be married."

He saw the trace of impatience.

"Get on with your career, get on with the living of your life . . . Pity it's raining, Mother."

Holt followed Jane's mother fast down the short path and through the front gate to the car. Jane's father carefully locked the door behind him. He sat with them in the back as they were driven to the crematorium that was away to the west, close to the river. They didn't talk on the journey, and Holt wondered whether they held their peace because of him or because of the driver. As soon as they had arrived at the crematorium, Holt removed himself from their side. There were cameras there, television and press photographers, and he felt that by hanging back he drew away from them the attention of lenses and the clicking shutters. Holt was good raw meat for the cameras. It had been leaked that they were close, that he had seen the killings. He tried to keep his head up, his chin jutting. He walked past the sprays of flowers and the wreaths. He saw the signature of the Foreign Secretary, and of the head of the Soviet Desk at FCO and there were four bundles of flowers which were simply signed with Christian names. Inside the porch of the chapel Holt saw a tall, austere man shaking the hands of Jane's mother and father. There had been FCO people outside, but Holt understood. The Director General of the Secret Intelligence Service could not stand in front of the cameramen, nor could his people sign their names on the wreaths. He wondered what had become of Jane's camera, what had happened to her photographs from the plane. He felt a surge of anger, as if these nameless men and the Director General of the Service were responsible for her death.

It was a short service. He sat alone behind her parents. He couldn't find his voice when they sang the 23rd psalm. He watched the coffin roll away from him, he watched the curtains close. He was crying in his heart. He remembered her voice, her grey eyes, her soft hair, and her lifeless hand. He remembered the man with the rifle. He saw her parents walk back up the chapel aisle and they didn't turn to him. He sat in his seat and stared at the closed curtain.

"You're young Holt, yes?"

He turned. The chapel had emptied fast. The man was thickset with a fine head of grey hair and the brush of a military moustache was squashed between nose and mouth.

"I am."

"We have to be moving. They'll be queuing up outside for the next one, damn conveyor-belt operation. Do you have wheels?"

He had steeled himself to spend the day with Jane's mother and father. He had made no arrangements to get himself away, and now it had been made plain to him that he was not expected back to the semi-detached home in Motspur Park.

"I don't."

"Have you the afternoon to spare?"

His studio flat in London was rented out. The tenant had signed for a year. Ahead of him was only a train journey back to Devon, plenty of trains, they ran all afternoon and evening. His father would come down to Exeter to collect him. An usher appeared beside the man, trying to hurry them.

"For what?"

"My name's Martins, Percy Martins, I'm from the Service. Your initial debrief by the FCO people landed on my desk."

He looked up at Percy Martins. He saw clear pale blue eyes that never wavered from his glance. "What is there to talk about?"

"What you saw, what happened."

Holt felt the control going, voice rising. "I thought everyone knew what bloody happened. I thought they all swallowed the Soviet crap."

"Not swallowed by everyone – come on."

Holt followed obediently. He noticed that Martins walked out of the chapel well ahead of him, so that he would not be included when Holt was again the cameramen's target. Holt reached a small estate car. Martins was already behind the wheel, engine started, pushing the door open for Holt.

"My son is at university in York. He's playing a match in London today, that's where we're going. My wife'll kill me if I get home tonight and haven't seen him. We can talk when we're there."

He drove fast and in total silence, occasionally peering down at the dashboard clock. On the M25 nothing passed them. Holt thought it must be a hell of an important game, a league decider or a cup final. He felt no urge to speak, was relieved to be left to his own company. He had had enough talking. Two whole days in London going through the programme that he had confirmed for the ambassador, and working over and over his description of the shooting, and each time he had questioned what appeared to be the general acceptance of the Soviet version of the killings he had just been shushed and assured that all was being put into place. They came to the playing fields. During the drive it had stopped raining, but now it had started again. Percy Martins flung himself out of the car and scampered round to the boot to fetch a pair of wellingtons. Holt saw that the back of the car was filled with fishing gear. An outsize rod bag, a cavernous landing net, a solid tackle box. He had to run to catch the man.

It was the farthest soccer pitch.

"Who's playing?" Holt said, when they reached the muddied touchline.

"York chemists against a gang of lawyers from University College, London."

"Is your boy good?"

"Bloody awful."

"Which one is he?"

"The one who can't kick with his left foot and hardly with his right."

"So what the hell are we doing here?"

They were the only spectators. There was no protection from the weather. Holt thought it was the worst game of football he had ever watched.

"As I told you, the report on your debrief landed on my desk."

Holt turned into the rain. He had to shout over the wind. "Why are you buying all this bullshit about a criminal robbery?"

"It suits us."

"Who can it suit?"

"Everybody – nearly everybody, anyway."

"Who is everybody?"

"Good question. Look at it, young Holt. There is a shooting in the Soviet Union, a highly embarrassing shooting, and they haven't a clue who is responsible. Best way to calm the matter down is to come up with a plausible story that cannot be disproved, that has the culprit removed and that does not show the Ivans in a particularly poor light. Just a bit of bad luck, wasn't it? Wrong place at the wrong time. They might just as easily have been walking along the pavement and a car had blown a tyre and swerved into them. Professionally speaking one has to see it as a successful exercise in damage limitation . . ."

"And everyone's so supine that they accept this convenient lie."

"I'm not everybody."

"Why aren't we saying out loud that this killing was the work of an Arab – that our ambassador and Miss Canning were set up by the Soviets to be murdered?"

"I think you've jumped too far. I believe you are right in thinking the killer was Arab, but not that the Soviets set it up. Highly embarrassing, as I said. In my opinion, this was an act of terrorism in Soviet territory. They can't admit that, can they? Oh Christ Almighty . . ."

One of the players had tried to kick the ball that wallowed in ankle deep mud, missed and fell on his back, and left the ball to be slotted into the net.

"That's my son and heir. God, he's pathetic, his mother's boy . . . FCO wouldn't see they've much choice but to go along with Ivan's version."

"So I've been brought to this absurd game to be given a lecture in Anglo-Soviet relations."

"You're being asked to help. Jane Canning was a member of the Service, and we will not take her death lying down."

Holt saw that the player who had given away the goal had been dismissed to the wing. The young man was pencil thin and pale. He was beginning to feel sympathy for the kid, particularly if his father was a pompous ass called Percy Martins.

"What does that mean in practice – not taking it lying down?"

"What it says. Holt, you were in the Crimea, in the centre of the Crimea is Simferopol. In Simferopol is a military academy which takes groups of foreign cadets for periods of up to . . ."

"Where is this getting us?"

"Listen, will you? . . . Among the foreign cadets are always Syrian-sponsored Palestinians. The shooting was at lunch time; that same Saturday evening a Syrian Air Force transporter put down at Simferopol and then flew on to Damascus . . ."

"How do you know that?"

"*Listen* . . . and that's none of your business. It is quite credible that a Palestinian, at least an Arab, shot the ambassador and Miss Canning and was flown back to the Middle East the same evening. It is even credible that the Soviets knew nothing of the plan."

"Why are you telling me this?"

"We need your help in identifying the man who killed Armitage and a member of our Service, your girl."

"And then?"

"That's none of your business either."

"I'd want him killed."

"So tell me what he looked like, everything."

Desultory cheers, H'ray, H'ray, H'ray; the game was finished. Martins's son tramped off the field. He didn't so much as look at his father. Martins made an attempt to greet him, but the young man kept walking. Holt thought Martins too proud to chase after him. And then it was too late. The two teams disappeared into the pavilion. Martins and young Holt paced the touch-line. They were still there after the groundsman had come out to unhook the goal netting and to gather up the flag posts. They were still there when the two buses with the chemists from York and the lawyers from London drove away from the pavilion. Holt poured out every detail from his memory on the man who had held the Kalashnikov assault rifle. The way he moved, height, weight, age, the clothes, the wig, the shape of the eyes, movement, features. Again and again, the crow's foot scar. Still talking when it was too dark for Holt to see Martins's face beside him.

Finally they walked back to the car.

"You never even spoke to your son."

"Watched him play, didn't I? That's what I promised his mother – how close would you have to be to him to see the scar?"

"Well, I was ten paces and could see it as clearly as I described it to you. I mean, you wouldn't miss it if you met him. You'll go after him?"

"She was one of ours."

Martins dropped Holt off at Paddington station, thanked him again and said he'd be in touch in a day or so. Then he crossed London and the Thames and parked his car in the basement at Century House. It was not unusual for him to be returning to his office as the commuters were heading for home. Martins lived in a torpid cul-de-sac in Putney, but his home was the seventh floor of Century. No need for him to ring his wife and tell her that he would be back late. She took it for granted that he would work eleven or twelve hours six days a week and that he would fish on the seventh. He had been 27 years in the Service. He had served in Amman and Cyprus and Tel Aviv. He was a graduate, years before the fighting ripped the city apart, of the American University of Beirut.

The debrief had taken days to reach him. It bore a string of FCO staff's initials and in Century it had come by way of the Soviet Desk. The seventh floor was Middle East. Martins was the Middle East Desk's third in the chain. The head of the Desk was twelve years his junior, his immediate superior was 14 years younger. Martins would climb no higher. Sometimes it rankled, most times in fact. His solace was his work.

On his desk was the debrief and transcripts of messages sent from an Antonov en route to Damascus. These had been intercepted by the Dhekelia listening post in Cyprus and deciphered at the Government Communications HQ in Cheltenham. It was indeed none of young Holt's business that the messages sent from the Antonov within minutes of its leaving Soviet airspace were in the code systems of Syrian Air Force Intelligence and not those of the regular Air Force.

For the next two hours he wrote down in neat longhand everything that Holt had told him. By the time he had completed seven foolscap sheets he believed he could build a picture of a face, a working likeness of a man. He was satisfied that he knew exactly where the crow's foot scar should be placed.

Later, at a time when the train carrying Holt was west of Taunton, Inter City 125 and hammering, Percy Martins took the lift two floors up the 19-storey building to a small cubby-hole of a room where a technician had been whiling away the hours making a balsa wood 1:50-scale replica of a vintage Churchill tank. It would be a late night. The technician would work with Martins to make a likeness of the face of an assassin.

The following evening the actual size portrait and the four typed sheets of briefing were carried in a large buff envelope in the nearly empty briefcase of a government messenger en route to Tel Aviv. For the duration of the flight, a little over four hours, the briefcase was attached to the wrist of the messenger by a length of fine steel chain. It would have been impossible for the messenger to eat the airline meal without his chain being noticed so he went without food.

At Tel Aviv the messenger was met by the Service's station officer. A docket was signed. The papers were exchanged. The messenger flew back on the return flight after killing four hours in the transit lounge, and twenty minutes in the restaurant.

Before dawn a light burned in the upper room at the rear of the British embassy on Hayarkon. This upper room had no view of the stretching Mediterranean sea. The walls of the room were of reinforced concrete, the windows were of strengthened glass. The room was reached by an outer corridor in which had been placed a gate of heavy steel vertical bars. Behind the locked door of the room, the station officer examined the face that had been built for him, and read Martins's brief.

The killer of Sir Sylvester Armitage and of Jane Canning was believed to be Arab, most probably Palestinian. The distinguishing feature of the Arab was a crow's foot scar of approximately one inch in diameter on the upper left cheek. The station officer smiled at what he called Martins's fingerprints all over the brief, his unlovely grammar, but the substance of it was good. Near the bottom of the third page was the text of the message – underlined in red, typical Martins touch – from the Antonov transporter after it had entered Turkish airspace.

"*The target is taken.*"

It was left to the discretion of the station officer as to whether he went for help to the Mossad, Israel's external Intelligence gathering organisation, or the Shin Bet, the state's internal counter subversion and counter terrorism apparatus, or to Military Intelligence. Since the trial of Nezar Hindawi and the severing by Britain of diplomatic relations with Syria, co-operation between London and Tel Aviv was unprecedentedly close. He had no doubt that he would get the help Martins requested.

As the low-level sunbeams rose above the squat, dun-coloured apartment blocks of Tel Aviv, the station officer dialled the private telephone line of the man whose friendship he valued most in Military Intelligence. He liked the hours they worked. He locked his room behind him, and with the photofit in his bag he drove to the Ministry of Defence on Kaplan.

As the crow flies, and nothing larger than a crow can make the flight without plucking up a barrage of ground-to-air missiles, it is 125 miles from Tel Aviv to Damascus. The principal cities of the old enemies are adjacent in the currency of modern warfare. Behind the frontier that divides them, Syria and Israel have massed divisions of armour and mechanised infantry, regiments of artillery, squadrons of interceptor aircraft. The two client states scowl at each other from the cover of curtains of state-of-the-art United States and Soviet equipment. Two great coiled armies awaiting the order to commence the blood-letting, poised to exploit the moment of maximum advantage.

In the waiting time, as the troops idle away the hours in their fox holes and base camps, the tanks are kept armed and fuelled, stacks of ammunition lie beside the heavy howitzers, the aircraft are loaded with their missiles and cannon shells and cluster bombs.

They wait, two nations obsessed with the need for one gigantic heave to ultimate victory.

For the Israelis the waiting is harder. They are the smaller nation and they are crippled by the cost of the feud.

For the Syrians the waiting is easier. They have a surrogate force obedient to their discipline. They have the Palestinians of the Salvation Front. The

Palestinians from their bases in Lebanon or from the camps around Damascus can be organised to strike at Israel, to harass Israel, to wound Israel. And the Palestinians are expendable.

It was a dry, dust-laden morning. It was a morning when the flies with persistence crawled at the eyes and into the nostrils of the men who paraded in the dirt yard of the Yarmouq camp. The sun climbed and shortened the shadows, and the stink of the shallow latrine pits lay across the camp.

The recruits had been standing on parade in the growing heat for a little more than an hour because the guests from Damascus were late and there was no explanation for the delay, and no one dared to stand the men down. They had come from the refugee centres in West Beirut, from Sidon and Tyre, and from camps in Jordan and South Yemen. They were aged between 17 and 19. They had joined the Popular Front for the Liberation of Palestine, because they believed that that organisation would give them the greatest chance to hurt the Zionist state. Some wore uniforms and boots that were Syrian army surplus, some wore jeans and T-shirts and pullovers. Some had already shaved their heads, some wore their hair to their shoulders. All held their unloaded rifles as if it were second nature to them. They were children suckled on conflict.

The commander was at the gate, fretting with his watch.

Abu Hamid stood in front of the squad of eighty recruits. His uniform fitted him well. He wore the tunic and top, camouflaged in pink and green and yellow, of a Syrian commando. He carried, loosely over the crook of his arm, a Kalashnikov assault rifle. Occasionally he barked an order at the recruits, ordered them to straighten up. He felt a new degree of authority. No one at the camp other than the commander knew his part in what had happened in Yalta, but there were other signs of the favour that had fallen into the path of Abu Hamid. Two days later than the others who had flown back from the Soviet Union, Abu Hamid had reached Yarmouq and when he had rejoined his colleagues he had been driven to the camp in a Mercedes Benz car by a chauffeur who wore Air Force uniform. Three times since then he had been off camp, and back late in the evening with the smell of imported whisky on his breath, and his girl had been allowed to the camp, and he had been promoted, which was why he now stood in front of the recruits.

The cars, when they arrived, billowed a dust storm. Abu Hamid yelled for his men to stand still, he aped the instructors at Simferopol. He saw the commander fawning a greeting to an officer who wore the insignia of a brigadier general.

The breath came in a sharp gasp from Abu Hamid's throat. He thought that every recruit behind him gawped at the officer who now climbed from the official car that had followed that of the brigadier general into the camp. The officer strode forward. He carried his cap in his left hand.

The officer's walk was normal. His torso was ordinary. He had no fingers on his right hand, a stump at the knuckle. It was his head that captured attention. There was nothing sharp in the definition of his features. The skin across his cheeks and his nose and his upper lip and his chin seemed fragile and tightly drawn, the opaque skin of a butterfly's or a moth's wings. The skin had a lifeless quality, dead skin that had somehow been reprocessed for further use, and stretched over the bones of the face and the muscles by a human hand and not by nature. The nose of the officer seemed a squashed bauble, and his mouth was a parched slit. The earlobes were gone. The eyebrows were gone. What hair there was seemed to have been planted behind a line drawn vertically down from the scalp's crown to the deformed ears. The hair was bleached pale.

A soft, small voice. A voice that he recognised. A voice with the lilt of a persuasive song.

"Good morning to you, Hamid."

He swallowed hard. "Good morning, Major Said Hazan."

He stared blatantly into the broken face. He saw the cracked, amused smile that rose in the expanse of skin. He saw the medal ribbons on the chest of the uniform tunic.

Major Said Hazan waved Abu Hamid forward. The commander was ignored as the major introduced Abu Hamid to the brigadier general. The ranking officer knew what Abu Hamid had achieved, it was there in his eyes for Abu Hamid to see, a shared secret.

Abu Hamid escorted the brigadier general and Major Said Hazan along the four rows of recruits. Only one cloud in Abu Hamid's mind that morning. Of course, he had expected that military security would check all the weapons issued to the recruits to ascertain that no live rounds would be carried on parade. He had not expected that his own AK-47 would be scrutinised, that he would have to clear the breach and show that his magazine was empty. One small cloud . . .

After the inspection the brigadier general called for the recruits to come close to him.

". . . In today's world no man can be neutral. A man is either with the oppressed or he is with the oppressors. We have to fight to our last breath. It is better to die with honour than to live with humiliation . . ."

When he was cheered, when the fists of the recruits were aloft, the brigadier general smiled his satisfaction. Abu Hamid clapped his hands, waved three of the recruits towards the administration building.

His remaining recruits formed a circle, facing inwards. A photographer edged forward, stretching on tiptoe to see into the circle. A European photographer. Abu Hamid saw the brigadier general gesture to the photographer to push harder. A dozen live chickens were brought to the circle, thrust into the ring. Abu Hamid shouted, "Death to all enemies of the Palestinian Revolution."

The circle closed. The chickens were caught, torn apart, wing from breast, leg from body, head from neck. Hands groping into a bedlam of movement.

The raw meat of the chickens, the warm flesh of the chickens was eaten, the blood drunk. Young faces frothing pink meat, spewing red blood.

It was a tradition of the Popular Front, designed as the first measure in the breaking down of the human inhibition against killing. For the first ritual a live chicken sufficed to play the part of an enemy of the revolution.

The photographer was on assignment from a news magazine in the German Democratic Republic. He took a roll of film on each of two cameras. Among his images was the man who wore a *khaffiyeh* headdress across his face, and who chewed at a chicken wing.

The brigadier general congratulated Abu Hamid on the dedication of his recruits, and Major Said Hazan clasped his shoulder in farewell. Abu Hamid was bathed in pleasure.

The Prime Minister's cars swept into Downing Street.

There were a few older men and women on the head of government's staff who could remember when a prime minister travelled with only a single detective and the chauffeur for company.

But over the wreckage of a seaside hotel from which a Cabinet had been pulled by firemen or dragged by police minders, a spokesman of Irish liberation had declaimed, "You have to be lucky every time, we have to be lucky once".

The Prime Minister detested the paraphernalia of the bodyguards, and the closed circuit cameras, and the alarm systems in Downing Street.

The Director General, who waited in the outer office, knew well the Prime Minister's impatience with security.

He saw the Prime Minister, hemmed in by Branch men, in the brief moment between the car and the doorway as he gazed down from the window above the street. The flash of the face that was reddened from the sunshine of the Asian tour and the jetlag. The Director General had the automatic right of access. He reported directly to the Prime Minister.

"It was a pretty dreadful funeral," the Prime Minister said, and shrugged off an overcoat. "Lady Armitage was first class, could have been welcoming us to a cocktail party, but there was a granddaughter there who cried her eyes out, noisily, rather spoiled things. What a thing to get back to, fourteen hours in the air and straight to church . . ."

The Director General knew the form. He allowed the talking to go on. Neither of the previous Prime Ministers he had served had exactly rushed to allow him to throw into the fray whatever hand grenade he was waiting to communicate.

". . . Do you know the Soviet ambassador read the second lesson, and read it pretty well. I thought that was a very spirited gesture . . ."

"He was badly overdue a spirited gesture, Prime Minister," the Director General murmured.

300

"I don't follow you."

"The deaths of Sylvester Armitage and Miss Canning are a considerable embarrassment to the Soviets. The killings were an act of political terrorism," the Director General said flatly.

"My brief from FCO said quite clearly that our diplomats were shot down by a common criminal."

"Which is regrettably untrue."

"Meaning what?"

"Meaning that the Soviet Union lied. Prime Minister, we are still looking for the last piece of evidence, but our belief is that the assassinations were the work of a Palestinian terrorist who was on a course in a military academy in the Crimea. We believe he flew out of the Soviet Union on the same day as the killings."

"Where does he lead us?"

The Director General said heavily, "The road goes directly to Damascus."

"Where he is beyond our reach."

The Director General produced a small leather notebook from his inside pocket. "They must never be beyond our reach, Prime Minister. May I quote you your words? I keep this with me always. You said two years ago, when speaking of the threat of terrorism, 'We need action, so that the terrorist knows he has no safe haven, no escape'. Your very words, Prime Minister. As I remember, you were heavily applauded."

"What do you have?"

"A face; we hope soon to have a name."

The Prime Minister's head was shaking, the eyes ranged anywhere in the room but back to the Director General's face. "We cannot just storm into Damascus, of all places."

"Miss Canning was a member of my team. I have never taken anything you have said, Prime Minister, to be empty rhetoric."

"He'll be beyond reach," the Prime Minister said.

"He'll have to hide well."

"There is something I have to know."

"Yes, Prime Minister?"

"Were the deaths of the ambassador and your Miss Canning condoned by the government of the Soviet Union?"

"We think that they knew nothing of it – may not know it now. Hence the embarrassment, hence the deception."

"I find it beyond belief that Syria, a client state, for God's sake, would instigate a terrorist outrage inside the Soviet Union."

"They may be a client state, Prime Minister, but not subservient. Their missile systems, for instance, won't allow Soviet personnel near Soviet hardware. Most certainly they do not take orders. They had a target – a motive too if you accept their twisted logic – and they would have believed with some justification that they could get away with it."

"I repeat myself . . . We cannot just storm into Damascus."

"And I repeat myself . . . We need action, so that the terrorist knows he has no safe haven . . . I will keep you fully informed."

The flies surged in the room, careless of the swatting irritation of the commander.

He gestured that Abu Hamid should sit. He brought him a can of Pepsi from the fridge. The sounds of the camp drifted through the windows.

"What do you want of me?"

"Major Said Hazan," Abu Hamid said.

"You have pleased him."

"His face."

"What of his face?"

"What happened to his face, his hands?"

"You are not a child to be frightened, Hamid. You are a fighter."

"Tell me what happened."

"He was a pilot, MiG-21. In combat over the Golan Heights in 1973 he was shot down, hit by a Sidewinder air-to-air missile fired from a F-4 Phantom. There was fire in the cockpit. He had to level out before he could eject. He is not a man to panic, he waited. He would not know the meaning of panic. When it was safe to eject, then he did so. His parachute brought him down behind his own lines. His face was rebuilt in Leningrad. Perhaps in the hospitals there they are not experienced in such injuries."

Abu Hamid drained the Pepsi. "I just wanted to know."

The commander leaned forward, his face close to Abu Hamid's. "You should understand, Hamid, that a man, with his face and his hands on fire, who does not panic, does not eject until the right time, that man is to be treated with caution."

"What are you telling me?" Abu Hamid's finger flicked at the scar hole on his cheek.

"That Major Said Hazan works now for Air Force Intelligence, that he has great influence . . ."

"I have performed a service for him. I am his friend."

"Be careful, Hamid."

"He told me today that I would be rewarded for what I did. He himself signed the chit for my girl to come to the camp. On his orders cars have been sent for me, bills have been paid."

"Then you are indeed his friend," the commander said softly.

He was a clever young man, with a bachelor's degree in physics from the Hebrew University of Jerusalem. In the reserve of the Israeli Defence Forces he held the rank of sergeant, in civilian life he was a research scientist for a company specialising in the manufacture of military electro-optics. He was said to have the most complete knowledge among all the reservists of the labyrinthine computer files held by Military Intelligence on Palestinian personnel.

The computer failed to throw up any reference to the crow's foot scar. The failure told the sergeant that the man of the photokit likeness had not been in IDF custody since the scar was acquired. A disappointing start . . . He was left with the computer and with thousands of IDF and Mil Int photographs. There were few concrete items in the information he had that would help him to reject material unlooked at. A flight to Syria told him that his subject would not be a member of the Palestine Liberation Organisation's Force 17. A man of Force 17 would never fly via Damascus. But the men had flaking allegiance. A fighter who was now in the Popular Front, or the Domestic Front or the Struggle Front, could have been in Force 17 a few years before . . . It would be a long slog with the green screen, and the photograph bank.

The sergeant reckoned from the age of the subject, and from the fact that he had been taken to Simferopol for a platoon leader's course, that it was possible he had been in Beirut when the Palestinians evacuated in the summer of 1982. There were 1787 photographs available from the days when the Palestinians had trooped down to the docks and boarded the boats that would sail them to exile. The photos were blown up from American newsreel coverage that had been purchased unedited by the Israeli Broadcasting Corporation. The sergeant put up every print onto a screen for magnification. Each photograph was studied meticulously.

For five days the photographs flashed in front of him in his room, the blinds drawn over the windows, a cone of light from the projector to the screen.

He had a dogged persistence.

After 1411 failures his squeal of triumph was heard in the adjacent rooms and corridors. He had found a thin young man riding on the top of the cab of an open lorry, a short-haired young man with a thinly grown moustache. A young man who had a rifle aloft in one hand, and whose second hand was raised in the Victory salute. He saw the wound on the upper left cheek. Standing close to the screen, a magnifying glass in his hand, he found the lines of what the report called the crow's foot . . . Back to the computer. The number of the photograph fed in. The search for cross reference information. Long moments of stillness and then the rush began.

Popular Front for the Liberation of Palestine.

Of the six men shown in the photograph, two had subsequently been identified.

One man in the photograph named after his capture in the security zone . . . but later released when 1190 Palestinians and Lebanese Shi'as were freed in exchange for three IDF soldiers. The sergeant cursed.

The second man who had subsequently been named . . . captured, a dinghy chased to the shore by a patrol boat. A night gun battle on the beach close to Nahariya, lit by helicopter flares. Four infiltrators dead, one captured. Link with Popular Front.

Late in the night, while the prison slept, two army interrogators drove into the floodlit courtyard of the Ramla gaol. A convicted prisoner was roused from his cot, taken to a room where no prison warder was permitted to be present.

The prisoner was shown the photograph. He knew the man. He remembered his name.

Four days later an East German news magazine appeared. The eighteenth page of the magazine showed a scrum of Palestinian recruits struggling for the privilege of ripping a chicken to pieces. One man in the photograph wore a *khaffiyeh* scarf around his throat, where it had slipped when he bit into the feathered wing of the chicken.

The face was in tight focus.

6

While his friend poured the coffee, the station officer peered down at the photograph.

His friend was Zvi Dan. The photograph from the magazine page had been enlarged and the scar was clear to the naked eye.

"You've done me damn well. A name for Chummy and a date and a place."

"But we have nothing much else with which to link him apart from the Beirut picture. Anything further can only be supposition."

Zvi Dan's career as an infantry officer had been cut short 15 years before when an exploding artillery shell on the Golan Heights had neatly severed his left leg immediately below the knee, and only two days before the cease-fire had wound up the battles of Yom Kippur. He had faced the prospect of civilian life or of finding military work that could be conducted away from the operational area. He had made major, Military Intelligence. He specialised in the study of Palestinian groups who were known to have firm links abroad, and whose operations against Israel were often far from his country's frontiers.

"I think that in London they are pretty concerned with this one. I think they'll take all the supposition they can get."

"Then we should begin to play the jigsaw."

Zvi Dan worked from an office in the Ministry of Defence. His quarters were apart from the main complex of buildings that stretched the length of Kaplan. His base was surrounded by a coiled fence of barbed wire and with additional armed guards on the gate. He had access to Mossad files and to Shin Bet interrogations of captured Palestinians. He read voraciously. In the small circle where his name was known he was credited with supplying the information that had led to the arrest of a Jordanian who intended to carry on board a Swiss airliner two hand grenades for a hijacking attempt on the Cyprus-Jordan leg of the flight. He had supplied the lead that enabled the Belgian police to raid a video arcade in a small town in the north of the country and arrest two Palestinians and a Belgian couple, and uncover 40 lbs of plastic explosive. His warnings had led to the interception at sea of two yachts being used by Palestinian infiltrators, the *Casselardit* and the *Ganda*. If he regarded these as little victories Major Zvi Dan could – and did – count as catastrophic defeats the assault on the synagogue in Istanbul, 22 Turkish Jews killed; the slaughter at Rome's Fiumicino airport, 86 killed and wounded; the massacre at Vienna's Schwechtat airport, 49 killed and wounded.

The station officer said, "I'll put my pieces on the board. The British ambassador in Moscow insults a Syrian diplomat, practically with a loud hailer, the entire diplomatic community looking on, right in the Syrian's master's sitting room. Claims of Syrian innocence in the El Al bomb laughed to scorn in public. Total humiliation of Syrians. Two: our man in Moscow is assassinated oblique stroke mugged in the Crimea, close to a military school where Palestinians are trained. Three: same evening a Syrian Air Force plane lands at the airport next door to the school and flies on to Damascus, en route sending a message saying in effect Mission Achieved. Four: our eyewitness at the shooting gets a clear view of Chummy and from that we follow through to the evacuation from Beirut in '82 and a member of the PFLP contingent. The last piece I can put on the board is what I'll call the Dresden photograph, that puts Chummy at a camp outside Damascus possibly seven, eight days ago. Those are my pieces."

"You want this Abu Hamid?"

"We want him, even if we have to go to Damascus to get him."

Zvi Dan laughed, a quiet croak in his throat, and the laugh brought on the hacking cough of the persistent smoker.

"Damascus would be easy. Damascus pretends it is an international city. There are businessmen travelling to Damascus, and there are academics, and there are archaeologists. It is a city of millions of people. In a city you can come shoulder to shoulder with a man. You can use the knife or the silenced pistol or the explosive under the car he drives. If it were Damascus then I would already offer you my felicitations, even my congratulations . . . the scar is only an inch across so you have to be close to identify the man you want."

"The girl who was killed, she was one of ours," the station officer said quietly. "Don't worry about getting close. We'll walk onto the bridge of his nose if we have to. That's the sense of the messages I am being sent from London."

The coughing was stifled. Zvi Dan beat his own chest. There was the rustle of the packet, the flash of the lighter, the curl of the smoke. The end of the nicotined finger stubbed at the Dresden photograph.

"Look at them. Other than the man you want they are all raw recruits. They are children who have joined the Popular Front and here they are participating in the first ceremony of induction. There will have been a parade, and there will have been a speech by a big man from the government. It is what always happens . . . They will have been in Damascus for a few days only. They will be moved on. They will go to a field training camp where they will be taught, not well, the art of small-unit operations. Your man, the man you want, the older man amongst them, he will travel with the children as their instructor. Possibly it is a reward for what he achieved in Yalta. They will go to a training camp with their instructor for perhaps half a year."

"Where would the camp be?"

"Where it is impossible for you to be close, shoulder to shoulder." For a moment the face of Zvi Dan was lost in a haze of smoke. "In the Beqa'a Valley."

"Oh, that's grand," said the station officer. "The 59 bus goes right through the Beqa'a Valley."

The valley is a fault, it is a legacy of rock strata turbulence of many millennia ago.

The valley floor is some 45 miles in length, and never more than ten miles in width. It is a slash between the mountains that dominate the Mediterranean city of Beirut, and the mountains that overlook the hinterland city of Damascus. It is bordered in the north by the ancient Roman and Phoenician city of Baalbeck, and in the south by the dammed Lake Quaroon.

The sides of the valley, deep cut with winter water gullies, are bare and rock strewn, good only for goats and hardy sheep. The sides cannot be cultivated. But the valley floor has the richest crop-growing fields in all Lebanon. The Litani river, rising close to Baalbeck, bisects the valley running south to Lake Quaroon. The valley floor is a trellis of irrigation canals, not modern, not efficient, but able to offer life blood to the fields. The best vines of Lebanon, the best fruit, the best vegetables, all come from the Beqa'a, and the best hashish.

The history of the Beqa'a is one of murder, conspiracy, feuding and smuggling. The people of the region whether they be Christian or Druze or Shi'a Muslim, have a reputation for lawlessness and independence. Government authority has always taken second place in the minds of the feudal landlords and the peasant villagers.

Times, of course, have not stood still in the Beqa'a. The villagers are better armed, each community now possesses RPG-7 grenade launchers, heavy DShKM machine guns, enough Kalashnikovs to dish them out to the kids.

The villagers are well off by the standards of torn, divided Lebanon, because when all else fails the hashish market bails them out. The trade is across the rifts of politics and religion. Druze sells to Shi'a who sells to Christian who sells to Syrian.

The Beqa'a now is a valley of pass papers and checkpoints. Shi'a checkpoints on the approaches to their villages. Druze checkpoints, Syrian army checkpoints on the main road from Damascus to Beirut, and more on the side roads that lead to their barracks, Palestinian checkpoints on the approaches to their training camps.

They had reached the high spot. Behind them were the customs buildings and the missile site. Ahead of them the ground, dun and grey, shelved away into the valley.

The recruits were in two military lorries, while Abu Hamid sat in the jeep driven by Fawzi, his liaison officer. Fawzi drove with enthusiasm, exhilarated in his role as middle man between the Popular Front training camp and the officers of Air Force Intelligence. Abu Hamid had thought that any man would be sick in his gut at such a job, but all the man cared for, all that he talked about on the climb to the mountain pass and the descent beyond, was the new-found opportunity for trade.

"Trade" he called it. Televisions and video cassette players and electric refrigerators would come to the Beqa'a from Beirut, freshly grown hashish would come from the valley, and Fawzi could take back to the old *souq* in Damascus as much as would cram into the covered back of his jeep. To Abu Hamid, the man was disgusting, the man was a criminal. He wondered how it was that Major Said Hazan would permit such a man to play a part in the Palestinian revolution.

But he had hardly listened to Fawzi. Yes, he had the babble from the man, from his thick spittle-lined lips, but after a while he had paid him no attention, thought only of Margarethe.

Abu Hamid did not know how long it would be until he next saw Margarethe. He had not been told. He fancied that if he put his hand under the vest below his tunic, and rubbed his hand hard against the skin, and that if he then put his hand against his nose, then he would smell the sweet scent of his Margarethe. With other women shyness made him brutal. It was so the first time with Margarethe, but she had slapped his face, right cheek and then left cheek . . . then come to him, rolled him onto his back, and loved him. He did not know where a woman had learned to love with such wild beauty. From that first time Margarethe made him love her with all the lights switched on; each time she stripped him, each time she straddled him. He could not comprehend why Margarethe Schultz worshipped the body of Abu Hamid, who did not have the money for shoes. He did not understand her dedication to the cause of a Palestinian homeland, did not understand the Red Army Faction of which she claimed to be a member. He had written to her on the last day of each month that he had been in Simferopol. And when she was naked she was beautiful to him . . .

What was wonderful was that she had waited for him, waited for six months for his return.

They were coming down into the valley.

He could hear the protests of the brakes of the lorries behind him.

"It is the hashish that gets the best price. I buy it here, I pay the major forty per cent of what I have paid. I double the cost of my outgoings and that is the price I will get in Damascus. I don't know what charge is made by the man who sells it on from Damascus. When it gets to Europe the price is fantastic. It amazes me that people in Europe will pay . . ."

They passed through two checkpoints manned by Syrian commandos. They crossed the floor of the valley. The road took them alongside a small village, and there were women out in the fields hoeing the damp ground between the first early summer wheat crop. They bumped off the road and followed a stone track for four or five miles. Much for Abu Hamid to see. There were old bomb craters still with the scorched blackness that years of rain had not discoloured. There was a tank regiment, hull down, in defensive position.

There's a network of slit trenches, newly dug and lined with the brightness of corrugated iron. There were areas that were marked by a single strand of barbed wire and the skull and crossbones sign designating minefields. They crossed two army engineers' bridges over irrigation ducts, and then traversed a rolling plank bridge over the main flow of the Litani river. They skirted a formation of camouflage-painted pillboxes. They were close to the far wall of the Beqa'a valley.

He saw the small tent camp ahead. A dozen tents. The camp nestled under the rising ground beyond. He winced. There was nowhere else that they could be heading.

"Is that the camp?" The disgust was rich in Abu Hamid's voice.

"You want orange groves and villas? You should go and fight in the Zionist state. You will find all the orange groves and all the villas that you could wish for there."

When darkness had fallen over the Yarmouq camp, when the perimeter flood-lights were reduced to small cones of light, a car drove through the gates and to the administration building. A runner was sent from the administration building to the hut where the commander had his quarters. The commander was seen by the runner to talk briefly to the men in the car, and then to get into the back seat. Two hours later the commander was dead, shot once in the head, and he was buried in a shallow grave beside the Quneitra road, beyond the airport, beyond the headquarters of Air Force Intelligence. When questioned by senior officials of the Popular Front investigating the commander's disappearance, the runner would be able to say in truth that the darkness prevented him from seeing the men inside the car, that they did not identify themselves.

For Major Said Hazan, the commander had outlived his usefulness. And he was a dangerous witness to a conspiracy, and he knew the author of that conspiracy. Of Abu Hamid, Major Said Hazan had no doubt.

Martins had come to the nineteenth floor.

He sat in an armchair with his papers on his lap. He sat uncomfortably upright. It was a strange habit of the Director General that he conducted his meetings from soft seating, never used the polished table and the straight chairs that were at the far end of the room. On the rare occasions that he was summoned to the Director General's office, Percy Martins was never at ease. The Director General seemed not to notice. Percy Martins read rapidly through the brief received from Graham Tork, station officer in Tel Aviv.

"So, it is his conclusion that Abu Hamid has by now either travelled to the Beqa'a, or is about to."

"Which makes it awkward for us."

"In Tork's opinion – rather an eccentric one, in my view – Damascus would be tolerably straightforward, the Beqa'a quite impossible."

"The Service doesn't believe in 'impossible', Percy."

Martins sucked at his teeth. "With respect, sir, the Beqa'a is virtually an armed camp. It is home for the Syrian army, at least one division of armour, regiments of artillery, units of commando forces. It's also home for a violently anti-Western Shi'a Muslim population in the villages. And for the Hezbollah Party of God fanatics, also for the units of Islamic Jihad who, although small, are strong enough to blast the Americans out of Beirut. And for half a dozen or more extreme Palestinian groupings . . ."

The Director General played with his pipe. "You're not addressing school-children and you're missing the point, Percy. You're providing me only with problems, but let me quote Sir Winston Churchill to you, 'Grass never grows under a gallows tree'. Hit the terrorist in his safe haven and you destroy not only him, but you do a greater damage to the morale of his comrades. Have we the location of this training camp?"

"Not yet, sir. Tork reckons his locals should be able to give it to him within a couple of weeks."

"We need that location, we need a target area."

"Are you considering requesting the Israelis to mount an air strike?"

"Waste of time." The Director General waved his hand dismissively. He had that habit. He was only two years older than Martins. The habit had the effect of making the number three on the Middle East Desk seem half-witted. "An airstrike tells the Syrians nothing. I want the man who tasked this Abu Hamid for his killing mission to know that we'll go to the ends of the earth to exact a specific revenge."

Martins read the familiar signs. The more he pointed out the objections the more annoyance he would cause. On the other hand, the less he objected the less cover he gave himself in the event of a foul-up.

"You'd actually consider sending a team into the Beqa'a?" Martins some-times wondered whether the Service activities were planned on a Christmas present pencil sharpener globe. "For all the reasons I have suggested, that Tork has set out, that is quite impossible . . ."

"Perhaps you didn't hear me the first time. That's not a word I care for. Get yourself down to Hereford, Percy."

Without invitation, Percy Martins heaved himself up from the low armchair. He strode round the room. Speak now, or for ever hold thy peace. He heard his own voice, raised.

"So I go and talk to the Ministry and then to Special Air Service, and what's the first thing they'll say? They'll say the scar on Abu Hamid's face is an inch across, they'll say how close do they have to get to identify a man with a one-inch scar on his face?"

"We've a witness, and I dare say we've got a pair of binoculars."

Martins hesitated. "Our witness is a diplomat, not a soldier, sir."

"In the words of your report when you met this young man: 'I'd want him killed' – it seems to me that he would be prepared to learn to be a soldier. A further point. The witness not only saw the scar, the witness saw Abu Hamid, saw his stance, how he moved, saw him run."

"To take a young man, untrained, into the Beqa'a, on a covert operation . . . . Sir, are you quite serious?"

"When we had Leila Khaled, Popular Front hijacker, in Ealing Police station I argued against swapping her for our airline passengers held hostage in Amman – I was overruled. When it was planned to fly a gang of Provisional IRA death merchants by Royal Air Force plane to London for a cosy chat with government, I argued against it – I was overruled. I was overruled then because I didn't have enough authority. Now I do, and the masters are going to learn how long and how ruthless our arm can be, and quite frankly, I hope they shit themselves in the knowledge."

Martins said, "I'll go and talk to Hereford."

"You'll do more than that. You'll get our witness down to Albury, dust the place out, get him up to the mark. No misunderstandings, Percy, this is going to happen."

They hadn't told her how long she had to make the rooms ready, nor how many people would be coming. She did not know whether they would be there in a day or a week.

She had her old vacuum cleaner, and a bucket of warm water with Jeyes fluid and a mop, and three ragged dusters, and a window cleaner aerosol spray. She had four sets of sheets ranged out in the frame in front of the Aga stove in the kitchen. It would be seven months since the house in the woods outside the Surrey village of Albury had been used. She had been afraid that if the house were not used then it would be sold off and she and George would be moved on.

There was no time for George's lunch that day. She had ordered him to fill each and every one of the coal hobs, light each and every fire on the ground floor, to split more logs, to find the fault in the hot water boiler, to go into Guildford with her shopping list, and to keep his brute of a dog off the floors she had washed.

Agnes Ferguson had seen it all. What a book she could have written. She had been housekeeper for the Service safe house at Albury for nineteen years. They had given it into her care in lieu of a widow's pension. She had kept the safe house for Eastern bloc defectors, for agents returning from imprisonment abroad while they were debriefed, for the preparation of men going into covert action overseas. It had been a long and anxious winter, and George not much company. The telephone call had seemed to breathe new life, new hope, into her that her future was assured.

"It's preposterous, no other word for it."

"It has the sanction of the Director General," Martins said grimly.

"It makes no difference whose sanction it has. It just isn't on," the brigadier said.

"Too dangerous, is that it?"

"It's not our way to duck a challenge, but nor is it our way to volunteer ourselves for a mission that has no chance of success. Understand me, no chance."

In the mist outside the brick bungalow, Percy Martins's car was parked beside the broad base of the clock tower. When he had locked the door he had noted the names inscribed on the stone plaque under the clock face, the fatal casualties amongst the men of the 22nd Regiment, Special Air Service. Had he not been under orders he would most probably have agreed with the brigadier.

"No chance of success, I'll report that back."

"Don't play clever games with me," the brigadier said. A hard man, piercing grey-blue eyes. "We have no experience of the Beqa'a valley. No man in the SAS has ever set foot in the Beqa'a valley. It is, and always has been, outside our theatre of operation. We are not talking about the Radfan mountain ops of the sixties, nor about Oman in the seventies. For both of those we had first hand experience to draw upon, and we had a wilderness area to work through. In the Beqa'a we have no experience and we have no wilderness. It would take us months of reconnaissance and preparation before we could walk in there with any reasonable prospect of survival."

"I'll convey your message."

"They keep their hostages in the Beqa'a. The reason they are there is that their captors believe it the most secure area in Lebanon. For strangers, the Beqa'a is a dangerous, closed valley. The stranger won't last long enough to pick his nose. To be frank, and it gives me no satisfaction to say so, we wouldn't stand a prayer."

"I'll report that you cannot be of help."

"But I can be of help," the brigadier said. "I can tell you who will get you into the Beqa'a, who might quite possibly even get you out."

Percy Martins felt the surge of excitement. A name was given. He wrote the name in his notebook, and then he asked for permission to use a secure telephone.

The last light of the afternoon.

The sun was an orange orb away to his left and sliding.

It was a good time for him because the ground ahead was cooling, and the haze that had distorted his vision was gone, and his barrel was no longer warm.

His right eye, peering into the 'scope, ached. That pain behind his eye stabbed at him. The pain was nothing new to him, but it was more frequent and more acute, and that worried him.

The target was six hundred metres away. Of course he had not measured

312

the ground. In two days and one night he had not moved in his hide except to raise his hips the few inches that enabled him to urinate into a plastic bag. He was good at measuring distance. Without his expertise at gauging a distance ahead of him then all his work would be useless. The chart in his mind told him the rate of the drop in flight of a fired bullet. He knew the figures by heart. The difference in a drop between 500 metres and 600 metres was 1.53 metres. The difference in a drop between 500 metres and 600 metres was the height of a grown man. But he knew the distance to his target, his experience had made the calculation, and he had adjusted his 'scope sight for that distance. Beyond the target, away to the target's right, was a small fire that had been lit by a shepherd. He had watched the shepherd all day, hoping that the shepherd would keep his flock close to the stream and far from the rock slope on which he had made his hide. He was grateful to the shepherd for lighting the fire. The fire smoked right to left. The movement of the smoke enabled him to gauge the wind speed that would deflect his bullet. Another graph. His estimate of the wind speed was five miles per hour. His estimate of the deflection was eleven inches, for a target that was six hundred metres away.

It amused him, the way that sometimes the figures in his head were metric, and sometimes they were yards and feet and inches, and sometimes the thoughts in his mind were Hebrew, and sometimes they were English. He reckoned that he was close now to the optimum moment, and so the throb of the pain behind his right eye was relegated in importance. He was old for work as a sniper. He was 48 years old, and the balance was delicately poised between his expertise at gauging the distance to the target and the wind speed, against the ache of a tired eye. On a range he could shoot well inside a melon-sized group at 600 metres. A man's head was wider than a melon. That he was not on a range made little difference to him. If he had been young, perhaps he would have been knotted in tension and he would have cramp in his leg muscles. He was not young, he was quite relaxed, and he had learned long ago to rotate his toes in his boots to beat the cramp. He was not looking for a head shot. His 'scope showed him, where the hair lines crossed, the upper arm of the target who was in profile to him. He waited for the target to turn, to face him, he waited for the hair lines to cross on the upper torso of the target.

Steady hands on the rifle. No shake in the elbow that supported the rifle. The target faced him, was gesturing. There was no caution from the target. The target had no need for caution. The target was standing on open ground that was four clear miles from the edge of the security zone, four clear miles beyond the stop point of Israeli patrols. He knew that the target, the man with the flowing beard and the old camouflage battledress, was a commander of a unit of the Hezbollah. He knew no more about him. He did not know why the man had been targeted. That concerned him not at all. He received his orders, he carried them out. He was only thankful that he still belonged, was still wanted, as a regular.

His finger slid slowly from against the trigger guard to curl around the curve of the trigger. The hair lines were full on the chest of the target, they wavered around the flash of a small gold pendant. He knew the men of the Hezbollah talked at length of the glory of martyrdom. There was a wry, cold smile on his dirt-smeared face.

Crane fired.

The crack of a bullet. The collapse of a man. The scream of the crows taking flight. The bleat of stampeding sheep. The yelling of the men who had been with the target . . . . And the great silence.

The sun slipped. The dusk gathered. A grey blanket sliding over the valleys and water courses and rock outcrops and *jebels* of south Lebanon. Shadows merging, features losing substance.

There would be no search, that was the advantage of firing in the late afternoon. There could be no search in darkness, and where to search? None of the men who had stood with the commander of a unit of the Hezbollah could have pointed out the source of the single shot.

In the black night, canopied by stars, Crane walked with his rifle and his backpack homewards towards the security zone. Each time he fired, each time he scored, he believed that he prolonged his life as a regular, he put off the day when life would mean little more than a seat at a pavement café on Dizengoff. In the darkness his strained right eye no longer throbbed, the stabbing pain was gone.

At the edge of the security zone an armoured personnel carrier waited for him. From a distance he shouted a password, and when the response was yelled back at him, he came forward.

The crew of the carrier were all youngsters, all conscripts. They stared in awe as Crane slept in the back of the lurching, pitching vehicle. Each one of the conscripts knew his name, his reputation. They saw the worn filthy boots, and the torn trousers, and the muddied camouflage tunic, and the smeared face, and the woollen cap into which had been inserted sprigs of thorn bush. He was a legend to them.

At the camp, on high ground outside the town of Kiryat Shmona, two miles inside the border of the state of Israel, Crane jumped easily from the tail board of the carrier. No backward glance, no thanks, no small talk.

He was told that a helicopter was standing by to take him to Tel Aviv.

"You've done well."

"I'll confess, sir, I had doubts at first. I'm losing them."

"That's what I like to hear, Percy. I am tired of the rubbishing of the Service by every newspaper in London. I'm looking for a result we can be proud of." The Director General shrugged into his overcoat. His briefcase was on the desk, filled with the evening's reading. His detective waited by the door.

"I'd like to be in charge, sir." Martins stuck his jaw forward.

"You'd *what?*"

"I'd like to run this show, sir – here and in Tel Aviv." He saw the Director General pause, take stock, then jerk the coat into place.

"I was thinking of Fenner."

"Hasn't my experience, sir. I'd give it my best shot, sir. You could depend on me."

"Bit old, aren't you, for running in the field?"

"It's my show, sir, and I want it, I want it badly."

The Director General wrapped his scarf across his throat. He pulled on his gloves.

"What would I tell Fenner?"

"That life doesn't end at fifty, sir."

The Director General laughed. "Bloody good . . . . It's yours, Percy. Get it in place."

Young Holt had been all day on the moor.

He came down the long straight road towards the village. All the time he was coming down the hill he could see the front garden and the front door of the house that doubled as his parents' home and his father's surgery. There was a car parked outside by the front gate. It had been there for as long as he could see the house.

He had caught every shower of the day, and the winds from the west had spurred him along. He had seen deer and he had seen a dog fox, and he fancied that he might have found the holt of an otter. And he had decided that he would return to London, end his indefinite compassionate leave. The decision made the wet and the cold worthwhile. Impossible to have made the decision at home, under his mother's watching eye.

He was coming fast down the hill, looking for a bath, looking for a mug of hot sugared tea. He could see her face, he could feel her arms round his neck, he could hear her voice. In the rain on the moor he had cried to her, in the wind he had shouted to her.

He saw the front door open. He saw his father come out, and look up the road and discover him and wave to him.

The front garden was a picture. Daffodils and crocuses, and the leaves sprouting on the shrub bushes, and the path cleanly swept. He reached the gate. He saw his father's wheelbarrow piled with winter debris and the fork and the secateurs and the broom leaning against the wheelbarrow, as if the work had been disturbed.

"Been waiting ages for you, Holt. There's a chap here who's driven down from London to collect you. A Mr Martins. Percy Martins, I think he said."

It was as if ropes tightened on his wrists.

He saw her face, felt her body, heard her voice.

"Don't be childish, Holt."

"Decent-seeming sort of chap," his father said. "Just a trifle impatient. Your mother's given him tea."

7

Holt walked gingerly down the staircase.

The carpet had had so much use that he thought his mother would not even have offered it to Oxfam. Most of the dull brass rods were loose. There were three oil paintings on the wall above the stairs just decipherable as Victorian military and all apparently smoked for years over a damp log fire. In the early morning light the house looked in even worse a state than it did by night. But he had had a good sleep, and at least the sheets had been aired.

Peeping through a door at the back of the hall was an elderly woman in a housecoat. She had a headscarf over her hair and the sharp angles told him that she had slept in her curlers and not yet removed them.

"Good morning," Holt said. He did his best to sound cheerful.

She told him that she was Mrs Ferguson, that she kept house.

He hadn't seen her the night before. It had been a five-hour drive from Exmoor, and when they arrived there was hardly a light on in the place, and no food waiting, and no sign of a welcoming drink, even. Martins had been true to form, hadn't talked all the way, having muttered right at the start that he wasn't going to go off half cock, that he would keep the mysteries until the morning. Better that way, that was Holt's opinion. He could be patient.

Away behind closed doors he could hear the muffle of Martins's voice, on the telephone.

"He'll be having his breakfast in fifteen minutes," Mrs Ferguson said. She seemed to reproach him, as if by coming downstairs he had caught her unprepared, as if he should have stayed in his room until called.

Holt prised open the bolts on the front door and slipped the security chain. He could still hear Martins on the telephone. Thirteen minutes until breakfast. He had the impression that breakfast was like a parade. The lock on the door was a new expensive Chubb, and he had seen the fresh alarm wiring at the windows.

He stood on the front steps. He gazed around him. The house was a tower at his back, faded red Surrey brick, probably sixty or seventy years old with rounded corners topped by farcical battlements. In front of him were lawns, uncut since the previous autumn, and daffodil swards and beds of daisies and rose bushes that had escaped a winter pruning. There was a clatter of pigeons in flight from the oak and beech and sycamore trees that fringed the grass. He heard the stampede escape of a squirrel in the overgrown rhododendrons that hid the curve of a shingle drive. Holt thought the garden could have been a paradise . . . . A dog was charging towards him. Heavy shouldered, black and tan, ears swept back, a mouth of white teeth. Holt was good with dogs. There had always been dogs at home. He stood his ground, he slapped his hand against his thigh, welcoming. He heard a bellow, a yelling for the dog to stop, stand, stay, come to heel. The dog kept on coming, stripping the distance across the grass. Holt recognised the markings and weight of the German Rottweiler. Round the corner of the house came an elderly man, built like his dog, hobbling in pursuit, and shouting his command, and being ignored.

The dog reached Holt. The dog sat in front of him and licked Holt's hand. The dog had dreamy pleasure in the wide mahogany eyes.

The man reached them. He was panting.

"You shouldn't be walking outside, not when her's out. Damn bastard spiteful she can be . . ."

He wasn't looking at the dog. The wet of the dog's tongue lapped the back of Holt's hand.

". . . She's a trained guard dog."

"She's soft as a brush, a lovely dog. My name's Holt."

"I'm George, and you'd best not be taking liberties with her. Vicious, she can be."

Holt was scratching under the dog's chin. He could see the rank happiness in the eyes. Holt believed there must be method in the madness. A dog that was loving and called vicious, a garden that was beautiful and left to sink to ruin, a house that was magnificent and nearly splendid but was obviously not cared for. He could be patient, but, by God, he'd require some answers by the end.

"Breakfast, Holt." The shout from the doorway. He saw that Martins wore corduroy trousers and a Guernsey sweater.

"And keep that beast under control, George."

Holt walked away. He turned once, briefly, to see the dog watching him going. As he went through the front door, Martins battered him across the shoulders with forced camaraderie.

"Sleep all right? Fine place. You shouldn't just take yourself outside, you were lucky that George was there to control that bloody animal. Word of warning about breakfast, eat everything, she takes it personally if you leave a crumb or a quarter of an inch of bacon rind. Straight after, we'll talk business."

They took breakfast in a dining room that could have, probably once had, housed a full-size billiard table, but the flooring was linoleum and there were five small square tables each covered with a plastic cloth. Holt thought it was a civil service canteen, and the food was right for a canteen, and the coffee was worse. Martins said that the house had been bequeathed to the nation in 1947, and that since no one wanted it the Service had been lumbered. He said that it cost a small fortune to run and to heat. He said that Mrs Ferguson was the widow of a Special Operations Executive agent who had been parachuted into France just before the invasion, captured and shot. He said that George was a former serviceman, wounded by mine shrapnel in the Cyprus

Emergency, and kept on by the Service as caretaker, gardener, driver, maintenance man. Holt wondered if Jane had ever been in a place like this.

Martins led the way across the hall and into a huge drawing room. The dustcovers were piled in the centre of the carpet, and the fire had not been cleared or laid again. Martins cursed. He lifted the pile of dust sheets, took them to the door, flung them out. At the fireplace he emptied the hod into the grate and then buried a fire lighter under the fresh coal, and lit it. When the smoke billowed across the room he cursed again and went back to the door and left it ajar.

"Typical of houses like this. You have to leave a door open if you want a fire, otherwise you're smoke gassed. Why the Service has to put up with it defeats me . . . . I imagine you're pretty cut up about Miss Canning."

They were there, the patient waiting was over. Martins was bent over the fire, prodding with a grimed poker. Holt stood in the centre of the room and stared through the windows. He could see the dog slouching disconsolately towards a rose bed, then squatting.

"I've done a fair amount of thinking while I've been at home."

"You must have been devastated, only natural."

"I was at first, but I've come to terms with it. I'm going back to FCO. Life is for living, that's what Jane's mother said to me."

"I don't quite follow you."

"I'm going back to work, I'm going to try to put Yalta out of my mind . . ."

Martins was up from the fire, and the poker was left across the grate. Shock in his eyes, the colour flushing to his face.

"Your girl killed, shot down in cold blood, butchered in broad daylight, and you're talking about 'life is for living', I don't believe my ears."

"Don't sermonise me, Mr Martins. My feelings are in no way your business, not anyone's business but mine."

"Oh, very nice. Hardly dead, and you're talking about forgetting her, abandoning her memory . . ." There was a waft of contempt in Martins's voice, and a tinge that Holt saw of anxiety.

"She was my girl, I loved her and she is dead."

"And to be forgotten?"

"You're an arrogant bastard, *Mister* Martins. What I said is that I intend to go back to work, to go on with my life."

"Then, young Holt, you are a selfish little creep."

"If you brought me half way across England to this slum to insult me . . ."

"I'm merely astonished to hear this gutless crap from a young man who said of his girl's killer, 'I'd want him killed'."

"And what bloody option do I have?"

"That's more like it. That's the question I wanted to hear." Martins smiled quickly.

"What the hell can I do?"

"Much better." Martins heaved the air down into his chest, like a great

318

weight had been lifted from him. "You had me rather worried for a minute, young Holt. You had me wondering whether there was an ounce of spunk left in your body."

"I don't see what more I can do for you," Holt said simply.

Martins spoke fast, as if unwilling to lose the moment. "You are, of course, a signatory to the Official Secrets Act, you are aware that such a signature places upon you an oath of silence on all matters concerned with the work of the Service. Everything that I am about to tell you is covered by the terms of that Act, and violation by you of those terms would lead, as night follows day, to your appearing in closed court charged with offences under Section One of the Act."

Just as if he were falling, as if the ground opened under him, as if he could not help himself.

"What can I do?"

Far in the distance the dog was barking. Holt could see the leaping body and the snarling mouth, and George waving a stick at shoulder height, teasing the animal.

"You can help the man who murdered your girl to an early grave . . ."

The turmoil rocked in Holt's mind. She had been the girl with whom he had planned to spend his youth and his middle years and the last of his life.

"And you can assist your country in an act of vengeance."

There had been no mention of Ben Armitage, no mention of an ambassador assassinated. But then the arm twist was on him, and Armitage was not personal to him.

The turmoil blasting him. He despised violence. He despised Jane's killer. But he had seen the eyes of the killer, he had seen the work of the gun of the killer.

"What are you asking of me?"

"That you join a team that will go into the Beqa'a valley in east Lebanon, that you identify Abu Hamid, the murderer of your girl."

"And then?"

"Then he is shot dead."

"And then we all just walk home?"

"You walk out."

"And that's possible?" Derision in Holt's voice, staring up into Martins's face, into the smoke cloud of the fire.

"If you've the courage."

"Who do I walk with and who fires the shot?"

"A man who is expert at crossing hostile territory, a man who is expert at sniping."

"One man?"

"So you're better off that way. He'd be better off alone, but you are the only man who saw the target. You have to go."

"Could it work?"

Martins waved at the billowing smoke. "We believe so."

"I'm a bloody puppet and you're a crude sod when it comes to manipulation."

"I knew I could depend on your help, Holt . . . We'll have some coffee."

"I don't have the chance to say no."

"We'd be disappointed if you did . . . I'll make the coffee. He's a first-class man that you'll be travelling with, quite excellent. He goes by the name of Noah Crane."

"*Catarracta* is the Latin word for 'waterfall'. Cataract is what you have in your right eye, it is an opacity of the crystalline lens of the eye. At your age it is not at all surprising that you display the early stages of what we call the senile cataract."

To the ophthalmic surgeon he was simply another patient. The examination was over. After the explanation, a cheque would be written out at the reception desk. He knew the man was from overseas, he assumed that he was required for diagnosis, a second opinion, not for treatment.

The patient lay back in the padded examination chair. He showed no emotion.

"In the cataract-affected eye there is a hardening and shrinking at the heart of the lens which in time will lead to the disintegration of the lens. The cataract itself will lead to a deterioration in your short sight. Now, Mr Crane, a cataract can be treated, but regrettably there looks like being another complication . . ."

They had been through the symptoms before the detail of the examination. Noah Crane had laconically described the frequency of the headaches while the viewing power of the eye was stretched, and the multiplication of bright lights in the distant dark. He had said that he saw better at dusk.

"The complication behind the cataract is – and I would have to carry out a further examination to be certain – that the retina of your right eye is probably diseased. I don't beat about the bush with my patients. Disease of the retina negates the type of successful surgery that we can carry out to remedy the cataract."

"How long do I have?"

"You have years of sight."

"How long do I have with my sight as it is?"

"You have no time. Your sight is already deteriorating. Everyone's is, of course, after a certain age. Mine is. Yours is. Without the problem of the retina I would say we could get you back to where you were a couple of years ago, but we have the retina, and that means your sight will gradually diminish . . . I should have qualified that. The affliction is purely in the right eye. Your left eye is in excellent shape. Do you work indoors?"

"Outside."

"Then you should not be unduly pessimistic. Outside you will be using your long sight, shortsightedness is not so important . . . . You should see a surgeon when you return home."

"I understand that there's a place in Houston . . ."

"But the American techniques of treatment are unproven. You could spend a great deal of money, Mr Crane, a huge sum, and have no guarantee of success."

The chair straightened to upright. Noah Crane sat for a moment with his head bowed and his hands clasped together. He could aim only with his right eye. He could not tell the ophthalmic surgeon that although he worked outside it was short range vision that mattered to him, was what his life depended on. No long range vision was required to peer into the magnification of the "scope sight". He climbed out of the chair, he walked out of the room.

So he knew. He had asked and he had been told. Time was slipping from him.

In the street he felt the bitter cut of the wind. The wind lashed from a side street into Wimpole Street. He wore light trousers and a light shirt that was open at the neck, and a light poplin anorak. Too many clothes for home in Kiryat Shmona at the base camp, not enough clothes for London in spring. In a small grip bag were all his possessions. A change of clothes, a wash bag, and a photograph in a leather wallet of his mother and her sister, and a small brown envelope. No other possessions, because everything else this man used was the property of the Israeli Defence Force.

He walked across central London, and then across the bridge to the railway station. He had seen his mother's sister, he had negotiated his price in the bare room on the third floor of Century, and the sight of his right eye was ebbing from him, he had no more business in London. He was ready to take the train.

The light was failing in the room, the shadows leaping from the fire. Percy Martins stood with his back to the flames.

"Crane being recruited was a master stroke . . . . You'll learn, Holt, that when the Service wants something it gets it. When the Service wants a man, it gets that man. You're to be a team, a two-man team. Neither of you can fulfil your task without the other. Crane cannot identify our target without you, you cannot eliminate the assassin without Crane. Two men with one aim, that's the way it has to be."

Holt was less than six feet from Martins, taking what heat he could that was diverted around the flanks of Martins's legs. He wondered why the man spoke as if lecturing to a full briefing room.

"Noah Aaharon Crane is 48 years old. I expect that's a relief, eh? No worries about keeping up with an old timer like that. His father was a British soldier stationed in Palestine at the outbreak of the Second War, married locally, got himself killed in Normandy."

"By the time he was 18 he had spent his childhood in Israel, and his adolescence in the UK. He joined the 2nd Battalion of the Parachute Regiment, that was 1959. He served with the Regiment in Borneo and Aden and in Northern Ireland, he made it to sergeant and his records speak of a first-class soldier. But his mother died in 1971, and for reasons that are close to him, Crane left the British army, flew to Israel and joined up with what they call the Golani Brigade. The file indicates that he had a sense of guilt at not having visited his mother – who was Jerusalem born and bred – for many years during the last part of her life, that a sense of blame took him back to her country. As an infantry man he earned a glittering record after his induction into the IDF. He was with the Golani at the retaking of Mount Hermon in 1973, he was in Lebanon in '78, he was a member of the assault squad on the old Crusader castle of Beaufort in '82. He was good enough to be a regular, he was hardened by combat experience, but he seems to have next to no interest in promotion. In fact it is difficult to locate what interests outside the IDF he does have. His only living relative is his mother's sister, living some-where in North London. He has never married. He refuses leave. There are men like that in our army, every fighting machine throws them up. They are difficult, awkward men. In time of war they are a godsend, in time of peace they are arseholes for nuisance value . . . I'm digressing . . . after the capture from the Palestinians of the Beaufort castle, twelfth century in origin but an excellent artillery spotting position, a particularly bloody battle, Crane's unit was pushed north and east into the Beqa'a valley, and he stayed there. He stayed put. He became a fixture for three years of Israeli presence there. Some inspired staff man back at the Defence Ministry seemed to have it locked into his head that the Beqa'a represents a back door to Damascus, a way round the Golan Heights. By the time that Israel abandoned its positions and retreated, Noah Crane had acquired as much knowledge of that valley as any man in the IDF. It is our assessment that he, alone, can get into the Beqa'a, do a job of work, and get out."

"Is this sanctioned by government?"

"Official Secrets Act, Holt – sanctioned from on high."

"You said 'difficult' and 'awkward'."

"You'll cope."

Holt stood. "I never had a chance, did I?"

"Of course you didn't. You have become, Holt, an instrument of government policy."

"And if I was to say I was frightened?"

"Frightened? You ought to be grateful. It was the girl you were screwing that was shot, Holt. I'd have thought you'd have been jumping at the chance to get stuck in."

"I'll do it," Holt said.

"Don't make a big song and dance about it," Percy Martins smiled.

"I will go into the Beqa'a valley and I will identify a Palestinian terrorist so that he can be killed with the sanction of my government."

"We don't play fanfares round here."

"And when I come back I will scrape my knuckles raw on the end of your nose."

A wider smile from Percy Martins. "You do just that."

Late afternoon came, and the crowds of the capital's workers were streaming towards the rail termini and the bus stops and the Underground platforms. It was the time of day when the Director General usually slipped anonymously into the Whitehall entrance of the Cabinet office to take the discreet tunnel to Downing Street.

The Prime Minister read the list. "Arson attempt on Israeli Tourist Office, Fateh responsible. Failed assassination attempt on Iraqi ambassador, Fateh responsible. Gun attack on El Al bus with fatalities, Wadia Haddad group responsible. Letter bomb sent to Iraqi embassy, source unknown. Iraqi arrested while carrying explosives and on way to IRA link-up, source unknown. Own goal as bomb explodes at hotel, Wadia Haddad group responsible. Shooting of Israeli ambassador, Abu Nidal responsible. Arson at Jewish Club, source unknown. Bomb explodes near Bank Leumi of Israel, source unknown. Bomb explodes near Marks & Spencer's main branch, source unknown. Thwarted attempt to buy sophisticated military sabotage equipment, PFLP General Command responsible. Bomb explodes at Jewish-owned travel business, source unknown. Interception of explosives courier, Abu Nidal responsible. Attempt to place live bomb on El Al jet liner, Syrian Air Force Intelligence responsible . . . . It's a truly sickening list."

"That's just Arab terrorism in London, Prime Minister, in the last several years. On top of that we should add attacks on British nationals abroad – the machine gun attack on the women and children of our servicemen in Cyprus – grenade attacks on hotels used by British tourists in Greece – that's a whole other list, which ends with the deaths of the ambassador and Miss Canning."

"Sir Sylvester Armitage was a fine man, a great servant of his country."

"Whose death should be avenged."

The Prime Minister hesitated. The suggestion had been made, but the decision was the Prime Minister's alone.

"It can be done?"

"A small surgical operation into the Beqa'a valley? Yes, it can be done."

"How many men?"

"Just two. A Jewish Briton who is familiar with the ground, skilled in covert work and a marksman, he will travel with young Holt who will identify the target."

"So few?" the Prime Minister murmured. "Would there be Israeli assistance?"

"Inside Israel, yes. Inside Lebanon, we would assume that also yes." The Director General stood at his full height, avuncular and confident. "But it would be our show, Prime Minister."

"Against the man who pulled the trigger on our ambassador?"

"Indeed that very man . . . . We would be acting in the very theatre where *others* talk about acting. We would not be scattering bombs over an international city in the hope they might find a target. We would be going for one man with whom we have a known score to settle."

"A marksman and a spotter," the Prime Minister mused. "Would they get out?"

"We've chosen the best possible soldier for the job."

The decision to be taken alone. The memory of sitting in a country church, hearing the tears of Armitage's granddaughter, of watching a coffin carried along the aisle, bedecked with spring flowers. The memory of many outrages, of television news clips of broken shop fronts, of blood smears on inner London pavements, of bodyguards crammed into armour-plated limousines.

"Bring me his head," the Prime Minister snapped.

The curtains were drawn, the fire smouldered.

Holt sat on a sofa. The light in the room was low as two of the five bulbs in the ceiling formation were dead.

Percy Martins was saying, "The Yanks cannot actually put this sort of operation together. You don't believe me? Well, I'll tell you. Their Special Forces have an annual budget of over a billion dollars, can you imagine that much money spent on one division-sized unit? No good, though. They have the Delta Force, and the helicopter Task Force 168, and the Air Force Special Operations Wing, but they're no damned good. They're more interested in saucy cap badges and expenses. Do you know that when they wanted to drop a squad on a hijacked liner in the Mediterranean, the Pentagon had to give permission for half the squad to leave United States' territory, and why? Because the squad was under investigation for fiddling expenses. Their kit doesn't work. They're too late on the scene. The Germans are fine, up to a point, but at Mogadishu when they stormed an airliner it was Britons who can-opened the plane for them and chucked in the stun grenades. When the Italians have a problem they get on the phone pretty damn quick and call up help from us . . ."

Holt wondered how Martins had ever made it into the Secret Intelligence Service. He thought he'd be better employed running the social calendar for an Ex-Servicemen's Club.

". . . When my Director General was on the phone just now he was really chortling. A dog with two bones."

"Is that all you care about?"

"Showing that we can do a job well, yes, I do care about that."

"So you can crow to the Americans, is that why I'm being chucked into Lebanon?"

"You're not being chucked, you volunteered. In case we misunderstand each other, young man . . ." Martins was striding the carpet, talking to the ceiling gloom and the cobwebs that were beyond the reach of Mrs Ferguson's feather duster . . . "In case we don't follow each other, let us be clear on something. You have been fortunate enough to have been chosen to carry out an operation of infinitely greater importance to your country's needs than anything you would have achieved in years of a career in the Diplomatic Service. Instead of a lifetime on your butt concocting reports that will have appeared better written and a month earlier in half of our daily newspapers, you are going to *do* something. You are going to *achieve* something about which you will be justly proud for the rest of your life."

There was the growl of a car engine. There was the scrape of the tyres on gravel. Holt heard the bellow bark of the dog.

He stood and went to the window. He pulled the curtain back. He saw the taxi pull up under the front floodlighting that beamed off the porch roof. The passenger must have passed his money inside the taxi, because when he climbed from the back the taxi drove away.

It was obvious to him that he was looking at the man called Noah Crane. He could be clearly seen in the light from the roof. He was a fleshless man. Skin on bone, physically nondescript, rounded shoulders, a cavern for a chest, and spindly arms. The wind flattened his cotton trousers and showed the narrow contours of his leg muscles. Cropped hair in a pepperpot mixture of brown and grey stubble, and below were hollow cheeks. Leather tanned skin over a jutting thin jaw lay tight on a beaked nose.

Holt watched as Noah Crane made no move towards the front door but gazed instead over the black shadow gardens, assimilating his whereabouts. The front door opened. The dog came out fast, and Holt could hear George yelling for it to stay, stop, stand. The dog went straight to Crane. Holt heard George shout a warning that the dog could be evil. The dog was on its back, and Crane crouched beside it. The dog had its four saucer paws in the air, and Crane was scratching the soft hair of its stomach. Crane picked up his grip bag and came evenly, not hurrying himself, up the porch steps, and the dog was licking his hand.

That was the truth for Holt. The dog recognised authority. When he came away from the window, Holt realised that he was alone, that Martins had left the room, gone to the hall to meet Crane. The dog had found the power and authority of the man. It was the moment when young Holt knew into what pit he had fallen, how deep was the pit, how steep were the sides. It was the moment that young Holt knew he stared at the face of a killer. It was the moment that young Holt knew the dangers, the hazards of the Beqa'a. He thought that Crane was unlike any man he had seen before. Something easy and untroubled about the way that Crane had walked up the old flagstone steps of the porch. He remembered how he had mounted those steps himself, in trepidation, anxious to please, fearful of what awaited him. Crane had come up the steps like a hangman, like an untroubled executioner.

God, but he was so frightened . . .

"Don't be childish, Holt."

The squeak of the swinging door.

The light flooding in from the hall.

"Holt, I'd like you to meet Noah Crane," Martins said.

Holt stood his ground, incapable of moving. He was taller than Crane, and he probably carried a stone and a half more in weight. He felt he was a beef bullock under market examination. Crane looked at him, head to toe. Holt wore a pair of well-creased slacks and a clean white shirt and a tie and a quiet check sports jacket, his shoes were cleaned. He felt like a schoolboy going for a first job. Crane wore dirty running shoes, his shirt was open three buttons from the neck. Expressionless eyes. Crane turned to Percy Martins. Martins stood beside him, playing the cattle market auctioneer.

"That's him?"

"That's young Holt, Mr Crane."

"Any military time?"

"No, he hasn't been in the armed services."

"Any survival training?"

"There's nothing like that on his record."

"Any current fitness work?"

"Not since he came back from Moscow, not that I know of."

"Any reason to take him other than the face?"

"He saw Abu Hamid, Mr Crane, that's why he's travelling."

"Any leverage put on him?"

"It was his girl friend who was killed, he didn't need persuading."

"Any briefing given him on the Beqa'a?"

"I thought it best to wait until you joined us."

The accent was London. Not the sharp whip of east, but more the whine of west London. Crane spoke to Martins from the side of his mouth, but all the time his eyes stayed locked on Holt. Crane came close to Holt. Close enough for Holt to see the old mosquito scars under the hair on his cheeks, close enough for Holt to smell the burger sauce on his breath, close enough for Holt to feel the coldness of his eyes.

It came from down by the side of Crane's thigh, no backlift, without warning. A short arm punch with the closed fist up into Holt's solar plexus. The fist pounded into Holt's jacket, into his shirt, into his vest, into his stomach. Gasping for breath, sinking towards the carpet.

Holt was on his knees.

"Nothing personal," Crane said. "But your stomach wall is flab."

Holt thought he was going to throw up. His eyes were closed tight shut. He could hear their voices.

"If he's not fit he's useless to me on the way in, useless on the way out."

"We'll get him doing some exercises."

"Too right."

Holt used the arm of a chair to push himself back to his feet. He forced his hands away from his stomach. He was swallowing to control the nausea. He blinked to keep the tears from his eyes.

"I don't apologise, Holt. If I have a passenger then I don't succeed. If I don't succeed you'll be dead, I just might be dead with you."

"I won't be a passenger," Holt croaked.

Major Zvi Dan waved the station officer to a chair. Pig hot in the room with the table fan burned out.

The walk from his car into the building, and then the trek down the corridors had brought the first sweat drops to the station officer's forehead.

"I'm sorry, but again they say they will not."

"Shit."

"I explained that the request for reconsideration came from the Director General of SIS – I knew what the answer would be. That's the Israeli way. We make decisions and we stick with them."

The station officer bit at his lip. "I think I knew that would be the answer."

"Before they make you their errand boy, have they any idea in London of what would be involved, logistically, in a helicopter pick-up deep in the Beqa'a?"

"Probably not."

"Then you should tell them."

The station officer reached for his notepad from his briefcase, he took a ballpoint from his shirt pocket.

"Fire at me."

"First, what is involved in a pick-up where there are no missiles, where there is only small arms fire. You will have stirred a hornet's nest the moment the killing is made. A similar situation last year – we lost a Phantom over the hills close to Sidon. We had a pilot on the ground with his electronics giving us his position. By fixed wing and by Cobra helicopters we put down a curtain of bombs and cannon fire around him, through which no human being could move. We did that for ninety minutes until it was dark. Phantoms coming in relays, gunships overhead the whole time. Do I have to tell you how many aircraft, how many 'copters that involved? Overhead we had a command aircraft the entire time. When we had night cover we flew in a Cobra to pick up the pilot, with more Cobras creating a sanitised corridor through which it could fly. At the pick-up there was no time to land, the pilot had to reach for the landing skids, hold onto them while he was lifted off and flown to safety. That is what's involved when there's no missile umbrella."

"They'll get it in London." The station officer was writing, grim faced.

"But in the Beqa'a you are under the missile umbrella. The Beqa'a is protected by the SA-2 Guideline for high altitude intruders, by the SA-8 Gecko for medium altitude intruders, by the SA-9 Gaskin for low level. If you put a helicopter in when there is a state of high alert, then you must also put in aircraft to protect it. Those aircraft in turn must be kept safe from the missiles. For that degree of protection you have to be prepared to assault the missile sites."

"In 1982 we destroyed the missile sites in the Beqa'a. To achieve that we had to do the following. We had to launch drones to fly where we thought the missiles were positioned, the drones have reflectors that make them show on the radar like full-sized piloted aircraft. When the Syrians switched on their radar fully and prepared the missiles, that was disclosed by the EC 135, a converted Boeing airliner, and the E2C Hawkeye. When we had exactly located the missile sites and had confused them with electronic jamming, then we hit them from the air with the Maverick missile, and the Walleye bomb that goes to the source of the missile's energy unit . . . . It was a big operation. You follow me? All that *had* to be done. On top of all that we were also obliged to fight off the Syrian interceptors. It was quite a battle . . ."

"I hear you."

"My friend, that is what is involved. That is what we have had to consider when you made a request for an airborne pick-up in the Beqa'a."

"No helicopter lift . . ."

"How could there be? It is not even our operation."

"Then they have to walk out."

"Our marksman and your eye witness, and the hornet's nest stirred . . . . Do you think in London that they appreciate the teeth of the Beqa'a?"

"Too late whether they do or don't, they're committed."

From a drawer in his desk Major Zvi Dan took a single plate-sized photograph. He told the station officer that the small pale patches in the magnified heart of the photograph were the tents of what was believed to be a Popular Front training camp for raw recruits. He went to his wall map and read off the co-ordinates for the position of the camp.

"We believe that is where you will find your man. It is a long way to walk to, a long way to walk back from."

The station officer dropped his notebook back into his case. He leaned over. "Crane is your soldier."

"He is seconded to you. He is paid by you. It is your operation."

The station officer thanked his friend for the photograph.

"I'll pass it on. Thank you, Tork."

"I thought you should know immediately, Mr Fenner. They'll be on their own in Lebanon."

They talked on a secure line. Henry Fenner, Number Two on the Middle East Desk at Century, and Graham Tork, station officer in Tel Aviv.

"I'll pass it on, but it's not my concern."

"Aren't you running this, Mr Fenner?"

"I am not. The Old Man's given it to Percy Martins."

"Is that a joke . . . ? He must be ready for going out to grass."

"I tell you, frankly, I'm not that sorry, not after what you've told me. And did you know that Hereford turned it down flat? For your ears, Mr Anstruther agrees with me, it's a no-no-hoper. My advice, meant kindly, is keep your distance. If Martins is going down the plug, where he should have gone years ago, make sure you don't go with him. Bye, Tork."

"Thank you, Mr Fenner."

In his office in the embassy, the station officer replaced his telephone. What a wonderful world . . . Anstruther and Fenner, high fliers on the Middle East Desk, giving him the nod and the wink. He had met Percy Martins on his last journey to London, thought he must have come out of the ark. He thanked the good Lord that he was posted abroad, that he didn't go each morning to a desk at Century.

He wondered if the young man, Holt, knew the half of it, and hoped to God that he did not.

It was the crisp snap voice that woke Mrs Ferguson. She stirred in her bed. Her eyes clearing, she peered at her alarm clock on the table beside her. It was 22 minutes past six o'clock, it was eight minutes before her alarm would ring.

She had good hearing, she could hear the words.

"At your age a fit soldier can do 50 sit-ups a minute, you managed ten. On your push-ups a fit man can do 30, you did eight. On your squat-thrusts you need to do 25, you got to six . . ."

She gathered her dressing gown around her shoulders, stiffly levered herself off the bed. She went to the window.

"You'll get fit and quick, or you're a burden to me . . ."

She saw Holt, wearing vest and underpants, lying spreadeagled on the terrace, his chest heaving. Mr Crane was standing over him and holding a stop watch.

"Now you do sprints, three times 40 metres."

She half hid her face behind the curtain. She saw Holt attempt to sprint between the edge of the terrace and the nearest rose bed, running like a drunk or a cripple, but running, not giving up.

"I reckon round this lawn six times is a mile and a half. If you do it in anything around eleven minutes that's excellent, anything over sixteen minutes is not good enough . . . . Get on with it . . ."

Holt was still running by the time Mrs Ferguson had washed and dressed and applied the thin pencil of lipstick, still on his feet, still moving forward.

8

A light wind caught at the tent flaps and swayed them. There were bell tents for the recruits. From the tent area a clear track had been trodden to a single smaller tent, and there was another path to the cooking area where a sheet of rusted corrugated iron, nailed to four posts, served as weather protection for the fire. Eight tents for the recruits, and a smaller tent for Abu Hamid and for Fawzi when he was there, and the cooking area, they were all in a tight group. Away from the tents and the cooking area, thirty yards away, was a stall with three sides of draped sacking that served as the latrine pit for the camp.

Near to the tents for the recruits were air-raid trenches that had been cut down through the topsoil and into the rock strata. They had been dug deep, approached by wooden slatted steps and covered over with tin to make a roof and then the displaced earth and stones. In one last trench slit a door had been made to fit close against the heavy wood of the surrounds, and in this trench were stored the Strela ground-to-air missiles that were a part of the camp's defence system. Further away, closer to the perimeter of the camp, were three separate ZPU-4 14.5 mm anti-aircraft multiple guns. The inner perimeter of the camp was marked by a close coil of barbed wire on which had caught fragments of paper and cardboard, and into which had been thrown the debris of old ammunition boxes and packing cases. The outer perimeter was a ditch, hewn out by bulldozers, and with steep enough sides to hinder the progress of a tank.

To the west of the camp was the wall of the side of the Beqa'a, to the north three miles away was a small Syrian camp housing a company of regular commandos, to the east was the full flat stretch of the width of the valley floor, to the south was a Shi'a Muslim village.

The camp had been sited 24 miles from the southern extremity of the Beqa'a. At its nearest point, the Israeli border was 36 miles from the camp. It was considered a safe haven.

Abu Hamid hated the place, hated the dirt and the filth and the smells of the camp. He hated the recruits who were his responsibility. He hated the flies in the day, and the mosquitoes that came at dusk from the irrigation ditch beyond the perimeter, and the rats that swarmed at night from the coiled wire. He hated the food that was cooked dry under the corrugated iron roof and over the open wood fire. He hated the relaxed calm of Fawzi who was the Syrian spy in place to watch over him. He hated the boredom of the training routine. Most of all he hated the isolation of the camp.

He had requested of Fawzi the necessary pass that would have enabled him to get to Damascus to see his Margarethe. Of course, the requests were not refused. Nothing was ever refused by the Syrians, the requests were only diverted, there was just the hinted promise that later everything would be possible.

For two weeks he had been a prisoner.

In two weeks he had not seen Major Said Hazan, nor had he seen any of the big men of the Popular Front. Of course, he knew that the Doctor, the inspiration of the Popular Front, could not travel into the valley, could not expose himself that close to the territory of the Zionist enemy, but there were others that could have come, others who could have demanded of the Syrians the right of access to himself and to the new recruits.

The place was hell to him. And there was a worm that ate at his confidence. Abu Hamid had performed a service to the Palestinian cause, to the government of the Syrian Arab Republic who were the sponsors of that cause. The service was secret, could not be spoken of. That was the worm. Of course, the recruits knew that he had taken part in the battles of 1982 in Tyre and Sidon and Damour and in West Beirut. But the recruits too, every last one of them, had been inside one or more of those battles. As young teenagers they had carried back the casualties, carried forward the ammunition. The young teenagers had been left behind in the Rachidiye camp, and the Ein el Helwe camp and the Miye ou Miye camp and the Sabra and the Chatila camps when the fighters had been given safe passage by foreign peace-keeping troops and sailed away. The kids had stayed, under the Zionist occupation. They showed him a degree of respect for having been to the military academy at Simferopol and having passed out as top officer cadet, only a degree of respect. If only they had known . . .

"When can we go to Israel?" was their sole concern. "When can we fight the real war?" the recruits pleaded with Abu Hamid. "When can we show that we have no fear?"

Abu Hamid had known men who had gone to Israel, fought the real war, shown that they had no fear. He had known them in the camps before the Israeli invasion of Lebanon in 1982. He had seen them go. He had never seen one of them return.

One fact alone mitigated the hatred he felt for this filthy, stinking camp. It was a secret to his recruits, but he had proved himself at Simferopol, and he would never be required to prove himself again. It would never be demanded of him that he should go through the security zone into Israel.

A very secret thought. A thought that he would never share.

They were coming down the gentle lower slope of the valley wall. The recruits were in a loose formation, twenty ranks of three abreast, and Abu Hamid played the part of a non-commissioned instructor at the military academy and strode at the side of them and shouted for the step to be maintained. The recruits were singing, with fervour, an anthem of the Popular Front, a song of killing and victory. The anthem was of death, was of battle, but the valley was a place of peace. From the elevation of the track, looking out across the cultivated floor of the valley, and across the sharp ridge lines of the irrigation ditches, and the light sweep of the unsurfaced road that fed their camp, Abu Hamid could see a scene of undamaged tranquillity. There were women from the Shi'a village pruning in the grove of olive trees, more women bent amongst the marijuana crop. There were men working between the lines of the vineyards, more men shepherding flocks of sheep towards brighter pastures amongst the gullies in the rock scrub. Smoke spirals drifted into the air above the commandos' camp.

He could hear birds singing. He could see two jeep vehicles kicking up short dust storms as they approached the camp along the unsurfaced road.

They came down the hillside. They reached the gate of the camp, the gap in the coiled wire, when the nearest of the jeeps was a hundred yards from the perimeter.

Abu Hamid gave his orders. The RPG-7 launchers to be returned after cleaning to the underground armoury. The rifles to be cleaned and inspected. The cooking for the midday meal to be started.

He waited at the entrance of the camp. The first jeep ground to a stop in front of him. The second jeep had pulled up fifty yards further down the track. The engines were switched off. Both jeeps carried the red and white flashes of the military police of the Syrian Army on their dust-coated flanks. He saw that the driver of the near jeep wore the white helmet of the military police, he saw Fawzi climb out from the passenger seat. Fawzi had been away for three days and three nights. He saw the grin, the expectant pleasure on Fawzi's face. Fawzi acknowledged Abu Hamid, a casual waft of the hand, then walked to the back of the jeep, threw it open.

The woman was chicken trussed. She was carried easily by Fawzi from the back of the jeep. Her ankles, below the length of the long hem of her skirt, were bound many times with the sort of twine that is used to bind straw or hay for cattle fodder. Her wrists were handcuffed behind her back. Fawzi carried her over his shoulder. She did not whimper, she did not writhe. Abu Hamid could not see her face which lay limp against the chest of Fawzi. She had no headscarf, her long hair was dirt-streaked, the pale soil of the Beqa'a smeared into the black tresses. He saw the military policeman, the driver, stay in his seat, light a cigarette. He followed Fawzi into the camp, behind the unmoving legs of the woman. The woman had no shoes and the soles of her feet were raw and blood-caked. Abu Hamid's finger flicked at the scar well in his cheek.

Beside the tents, Fawzi heaved the woman to the ground. She fell hard, on her hip and her shoulder. No sound from her lips, only the heave of her lungs to replace the breath punched from her body.

Abu Hamid swallowed. The recruits were gathering, forming a hesitant circle around Fawzi and Abu Hamid, and the woman. Fawzi was panting, but silent, preparing his speech. Abu Hamid saw the face of the woman. He thought that her nose was broken because of the twist of the point of her nose as if it were putty and could be moved easily sideways. Her eyes were closed, perhaps she did not care to open them, perhaps the bruising was too heavy for her to be able to open them; there was dark vivid bruising on the soft sallow skin. He could see that the buttons of her heavy blouse had been torn away, he could see the sears on her throat and on the upper skin of her breasts. Abu Hamid thought that she had been burned with cigarette butts. He was struggling to suppress his vomit nausea.

"This woman is Leila Galah," began Fawzi. "Her parents live in Nablus, in the Occupied Territory. She herself comes from the Bourj el Barajneh camp in Beirut. She is 23 years old. She left the Occupied Territory seven years ago to join the Popular Democratic Front – all this she has told us."

No one looked at Fawzi. Every eye in the circle of recruits was fixed on the still body of the woman lying at Fawzi's feet.

"Also she has told us that for two years she has been an agent of the Zionist enemy . . ."

Abu Hamid heard the anger growl from his recruits. He heard the sucked breath. He saw the smile sweeping Fawzi's face. He wondered if the woman heard her denunciation.

"She has told us that she is a spy."

Abu Hamid had gone, after the evacuation from Beirut, to the port of Aden, the capital city of the People's Republic of South Yemen. He and friends had once gone in a fishing boat out to sea, beyond the sight of land, and they had tossed over the side a sack of offal and entrails, and when the sharks had closed on the blood-soaked meat, they had fired at them with their automatic rifles . . . for sport. He could remember the surging interest, the relentless approach of the sharks to the meat and the blood and the skin. The woman was the meat, that she was a spy for Israel was the blood scenting the water, the recruits were the sharks of the scarlet-streaming Red Sea.

"From her own mouth, she is an agent of the Shin Bet. She has taken the shekels of the Israeli security service. She has betrayed her name, the name of her father and of her mother. She has betrayed her own people, the Palestinian people. She has betrayed you, the fighters and defenders of the Palestinian revolution."

The circle was closing, tightening. The growl had become a scream. Abu Hamid looked from the face of the woman to the faces of the recruits. Eyes ablaze, mouths cracked with hate, fists clenched tight and shafting the air in fury. He saw himself walking across the street in front of the Oreanda Hotel of Yalta, and discarding the light anorak that covered the Kalashnikov. He saw himself gazing at the features of the girl as she came through the door that was held open for her by the man who was his target. He saw himself raising the extended shoulder stock to fit hard against his collar bone. He saw himself squeezing the trigger of the Kalashnikov . . . He thought he was going to vomit . . . He saw the girl flying back, lifted from her feet, flailing against the body of the target, and then the target going down. He had felt no rage . . . He had not felt the tempest emotion of the recruits.

He thought the woman was beautiful, even with the bruises and the burns. He saw the dignity of her quietness, her silence in pain.

"She was arrested by the agents of the military eight days ago. She has

333

been interrogated, she has made a full confession of her criminal betrayal, she has been sentenced by a tribunal. She is to die."

Because he wanted to be sick, because he thought the woman was beautiful, because the target was bound tight and not free to walk through the glass doors of the Oreanda Hotel, because there was not the adrenalin excitement of the escape from the streets of Yalta, he knew the squeal of weakness in his body.

Abu Hamid shouted, "We will kill the spy pig." The shout was the hiding of his weakness.

The baying for blood boiled around the woman. The shout of Abu Hamid for the right to slaughter her, the shouts of the recruits for the right to participate in the letting of blood.

Fawzi stood now over the top of the trussed woman. His straddled legs were over her hips. The woman showed no fear. The woman was a clinging fascination to Abu Hamid. Why did she not beg?

". . . Because she endangered you, it will be you that carry out the sentence of the tribunal."

Why did she not spit at her tormentors? Why did she not shriek in fear?

"Remember this. You are here under the protection of Syria. You are safeguarded by the vigilance of the Syrian security service. There is no safety for traitors in the Beqa'a. Traitors will be rooted out, destroyed."

Inch by inch, stamped foot by stamped foot, the circle was closing on the trussed woman. Abu Hamid gazed into her face. For a moment he saw a flicker of animation from her eyes, he saw the curl of her lips. She stared back at him. If it had been himself . . . If it had been Abu Hamid tied at the ankles, handcuffed at the wrists, waiting for the lynch death, would he have been able to show no fear? Abu Hamid understood the power of Syria over the recruits of the Popular Front. A spy had been brought for them to revile, to massacre, just as the Syrians had provided the chickens for those same recruits to despoil at the Yarmouq camp. The power of Syria mocked them, made scum of them. The means of their learning was a bound and handcuffed woman. She stared back at Abu Hamid. At last he saw the contempt in her eyes, the sneer at her mouth.

Abu Hamid wrenched back the cocking arm of his Kalashnikov.

Into the contempt and sneer of the woman's face he fired a full magazine. He raked the body of the woman long after the life had been blitzed from her. The gunfire boom had died, died with the life of a woman branded a spy. The barrel of the rifle hung limp against his thigh and his knee. The body was a mess of blood and cloth and flesh. The circle had grown, had widened. The recruits had seen the trance in which Abu Hamid had fired – none had felt safe to stand close to the shooting. He saw the tremble at Fawzi's jaw.

He walked away. He left the circle and the Syrian and the body of the woman. He walked to the wire coil at the perimeter.

Down the unmade track, leaning on the bonnet of the second jeep, was Major Said Hazan.

Major Said Hazan was clapping the palms of his hands, applauding.

Abu Hamid turned away. He walked to the far side of the camp. The moment before he was lost behind a wall of tent canvas he looked back to where he had shot the woman. He saw the bouncing shoulders and the leaping heads, and he knew that the recruits danced on the bloody corpse of the woman who had been a spy for Israel.

He went behind the tents and vomited until his stomach was empty, until his throat burned.

He wiped his lips with the back of his hand, then he went through the camp entrance gap and down the track.

He gasped the question to Major Said Hazan.

"Why was she here?"

"The Israelis always want to know what is the situation in the Beqa'a."

"Why my camp? Why the camp where I am?"

"Chance, nothing more than chance."

"Was she searching for me?"

"You should not acquire for yourself too great an importance. You are as a flea on a dog's neck. Your bite has been felt, but you cannot be found . . ." The voice of Major Said Hazan steeled. "Why did you not permit your young men to execute the spy?"

"It is my role to lead, to lead by example," Abu Hamid said.

"A fine answer . . . in a few days you will be brought to Damascus."

He saw the smooth skin of Major Said Hazan's face wrinkle in the attempted warmth of a smile.

"Why did you choose me for Yalta, Major?"

"I knew of you."

"What did you know?"

"Had you ever killed, Hamid, before Yalta?"

He blurted. "I fought at Bent Jbail in 1978. I was young then. I fought in 1982. I was at Tyre and then at Sidon and then at Damour and then at Beirut city. Many times . . ."

"Answer the question I asked."

"I have fought many times."

"The question is so very simple. Had you ever killed, Abu Hamid?"

"I have fought the Israeli . . . of course, I have killed the Israeli . . ."

The calming voice. The voice of endless patience. "Had you looked into a man's eyes, a man who is alive, looked into his eyes and then killed him? Tell me, Abu Hamid."

He could not control his stammer. "When you are fighting the Israeli you cannot stand about, look for a target . . . It is necessary to use a great volume of fire."

"Into his eyes, and then killed him?"

"If you are that close to the Israeli you are dead."

"Seen the fear in his eyes, because he has the certainty you will kill him?"

"Once." Abu Hamid whispered.

"Recall it for me."

The words in a rush, a torrent flow. "When we had left Beirut, after we had evacuated, we went to South Yemen. We were allowed to take out only one small bag and our rifle. The great men of the Arab world let us be humiliated, after we had fought with sacrifice the battle of the whole Arab world . . ."

"In South Yemen . . ." An encouragement, not a rebuke.

"We were in a tent camp, I had a transistor radio and one day my radio was taken. I found the thief. I went into his tent. He was playing a cassette tape on my radio. First he laughed at me, I waited until he was crying – yes, until he was certain, and then I shot him."

His hand was taken, gripped between the stumps and the thumb. He closed his eyes. He felt the brush of the silk skin across his face. He felt lips that had no moisture kiss his cheek.

"I had heard of it. It was why I chose you."

For a long time he watched the dust cloud spurting up from the back wheels of the jeep as it drove away.

The merchant had been through two road blocks of the Syrian army. He travelled the route every Monday and Saturday from Beirut, and returned by the same road to the capital every Tuesday and Sunday. He was well-liked by the commando sentries. The main trade of the merchant was in small electrical components, anything from light bulbs and plugs to drums of flex wire to parts for the small generators that provided much of the power in those areas of the Beqa'a that were off the two main roads and distant from the main supply. The merchant always offered the soldiers insignificant gifts, crates of soft drinks, throw-away lighters. Beside the wind-blown, weather-blasted and cardboard-mounted photograph of the stern-faced President of the Syrian Arab Republic at the road blocks he had made his small talk, offered his passes for cursory inspection, and been waved on. He was lighter in his load by two cartons of Camel cigarettes.

The merchant drove south, taking the straight main road, the eastern side of the Beqa'a. His car was a Mercedes, eleven years old and with 180,000 kilometres on the clock. The back seat had been torn out to provide him with additional carrying space for his wares. He always drove slowly, and would tell the sentries at the road blocks that he thought his motor was on the last legs and close to collapse. He always made a joke of it. The snail speed of the laden, rust-coated Mercedes was a familiar source of amusement. By travelling slowly the merchant observed so much more.

He was south of the village of Haouch el Harime, he was north of the small town of Ghazze. He slowed the car, drove off the tarmac and came to stop on the hard shoulder. He walked from his car to a small clump of olive trees. He pulled down the zip of his trousers. While he urinated he had the time to check that the old upturned bucket beside the tree in front of him had not been moved since the previous time that he had checked. There was no need for him to check the hidden space under the bucket. If the bucket had not been moved then no message had been left. He shuddered. If any man had watched him, from a distance with the aid of binoculars, they would have thought that he merely finished by shaking clear the remnant droplets. He shuddered in sadness and in fear.

The merchant had known since his last journey back from the Beqa'a to Beirut that an agent had been held. The conversations at the road blocks had given him the bare information. The unmoved bucket told him which agent had been taken. The spy would not know the identity he assumed, but the spy could have revealed the location of the dead letter box under interrogation. He turned. If any man watched him through the magnification of binoculars he would have seen the merchant pull back up the zip of his fly before shambling back to the Mercedes. He would not again break his journey by the clump of greening olive trees.

The merchant drove on through Ghazze, and took the winding road south of Joub Jannine that climbed the Jabal Aarbi hills, until he came to the village of Baaloul. At the village he was welcomed like a hero because he brought a new magneto for the petrol driven pump of the community's drinking well. In the morning, after talking late with the villagers, after sleeping in the concrete block house of the head man, he would go south again. He would drop his own message beyond the town of Qaraaoun, and then swing first west and then north for his return to Beirut.

The merchant was a man of middle age, grossly overweight, a man of Moroccan origin and of the Jewish faith, a citizen of the state of Israel, and in the employ of the Mossad.

In the house of the head man of the Shi'a village of Baaloul, the merchant had slept poorly. His mind could not escape from the vision of a tortured colleague, of the fate of a captured agent.

Major Zvi Dan said, "We cannot confirm that the recruits are at the camp, nor that they are under the command of Abu Hamid."

"You didn't tell me that you were trying to confirm it," Tork said.

"We were trying to, but sadly we did not succeed. We had an agent in that region, but the agent has been taken . . ." Major Zvi Dan sighed, as if this were a matter of personal grief.

"You had someone in that camp?"

"We had an agent in the area."

"That's insanity. You may have alerted them, blown the whole show."

"We committed a valued, trusted agent, now lost. Don't shout at me."

"Shit . . . you may have blown it,"

"Wrong. The information requirements given to the agent were vague and covered various areas. Whatever those pigs beat out of her will not identify our target."

"*Her?* You sent in a woman?"

Major Zvi Dan slammed his fist onto his desk. "Spare me your British chivalry crap. We are at war. We use what we have. Old men, women, children, what we have. You miss the point."

"The point being . . . ?"

"My friend, you may make all your preparations, you may – Crane may and the boy may – walk into the Beqa'a, take up a sniping position above the camp, and find that your target isn't there, perhaps never was there. That is what I tried to save you, that chance."

"I'm sorry," the station officer said softly.

"For what?"

"That you lost your agent."

"Friend, do not be sorry for me. Be sorry for her, a human being taken by animals. I will have lost a skirmish, she will lose her life, maybe already has."

"London will be grateful," the station officer said softly.

"That'll be nice," Major Zvi Dan said, "but I don't want their gratitude. What I want is that your people will very seriously weigh the risks before it is too late. Tell them, so that they understand about real war."

"I'm better than I was." The sweat soaked into his tracksuit top. "Can't you admit I'm improving?"

"Your sit-ups are average, your push-ups are average, your squat-thrusts are average. And all the time you're yapping, you're losing strength," Crane said. "You're still a passenger, Holt, so work."

"I'm fit, and you haven't the decency to admit it."

"Is that right?"

"Too damn right. You've such a bloody ego on your shoulders that you can't admit that I'm fit to walk with you. I know your sort, Crane, you're the sort that hasn't the bigness to admit that I've done well."

"Done well, have you?" Crane smiled grimly.

Holt gazed up at the wall of the house. He saw Mrs Ferguson's face at the upper window. She was always there when he was performing his morning exercise ritual, when he went for his shower she would go down to the kitchen. The start of every day.

"I tell you what I think, I think I'm a bloody sight fitter than you are . . ." Christ, that was stupid. "I'm sorry," he said, sagging back on the damp slabs.

"Wait there." Crane snapped the instruction. He strode away, into the house.

Holt lay on his back. The sweat was cooling on his skin. His anger cooled too, but he knew what had scratched him. Planning and logistics were between Percy Martins and Crane. They huddled in front of the living room fire, they pored over the maps and over the inventory of required equipment, and over the aerial photographs. Never was Holt asked for his opinion. He *was* the bloody passenger. He had not even been shown the aerial photographs of the camp. He had not been lectured on the Beqa'a, what he would find there. He had not been told how they would go in; he had most certainly not been told how they would get out.

George was standing a few yards from Holt and watching him. He had a sly smile, as if there were some sport to be had. The dog was sitting beside George, quiet for once, interested. Martins had followed George out of the house. He was sniffing at the air as if that would tell him whether it would rain this day. Neither George nor Martins had the time of day for Holt. Something they thought bloody clever was being cooked. Holt stood. He rocked. His legs felt weak. Of course he was weak, he had done the circuit of the sit-ups, push-ups, squat-thrusts, he had done the triple sprint, he had done the endurance run. He breathed deep, he pulled the oxygen back into his body, down into his lungs, deep into his blood stream . . .

Crane came through the French windows, out onto the patio. He carried an old rucksack and a set of bathroom scales. He put the scales down and walked into the garden. George was laughing quietly. Martins had the look of a headmaster who has to punish a boy caught smoking – this hurts me more than it will you. Crane was in the rockery, tugging loose the stones. Crane loaded stones into his rucksack. When he had brought it to the scales Holt saw that it weighed five and a half stones, 77 lbs. Crane swept the rucksack onto his shoulders.

"You say that you are fitter than I am. When we are in the Beqa'a this is what I carry, and you will carry the same. Now we shall go six times round the lawn, the endurance . . . but you won't have the weight, and I shall beat you."

"I already apologised."

"I don't hear you." Crane growled.

Holt led the first time round. He tried to run easily, loosely, he tried to save himself. Past the decaying summer house, past the bare beech tree, past the rose beds, past the rhododendron jungle, past the straggling holly hedge, past the patio where George was smiling, where Martins was still looking pained. All the time the pounding feet of Crane behind him.

The second time round, Holt led.

The third time round, Holt led. The third time round hurt him, because he tried to increase his speed. Ten years since he had run competitively, school sports, and even then he hadn't cared for it. Stepping up the stride, trying to break Crane, trying to open the gap. Legs hurting, guts hurting, lungs hurting, and all the time the stamping tread of the man behind him, and the bastard carried 77 lbs weight on his back.

The fourth time round, Holt led. As though they were held together by elastic, when Holt lengthened his stride, Crane stayed with him. When Holt slowed then Crane stayed back. The fourth time round and Holt understood. He was a plaything.

The fifth time round, Holt led. His own breath coming in hurt surges, his legs leaden, his head rolling. Crane was behind him, struggling more now, but in touch. No chance now of Holt running him out. Survival was the game. Survival was keeping going. Survival was pride. He could not win, he knew the bastard would take him on the last circuit. Jane's face was in his mind. Jane's face back in his mind after being gone, absent, for days . . . Jane, darling, lovely Jane . . . Jane whose body he had known . . . Jane who was going to share his life . . . Jane who was watching him . . . Jane who was now . . . He was screaming, "Why did you have to stand in front of the old fool?" Couldn't hear his own voice. Could only hear the beat of Crane's feet, and the wheeze of his breath.

The sixth time round, Holt led. He led at first. He led past the summer house. He led past the beech tree. He led past the rose beds, but Crane was at his shoulder. He led past the rhododendrons, but Crane was beside him, only fractionally behind. He saw Crane's face. He knew he had lost when he turned his jerking head to see the composure of Crane's face. Past the holly hedge and he was following Crane home. His legs were jelly. When he reached the patio, Crane was already unslinging the rucksack. He lay on the grass, beaten.

"Put those stones back where I found them," Crane said. "Then go take a shower."

The dog was licking his face, large and gentle strokes of the dog's tongue. The patio was empty. Crane and Martins and the grinning George had left young Holt to his self pity, to his picture of his girl. He retched, he had nothing to lose. It was raining. At first he could not lift the rucksack. He crawled to the rockery, dragging the dead weight behind him with the dog nuzzling at his ears. He tipped the stones out of the rucksack onto the wild strawberry strands.

The dog followed him inside and he didn't care that the dog, with muddied feet, was not allowed in the house, didn't give a damn.

Holt stood at the door of the dining room.

Martins and Crane sat at a table at the far end of the room. Crane was wiping the perspiration from his neck with his napkin.

His voice was a stammer, the weakness of it betrayed him.

"Why, Mr Crane? Why was that necessary?"

"So you get to understand my meaning of fitness."

"What happens if I am not fit?"

"On the way in, you slow me down because I have to travel at your speed. On the way out if you are not fit, I ditch you. And if I ditch you, you're dead or you're captured. If you're captured you'll wish you were dead."

Martins said, "You're making a fool of yourself, Holt."

"I'm not your son, *Mister* Martins. Don't talk to me as if I were your poor bloody son."

"Watch your mouth, and remember that I was a field operative for the Service before you were born. I won't get another show like this, I'm going to make damn certain this one works. So get a grip on yourself. She was your girl, and you never heard me say it would be a picnic. And get that bloody dog out of here."

9

It was a miserable drive for Holt.

He was relegated to the front seat with George at the wheel and taciturn. Martins and Crane were in the back of the old Volvo, and behind them, separated by stout wire mesh, was the Rottweiler. George was disgruntled because Martins had told him that the state of the car was a disgrace and had refused to leave until the sides had been hosed down and the floor mats shaken out and the ashtrays emptied. Martins was deep in his papers and Crane slept beside him with the ease of a man who catches his rest where, whenever, he can find it.

George drove well – as though it was the only thing he was good at – and he concentrated on the road ahead. Holt was on his own again.

But then for eleven days he had effectively been on his own, and he had given up the struggle to be party to the planning of the operation. He could cope. He was good at being alone, had been since childhood. Childhood in a country general practitioner's home, with Mum doubling as receptionist/secretary and nurse, had dictated that there were long times during the school holidays when he was left to his own devices. Being alone was not being lonely, not in Holt's book. Being alone, being able to live in a personal capsule, was fine by Holt. Noah Crane was another loner, Holt thought; they should have had a rapport, except that Crane was too damned good at being alone to share even a common purpose. It had been good last night in the drawing room, after another awful Mrs Ferguson supper, when Martins had launched into a sermon about "the long arm of vengeance" and "the moral evil of terrorism", about "those who have deeper convictions, stronger wills, greater determination, will surely triumph", about "the satisfaction of going the other side of the hill to strike with a mailed fist". High grade crap, and Crane had shown what he thought of it. He closed his eyes and fell asleep. They should have been friends, young Holt and old Noah Crane. That they were not friends was a pity, nothing more, and he'd get there, sooner or later, if it killed him.

He knew they were going to an army camp. He didn't know more because he hadn't been told, and by now he had stopped asking. For a change it was a crisp and clean morning, bright and fine. A good morning for a walk on the wilderness wildness of Exmoor, even a good morning for sitting next to George who spoke not a word and sucked peppermints. They went west across Salisbury Plain, past the ancient hulks of Stonehenge, across the great open spaces that were criss-crossed with tank tracks, past small stone villages with neat pubs and Norman churches. The first time in eleven days he had been

342

away from the crumbling damp pile and the overgrown garden that was encircled by the ten foot high chain-link fence set along concrete posts. Thank God for it, being away. They came to the small, bustling town of Warminster and they followed the red painted signs towards the military camp.

They were checked at the gatehouse. They were saluted as they drove through. Holt didn't turn to see, but he fancied from the rustle of movement behind him that Martins would have given the sentry an imperial wave of acknowledgement. They pulled up outside a square red brick building.

They were escorted to an upper room that was filled with the warm smell of fresh coffee, all except George. They were in the military world. Friendly handshakes, warm greetings. There was a long heavy box on the floor, half pushed under the table from which the coffee and biscuits were served.

The cups and saucers were back on the table. Three officers in smart pressed uniforms and polished boots, and Martins in a tweed suit, and Holt wearing his sports jacket, and Crane in the same trousers and the same poplin anorak that he had worn since he had arrived. Ready for business.

"How many marksmen?"

"Just one," Martins said. "Mr Crane is the marksman."

Holt thought the soldiers had assumed that he, Holt, was the marksman. Surprised, they stared at Crane. Another day that Crane had not bothered to shave.

"What weapon are you familiar with, Mr Crane?"

"More weapons than you've handled," Crane said, indifferent.

Holt saw the glint in the officer's eyes. "I see. Let me put it another way. What sniper weapon are you most familiar with, Mr Crane?"

"Galil 7.62 mm semi-automatic."

"We think ours is better."

"I don't need a sales pitch – I'm using yours because that's what I've been told to use."

Holt chuckled out loud, involuntarily, couldn't help himself, then bit his lip to silence. He wondered if the man had been born to whom Crane could be civil.

Martins said, "It's a British show, British equipment will be used."

Holt reckoned he had the drift. British equipment to be used, and no one too sorry if after a successful snipe the British equipment could be left behind. British ammunition cases . . . a calling card for the Syrians.

The case on the floor was pulled clear of the table. Holt saw the rifle lying on its side in a cut-out bed of foam rubber. The rifle was painted in green and brown shades of camouflage. He saw the telescope sights snug in their own compartments.

For the officer it was a labour of love. "It is the Parker-Hale M.85 bolt action, detachable box magazine, militarised bipod with provision for either swivel or cant adjustment. It will travel with a 6 × 44 daylight 'scope sight, and also the passive night vision job. We reckon it, in the right hands, to have a hundred percent success ratio at a first shot hit at anything under 650 yards, but the rear aperture sight has the capability of up to 975 yards."

"What's the weight?"

"With one magazine full and the telescopic sight it comes out at a few ounces under fourteen pounds . . . Going far, is it?"

"Not your concern," Martins said.

"Far enough for the weight to matter," Crane said.

"You want to fire it?"

"Prefer to fire it than have lunch."

"Then you'll want some kit."

"Right, and I want kit for him." Crane jerked his thumb at Holt, then turned to him. "Go and have the best shit and the best piss you've had all week, and get back here smartish."

Holt would have been gone ten minutes.

He came back into the room. Crane already wore camouflage battledress and his clothes were in a neat folded pile on the edge of the table. Crane tossed a tunic and trousers to Holt, pointed to a pair of boots and a pair of heavy khaki socks.

They walked for half an hour till they reached a place that satisfied Crane. Out of the camp, away up on the plain, beyond the red flag flying a warning of live shooting. They settled into beaten-down bracken. Crane said that Holt wasn't to talk, wasn't to move. Hundreds of yards ahead of them, across a shallow valley of young trees, Holt could just make out the barricade of sandbags and in front of it the human-shaped target.

Five hours and thirty-five minutes after they had taken their positions, Holt lying half a body length behind Crane and a yard to his right, the marksman fired.

One shot. No word, no warning that he was about to shoot.

Holt's legs were dead, his bladder was full, his mind was numbed.

They lay in the bracken a full ten minutes after the single shot, then Crane stood and walked away with the rifle on his shoulder, like he had been out after wood pigeon or wild duck.

Holt stumbled after him, bent to massage the circulation back into his legs.

Crane had his head down, was walking into the wind. "The way you fidgeted we wouldn't have lasted an hour."

"For Gods sake, I hardly moved."

"*Hardly* isn't good enough, not in the Beqa'a."

They were picked up by a waiting Land Rover and driven back into the camp.

By the time that Holt and Crane had peeled off their battledress, the human-shaped target had been carried into the room.

Holt saw the single bullet hole. The hole was central upper chest. A group formed. Two of the officers and Crane and Martins, with an inventory sheet, ticking off a list. The talk was in a jargon shorthand which Holt did not understand. As he dressed he found that his eyes always strayed back to the single hole on the target, a single killing shot. God, he could hardly tie his shoe laces. And he was making a mess of knotting his tie. He had his shirt buttons out of kilter. As if at last it were serious . . . as if every other thing since the steps of the Oreanda Hotel had been a cartoon for a comic paper.

Grown men discussing in low voices the grained weight of specific bullets, and the holding capacity of a Bergen, and night walking speeds, and the quantity of "compo" rations required. Grown men talking through the logistics of a killing snipe . . . that was bloody serious, young Holt.

The third officer stood beside him.

"We let you loose for an hour then we went onto the hill-top above and had a look for you. How far were you apart?"

"Why?"

"We saw you pretty quick, we never saw him. Was he far away?"

"Pretty far," Holt lied.

"It was a hell of a shot, 750 yards. Incredible. You know in one week in Belfast I once had seven hits, all between 600 and 1,000, but I knew the weapon, always used the same one. I tell you, to get a perfect hit with the first shot with a new weapon, unbelievable."

"Perhaps he just likes killing people," Holt said.

"Don't we all? My sweat is that all I get to blow away these days is pheasants . . . I envy you. I envy him more."

"Then you're out of your mind."

"Just trying to make conversation," the officer smiled.

Across the room the murmur of voices was uninterrupted. Holt caught occasional phrases, descriptions. Something called a Rifleman's Assault Weapon, something about low day/night signature, something about standoff demolition, something about minimal training, something about a Rifleman's Assault Weapon being right for young Holt. But Crane shook his head, didn't look at Holt, just indicated that he wanted none of that for Holt.

Holt's hands flickered uselessly at his tie. The officer knelt in front of him and without fuss tied Holt's shoelaces.

"You're fortunate to be with him. Marksmen are a rare breed. They tend to survive. Wherever you're going, whatever the opposition, they'll regret that guy ever turned up. Good luck."

"Mr Crane doesn't trust luck."

"I hope you win."

"I'm scared out of my mind."

The officer looked embarrassed, finished with the shoelaces, stood and smiled awkwardly.

When they went down the stairs, out to the Volvo, George was holding the Rottweiler back from the opened hatch of the car and three private soldiers under the supervision of the quartermaster sergeant were loading equipment, wooden and cardboard boxes and two Bergens. When they had finished, George had to rummage in the load to make a space for his dog.

Martins signed three sheets on the quartermaster's clipboard.

The officers waved them away, waved to them until they were round the corner, gone from sight.

Out onto the main road.

George driving fast. The dog snoring again.

"You're off tomorrow, Holt," Martins said.

He didn't ask whether he could telephone his parents when he was back at the house, tell them he'd be away for a few days.

He didn't even ask what was a Rifleman's Assault Weapon, and why it needed minimal training and why it was not right for young Holt.

He thought about a young man from the far side of the world, a young man of his own age. A young man with a crow's foot scar on his left upper cheek.

They drove in silence.

It was evening when they reached the house.

George was left to park the car, unload the equipment, exercise the dog. Martins hurried to the telephone. Crane said he was going to have a shower. It was as if everybody had too much work on their hands to concern themselves with young Holt, so scared he could scream and starting the journey for the Beqa'a the next day. Everyone too busy.

Holt sat in the living room, turned the pages of a magazine, didn't read the text, didn't register the photographs.

He heard Martins stamp into the room.

"It's too damned bad. She is becoming quite impossible . . ."

He didn't take the cue, didn't ask what was bad, who was impossible. Too bitter to be feed man for Percy Martins's little act.

"She is cooking for a dinner in the village hall, not for us. We come second to the village hall social evening. Sometimes that woman goes too far."

"I fancy a night out," Holt said.

"A cabaret at the village hall? That's a poor joke, Holt."

"It's all a piss-poor joke, Mr Martins. I fancy a night out."

"Now, wait a minute . . ."

"Alone. Don't worry, Mr Martins, I won't run away. You can tell the horrible people who run you that young Holt says you've done a hell of a good job in trapping him."

"Don't you understand, it's for your country."

He had drunk seven pints of best bitter. He had drunk three whisky shorts.

He stood on the stage.

The comedian was long away. The magician had packed and gone.

There was an untouched pint and another whisky on top of the piano.

The clock on the square tower of the village church that was across the road from the hall chimed the strokes of midnight.

He had given them his whole repertoire. He had led them in his *South Pacific* selection, his Presley impression, his Jim Reeves collection. He had them going with his choruses, he had them clapping to the hammer thump of the pale young rector on the piano beside him.

He rocked on his feet. His face was flushed. He could hear the shouting and the cheering from the audience. He understood his audience. It was an audience that he recognised from his village at home. They were the farm workers and their wives, and the Post Office staff and their wives, and the council workers and their wives, and the builders and joiners and their wives. Because he had drunk too much he had pushed his way forward and climbed the steps to the stage after the magician had taken his bow, he had offered himself when he had thought the evening was flattening out.

"Give us one more, young 'un." The shout from the back, from the darkness beyond the footlights and the smoke haze.

The rector shrugged. Holt whispered in his ear.

Holt sang.

> " 'Wish me luck, as you wave me goodbye,
> With a cheer, not a tear, make it gay.
> Give me a smile,
> I can keep all the while,
> In my heart while I'm away.
> Till we meet once again you and I,
> Wish me luck, as you wave me goodbye,' "

How many of them knew where the Beqa'a valley was? How many of them had any idea what the Popular Front for the Liberation of Palestine was? They joined in for the chorus.

> " 'Wish me luck, as you wave me goodbye,
> Cheerio, here I go, on my way.
> Wish me luck, as you wave me goodbye . . .' "

Holt was not aware of the spreading quiet. His song, his voice filled his head. A young man saying his farewells, heading for the Beqa'a with a marksman who could kill with a state-of-the-art rifle at 750 yards. A young man who had been told he was going to the Beqa'a to have a man killed for his country. Did any of them care? Small safe people, living small safe lives, in a small safe community. A lone voice, and a piano, desperate for tuning, echoing through a tin-roofed village hall in the English countryside.

> " 'Wish me luck, as you wave me goodbye.
> Wish me luck,
> Wish me luck,
> Wish me luck . . .' "

As the morning sun, brilliant bright, hugged the rim of the valley, the jeep pulled away from the camp.

No heat yet in the air, and Abu Hamid was cold in the passenger seat. He did not know for how long he would be in Damascus, he had not been told. He knew only that he was escaping from the camp and the firing range in the wadi cut into the hillside, and that, along with the possibility that he would have the chance to be with Margarethe, was sufficient to lift his spirits.

While they still crawled over the ruts and stone chips of the unsurfaced road he saw the cluster of dogs.

He knew at once. He should have stood over them when they dug the grave. Slowly they passed the dogs. There were six, seven, of them, perhaps more. There was no window on the side of the jeep. He heard the snarling, selfish anger of the dogs. The dogs were pulling, snapping, tugging at the dark-stained bundle. Beside him the driver grinned. They drove on. The fighting dogs were left in the dust thrown up by the wheels of the jeep.

They crossed the valley. They were waved through the checkpoints. They reached the fast, tarmacadamed road to Damascus.

What the wandering Lawrence called a pearl in the morning sun is a vast archaeological treasure ground. It is also the oldest continually inhabited city in the world. The present population, numbering 7,000,000, are the successors of those who first settled south of the Jebel esh Sharoi, east of the Jebel Khachine, five thousand years ago. Damascus has seen the worship of pagan gods, and of the Roman Jupiter. Damascus was the settling place of St Paul and the budding spirit of Christianity, it was the centre of the world of Islam, it was a great city of the Ottoman despots, it was a fiefdom of European France. Now it is a bastard mixture of cultures. On the broad French-style boulevards of Damascus walk the covert fundamentalists of the Moslem faith, discreet and quiet-living Jews, Sunnis, ruling Alawites from the northern coastline, Soviets from the east, eye-catching prostitutes aping what they believe is the Western way of provocation. The regime, which is bankrupt and sustained by loans from the oil-rich Gulf, is headed by a man whose Air Force career was undistinguished, who had levered himself to Defence Minister in time for the catastrophic defeat at the hands of Israel in 1967, who had then climbed to President in time for the greater military disaster of Yom Kippur. The regime lives on a foundation of terror and repression. There are eight separate organisations responsible for internal and external security. The security men are the new masters of modern Damascus; they and their regime are without mercy. Orders are issued for public hangings on the portable gallows in Semiramis Square. Orders for 200 supporters of the Muslim Brotherhood to be brought by the lorry load to the centre of Aleppo and executed by firing squad. Orders for 300 Islamic fundamentalists to be taken from the Tadmor prison in Palmyra to a trench dug by bulldozers, and there to be buried alive. Orders sent to Hama, after the suppression of revolt, for the killing of 15,000 males over the age of ten. Orders for torture, orders for murder. Mercy is a stranger in Damascus today; perhaps it was always so.

*

He knew enough of the geography of Damascus to know that they had entered the southern district of Abu Rummaneh.

He was being taken to the Air Ministry complex. They were approaching the Avenue El Mahdy. The driver said nothing. Abu Hamid was familiar enough with men such as his driver. A Palestinian learned in Damascus that he could expect no warmth from a Syrian, not unless he had favours to offer.

He had never before been to the Air Ministry complex, sprawling, five storeys high, he had had no reason to.

Close to the Air Ministry, Abu Hamid saw the security presence on the pavements. Young men in street clothes lounged under the trees, leant on the lamp posts, sauntered beside the road. All the young men carried Kalashnikov rifles. When he had first lived in Damascus he had heard the rumours. Even out at the Yarmouq camp he had heard the explosions in the night of roadside bombs detonated against six army lorries in different locations and, so the rumours said, 60 had been killed; a car bomb in the city centre, and 40 killed. He understood why the security men lounged on the street corners, leant against the lamp posts, sauntered on the pavements.

There was a concrete chicane pass inside the gates of the Air Ministry. Abu Hamid was dropped off in front of the gate. He still had his leg in the jeep when the driver gunned the engine. Bastard . . . He hopped clear. He endured the suspicion of the sentries, shining helmets, immaculate uniforms. He felt unclean from the dust of the Beqa'a. He could smile as he was body-searched. If there were a car bomb at the Air Ministry then it would be the supercilious sentries at the gate that would catch the flying axles and radiator and gear housing.

He was escorted inside. It had taken twenty-five minutes to establish that he was expected.

A new experience for Abu Hamid, walking the scrubbed, airy, painted corridors and staircases of the Air Ministry. The first time he had ever stepped inside such a place. A new world to him. At the end of a long corridor was a gate of steel bars, guarded. The gate was opened, he was taken through, the gate clanged shut behind him. Into an inner sanctum.

He could shiver, he could wonder what was wanted of him.

A door subserviently knocked by his escort. A uniformed clerk greeted Abu Hamid, ushered him inside, crossed to a door beyond a huge desk, knocked. A shout. The space of the room emerged in front of him.

In all the years of his young life Abu Hamid had never seen such luxury. He stared around him. His eyes roved from the whispering hush of the air conditioning machine in the wall to the heavyweight softness of the leather sofa to the teak table to the sparkle of the decanter and glasses to the fitted pile carpet to the hi-fi cabinet to the dull true silver of the photograph frames . . . could not help himself, a child in a glittering treasure land.

He saw the welcome smile of Major Said Hazan. The major was far back in a tilted chair, his polished shoes on the polished desk top. The major was waving him inside, waving with his stumped fist for him to cross the carpet pile in his dust-laden boots. Abu Hamid knew the man who sprawled in the depths of the sofa. He knew the man only by a given code name. He knew that the man was designated as the head of the military wing of the Popular Front. He knew that the man was believed to be at least number three and possibly number two in the command ranking of the Popular Front. He knew that the man had once himself opened a package sent from Stockholm to the offices of the Popular Front in Beirut . . . that was many years before, but many years did not restore a right arm taken off at the elbow, nor three fingers amputated from the left fist, nor smooth away the wounds of the shrapnel in his neck and jaw.

"Of course you know our Brother. You are welcome, Hamid. I hear good things of what you are achieving with the young fighters. I hear only good things of you . . ."

He stared at them both, in turn, these veterans of the war against the state of Israel, and the scars of their war. A ruined face, a lost arm and a lost grip of fingers. Was that how he would end? A face that his Margarethe would shrink from, hands that could not caress the white smooth skin of his Margarethe . . .

"Come, Hamid, sit down."

The door was closed behind him. He sat on the edge of the sofa, he felt the feather sink under him.

"I have sad news for you, Hamid. Your commander in Simferopol has gone to a martyr's resting place, but he died in his uniform, his life was lost in the service of Palestine . . . A car accident . . . most sad. We all grieve for his passing."

No expression was possible on the unlined skin of the major's face. Abu Hamid saw no change in the eyes or at the mouth of the Brother. The understanding came as a fast shaft. The commander and Abu Hamid and Major Said Hazan had been the only persons directly involved in the shooting at Yalta. Three persons, now two persons.

"I want two men, Hamid. I want two of your best recruits."

Abu Hamid looked across the width of the sofa to the Brother. Their eyes did not meet. Again he understood. They were the proxies, the Palestinians. He was learning, sharply, quickly.

"What skills would the two men have?" Abu Hamid's recruits were raw, not yet expert in weapons or explosives.

"Courage, commitment. They will join others. You will go back to the Beqa'a this morning. You will choose the two men. You will take them to the Yarmouq tomorrow . . . What is it, Hamid? I can see your impatience. Anger, is it? Or passion, is it? Tomorrow, Hamid, you will have the time to attend to your lady. Today the revolution has need of you . . . your best men, remember."

"It will be done, Major."

Holt had a sore head. He walked half a pace behind Martins and Crane. It was a part of the airport that was new to him. He hadn't been to Israel before, nor had he been to South Africa, so he had never come this way. It was the airport high-security corridor, quarantined from "ordinary" flight passengers, reserved for the two flights thought to be most greatly at risk from terrorist attack. He had seen it on television, of course, but the sight of the police and the dogs and the Heckler and Koch machine pistols still startled him. Policemen patrolling and parading in front of him with attack dogs on short leashes, with machine pistols held in readiness across their chests. He wondered how long they would have, how many fragments of seconds in which to beat off an attack. He wondered how long it would take them to snap out of the Musak swimming calm of the corridor, how long to get the safety to Off, to get the finger from the guard to the trigger. He wondered how they slept at night, how they rested, relaxed with their kids. And if he found the man in the Beqa'a, and Crane shot him, would that make their lives easier?

They settled into the chairs of the departure lounge, the same departure lounge in which, months before, an alert El Al security man carrying out the final personal baggage checks had been suspicious of a bag carried by a 32-year-old Irishwoman, Anne Murphy. When the security man emptied the bag he believed it still too heavy. When he stripped up the bottom of the bag he found underneath three pounds of oily soft orange-coloured plastic explosive, manufactured in Czechoslovakia. The potential of the explosive was equivalent to the simultaneous detonation of 30 hand-grenades. The explosive, the timer, and the detonator had been supplied to a plump-faced Jordanian called Nezar Hindawi by senior officers of Syrian Air Force Intelligence. It was intended that the pregnant Miss Murphy would be blown out of the sky along with all the passengers and crew, that the disintegrating aircraft would crash in the mountains of Austria, that all evidence of guilt should be destroyed.

Holt's mind was dead to his surroundings. His head ached from the excess of alcohol that he had consumed the night before. But sitting in that same departure lounge should have made him think of those events. In reprisal the government of the United Kingdom had broken diplomatic relations with the Syrian Arab Republic. Sir Sylvester Armitage had gone into the folklore of Foreign and Commonwealth with his booming "Bloody Nonsense". Sir Sylvester Armitage had been targeted, and Miss Jane Canning had walked in front of him onto the steps of the Oreanda Hotel in Yalta. The beginning of this story was in this departure lounge, leading to Gate 23 of Terminal One, months before. Holt sat with his chin on his chest and the throb in his temples. Crane sat and slept. Percy Martins sat and pondered the final elusive clues of the day's crossword.

A little before 5.00 a.m., in a deep grey dawn haze, a British Airways Tristar slammed down onto the tyre-scarred runway of the international-airport east of Tel Aviv.

It was just 29 days since a trio of British diplomats had boarded an aircraft at Moscow's Vnukovo airport for a flight to the Crimea.

10

In the same jeep, with the same silent driver, Abu Hamid escorted his two chosen recruits to the Yarmouq camp.

Both were 17 years old. All of the way back from Damascus the previous day he had considered which of his sixty he should proposition.

Mohammed was the most obvious choice because he was always the loudest to complain at the boredom of the training, to harangue his fellow recruits of time wasted when they should have been carrying the war into the Zionist state; he would eat, chew, choke on his words. The second, Ibrahim, had been brought to Abu Hamid's notice by the murmured accusation that he was a thief, that he pilfered the paltry possessions of his fellow recruits. Well, he could thieve to his content in the state of Israel. The choice had been made by Abu Hamid alone. He had found Fawzi gone when he had returned to the camp. Gone smuggling, the bastard, gone to organise the early summer cropping of the hashish fields, to gather his cut from the merchants who traded in transistor radios and Western liquor and fruit and vegetables out of the Beqa'a. He had seen both men separately in his tent. He had spoken to them of the glory of the struggle against Israel, and of the love of the Palestinian people for the heroism of their fighters, and of the money they would be paid when they returned. Both men, separately, had agreed. Easier for Abu Hamid than he could have dared expect. The exhortation and the bribe, good bedfellows, working well together. He had wondered if they were frightened, if they dreamed of death. He wondered if the one guessed that he had been chosen because he had made a bastard nuisance of himself in the tent camp, the other because he was whispered to be a thief.

Abu Hamid cared not at all what they knew.

The jeep was stopped at the entrances to the Yarmouq camp: the sentries radioed to Administration for an officer to come.

Abu Hamid whistled quietly to himself. He had the statistic in his head, their chance was one in 100. A one in 100 chance of his seeing them again.

It was the Brother who came to the gate. Abu Hamid saw the loose empty sleeve of the Brother's jacket. He told the Brother the names of the two men that he had brought, he watched as the Brother peered inside the jeep at the two men, weighing them. The Brother gave Abu Hamid two sealed envelopes, then politely asked Mohammed who was the boaster and Ibrahim who was the thief to come with him.

He watched them go. He watched the barrier lift for them, fall after them. He saw the camp swallow them.

He tore open the first envelope. The form carried the heading of the Central

Bank of Syria. It told him the number of an account in which the sum of 5000 American dollars had been lodged in his name. His chortling laughter filled the front of the jeep. Abu Hamid owned nothing. He had no money, no things even that were his own. He felt his chest, his lungs expand with the excitement; his head sing. He ripped open the second envelope. A single sheet of paper, a handwritten address.

He pushed the form of the Central Bank of Syria into the breast pocket of his tunic and buttoned it down, he thrust the address into the driver's face. The driver shrugged, started the engine, turned the wheel.

When Abu Hamid looked back at the gate he could no longer see the backs of the Brother or of Mohammed and Ibrahim.

He was driven into the centre of Damascus.

The jeep driver seemed to pay no attention to traffic lights at Stop or to pedestrian crossings. Away from the wide streets, into the warren alleys of the old city. Past the great mosque, past the colonnade of the Roman builders, past the marble Christian shrine to John the Baptist. Through the narrow roads, weaving amongst the cymbal clashing sherbet sellers, past the stalls of spices and intricate worked jewellery, past the tables of the money changers, past the dark recesses of the cafes, inside the vast sprawl of the Souq al Hamadieh. Only military vehicles were allowed inside the tentacles of the *souq* lanes, and only a military vehicle would have had the authority to force a way through the slow shuffling morass of shoppers, traders. He supposed he could have bought a street, he thought he could have cleared a table of jewellery, a shop window of stereo equipment, a clothing store of suits, he had in his tunic breast pocket a bank order form from the Central Bank of Syria for 5000 American dollars. He could have bought flowers for Margarethe, champagne for Margarethe. He could take her to restaurants, the best, and order a feast of *mezza* and the *burgol* dish of sweet boiled crushed wheat and the *yalanji* dish of aubergines stuffed with rice and the *sambosik* dish of meat rissole in light pastry and unleavened bread and as much *arrack* as they could drink before they fell.

He could buy her what she wanted, he could buy himself what he wanted. He had been paid for the success at the Oreanda in Yalta.

The driver stopped. He pointed. He pointed down an alley too narrow for the vehicle. He wrote on the paper beside the address a telephone number to call for transport back into the Beqa'a.

Abu Hamid ran. Shouldering, pushing, shoving his way through the throng.

He saw the opened door, the stone steps.

He ran up the steps. The wooden door faced him. The handle turned, the door swung.

"Well done, sweet boy, well done for finding me."

His Margarethe, in front of him. Her fair hair flopped to her shoulders, her body sheathed in a dress of rich wine–coloured brocade. His Margarethe standing in the heart of a quiet oasis, in a room of cool air, standing in the centre of a faded deep sinking carpet, standing surrounded by hanging dark drapes and the heavy wood furniture, intricately carved. He thought it was the paradise that the Old Man of the Mountains had spoken of, the paradise of the Assassins.

"Wasn't I good to find it, wasn't I good to find such a place for us?"

No questions in his mind. No asking himself how a foreigner with only the handout crumbs from the table of the regime could find paradise, quiet, clean comfort, amongst the alleys of the *souq*. He was kissing her, feeling the warm moisture of her lips, scenting the hot skin of her neck, clutching the gentle curves of her buttocks then her breasts.

The news was bursting in him. He stood away from her. He beamed in pride. He pulled the form from the Central Bank of Syria from his pocket.

"A piece of paper . . ."

"Read the paper."

He saw the moment of confusion, then the spread of concentration, then the drift of disbelief.

"For what?"

"It is *five thousand dollars*, for me."

"For what?"

"For what I have done."

"It's a joke, yes? What have you done?"

"Not a joke, it is real. It is for me. It is the paper of the Central Bank of Syria."

"You have not done anything, sweet boy. You are a revolutionary soldier . . . why is this given to you?"

Abu Hamid stood his full height. He looked up, into the eyeline of Margarethe Schultz. He said sternly, "For what I have done this is the reward of the Syrian government."

She blinked, she did not understand. "You have done nothing. You came to Syria, you lived in a camp. You went to the Crimea, you were one of many, you came back. Now you are in a camp in Lebanon. What in that history is worth five thousand dollars?"

"It is payment for what I have done for the Syrians."

"Sweet boy, you are a fighter of the Palestine revolution, not an errand kid of the Syrians."

"You insult me. I am not an 'errand kid'."

"Hamid, what did you do for the Syrians?"

She was close to him, she stroked the hair of his neck.

"Hamid, what did you do?"

"I cannot . . ."

"Damn you, what did you do?"

"Don't make . . ."

"What?"

It came in a blurted torrent. "In the Crimea I killed the ambassador of Britain, I killed also one of his aides . . ."

"For that they pay you?"

354

"For that they reward me."

She stood straight, contemptuous. He saw the heave of her breasts under the brocade of her dress.

"Which is more important to you, the revolution for Palestine, or dollars earned as a hireling?"

He said meekly, "I was going to buy things for you, good things."

"I fuck you, sweet boy, because I believe in you I have found a purity of revolution."

He handed her the bank order for five thousand American dollars. He watched as she made a pencil thin spiral of it, as she took from the table a box of matches, as she lit the flame, as she burned the wealth he could barely dream of.

"You are not a hireling, sweet boy. In the purity of fire is the strength of the struggle of the Palestinian people."

She lifted her dress, pulled it higher, ever higher. She showed him the spindle of her ankles, and her knees, and the whiteness of her thighs, and the darkness of her groin, and the width of her belly, and the operation scar, and the weight of her breasts. She was naked under her dress. She threw the dress behind her.

She took him to her bed. She took the clothes from his body, kneeling over him, dominating. She straddled his waist.

When he had entered her, he told her of the woman who had been a spy, the woman he had shot. As he told her of the killing, she pounded over him, squealing.

Later, when he rested on the bed, when she had gone to the bathroom to sluice between her legs, he would reflect what her ardour for the clean struggle, the pure revolution, had cost him.

Abu Hamid lay on his side on the bed. If an *Arab* girl had burned five thousand American dollars he would have killed her. He worshipped this European. Could not understand her, her love of his revolution, but could worship her. And she had waited for him, he thought she was a dream of pleasure.

Her soft voice in his ear. "Will they hunt you?"

"Who?"

"The English whose ambassador you killed, the Israelis whose spy you killed."

"In Damascus, in the Beqa'a, how can they?"

"You will not be for ever in the Beqa'a. You will take the battle of the Palestinian revolution into Israel."

If he told her of his fear, then he would lose her, he would be the assassin dismissed from paradise. He lied his courage.

"I believe in the inevitability of victory."

She kissed his throat, and the hairs of his chest. With her tongue she circled the crow's foot scar on his upper left cheek.

*

He was a good looking boy, blond sun-bleached hair, a wind tanned face. The uniform looked well on him.

He wore jauntily the sky-blue beret of a soldier on United Nations duty, and his shoulder flash denoted that he was a private soldier of NORBAT.

He was Hendrik Olaffson. He was 23 years old. He was a nothing member of the Norwegian Battalion serving with the United Nations Interim Force in Lebanon. He had been eight months with NORBAT in the north eastern sector of the UNIFIL command.

Intellectually he was a nothing person, militarily he was a nothing person. To Major Said Hazan he was a jewel. Only to Major Said Hazan was Hendrik Olaffson any different to the thousands of private soldiers making up the UNIFIL force from France, Ireland, Ghana, Fiji and Nepal, men stationed in a buffer zone separating southern Lebanon from northern Israel.

At the NORBAT checkpoint on the Rachaiya to Hasbaiya road, it was usual for the UNIFIL troopers to talk to the travellers as they searched the cars for explosives and weapons. The common language of conversation was English, and it was unusual for the troopers to find a traveller who spoke English as well as they did themselves. From a first conversation four months earlier had come the promise of a small quantity of treated marijuana. Enough for one joint each for Hendrik Olaffson and the two soldiers who shared the next night sentry duty with him. The traveller was regularly on that road, the conversations were frequent, the marijuana became plentiful.

In due course Major Said Hazan, who received a report each two weeks from the traveller, had learned of the political views of Hendrik Olaffson. One quiet day at the road block the traveller had heard the gushed hatreds of Hendrik Olaffson. The hatreds were for Jews. The hatreds went far back beyond the life of Hendrik Olaffson, to the early life of his father. The grandfather of Hendrik Olaffson had been on the personal staff of Major Vidkun Quisling, puppet ruler of Norway during the years of German occupation. In the last days, as the Wehrmacht had retreated, the grandfather of Hendrik Olaffson had taken his own life, shot himself, spared a post war tribunal the job of sentencing him. The father of Hendrik Olaffson had been brought up as a despised, fatherless child in Oslo and had died young, consumptive and without the will to live. Many years ago. Too many years for any stigma to survive on Hendrik Olaffson's record. But the boy burned with what he believed to be the injustice that ruined his family. All this had been vouchsafed to the Arab traveller at the road block.

He drove a three-ton Bedford lorry, painted white, marked with the sign of UNIFIL. He drove the lorry from the Lebanese side of the security zone that was patrolled by the IDF and their surrogates, the Christian South Lebanese Army, through the zone and into Israel. A UNIFIL lorry was not searched.

He drove the lorry from the NORBAT area to collect 15 soldiers from his country's contingent who had been enjoying four days' rest and recreation in Tel Aviv. On the way south, in darkness close to Herzilya which was a northern suburb of the coastal city, Hendrik Olaffson dropped off the two recruits who had been selected by Abu Hamid. They had travelled in the back of the lorry hidden behind packing cases.

Of course Hendrik Olaffson was a jewel to Major Said Hazan. The major believed he had found the crack in his enemy's armour, a crack he could exploit.

When they ran from the road, into the night, when they watched the disappearing tail lights of the white lorry, it was Ibrahim who led, Mohammed who held the strap of the grip bag.

"Your man isn't the great communicator, our man hasn't much to say for himself. They're an odd pair of birds," the station officer said.

Major Zvi Dan shrugged. "Whether they can talk to each other is hardly important. What matters is whether they listen to each other. What is critical is that they have respect for each other."

"When I saw them at the hotel yesterday, and the day before, the impression I had is hardly one of respect. Our man's very quiet, like he's out of his depth and doesn't know how to get into shallow water. Crane speaks to him like he would to a child."

"Respect is difficult when the one has so little to contribute."

The station officer glanced down at his watch. "This Percy Martins will be here soon, he's a crochety old wretch . . . the word from London is that he was damn near on bended knee to the Director to get this trip . . . He's bringing Crane."

"And your young man?"

"That pleasure must still await you, Crane's sent him to the beach for a week, and told him he'd kick his arse if he got sunburn."

"Mr Fenner is not coming to grace your mission with his presence?"

"Staying in London, sadly." The station officer did not expand, did not feel the need to explore the grubby departmental laundry with his friend.

The girl soldier who did the typing and filing in the outer office put her head around the door. Dark flowing hair, sallow skin, tight khaki blouse. The station officer wondered how elderly crippled Zvi Dan attracted such talent. "Martins has arrived," she said languidly.

Holt lay on the beach.

There was a hotel towel over his legs, draped up to the swimming trunks he had bought at the hotel shop. He wore a shirt, with the sleeves down. He checked the time every half an hour, so that he could be certain that he kept to the schedule Noah Crane had given him. Half an hour with his skin exposed lying on his back, half an hour with his skin covered lying on his back. Half an hour with his skin exposed lying on his stomach, half an hour with his skin covered lying on his stomach.

It was the third morning. He was settling to the routine.

The first morning he had been allowed to stay put in his bed. The last two mornings his alarm call had gone off beside his head at 5.30. Breakfast was tea, toast. Out onto the beach, a lone figure working at sit-ups, push-ups and squat thrusts, and then repeated sprints, and then the endurance run. However bad the endurance run had been on the soft grass of the country house, it was hell's times worse on the dry sand of the beach. Exposure to the sun all morning, then a salad and cold meat lunch, and then the repetition of the exercises in the full heat, and then recovery on the beach. A final repeat of the exercises as the sun was dipping. After that, the time was his own, that's what Crane had said.

So young Holt had stayed the daylight hours on the beach in front of the row of tower block hotels.

But he had started to walk the streets of Tel Aviv in the evenings, after he had showered the sand and the sweat off his body, before he was due to attend dinner with Crane and Martins.

He thought Tel Aviv ugly and fascinating.

Perhaps there had never been time at the country house for him to consider what he would find there, but nothing about it was as he had expected. He had walked the length of the seafront promenade, past and beyond the hotels, past and beyond the fortified American embassy, past the scorched grass of Clore Park, he had tramped to the old Arab town of Yafo. He had walked down Ben Yehuda, past the small jewellery shops and the shops that sold antique Arab furniture. He had walked back on Dizengoff, past the plastic-fronted pavement cafes. He thought it was a country of beautiful children, and a country of olive green uniforms and draped Galil and Uzi weapons. That the state was not yet 40 years old was apparent to Holt from the ramshackle development of building, fast and unlovely construction. Dusty dry streets, unmended pavings, peeling plaster on the squat blocks of apartments. He thought he understood. Why build for the future when your country is targeted by long range Scud missiles, when your country is nine, ten, eleven minutes' flying time away from hostile air bases, when your country is flanked by enemy armies equipped with the most modern of tanks, artillery and helicopters?

When he worked at his exercises, when he walked the streets, then his mind was occupied. When he lay on his back or his stomach on the beach, when he lay on his bed after supper, then his mind swam with the character of Noah Crane.

He hated to think of the man. He had tried with eagerness, with humour, with achievement to break into the shell defence of Noah Crane. God, had he failed.

"I find the attitude of the Israeli Defence Force quite incredible," Percy Martins said.

"Not incredible, entirely logical," Zvi Dan said quietly.

"This ground was all covered in my report, Mr Martins," the station officer repeated soothingly.

"It is most certainly not logical that the Israeli Defence Force will offer no facilities for extracting Crane and Holt."

"Mr Martins, if we wished to make an incursion into the Beqa'a we would do so. It is you who wish to do so."

"There has to be a plan for the extraction of these two men in the event of difficulties. They have to be able to call by radio for help."

"Israeli lives, Mr Martins, will not be put at risk for a mission that is not ours."

"Then I will go higher in the chain than you, Major Dan."

"Of course, you are free to do so. But may I offer you a warning, Mr Martins? Create too many waves and there's a possibility that the co-operation already offered you will be reduced . . . but you must decide for yourself."

"Dammit, man, would you turn your back on them, would you see them die out there?"

Percy Martins took the handkerchief from the breast pocket of his suit jacket. It did not seem strange to him that he wore a suit of light green tweed plus matching waistcoat with the room temperature close to 100 degrees Fahrenheit. It was one of perhaps six more or less indistinguishable suits that he always wore, winter and spring and summer and autumn, except on Sundays. There was a watch chain across the buttons of the waistcoat, given him by his mother after his father's death, and the timepiece was more than sixty years old and kept good time if it was wound each morning. He mopped the perspiration from his forehead. He disapproved of the designer safari suit in which Tork was dressed, and he disapproved more of the lack of support he was getting from his colleague. His career in the Service had been a lifetime of struggle. His response to all obstacles was to lower his head and raise his voice. There was not one colleague in Century who could level against him the accusation of subtlety.

"I have to believe, Mr Martins, that the hazards of a mission into the Beqa'a were fully evaluated."

The station officer saw Percy Martins blanche. He saw the tongue flick across the lips.

"We *must* have back-up."

The station officer had been long enough away from Century to recognise the signs. He felt as if he had eavesdropped a conversation on the upper floor of Century. Naturally, the Israelis would jump to the bidding of the men from the Secret Intelligence Service. Take it for granted that the Israelis would be grateful to help in every possible way.

"I think that what the major is trying to say, Mr Martins, is . . ."

"I know bloody well what he's trying to say. He's trying to say that two men would be left to rot because the Israeli Defence Force is not prepared to get off its backside and help."

Major Zvi Dan said, "Mr Martins, allow me to share with you two facts of life in this region. First, for years Israel has pleaded with Western governments to take action against international terrorism, and for years we have been rebuffed. Now, you are in our eyes a Johnny-come-lately, and you expect after years of rejecting our advice that we will suddenly leap in the air at your conversion and applaud you. We think of ourselves first, ourselves second, ourselves third, it is what you have trained us to do. Second fact: in Lebanon in the last five years we have lost close to one thousand men killed. If our population were translated to that of the United States then we would have lost more men killed in five years than died from enemy action in the whole of the Vietnam war that was of double the duration. If our population were that of the United Kingdom, then we would have lost, killed, some 17,000 soldiers. How many have you lost in Northern Ireland, four hundred? I think not. How many were killed in the South Atlantic, 350? Not more. Mr Martins, had you lost 17,000 servicemen in Northern Ireland, in the South Atlantic, would you rush to involve your men in further adventures that would end in no advantage to your own country? I think not, Mr Martins."

Percy Martins sat straight backed.

"In the event of a crisis the abandonment of those two men would be contemptible."

"Not as contemptible as the appeasement of terrorism that has for years been the policy of your government, of the governments of the United States, of France, of Germany, of Greece. We have offered and already given considerable co-operation. You should make the best of what you have."

There was the scrape of the chair under Percy Martins. He was red-faced from the heat, flushed from the put-down. He stood, turned on his heel. No hand-shakes, no farewells. He strode out of the room.

A long silence and then the major said, "Before he leaves, I should see Noah Crane."

The station officer reached for his hand, clasped it, shook it in thanks.

They took a bus through the snail slow raucous rush hour of the late afternoon. She clung to him to avoid being pitched over in the jerking progress of the bus. They raised eyes. Margarethe was the only woman on the bus, and a white woman at that. Her Arabic was uncertain, good enough for her pithy comment about the coming role of women in a socialist democracy to be heard, good enough to check the blatancy of the gaze she was subjected to when her hands were held behind Abu Hamid's neck.

She had been coy. She had not told him where she was taking him. It was three days after he had found her in the shaded room above the alley in the Souq al Hamadieh. It was the first time in three days that he had left the room, the first time in three days that he had dressed, the first time in three days that he had moved more than a dozen paces from the dishevelled bed.

He was returning to the Beqa'a in the morning.

She released her hands from his neck. She pecked at his cheek. She horrified the men on the bus. He loved her for it. He kissed her. He offended the passengers and gloated. He showed, in public, for all to see, his love for a woman, for an infidel.

They stepped off the bus.

A dark wide street. High walls to the sides of the dirt walkway along the road. He did not know where they were. She held his hand. She led him briskly.

The gate was of thin iron sheet, nailed to a frame, too high for Abu Hamid to see over. She pulled at a length of string that he had not seen and a bell clanked. A long pause, and the gate was scraped open.

She led him forward. They passed through a gloomy courtyard. She had no word for the old man who had pulled back the gate for her. She walked as though she belonged. They climbed a shallow flight of steps, the door ahead was ajar.

Through the doorway, into a cool hallway, on and down a dim lit corridor, into a long room. His shadow, her shadow, were spread-eagled away down the length of the room. He saw the blurred shape of a robed woman coming towards him, and the woman took the hands of Margarethe in greeting and kissed her cheeks.

He saw the lines of tiny cot beds that were against the walls on both sides of the long room. His vision of the room cleared. He saw the cot beds, he saw the sleeping heads of the children. Margarethe had slipped from his side. She moved with the woman, deep in whispered conversation, Margarethe using her flimsy Arabic in short pidgin sentences; they paused only in their talk to tuck down the sheets that covered the children, to wipe perspiration from the brow of a child with a handkerchief. He looked down on the faces of the nearest children, took note of the gentle heave of their breathing, of their peace.

From the far end of the room she summoned him. Without thinking he walked silently, on the balls of his feet.

A child coughed, the woman in the robe slid away from Margarethe, went to the child.

Margarethe said, "It is where I work, it is the new place that I work."

"Who are the children?"

"They are orphans."

He saw the robed woman lift the child from the cot and hug it against her chest to stifle the coughing fit.

"Why did you bring me?"

"They are the orphans of the Palestine revolution."

He looked into her eyes. "Tell me."

"They are the future of Palestine. They were orphaned by the Israelis, or by the Christian fascists, or by the Shi'a militias. They are the children of the revolution. Do you understand?"

"What should I understand?"

He saw the woman return the child to the cot bed, and smooth the sheet across its body.

"Understand the truth. The truth is these children. These children lost their parents at the hand of the enemies of Palestine. These children are truth, they have more truth than the baubles that can be bought with five thousand American dollars . . ."

He closed his eyes. He saw the flame crawling the length of the spiral of paper.

"What do you want of me?"

"That you should not be corrupted."

He saw the radiance in her face, he saw the adoration for the great struggle to which she was not bound by blood.

"You want me dead," he heard himself say.

"The man that I love will not be a hireling who kills for five thousand American dollars."

"You know what is Israel?"

"The man that I love will have no fear of sacrifice."

"To go to fight in Israel is to go to die in Israel."

"The man that these children will love will have only a fear of cowardice."

"To go to Israel is to be slaughtered, to be dragged dead in front of their photographers."

"These are the children of the revolution, they are the children of the fallen. They must have fathers, Hamid, their fathers must be the fighters in the struggle for Palestine."

"Have I not done enough?"

"I want you to be worth my love, and worth the love of these children."

She took his hand. He felt the softness of her fingers on his. She shamed him.

"I promise."

"What do you promise, sweet boy?"

"I promise that I will go to Israel, that I will kill Jews."

She kissed his lips. She held his hand and walked him again down the room, past the long rows of sleeping children.

They settled to sleep in a grove of eucalyptus trees near to the north bank of the Hayarkon river. They were at the very edge of the Tel Aviv city mass.

They had eaten the last of their food on the move, as they made their way through Herzilya and Ramat Ha-Sharon.

They had the map of the streets. They would start early in the morning. They had decided it would take them more than an hour and a half to walk from where they were to the bus station off Levinsky on the far side of the city.

With the food gone, the grip bag contained only the three kilos of plastic explosive, plus the detonator and the wiring and the timer. As they lay under the ripple rustle of the trees, Mohammed and Ibrahim talked in whispers of what they would do with the money they would be paid, what they would buy in the stores of Damascus when they returned.

*

362

A light wind brought the scent of oleanders in bloom and the rumble of the lorry traffic in from the street. They were sitting near to the door of the dormitory room, their backs against the wall.

Margarethe said, "When I am here I am at peace."

Abu Hamid said, "I have no knowledge of peace."

Lying on her lap, huddled against her breast was a girl child who had vomited milk. On his shoulder, his hand gently tapping its back, was a boy child now quietened from crying.

They were in darkness. The shaded nightlight was at the far end of the room.

"When you were like them, was there no peace?"

He whispered, "There was no peace in the tent camps. When I was like them there were only the camps for refugees, for my people who had fled from the Israeli."

"But you had what they do not have, you had the love of your mother."

"Who struggled to survive with a family in a tent."

"What is the future of these little ones, my sweet boy?"

"Their future is to fight. They have no other future."

"What do you remember of when you were a child?"

He grimaced. "I can remember the hunger. I can remember the drills to get us to run fast to the ditches so we would be safe if their aircraft came."

She watched the boy child's fingers clutch and free and clutch again at the collar of Abu Hamid's tunic. She asked, "You surely do not regret being a fighter?"

"I do not regret it, but I never had the chance to be otherwise. So, there are Palestinians who have gone to the Gulf and to Saudi and to Pakistan and to Libya, and they work for the people there. I do not have that chance. Margarethe, I can write only my name. I can read a little, very little . . . I tell you that in honesty. I cannot go to Bahrain or Tripoli to work as a clerk. There is no employment for a clerk who can read very little. There were not schools at the tent camps which taught reading and writing and making arithmetic. We were taught about the Israelis, and we were shown how to run to the air raid shelters . . ."

She saw the boy child's fingers grasping at his lips and his nose. He made no attempt to push the boy child's fingers away.

". . . and if we have not succeeded in our lifetimes in freeing our homeland from the Israelis, then these little ones also must be taught to be fighters. We cannot turn our back on what has happened to us."

"You said two hours ago that you had done enough."

"Do you try to make me ashamed?"

"You are a fighter, that is why you have my love."

The boy child's fingers had found the small well hole of the crow's foot scar. There was a gurgle of pleasure. He suppressed the memory of the stinging pain as the artillery shell shrapnel had nicked across his left upper cheek, the memory of the last days of the retreating battle for West Beirut.

363

"It is all I know. I know nothing of being a clerk."

Major Said Hazan made up a rough bed of blankets on the leather sofa in his office, then undressed.

When he had folded his clothes, when he stood in his singlet and shorts, he went to the Japanese radio behind his desk and tuned to the VHF frequency of the Israeli Broadcasting Corporation. He smoked another cigarette. He searched his way through the file on his desk, the file that obsessed him. He listened to the news broadcast in the English language. It was a powerful radio, it guaranteed good reception.

The radio, in his opinion, broadcast a news bulletin of irrelevant crap. It said that "orthodox" Jews in Jerusalem had again been stoning bus shelters that carried advertisements showing women in bathing suits. The pipe line feeding the Negev irrigation system from the Sea of Galilee had closed down because of shortage of water. The triumph of a rabbi who had come up with the solution of self-propelled tractors to work on the Golan Heights during the fallow year when the Commandment dictated that a farming Jew should not work his fields. The rate of inflation. The public squabbling between Prime Minister and Foreign Minister. New figures showing the decline of young people seeking a kibbutz life. The performance of a Tel Aviv basketball team in New York . . . But the bulletin pleased him.

If the recruits had been taken he would have heard it on the radio. The IBC was always quick to report explosions, arrests. If they had been taken it would have been on the radio that evening. He switched off the radio and lay on the sofa.

Major Said Hazan laughed and the shiny skin on his face buckled in his mirth. His own secret, his own reason to laugh. The secret of the timer was shared only between himself and the technician in the basement technical laboratory of the Air Force Intelligence wing. Not shared with the Brother of the Popular Front, not shared with the cattle who had been brought from the Beqa'a. The cattle believed the timer was set for 45 minutes, the cattle believed they would be off the bus at the Latrun Monastery and that the explosion would follow when they were legging it hard to Ramalleh, cross country into the Occupied Territories. The setting of the timer was the secret he shared only with his technician.

When his laughter subsided, he concentrated on the file.

The first page of the file showed in detail a plan of the layout of buildings of the Defence Ministry on Kaplan.

Major Said Hazan was half in love with the file.

He was in singlet and running shorts and track shoes, and washing his stubbled face when the telephone rang in the bedroom. He wiped his eyes. Water splattered on the tile floor. The telephone yelled for him.

It was not yet a beard, just a dark rash over his colouring face.

He picked up the telephone.

"Holt?"

Crane's gravel voice in Holt's ear. "Get your clothes on, get downstairs."

"What's the panic?"

"We're going out."

"Where?"

"Travelling."

"What do I need?"

"Just yourself, dressed."

"For how long?"

"A few days."

"For God's sake, Crane, you could have told me last night . . ."

"You're wasting time, get down."

He heard the purr of the telephone. He slammed his receiver down. He chucked on his trousers and a shirt. Holt steamed. He had had dinner with the monosyllabic Crane and Percy Martins. Crane had hardly spoken beyond asking for the salt to be passed him, and sugar for his coffee. Martins had been bottling some private anger. Nobody had told Holt anything.

He ran down the service stairs and strode into the hotel foyer.

Up to Crane who was standing by the glass front looking out, bored, onto the street.

"Will you start treating me like a bloody partner?"

Crane grinned at him. "Come on."

They walked past the hotel's taxi rank. They walked all the way to the bus station. Crane had the decency to say that a walk would do Holt good if he was missing this morning's work-out. Crane set a fierce pace. That was his way. Three times Holt tried to batter his complaint into Crane's ear, three times he was ignored.

It was a dingy corner of the city. Noisy, crowded, dirty, impoverished. And this was the new bus station. Holt wondered what the old one had looked like. Sunday morning, military travel day. To Holt, it seemed that a full half of Israel's conscript army was on the move. Young men and young women, all in uniform, all with their kit, most with their weapons, rejoining their units after the weekend. Crane moved fluently through the crowds, through the queues, as though he belonged, and Holt trailed behind him.

There were buses to Ashkelon and Beer Sheba and Netanya and Haifa and Kiryat Shmona and Beat Shean. Buses to all over the country. Buses to get the army back to work. So what the hell happened if the enemy came marching in at a weekend? Holt caught Crane, grabbed his arm.

"So where are we going?"

"Jerusalem, first."

"Why don't you tell me what we're doing?"

"Surprise is good for the human juices."

"Why don't we drive?"

"Because I like going by bus."

"When do we start being a partnership?"

"When I start telling you where you're going you'll start messing your pants."

Crane grinned, shook himself free.

He pointed to a queue. He told Holt to stand there.

Holt stood in the queue. It stretched ahead of him. He was wondering whether they would get two seats when the driver deigned to open the door of the single decker bus. There were soldiers in front of him, men, women, there was a woman with four small children, two in her arms, there was an elderly couple arguing briskly.

There were two young men.

There were two young men who looked, moved, seemed different. Holt could not say how they looked, moved, seemed different. He was the stranger . . . Light chocolate skins, but then the Arabic Jews had light chocolate skins . . . Long dank curly hair, but then there were Arabic Jews of that age who would be in their last year of school, or who had some exemption from the military . . . Nervous movements, anxious glances over the shoulder, snapped whispers to each other . . . looking, moving, seeming different. And then the queue started to move, and the soldiers were surging and the woman was shouting for her stray children, and the elderly couple were bickering away their lives.

Alone in the queue, Holt saw two young men who looked, moved, seemed different.

He was a stranger. He took nothing for granted. He saw nothing as ordinary.

He watched. He was edging forward. He just knew that he would reach the steps into the bus, the driver, and Crane would not be back with the tickets. Holt moved a little out of the queue, so that he could watch for Crane more easily, so that he could shout to him to hurry. He was only half a step out of the queue. It gave him sight of one of the young men with his hand in a cheap grip bag, fiddling. He saw the frown of concentration on the forehead of one of the young men, and he saw the strain of the other young man who bent close to his friend. He saw that the two had their hands in the bag. Relief on their faces, hands out of the bag. He saw their hands clasp together, as if a bond was sealed, as if a mountain were climbed.

He was alone beside the bus, alone he saw them.

The taller of them slipped away. The shorter climbed the narrow steps onto the bus. Holt was looking for Crane – wretched man, as if the man enjoyed making Holt sweat . . . Holt saw the taller of the two young men standing at the ice cream kiosk. The one moment frantic because of something in a grip bag, the next moment buying ice cream . . . Crane walking unhurriedly back from the ticket booth, Holt waving for him to hurry.

He saw the taller man skipping across the road from the kiosk towards the bus.

The queue was formed alongside an all-weather shelter. A stout graffiti-covered brick wall masked the windows of the bus from Holt. He was buggered if he were going to stand like an obedient dog waiting on Crane. Holt was moving towards Crane . . .

He felt the hot wind. He heard the roar of the fire wind. He was off his feet, flying. Could not get his feet to the ground, could not control his body, mind, arms. Moving above the road, moving towards the ice cream kiosk. He could see the kiosk, he could see the taller man with the ice creams splattering across his chest. He felt the snap cudgel blow of the bricks at the back of his legs. He heard the thunder blast of the explosion.

Holt careered into the taller man, hit him full in the body, smashed against the splattered ice cream cones.

Eyes closed. The knowledge of fire, the certainty of calamity. Ears blasted, ringing from the hammer strike of plastic explosive.

The body was under him. The body of the taller man was writhing.

Holt did not understand. Explosion, fire, demolition, he knew all that. He did understand that the taller man on whom he lay had wriggled clear of his belt a short double edged knife. Could not comprehend, why the taller man on whom he lay held the double edged knife and slashed at him. All so bloody mad. Mad that he had flown, that he could not control his legs, that debris lay around them, that the taller man slashed at him with the bright blade of a knife. The knife was at full arm stretch. The taller man screamed in words that Holt did not know.

He saw the knife closing on him. He saw the old dirty running shoe. He saw the knife part from the fist, clatter away. He saw the tail end swing of Crane's kick.

Holt blurted, "His friend took the bag. He went to get an ice cream. He tried to knife me."

The breath was crushed out of Holt's chest. Crane had smother dived onto him. He was gasping for air. He felt himself pushed aside, rolled away, and Crane had twisted the taller man onto his stomach and hooked an arm behind the back, held it, denying the taller man any freedom of movement. Holt saw the spittle in the mouth of the taller man and heard the frothing words that he did not understand.

Again the staccato explanation from Holt. "There were two of them in the queue. They had a bag. One climbed onto the bus, the other went for ice creams. I was just picked up, I was chucked across the road. I hit him, fell on him. He pulled the knife on me."

"Bastard terrorist," Crane said, a whistle in his teeth. "Arab bastard terrorist."

Holt looked into Crane's face. It was the eyes that held him. Merciless eyes. As if the anger of Crane had killed their life; ruthless eyes.

"He was shouting in Arabic at you," Crane said.

Crane moved fast. Holt left to fend for himself. Crane moving with the Arab propelled in front of him by the arm lock, and Holt crawling to his feet and struggling to follow. Crane driving the Arab forward as if his only concern was to get clear of the bus station. Holt thought he would be sick. His foot kicked against a severed leg. He stepped over the body trunk of the elderly woman who had been arguing with her elderly husband, he recognised the shredded remnant of her dress. His shoe slid in a river of blood slime, and he careered sideways to avoid a young girl soldier who dragged herself across the road on her elbows and her knees, and who tried with her hands to staunch the blood flow.

There was the cut of the screams in the air, and the first shrill pulse of the sirens.

Holt lurched, staggered after Crane and the Arab. They were going against the tide surge of shoppers, shop keepers, taxi drivers, passengers from other queues who ran towards the smoking skeleton of the Jerusalem bus.

A police car swung a corner, tyres howling. Crane put himself into the road in front of it, forced it to stop. All so fast. Crane jabbering at the driver and his crew man and wrenching open the rear door and dragging the Arab inside after him, then reaching out to pull Holt aboard. The door slammed shut.

The police car reversed, turned, sped away. Holt smelled the fear scent of the Arab who was squashed against him, pressed between himself and Crane.

"Tell me I did well, Crane."

"Nothing to boast about."

"I did well."

"You did what any Israeli would have done. Nothing more, nothing less."

They had left him in the corridor that led down to the cell block. He had been there for more than three hours. He was ignored. He sat on a hard wooden bench and leaned exhausted back against the painted white brickwork of the corridor walls.

Through all the three hours a procession of men passed up and down the corridor. There were soldiers, officers with badges of rank on their shoulders, there were senior policemen in uniform, there were investigators of the Shin Bet in casual civilian dress. He was never spoken to. He was brought no coffee, no tea. The heavy wooden door with the deep key setting and the small peep hole was left empty. Holt heard the questioning, and he heard the thumping and the beating, and he heard the screams and the whimpering of the Arab. The screams were occasional, the whimpering was all the time. Holt could recognise the battering of the fists and the boots, could find images for those sounds.

Crane came out of the cell block.

Holt stood. "I have to say, Mr Crane, that whatever was done at the bus station I do not approve of the torture of prisoners . . ."

Crane stared at Holt. "There are five dead, two of them children. There are 51 injured, of whom eight are critical."

"You win against these people by a rule of law, not a rule of the jungle."

"Is the need for a rule of law taking you into the Beqa'a?"

"Abu Hamid in the Beqa'a is beyond the law, this man is in the custody of the law."

"Neat, and pathetic. Whether or not you'll be alive in two weeks' time may well have depended on the thrashing that Arab shitface is getting right now."

"How?"

"I fancy coffee."

"How?"

"Because we've kicked him and belted him and he talked to us. Abu Hamid selected him for the mission. He was a Popular Front recruit at a camp run by Abu Hamid. Considering the state of his hands he's drawn us a damn good layout of the camp and he's done us quite a good map of where the camp is. Fair exchange for handing out a thrashing, don't you think, knowing where to find Abu Hamid in the Beqa'a?"

"I just meant . . ."

"Close it down, Holt. I don't think I fancy walking into Lebanon with you bleeding a damn great trail of your sensitivities."

"I hear you," Holt said.

A police car drove them back to the bus station.

The building was Beit Sokolov, on the far side of the road and down the hill on Kaplan from the Defence Ministry complex.

The chief military spokesman was a barrel-chested bustling man, wearing his uniform well, showing his para wings on his chest. He strode into the briefing room.

He walked to the dais. His entry quietened them. He faced his audience. They sat below him, pencils and pens poised over the blank sheets of their notepads. They were the military correspondents of the Israeli Broadcasting Corporation and *Maariv* and *Yediot* and the *Jerusalem Post*, and the bureau chiefs of the American and European broadcasting networks, and the senior men of the foreign news agencies. He checked around him. He was satisfied there were no microphones to pick up his words.

"Gentlemen, on a matter of the greatest importance to us, a matter directly affecting the security of the state, we demand your co-operation. Concerning the terrorist bomb explosion in the New Central bus station this morning, you will be handed our statement at the end of this informal briefing. The statement will say that two members of the Popular Front for the Liberation of Palestine terrorist organisation were involved in the planting of the bomb, and that *both* died in the explosion. Your reporters may, in conversation with eye witnesses, bring back stories of one terrorist being arrested and driven away from the scene of the explosion. We demand that that information does not appear. It is of the uttermost importance that the terrorist leaders who despatched these two men do not know that we are currently interrogating one survivor. A matter of life and death, gentlemen. Any attempt to smuggle information concerning this survivor past the censors, out of the state, will lead to prosecution and harshest penalties of the law. Questions . . ."

The bureau chief of the Columbia Broadcasting Systems drawled, "Have we gotten involved in another bus ride cover-up?"

The military spokesman had anticipated the question. Four years before, four Arabs from the Gaza Strip had hijacked a crowded bus in southern Israel, and threatened to kill the passengers if 25 Palestinians were not released from Israeli gaols. The bus had been stopped, and stormed. Two Arabs had died in the military intervention, two others had been seen being led away into the darkness at the side of the road by the Shin Bet. In a field, out of sight, these two were bludgeoned to death. Senior officials of Shin Bet were subsequently granted immunity from prosecution, and resigned.

"The move is temporary. There will be no cover-up because the survivor is alive. Within a month he will be charged with murder and will appear in open court. Questions . . ."

The senior Tel Aviv-based reporter of the Reuters news agency asked, "Will we ever be told what it is that is a matter of life and death?"

"Who can tell?"

The briefing was concluded.

Within fifteen minutes the IBC had broadcast the news that according to the military spokesman it had now been ascertained that two Arabs, thought to be the bombing team, had died in the explosion.

Because of the deformity of his features it was difficult for the other officers in the room to ascertain the feelings of Major Said Hazan.

The major had pulled his chair away from his desk. He was bent over his radio set, listening intently, as he had been for every one of the news broadcasts from Israel that morning.

He switched off the radio. He resumed the course of the meeting. He knew the scale of the casualties. He knew the fate of the two recruits. He knew that the trail of evidence to the Yarmouq camp on the outskirts of Damascus was cut.

More martyrs for the folklore of the Palestine revolution, more casualties for the enemy that was Israel.

The station officer rang Major Zvi Dan immediately after the news broadcast.

"I just want, again, to express my gratitude. If they had known there was a survivor . . ."

". . . They would have moved the camp, the contact would have been lost. We have given you the chance, we hope you can use it."

11

They had slept in a hostel for soldiers in transit.

No explanations from Crane, and Holt was less bothered at the silences with each day he spent in the man's company. He was into the rhythm of tagging along, speaking when he was spoken to, following Crane's lead.

They had had fruit and cheese for breakfast. He thought his beard was beginning to come, slowly enough, but starting to appear something more than just a laziness away from the razor. When he had stood in front of the mirror, when he had taken his turn at the wash basin, when he had looked at himself, then he had wondered how Jane would have liked his beard . . . only a short thought, a thought that was cut before being answered because Crane had been behind him and told him to put away his toothpaste, told him to get used to life without a toothbrush. No explanation, just an instruction.

It beat him, why they could not stay in a hotel when they had all the expense money available to pay for a suite at the Hilton, why they had to sleep in a hostel at eight shekels a night.

He had reflected. His mind had cast back to the Crimea journey, to the field of the Light Brigade on which he would have walked with Ben Armitage.

"Ours not to reason why."

That was life with Noah Crane.

"Ours but to do and die."

Pray God that was not life with Noah Crane.

When he had finished his breakfast Crane stood and walked away from the table. He wouldn't wait for Holt to finish what he was eating. Holt stuffed two apples into his trouser pockets, grabbed a slice of cheese and followed him out. At a table in the hallway Crane put down his bank notes, and waited for his four shekels of change. No tip.

They walked. Crane said that Holt was missing his morning exercises, so they wouldn't take a bus. Holt was used now to Crane's stride, his cracking pace. They started from old Jewish Jerusalem, with the walls of the old city behind them and the golden semi orb of the Dome of the Rock. If he ever returned to London . . . of course he would . . . When he returned to London no-one would believe he had been in Jerusalem and never visited the old city, never walked the route of the Cross. And he was fitter. He could tell that, he was beginning to match Crane stride for stride. Away along wide streets, under gently leaved trees, over steep hills, and into new Jewish Jerusalem, through suburbs of villas constructed of clinically cut sand rock.

They were on the fringe of the city, they climbed the last hill.

They were overtaken by the tourist coaches as they approached the memorial.

"Yad Vashem, Holt," Crane said. "It's where we remember the six million of our people that the Hun slaughtered."

"History makes man complacent, doesn't get people forward. Take the Irish . . ."

"Don't give me university crap. Isaiah, 56,5. 'Even unto them will I give in mine house and within my walls a place and a name better than of sons and daughters: I will give them an everlasting name, that shall not be cut off.' We do remember what happened to our people. If we ever forget them then that will be the day that the same can happen to us."

"I don't believe history tells us . . ."

"Holt, six million of our people went to the gas chambers and the furnaces. They didn't fight, they lay down. Because we remember what happened, today we will always fight, we will never lie down. I don't want a debate, I'm just telling you."

They went into the low ceilinged bunker that was the heart of the memorial. They stood at the rail, they looked down on the stone floor in which were carved out the names of the 21 largest concentration camps. Further from the rail were fading wreaths, and near to the back wall of rough cut lava rocks there burned a flame. Holt was the tourist, he gazed around him, as if he stared at the Kremlin cupolas, or the arches of the Coliseum, or the Arc de Triomphe, or the Statue of Liberty. He turned back to see if Crane was ready to move on. He saw the gleam of a tear rolling on Noah Crane's cheek. He could not help himself, he stared blatantly. He read the names . . . Treblinka, Auschwitz, Dachau, Belsen, Lwow-Janowska, Chetmno . . . He stood behind Crane so that he should no longer intrude into the privacy of his vigil.

Abruptly Crane swung away, marched out into the sunlight. They walked quickly.

Crane leading, Holt following.

They walked through a garden parkland that was laid out in memory of Theodor Herzl, the originator of the concept of a Jewish state. They went past the young sprouting trees and bank beds of flowers, and down avenues of bright shrub bushes. When they had crossed the parkland, when they looked down the hillside, Holt saw the terraced rows of graves with their slab stone markers. He stood on the high ground, he left the neat chip stone paths to Noah Crane. It was a personal pilgrimage. For a long time he watched the slow lingering progress of Crane amongst the graves.

Holt brushed the flies from his forehead. He was being given a lesson, that he was aware of. He thought that Crane did nothing by chance.

At the far end of the graveyard, Noah Crane looked up, shouted to Holt, "They're all here, Holt, the high and mighty and the unknowns. Men from the Stern Gang, from the Liberation War of '48, Sinai, Six Days, Yom Kippur, Netanyahu who led the raid to Entebbe, Lebanon, all the men who've given their lives for our state. We value each one of them, whether he's a hero like

Netanyahu, whether he's a spotty faced truck driver who went over a mine in Lebanon. Whatever happens to me in the Beqa'a they'll get me back here, that's the best thing I know."

"That's mawkish, Crane."

"Don't laugh at me. This isn't a country that's going soft. You know, Holt, in the President of Syria's office there is one painting, one only. The painting is of the Battle of Hattin. You ever heard of that battle, you with all your history? 'Course you haven't . . . At the Battle of Hattin the great Saladin whipped the arse off the Crusaders. The President of Syria aims to repeat the dose. He aims to put us to the sword, and the rest of us into the sea. Got it?"

"Got it, Mr Crane."

"It's not my intention to end up here, Holt."

"Glad to hear it, Mr Crane."

"So you just remember each damned little thing that I tell you, each last damned little thing. You do just as I say, without question, no hesitation," Crane's voice boomed on the hillside. "That way I might just avoid the need of them cutting a hole for me."

"Let's hope we can save them the trouble, Mr Crane."

Later, towards the end of the morning, with their kit, they were dropped off at the start point chosen by Noah Crane.

They were going walking in Samaria, north from Ramalleh towards Nablus, in the Occupied Territories.

Via a scrambled telephone link, Percy Martins reported progress to the Director General.

From Tork's office in the Tel Aviv embassy he spoke directly to the nineteenth floor at Century. By protocol he should have talked to Fenner. He hoped, fervently, that Fenner would hear he had bypassed him.

"Crane's taken the youngster for a few days into the Occupied Territories to get him thinking the right way, used to the equipment, used to the movement."

"And then they go?"

"They're going to be picked up near Nablus, they'll be taken to Kiryat Shmona, rest up for a few hours, then off."

"What state is the eye witness?"

"Holt's in a good state. He'll do well."

"How are they coming out?"

"They're going to have to walk out."

"Haven't you bent a few backs?"

"God knows, I've tried, but they're going to have to walk out."

"Anything new?"

"We have a fix on a training camp that is being run by Abu Hamid. We know exactly where to go for him."

"The Prime Minister wants it for Sylvester Armitage's memory. I want it for Jane Canning's memory. I'm relying on you, Martins."

Martins, hired hand, third man on the Desk, first time running his own show, said defiantly, "You can depend on us, sir."

Crane was on watch, Holt drowsed.

For Holt, the night march with the laden backpack was the most exhausting experience of his life.

"They're going, Prime Minister, within a week."

"To bring me his head?"

"Regrettably not on a salver, but his head for all that." The Director General smiled.

"He's terribly lucky."

"Who is, Prime Minister?"

"This young man we've sent out there."

"The eye witness."

"Exactly, terribly lucky when so few people of his age have the chance afforded them of real adventure."

"Let us hope he appreciates his good fortune, Prime Minister."

"I have to tell you, I would be less than honest if I did not. I am already savouring the moment when I can recount this small epic to our friends in the States . . ."

"Forgive me, but they have a long road to walk."

"If I do not have the head of this Palestinian wretch, then most certainly I will have another head. It's your plan and your advice I'm taking."

The Director General smiled comfortably across the Downing Street sitting room.

"It was a very fine calculation then, Prime Minister, and in a number of particulars it is finer still."

The Prime Minister was gathering papers. The meeting was over. "His head or yours. Goodnight."

The second night out, and they had not been walking more than an hour and a half, and it was the third time that Holt had fallen, pulled over onto the rocks by the weight of his pack the moment he had lost his balance.

He heard the stones rumbling away on the hillside. He could have cried in his frustration. He could hear the venom of Crane's swearing from in front.

Abu Hamid watched them coming.

He stood at the flap of his tent and studied the slow progress towards the camp of the girl who led the donkey, and behind it the crawling jeep. He could hear the soft cough of the jeep's engine as it idled. At that distance, even, more than half a mile, he knew that it was Fawzi's jeep.

She wore the floppy trousers of the Shi'as, and the short cotton skirt, and the full loose blouse, and the scarf tied tight over her head and then wrapped across her mouth to mask her face. She dressed in the clothes of a village girl of the Beqa'a. The jeep was a dozen paces behind her, but she made no effort to quicken her pace, or to move aside.

Abu Hamid sucked at a hardly ripe peach, swirling his tongue over the coarse surface of the stone. He knew that in the Beqa'a, under the eye of the Syrian army, under the control of the Syrian Intelligence agencies, nothing would happen by chance. He knew that it would not be by chance that a girl walked a donkey along the track that led only to the tent camp, and that the girl was followed by Fawzi's jeep. She was young, he was sure of that, he could see the smooth regular flow of her slim hips, the trousers and skirt could not hide the slender outline of the young body.

Abu Hamid took the peach stone from his mouth, threw it high into the coiled wire of the perimeter fence. He called for the recruits to come forward, to break from their meal, to get off their haunches, make a formation. He lined them up, three untidy rows.

He turned to face the entrance to the camp.

Now the jeep accelerated and swung past the girl. The donkey shied, and the girl held her course and seemed unaware of the jeep. She was lost for a moment in the dust thrown up by the jeep's wheels, and when she appeared again she still walked forward, light step, leading the donkey. Abu Hamid saw that the donkey had a pair of old leather pannier bags slung down on its flanks.

With a swaggering step Fawzi walked towards Abu Hamid. His hands rose to grip Abu Hamid's shoulders, he kissed him on both cheeks. Abu Hamid smelled the lotion that crept to his nostrils. Fawzi clapped his hands for attention, played the big man. For Abu Hamid it shamed the Palestinian revolution that Fawzi and his clumsy conceit should have control of the recruits, of himself. He watched the girl and the donkey approach the camp entrance. Fawzi had his back to the girl and the donkey, as if their time had not yet come. Fawzi addressed the recruits.

"Fighters of the Palestine revolution, I have news for you of an epic attack by the Popular Front deep into enemy territory. A commando force of the Popular Front has travelled to the heart of the Zionist state, and in so doing has disproved the claim of the Zionists that their borders are secured. The target was the principal bus terminus in Tel Aviv. The attack was timed for last Sunday morning, at the moment when the maximum number of enemy soldiers would be boarding transport to return to their units. The Zionists, of course, have attempted to minimise the effectiveness of our commando strike by releasing ridiculously false figures of the casualties inflicted. Their lies will not deflect the truth. Forty-eight of their soldiers were killed, more than a hundred were wounded. The heroism of the commando knew no limitations.

They carried out, our men, an attack of greater pain to the enemy than the successful assault by hand grenade at the Dung Gate in Jerusalem against a military parade. Fighters, I said to you that the heroism of the commando knew no limitations. I grovel in admiration at such heroism. The plan of the attack allowed for the commando to place a bomb on the Tel Aviv to Jerusalem bus. The bomb was fitted with a timing device that would permit the commando to leave the bus en route with the bomb left under a seat. That was not good enough, fighters, for this heroic commando. They feared that after they had left the bus that there would be a small chance of the discovery of the bomb that would negate the attack. Such heroism, fighters . . . The commando was governed by total commitment to the cause of the Palestine revolution . . . They set the timer early. They stayed with the bomb until it exploded. By their selfless action they determined that there was no possibility of the bomb being discovered and rendered harmless. For the success of the revolution they gave their own lives. Fighters, the strike force of the commando came from this camp. They were your brothers in arms. Fighters, Mohammed and Ibrahim were of your blood. They shared your hardships, they shared your food, they shared your tents. They were given the chance to wage total war against the enemy, against your enemy, they did not fail the cause of the Palestine revolution."

Abu Hamid stood numbed. The man who was an incessant pain in the arse was now a hero. The thief was now a martyr.

The girl with the donkey walked slowly through the entrance gap in the wire.

The recruits gazed awestruck at Fawzi. They had clung to each word he had spoken. As if each man yearned for himself the admiration now settled on Ibrahim and Mohammed.

The girl now stood beside Fawzi. She held loosely in her hand a length of rope that was fastened to the bridle. The donkey was old and patient.

Fawzi looked to the girl with pleasure.

"Without great courage, without great bravery, the Palestine revolution will not be won. But we have the courage, we have the bravery, and so the victory of the revolution is inevitable. Look at her, fighters, look at her and rejoice in the courage and bravery of the revolution. She is sixteen years old, she is in the full flower of youth. She has no ambition other than to give her life, her breath, her spirit, to the revolution."

Abu Hamid stared at the girl. He could not tell whether she heard Fawzi. Her face was blank, her eyes were dead. He had seen men who habitually smoked the poppy, or dragged on cigarettes made from the marijuana crop, and their eyes, too, were dead, their faces were without expression. He could not say whether her love was for the revolution or whether it was for the poppy and the hashish fibre.

"This girl is going alone to the security zone. Without the support of comrades, with the help only of a fervent faith in the ultimate success of the revolution, she is going into the security zone with her donkey. The donkey is her friend. The donkey has been with her since she was a child at her mother's breast. In the bags carried by the donkey will be one hundred kilos of industrial dynamite. Do you understand me, fighters? This girl will go to the checkpoint at the entrance to the security zone, where there are the Israeli surrogates of the fascist South Lebanese Army, and the Israelis with their personnel carriers, and the torturers of the Shin Bet. When she is amongst them she will fire the explosives. They will go to their hell, she to her paradise."

His eyes never left the girl. She was a wraith. What Abu Hamid could see of her face was dry and pale. He could not see fear, he could not see boredom. Could it be real? Could a girl have such love of martyrdom that she would lead a donkey laden with explosives amongst the enemy, that she would obliterate herself and her enemy? He knew of the Shi'a car bombers, the heroes who had ploughed their vehicles into the American embassy, and the French embassy and the Marine camp in Beirut. He knew of the car bomb that had been driven against the walls of the Shin Bet headquarters in Tyre during the enemy's occupation of the city. He knew that the cars approaching the security zone were treated with such suspicion that a better chance now existed for approaching close with a donkey or a mule or a pack horse. Could a girl have such little love of life?

"She is an example to us all. By seeing her, by knowing of her, we are honoured. She visits you in order that you may be encouraged by the memory of her bravery, when the time comes for you, yourselves, to go south and fight the enemy who denies you your rightful homeland. Show her your love, show her your admiration."

Abu Hamid raised his fist in the air. White knuckles, the fist punching.

"Long live the Palestine Revolution."

The recruits shouted their answer, echoed his words.

"All glory to the martyrs of the Palestine Revolution."

The cheering soared.

"Strength to the enemies of the state of Zion."

"Courage for the fighters whose cause is just."

The girl did not smile. Slowly she rolled her head so that she gazed flatly at each and every one of the recruits who yelled their support of her. She turned. She seemed to speak a word into the ear of the donkey. She stood for a moment in profile to Abu Hamid. He saw the bulge, he saw the weight forward and low on her stomach. He knew she was pregnant. She led the donkey away and out of the camp. The recruits cheered her all the way, but she never looked back.

Abu Hamid dismissed the recruits and they stood silently at the camp gate as the girl and the donkey became small figures on the rough track.

Fawzi beamed. He walked to Abu Hamid.

"She is to go through all the villages between here and the security zone. It has a great effect on the villagers, just as she has made a great impression on your men. When she has made her attack, a film of her will be shown on the television, it is already made."

"Is she . . . ?"

"Drugged? You surprise me, Abu Hamid . . . She is a fighter, she is like yourself."

Fawzi drove away in his jeep. He caught up the girl and her donkey before they reached the tarmac road.

When he strained his eyes, Abu Hamid could see them. A girl and a donkey, and just behind them the jeep of the Syrian army.

They worked hard at their training that morning. No back-chat, only studied concentration. They worked at the lesson of the platoon in attack on a hillside against a defended position, with the support of .50 calibre machine guns and RPG-7 launchers.

That morning Abu Hamid did not find the need to repeat any part of his teaching.

Holt drank his water. It was a new discipline to him, to ration himself. He must have looked with obvious longing at his water bottle, because he was aware of the smear of amusement at Noah Crane's mouth.

The merchant braked, slowed his Mercedes.

Ahead of him, down the straight road running from north to south under the east slope of the Beqa'a valley, was a column of Syrian army trucks. The trucks, more than a dozen of them, he estimated, had pulled across onto the hard shoulder of the road. He came forward slowly. Always his way to pass a military convoy slowly, so that he could see what the convoy carried. And always better to go slowly past the Syrian military, with the window wound down the better to hear any shouted instructions – they would only shout once, they would shout and if their shout was ignored they would shoot.

There was a jeep stopped at the head of the convoy, and he saw a very fat young lieutenant talking, arm waving, to another officer. Heh, who was he, Menachem, to laugh at the grossness of a young soldier? The merchant weighed on the scales some nineteen stone . . . He saw a young girl leading a donkey.

The girl and her donkey were at the far end of the convoy, coming past it. He drove onto the same hard shoulder, he switched off his engine. No one looked at him. He listened but there was no shouted instruction. The canvas roofing of the lorries had been rolled down. He saw that they carried troops. A dozen lorries could carry two companies of infantry, the mental arithmetic was second nature to the merchant. The troops crowded to the sides of the lorry and watched the girl and her donkey come alongside them, move forward. Faintly, he could hear the shouting voice of the gross young lieutenant who had gone from the side of the officer and now offered explanation to the soldiers. As the girl led her donkey past each truck, so the soldiers cheered her.

Deep in his mind where the truth of his existence was hidden, the merchant swore. He recognised the signs, and it would be two days before he was again in a position to make a drop. A long time ago he had been offered a radio.

He had declined, he had said he would not be able to learn how to use it, and anyway he had known that a signal sent to Israel was a signal sent also to the men of Syrian Intelligence. He preferred the dead letter.

The bomber would be paraded through the Beqa'a. The bomber would be used to jolt the commitment of the young. He could see that the bomber was herself scarcely more than a child.

The merchant, Menachem, saw his controller, Major Zvi Dan, rarely. Never more than twice a year. The last time, smuggled by the IDF through the night across the border, he had talked to Zvi Dan about the bombers.

The bomber was just a slip of a girl. He could piece together what Zvi Dan had told him, late and over whisky, about the bombers.

"You know, Menny, the IRISHBAT found a car bomb in their sector, abandoned. They made it safe, and then they looked to see why it was abandoned. You know why, Menny? It was abandoned because it had run out of petrol . . ." The merchant could remember how they had laughed, hurting their stomachs laughing. "They are not all suicide people, we had one who came up to the checkpoint and surrendered, and said that the girl who was with him had already run away. Do you know with another, Menny, the bastard Syrians gave him a flak jacket to wear and they told him that way he would survive the explosion of his own car, and in the car was more than 150 kilos of explosive. More recently, they have taken to a remote firing. The bomber goes to the checkpoint, but the detonation is remote, from a command signal, from a man who is hidden perhaps a kilometre away. That is because they know that not every recruit wishes to hurry to martyrdom. We have learned, Menny, that the bombers are not so much fanatics, as simple disturbed kids. There was one who was with child and did not dare face her father, there was a boy who had quarrelled with his father and run away, there was one whose father was accused by the Syrian military of crimes and who volunteered to save his father from gaol. Believe me, Menny, they are not all Khomeini fanatics. Most are sick kids. We know, we have captured eleven of the last sixteen sent to the security zone. I tell you what is the saddest thing. They make a film of the kids, and they show it on the television, and they make great heroes of the kids. There is a village in the security zone where live the parents of a boy who drove the car for one of the big Beirut bombs, and now it is like his home is a tourist attraction, and his father is a celebrity, and the kid's picture is everywhere on the walls. Heh, Menny, what sort of cretin takes a holiday in south Lebanon? Only a Jew, if the discount is good." More laughter, more whisky. A conversation of many months back.

There were times, in the loneliness of his subterfuge life, that the merchant doubted his own sanity. There were times when his mind ached for a return to the buoyant, carefree students on the campus in the Negev desert. He saw the girl leading the donkey. Zvi Dan had told him that the men of Syrian Intelligence scoured the villages of the Beqa'a for kids who would drive a car bomb, for kids who would lead a donkey bomb. He thought that the girl and the donkey and the heavy bags slung on the rib cage of the beast were an abomination. One day he would go back to his students . . . on a day when there were no more donkey bombs, no more car bombs, Menachem would go back to his lecture room.

Whatever he saw, whatever its importance, he would not break his routine. It would be two days before he could report the coming threat to a road block leading into the security zone.

She had passed the parked lorries. He could hear the shuffle of her feet, the clip of the donkey's hooves. He saw the sweating lieutenant amble towards his jeep. For the soldiers the parade was over.

He saw the face of the girl, devoid of expression.

He shouted through his opened window.

"God is great."

They were high above the village. Crane had pointed to it on his map, 'Aqraba. Holt watched through binoculars as the kids launched their rocks and Molotovs at the troops. It was like something he had seen on the television from Northern Ireland. From their vantage point, Holt not daring to move for fear of Crane's criticism, they watched a day-long battle between the kids and the soldiers, fought in a village square that was wreathed in tear smoke, and in the alleys behind the mosque. Sometimes, when the fight went against the soldiers, Holt heard Crane's chuckle. Sometimes, when the soldiers caught a youth and battered him with their rifle butts, Holt ground his teeth.

He heard the voice in the corridor, and the clatter of feet.

Martins tidied the newspaper. He had been through yesterday's *Times*, and the *Herald Tribune*, and that day's *Jerusalem Post*. Read them all from cover to cover, right down to the cost of a ten-year lease on a two bedroomed flat in West Kensington, to the discounts available in a jewellery store's winding up sale in Paris, to the price of a second hand Subaru car in Beer Sheba. He was nagged by frustration. Martins could recognise that he was the outsider, he was an intrusion in the smooth dealings between Tork, station officer in Tel Aviv, and his local contacts.

He tidied his paper. He scraped out the debris from the bowl of his pipe into the saucer of the coffee cup that he had been given three hours before. He ignored the No Smoking sign stuck onto a window of the station officer's room.

The door opened. Martins saw the station officer blink as the smoke caught his eyes. Sod him . . . The station officer tugged in with him a shallow long wooden box, olive green. No greeting, not as yet. The station officer's priority was to get to the window, shove it open, then to the air conditioner, switch it off.

"Been able to occupy yourself?" the station officer asked curtly.

"I've passed the time. What have you brought?"

"A rifle."

Martins tried to smile. "A present for the Ayatollah and the Mullahs?"

"I beg your pardon?"

"Just a joke."

"Actually it is the rifle for Crane."

"We brought Crane's rifle out from England – rather a lot of paperwork."

"It wasn't the rifle he wanted."

"Why didn't the bloody man say what he wanted? He test fired the Parker Hale, he didn't complain."

"Perhaps you never asked him what he wanted. Perhaps you just told him what he was getting."

"The man's impossible."

"Just doesn't waste time arguing. What he would have told you he wanted if he had been asked was a model PM from Accuracy International, small firm down in Hampshire."

"How did it get here?"

"Israelis picked it up yesterday, shipped it out in their DipCorps bag to save time, avoid the export licence. I collected it this morning."

Martins puffed, "That makes me look a complete fool."

The station officer asked, "Would you like some more coffee?"

"There are more important things than coffee. If it has not escaped you, I am in charge . . . Damn it, man, I didn't know you were smuggling a rifle out of the UK, I don't know where Holt and Crane are, I don't know when the jump off is, I have not been given access to the latest intelligence on the camp."

"Unfortunate."

"Meaning?"

"You're going to have to live with it."

"I'm a senior man in London, Tork . . ."

"And this is Israel. Sorry . . . Decision taking is in Crane's hands, and stays there. Crane will decide on the jump off, on the route. He will make the decisions because he is going to be in the Beqa'a, and we are not, for which in all sincerity I thank God."

"You and I are going to have to get one or two things straight."

The station officer glanced up, heard the rasp in the voice. He thought a man who wore a three piece suit in the heat of Israel to be a fearful ass.

"As I understand it, Mr Martins, you got the job, were sent out here, because there were no decisions to be taken – sorry."

"Fenner told you that . . . ? Well, you've got a nasty surprise coming to you. Control of this mission has been entrusted to me by the Director General, and I mean control. And one more thing: there is more to the work of the Service than the analyses that you fill your day in writing. I've read some of your stuff – 15 pages on the future of the Coalition here, eight pages on the prospect of a right wing backlash, 21 pages on future settlements on the West Bank, all the sort of crap that Fenner wants, the sort of gibberish that keeps Anstruther happy."

"I am sorry if my material is too *complex* for you, Mr Martins."

"You can think of it as complex if you wish, Tork, but you'd better get it into your head that this mission into the Beqa'a is of infinitely greater importance to the interests of the United Kingdom than the trivia with which you spend your days, and if this goes wrong, for your lack of co-operation, I'll have you gutted," Martins said.

The station officer peered down at him. Twice in the last week his wife had asked him whether they were not duty bound to invite Mr Martins, out from London, to their flat for dinner. Twice the station officer had told his wife to forget it, leave the man to his hotel room. The station officer fancied he could hear the boastful chat in London on the upper floors of Century. Problems, why should there be problems? Difficulties? Difficulties only existed to be overcome. A good show, a super big show.

As if it was a gesture of defiance, Martins shovelled tobacco from his pouch and into the bowl of his pipe.

"I'm going to be in Kiryat Shmona."

"What for?"

"Because I'm bloody well responsible."

"Once they're over the frontier, once they've gone there's nothing you can do."

"I have to be somewhere, and that's where I mean to be," said Martins.

The station officer considered the alternative. He thought of having him fretting in his office for the next week, perhaps longer.

"I'll take you up."

Rebecca was the personal assistant to the major. She had been with him for more than two years. Major Zvi Dan liked to say, when he introduced her, that she was his eyes and his ears, that she alone understood the mysteries of the now computerised filing system. She was blessed also, he claimed, with an elephantine memory. At the end of each working day he would share with her his thoughts, his new found information, and they would be stored electronically in the computer and mentally in her head.

Rebecca sat in the front passenger seat of the pick-up truck. She was out of uniform. She wore jeans and a blouse of brilliant orange. First she had smoothed her nails with a manicure stick, now she painted them purple, fingers and toes.

Rebecca was a fixture in Major Zvi Dan's life. Perhaps he relied too greatly on her, on her memory and her organising skills. She bullied him – not that he complained other than to her face. She made him go to the doctor at Defence when his leg stump ached intolerably, she forced him to eat when the work load bowed him down, she came once a week to his bachelor flat, high and overlooking the Ramat Gan quarter, to collect his dirty clothes and take them to a launderette.

They had been parked at the side of the Nablus to Jenin road for a little more than an hour.

Rebecca glanced up occasionally from her concentration to amuse herself at the growing anxiety of Major Zvi Dan. The major paced around the pick-up. He looked down at his watch. He fingered the automatic pistol that was tucked into the belt of his slacks. With binoculars he studied the pale rock strewn hills, and the small terraced fields from which the stones had been lifted to make walls.

She heard the snort of Major Zvi Dan's exasperation. When they had first stopped, he had told her that within five minutes they would be making the rendezvous with Crane and the English boy. Five minutes drifting into more than an hour. He was cursing quietly, he was staring up the road, he was searching for the approach of two small and distant figures.

"You should get something done about those eyes, Major."

She heard the voice. She swung her head. Major Zvi Dan was rooted, peering down the rough hill slope that fell from the road. Small rocks only, low and hardy scrub bushes. She watched the head of the major tilt and twist as he tried to find the source. She could see no hiding place.

"Crane?" Major Zvi Dan shouted. "Get the hell up here."

The ground seemed to rise. The figure seemed to materialise. Where there was dung grey rock there was a standing man.

"You need to get them looked at, Major."

She laughed out loud.

"Move yourself, Holt."

A second figure appeared. They stood together some fifteen yards from the road, level with the pick-up.

They were in uniform, their skins were dirt smeared.

"I am a busy man, Crane. I have better things to do."

Crane came forward.

"You should meet Holt, Major."

Major Zvi Dan stared Holt up and down. "How's he done?"

"Acceptable."

"Is he good enough to go?"

"The first day he'd have had us identified three times. Second day once, third day once. He's just been under your glasses for an hour, that makes him acceptable."

"Get in the back," the major said coldly.

Rebecca watched. She saw that Crane carried his back pack easily, like it was a part of his body, along with the rifle with the elongated telescopic sight. She saw that the younger man came more slowly, as if the back pack were a burden, as if he had never before carried an Armalite rifle.

"What's your time table, Crane?"

"Shit and shower first, long sleep. Tomorrow, aerial photographs and maps, pack the kit. Move tomorrow night."

She watched Crane climb easily into the open back of the truck, slinging his backpack ahead of him, she saw the young man struggle to scramble aboard and get no help.

The Mercedes was clean, the merchant carried the code in his head.

In the darkness of early night, before the stars were up, the merchant had lifted the bonnet of the car and loosened a battery cable.

He was a little off the main road. He was parked above the sparse lights of the village of Qillaya.

It was a routine for him. If he had been bounced by a Syrian patrol or by a group of Shi'a militia, or by a band of the Hezbollah, then he would have had the explanation that his car's engine was broken, that he could not put it right in the darkness.

He wrote his message, a jumble of numerals on a scrap of paper.

He had to walk some fifty yards from the car to the angle of the road. There was always danger in these moments, on the approach to a dead letter drop. He could take every precaution during his travelling, during his halts, but the moment of maximum danger was unavoidable. If the dead letter drop was compromised he was gone. He was breathing hard. On the angle of the road was a rain ditch, cut to prevent the tarmacadam surface being eroded during the spring floods when the higher snows melted. In the ditch was a rusted, holed petrol drum. He left his messages in the drum, he received his messages from the drum. He was not more than 2000 yards from the UNIFIL zone, there was a checkpoint of NORBAT 2000 yards down the main road. He was eleven miles from the Good Fence, the Israeli frontier. He was a few minutes' walk, a few minutes' drive, from the sanctuary of the NORBAT checkpoint, from the safety of his country's frontier. It was always the worst time for him, when he was within touch of sanctuary, safety, when he was short moments from turning his back on the checkpoint and the Good Fence and starting the drive back into the Beqa'a.

He had the paper in his hand. The merchant bent over the drum, searched for the hole into which he would place his coded report of the progress south through the valley of a girl with a donkey bomb.

The torch light flooded his face.

He thought he was losing his bowels.

He could see nothing behind, around, the blinding beam of the torch.

He waited for the shot.

The urine was driving from his bladder.

"It's Zvi, Menny. Heh, I am sorry."

The torch light went out. The merchant stood his ground, could see nothing.

There was an arm around his shoulder, stifling the trembling of his body.

"I think you pissed yourself. Heh, I am truly sorry. There was someone who had to see your face."

The merchant saw the shadow looming behind the shape of his friend, but the shadow came no closer.

The merchant whispered, "Couldn't you have used a night sight?"

"He wanted clear light on your face, it was important . . ."

For ten minutes the merchant and Zvi Dan sat by the rain ditch. The merchant made his report in incisive detail. Zvi Dan gave his instructions, handed over the package.

The merchant went back to his car. First he collected an old pair of slacks from the boot and quickly changed into them, then he refastened the battery cable. He drove back to the main road and then on to the village of Yohmor where he would spend the night. In the morning he would advise the elders of the village on the spare parts they needed to buy for the repair of their communal generator, and how much those parts would cost.

Holt started up in his chair. He had been dozing. He was brought back to life by the thud of the boots on the plank slats of the verandah. God, and was he lucky to have dozed. Percy Martins was still in full flow and the station officer seemed to suffer from a private agony, and the girl was reading a Hebrew romance with a lurid cover.

The verandah was outside the officers' canteen at the army base. There were pots of flowers, and a jungle of vine leaves overhead, and there was coffee and Coca-Cola to drink if anyone could be bothered to go inside to the counter to get it for himself.

The girl was reading the book and ignoring Martins like Jane had been able to do when they were in his or her London flat and he was watching the cricket on television. The station officer hadn't quite the nerve to turn his back on the reminiscing. Martins was remembering his time in Cyprus, spook on the staff of Government House, recommending his old strategies for application in the Occupied Territories.

Holt looked behind him, turned in his chair. He could see that both the major and Crane were still wet from face washing, and he could see that it had been a fast job because there were still smears of dark camouflage cream under the ear lobes and down at the base of their throats.

Crane said, "Long day tomorrow, Holt . . ."

Martins said, "Pleased you've returned from wherever, Major. Something I'd like sorted out. I am informed I have to sleep in an hotel. I would have thought you could put me up on camp."

Major Zvi Dan said, "Not possible."

The girl, Rebecca said, "Do you like cocoa?"

Holt said, "Ages since I've had it. Quite."

Crane said, "Get to your bed, Holt. Now."

The station officer said, "I'm off early in the morning, back to Tel Aviv, I'll be gone before you've surfaced . . . Give it your best effort. Look forward to welcoming you back. Holt. Sergeant."

Holt stood and shook the station officer's hand, a damp hand and a limp grip. Crane wandered off towards the counter in search of food.

Percy Martins drummed his fingers on the table. "I would like to discuss the matter of my accommodation further."

The girl, Rebecca, was back in her book. Holt saw the mud dirt on the major's boots.

"Goodnight all," Holt said.

He went to the room they had allocated him. A white painted cubicle, with a bed and a table and a chair, and three hangers on a nail behind the door. He didn't bother to wash, and he wasn't allowed to use toothpaste. He peeled off his jogging shoes and his shirt and trousers. He switched off the light, flopped on the bed. He had slept fourteen hours the night before, and he was still tired. The day had been divided in two. There had been the kit part of the day, and there had been the route planning part of the day. He didn't think it was from choice, he assumed it was from necessity, but at least Crane had talked to him, at him. Down the corridor was Crane's room, and next door to that the kit was laid out for packing in the morning. Crane had talked to him, at him, when they were with the Intelligence guys, when they were looking at the aerial photographs that foot printed the Beqa'a.

He heard the knock at the door.

He didn't have the time to reply. The door opened.

He saw the silhouette of the girl against the lit corridor. He saw that she carried a mug, steaming.

Holt laughed out loud, "Not the bloody cocoa?"

She laughed back at him. The curtains were thin, and when she kicked the door shut behind her, the floodlights outside streamed through. He could see that she was laughing.

"It's the best thing to make you sleep."

"You're very kind."

"And you are going to Lebanon tomorrow, so you need to sleep." She sat on the bed. She wore a deep cut green blouse, and a full skirt.

He thought her laughter was an effort. He thought she had sad eyes, and there were care lines on the edge of her mouth. He took the mug from her, held it in both hands, sipped at the thick stirred cocoa. He had not had cocoa since before he went to boarding school, since his mother used to make it for him on cold winter evenings when he was a small boy.

Holt tried to smile. "It's supposed to be a secret, me going into Lebanon tomorrow."

"My husband was in Lebanon. He went with the first push, and then he went back again in the last year of our occupation. After the first time he was a changed man. He was very bitter when he came home to me. Before he went he used to play the saxophone in a small jazz band where we lived. He never played after he came back. He was an architect, my husband. There were many casualties in his unit, tanks. I used to wonder what an architect, a saxophone player, was doing driving a tank in Lebanon. My husband said that when the IDF first went into Lebanon they were welcomed by the Shi'a people, the people in the villages threw perfumed rice at the tanks, by the time they left that first time they were hated by the same Shi'as. The mines were in the roads, the snipers were in the trees. He was called up again for Lebanon in '85, just before the retreat started. The leaders, the generals, of course they didn't call it a retreat, they called it a redeployment. He used to write to me. The letters were pitiful. He used to say he would never go back again, that he would go to prison rather than serve another tour in Lebanon. He used to say that the basic rule of survival was to assume the worst, at every moment, to shoot first. Lebanon brutalised him. A week before he was due to come out, from the second tour, he wrote to me. He wrote that they had painted on their tank the words, "When I die I will go to Heaven, I have already been through Hell." He was killed the day after. He was shot by a village boy near Joub Jannine. They knew it was a village boy because they caught him in their follow up search, he was 13 years old. He was 13 years old and through hate he shot my saxophone player, my husband. That is Lebanon, Holt."

"I am sorry."

"It is the way of life for us. We are Jews, we are condemned to a permanent perdition of warfare."

"I'm sorry, but my viewpoint is from a long way away. I'm not trying to be an impertinent outsider, but I think you've brought much of it on yourselves. Again, I'm sorry, but that's what I feel."

"When you go into Lebanon you will be part of us. There is no escape from that."

"You know my quarrel, why I go?"

"I've been told. Your leaders, your generals, want a man killed. They need you for assistance at the execution."

"The man killed the girl I loved," Holt said. He raised the cocoa mug to his mouth. The cocoa spilled from his lips, dribbled down onto his new found tan from the beach at Tel Aviv.

"Do you go into Lebanon for the girl that you loved, or for your leaders and your generals?"

Holt shook his head. He said softly, "I don't know."

"Better you go for your girl."

"Did he love you, your husband, when he died?"

"He wrote in his letters that he loved me."

"My girl, she snapped at me, the last words that she spoke. We were quarrelling . . . Can you see what that means? The last time we spoke, the last memory I have of her, is of argument. That's a hell of a weight to carry."

"Close your eyes, Holt."

His back was against the pillow that was propped up against the wall. His eyes closed. He felt her movement on the bed. He felt the softness of her lips on his cheek. He felt the moisture of her lips on his mouth. He felt the gentleness of her fingers on the bones of his shoulder.

"My husband, Holt, my saxophone player, he used to write to me from Lebanon that the feel of my mouth and my hands and my body was the only sanity that he knew."

With the palms of his hands he reached to the smooth angles where her cheeks came down to her throat. He kissed her, as if with desperation.

"Remember only her love, Holt. Make her love your talisman."

The memories were a rip tide. Walking with Jane in the sunshine of spring on the moorland hills. Sitting with Jane in the darkness of a London cinema. Lying with Jane in the wet warmth of her bed.

His eyes were tight shut. He moved aside in the bed. He heard her peeling away her blouse, pushing off her shoes, dropping down her skirt. He felt the lovely comfort of her against his body.

He cried out, "It doesn't help her, cannot help her, killing him."

"Until he is dead you have no rest. Her memory will only be torment. Love me, Holt, love me as you would have loved her. Love me so that you can better remember her when you are in Lebanon."

When he woke, she was gone.

As if she had never been there. As if he had dreamed of Jane.

12

His eyes ached, his forehead hurt.

Crane had the maps in front of him, and the aerial photographs. An Intelligence officer took Crane through the photographs.

It was the close work that pained him, caused him to blink, but this close work was inescapable, critical. The pilotless drone had flown the previous day. The Delilah drone had flown from inside Israel, and taken a route north from Metulla and over Marjayoun in the security zone. The drone had clipped the edge of the NORBAT sector and flown on at a height of 15,000 feet towards Yohmor. By the time that it cleared Lake Qaraaoun at the southern end of the Beqa'a valley, the camera set in the belly of the Delilah was picturing the ground beneath. The drone's flight path had taken it along the western side of the valley, over small villages, over goat herds and the boys who minded them, over women hoeing the weeds out of the stony fields in preparation for the planting of corn crops, over the steep sloping tiled roofs of Shi'a villages, over Syrian army positions, over the main road running north east from Khirbet Qanafar to Qabb Elias, over the small vineyards from which would come in the autumn the delectable bottles of Cabernet Sauvignon and Pinot Noir, over the Syrian headquarters garrison at Chtaura across the Beirut to Damascus road, and then east, and then south along the Bar Elias to Ghazze road. And, of course, Delilah, a speck in a clear midday sky, had passed over a tented camp that was surrounded by a fence of coiled barbed wire and a bulldozed ditch. The drone had been seen by many people. It had been seen by the boys with the goats, and by the farming women, and by the men sitting outside their village coffee houses, and by bored Syrian soldiers, and by Abu Hamid as he lectured his class in the workings of the DShKM heavy anti-aircraft machine gun, and by Fawzi as he negotiated a transaction with a headman, and by a merchant who drove an old Mercedes car. Seen by many people, but unremarkable to all of them. The drone flew twice a week, it was accepted.

The photographs had been taken especially for the benefit of Sergeant Crane.

He studied each one with the help of a stereoscope. It was the stereoscope that killed his eyes, brought the throb to the deep recess where his retina was diseased. Had to use the stereoscope, because that was the instrument that threw the flat vision of the photographs into a three dimensional reality.

Crane spoke only rarely to the youngster. He thought of him as the "youngster". He believed that he was not a nursemaid, and his experience of handling novice troops had taught him that to talk too frequently was to confuse. He expected that Holt should listen, and above all that he should watch. Noah Crane did little by chance. He demanded that Holt should concentrate, watch everything, react on it, remember it.

Most times his conversation was with the Intelligence officer. He trusted the man. The planning of the route required trust, and the man had served him well. Most recently this gawky, spider-like Intelligence officer had carried out the detail of the planning for the sniping of a Hezbollah unit commander. His care had earned the trust of Noah Crane. They talked in the Hebrew tongue. Crane had two maps on the table in front of him. The one he marked, bold lines for the route, decisive crosses for the stop positions, the other he left clean.

The Intelligence officer gathered up the photographs. Noah Crane folded the map that was not marked. He spoke from the side of his mouth to Holt, staccato, as if it were obvious.

"See the way I fold it. The way I fold it doesn't show which section interests me, it concertinas out. And I never put my fingers on it. When we're out there, when we're using it, we will always use a pointer, like a stick, to indicate. We never leave marks on the map, finger marks."

"So that if we are captured they don't know what our target was?"

Crane said, matter of fact, "We don't talk about capture. Capture is not thinkable. It is in case we lose the map."

He saw the youngster look away.

He led Holt to the kit room, the room beside his own. He was a loner. For years, as a sniper, he had taken responsibility for himself, for his own skin. Noah Crane had never gone after promotion, he had shunned taking novice soldiers under his wing. He didn't bloody well know how to raise the spirits of the youngster, didn't bloody know. He could see the youngster was scared witless, standing close to him, walking close to him, but he didn't bloody well know how to breathe confidence into the youngster. And it worried him. He needed the youngster to begin well . . . and how? How to get the youngster doing it right. That was an agony to Noah Crane, a second agony to the pain behind the tiredness of his shooting eye.

Holt was young enough to be Noah Crane's son, and he had never fathered a son, never brought up a son. 'Course he didn't know how to communicate with the youngster.

He had laid the kit out in the same way he always did.

Two Bergen packs nearest the door, the kit stretching away.

"You'll know him, won't you?"

"I'll know him."

"I'd skin you, if we went that far and at the end you didn't know him."

"Mr Crane, I see him just about every hour of my waking life. I see his face, I see his movement, I see him running. There's no chance, if he's there, that I won't know him."

"Not personal, I just had to be sure."

"Mr Crane, has it ever crossed your mind that I might not be sure of you?"

"You cheeky brat, you know about nothing."

"I know about plenty. About the things normal people know. I'm just weak about going into other folks' back yards and killing people . . . They don't do degree courses in that."

"Everything I do you copy. You do everything I say, and we'll make it back."

"I hear you, Mr Crane, and is there something I can say?"

"What is it?"

"It would be great to see you smile, and to hear you laugh would be quite marvellous."

Crane scowled.

"We're taking more than we had on the warm up hike. We're taking what I can carry, which means you have to manage with the same. We are taking five days' water, which is 50 lbs weight. We are taking rations for five days. We will have first aid and survival gear. We will have a sniper rifle with day vision and night vision sights, and we will have an Armalite rifle with six magazines. Watch the way I pack your kit, I won't pack it for you again . . . It's not easy for me, you know, having a green arse."

"I'll do my best, Mr Crane."

"Too right you will, 'cos I kick hard."

When the Bergens were packed, and the weapons had been cleaned one more time, Crane dressed in olive green military trousers and shirt. He saw that Holt watched the way he pulled the sleeves down and buttoned them, hid the forearm skin. He saw the way Holt copied him as he threaded the hessian lengths of brown and yellow and black material into the rubber straps sewn into the uniform, to break down the body's outlines. He saw that Holt imitated him as he smeared the insect repellent cream on his face and throat, but not on his forehead. He could have explained that creams were never put on the forehead, because the sweat would carry it into the eyes, but he saw no point in explaining. The youngster just had to watch, copy, imitate. When Holt was dressed, he hoisted the Bergen pack onto Holt's shoulders, told him to walk around, told him to get the feel of the pack that was half as heavy again as the one that Holt had struggled with in the Occupied Territories. Six times round the room, and then the adjustments that were necessary on the straps. More adjustments for the waist belt. And adjustments for the sling strap of the Armalite.

Holt said, "Why haven't you given me a practice with the Armalite?"

"Because if our lives depend on you with the Armalite, then they're not worth much."

"I have to be able to fire it."

"If it has to be fired then it'll be me that's firing it. You're just there to carry it."

Crane reached out. He took the wrist watch off Holt's arm. For a moment he read the inscription on the back. "Our dearest son, 21st birthday, Mum and Dad". He felt a vandal. He tore off the strap. He looped a length of parachute cord through the slots, knotted the ends. With adhesive tape he fastened two morphine ampoules to the cord, one each side of the watch. He hooked the cord over Holt's neck, saw the watch sink with the ampoules down under Holt's shirt front.

Like he was dressing a kid for a party, he tied a dull green netted cloth around Holt's forehead. He stood back, he looked Holt up and down.

"You won't get any better," Crane said. He punched Holt in the shoulder, he made a rueful grin.

"If they ever audition for the lead in the Great Communicator, you'd be a certainty, Mr Crane. You might even end with an Oscar."

"Let's move."

He thought the youngster was great, and he did not know how to tell him. He thought that he was not alone. He had seen the way Percy Martins looked at Holt, when Holt didn't see him. He thought they were both trying to reach the youngster, and both failing, both too bloody old.

Crane said, "You won't have noticed, Holt, but there is no magazine on the Model PM Long Range. It's one shot only. You don't get a chance to reload. You have one chance, one shot. I have to get into a five-inch circle at around a thousand yards with a first shot, an only shot."

He saw the sincerity in Holt's eyes. "That's why they had to dig out the best man, Mr Crane. Thank God they found him."

They went through the door.

Holt's own clothes and Crane's were left folded in separate plastic bags, each with a name-tag.

Loaded down by the Bergens they walked down the corridor, out to the transport.

Percy Martins was talking to him, pacing alongside Holt. He was following Crane out into the sunshine and towards the mine-proofed Safari truck.

"I'll be here, Holt, I'll be at Kiryat Shmona, and via Tel Aviv I'll have secure communications with London. Everything that I can humanly do for you will be done, rest assured on that . . ."

He saw the girl standing on the verandah of the officers' canteen. She wore scarlet this morning. He would like to have gone to her, kissed her his thanks for what she had given to him. She looked straight through him, as though he were a stranger.

"You're going to help to make the world a better and a safer place for decent folk, young Holt. Go in after that bastard and blow him away. Let them know that there are no safe havens, no bolt holes, that we can see them and reach them even when they're the other side of the hill. I'll be waiting for you."

"Great, Mr Martins."

He followed Crane into the back of the Safari, the major gave him a hand up, pulled him over the tail board.

"God speed . . ."

Holt didn't hear any more. The Safari lurched forward. Martins stood in the road, shouting silently, waving as if it were important, with the white plastic nose shield set as a bullseye in the centre of his sun red head, and the light catching the watch chain across his waistcoat. When he looked to the verandah the girl was sitting and her head was in her book.

He felt the sharp finger tap on his arm.

Crane said, "Forget it, right now you've more to think of than some doe-eyed fanny."

He didn't think any woman had ever loved Noah Crane. He thought Noah Crane was in pain because of the way that his face was screwed up, and his forehead was cut with lines. The back of the Safari was covered with a canvas roof and sides, and the three of them sat as close as was possible to the driver's cab. To other cars, to people walking on the road, they were unseen. Their own vision was through the open back. The major and Noah Crane sat on the slatted seats, facing inwards, and Holt was down on the floor between them and sitting on sandbags. The sandbags covered the whole of the floor of the back of the Safari. Holt understood they were there to cushion a mine explosion. He smiled to himself, did not show his black amusement to the others. He had once read of a man who was shipwrecked and alone in a rubber dinghy, and the man had said that the worst aspect of his 100-day drift before rescue was when the sharks came under the dinghy and prodded the thin rubber base with their snouts. He wondered which would be worst, the snout of a tiger shark under his backside, or the blast of a land mine – great choice, beautiful options.

He held the Armalite rifle upright between his knees, and he didn't even know how to maintain it, how to strip it, how to clean it. He was young Holt. He was a young diplomat of Third Secretary grade. All so wretchedly unreal.

They went through the village of Metulla, and through the back of the Safari Holt saw that almost immediately they drove past a border checkpoint and through a wide cut gap in a high wire fence. Crane reached out, no preliminaries, took the Armalite and with fast hand movements cocked it. Holt heard the clatter as the escort sitting in front beside the driver armed his weapon.

"Welcome to our security zone, Holt." The major seemed to smile, and he creaked his leg as he shifted to take more easily a Service pistol from the leather holster at his waist. "It is our buffer or protection strip. At the fence we have our last line of defence to keep the swine out of our country. At the fence we have the electronic beams, body heat sensors, TV camera fields, mined areas. But that is the last line. We try to halt them, the infiltrators, here in the security zone. You know we have around ninety attempts each month to get through the security zone but they don't get through. The security zone is of the greatest importance to us. We are indeed lucky, Holt, that we have in the security zone several thousand armed men of the South

Lebanese Army, they are Christians who were isolated down here when Lebanon fragmented. We pay them hugely, much more than we pay our own soldiers, and because they have to fight for their own survival they protect us well. The security zone, Holt, is a place of enclaves. Apart from the Christian enclaves, there are groupings of Shi'a Muslim, and Islamic Fundamentalist Muslim, and Hezbollah Muslim. The Shi'as and the Fundamentalists and the Hezbollah have in common a hatred of everything Jewish and everything Christian. It makes for an interesting zone. But we have cut our funerals. The funerals of our soldiers were destroying our nation. The SLA now die on our behalf, handsomely rewarded for their sacrifice. Our men are more precious to us than shekels, we can pay the price."

They drove on. Over the lowered tail gate Holt saw that they were climbing through a dry and barren landscape. He saw road blocks that they sped through without checking. He saw a Subaru saloon, with no identifying number plates, parked on the hard shoulder, and there were two men in civilian clothes sitting on the bonnet and one cradled a sub-machine gun on his lap and the other had a Galil rifle slung from his shoulder. The car was low on its suspension. He presumed they were Shin Bet, that the car was armour plated. They passed the turning to Khiam, and Holt saw the fences and watch towers of what seemed a prison camp. They passed the turning to Marjayoun, which Holt knew was the principal Christian town in the zone.

They climbed.

The major and Crane talked fast now, in Hebrew. They talked over the top of Holt, as if he were not there, and twice the major leaned over Holt and tapped energetically with his finger at a piece of equipment on Crane's belt harness. It was the one piece of equipment that was not duplicated on his own belt harness.

The truck was slowing, changing down through the gears. There was the rocking motion of the vehicle as it pulled off the road, and headed up to a steep incline on a rough track.

They lurched to a halt.

"Where you walk from, Holt," the major said.

Crane disarmed the Armalite, cleared it, then handed it to Holt. He carried his Bergen and his Model PM to the tail board, jumped down. The major clumsily followed him. Holt lugged his Bergen the length of the Safari and swung himself off the end. All three ran the few yards into a concrete and stone built observation post. It was early afternoon. It was sickeningly warm in the observation post, as though the reinforced walls held the heat.

He sensed the tension immediately.

There were two soldiers and an officer. There was a radio squawking with bursts of static, and one of the soldiers sat by the radio with his earphones clamped on his head and held tight by his hands. The other soldier and the officer raked with binoculars the ground ahead of their split vision port holes.

He saw the major speak to the officer, saw the officer shake his head, resume his watch.

Holt came forward. He placed himself at the officer's shoulder. He stared out.

The checkpoint was about a hundred yards down the road, a chicane of concrete blocks positioned so that a vehicle must slow and zigzag to pass through. The road stretched away, winding and falling towards the green strip of the Litani river bed. The observation post was, Holt estimated, a hundred feet above the road. A great emptiness. A silence stretching up the road that led north. Down at the checkpoint he could see that the soldiers all peered up the road, some through binoculars, some holding their hands flat against their foreheads to protect their eyes from the sun.

"When do we go?" Holt asked, irritated because he was ignored.

"When it is dark," the major said, all the time gazing up the road.

"So why are we here so early?"

"Because the transport has to be back before it is dark."

"So what do we do now?"

"You wait, because I have other things to consider."

Holt flared, "Why can't someone tell me . . . ?"

"Leave it," Crane snapped.

He felt like stamping his foot, furious and apparently powerless. The officer had turned away from the vision slit he watched through, and had gone with quick, nervy movements to the table where the radio operator worked. The officer pulled a cigarette from a packet beside the set, lit it, puffed energetically on it, then offered a cigarette to him. Crane was looking at him. Sulkily he shook his head. Cigarettes were banned. Toothpaste was banned. Soap was banned . . . Crane had said that cigarettes and toothpaste and soap were all banned because they left a smell signature. What the hell was a smell signature? What sort of language was that? *Smell signature*. He looked up, it was on the end of his tongue to argue what difference it would make if he had one cigarette.

They had their backs to him. He stared at the backs of the officer, and the soldier, and the major, and Crane. Hunched backs, heads pressed against the wood surrounds of the vision slits.

He could see over Crane's shoulder.

In the bright light of the afternoon he had to blink to make anything from the sunswept rocky ground and the narrow grey pencil line of the road.

The radio operator was scribbling, then tearing the paper off his pad, holding his arm outstretched for the officer to take the message.

He could see a girl leading a donkey.

The soldiers at the road block were running to take cover behind the blocks of the chicane, and two men were crouched in the cover of their car back from the roadblock.

Unbelievable to Holt. The soldiers had taken cover because there was a girl a thousand yards down the road leading a donkey. A girl and a beige brown donkey, and this Man's Army was flat on its face. A girl and a donkey, something out of a Sunday School lesson when he was still in short trousers. A small boy's idea of the Holy Land – bright and sunny, and yellow rock, and a girl with a donkey.

The major spoke to Crane. Crane shrugged, nodded. The major spoke to the officer. The officer went to the radio, took the earphones from the operator, spoke briefly into the microphone.

A girl coming up the road and leading a donkey. The only movement Holt could see through the vision slit. Crane had gone to the back of the observation post, was rooting in his kit. Holt saw two of the soldiers who had been behind the cement blocks were now scurrying, bent low, to get further back. All unbelievable. Crane pushed Holt aside, wanted the whole of the vision slit to himself, and he was jutting the barrel of the Model PM through the slit.

"For God's sake, Mr Crane, it's a girl."

"Don't distract him," the major said quietly.

"So what in God's name is he doing?"

"Be quiet, please."

A girl with a donkey, something sweet, something pastoral.

Crane slid a bullet into the loading port forward of the bolt arm, settled the rifle into his shoulder.

"What in bloody hell gives? It's a girl. Are you sighting your rifle? Can't you see it's just a girl? Is this your idea of a test shot?"

"Quiet," the major hissed. Crane oblivious, still.

"It's a bloody person, it's not just a *target* . . ."

Crane fired.

There was the rip echo of the report singing around the inside of the observation post. Holt's eyes were closed involuntarily. He heard the clatter of the ejected cartridge case landing.

He looked through the vision slit.

The donkey stood at the the side of the road beside the small rag bundle that was the girl.

Holt looked at them, looked from one to the other.

"Bloody well done, so you've got your rifle sighted. Only an Arab girl, good target for sighting a rifle. First class shooting."

Crane reloaded.

The donkey had moved a pace away from the girl's body, it was chewing grass at the side of the road.

"I didn't know it, Crane, I didn't know you were a fucking animal."

Crane breathed in hard. Holt saw his chest swell. The rifle was vice steady. Crane breathed out, checked. Holt watched the first squeeze on the trigger, saw the finger whitening with the pressure of the second squeeze.

Again the crash of the shot echoed in the confines of the observation post. Crane spurted out his remaining breath.

Holt saw the orange flame.

Holt saw the flame ball where the donkey had been.

There was a thunder rumbling. There was a wind scorching his face at the vision slit.

The donkey had gone. The girl had gone. There was a crater in the road into which a big car could have fallen. Holt stared. God, and he felt so frightened. He was naked because he knew nothing.

Crane ejected the cartridge case. His voice was a whisper, a tide turn over shingle, a light wind in an autumn copse. "Did you watch me?"

"I'm just sorry for what I said."

"As long as you watched me, saw everything I did."

He had seen that Crane's head never moved. He had seen the breathing pattern. He had seen the way Crane's eyebrow and cheek bone merged into the tube of the telescopic sight. He had seen the two stage squeeze on the trigger.

"I saw everything that you did."

The major said, "You are in Lebanon here, Holt, nothing is as it seems."

They were given tea.

Crane cleaned the rifle, unfastened the bolt mechanism to pull the cloth through the barrel.

Major Zvi Dan crouched beside Holt.

"I don't think, and this is not criticism, that you know anything of the military world."

"I'm not sorry."

"If you had been born an Israeli you would have been in the army."

"Not my quarrel."

"You may not think it your quarrel, but when you walk from here, when you walk away from our protection, then every man and woman and child in the villages and towns of the Beqa'a would hate you if they knew of you. Would you believe me if I told you, Holt, that in the Beqa'a they do not acknowledge the Geneva Conventions on the treatment of prisoners . . . ?"

Holt grimaced, he liked the man. "I believe you."

"I am so very serious. It is a place without conventions. There would be no officers to safeguard you. Your life would be worthless after the sport of torturing you."

Holt said softly, "I'm scared enough, no need to make it worse."

"I do not try to frighten you, I try only to stress that you should follow Noah, exactly follow him. Noah is a marksman, he is a sniper. Do you know that in your own army for many years sniping was frowned on? It was not quite right, it was even dirty. Examine the job of the sniper. He shoots first against an officer. When does he shoot the officer? He kills the officer when he goes for his morning defecation. The officer is dead, his men are leaderless, and they dare not leave their trench for the call of nature. They make their mess in their trench, which is not good, Holt, for their morale. The sniper is hated by his enemy, he is prized by his own forces who are behind him. Often they are far behind him, where they cannot be of assistance to him. It is a peculiar and particular man who fights far beyond help. Your Mr Crane, who has never accepted a medal, is peculiar and particular. Follow him."

Holt sat on his backside as far as he could be from the vision slits. For as long as he could avoid it, he wanted to see no more of a battlefield where the enemy was a young girl, and her arsenal was a donkey.

The aircraft was late.

The aircraft was at the end of its flying life. At every stopover it required comprehensive maintenance testing. The aircraft was elderly because that way the premiums paid to Lloyds of London by Middle East Airlines for comprehensive insurance cover could be kept to a reasonable figure.

The aircraft landed from Paris in the middle of the afternoon. It had come in over the sea, the view of Beirut had been minimal in the heat haze.

He was Heinrich Gunter, the passenger who was eager to be free of the passport queue in the bulletpocked airport terminal.

He was 45 years old, and this was the thirty-ninth visit he had made to Beirut since the shooting and shelling had started in 1976.

He was a middle-management employee of the Credit Bank of Zurich, and he was personally responsible for the administration of many millions of United States dollars invested with his bank by wealthy, quiet-living Lebanese entrepreneurs.

He was married, with three children, and he had told his wife that morning that Beirut was fine if you had the right contacts, made the correct arrangements.

He was expecting to be met. He was not to know that the airport road had been closed for three hours, that a rising of tension between men of the Druze militia and of the Shi'a Amal militia had prevented his agent from getting to the airport to meet him.

He hurried away from the passport control. He collected his one suitcase that was adequate for a two day stay, maximum. He moved through the frequently repaired glass doors at the airport's main entrance. He could not see his agent.

After waiting for 25 minutes, Heinrich Gunter agreed with a persistent taxi driver that he would pay the fare asked, in hard currency. He was told that the driver knew a safe way, avoiding the area of tension, to the hotel into which he was booked. It was already a long day. A row with his wife over his breakfast because he was going to Beirut, an argument at Zurich airport because the Swissair flight was overbooked and he was a late arrival, drinks in the airport bar at Charles de Gaulle because Middle East Airlines was leaving late, more drinks on the flight because he was going to Beirut. It had been a long day, and he had been drinking, and he took the taxi.

Heinrich Gunter never really saw what happened. In the back seat of the taxi Heinrich Gunter lolled back, the whisky miniatures of the Paris airport and the Middle East Airlines first class cabin had taken a gentle and gradual toll.

By the time that his eyes opened, the taxi had been waved down to the side of the road, the back door had been wrenched open, a hand had grabbed for the sleeve of his jacket. The first thing he clearly saw was the barrel of a rifle half a dozen inches from his chest. The first thing he felt was himself being propelled out of the car. He lurched to the pavement. He was grabbed under each arm and rushed down an alley way. He had seen a flash of two slimly built young men, each wearing a cotton imitation of a balaclava face mask, each carrying a rifle. In the alley a length of cloth was wrapped around his face, covering his eyes. He was kicked hard in the leg, the back of his head was cudgelled with the butt of a rifle.

There was no fight in Heinrich Gunter as he was dragged away.

He knew what had happened to him. He was sobbing as his shoes scuffed the surface of the alley way. He had not even shouted for help. He knew he was beyond help.

Fawzi showed his papers to the NORBAT sentry. The papers identified him as a Lebanese dentist.

He drove out of the UNIFIL sector. The checking by the sentry of his car had not been thorough. A thorough check would have discovered the dirtied overalls in which he had lain on the hillside a mile and a half from the road block. It would also have discovered a powerful pair of East German binoculars. Had the car been stripped to its panels, then the sentry would have unearthed the radio controlled command detonator that would have fired the explosives in the pannier bags slung against the donkey's sides.

He went fast, angrily.

He had seen weeks of manipulation destroyed by a long range marksman.

He had failure to report to Major Said Hazan.

He had seen the girl as a gem, and her long triumphant journey had been ended several hundred yards short of her target. Fawzi could taste the humiliation.

Percy Martins wrote his occupation as "government servant", and the reason for his visit as "vacation", when he filled in the registration form at the guest house.

He had not been asked where he wanted to stay. He had been driven from the army camp at Kiryat Shmona to the Kibbutz Kfar Giladi. He was not that disappointed. He was greeted at the reception desk as a V I P. His bag was carried. He was treated with respect. The guest house, six stories high, set in flowering gardens, appealed to him.

He was given his key.

"I was wondering," he said to the raven haired, raven eyebrowed, receptionist, "would there be any fishing in these parts? Would one be able to hire a rod?"

Percy Martins was nothing if not a pragmatist. He understood that his marriage was in terminal collapse, that his relationship with his son was as good as finished. He could look clear-headed at his career, twice passed over for promotion to Deputy or In Charge of the Middle East desk. But he was no longer wounded by setbacks. He could cope with his home life. He could live with what to other men would have been humiliation in the office. He could endure the taciturn Holt and the imperious Israelis. That is what he told himself. He said to himself, Sod the lot of them. He would bloody well go fishing.

"I would have thought there would be some trout in those nice little streams running down from Mount Hermon. Now trout isn't what I usually go for – I'm a pike man actually. I don't suppose you know about pike. If you're into trout then you would regard pike as something akin to vermin. You'll see what you can find out for me, of course you will. You're very kind."

With his key in his hand he trudged up the stairs to his second floor room. He imagined himself ushering young Holt into the Director General's office, and of standing quietly at the back of the room. Very well done indeed, Percy. We are all proud of you.

He sat down on the bed. He unbuttoned the front of his waistcoat. He loosened his tie. Sod the lot of them. He held his head in his hands. Unseen, alone, close to tears.

There was a crushed ball of paper on the pile carpet beside the chair of Major Said Hazan. It was the clean sheet of paper he had crumpled with all the strength of his fist when the telephone call had informed him that the girl and her bomb had not reached target.

He had given his instructions. On the evening television news broadcast, transmitted by the Syrian state station, a statement would be made by the girl. She would talk of her commitment to a Lebanon free of Israeli terror, and of her commitment to the Syrian cause and the Palestine revolution. And then the news reader would give factual information of the heavy casualties inflicted on the IDF and their surrogate SLA by the sacrificial heroism of the girl.

The truth, and this was clearly recognised by Major Said Hazan, was an irrelevance. The northern boundary of the security zone was a closed area, there would be no independent witnesses. More of the Arab world would believe the claim of the Syrian state station than would believe the denial put out by the Israeli Broadcasting Corporation. The message would go on the airwaves that a young Muslim girl of exemplary purity had given her life in the struggle against the Zionist brutes – she had been photographed with care by the camera, her pregnancy would not be seen. It was the estimate of Major Said Hazan that a car bomb or a donkey bomb had more effect on the anxious sheiks and emirs and sultans of the oil wealthy Gulf than any other lever for the extraction of funds. Great truth in the ancient Arab proverb, The enemy of my friend is my enemy, the enemy of my enemy is my friend. His country needed the funds of the Gulf. The route to those funds was through constant, daring attacks against Israel carried out by the young vanguard of the Arab peoples.

The truth might be an irrelevance, but he hated to know that the bomb had been stopped short of its target. The crushed, crumpled paper lay beside his feet.

He reached for the telephone. There were some who came to his office who marvelled to find four telephones on the table beside his desk. A joke had once been made that he had only two ears, two hands. A poor joke, because his ears had been burned away, leaving only stumps, and the fingers of his right hand had been amputated. One telephone gave him access by direct line to the desk of the brigadier general commanding Air Force Intelligence. A second telephone gave him scrambled communication with military head-quarters at Chtaura in the Beqa'a valley. A third telephone gave him an outside line, the fourth put him into the exchange system of Air Force Intelligence. He lifted the third telephone.

He dialled.

He spoke with silk. "Is it you? . . . A thousand apologies, I have been away, and since I have been back just meetings, more meetings. Too long away from you . . . How was he, my pet? . . . How was his spirit? How was his resolution? . . . My pet, you would lift the organ of the dead . . . Excellent. I will see you, my pet, as soon as I can turn away this cursed load of work. Goodbye, my pet."

There had been the knock at his door which caused him to ring off. He loved to hear her guttural foreign voice. He loved to linger with his thoughts on the smooth clean curves of her flesh . . .

He called for his visitor to enter.

Major Said Hazan stretched out his left hand in greeting.

"My Brother, you are most welcome . . ."

For an hour he talked with this military commander of the Popular Front over the plans for an attack on the Defence Ministry complex in Tel Aviv. That section which housed the rooms of the Military Intelligence wing was ringed in red ink. They discussed the method of infiltration, and leaned towards a seaborne landing, and they pondered over the sort of man who might have the élan, the resolution, to lead such a mission.

After an hour Major Said Hazan had quite overcome his sharp fury at the failure of the girl and her bomb at the checkpoint in the security zone.

Far behind them, far from sight, came the dulled reports of the artillery, and far ahead of them there was the brilliance of the flares bursting and then falling to spread their white light against the darkness.

Holt tugged at the Bergen's straps, wriggled for greater comfort. They were outside the observation post.

Crane said, "I told you not to look at them."

Crane had his back to the flares.

"And you haven't told me what they're for."

"I'm not a bloody tourist guide."

"Why are they firing flares, Mr Crane?"

"Because you're looking at the flares you're losing the ability to see in darkness. We have to pass through a chunk of NORBAT ground, so we are putting flares up for illumination between NORBAT positions and where we're walking, we're burning out their night vision equipment. Got it?"

"Would have helped if you had told me in the first place."

"Piss off, youngster."

"Let's get this show on the road, then."

They hugged each other. A brief moment. Arms around each other, and the belt kit sticking into the other's stomach, and the weapons digging at each other's rib cages, and the weight of the Bergen packs swaying them.

They were two shadows.

The stars were just up. The moon would be over them at midnight, an old moon in the last quarter.

They crossed the road beneath the observation post. They headed into the darkness, away from the road, away from the slow falling flares.

They were gone from the safety of the security zone. Nothing in his mind except concentration on his footfall and the faint shape walking in front of him. Nothing of Jane who had been his love through his life before, nor of the girl who had been his comfort the night before, nor of the leaders and the generals, nor of his country. Only the care of where he laid his boot, and his watch on Noah Crane ahead.

13

It started as a casual conversation.

At the airfield south of Kiryat Shmona there was a hut where helicopter passengers could wait, sit in comfortable rattan style chairs, for their flight. There was a steward dispensing orange juice, there was a radio tuned in to the army station, there were some pot flowers which had even been watered.

The pilot came into the hut to advise Major Zvi Dan that there would be a short delay before he could lift off with the major and the major's assistant.

"Up to your ears?" the major asked.

The pilot knew Zvi Dan. The pilot sometimes joked that he was a bus driver, that Zvi Dan travelled more often from Tel Aviv to Kiryat Shmona than any grandmother in search of her grandchildren.

"I'm down the queue for refuelling, for maintenance checks. Ahead of us are the choppers going tomorrow."

Because the pilot knew Zvi Dan, he knew also that the major worked in military Intelligence. He could talk freely.

"Where?"

"Big show up the road."

"I've been out of touch." Zvi Dan sipped at the plastic beaker of juice.

"Bombers are going up the road in the morning, we're down for rescue stand-by."

"So we're in the queue, and what's new? That's the old army motto, Hurry up and Wait."

Rebecca read her book, almost at the end, rapt attention.

"There's to be a big chopper force on rescue standby, it's a difficult target they're going for."

"How so?"

"The Beqa'a, not under the missile umbrella directly, but the fringe area. It's not the missile that's the problem, the target's just small, and for small targets they have to line up more carefully, all the usual gripes from the bombers."

"What's the target?"

The pilot leaned forward, said quietly. "We were told that they had good interrogation of one of those shit pigs that did the bus station – well, you'd know more of that than me, that it was all hocus them both being killed. Seems they came out of a training camp in the Beqa'a, that's where the bombers are going . . ."

Major Zvi Dan was rigid in his chair. His orange juice had spilled on his tunic.

"Heh, have I said something?"

He saw the major's back going out through the door.

Rebecca looked up, grimaced. She had not been listening. She went back to her book.

Major Zvi Dan, anger mad, pounded into the night.

He swung through the door of the airfield's flight operations room. He stomped to the chair of the flight operations officer. He pulled the chair round, swivelled it to face him.

"I am Major Zvi Dan, military Intelligence. I am an officer with an A level category of priority. On a classified matter of importance I demand an immediate takeoff for Tel Aviv."

He cowed the flight operations officer into submission.

He could barely believe it: two men had started to walk towards the Beqa'a, to walk towards a tent camp, to identify a target, to take out a terrorist, and the Air Force were planning to beat them there by two days and scatter the ground with cluster bombs. Right hand and left hand, light years apart. Why couldn't his bloody country put its bloody act together?

He stormed back into the hut. He limped up and down the floor space, pacing away his impatience.

The pilot came in. "You put a bomb under somebody, Major. We have clearance for lift-off in ten minutes."

It was the same rhythm of advance that Holt had learned during the hike in the Occupied Territories. But that had been only rehearsal. Different now. In the Occupied Territories Crane had hissed curses at him when he kicked loose stones, when he stood on dry wood, when he stumbled and stampeded away small scree rock. On his own now, wasn't he? Had to make do without help. Not that he needed cursing when he scuffed a stone, he wanted to punch himself in frustration each time.

Holt knew that the pace that had been set was aimed to cover one mile in each hour. It had been dark at six, it would be light again at six. They had moved off an hour after darkness, they would reach their LUP an hour before dawn. He was unconsciously soaking up the jargon, a Lying Up Position had become LUP. Ten hours on the move, ten miles to cover. Stripped, Holt weighed 168 pounds. He carried a further 80 pounds' weight in his clothing, his Bergen and his belt. In addition he was ferrying the Model PM, because Crane had the Armalite. He remembered the race around the lawns of the house in England, when he carried nothing, when Crane had a backpack full of stones. Christ, there was a weight on his back, on his hips, on his arms.

The first hour he had kicked stones, the second hour fewer. They were in the third hour and he moved as Crane had shown him. His booted foot edged forward, found the ground, the ball of his foot rolled, tested. If the test was fine, if the stone held fast, then the weight followed. It was the rhythm of each pace, every footfall tested.

There was just the starlight for them to move under. Crane was fifteen yards in front. It was Holt's job to follow Crane's speed. Crane set the pace, Holt had to follow. Crane was an outline ahead of him, blurred at the edges by the hessian tabs on his body shape and on the bulk of his Bergen. All the time he had to be within sight of Crane, because Crane would not stop each few yards and turn to see if Holt kept contact.

A week before, before the hike into the Occupied Territories, Holt would not have credited that so much skill, so much care, would be involved in moving across ground at night.

It was indeed a rhythm.

It was the same rhythm from the moment they had crossed the road under the observation post, headed away.

Every 30 minutes they stopped. Holt would see Crane hold up his hand and then drift to the side off the line of march. A few moments of listening, looking into the darkness, with Crane and Holt sitting back to back, each covering a 180 degree arc of vision. No talking, no whispering, just the straining of the ears and the eyes. In the Occupied Territories, Crane had told Holt that they should always be low down when they were listening, looking, seeking for information that they were followed or that there was movement ahead of them. Crane had said that a dog or a cat had good vision at night because its low eye line permitted it to see most shapes against a skyline in silhouette. In the short moments when they were stopped, Crane would check his map, holding over it the lens of his Beta light, powered by tritium, giving him the small glow that was hidden from view, sufficient for him to see by.

During the third hour they crossed the Litani river. Waist deep in fast water, going off rocks and climbing back onto rocks, so that they left no footprints in mud. There were no roads, and Holt saw that Crane avoided even rough tracks that could have been used by the villagers of Qillaya that was across the river to the east, or Qotrani that was beyond the hill summit to the west. It was strange to Holt how much he could see with the help only of starlight, something he had never thought to learn before. He supposed the trail they took might have been made by wild animals, perhaps an ibex herd, perhaps the run of the low bellied hyrax, perhaps the regular path of a scavenging hyena or a fox.

North of the narrow road between Qillaya and Qotrani, in the fourth hour, they were high above the Litani, traversing a steeply sloping rock face. On the slope face they moved sideways, crab-like. When they had to cross the upper lines of a side valley, Holt saw that Crane immediately changed direction as soon as they had been outlined. He had been told why they did not climb to the upper ridges of the hills, Crane had told him that the military were most likely to be on the high ground, basic officer training was to seek out the greatest vantage point. A hellish strain on Holt's leg muscles as he fought to hold his balance against the sway of the Bergen weight when they crabbed on the sloping, uneven ground.

By the fifth hour he was sagging down at the RP. The Rally Points, where

405

they stopped for the few moments each half hour, seemed to him to be drifting further apart. He knew that was eyewash, he knew he was feeling the exhaustion of the night march. At the RPs he sat against Crane's shoulder, and had to be elbowed hard in the ribs to remind him that the stop at the RP was not for recovery, but for checking that the way ahead was clear, that the way behind was not compromised.

He was halfway through the first night, and there would be three nights of marching to get to the tent camp, and then there would be the stampede march back. God, and he was tired, and he was only halfway through the first night. He could hear his chest heaving, he could feel the gasping pant in his lungs. Silence from Crane, as though he were out for a stroll in the park . . . Bloody man.

Rebecca drove from the Sde Dove airport on the north side of Tel Aviv, across the city.

Major Zvi Dan sat beside her, still angry, silent. The streets were fully lit. Bright shop windows, pavement crowds, café's packed. The anger corroded him. The old and the young strolling the streets, examining the windows, laughing and joking and singing, and two men not quite a hundred miles to the north were struggling in the darkness through rivers, over rock slopes, further and deeper into the territory of the enemy. The logic was gone from his mind, blown away by his temper. He wouldn't have said that he wanted the citizens of Tel Aviv to hot tail it to the synagogues and offer prayers, nor that they should shut their mouths, shut off their music, tiptoe down Dizeng-off, but it fuelled his anger to see so many who knew so little, cared less.

She dropped him on Kaplan, outside the David Gate of the ministry. She said something to him about what time she would arrive in the morning, but he didn't hear her. He ran, as fast as his imitation leg would allow him, towards the barrier and the night sentries. And he couldn't find his pass . . . and his pass wasn't in his breastpocket . . . and his pass was in his bloody hip pocket. He could have been the Prime Minister, could have been the Chief of Staff, he would not have entered the David Gate if he had not found his pass in his wallet in his hip pocket.

He was allowed through. They didn't hurry themselves. It was the way of sentries, little men with power, that they never scrambled themselves for a man who was hurrying.

He headed for the wing building occupied by the IAF staff.

And how his leg hurt him when he tried to run. . . . Into the building, another check on his pass. . . . Up the stairs and into the access corridor used by night duty staff, one more check on his pass . . . along the corridor and into the fluorescent lit room that was the war management section of the Israeli Air Force. A big, quiet room, where the men and the women on duty spoke in soft whispers, where the radios were turned down, where the teleprinters purred out their paper messages. A room flanked by huge wall maps, and dominated in the centre by the operational console table. It was from this room that the long range voice contact had been kept with the Hercules transporters flying the slow lonely mission of rescue to Entebbe, and from this room also that the F16s had been guided the thousands of miles to and from their strikes against the Palestine Liberation Organisation headquarters in Tunis and the Iraqi nuclear OSIRAK reactor outside Baghdad. Those who worked in this room believed themselves to be an elite back-up force to the elite arm of Israel's retaliatory strike capability. Those who worked in the room looked first with puzzlement, then amusement, at the hobbling army major making his entry.

It was a room of great calmness. Low key calmness was the strength of the men and women who supported the combat pilots. Major Zvi Dan had abandoned calmness. He was dirty, he was tired, his hair was dishevelled.

All eyes were on him.

A girl officer, wearing lieutenant's insignia on her shoulder flaps, glided from a chair to intercept him.

"I need to see, immediately, the duty brigadier." Major Zvi Dan breathed hard. In no condition, not with the imitation leg.

"In connection with what, Major?"

"In connection with a classified matter."

"Believe it or not, Major, all of us who work in here have a degree of security clearance."

There was a tiny surf of laughter behind her. She was a pretty girl, auburn hair gathered high onto the crown of her head, a tight battledress blouse, a skirt that was almost a mini, and short white socks, carefully folded over.

"Please immediately arrange for me to see the duty brigadier."

"He is sleeping."

"Then you must wake him up," Zvi Dan growled.

"Regulations require that . . ."

Zvi Dan glowered over her. "Young lady, I was fighting for this God-forgotten country before you were old enough to wipe your own tiny butt. So spare me your regulations and go at once and wake him."

This last he bellowed at her, and she did. She spat dislike at him through her eyes first, but she went and woke the duty brigadier.

He was in poor humour. He was a tired, pale man, with grey uncombed hair and a lisp in his voice.

"Major, I do eighteen hours on duty on a night shift. During that time I take two hours' rest. My staff know that I am to be disturbed from that rest only on a matter of the highest importance. What is that matter?"

"You have a strike tomorrow against a Popular Front camp in the Beqa'a, located at 35.45 longitude and 33.38 latitude."

"We have."

"It has to be cancelled."

"On whose say?"

"Mine."

"The strike was authorised by the Chief of Staff."

"Then he didn't know what he was doing."

"Tell me more, Major."

"That camp must not be attacked."

"What is it? Do we have prisoners there?"

"No."

The duty brigadier gazed shrewdly at Major Zvi Dan, as if his annoyance was gone, as if now he were amused at the puzzle.

"Do we have a ground mission going in – which the Chief of Staff does not know about?"

"There is a mission. The Chief of Staff would not be aware of the fine detail."

"To that camp?"

"There is a mission in progress against that camp."

"An IDF mission?"

"No."

"Fascinating. . . . So, who can that be? The Americans, the doughnut boys?"

"The British."

"So the British have gone walking in the Beqa'a, have they? How many of them?"

"Two."

"Two British are in the Beqa'a. What have they gone to do, to pick grapefruit . . . ?"

"There is nothing in this matter that should amuse you." Major Zvi Dan stared coldly for a long time into the face of the duty brigadier. The coldness came from the freshness of his memory. Two men battleclad, their heavyweight Bergen packs, their bearded dark, creamed faces, their killing weapons. "In liaison with our Military Intelligence section, the British have two men walking into the Beqa'a to get above that camp, to identify the assassin of their ambassador to the Soviet Union, to shoot that man."

"It is the policy of Israel, Major, the policy of the country that pays your wage, to hit the source fount of terrorism. From that camp an attack was launched against your country. It is expected and demanded of us that we strike back."

"You scatter a few bombs about, you may inflict casualties, you may not."

"It is expected of us."

"You will break up the camp. You will destroy a real chance of the killing of a single man whose death is important. Send that attack tomorrow morning and you ensure that two days later a brave pair of men will arrive at their target position to find nothing to fire upon. Brigadier, how many times do you kill the people you want killed, for all the Phantoms, all the bomb weight?"

"Thank you, Major."

"Which means?"

"That I shall wake the Chief of the Air Staff. Where will you be?"

He wrote on his notepad his extension number. He tore the page off, handed it to the duty brigadier.

"All night."

"I make no promises, I merely pass the problem higher."

The quiet returned to the room.

All of them, at their desks and their consoles and tables and maps, watched with the duty brigadier the flapping swing door, and heard the uneven diminishing footfall.

The girl officer asked, "What do we owe the British, sir, with their arms embargo, their criticism of us?"

The duty brigadier said, "The British were going to hang my brother in 1947 when he was in the Irgun. They reprieved him 48 hours before he was to go to the hangman. I was a small boy then . . . The first people that I learned to hate were the British soldiers, who had captured and tortured my brother, and twenty years later I was a guest at their staff college, the staff college of the Royal Air Force. We owe them only what is best for us, and that decision mercifully is not mine."

In the small night hours, Major Zvi Dan's head lay on his hands that were spread on his desk.

The telephone was close beside him, and stayed silent.

The end of the seventh hour of the first night march, the time of the fourteenth rest moment at a rally point.

Above them, aloft on the steep slope, were the lights of the village of Meidoun. At the previous rally point Crane had shown the marking of the village on the map, used the Beta light for Holt to see it, and then Crane had shaken his head, as though the place was bad news. Holt knew that already Crane had broken one of his bible laws. The bible according to the prophet Crane stated that they should not pass within a thousand yards of a village. But no damned option. They had been moving on the slope below the village and above the Litani where it ran fast in a narrow gorge. They were sandwiched. It was a bastard place, and the rules were broken. On the far side of the gorge Holt could follow the movement of headlights snaking on the road, going north. To the west was a Shi'a village, below them was the rushing river. To the east was the main military road.

Holt heard a stone fall. He heard a stone dislodged below him. After the long silence of the walk in the night his hearing was clearer than he had ever known. He froze. Crane, beside him, had half risen. Crane was now a bent statue. There were the sounds of more stones slipping on the slope below. Crane showed Holt the palm of his hand, the gesture that he should not move.

There were the sounds of a young shrill whistling voice, and then the sharp bark of a dog. The whistling and the barking and the falling stones were closer.

Crane's hand was on Holt's shoulder, urging him down, down until his face ate at the cool dust of the rock slope.

God, was this where it ended? Not a third of the way in, not eight miles from the jump-off. Pray God that it didn't end because a village kid had gone after rabbits with his dog down to the scrub at the side of the Litani river. He tried to control the pace of his breathing. Breathing was another of the chapters of Crane's bible. Everything was down to control of breathing, keeping it regular, keeping it smooth, swallowing it down. He smelled the boy first, then he saw him.

The smell was of urine and animal fodder. It was a fecund sweet smell. No cigarette taste in his mouth, nor the cloy of toothpaste, nor the scent of soap on his face. He could smell the boy clearly moments before he saw him.

At first the boy was a shadow shape. The boy materialised as a wraith out of the darkness below, but coming fast, climbing easily on a steep pathway running down from the village to the river gorge. It was the moment it could all end. A shout would have been heard in the village, a scream would have roused the village. A fear yell would have brought the men of the village running, scrambling for their weapons. And there was the dog. The dog was close to the heels of the boy, skipping after him then stopping to sniff or lift a hind leg, then catching the boy. He knew that each village was an arsenal. Each village community would have automatic rifles and rocket propelled grenade launchers and machine guns. He wondered if Crane had his hand on the whipcord handle of his knife. He could follow the line of the boy's climb, he saw that the boy with the dog at his heels would pass less than a dozen yards from them. He tried to slow his breathing, tried to master the battering heave of his heartbeat.

The boy was level with them, no break in his pace. The boy was unaware of them. Long seconds in the life of young Holt. Didn't want to look, didn't want to see. Had closed his eyes. Didn't want to know the moment of discovery if that were to be their fate. If Crane knifed the boy then the boy would be missed and searched for, and when he was found then the trail of his killers would be tracked. The rock that seemed to penetrate into the flesh of his groin grew sharper, more cutting with each moment that he lay prone on it. He was against Crane's body and there was not the slightest flicker of movement. His bladder seemed to have filled to aching point. There was the first whisper of cramp behind his knee. There was a dried leaf teasing at his nostril. He wanted to pee, wanted to jerk his leg straight, wanted to sneeze, and if he wet himself or moved his leg or sneezed then the mission was gone before it had begun.

He heard the growl of the dog.

The boy was above them, going quickly. The boy called for the dog to catch him.

410

Holt fractionally opened his eyes. The dog was two, three yards from them. The dog was thin as a rake, brindle brown he reckoned, and back on its haunches in defence, and growling at Crane.

The boy threw a stone, and called louder for the dog.

The growl was a rumble of suspicion. His bladder was bursting, cramp pain spreading, his sneeze rising.

The dog yelped. The second stone thrown by the boy hit it square in the neck.

The boy raised his voice to shout for the dog to come.

He heard the sounds going away. He heard the sounds of the boy and his dog dwindling away up the hillside path. He lay on his face. He felt only exhaustion, he felt too tired to know relief.

He felt Crane's hand on his shoulder pulling at him to get upright.

Crane's mouth was at his ear, a near silent whisper, "We've time to make up."

"Did I do all right?"

"That wasn't militia, not soldiers, just a kid. That was nothing."

Crane rose to his feet, headed away. Holt let him go fifteen paces then took his own first step.

He remembered the words of the song, mouthed them silently to himself,

" 'Wish me luck, as you wave me goodbye,

Wish me luck, wish me luck, wish me luck . . .' "

And he seemed to hear her voice.

"Don't be childish, Holt."

He thought that he hated himself. He could have seen the boy knifed to death. He had never seen the face of the boy, he did not know the name of the boy. He was totally ignorant of the boy, and he could have cheered if Crane had felt the need to slide his short-bladed knife into the stomach of the boy, if Crane had drawn the sharp steel across the throat of the boy. If the boy had turned off the path, if the boy had come to see why his dog growled, then Holt would have cheered the boy's murder. As if a sea change had passed through him, as if he were no longer the man who had complained to Noah Crane about the torture of a Palestinian. He was dirtied in his soul.

He could remember, like yesterday, when he was ten years old, three days past his tenth birthday, and he had been walking with a holiday friend beside the river that ran close to his home. He had found a fox with a hind leg held by the thin cutting wire of a rabbit snare. There had been a blood smear around the wire, a little above the joint of the hind leg of the dog fox where the wire had worked deep through the fur and skin. Below the wire the hind leg hung at a silly angle. He had known, and he was only three days past his tenth birthday, that the dog fox was beyond saving because the leg was impossibly damaged. And he could not have freed it anyway because the dog fox snarled its teeth at him and at his friend, and would have bitten either of them if they had come close enough to release the other end of the wire from the hazel stump around which it was wound. They had taken smoothed rocks from the river shore, and they had thrown them at the fox until they had stunned it, could approach it, and with more stones they had battered the fox to death. All the time that he had killed the fox he had cried out loud. He could still remember how he had cried, childlike, in his bedroom that night. And now he could have cheered if the boy had been knifed.

He followed Crane. More of the Crane bible. He kept his eyeline to the right of Crane so that the moving shape was in the periphery of his vision. Crane had said that that way he would see better.

He was learning. He was changing.

Every late spring and every late autumn the ambassador of the United States entertained the Prime Minister of the United Kingdom to dinner in the splendour of the official residence in London's Regent's Park. For those two evenings of the year the lights blazed, the drink flowed, the hospitality was warm. It was the style of these two evenings that the Prime Minister would attend in the company of selected Cabinet ministers with responsibilities particularly affecting relationships "across the drain", along with principal industrialists with commercial links to the United States. On the American side a secretary of state would make the flight across the Atlantic. They were social occasions primarily, but permitted the free exchange of ideas and views.

A warm damp night. A fog rising from the park's grasslands. The mist outside was thickened in the driveway by the exhaust fumes of the chauffeur-driven cars. The night air was rich with good humour, noisy with guests making their farewells.

The Prime Minister warmly shook the hand of the ambassador.

"A wonderful evening, as always."

"A good night for a celebration, Prime Minister."

Below the steps the Branch men surrounded the Prime Minister's car, the lit interior beckoned. There was the warble of the radio link in the police back-up car. If there was a weakness in the make up of the evening it was that the ambassador and the Prime Minister had sat at dinner at opposite ends of the table, had barely exchanged words.

"You have the advantage over me, what is there in particular to celebrate?"

"An American triumph in the war against terrorism. We're very proud, I've wanted to tell you all evening."

"What triumph?"

"We have an Air Force base at Vicenza in northern Italy. Two nights ago our base security, American personnel, picked up a Lebanese male on the perimeter fence. He was in a hide and checking out the wire security with a PNV pocket 'scope. Sorry, that's Passive Night Vision. Our guys whipped him straight inside, straight into the guard house."

The Branch men fidgeted. Other guests stood respectfully out of earshot and in line to offer their thanks.

"What do the Italians say?"

"There's the beauty of it. About now my colleague down in Rome will be informing the Italians that our captive is currently on a USAF transporter and heading Stateside. No messing this time. But I'm jumping . . . I haven't got to the choice part."

The guest line grew. The Prime Minister's driver switched off the engine of the Rover.

"The choice part is this . . . TWA flight 840, Rome to Athens in the spring of '86, an explosion at 15,000 feet takes a hunk out of the fuselage through which four passengers are sucked. Three of those four are American citizens. The source of the explosion was under a seat occupied by a Lebanese woman who had hidden the explosives before getting off in Rome. Okay, you're with me? Choice bit. That woman boarded at Cairo for the leg to Rome. She was seen off by a male, tagged as Palestinian, we have his description, we have his finger marks on the ticket stubs left at Cairo TWA check-in. We have him as the organiser, and the woman just as the courier. That man is one and the same as the joker on the fence at Vicenza. The prints match. That bastard is up in a big bird right now, Prime Minister, he's going to Andrews base then a tight little military cell. That's why you can join me in celebration."

"Remarkable," the Prime Minister said softly.

"You'll remember what the President said. He said to these swines, "You can run, but you cannot hide". That's what we're proving. It's the first time we're able to put deeds to words, make action out of talk. We reckon this to be the turning point in the war against international terrorism. You're not cold, Prime Minister . . . ?"

"Not cold."

"It's the first time this has happened, and it's the first time that counts. Sam leads the way, Sam is first in, that's our celebration."

"A fine stroke of luck," the Prime Minister said distantly.

"In this game you earn your luck. Look, we've known for a year this man was in and out of Lebanon, in Damascus or in the Beqa'a valley. We went through all the military evaluations about getting a force into the Beqa'a to drop him there. Can't be done, no way. The Beqa'a would swallow a marine division, that was our best advice, and even if we got in we'd never get out."

"You're very well informed."

"Secondhand, my number three here was in Beirut previously . . . we would have faced the risk of prisoners being paraded through Damascus, hell of a mess. Going into Lebanon wasn't on . . . that's diversion. It's being the first that matters. Prime Minister, not at your expense of course, but we're feeling very comfortable at this moment, very bullish. You see, what really matters is not just confronting these people, it's putting them into court. Assassination is small beer when set against the full rigour of a court of law."

The Prime Minister smiled congratulation, and walked away down the steps to the car. The engine coughed, the doors slammed shut. The car pulled away, trailed by the back-up.

The Prime Minister's age showed, the tiredness of office and responsibility. There was a long sigh of weariness.

"Inform my office to have the Director General stand by. I'll be calling him from Downing Street as soon as I get there."

The Prime Minister sagged back in the seat. The Branch man in the front passenger seat relayed the instruction.

"What have you to do?" the private secretary asked quietly.

"I just have to cancel something. Nothing for you to worry about."

He had been dreaming of the fish he would catch, in the sleeping recesses of his mind was the recollection of the conversation he had had in the guest house bar with a tractor driver from the Kibbutz Kfar Giladi. Not a fast river to fish in, but a fish farm pond, not flies nor lures for bait, but worms from a compost heap. And to hell with tradition. Percy Martins dreamed of tight lines . . . until the bell exploded in his ear, like a big rainbow jumping.

He groped, he found the light. He lifted the telephone.

"Martins."

"Is that a secure line?"

"No."

"DG here."

"God . . . good evening, sir."

"Good morning, Percy. Our friends, where are they?"

"Gone."

"Can you reach them?"

"No."

"Why not?"

Martins sat straight up in his bed. "Because sir, they have no, ah, telephone. As it is they are carrying in excess of eighty pounds weight. I would hazard, sir, that you or I could barely lift eighty pounds weight, let alone walk a long way with it."

"Thank you, Percy. That's all the detail I need. Just confirm for me that you've some means of communicating with them in case you wanted them back in a hurry."

"That's not on, sir. In fact it's quite out of the question. We've no means at all."

"Thank you, Percy. Keep up the good work. And goodbye."

Martins replaced the telephone. He switched off his light.

He could not find again for his mind the pleasure of an arching rod. He thought of two men struggling through the night, moving further from safety, and he was damned pleased those two men carried no radio transmitter/receiver, were beyond recall.

Slowly, like a cat beside a fireplace that is minutely disturbed, Major Zvi Dan opened his eyes. He looked from just above his hands across the room.

The girl, Rebecca, sat on the one easy chair in the room, a new book was in her hands.

"Message?"

She shook her head.

He grimaced. "There is nothing more I can do. If I go higher then I antagonise."

"You have to wait. Coffee?"

He moved his hand, declined. They would not be drinking coffee, Noah Crane and Holt who were heading towards the Beqa'a.

"If they hit the tent camp, I quit. If they bomb that camp, they'll have my resignation."

She looked at him curiously, "Why does it matter to you?"

"Because . . . because . . ." Major Zvi Dan rubbed hard to clear his eyes of sleep. He coughed at the phlegm in his throat. "Because . . . because of that boy, because of Holt. He shouldn't be there, he is not equipped to be there. It would be a crime if we screwed up their effort."

He let his head fall back to his hands. His eyes closed. Beside him the telephone stayed silent.

"Prime Minister, they cannot be recalled because they have no radio transmitter/receiver. Each of them, without a radio transmitter/receiver, is carrying in excess of eighty pounds weight. I would hazard that you or I could barely lift eighty pounds weight, let alone walk across country with it."

The Prime Minister sat in a thick dressing gown before the dead fire in the private sitting room. The Director General had lit his pipe, was careless of the smoke clouds he gusted around the small room.

"They are not carrying a radio because a radio and reserve batteries would have increased each man's weight burden by at least 10 pounds. In addition, radio transmissions, however carefully disguised, alert an enemy. . . . Am I permitted to ask you what has undermined your enthusiasm for this mission?"

The Prime Minister fumbled for words, stumbled in tiredness. The conversation with the American ambassador was reported. The Prime Minister slumped in the chair.

"I want them called back."

"And you cannot have what you want."

Four o'clock in the morning. The chimes of Big Ben carried on the squalling wind, bending around the great quiet buildings of Whitehall.

"I was talked into something that I should never have allowed myself to accept."

"We are an independent country, we are not beholden to the opinions of the United States of America."

"I was beguiled into something idiotic, by you."

"You told me that then you would claim my head." The Director General had no fear of the head of government. A wintry smile. "Would it be your head you are nervous for?"

"That's impertinent."

"Prime Minister, it would distress me to think that the sole reason for your authorising this mission was to enable you to brag to our cousins over the water."

"You have made me a hostage."

"To what?"

"To the fortune, the fate, of these two men. Think of it, think if they are captured, think if they are paraded through Damascus, think what the Syrian regime can make of that, think of the humiliation for us."

The Director General stabbed the air with his pipe stem. "You listen to me. This is nothing to do with point scoring over our American allies, with boasting to the Oval Office . . . Listen to me. Your ambassador was assassinated. That would be enough, enough to justify much more destructive a response than this mission, but Miss Jane Canning was one of mine. Miss Jane Canning too was murdered. I do not tolerate the murder of one of mine. The arm of my vengeance reaches to the other side of the hill, reaches to the throat of a wretched man who was stupid enough to murder Miss Jane Canning. Do you hear me, Prime Minister?"

He towered above the Prime Minister. He glowered into the face of the Prime Minister. He sucked at his pipe. He reached for his matches.

"How soon will I know?"

"Whether it is Abu Hamid's head that is on a salver, whether it is my head or yours?" The Director General chuckled. "Three or four days."

He let himself out. The Prime Minister thought the door closing on his back was like the awakening from a nightmare.

Exactly an hour before dawn they reached the first lying up position.

The LUP had been chosen by Crane from the aerial photographs. The photographs of this stretch of upper ground high over the Litani and the village of Yohmor had shown no sign of troop tracks, nor of grazing herds. There was a mass of large, jagged wind- and snow-fractured rocks.

They went past the LUP, moved on another two hundred yards and then looped back in a cautious circle. According to Crane's bible, the way to make certain that they were not followed.

Amongst the rocks Crane helped Holt to ease off the Bergen. For an hour they sat back to back, alert, listening and watching.

Crane whispered, "I suppose you think you've earned some sleep."

Holt was too tired to punch him, too exhausted to laugh.

The dawn came fast, a spreading wash of grey over the rough ridges of Jabal bir ed Dahr. A new morning in Lebanon.

14

Abu Hamid stretched, spat onto the dirt floor beside his camp bed, and shook himself awake.

The light knifed through the poorly fastened join in the tent flaps. He glanced across the short interior, saw that Fawzi's bed had not been slept on.

There was never any explanation of Fawzi's coming and going. Abu Hamid spat again, then untied the strings that held the flaps together. He yawned, arcing his head back. He had slept for seven hours and was still exhausted. He had slept but not rested because his mind had turmoiled through the night, scattering thoughts with the drive of an old engine. His mind had clanked with memories spread out over many years of his life.

The sun beat into the tent. His opening the flaps was a signal for the flies to begin their daily persecution. From under his bed he took his personal roll of lavatory paper. He had so little in the world that was his own, he valued his personal lavatory paper so greatly. He set off for the latrine.

The fire was alight in the cooking area. There was the rich smell of a slowly simmering meat stew, and the dry aroma of cooking bread. He had chosen well with their cook, a good boy who earned his absence from the firing range and from the day-long exercises out on the hill slopes and the wadis. He might make every last one of them a fighter, except the cook. The cook would never be a fighter against Israel, but not one of the other recruits would prepare goat stew like this boy. He deserved to be left to forage for wood, to snare rabbits, to dig out a cold store, to go to the village to buy vegetables. He walked by the cooking area. He dipped a finger into the slow-bubbling whirlpool of the pot. He bowed his head, he made a play of his satisfaction, and the cook inclined his head with a wide grin to take the compliment.

There was a line of recruits waiting outside the latrine's screen. From yards away Abu Hamid could hear the howl of the flies.

His memories were of what he had been told of the times long past, the times before he had been born, of his grandfather who had been a corn merchant, sufficiently successful to have owned a villa near to the sea in Jaffa, the town that was now called Yafo by the Zionists and which had been swallowed in the spread of Tel Aviv. From the time he was a small child he had been told of his grandfather's home in what was now Israel. His father had told him that the building was now a restaurant serving Italian food. In his family there had been no photographs of the house, but he had been told that the rooms led off a small courtyard that in the times long past had been shaded with a trellis of vines. He had told his father once, years back, that he would one day set foot in that house, he would stand in that courtyard or he would die on the route to that house. His father had shrugged, muttered the words "If God wills . . ." and kissed his cheek as he had gone away to the ranks of the Popular Front.

His inherited memory told him that his grandfather and his grandmother, and his father and his mother, and his uncles and his aunts, had been put out of their homes in Jaffa in 1948 when the war had gone against the Arab armies. The house of his grandfather was left behind, the grain storage warehouse in the docks had been forsaken and was plundered to feed the flood of Jewish settlers arriving from Europe.

Abu Hamid arrived at the line waiting to use the latrine. He went to the front of the line, he stood at the head and he yelled for the recruit inside to stir himself and get out.

His grandfather and the tribe that he led had settled in a refugee camp on the hills above Jericho in the winter of 1948. He had learned of the hunger and cold and lack of shelter in the camp on the West Bank of the Jordan river, of the lack of funds from the government of the boy king Hussein, of the lack of materials provided by the fledgling relief organisations. His parents had been married in Jaffa, little more than children, his father had worked for his grandfather in the accounts office of the business, but their own first children had not been born until they had reached the damp cold of the refugee camp. He had been told that he had been born in 1960 in a tent, that his mother had nearly died of pneumonia after his birth.

The recruit came out of the latrine. The smell billowed with him, as if released from behind the screen. He took a deep breath, hurried inside. He squatted over the pit. He held his breath. He clutched the roll of soft yellow paper.

The first memories were of the refugee camp. Of the fierce heat of the summers when the sun spread down from clear skies onto the dust and the rock of the hillside, the chill and rain and winds of winter when the pathways of the camp were river races and the cesspool drains overflowed, and there was no school for the kids and no place for them outside the wire on the edges of the camp. There was a memory that was clear, of the fighting on the hills above the camp when he was seven years old, and the sight of the Jordanian troops in retreat, and the billowing dust clouds of the Israeli tanks and half tracks in pursuit. Sharp memories now of his grandfather leading his tribe a further step away from the house that was now an Italian restaurant. They had joined the refugee swarm – his feet blistered and his belly swollen in hunger – that had crossed the Allenby bridge over the river Jordan, under the guns of the Israelis, and climbed to new tents in a new camp, on the outskirts of the city of Amman.

There was the gleam of two pin heads of brightness. Two ruby red lights beaming at him. The lights were in the shadow fold of the screen where it reached the ground around the pit. He knew what he saw but he peered with fascination, compulsion, down at the lights until he saw the yellowed stumps of the bared teeth and the grey needles of the whiskers. A rat. The breath burned out of his body. He had to gulp again for air, foul air within the screen. He watched the rat, he prayed the rat would not go behind him where he would not be able to see whether it came closer to the dropped trousers at his ankles.

He picked at the scar well on his face. He was afraid of the beady eyes of the rat. With his trousers at his ankles he did not have the freedom to kick out at the rat.

He remembered the school in the camp called Wahdat. He could remember the encouragement of the blond haired teacher from Switzerland, and the care of the lady from France who ran a clinic in Wahdat. He could remember the day that the tanks of Hussein had battered into Wahdat. He was ten years old, his memory was quite clear. He could picture in his mind the tortoise shapes of the tanks grinding into Wahdat, blasting at the school house which was built of concrete and therefore defended by the Palestinian fighters, hammering at the clinic because that too was defended as a fortress. They were Palestinians, they were Arabs, they were the citizen families of Wahdat. Their enemy was not the Israelis, their enemy was the army of an Arab king.

He moved slowly. He thought that a sudden movement might startle the rat, provoke it.

They were memories that had denied him rest when he had slept in his tent. Ten years old, and a refugee again. His grandfather did not lead the tribe out of the Wahdat camp, his grandfather was buried in a shallow grave on the edge of the camp, one amongst many. His father led the exodus of the family away from Amman. The ten year old boy was of an age to know the glory of the struggle as fought by the Popular Front of Doctor George Habbash. The Popular Front had brought the aircraft of the imperialist enemies to the desert landing strip at Ga'khanna, they had brought to Jordan the airliners of the Americans and the British and the Swiss. A boy of ten years could understand the success of the Popular Front in capturing airliners of enemies, but a boy of ten years did not understand that such a capture could be regarded as a legitimate provocation by the king of Jordan, justification for terminating the state within a state, the Palestinian autonomy inside the kingdom. His grandfather was dead, his grandmother was blinded, the family tribe was again destitute, again uprooted.

Abu Hamid was pale faced when he emerged from the latrine. He left the rat to eye the next man. He walked away towards the perimeter fence, sucking in the clean air. And it was the same each morning. Each morning he thought he would be sick, throw up in front of the recruits, when he came out of the latrine.

Memories of the family settling in another tent on the edge of the Rachadiye camp outside the Lebanese coastal city of Tyre. The family tribe was a rolling stone, tumbling from a tent at Jericho to a tent at Amman to a tent at Tyre. By the time he was aged 15, by the time that Abu Hamid took the oath of the Popular Front, his unseeing grandmother had died. It was the end of 1975.

He knew all the events of that year. He knew of the martyrdom of the Comrades who had captured the Savoy Hotel in Tel Aviv and given their lives at cost to the enemy. He knew of the heroism of the commando who had killed and wounded nearly a hundred enemy with his bomb in the café by Zion Square in Jerusalem. He knew of the men who had captured the OPEC conference and turned the eyes of the world on the suffering of the Palestinian people.

He gazed out over the quiet hillside beyond the perimeter fence. He watched the stillness. He listened to the silence. So great a stillness, so great a silence, as if the possibility of warfare did not exist.

His memories told him of the dispersal of his family tribe. He did not know where were his uncles and his aunts, his cousins, his nephews and his nieces. He knew that his brother, two years older than himself, had died fighting the Israelis in 1982 at Sidon. He knew that his sister had been wounded at Damour that same bitter summer. He knew that his parents were besieged by the Shi'a militia in the camp at Rachadiye.

He walked slowly along the perimeter fence. He saw the rat holes and the paper rubbish caught on the coiled wire. Since he had joined the Popular Front, twelve years ago, he had suffered the dream. The dream was to walk the street in Jaffa until he came to the house that was now an Italian restaurant. The dream was to put out of his grandfather's house those who had made a home into a restaurant, put them out on the street and there bayonet them. The dream was to take the hands of his father and mother and to lead them from Rachadiye to Jaffa and to take them to the house that had been his grandfather's and to give them the key and to tell them that what was rightfully theirs was theirs once more.

The dream was in his mind as he walked the fence. When he had the dream he had strength. The girl had given him the strength to dream of the house in Jaffa. The girl had taken the promise from him, the promise to go to Israel, the promise to kill Jews. As if he had never wavered. Margarethe had fashioned the courage for him to dream of walking on the street in Jaffa. He saw her in the badly lit dormitory for the orphans.

He was jolted from his thoughts.

He had stumbled against the rail post that marked the entrance to an air raid bunker.

Abu Hamid looked at the filled sleeping bag at the bottom of the steps, he saw the black hair that was the crown of a head peeping from the bag.

His anger flashed. He thought a recruit was hiding in the bunker to avoid duties. He scratched up a handful of small stones, threw them down on the head. He heard the oath, he watched the convulsive movement, he saw Fawzi's face.

He almost laughed, whatever his own instinctive anger had been was nothing set against the disturbed fury of the Syrian officer.

"I thought you were a malingerer," Abu Hamid said. "I did not think to find our Political Liaison hiding in an air raid bunker."

"That stuff's in my eye."

"You sleep better there than in a bed?"

"Are you a fool or are you still asleep?"

"Are you telling me that if I don't take my sleeping bag into a bunker then I am a fool?"

Fawzi wriggled his shoulders clear of the bag. He was shouting up from the dank dark of the bottom of the steps. "I was back late last night. I walked into this place, like it was a hotel on the Beirut Corniche. Try getting out of your bed in the night, hero, and try checking your sentries. Try counting how many are asleep. I walked in here, if I had been an enemy you would have been dead."

Abu Hamid sneered, "I thought we were under the protection of the omnipotent forces of the army of the Syrian Arab Republic. Do you think so little of that protection that you sleep in a bunker?"

"When I sleep in this camp, now that I am back with you, I will sleep in a bunker until . . ."

"Until what?"

"Until the air raid."

"What air raid?"

"Then you are a fool, Abu Hamid, you are stupid."

"Give me the breadth of your wisdom."

"Even a fool knows there will be an air raid . . . Six days ago a bomb was exploded at the bus station in Tel Aviv . . . A fool knows that each time there is a major attack inside Israel that they retaliate with their aircraft, or has Abu Hamid forgotten? We have not yet had the air raid, but do not think the Israeli sleeps, he never sleeps. The Israeli will bomb us. The Israeli has to find a target. I do not want to be woken to the sound of you idiots trying to launch Strelas, trying to fire the DShKMs. I want to be able merely to crawl a few metres into the depths of a bunker should they strike our camp. Until they have bombed only an idiot would choose to sleep in a tent."

The fight was gone from Abu Hamid. He asked quietly, "Why our camp? They died both of them, they were not interrogated."

"I am just careful, because I am careful I will live to be an old man. It is my intention to die in my bed, Abu Hamid."

He saw the surprise cloud fast across the face of the old man on the steps of the Oreanda Hotel. He saw the shock spread into the eyes of the girl who walked in front of him. He could not know whether he was marked, whether he was identified. He trembled.

"If we hide in holes in the ground we show them our fear."

Fawzi rolled his bag, climbed the steps, belched. "And that to me is a small matter."

"Then you are a coward."

"Then I am a survivor."

Abu Hamid gazed into the clearness of the skies. He saw an eagle wheel, high on a thermal draft. He saw the peace of the valley.

*

The telephone rang.

Rebecca reached for the receiver.

She wrote on her notepad. She never spoke. She put down the telephone.

"The Chief of the Air Staff will see you in his office, immediately," she said. "And for love's sake, tidy yourself."

"So they both died, brave boys."

"They died in the cause of freedom."

The Arab traveller shrugged. He leaned against the wall of sandbags. The marijuana had been passed, a package hidden in rolled newspaper, for circulation amongst the NORBAT platoon.

The traveller and Hendrik Olaffson talked quietly. The other troops manning the UNIFIL post were engaged in searching vehicles. They talked without being overheard.

"From our position we were able to see the girl who came with the bomb on her donkey, yesterday. She had not come through our check, she must have skirted us and gone across country, but we could see her getting towards the SLA and Israeli block. I tell you this, friend, they were waiting for her. That is certain. Even before she came within sight they had moved their people back behind the fortifications, as soon as she appeared, when she was hundreds of metres away, they were all behind cover. For certain they were waiting for her, ready for her."

"A sweet child of courage."

Hendrik Olaffson murmured, "They had a marksman in position. We worked it out afterwards. They shot her at a range of at least one thousand metres. One bullet, one firing, she went down. Then one more shot to detonate the donkey. It was incredible shooting."

"You are observant, friend."

"More, I have more to tell you."

"Tell me."

"Last night, just after dusk the Israelis fired many flares to the west of our OPs. There was no artillery, just flares. Now that is not usual for them. Yes, often it is flares and then artillery, but this time only the flares."

The traveller gestured with his hands. "I am just a humble traveller of the road while you, friend, are a trained and educated soldier. What does the firing of the flares tell you?"

The young Norwegian leaned forward. He did not say that the explanation offered for the firing of the flares was the opinion of his company commander, a regular officer with the rank of captain and fourteen years in the military. He gave it as his own. "They blinded our equipment. If they believe there is an incursion of the Palestinians or the Hezbollah then they would also have fired shells. They made useless our night viewing. My assumption, they acted to prevent us seeing what they were doing. Why should they do that? My assumption again, they were passing through the NORBAT area. I offer you something else. During the night no transport left the checkpoint for Israel, so there is no indication that men coming from Lebanon were awaited and then taken back to Israel. I believe that the Israelis were inserting a squad *into* Lebanon."

"You believe that?"

"I am certain of that."

"Friend, you are a great help to the cause of freedom." After he had drank the dregs of a mug of thick, sweetened tea, the traveller waved his farewell.

The marijuana was dispersed among the NORBAT men at the checkpoint, hungrily broken down for sale onwards amongst those men of the battalion who needed the treated weed to make bearable service with UNIFIL.

Hendrik Olaffson was becoming by the standards of a private soldier in the Norwegian army a wealthy young man. There was money in excess flowing inside NORBAT, there were only occasional four day visits to Tel Aviv and more frequent evening visits to northern Israel for the soldiers to spend their wages. He kept his money, Norwegian bank notes, hidden in a slit in the base of his kitbag.

He had neither a sense of guilt, nor any fear of discovery.

"That's him."

"You are certain?"

"It is the one against the sandbags."

"No doubts."

"I am certain."

For three days the two men from Shin Bet had escorted the tall Arab teenager, Ibrahim, from vantage point to vantage point on the extremes and slightly into the UNIFIL sector controlled by NORBAT. The Shin Bet men were both fluent Arab speakers, both armed with Uzi submachine guns. All the time one of them was linked by handcuffs to Ibrahim.

They were a kilometre and a half from the NORBAT checkpoint, on rough raised ground, and across a valley from the sandbagged position.

It was of no surprise to the Shin Bet men that the teenager was eager to co-operate in their investigation. It was their experience that the fervour of an attacking commando was quickly dissipated by the despair brought on by capture. The interrogators who had beaten, kicked, punched the initial information out of Ibrahim had been replaced days before. They had done their work, they were not a part of the new scene around the teenager. In his early statements, between the screams, of course, Ibrahim had told the interrogators how he and Mohammed had reached Israel, had told them of the UNIFIL lorry. For the last three days, aided by high powered Zeiss binoculars, the two Shin Bet men and their prisoner had scoured through the magnifying lenses for the driver of the UNIFIL lorry.

The binoculars showed a well built and pleasant faced young soldier, with a shock of fair hair streaming from below a jauntily worn blue beret.

"Absolutely certain?"

"That is the one who drove the lorry to Tel Aviv."

They praised the teenager. They made him believe they were his friends. They made a pretence to him that his future might lie other than in a maximum security wing of the Ramla gaol.

They led him back into the security zone. They drove him into Israel with his head masked by a blanket. When they had returned to their base, reported their findings, a second team was infiltrated forward to maintain surveillance from a distance on the Norwegian soldier.

"I gather that last night, Dan, you went barging into Air Operations, demanding that a mission be cancelled."

"Correct, sir."

The Chief of Air Staff looked coolly at Major Zvi Dan. "I assume this was not a flippant request."

"It is critical that the mission be cancelled."

"They fly in ten minutes . . ."

"Criminal."

". . . unless I am given reason for cancellation. You have one minute, Dan."

Major Zvi Dan looked at the face of his watch. He waited for the second hand to climb to the vertical.

"First, a raid on the camp from which the bus station bombers were launched will tell the Popular Front military command that at least one of their men has been captured and successfully interrogated, which would lead to the dispersal of the camp. Second, such a dispersal would mean the disappearance of Abu Hamid, the Popular Front commander at the camp. Third, last night a two-man team left Israel to walk into the Beqa'a with the specific and only task of sniping Abu Hamid who was the murderer, with Syrian connivance, of the British ambassador in the Soviet Union. Fourth, the team is British, and our country needs friends where it can find them. If we foul that mission we hardly have Great Britain in our palm. Fifth, a planned snipe offers a greater guarantee of taking out a known and effective terrorist whereas an air-strike may kill some second-grade recruits but offers no certainty of success. Sixth, I would hate two very brave men, one a Jew, to walk into that danger for nothing . . ."

He paused. The second hand of his watch crawled again to the vertical.

He breathed in deeply.

The Chief of the Air Staff reached for his telephone, lifted it, waited for a moment for it to be answered. He glanced at the major, his smile wintry.

"The tasking of callsign Sierra Delta 6, the target should be the second option."

The telephone was replaced.

"Thank you, sir."

"You should not thank me, you should thank your own major general. Last week I attended a briefing given by our head of Intelligence. In his address he referred back to what he had said at the time of the synagogue massacre in Istanbul, where 22 Jewish lives were taken by the Abu Nidal group. At the time he said, and he repeated it for us, 'You cannot lash out blindly. This is not a war of days, weeks, even months; those responsible will be pursued to the ends of the earth. But we must have a clear address before we act, then act we will.' I appreciated what he said . . . You have an address, you have a name. I pray to God that you can deliver to that address."

Major Zvi Dan ducked his head in acknowledgement.

He walked out of the office. He felt a huge exhaustion sweeping over him.

Holt lay in the rock cleft and slept. He was huddled tight, a foetus in the womb, his knees up and as close to his chest as the bulky shapes on his belt would allow. The sun was rising, close to its zenith, but he had discarded none of his clothes, nor his chukka boots. A lightweight blanket was laid over him.

He was too tired to dream. He lay in the black abyss of sleep.

From a short distance the fact that two men rested up in the rock cleft could not have been spotted. Neither could it have been seen from the air as this small gap in the yellowed rock was covered by a drape of olive green scrim netting. His Bergen pack was beside his shoulder, he was not allowed to sleep against it for fear that his body weight could damage the contents.

Holt woke when Crane shook his shoulder.

There was the moment when he did not know where he was. There were the few seconds of slow understanding. Not in his bed in the doctor's house on Exmoor, not in his bed in the London flat, not in his bed in the Moscow apartment, not in his bed in the Tel Aviv hotel. Crane's hand was relentless on his shoulder, urging him awake.

Because they were trapped under the scrim net, the fumes of the hexamine solid fuel cubes permeated to his nostrils. The fumes told Holt where he was. The first time in the hike in the Occupied Territories that he had known the hexamine stench under the scrim netting he had nearly gagged. He heard the bubbling of the water.

"Time for a brew up, youngster."

He saw the two tea bags cavorting in the boiling water.

"How long have I been out?"

"I let you have two hours, you looked like you needed two hours."

"I can do the same as you."

"No chance," Crane dismissed him.

They spoke in low whispers. Each time Crane spoke Holt had to lean towards him to understand what he said.

Crane passed him the canteen and began to anoint himself with the mosquito cream. Holt drank fast from the scorching tea, burned the soft tissue on the inside of his mouth, gulped. While he was smearing the cream on to his skin surfaces Crane was tracking with his binoculars backwards and forwards searching over the ground below them, around them.

"Clear?"

"So far."

Holt handed back the canteen. "I want to pee, where do I go?"

"You don't just go for a walk."

"Where?"

"You roll on your side, you undo your flies, and you piss. Simple."

"Then I have to sleep on it, and sit on it."

"Then you get to learn to piss when it's dark, before we settle and before we move off. That's when you piss and that's when you crap, like I showed you . . . and wake me in an hour, and don't do anything stupid. Just do what I've told you."

"If I've had two hours' sleep you can have two."

"You think I'll sleep two hours knowing you're watching my back?"

Crane was gone. Blanket over his head, curled into a ball, breathing regular, the low growl of a snore.

God, and it was blessed uncomfortable in the cleft. He must have been dead tired to be able to sleep on those rocks, and a separate ache was in every inch of his side, in his shoulder and in his ribs and in his hip and in his thigh.

Before, before he had known what it was to walk through a night and to get to a lying up position for the day, he would have thought that night was the enemy and daytime was the ally. Not any more. Night was the friend, darkness was the accomplice. At night and in darkness he could melt into the shadows, he was on his feet and able to move. Daylight was the bastard, in daylight he was tapped down into the cleft of two rocks and he couldn't stand and he couldn't walk. The cover was waist high, and if he stood or he walked then he would be seen. For a long time he looked across the few inches at Crane. Christ, wouldn't he have liked to have woken him, talked to him? Not half a chance of that. Just time for a few words in the moments between sleeping and sentry duty, and another few words before moving off, and another few words before lying up for daylight. It was a bastard . . . and he watched the calm heave of Crane's breathing.

First job of the day. Crane's bible. Holt laid out the six magazines for the Armalite which were carried between them. Only five were loaded. Holt's job was to change the thirty rounds of ammunition from one magazine to another, so that each time he carried out the manoeuvre a different magazine would be left empty. Crane's bible said that magazines left full led to the weakening of the spring. Crane's text said that most firing failures were in fact magazine failures. The first time in the Occupied Territories it had taken Holt close to an hour to reload the 150 rounds; now he was going at twice that pace.

Second job of the day. Clean with dry cloth and graphite grease the outside surfaces of the Armalite and the Model PM. Crane's text said that cleaning oil should never be used because it would leave a smoke signature of burned off oil in the firing heat. He checked that the condoms were tightly fastened over the barrels of the two weapons.

He was painfully hungry. Might have sold his mother for a bar of chocolate, well, pawned her for sure. Crane's bible said no sweets to suck, because when you sucked sweets you also bit them, and when you bit them you made such a noise in your head that you knocked out your hearing, no boiled sweets. He had had a biscuit and a piece of cream cheese before going to sleep. They would have their main meal at the end of the afternoon, Crane had said. The old goat had said it would be a proper bloody feast. Crane had said that it was a good thing to be hungry, that hunger bred alertness.

He heard them a long way off. He thought he could hear the aircraft from a hell of a long way off because he was so hungry.

Through the squares of the scrim net he thought he could see the silver shapes leading the run of the vapour trails, flying south to north. It was strangely disconcerting to him to know that Israeli aircraft were overhead, flying free, while young Holt was down on his backside in the cleft in the rock. He watched the trails until they were gone from sight.

He had the binoculars. He looked down on the village of Yohmor. He could see the men moving listlessly between the houses and the coffee shop in the centre of the village. He could see children scampering down to the Litani river to swim and dive. Between the rock cleft and the river he could see a lad herding sheep, tough little blighters and sure-footed, scrambling towards a small plateau where water must be held, or where there must be a spring, because there was green on the handkerchief of level ground.

Beyond Yohmor, higher up the far valley, was the winding road. It was the dirt cloud that he noticed first, and then the rumble of the engines travelled across the valley to him. Six tank transporters, each loaded, and a couple of lorries and a couple of jeeps. Through the glasses he studied the tanks. With the glasses he could see the unit markings on the turrets. He had never seen tanks before, not the 60-ton main battle tank jobs. He saw the long lean barrels of the tanks. Holt seemed to crush himself down against the rock base of the cleft. Over the battlefield had flown two pairs of multi million pound strike aircraft, across the battlefield were being hauled six tank monsters. They were the bloody currency of the battlefield. Holt wasn't. Holt was just ordinary. Holt didn't even know how to fire a damned Armalite . . . Crane slept. Holt hadn't known anyone who could sleep as easily as Crane before. Right, the man kicked, and he stirred. Right, the man snored. But he slept.

Crane coughed, guttural. He turned from his side to his back and then shook himself, coughed again. Holt would speak to him about that. Crane moved onto his other side. Have to speak to the prophet Crane about making so much noise coughing. Holt would enjoy that. He'd enjoy it, because he could pull a suitably aggrieved face and say in all seriousness that Crane's coughing was putting the mission in jeopardy . . .

So still.

Holt not moving. Holt grabbing to halt his breathing.

Not daring to move, not daring to breathe.

Crane's heel had moved the stones.

Holt watched the snake emerge from its disturbed hole.

Crane had been lying on the stones, and hidden under the stones had been the snake.

Holt had a knife in his belt, he had the binoculars in his hand.

Crane's body rolled.

If Crane sagged again on to his back then he would lie on the snake.

Holt had had all the books when he was a kid. Holt knew his snakes. There were snakes on Exmoor, kids always knew about snakes.

Saw-scaled viper, *Echis carinatus*. Vicious, a killer, common all over North Africa, the Middle East, across to the sub-continent.

The snake slithered slowly over the rock at the small of Crane's back.

God, don't let him roll. God, don't let the old goat cough.

The snake was a little less than two feet long. It was sandy brown with pale blotches and mahogany brown markings.

Holt saw the flicker of the snake's mouth.

He thought Crane slept deeply. He thought that if he called to him to wake that he would start in a sudden movement. He couldn't lean across to him, couldn't hold him as he woke him, because to lean forward would mean to cover the snake with his body.

The damn thing settled. The bloody thing stopped moving. Sunshine filtering through the scrim net. Two warm stones for the snake. Holt thought the snake's head, the snake's mouth, were four or perhaps five inches from the small of Crane's back.

Couldn't go for his knife. To go for his knife was to twist his body, to unhook the clasp that secured the knife handle, to draw the knife out of the canvas sheath. Three movements before the critical movement, the strike against the neck of the snake. Couldn't use his knife.

Crane grunted. Holt saw the muscle tighten under the light fabric of Crane's trousers. The old goat readying himself to roll, the prophet winding himself up to change position.

The bible according to Crane. When you've got something to do, do it. When you've got to act, stop pissing about.

Holt looked at his hand. Quite surprised him. His hand was steady. Shouldn't have been, should have been shaking. His hand was firm.

Do it, stop pissing about.

The snake's head was over a stone. He marked the spot in his mind. The spot was an inch from the snake's head.

One chance for Holt. Like the one chance that Crane would have when he fired.

His hand was a blur.

The binoculars were a haze of movement.

He felt the bridge of the binoculars bite against the inch thick body of the snake.

All the power he had in him, driving against the thickness of the snake at a point an inch behind the snake's head. The body and the tail of the snake were thrashing against his arm, curling on his wrist, cold and smoothed dry. The mouth of the snake was striking against the plastic covering of the binocular lenses. He saw the spittle fluid on the plastic.

When the movements had lessened, when the body and the tail no longer coiled his arm, he took his knife from his belt and sawed off the head of the snake at the place where it was held against the stone by the bridge of the binoculars.

The head fell away. With his knife blade Holt urged the head down between the stones.

He was trembling. He saw the blade flash in front of his eyes. He could not hold the blade still. His hands were beginning to shake.

His eyes were misted.

Holt heard the growl whisper.

"Can I move now?"

"You can move."

"What was it?"

"Saw-scaled viper."

"I can move?"

"You can get into a dance routine if you want to."

Crane's head emerged from under the blanket. Steadily he looked around him. Holt saw that when Crane focused on the snake's body, sawn to a stump, that he bit at his lip.

Holt moved the stones with the tip of his knife blade, exposed the snake's head, and the bite on Crane's lip was tighter.

"Do you fancy a brew, youngster?"

Holt nodded.

"Youngster, don't let anyone ever tell you that you aren't all right."

15

When they had eaten, when they had wiped clean their canteens and stowed them again in their belt pouches, Crane talked.

His voice was always a whisper, low pitched. There were times that Holt interjected his questions and in the excitement of the communication he lost control of the pitch in his chords and then Crane would silently wag a finger to show his disapproval. But the disapproval was no longer the put down. It was as if young Holt had proved himself in Crane's eyes.

They sat back to back. With the food eaten the daytime sleeping was finished. Their heads were close, mouth to ear in close proximity. The debris of the food wrapping had been collected by Holt and put into the plastic bag reserved for rubbish. It would be dark in an hour, when it was dark they would wait a further hour to acclimatise their eyes and ears to the night, then they would move off.

Crane faced down into the gorge, and watched the main road leading into the Beqa'a. At their next lying up position they would be overlooking the valley. Holt's attention was on the steep slopes above and to the west, looking into the sun that would soon clip the summits on the Jabal Niha and the Jabal el Barouk that were six thousand feet above sea level.

They were for Holt moments of deep happiness.

Mostly he listened, mostly Crane talked, whispered.

Crane talked of sniper skills, and survival skills, and of map reading skills and of evasion skills. He took Holt through the route of the coming night march, his finger hovering over but never touching the map. He showed him the next LUP, and he showed him then the track they would follow for the third of the night marches, and where they would make the final LUP on the ground above the tent camp. He showed him by which way they would skirt the high village above the valley of Khirbet Qanafar, how they would be sandwiched between Khirbet Qaafar and the twin village of Kafraiya, he showed him where, above them on the Jabal el Barouk, was positioned the sensitive Syrian listening and radar post. He showed Holt, on the map, from where he would shoot, with the sun behind him, with the sun in the eyes of those in the camp.

Happiness for Holt, because he had won acceptance. He was trusted.

"And you want him dead, Mr Crane?"

"Just a soldier, being paid to do what I'm told."

"Being paid a hell of a lot."

"A chicken shit price for what I'm doing."

"I'm not being paid," Holt said.

"Your problem, youngster."

"I saw your room back at base camp, I couldn't see what you'd spend your money on."

Crane smiled, expressionless, but there was a sharp glint in his eyes. "Too long to tell you about."

A curtain fell in that moment, then Crane's face moved. Holt saw the flicker of regret. He thought a scalpel had nudged a root nerve.

"Have you ever been paid before, to kill a man?"

"Just taken my army pay."

"Have you killed many men, Mr Crane?"

"Youngster, I don't notch them up . . . I do what I'm paid to do, I try to be good at what I'm paid for doing."

"Is it a few men, is it a lot of men, that you've killed?"

"Sort of between the two, youngster."

Holt watched him, watched the way he casually cleaned the dirt out from behind his nails, then abandoned that, began to use a toothpick in his mouth.

"Is it different, killing a man in battlefield conditions to killing a man that you've stalked, marked out?"

"To me, no."

"Do you think about the man you're going to kill at long range? Do you wonder about him, about whether he's guilty or he's innocent?"

"Not a lot."

"It would worry me sick."

"Let's hope you never have to worry yourself. Look at you, you're privileged, you're educated, you're smart, people like you don't get involved in this sort of dirt."

"This time I have."

". . . most times people like you pay jerks to get these things done. Got me?"

"But don't you feel anything?"

"I kind of cover my feelings, that way they don't get to spit in your face."

"What's your future, Mr Crane?"

Again the quiet smile. "What's yours, youngster?"

Holt was watching a bird like an eagle soar towards the summits above him. A beautiful, magnificent bird. He thought it must be from the family of eagles. No flap of the wings, just the drifting glide of power, freedom.

He grinned, "I suppose we get out of here?"

"Or I wouldn't have come. I don't buy one way tickets, I came and I aim to leave."

"I'll go back to England, then I have to make the big decision of where the next move is. I can stay in Foreign and Commonwealth, as if nothing had ever happened, as if Jane Canning hadn't existed. Or I can quit . . . I could walk out on them, I could teach, go into business. Now, I don't know. Where I came from is rough, wild country. It's at peace. Nothing ever happens down there. In our village, if they knew I was in Lebanon, well, half of them wouldn't know where it was."

"You're lucky to have options," Crane said.

"What's your future?"

"I'm getting old for this rubbish."

The bird was brilliant against the fall of the sun. The light in the gorge behind him was greying. The bird was the size of the lofty buzzards that he knew from Exmoor.

"What does an old sniper do in his retirement?"

"Sits at the pavement cafés on Dizengoff, listens to all the talk, and has nothing to say. You can't boast about my work, my work never existed. An old sniper in retirement, youngster, is a lonely bastard."

"Come to England."

Crane snorted.

"Where I live, you'd like that."

"Leave it, Holt."

He persisted. "It would be fantastic for you." He smiled as he planned Crane's retirement. "You could work for the water people, a bailiff on the salmon runs. You could be a gamekeeper. It's a huge park area, they need rangers for that . . ."

"You're all right, youngster, but not all right enough to organise me."

"You'll have the money to set yourself up, you could buy . . ."

"The money's spoken for."

He searched for the bird, couldn't find the damned thing. His eyes raked the crest of the hill. He looked into the sun. He cursed. Eternal damnation in Noah Crane's bible was to look directly into light, self inflicted blindness.

Crane said, "It's a difficult walk tonight, youngster. It's where we can hit Syrian regular army patrols, or Hezbollah, or just Shi'a village trash. Tonight it starts to get serious."

"I hear you, Mr Crane."

There was the start of a blister coming on his left heel, Holt didn't mention it, nor did he speak of the sores coming on his shoulders from the Bergen straps. He started to change the rounds in the magazines for the Armalite.

Later, when it was fully dark, he would move away from the rock cleft and squat down, and then he would learn to wipe his backside with a smooth stone. Bloody well looking forward to that, wasn't he?

The deal was struck in the hallway of the house, not that Heinrich Gunter knew of this transaction.

Heinrich Gunter, banker from Europe with a fine apartment and a salary and pension scheme to match, lay tightly bound on the cellar floor below the hallway. He knew he was in a cellar because almost as soon as he had been brought in from the street he had been bustled down a stairway. He was still blindfolded. His wrists were securely tied behind his back. There was lashed rope biting into the skin of his ankles. He had lost his spectacles when he had been hauled out of the taxi. His tongue could run on the chipped edge of his broken tooth, behind the swelling of his bruised lip.

In the hallway of the house, Gunter was sold on. There was a gentle irony that amongst the men who regarded the United States of America as the Great Satan the currency of the transaction should be American dollars, cash.

For 25,000 American dollars, the Swiss banker became the property not of the freelancing adventurers who had kidnapped him, but of the Party of God, the Hezbollah.

The money was passed in a satchel, hands were shaken, kisses exchanged. Within a few minutes, the time taken to swill a bottle of flat, warm Pepsi-Cola, the cellar had been opened, and Gunter lifted without ceremony or consideration up the steps, into the street, down into the boot of a car.

He was in darkness, in terror, half choking on the exhaust fumes.

Because the information provided by the traveller moved raw and unprocessed by any other Intelligence officer direct to the desk of Major Said Hazan, the call that he made gave him pure satisfaction.

In the Syrian Arab Republic of today there are many competing Intelligence agencies. That, of course, was the intention of the President, that they should compete, that each should derive pleasure from a coup. It is the belief of the President that competing powers deny any single agency too great an influence. Too considerable an apparatus might threaten the stability of the President's regime. But the President had been a pilot, and in the Syrian Arab Republic of today the Intelligence gathering organisation of the Air Force ranks supreme.

Major Said Hazan used his second telephone. This telephone was the one with a scrambler device and gave him a secure line to the military headquarters at Chtaura on the west side of the Beqa'a.

"The interception of the girl with the donkey leads us to believe that the enemy has an agent free in the Beqa'a, also that this agent has frequent communications with a controller. An especial vigilance is required . . ."

He drew deeply on his cigarette. He smoked only American Marlboro that were brought to him, free of charge, by the toad Fawzi. Major Said Hazan thought of him as no better than a reptile to be squashed under foot because he had never faced combat. He brought Major Said Hazan cigarettes and much more in return for his licence to move backwards and forwards between Beirut, the Beqa'a and Damascus. The toad was a kept man, as much a harlot as his own foreign sweet pet.

". . . We also have reason to believe that some 24 hours ago the enemy infiltrated a group from a checkpoint north west of Marjayoun into the NORBAT area between the villages of Blat and Kaoukaba. It is to be presumed that this group has gone through the NORBAT sector and will be moving towards the Beqa'a. Maximum effort is to be given to the interception of this group."

In front of him the desk was clear. His papers, and most particularly the plan of the Defence Ministry on Kaplan in Tel Aviv, were locked away in his safe. His evening was free for his sweet pet. The good fingers of his left hand toyed with the clip fastening of the leather box. He thought the pendant, the sapphire jewel and the diamond gems would be beautiful on the whiteness of her throat. The pendant had cost him nothing. There were many merchants in Damascus who sought the favour of Major Said Hazan.

"I would stress that both these matters have the highest priority. We shall be watching for results."

He saw nothing strange, nothing remotely amusing, in the fact that he handed down instructions for action to a full brigadier of the army. Major Said Haza was Air Force Intelligence.

If the spy were caught and the incursion group intercepted it would be the triumph of Major Said Haza. If they were not caught it would be the failure of headquarters in the Beqa'a.

Now for his sweet pet, the only woman who did not stare at him, did not flinch.

They came back by truck.

Abu Hamid was the first off the tail board. As the chief instructor, he had the right to wash first.

He was filthy. The dust caked his face. His uniform denims were smeared black from handling the collapsed beams that had caught fire.

He had seen the results of air raids in Tyre, Sidon, Damour and in West Beirut, but that had been years before. Many years since he had stood in a line of men manhandling the sharp debris of fallen concrete. Many years since he had helped to manoeuvre the heavy chains of the cranes that alone could lift whole precast floors that had fallen in the blast of the high explosive.

They had been ten miles to the north. They had tunnelled into a ruin in the village of Majdel Aanjar. Once the building had been a hotel; until that morning the building had been the sleeping quarters of a unit of the Popular Struggle Front. They had been amongst many, digging at the rubble, gently pulling out the bodies. There had been squads of the army with heavy lifting equipment, there had been the local people, there had been men of the Democratic Front and the Abu Moussa faction and from Sai'iqa. Those from the Democratic Front and the Abu Moussa faction and Sai'iqa had been trucked in as much to help in the recovery of the casualties as to witness the damage done by the air strike of the enemy.

When they had finished, when the light was failing, Abu Hamid had called his own recruits together. Forcefully lectured them on the barbarity of the Zionist oppressors, told them that their time would come when they would be privileged to strike back.

He was heading for his tent, he was shouting for the cook to bring him warm water, he was intent on dragging off his clothes. He rounded one of the bell tents.

434

He saw Fawzi sitting in front of the flaps of his own tent.

Abu Hamid said, "From what I saw you could have been sleeping in the bunker and you would not have been saved."

Fawzi said, "Tonight I sleep in our tent, the Zionist gesture has been made."

"It was horrific. Pieces of people . . ."

"We are lucky that our comrades martyred themselves, or it would have been us."

Abu Hamid said, "We are the more determined, we will never give up our struggle. Tell that to them in Damascus."

"Tell them yourself, hero, there is transport coming for you in the morning."

Inside his tent, Abu Hamid stripped off his filthy clothes. He stood naked. The galvanised bucket of warm water was brought into his tent. He thought of the orphan children. He thought of the mutilated bodies. He could not believe that he had ever hesitated through fear. He thought of his grandfather's home. He thought of the blood that would gush from a bayonet wound.

"I don't have any feelings for him," Holt said.

"For who?" Crane helped him to ease the weight of the Bergen high onto his shoulders.

"For Abu Hamid. I don't loathe him, and I don't feel pity for him."

"Better that way."

"If I'm going to help to kill him, then I should feel something."

"Feelings get in the way of efficiency," Crane said.

They moved out.

There was a faint light from the stars to guide them.

It was the boast of the technicians who worked in the small fortified listening post astride the top of the third highest peak of the Hermon range that they could eavesdrop the telephone call by the President of Syria from his office in Damascus to his mother, telling her when he would call to take a cup of lemon-scented tea with her.

The listening post of prefabricated cabins and heavy stone fort circles was 7,500 feet above sea level. In the Yom Kippur it had been captured. The girl technicians had been raped, slaughtered. The boy technicians had been mutilated, tortured, murdered. On the last day of the fighting, after a battle of intense ferocity, the listening post had been recaptured. The listening post was of immense strategic and tactical value to the military machine of Israel. Beneath its antennae was the most sophisticated electronic Intelligence gathering and signals equipment manufactured in the United States of America and in the state's own factories. The listening post was situated some 35 miles from Damascus, and some 40 miles from Chtaura on the western side of the Beqa'a alley.

The Hermon range marked the north eastern extremity of Israelite conquests under the leadership of Moses and Joshua. The eyes of Moses, the ears of Joshua, that was how the present-day technicians regarded their steepling antennae towers concreted into the bed rock of the mountain top.

The problem lay not with the interception of telephone and radio messages from Damascus to military headquarters at Chtaura, more in the analysis and evaluation, carried on far behind the lines inside the state of Israel, of the mass two-way traffic.

In full flow, untreated data swarmed from Damascus and the Beqa'a to the radials of the antennae before the computers of the Defence Ministry on Kaplan attempted to make sense from the jargon of coded radio messages, scrambled telephone conversations.

Some communications received by the eyes of Moses and the ears of Joshua were more complicated in their deciphering than others. A telephone call from Damascus to Chtaura via a scrambled link offered small scope for interpretation. But radio messages fanning out from Chtaura to battalion-sized commando units stationed at Rachaiya and Qaraaoun and Aitanit gave easier work to the computers.

The orders coming from Chtaura to Rachaiya and Qaraaoun and Aitanit made plain to the local commanders that their origin was Damascus. The orders were acted upon.

That night, patrols were intensified, road blocks were strengthened.

It had been the intention of Major Zvi Dan to work late in his office, to delve into the small hillock of paper that had built up on his desk while he had been in Kiryat Shmona.

Behind him was a wasted day. He had failed to beat off the lethargy that had clamped down on him after the tension of his early morning battle to have the airstrike diverted. He was slow with his work, but he would work through the night, and then return to Kiryat Shmona in the morning. The girl, Rebecca, had gone home. Sometimes when she was gone he felt as crippled by her absence as he was crippled by the loss of his leg. He read for the third time the evaluation by the Central Intelligence Agency, newly arrived, of a preliminary debrief of a Palestinian captured in northern Italy. Israel for so long had stood alone in the front line of the war against international terrorism that it amused him to notice how the Western nations were now queuing to demonstrate their virility.

He could remember the carping response of those same nations when the IAF had intercepted a Libyan registered Gulfstream executive jet en route from Tripoli to Damascus. Intelligence had believed Abu Nidal to be aboard. The previous month the jackals of Abu Nidal had killed and wounded 135 civilians at the check-in counters at the airports of Rome and Vienna. Those Western countries had issued their sanctimonious disapproval because the intelligence had been ill founded. He could recall numerous instances of public criticism from the government of the United Kingdom for Israeli retaliatory strikes, yet now they had men slogging into the Beqa'a . . . Of course it had been bluff. He would never have resigned. Of course he would just have gone back to his desk and started to work again, had the jets hit the tent camp. He knew no life other than the life of defending his country – had he been a Christian – and he had many friends who were Christians – then he would have said that that was the cross he had to bear.

He wondered if the Americans had the guts to stand in the front line. He thought of the thousands, tens of thousands, of American citizens living abroad who would be placed at risk when a Palestinian went on trial in Washington, went to death row, went to interminable lawyers' conferences, went to the electric chair.

There was a light knock on his door.

He started. He had been far away.

He was handed a folded single sheet of teleprinter paper.

The door closed.

He read the paper.

He felt it like a blow to his stomach, like the blast that had carried away his leg.

He reached for his telephone, he dialled.

"Hello, This is Zvi. You should come to my office straightaway . . ."

He heard the station officer wavering, there were people for dinner, could it wait until tomorrow.

"It is not a matter for the telephone, and you should come here immediately."

Men from the Shin Bet watched the Norwegian leave his company head-quarters. He was clearly visible to them through the 'scope of the night sight. They saw that he had changed from his uniform fatigues into civilian dress. In a white T-shirt and pale yellow slacks, the young man showed up well in the green wash of the lens. They watched him, with three others, climb into a UNIFIL-marked jeep and head south towards the Israeli border.

The car took side lanes to skirt Syrian army road blocks on the highway leaving Beirut. From a post that was jammed sturdily through the top gap in the front window flew the flag of Hezbollah. On a white cloth had been painted the word "Allah", but the second "l" had been transformed to the shape of a Kalashnikov rifle. The car used a rutted, deserted road and climbed, twisted, towards the mountains to the east.

The station officer read the teleprinter sheet. At home the local wine had been flowing free. His suit jacket was on the back of the chair. He took off his tie, loosened his collar.

"Shit . . ."

He did not concern himself with the demand for "especial vigilance" for a spy in the Beqa'a. He read over and over the order for "maximum attention is to be given to the interception of this group".

". . . So bloody soon."

"For Crane it would be natural to assume that the enemy is alert." Major Zvi Dan hesitated. "But he has Holt."

"And the boy's green. I shall have to tell them in Century . . ."

"Tell them also that there is nothing you can do, nothing we can do."

It would be two hours before the station officer returned, sobered, to his guests.

His message, sent in code from his embassy office, reported the probability, based on intercepted Syrian army transmissions, that the mission of Noah Crane and Holt was compromised.

He thought that he had made a fool of himself at the fish pond.

The first fish was exciting, the second fish was interesting, the following 34 fish were simply boring. If he had not pulled out the pellet-fattened trout then they would have used a net for the job.

But time had been killed, and it had been made plain to him that he was denied access to the Intelligence section at the Kiryat Shmona base, and that news – whatever it might be – would reach Tel Aviv first.

He had taken a bath. He had put on a clean shirt and retrieved his trousers, pressed, from under the mattress of his bed. Percy Martins had smoothed his hair with his pair of brushes.

Dinner in the dining room. Trout, of course. A half a bottle of white Avdat to rinse away the tang of the artificially fed rainbow.

Before dinner and after dinner he had tried to ring the station officer. No answer from his direct line at the embassy. No help from the switchboard. Inconceivable to him that the station officer would not have left a contact number at the embassy's switchboard, but the operator denied there was such a number. He walked to the bar. He could read the conspiracy, those bastards at Century in league with that supercilious creep, Tork, a mile off. They had shut him out. Actually it was criminal, the way that a man of his dedication to the Service and his experience was treated. The Service was changing, the recruitment of creatures like Fenner and Anstruther, and their promotion over him, that showed how much the Service had veered off course. Good work he had put in over the long years of his time in the Service. He had had his coups, and damn all recognition. He reckoned that his coups, their full extent, had been kept from the Director General . . . if the Director General only knew the half of it, Percy Martins would have been running the Middle East Desk long since, sitting in Anstruther's chair, kicking the arse off Fenner. He would have bet half of his pension that the Director General had never been told that he had crowned his Amman posting with, as near as dammit, a prediction that the Popular Front were about to launch a hijack fiesta. In his three years in Cyprus he had actually gone to his opposite number at the American shop, warned him of the personal danger to the ambassador, all there in his report – he bet the Director General had never been told, certainly never been reminded when the ambassador had been shot dead. First categoric and specific news of the Israeli nuke programme out of Dimona, that had been his climax on a Tel Aviv tour – he hadn't had the credit, the credit had gone to the Yanks. God, and he had made sacrifices for the Service. Sacrifices that started with his marriage, followed with his son. He hadn't complained, not when he was given his postings, not when his wife had said she wasn't going Married Accompanied, not when his son had grown up treating him like an unwanted stranger. A record of total disappointment at home, and he had never once let it show, hadn't let his work suffer.

Holt and Crane into the Beqa'a, Percy Martins's last big one, by Jesus, he would not let the last big one go unnoticed on the nineteenth floor of Century.

He had a good record, nothing to be ashamed of, and less recognition for it than the man who sat behind the reception desk at Century. Meanwhile he was stuck in a kibbutz, where there was no fishing, where there was no access to a damn good mission going into Lebanon. Of course, he should have insisted that there was proper preparation of the ground rules before he ever left London. And no damned support from the station officer. The station officer's balls would be a decent enough target when he made it back to Century . . .

He had signed his bill, should have had a full bottle of Avdat but he had never gone over the top with expenses, he had strolled to the bar.

Percy Martins had never been able to understand why so many hotels dictated that drinking should be carried out in semi-darkness and to the accompaniment of loudspeaker music. There were Americans in the shadows, from the air-conditioned bus that had arrived in the afternoon. He preferred solitude to them. Blue rinse, check trousers and damn loud voices for both sexes. The Americans had all the tables except one. Two men sat at the table, and bloody miserable they seemed to Martins because in front of each of them was a tall glass of fresh pressed orange juice. Not young and not old, the two men. Obviously Israelis. One wore an old leather jacket, scarred at the cuffs and elbows, the other wore a bleach scrubbed denim jacket. They were not talking; they looked straight ahead.

And there were the young Scandinavians. He knew they were Scandinavians, impossible language they were speaking, like English taped and played backwards. And drinking, and loud. All that Martins associated with Scandinavians.

There were four of them. He had the choice between several loud American women and their husbands, the teetotal Israelis, and four merry Scandinavians. They were at the bar, they were ordering another round. He assumed them to be UNIFIL. At the bar he nodded to them, made his presence known, then ordered himself a beer.

He had drunk half his beer, not made contact, when the young man closest to him lurched backwards on the punchline of a joke, stumbled against Martins' elbow while he was sipping, spilled a mouthful down the laundered shirt.

It was the beginning of the conversation. Handkerchiefs out, apologies first in Norwegian and then English when Martins had spoken. Introductions.

He learned that the young man who had jogged him was Hendrik. He learned that Hendrik was with UNIFIL's NORBAT. He learned that Hendrik and his friends were allowed one evening a week in Kiryat Shmona.

He was rather pleased. A stained shirt was a cheap price to pay for introductions.

A replacement beer was called for by Hendrik.

"You are English, Mr Martin?"

"Martins. Yes, I am English . . . Cheers."

"Here for holiday?"

"You could say I am here for a holiday, Hendrik."

"For us it is not a holiday, you understand. No holiday in south Lebanon. What does an Englishman find for a holiday in Kiryat Shmona?"

"Just looking around, just general interest . . . Your glass is empty, you must allow me."

Martins clicked his fingers for the barman. Had he looked behind him, he would have seen that the two glasses of orange juice remained untouched, that the Israelis leaned forward, faces set in concentration. Four beers for the soldiers, a whisky and water for Martins.

"So how do you like it here, Hendrik, serving with the United Nations?"

"Are you a Jew?"

The young man's face close to his own. "Most certainly not."

"The Jews treat us like filth. They have so great an arrogance. They make many problems for us."

"Ah yes. Is that so?"

His whisky was less than half drunk, but the barman had reached for it, prompted by one of the soldiers. The glass was refilled.

"That's most civil of you. You were saying, Hendrik . . ."

"I was saying that the Jews make many problems for us."

"Not only for you, my boy," Martins said quietly, the first trace of a slur in his speech.

"Every day they violate the authority of the United Nations."

"Is that so?"

"Every single day they come into the UNIFIL area."

"Indeed? Do they indeed?"

"They come in and they make trouble, but it is us who have to mend the damage."

"Absolutely."

There was an appealing candour to the young man, Martins thought, compared to his own callow son, miserable little brat, without a polite word for his father.

"That's very decent of you . . ." The whisky glass was gone again. Percy Martins felt the warm careless glow in his body.

"They've always made trouble, the Jews. Since way back, since before you were born, my boy. Part of their nature. Now, don't get me wrong, I'm not an anti-semite, never have been, but by God they tax my patience. They always have done, damn difficult people to do business with when you need co-operation."

"Business or holiday?"

Martins leaned forward, avuncular, confiding. "A little more business than holiday."

"What sort of business?"

Martins swayed, "Careful, my boy. Over your young head . . ."

He seldom drank in London. A pint in the pub or a quick Scotch when he slipped out of Century in the evening to get some fish and chips or a takeaway pizza before going back to work late. He kept no alcohol at home. If he left alcohol in the house it would be drunk by his wife, or by the boy when he was home from college. But this was a first class young man, with a good reading of events, a very level headed young man. God, why did they have to have that bloody music? And why did those bloody Americas have to address each other as though they were in the next state?

"Like last night."

"Sorry, my boy, what was last night?"

"They sent an infiltration team through our lines . . ."

Martins reeled back. "How did you know about that?"

He was close to losing his footing. He hung on the edge of the bar.

"They sent an infiltration team through last night."

Martins shouted. "I bloody heard you, don't repeat yourself. I asked you a question. How did you bloody know what happened last night?"

He was not aware that his raised voice had quietened the Americans. He did not see the man behind him, the one who wore the leather jacket, slide from his chair, go fast for the door.

"Why do you shout?"

"Because I want an answer, my boy."

"To what, an answer?"

"How you knew about an infiltration team moving off last night."

"Does it concern you?"

"Your answer, I want it."

His vision was blurred. He could not register the curious concentrated interest of the boy Hendrik.

"An Englishman, on holiday – why does an infiltration concern him?"

"It bloody well concerns me, how you knew."

"You are drunk, mister."

In front of him the young man turned away, as if no longer interested. Martins caught at the white T-shirt, spun him round.

"How did you know about the infiltration last night?"

"Take your hands off me."

"How did you know . . . ?"

There was quick movement. As though the Norwegians were suddenly bored with the elderly Briton. Martins's shout still hung in the air as they pushed past him, away from the bar, out through the swing door.

The music played was ragtime.

The man sitting at the table behind abandoned the two orange juices, hurried out through the door to drag his colleague off the telephone.

There was the sound of the UNIFIL transport roaring to life in the car park.

"What did he say, Hendrik, that pissed fart?"

Hendrik Olaffson drove. "Heh, thanks for pulling the asshole off me."

"What was it about?"

He spoke slowly. "He was English. He said he was a tourist, but he did not dress like a tourist and there is no tourism here, that is the first. Then the second, he went stupid when I said that the Israelis had infiltrated through our sector last night. He said, 'How did you know about an infiltration team last night?', those were his words."

A voice from the darkness in the back of the jeep. "Hendrik, is it possible that the British have pushed an infiltration group through our sector, going north?"

"Into the Beqa'a? It would be madness."

"Madness, yes. But worth much weed, Hendrik . . ." They were laughing, full of good humour.

They were waved through the checkpoint at Metulla.

In the foyer of the guest house of the Kibbutz Kfar Giladi, the receptionist passed the man who wore the frayed leather jacket her guest book. Her finger pointed to the name and the signature of Percy Martins, British passport, government servant.

They were moving on an animal track. He thought it could be a goat track. There were wild goat loose on Exmoor and Holt knew their smell. He reckoned it was a regular track. It was the fifth hour of the night march and the old moon was up, in the last quarter which was the best time for night infiltration according to Crane's bible. Maximum safe light for them to move under, and it was a hell of a job for Holt to follow the track. Would have been impossible for him if he had not had the guiding wraith of Crane ahead. Damned if he could figure how Crane could have able to identify the animal track from the high-up aerial photographs.

The fifth hour, and the march was now going well. Two hours back it had not been good, they had scampered across the tarmac road in their path. A bad bit, the road, because they had had to lie up for quarter of an hour before moving into the open, and in the waiting Holt had felt the fear pangs. Gone now, the fear, gone because the road was behind them and below them. The hillside was steep, and much of the time Holt walked crab style going sideways, because that was the easiest way with the weight of the Bergen. The Bergen should have been easier. He was a gallon of water down, ten pounds weight down, didn't seem to make any difference. He was feeling good and the blister hadn't worsened, and he thought he could live with the sores under the backpack straps. He was the son of a professional man, he had been to private school, he was a graduate in Modern History, he had been accepted via the "fast stream" into the Foreign and Commonwealth Office. And no bloody way any of that had fitted him for crab walking along a hillside in south Lebanon, no bloody way it would help him if the blister on his heel burst, if the sores on his shoulders went raw.

He thought he was beginning to move by instinct. He thought he was getting into the rhythm of the march.

He tried to think of his girl. So hard to see his girl in his mind, because his mind was taken up with footfall, and lying up positions, and water rations, and watching and following Crane up ahead. The old goat on an old goat track . . . Hard to think of Jane. It seemed to him like a betrayal of her memory, of his reason for being there. She was just a flicker in his mind, like the bulb going in a striplight. The good times with Jane, they didn't have anything to do with changing the ammunition twice a day in the magazines, nor with squatting in the lee of a rock after dark using smooth stones to wipe his backside, nor with cleaning his teeth with a pick because paste left a smell signature, nor with carrying a Model FM long range sniper rifle that gave one chance, one shot. He could feel his Jane. She could be against his skin, like the pain of the pack straps was against his skin, like the heel of his right chukka boot was against his skin, he could feel her, but he could not see her. Each time he tried to see her then he reckoned it was the girl, Rebecca, that he saw.

He didn't know whether Crane had quickened his pace, or whether he himself was slowing. Feeling Jane's body against his skin, seeing Rebecca's body against his skin. That was a bastard, like he was selling his Jane short.

He was struggling to keep pace with Crane, he was struggling to see the soft face, lips, throat, eyes of his girls.

He kicked the stone.

The track was not more than foot wide. There was a sloping black abyss to his right. His left hand was held out to steady himself against the rock slope soaring above him.

He had gone straight through the stone. He had not paused, he had not tested the ground under his leading foot. He had begun to move by instinct.

The loose stone rolled.

The stone slid off the track.

The stone seemed to laugh at him. The stone fell from the track, and bounced below, and disturbed more stones. More stones falling and bouncing and being disturbed.

He stood statue still. The vertigo seemed to pull at him, as if trying to topple the weight of the Bergen pack down into the abyss, after the tumbling stones.

Snap out of it, Holt. Get a grip, Holt. No room in his mind for his girl, any girl. No room for pack strap sores, nor heel blisters. Get yourself bloody well together, Holt. He jerked his foot forward. He rolled the sole of his boot on the ground of the track ahead. Tested it, eased onto it. First stone he had kicked all night. Crane hadn't stopped for him. Crane's shadow shape was smaller, moving away.

All the time the echoing beat of the stones skipping, plummeting, racing, below him.

He was into his stride again when the flare went up.

A thump from below and behind. A white light point soaring . . . Crane's bible. Trip wire ground level flare, freeze into tree shape and sink ever so slow. High level flare, drop face down like there's no tomorrow.

The moment before the flare burst into brilliance, Holt was on his face, on his stomach, on his knees.

The flare when it burst seemed to struggle against gravity. It hung high. A wash of growing light on the hillside. The epicentre was behind him, but he could sense the light bathing his hands and the outline of his body and his back, and niggling into his eyes. He lay quite still. Ahead of him he could see the exposed soles of Crane's boots.

The flare fell, died.

There was a hiss from Crane. Holt saw the fast movement of Crane's arm, urging him forward. He was half upright,. and Crane was moving. He was trying to push back the weight of the Bergen holding him down, and the weight of the Model PM, and the weight of his belt kit.

Crane gone. Blackness where there had been light. Should have bloody closed his eyes. Shouldn't have let the light into his eyes.

The second flare was fired.

Holt dropped. Eyes closed now, squeezed tight.

Trying to do what Crane had told him, trying to follow verse and chapter of Crane's bible. Nothing over his ears, his hearing was sharp, uncluttered. He heard the voices below. No bloody idea how far below. Voices, but no words.

When the light no longer hurt his eyes he looked ahead. The flare was about to ground. The path ahead was clear. He could not see Crane.

There were two more flares.

There were bursts of machine gun fire against the hillside. The strike of the tracer red rounds on the hillside seemed to Holt to have no pattern, like it was random firing. He had grown to know the jargon. He reckoned it was *prophylactic* firing. He wondered to hell whether they had *thermal imagery* sights, whether they had *passive night* goggles. There was movement below him. He thought he heard the sounds of men moving in the darkness, scrambling on the slopes. He could hear the voices again. Christ, he was alone. His decision, alone, to move or to stay frozen. His decision, whether to reckon he was invisible to the men below so that he could move, whether the firing had been to flush him out into the view of the TI sights and the PN goggles.

Hellishly alone. He could not crawl, if he crawled he would make the noise of an elephant. If he were to move he had to get to his feet, he had to walk upright, slowly, weighing each step.

He lay on his face. He thought of how greatly he depended on the taciturn goading that he had from Crane. He pulled himself up. He listened to the voices and the movements on the hillside. The thought in his mind was of being alone on the hillside, of being discovered, of being apart at that moment from Noah Crane.

The aloneness drove him forward.

There was no more shooting. There were no more flares. The voices faded, the footfalls died.

He tried to remember how far it would be to the next halt position. He tried to recall the map that Crane had shown him before they had moved off. They were now in the sixth hour. Holt had not taken much notice of the map, didn't have to, because he had Crane to lead him.

Alone, Holt resumed his night march.

It might have been five minutes later, it might have been half an hour, he found Crane sitting astride the animal track.

He could have kissed him.

Crane whispered, "Syrian regular army patrol."

Holt spoke into Crane's ear. "Routine?"

"They're not usually out at night. Usually tucked up, holding their peckers."

"Why would they have been out?"

"You're the educated one, youngster."

"Were they waiting for us?"

"You went to university."

Holt hissed, "Tell me."

"Just not certain that one kicked stone was it, but waiting."

"Are we blown?"

Holt saw, in the fragile moonlight, Crane's smile without humour. "They're behind us, there's only one sensible way to go."

They moved off.

He was unaware of his shoulder sores and of his heel blister. Holt was aware only of each single, individual footfall.

They bypassed the sleeping village of Aitanit, and the silent village of Bab Maraa, they climbed high to avoid the village of Saghbine where dogs broke the quiet of the night.

Below him to the east was the moon-draped flatness of the floor of the Beqa'a valley. Holt thought of the valley as a noose.

445

16

In front of him, below him, in brilliant sunshine, lay the valley.

He could see right across to the grey-blue climb of the far wall. In the soft haze it was hard for him to make out clean-cut features in the wall. Behind the rising ground were the *jebels* that marked the line of the border between Lebanon and Syria. With difficulty, he could make out the far distant bulk of the Hermon range.

Holt and Crane had reached the lying up position in darkness, and Holt had taken the first guard watch, so that he had taken his turn to wrap himself in the lightweight blanket and tried to sleep under the scrim net while the dawn was spreading from the far away hill slopes. Crane must have let him sleep on beyond his hour. They were above the village of Saghbine. Crane had set his LUP in an outcrop of weathered shapeless rock over which the scrim net had been draped. Holt knew that Crane's bible decreed that they should never make a hiding place in isolated, obvious cover, but there was a scalped barrenness about the terrain around them. The nearest similar outcrop would have been, he estimated, and he found it difficult to make such estimates over this ground, at least a hundred yards from their position. Lying among the rocks, in the filtered shade of the scrim netting, he felt the nakedness of their hiding place. It seemed impossible to him that they should not be seen should an enemy scour the hillside with binoculars. But Crane slept and snored and grunted, like a man for whom danger did not exist. There was room between these rocks, under the scrim netting, for the two of them only if they were pressed against each other.

Their valley wall, on which jutted the occasional rock outcrop, shelved away to the floor. He could see that the rock of the sides gave way to good soil at the bottom. The fields were neatly laid out, delineated by the differing crops. The valley walls were yellowed, browned, the valley floor was a series of green shades, and Holt could make out the flow of the Litani winding, meandering, in the middle of the valley, and he could see also the straight cut ditches that carried the irrigating life run of water from the river into the fields. He played a game to himself and tried to make out the produce of the handkerchief fields. He could see the posts supporting the vines that were just beginning to show their spring shoots, and the cutback trees of the fruit orchards, and the hoed-between lines of the grain crop, and the more powerful thrusting traces of the marijuana plants, and the white streamers of the plastic tunnels under which the lettuces flourished.

Holt thought that luxury was a warm bath, and a razor, and a tube of toothpaste . . .

What few trees there were, pine or cypress, were in small clumps on the valley floor. He reckoned the village of Saghbine was about a mile away below them. The village was clear enough through the binoculars, but it was hard for him to make out the individual buildings when he relied only on his eyesight. He was interested in the village because in his imagination he exchanged the village houses for the aerial photograph he had seen of the camp, and he tried to imagine how it would be when they came to lie up a thousand yards from the camp. Terrifyingly open . . . If the camp had been where Saghbine was . . . if they had had to manoeuvre to within a thousand yards of Saghbine and rest up through long daylight hours . . . he couldn't see how it could be done. And Crane, snoring and nestling against him, just slept, slept like tomorrow was another day, another problem.

The village was a sprawled mess of concrete block homes and older stone buildings with a mosque and minaret tower in the centre. The high pitched chanted summons to prayer from the minaret tower reached him.

"Fancy a brew?"

Crane had an eye open. Snoring one moment, thinking of tea the next. Holt thought that Crane might just turn over and give up the ghost if the crop failed in Assam and Sri Lanka.

"Wouldn't mind."

"Done the magazines?"

"Done them."

"What's new?"

"Place is like the grave."

Crane stretched himself full length. Holt heard his joints crack.

"Then you're a danger to me, youngster."

"How come?"

"Because, youngster, when you start thinking the Beqa'a is quiet as the grave then that's the time you start to get careless."

"I just said the place was pretty peaceful, which it is."

Crane took the binoculars. Tea was going to have to wait. Holt bridled, and Crane didn't give a damn.

Crane started by looking south.

"Pretty peaceful, eh, that what I heard? Back where *you* kicked the stone last night, where they fired the flares, there's troops out there. Pretty blind if you didn't see them, but they're there . . ."

His head turned, his gaze moved north.

". . . There's a kiddie with some sheep, or didn't you see him? He's a mile back, not much more, he's about four hundred feet below us. He'll be watching for hyena because he's got lambs with him. If he sees anything that adds up to hyena then he'll yell, bet your backside . . ."

Again the twist of the head. Crane peered down at the village.

"Gang of guys going into the mosque for a knees down, or didn't you see them? They're in fatigues, or didn't you see that? They'll be Hezbollah, or didn't you know that? If the troops find a trail, if that kiddie spots you when you go to scratch your arse, then the God men'll be up here, too damn right."

"I hear you, Mr Crane."

"So, don't go giving me crap about it being quiet."

"It looked quiet."

"Looked? Heh, watch the kiddie . . ."

Crane passed the binoculars to Holt. He gestured where Holt should look. To himself, Holt cursed. When the boy and the sheep were pointed out he saw them. Could have kicked himself. The boy with the sheep wore flopping dun-coloured trousers and he had a grey blanket over his shoulders, and the sheep and the lambs were dirty brown-white with black faces. He hadn't seen them, wouldn't have seen them without the prompting.

"I'm sorry."

"Doesn't help you, youngster. Waking up is what helps."

Holt watched the boy with the sheep. It was as if he were dancing to the music of a flute. Private dancing, because the boy was sure that he was not watched. The boy tripped in the air, and his arms circled above his head, skipping from foot to foot, bowing to something imaginary.

Crane whispered, "If he stops his act, if he starts running, then I get the shits. Do I piss you off, youngster?"

Holt grinned, "Why should you do that?"

"I'll give you a lecture. The troops back there, they hate you. The kiddie with the sheep, he hates you. The guys in the mosque, they hate you. Out here, I'm the only one on your side. Don't get a clever idea that somehow because you're a Brit, because you're not Yank and not Jew, that the troops and the kiddie don't hate you. Our problem was, before we came here in '82, that we never worked out just how much they'd hate us. When they started to mess with us we kicked their arses, we blew up their houses, we carted their guys away to prison camps. They hate us pretty deep. They're dangerous because they've this martyr crap stuck in their skulls, aren't afraid of biting on a .762 round. Fight them and you're in a no win, you kill them and you've sent them to the Garden of Paradise which they don't object to. They go in hard. Kill 'em, and more come, there are more queuing up to get to that Garden. They made our life a three-year misery for sinners when we were in the Beqa'a. They sniped us, they mined us, they never let go of us. Bombing them is the same as recruiting them. And they don't fight by your nice rules. When I'm in the Beqa'a I forget everything, every last thing, that I learned about Hearts and Minds when I was in the British Paras. Treat each last one like he's an enemy, like he wants your throat, that's what I learned here. Don't ever hesitate, just kill, because they have no fear. The girl with the donkey, she had no fear . . ."

"Do you have fear, Mr Crane?"

"Only when I've got you hanging on my tail, telling me it's all peaceful."

The chanting from the minaret had stopped. In the fields work was resuming. Holt could see the women with their hoes, forks, spades, shovels.

448

Crane grabbed the binoculars from Holt.

He gazed down at the approach road into Saghbine.

He seemed to smile.

There was a billow of dust on the road. Crane passed the binoculars back to Holt.

Holt saw the car with the dust streaming from its wheels.

"Don't ever forget what that car looks like."

"Why?"

"Because I say don't ever forget that car."

The car was an ancient Mercedes. Holt thought it not much less than a miracle that it still moved. The panels were rusty ochre. The front wing looked to have been in an argument. There were white smears of filler in the roof. He could see packing cases in the back, that the seats behind the driver had been stripped out. At his angle he could not see the face of the driver, only the width of his gut.

"I see the car."

"About time you learned how to make a brew. Get on with it."

The phone trilled on Major Zvi Dan's desk. Rebecca picked it up.

She listened, she passed it to him.

She saw the annoyance, because he liked to be told first who was calling him.

"Dan here . . . What name? Percy Martins. Yes, I am aware of the presence of Percy Martins at Kfar Giladi . . . What do you mean, is he sensitive? . . . No, I will merely confirm that he is sensitive, but also that his role in Israel cannot be regarded as the legitimate business of the Shin Bet . . . I don't believe you . . . You have to be joking . . . I had a flight for this evening – but I'll drive . . . listen, listen, everything to do with that man is sensitive . . . three hours."

He replaced the telephone. His head sank into his hands.

Rebecca looked at him. "Is it bad?"

"Unbelievable." As though the wound were personal to Major Zvi Dan.

"Is it bad for the young man?"

"The roof is falling in on him."

Mid-morning, and Percy Martins lay in the bed in his darkened room. He had bawled out the woman who had come to clean and change his bedclothes, sent her packing. He had ignored his wake-up call. There was a drumbeat behind his temples. He knew there was a calamity in the air, couldn't place the source of it. He seemed to think that if he got up and washed and shaved and dressed, then he would get to the bottom of the catastrophe . . . and he didn't want to. He shirked the discovery.

While he remained in his room, while he lay in his pyjamas, he was unaware that a man from Shin Bet sat on a chair beside the staircase where he could look down the corridor, watch the door of Percy Martins's room.

A quiet morning in the NORBAT sector.

The troops had checked and searched only four cars and two cartloads of market produce in the previous three hours. The sun was sprawled in the skies, a lethargy hung over the road block, a shimmer burnished up from the roadway. Two of the Norwegians dozed in the oven area under the tin roof that topped their sandbagged position, a third played patience at the lightweight table beside the entrance to the position.

Hendrik Olaffson, smartly turned out in a freshly laundered uniform, carried his NATO self-loading rifle easily on the bend of his elbow. He stared up the road. He watched the bend. He waited to see if the traveller would come to visit.

He realised they had taken a diversion.

The driver of the jeep turned frequently to give the face of Abu Hamid a sharp glance, as though he was the possessor of a private joke. The driver had few teeth. A grin for Abu Hamid to see, and foul breath seeping through the gaps above and below the few there were. Abu Hamid was not familiar enough with Damascus to know where they went. He would not ask why they had taken a diversion from the usual roads they used to get from the Beirut road across the city to Air Force headquarters, would not give the bastard the satisfaction.

They were in narrow streets. Abu Hamid thought the driver a lunatic. He had the belt on, and that had been a sign of fear, and he knew that he would be ignored if he asked the bastard to go more slowly, or to pay heed to the pedestrians and cyclists. He would just give the bastard pleasure if he told him to pay attention to the traffic signs.

In surges that shook Abu Hamid, lurched him forward against the belt, the jeep hammered down narrow streets, scattered women with their shopping bags, grazed a cart drawn by a ragged, thin horse.

They came into a square. The square seemed overhung, squashed in, by the buildings around. It was a dark square because the buildings were tall and cut out the sun. Abu Hamid thought that only at the middle of the day would the sun fall into the cobbled centre of the square. There were balconies at many levels of the surrounding buildings, with washing suspended from them, and the stucco facades were peeled raw.

He felt the tug at his sleeve. He realised the driver had slowed. He saw the squinted amusement in the driver's eyes. The driver jabbed with the nicotined tip of his finger, showed Abu Hamid that he should look to the centre of the square.

He was not prepared.

He retched, choked, he tried to swallow down the bile that pitched into his mouth.

There were three men suspended from the gallows beam.

It was late morning. There was the bustle of traffic, and the cries of the hawkers, and the shouts of the traders, and there were three men hanging from three ropes from the scaffold. Their heads were hooded, their arms were pinioned behind their backs, their ankles were tied with rope. He knew they were men because under the long white robes in which they were draped he could see the ends of their trousers, and he could see also that they wore men's shoes. There was no movement in the three bodies because no freshness of wind could enter the confines of the square. Fastened to the robes on each man was a large black painted sign. The driver split his face in a delighted grin.

"You like it?"

"Who are they?"

"Can you not read?"

"Who are they?"

"They are Iraqis."

"What did they do?"

"Who knows what they did? They were accused of 'jeopardising state security to the Israeli enemy'. They are Iraqis, they let off bombs in Damascus, they killed many people . . ."

The jeep idled past the rough cut, fresh wood gallows. Abu Hamid stared. He saw that the shoe lace of one man was undone, that his shoe was all but falling from his foot. A fast flash thought for Abu Hamid. He saw a man in terror, crouched on the floor of a cell. He heard the tramp of feet in a passageway. He felt the shame of a man who was to be taken out to be hanged in a public square and whose fingers would not allow the small dignity of retying his shoe lace.

". . . That is what I heard, that they set bombs in the city. The government says they are agents of Israel. Who am I to say they are not? They were hanged at dawn. You like to see it?"

The driver chuckled. Abu Hamid saw the stains at the groin of each man. Abu Hamid nodded dumbly.

"It is good," the driver said. "It is not often that they hang the enemies of the state where we can see them. It should be more often . . ."

The driver slammed his foot down onto the clutch, went up through his gears. He hit the horn.

They went fast out of the square. Within a few minutes they were back into the system of wide boulevards that were the public face of Damascus. They were heading for the air ministry headquarters.

"Did Major Said Hazan give orders that I was to be brought this way, that I was to see them?"

Abu Hamid saw the black tooth gaps, and the yellowed stumps, and he heard the cackle of the driver's mirth.

"Ourselves, we are not sure of him," the Brother said.

"He has proven himself."

"We are not certain of his determination."

Major Said Hazan wriggled in his chair. He fancied he could still feel the sharpness of her nails in the skin at the small of his back. The skin on his back and down over his buttocks was of an especial sensitivity, because it was from there that the surgeons had taken the live tissue for grafting onto the uncovered flesh of his face. "He was the top student in Simferopol, and in the military academy he showed us the extent of his determination."

The Brother shrugged. It was many years since the Popular Front had been able to take decisions for themselves.

"If you are certain . . ."

"It is what I have decided."

Major Said Hazan went to the door of his office. In the outer office he saw the young Palestinian sitting with his head drooped. He thought the young man seemed tired. He made his pretence of a welcoming smile, he waved Abu Hamid into his office.

"You had a good journey, Hamid?"

"I had a good journey," Abu Hamid muttered.

"You saw the sights of Damascus?"

"I saw the hanged bodies."

Major Said Hazan stretched out his arms, rolled his shoulders. "We are like an old city, Hamid, with enemies at every gate, but if we are ruthless in our struggle our enemies will never scale our walls nor force our gates. Please, Hamid, be seated."

Major Said Hazan took from a cabinet refrigerator a chilled bottle of fruit juice and poured it for Abu Hamid. He went back to his desk, he took from a drawer the plan of the Defence Ministry on Kaplan, and spread it over the surface of the desk. With the heel of the hand that had no fingers he smoothed the plan flat.

"You are a fortunate young man, Hamid. You have been chosen ahead of others. You have been chosen to strike a great blow for your people . . ."

The Brother said, "We ask you to lead an attack into Israel."

Major Said Hazan watched the young man's jaw tremble. He saw that the soles of his boots fretted on the pile of the carpet.

There was a syrup in the voice of Major Said Hazan, "You hesitate, Hamid, of course you hesitate. You wonder to yourself, are your shoulders sufficiently broad to carry the weight of such responsibility? Your immediate concern is whether you have the competence to carry out a mission of this importance . . . Hamid, because you hesitate there might be others who would take such hesitation as a mark of cowardice, not I. Hamid, it is I who have faith in you.

I could not believe that you have less courage than a girl child who would walk against her enemy with a donkey and with explosives."

He saw Abu Hamid's eyes waver, stray to the Brother.

"I would refuse to believe that you had less courage than had Mohammed and Ibrahim, chosen by yourself, for the glory of carrying a bomb onto the Jerusalem bus . . ."

He saw that the young man now held his head in his hands.

". . . Look at me, Hamid, look at my face. I carry the scars of being in the front line of the struggle against Israel. I would not be amongst those who might say that because you hesitate you do not have the courage to follow where I lead . . ."

He saw Abu Hamid's head rise. He held him, eye to eye.

"I know, Hamid, that the money draft of the Central Bank of Syria has never been cashed. I know, too, that in the presence of the orphans of the Palestine revolution you pledged your loyalty to the struggle . . ."

He saw Abu Hamid's eyes gape open. He saw the confusion spread.

"Because I know everything of you, I have chosen you."

"We ask you to lead an assault against the Defence Ministry of the Zionist state," the Brother said.

"You would go from here to the bed of your girl. You are the modern day inheritor of the mantle of the Assassins, Hamid. You are honoured amongst your equals, you are loved by the weak and the young and the aged who cannot fight, but who stand behind you, who pray for you."

"We have to have your answer, Hamid," the Brother said.

"You would go from the bed of your girl, from the perfume of her body . . . There is a clear choice, Hamid. Either you are worthy of the love of your people, or you are branded a coward. You would not prove me wrong, Hamid, I who have trusted you."

Major Said Hazan saw the trance in the eyes of Abu Hamid. He knew that he had won. He wondered why the shit scared bastard took so long to clear away his hesitation. It did not concern him that Abu Hamid would be shit scared when he led his squad against the Defence Ministry in Tel Aviv. No way out, no escape then, a rat under a boot, and the rat would fight. The rat would claw and bite for survival. Shit scared was desperate, shit scared was good. He thought the boy would fight well.

"I will," Abu Hamid said.

It was over. Major Said Hazan said that the Brother could take Abu Hamid for an initial planning briefing, that he should stay the night in Damascus, that he should return to the camp in the Beqa'a and choose ten men who would accompany him into Israel.

Major Said Hazan turned briskly back to his desk. "I have work," he said curtly.

He had eaten only bread in the last 24 hours, he had drunk only water. He was moved in the black boot of a car, his eyes hidden in darkness by the hood, every few hours. He spoke no Arabic, so he did not understand the low voices of his captors. Heinrich Gunter, trussed, strapped, blind, had long since ceased to concern himself with the outside world, the world beyond the boot of a car and the basement of a building. He no longer thought of his wife and his children, nor the actions of his government, nor the position that his bank would have taken. If his hands had been free, if his tie had still been around his throat collar, he would have attempted to end his life. He knew enough to recognise that he was the classic kidnap victim. He was the man who had disregarded the warnings, who had thought that he had arranged the safe passage into the city.

Rolling painfully in the boot of the car Gunter knew the pit depths of despair. He could think of no corner into which he could crawl in his mind, where he would find comfort. He could think of no power to help him. Into the coarse material of the hood he sobbed his tears. He had seen on the television back at home the photographs of the men held hostage. Cheerful, smiling faces from family snapshots and company archives of journalists and business men and priests and academics. He had also seen the photographs of those few who had returned from captivity, haunted men whose cheeks had sunk and whose eyes were buried in dark sockets. The rare few who had been brought out to freedom.

But Gunter no longer cared about the many who were held, or the few who had been freed. He did not believe in the possibility of freedom, he believed only in the blessing of death.

In the middle of the day, when the car had halted, bumped off a road, he was given food. The hood was lifted an inch or two. Bread was fed to him, given him in small pieces, each piece replaced when he had chewed and swallowed.

He had no idea where he might be, what part of Lebanon he was in, and it did not seem to him to matter.

Holt played the chef. It had been a bit of a joke between them that Holt had been allowed to plan the menu for the main meal of the day.

His gut ached with hunger. More of Crane's bible. The bible said it was good to be hungry. If you were hungry you weren't drowsy. If you were drowsy you were halfway to being ambushed.

Crane sat under the scrim netting with his legs folded and his back straight and the binoculars at his face. Holt was on his hands and knees over the hexamine tablets heating in their frame, and on the frame the canteen of water boiled. Crane's bible said that the hexamine tablets were the only source of fire they could use, anything else would give off a smoke signature and a smell signature. Two tablets the size of the firelighter pieces that his mother used at home to get the sitting room logs alight.

They were going to have a hell of a good meal. Had to be a good meal.

God alone knew where they would be in 24 hours' time. Overlooking the camp, that's where they should be all through tomorrow, watching for Abu Hamid on the binoculars. Crane's plan said they should go for a dusk shot. Holt couldn't imagine having much room for stewing up a meal, or much appetite for it, when the time was getting close for action with the Model PM. So a good meal, that afternoon, a long rummage round the Bergen for the ration packs, all that was choice and best in the sachets.

Holt heard the low whistle between Crane's teeth. He looked, he saw Crane had the binoculars away from his face, that his lower lip was bitten white by his upper teeth. Crane saw Holt's attention, relaxed his mouth, returned the binoculars to his eyes. Holt looked away.

It wasn't the first time, nor the second nor the third that Holt could recall the sight of screwed up pain on Crane's forehead, in Crane's eyes, at Crane's mouth. He looked away. He didn't want to look into Crane's face because he was afraid.

It was the best menu he could manage.

Not a prawn cocktail or marinated mackerel for *hors d'oeuvre*, but a sachet of izotonic powder mixed with water to give a lemon-tasting vitamin boost. Not a bisque or a consommé for the soup course, but a short and stubby stick of peperone to chew. Not steak and chips or lamb cutlets for *entrée*, but the boiling water into the plastic sac that held the dehydrated chicken and rice flakes. Not a strawberry flan or a sherry trifle for dessert, but a granola cereal bar that seemed to explode and expand and bulge the mouth full. Not coffee to wash it down, but a brew with a teabag. And a piece of chewing gum to wind up the feast. That added up, Holt reckoned, to a hell of a meal.

He had the powder ready mixed, he had the peperone laid out, he had the granolas ready. When he had mixed the chicken and rice they could get stuck in while the water heated for the tea bags.

Holt looked up. He saw Crane's head, bowed, his eyes closed tight. Shouldn't have bloody looked . . .

"Dinner is served, Mr Crane."

He saw the face snap back to life, saw Crane grin, as if there was no problem.

"Brilliantly done, young Holt."

They ate. Holt was learning from watching Crane. The izotonic drained, and the sachet held upside down over the mouth for the drips, and the peperone lingeringly held on the tongue for the spice taste, and the fingers wiping the remnants of the chicken and rice from the sides of the canteen, the tea drunk.

"What's your problem, Mr Crane?"

Crane twisted his head, as if he were caught on the wrong foot. "I've got no problem."

"Give it to me."

"Being in fucking Lebanon, is that a problem . . . ?"

"If you've got a problem then I've a right to know."

Crane snarled, "Being here with you, that's enough of a problem."

"Mr Crane, we are together and you are in pain. It seems to me you have a pain in your eyes . . ."

"Get the canteens cleaned, get the rubbish stowed."

"If you have a problem with your eyes then I have to help."

Crane was close to him. Holt saw the anger in his face.

"How are you going to help?"

Holt shook his head. "I don't know, but I . . ."

"What do I need eyes for?"

"For everything."

"To shoot, crap kid. I need eyes to shoot. I need eyes that can put me into five inches at a thousand yards."

"What is it with your eyes?"

Crane slumped back. He rubbed the back of his hand across his eyes, like he was trying to gouge something out of them. "Disease of the retina."

"Can you shoot?"

"I shot at the road block."

"You had two hits at the road block."

"I don't know why, truly. Okay, I had two hits, but she wasn't going anywhere. I suppose it didn't matter. Perhaps that's why I had the hits . . ."

"Is that why you took the job, for the money, for treatment?"

"There's a place in Houston. They have a one in five success rate, that's one more than anywhere else. It's my shooting eye, youngster."

"Mr Crane, if you can't shoot, then what's going to happen?"

Holt looked into Crane's right eye. He saw the blood red veins creeping towards the iris.

"Bet your life, Holt, I'll shoot one last time."

Holt wiped out the canteens. He cleared up the rubbish and put it in the plastic bag. He rubbed down the Model PM and the Armalite. He changed the ammunition rounds in the magazines. He felt the light had gone out. He smeared insect repellent cream onto his cheeks and his throat and onto the backs of his hands. He felt that he had been tricked. He took off his boots and peeled down his socks so that he could renew the plasters across his blister. They had given him a man who was over the hill. He let a glucose tablet dissolve in his mouth. He had gone into the Beqa'a with a marksman whose sight was failing. That was a good laugh.

"It's worse, isn't it, worse than it's been before?" Crane nodded.

Inside the perimeter of the base camp at Kiryat Shmona, in a position far removed from the sight of the camp's main gate, were the prefabricated offices used by the Shin Bet. In previous times the principal occupation of the Israeli internal security apparatus had been to watch over the Arab population of the West Bank of the Jordan river. Since the invasion of Lebanon in 1982, the main thrust of Shin Bet work had been in the northern frontier and the security zone. Building had not kept pace with the development of the new and onerous duties. It was as if the prefabricated, sectionalised buildings represented a pious hope that the diversion of resources to matters affecting Lebanon was merely temporary. A hope only. The men of the Shin Bet found their resources absorbed by the fierce thirst for violence and revenge among the Shi'a villagers of the security zone and the countryside to the north. There was no sign that the crowded offices in the base camp would in the near future be emptying.

Major Zvi Dan had left Rebecca outside, left her to sit in the afternoon sunshine on a concrete step. He was in a cubbyhole of a room with three officials of the Shin Bet. He brooded miserably that in their temporary quarters they had failed to install a halfway decent coffee machine.

He was hellishly tired from the drive out of Tel Aviv.

". . . So that is the situation, Major, concerning the Norwegian soldier and the situation concerning the Briton, Martins."

"Martins is mine."

"The case of Private Olaffson is a very delicate matter."

"I don't know what you do. While he is in the UNIFIL area we have no jurisdiction over him, and the UNIFIL command will not respond favourably to a request that he be interrogated."

The senior Shin Bet man tidied his papers together. "This Olaffson, he drove the two Popular Front bombers to Tel Aviv?"

"Confirmed."

"He knew their mission?"

"Probably not, but he would have to have assumed that they were heading towards a terrorist target."

"Then Private Olaffson will have to discover at first hand what is a terrorist target."

Major Zvi Dan was passed the report compiled by the two agents who had tailed Olaffson to the guest house of the Kibbutz Kfar Giladi, who had sat in the bar, who had listened to the conversation between the Norwegian soldier and a member of the British Secret Intelligence Service.

He read fast. He winced.

"Martins I will deal with."

"Friend, you are a warrior of the cause of freedom."

"I only tell you what I heard."

"Repeat it for me, friend."

"He said, 'How did you know about an infiltration team moving off last night?', that was what he said." Hendrik Olaffson spelled it out. He spoke slowly. He gave time for the traveller to write the words on a sheet of paper.

The traveller put away his paper. He took the hands of the young man and he kissed him on each cheek.

"It is worth something?"

"It is worth much," the traveller said. "We will show you our gratitude."

When he had gone, the four soldiers at the checkpoint huddled together. They talked about quantity, they talked of the monies that could be charged for the quantity of hashish that would be supplied as a matter of gratitude.

Far away across the valley, invisible amongst scrub bushes, a photographer bent over the camera on which was mounted a 2000 mm lens and carefully extracted a roll of film. Martins had made himself a prisoner in his room, he had not drawn the curtains back. Through the centre gap he had seen the start of the day and the middle of the day and then the end of the day. It was dark now and he had abandoned his unmade bed and sat cross-legged on the floor, his back against the furthest wall from the door. He knew they would come for him. He wore his suit trousers and his shirt and his socks, and he had not shaved. Though he had eaten nothing during the day he felt no hunger. He was cocooned in pity for himself.

When there came the knock at the door he flinched. Not the chambermaid's inquiring tap, but the thump of a closed fist on the door panel.

He didn't reply.

He watched as the door crashed open, and as the man whose shoulder had been against it lurched into the room. The man wore a leather jacket, scuffed at the wrist and the elbows. He knew the man from somewhere, his jaded memory could not tell him from where. There was another man framed in the doorway. Slowly, Martins pushed himself upright. There were no words necessary. Martins went to his disturbed bed and bent to find his shoes. He wondered if they knew yet at Century. He wondered how many of them would be celebrating his fall from grace.

He walked to the door. As they moved into the corridor the man who wore the leather jacket laid his hand on the sleeve of Martins's shirt and he shook it away.

There was one of the men ahead of him and one behind. He walked free of them. He felt a great tiredness, a great sadness. They went out into the fresh air, onto the fire escape. Martins understood. If he had been the man in the leather jacket he would have done the same.

He was driven to the base camp at Kiryat Shmona. There was a standard procedure used. He had ducked into the back seat of the car and been waved across towards the far door. He knew the door would have a locking device. The man with the leather jacket sat beside him. He thought that this was the way a traitor or a dangerous criminal or a sex offender would be dealt with. He stared straight ahead of him. He shook his head when the man in the leather jacket offered him a cigarette.

Once in the camp he was taken into a small, bare room. He sat at a table. He stared across the surface of the table at Major Zvi Dan. Two men sitting on hard chairs separated from each other by a narrow plastic-topped table. He heard the door close behind him.

Martins thought he had never stared into eyes so filled with contempt.

"Are we to be taped?"

"Of course."

458

"I don't think that's really appropriate."

"Mr Martins, in your position you should not presume to tell me what is appropriate."

"I should not be treated as an enemy agent." He felt the confidence slowly ebbing back to him. He sat straighter in his chair.

"That is how we view you."

"That's preposterous."

Major Zvi Dan spoke very quietly, he spoke as though he were nervous that he might lose control of his temper. "You have behaved like an enemy agent. You have endangered lives."

"Rubbish. I was merely foolish. I drank too much."

"You endangered the lives of Holt and Noah Crane and at the very least you put their mission at risk."

"Quite ludicrous. I was drunk, men get drunk. I was indiscreet, it happens. Whatever I said would have been gobbledygook to that Scandinavian, he wouldn't have understood a word of it."

"You passed information of vital importance to the enemy."

"The enemy?" Martins snorted. "Your sense of the theatrical does you credit, Major. I was talking merely to a private soldier of the NORBAT . . ."

"To an agent of the enemy." There was the appearance on Major Zvi Dan's face that he thought he was talking to an idiot, a retarded creature. He spelled out each word. "A bomb exploded in the central bus station in Tel Aviv, you may remember. Holt and Crane will not have forgotten. Two terrorists were responsible. The terrorists travelled into Israel via the Beqa'a valley in Lebanon . . ."

"Don't give me a yesterday's newspaper lecture."

". . . in Lebanon. They were brought through the UNIFIL sector, through the security zone, across the border, hidden in United Nations transport."

"So?"

"Your private soldier drove that transport."

"God . . ." The breath seeped from Percy Martins.

"Your private soldier, to whom you confided the existence of an infiltration team, is an agent of the enemy."

"Christ . . ." Martins slumped. He felt the looseness in his bowels, a feebleness in his legs. "I don't suppose . . . he didn't understand . . ."

"It is our belief that the information you provided him with is already en route to Damascus."

Martins said, "You cannot know that."

With great deliberation, Major Zvi Dan lifted from the floor a brown paper envelope. From the envelope he spread out on the table a series of photographs. His finger settled on one, and he pushed it towards Martins.

Martins saw the back of the head of the UNIFIL private soldier. He saw a man leaning forward to kiss the cheek of Olaffson.

"It is how they show their gratitude," Major Zvi Dan said.

"I couldn't have had any idea," Martins said.

"You were drunk, you knew nothing." The savage reply.

"What can I do?"

"If you are not too proud to pray, you can pray. You came here in your naïveté to play a game of political chess. You came here to further your career. Now all you can do is to pray for the lives of the men you have criminally endangered."

"Will you tell them in London?"

"That they sent an idiot here? Maybe they are all idiots in London, maybe they all seek to play games."

"What do you propose to do with me?"

"You will be confined in the camp area, where you can do no further damage."

"And afterwards?"

"Afterwards you will live with your shame."

"What have I done?"

"You have confirmed to the Syrians that there is a mission. You have told the Syrians of British interest in that mission. If the Syrians can make an equation between the mission and the killings at Yalta then they will know the target. They will remove the target from view, and also they will ambush your man and my man. If the Syrians make the equation then the mission is lost, our men are lost."

Martins murmured, "God, I am so sorry."

"Pray that the Syrians are as idiotic as you are . . . Myself, I do not think it likely."

There was the scratching of Major Zvi Dan's chair as he stood up. The door opened. The two men led Martins away to confinement, his head sagging.

They had studied the map, they had covered the trail they would use and the position of the rally points.

"How long tonight?"

"Eight hours."

"And then the camp?"

"In eight hours we should be above the camp, youngster."

"How are the eyes?"

"Just stick to worrying about yourself, whether you'll recognise the target. I don't need your worry."

"You should come back with me, Mr Crane, afterwards, back to England."

"You talk too much, Holt."

"I've done nothing in my life. If I'd done everything you've done in your life there's nothing I'd want more than to go away, bury myself, live on the moor, walk beside the rivers, know the peace of where I live. I haven't earned that peace, Mr Crane. You have."

"Is it that good there?" Crane asked.

"You could walk free. The animals are free, the people are free, the light and the air are wonderful. No rifles, no fighter bombers, no bloody minefields, you deserve that peace, Mr Crane. Will you think about it?"

"Might just."

They had the Bergens high on their backs. Holt let Crane get fifteen yards ahead, then moved out after him. The start of the last night march.

As a matter of routine, Major Said Hazan received in the early evening a report covering the previous 24-hour period as prepared by army headquarters at Chtaura. He read every detail of the report, as he always did. Far down in the list he read that a patrol in position west and south of the Beqa'a village of Aitanit had fired flares in response to unidentified movement further west of them. The report stated that a follow-up search in daylight centred on an animal track, but had failed to provide evidence that would justify further sweep searches of the area.

The major went to his wall map. He put a red-headed pin into the map over the area of the UNIFIL sector through which it had been reported that an infiltration had been made. He drove in another red-headed pin at the point of the unconfirmed contact with the patrol. He stood back. He extended a line from the infiltration point to the supposed contact. They were going north, the shortest possible route into the foothills on the west side of the Beqa'a.

In the valley, marked on his map, were the camps of 18 different Syrian army concentrations, and in addition the camps of the Popular Front, the Democratic Popular Front, the Abu Moussa faction, the Sai'iqa group, the Popular Struggle Front. There were also the villages used by the Hezbollah, and the houses occupied by the men of Islamic Jihad. There were the communities that played host to the revolutionary guards who had sat in the Beqa'a unmoving after their despatch from Iran. In all, indicated on his map, there were 43 locations that could prove of interest to an infiltration team of the enemy.

At the moment he was helpless. But he was a man of patience.

In the camp the cook's fire guttered. The cook thought that in the morning he would use the last of his wood to prepare the breakfast, that he would spend the morning scavenging for more.

17

It was a crisp, sharp night.

The heat of the day had dissipated into the rocky slopes. In the night there was a fresh wind that caught at the sweat that ran in rivers on the throat and chest of young Holt. The pace of the night march was no greater and no less than it had been on the two previous nights, but he sweated, as he thought, like a pig. The pace of the night march remained, give or take a few yards or a few minutes, at one mile in one hour. The going should have been easier because each man was lighter from the consumption of water, close to a half of the water had been used, but still he sweated in the cool of the night march. He felt as if, along with the perspiration, the strength oozed from his body. When they reached there, when they were on the high ground overlooking the tent camp, Holt thought he would be reduced to a wrung out rag. There were no more kicked stones, there were no cracked twig branches, there was no scuffling through sun crisped leaves. Each step was concentration, each short checked stride was care.

Crane was a shape ahead of him. It was a blurred shape that only came to life at the rally points when Crane stopped and squatted and Holt reached him to slump beside him. They did not speak at the first rally points of the night. They sat and allowed their leg muscles to soften and Holt let his mind wander from the concentration and care and exhaustion of the march. There were no words, no whispers, because Holt did not have to be told that they were now deep behind the lines. It was all in his head, it had all been told him and was remembered. They were moving north on the hill slopes between the valley floor and the peaks of the Jabal al Barouk. On the Jabal al Barouk was a state-of-the-art Soviet-built complex of radar dishes and antennae manned by the Syrian air force. Sensitive country. The dishes and antennae were protected from surprise attack. Scattered round the air defence and signals listening equipment would be, according to Crane's bible text, the GS–13 divisional level surveillance radars operating from 50 kW power packs and with a twelve kilometre competence to detect personnel and a 25 kilometre range for seeing the movement of vehicles. Moving on the slopes above the valley and below the installations on the summit of Jabal al Barouk, Crane led Holt in darted spurts as a sailor would tack before the wind. They changed the angle of their progress every fifty, sixty, yards, as if by that manœuvre Crane believed he could throw the attention of a drowsing ground surveillance radar screen operator. Of course, it would have been faster to have moved lower down onto the gentler slopes of the valley sides, but Crane had explained at the last lying up position that further behind the Syrian positions the risk increased of blundering into mine fields, of drifting into the wadis where the anti-personnel mines would be set around the heavy pressure anti-armour concentrations. That night, on the marches between the rally points, Holt learned much. He learned of the methods of evasion from the dishes of ground surveillance radar, and of the way in which the cover of the terrain could be used to prevent discovery of their progress at the hands of thermal imagery equipment. He learned of the hazard of a low flying aircraft, droning above them without even navigation lights, when Crane had plotted the aircraft's path and scuttled to get clear of its flight line in case it carried infra-red targetting screens.

They moved on. Holt could not assess the threat. He could only remember the warnings that had been given him in a gravel whisper before they had left the lying up position. They lurched from rally point to rally point. The exhaustion spread through Holt's legs, through his back, through his shoulders. His recovery in the short breaks at the rally points became steadily less restorative.

He understood why the exhaustion seeped through him . . . He was helpless . . . He was led on and on by a man with disease clawing at the retina of his right eye. He was with a marksman who had taken a contract in order to finance a one in five chance operation to reverse the decline in the sight of the shooting eye. He himself was blind, his king's good eye was done for . . . and he had to live with it. In the first part of that night's march, up to the first rally point, he had felt a bursting anger towards Crane. The anger was gone, knocked away by the tiredness in his legs, the soreness of his feet. He felt a sort of sympathy. But it was bloody pointless, feeling sympathy for Crane. Sympathy was no salve for the disease in the retina.

They went west and high to bypass the village of Ain Zebde. They would climb to avoid the village town of Khirbet Qanafar. Beyond the glow of Khirbet Qanafar, two and a half miles ahead, they would come down the hill slope until they overlooked the tent camp.

It was late into the evening.

The city was a mysterious place of flickering headlights and of candle-thrown shadows.

Another power cut in Damascus. The cutting of the electricity supplies was more frequent that month, a cut that would last five hours and there was nothing remarkable in that. The traffic moved through a wraithlike haze of exhaust fumes. The cafés were lit by the wavering flames of the candles. Abu Hamid saw that few of the cafés had lanterns lit. There was a shortage of oil for the power station, also a shortage of paraffin for the public.

His mind was bent by the weight of detail forced upon him by the Brother. Through the afternoon, through the evening, he had listened and attempted to absorb the attack plan against the Defence Ministry on Kaplan as described to him by the Brother. He had been allowed to write nothing down, everything he had been told had to be committed to memory. He knew the numbers of the men involved. He knew the fire power they would carry. He knew the harbour from Cyprus out of which he would sail, he knew the times of the tide changes that would dictate the time of sailing. He knew the speed at which the coastal tramp ship would travel. He knew of the diversionary tactic that had been planned to draw away the patrolling missile boats. He knew of the two closed vans that sympathisers would drive to the shore line at Palmahim, south of Tel Aviv. He knew of the driving time from the shore line to the buildings on Kaplan. He knew of the defences of the ministry complex.

Through the cacophony of the horns, through the darkened traffic lights, through the swirling crowds of the *souq*, the jeep pressed its way towards the alley.

The jeep shuddered to a halt. The headlights lit a drover who flailed at the back of a horse that refused to pull further a cart laden with vegetables. From the way the horse refused to ground its left front hoof, Abu Hamid thought the horse to be lame. The jeep driver was shouting at the drover. The drover was shouting at his horse. He slipped open his door. He slammed the door shut after him. He was gone into the night, into the flow of the crowds. He was no longer the Palestinian who had been chosen to sail onto the beach at Palmahim which was south of the city of Tel Aviv. He was no longer the man on whose forehead the spot of the martyr had been painted. He could have turned, he could have cut into the narrow lanes. He could have fled. He was a moth, the alley was the lamp, the woman was the light.

When he knocked at the door, she opened it to him. She wore the loose dress of an Arab woman.

He saw the soft whiteness of the skin on her throat. He saw the curved fullness of her breasts and of her hips. He saw the hands that reached for his face in welcome.

She was Margarethe Anneliese Schultz.

At Wiesbaden in the Federal Republic of Germany, in the computerised records section of the *Bundesamt für Verfassungsschutz*, the printout directly relating to her history, biography and activities would, on a continuous roll of paper, stretch to 235 inches. That part of the Federal Internal Security Office devoted in its work to the destruction of urban guerrilla movements inside the state was indeed familiar with Margarethe Anneliese Schultz.

She was now 33 years of age. She had been born the only daughter of a pastor serving a small community a few kilometres to the north of Munich. As an only daughter she had been a spoilt and privileged child. Early in her life she had learned the art of winning her way either by tantrums or by sweet smiles. Within the budget of her parents' household her every whim had been granted.

Excellent grades in her final school examinations led to her admission as a student of social sciences to the Free University of West Berlin. Her father had a married cousin living in the city. Her father had believed that it would be a good thing for the young girl to continue her education away from home, while at the same time remaining under the eye of the family. It had been the summer of 1974 when Margarethe Anneliese Schultz had left home with her two suitcases to take a train to Frankfurt, and another train to West Berlin. That late summer the Federal Republic recovered from the excesses brought on by victory in the World Cup soccer tournament, and awaited the death of a judge shot dead at his front door, and the death of Holger Meins from self-inflicted starvation, and the sentencing of Ulrike Meinhof.

From the day they waved their goodbye, as the long distance express train pulled away from the platform at Munich's *Hauptbahnhof*, Doktor and Frau Schultz had not set eyes on their beloved daughter. One letter only had been received by them, written a week after her arrival in West Berlin. Margarethe Anneliese Schultz had within a month of her arrival in West Berlin dropped out of her course, dropped into underground cover. She had been recruited into a cell of a Red Army faction that sought to revive the drive of armed insurrection on behalf of an oppressed proletariat as first initiated by Ulrike Meinhof and Andreas Baader and Jan-Carl Raspe and Gudrun Ensslin and Holger Meins. In a world of heady excitement she became a part of the small core of revolutionaries living in sympathisers' apartments, stretching her legs to the newest young man who carried a Firebird 9 mm Parabellum pistol, eating in restaurants on the proceeds of bank robberies, moving in stolen BMWs and Mercedes saloons.

Her parents had reported her missing to the Munich city police.

Eight months after she had left them, men of the "PoPo", the political police, had called on the pastor, had interviewed him in the living room of his home, and after 35 minutes had left him in prayer on his knees and with the comfort of his wife.

The pastor's daughter was a bank robber. The pastor's sweet child had driven the getaway car from a robbery in which a policeman had been fatally shot. The pastor's angel was on the list of those hunted by the political police, the criminal police and the security police.

Her induction had been through a working circle, photography. It had been her initial role to photograph targets for assassination, targets for bombing. Her hand was steady. Her photographs were crystal sharp in focus. The years passed. The Red Army faction slaughtered the high and the mighty of the state. The capitalist exploiters were cut down. Chief Federal Prosecutor Siegfried Buback, executed. Chief Executive of the Dresdner Bank Jurgen Ponto, executed. Military attaché to the FRG embassy in Stockholm, Baron von Mirbach, executed. President of the Federation of Industries Hanns-Martin Schleyer, executed. The government stood firm. The killings did not win the freedom of the founding fathers and mothers of the movement. There was a week when despair became a plague. A Lufthansa holiday jet hijacked to Mogadishu in the African state of Somalia was retaken by the intervention of the *Grenzschutz Gruppe Neun*. The principal imprisoned activists hanged or shot themselves in their cells. The movement sagged under the failure of action and the loss of the star participants. Margarethe Anneliese Schultz, her face on the wanted posters, her name on the charge sheet of a Federal court, her future likely to be 20 years behind bars, drove into Switzerland, took a train to Italy, bought an airline ticket to Damascus.

She threw off the cause of the bovine proletariat of her homeland, she embraced the cause of the Palestinian people. She was careful with her favours, she dispensed them only where they could be of advantage to her.

She had sought out a protector, a man of such influence that she would not be repatriated to the maximum security women's prisons of West Germany.

He was a repulsive bastard, the major in Syrian Air Force Intelligence, but he had influence. She warmed his bed. She worked hard to please him. In obedience to the wishes of Major Said Hazan, she had, many months before, given herself to a young Palestinian fighter of the Popular Front.

The pendant hung at her neck.

The pendant was a sapphire held by a fastening crescent of diamonds.

The pendant hung at her neck from a gold chain of close, fine links.

He heard the words. The drooled words slipping from the rebuilt mouth of Major Said Hazan ... "in the presence of the orphans of the Palestine revolution you pledged your loyalty to the struggle" ... He heard the words that had been used to taunt him.

The chain that supported the pendant lay on the smooth skin of her throat.

She was kissing his mouth, and the lobes of his ears. She told him of her love. The flatness of her stomach undulated against his groin. The warmth of her breasts drifted through the cotton of his shirt.

Abu Hamid, standing just inside the room, leaning back against the closed door, hearing the muffled raucous sounds of the *souq*, knew that he would kill the girl he had loved.

He was calm. He felt no fear. It was not as it had been when the woman who was a spy for the Israelis had gazed back in contempt into his face. It was as it had been when he had gone to seek out the man who had stolen his transistor radio. It was as it had been when he had eased himself up from the bench outside the Oreanda Hotel, when he had walked, filtering between the traffic, towards the hotel steps. As it had been when he had raised the assault rifle to confront the old man and the young woman pushing through the glass swing doors.

Major Said Hazan had played with him as a child. The toy that had won him had been the breasts and the cleft of Margarethe Schultz. He held her in his arms. He smelled the cleanness of her hair and the dry pleasure of her body.

"I love you, brave boy."

"As you love him?" Abu Hamid murmured from the pit of his throat.

"I love you for your courage, brave boy."

466

She arched her head upwards, she stretched to kiss his forehead. Her neck was pulled taut. The pendant seemed to him to dance on her skin, and the candlelight caught the kingfisher brilliance of the sapphire and flashed upon the wealth of the diamonds.

"As you love him?"

He held the back of her head in his left hand, the fingers tight into the looseness of her hair. He held the back of her neck in his right hand, the fingers twined into the slender strength of the chain.

"I love only you, brave boy."

She had not looked into his face. She had not seen his eyes. She had not seen the smile curve at his lips. He thought of her cheeks against the reconstructed atrocity that was the face of Major Said Hazan. He thought of the fingerless hand groping to the smoothness of the skin of her thighs.

The fingers of his left hand that were tight in her hair jerked Margarethe Schultz's head back. He saw the shock sweep into her eyes. With his right hand he tore the pendant from her throat, snapping the chain clasp on her neck. He bent her head down so that it was lower than the level of his waist, so that she could see only his feet. In front of her, between her bare feet, between his boots, he dropped the pendant. He stamped on the sapphire, on the diamonds of the crescent. He thought of how she had shamed him from taking money, how she had burnt the letter from the Central Bank of Syria. She had taken a pendant of sapphire and diamonds, she had taken the body of Major Said Hazan. He ground with his heel into the carpet. He heard the wincing gasp of her breath as he moved his foot aside, forced her head lower so that she could see the shattered pendant.

She had taken the love of Abu Hamid. She had taken his pledge that he would go into Israel, take the war into Israel, take his death into Israel.

When he pulled her head up, when she could look into his face, she spat.

She snarled, "You are scum . . . You are not even a good fuck, not even as good as him . . ."

He saw her eyes bulging towards him. He saw the blue sheen at her lips. He saw her fingers scrabble to hold his wrists. He saw her tongue jumping from her mouth.

When he let go of her throat, when she slid to the carpet, he crouched over her.

He could hear the choking of his tears. He lay across her. He could feel the wetness of her skin where his tears fell.

Percy Martins was on his bed.

It was hours since he had walked around the bare room. He had only had to walk round once to understand the nature of his confinement. Behind the curtains over the windows he had found the metal bars. He had noted that there was no light through the keyhole of the door. He had heard the coughing of a man in the corridor.

He was on his bed.

He was close to sleep when he was roused into alertness by the muffle of voices behind the door. He heard the rasp of the turning key. He sat upright on his bed.

It was the girl, Zvi Dan's assistant, Rebecca. She carried a mug of tea. He could see that it was freshly made, that it steamed in her hand. She passed him the mug.

"That's uncommonly civil of you."

"It is nothing."

"Why?"

"I thought you had been kicked, I thought they were queuing to kick you again. There were plenty of them in line to kick you."

"People like to kick a fool, when a fool is down." Martins drank the tea, scalded the roof of his mouth.

"Kicking you does not help Holt."

He gazed into her face.

"I suppose it's stupid to ask, but there hasn't been any news?"

"There could only be news from the Syrian radio. We are monitoring their transmissions, there has been nothing on their radio."

Martins slumped back onto his bed. "The waiting, it's so bloody awful, waiting for news of catastrophe, and for the inevitability of disgrace."

"What are your feelings for Holt?"

"He's one of the finest young men I've ever met, and I never got round to telling him."

She turned away, went out through the door. He heard the key turn. He lay in the darkness and sipped at the hot sweetness of the tea.

With three men to escort him Heinrich Gunter stumbled, tripped through the darkness over the rough ground on the slope of the hillside.

He was handcuffed to one man.

He had been given back his shoes, but they rubbed and calloused his feet and it was more years than he could remember since he had last worn lace up shoes without socks. He had been given back his shoes, but they had retained his shirt and his suit jacket and his trousers. He wore his vest and his underpants that now smelled and over his shoulder was draped a coarse cloth blanket.

Where they had left the car, his photograph had been taken. All very quick, and he had hardly been aware of the process. The hood had been snatched up from over his face, the light had blasted him. Time for him to identify the gun barrel that had been the sharp pain under his chin, and the face mask of the one who held a camera level with his eyes. Two workings of the camera, and the flash, and the hood retrieving the darkness and falling. The taking of his photograph had disturbed him. As if the photograph brought him back towards a world that he understood, a world of ransom demands and bribery, and of newspaper headlines and radio bulletins, and of the government in

Bonn, and of the helplessness of the world that he knew. The taking of the photograph had forced his mind to his family, his wife and his children, and his home. Forced him to think of his wife sitting numb in their home and of the dazed confusion of his children.

It was easier for him when he was in their world, not his own, when he lived the existence of his captors. Their world was the gun barrel and the handcuffs, taking a hooded hostage across the rough sloping ground below the Jabal al Barouk.

Crane froze.

Holt, behind him, had taken three more steps before he registered Crane's stillness.

Crane held the palm of his hand outstretched, fingers splayed, behind his back, so that Holt could see the warning to stop.

It was the fifth hour of the night march. Holt was dead on his feet. The moon, falling into the last quarter, threw a silver light on them.

Crane, very slowly, sunk to his knees and haunches. A gentle movement, taking an age to go down.

Holt followed him. The Bergen straps cut into his shoulders. Pure, blessed relief, to sink low and not to have to jar the Bergen on his back.

Crane turned his head, his hand flicked the gesture for Holt to come forward.

Holt sensed the anxiety growing in his body. When Crane had first stopped he had been walking as an automaton, no care other than not to disturb a loose stone or tread on a dried branch. Gone from him, the sole concentration on his footfall. He came forward, he strained his eyes into the grey-black stillness ahead, he saw nothing. He found that his hands were locked tight on the stock of the Model PM and the bloody thing was not even loaded and the flash eliminator at the end of the barrel was still covered with the dirt-stained condom. Hell of a great deal of use young Holt would be in defending the position . . . He was close to Crane, crouched as he moved, close enough for Crane to reach back and with strength force him lower.

Crane had him down, pushed Holt so that he lay full length on the narrow track.

Holt heard the stone roll ahead of them. A terrible quiet was in him, the breath stifled in his throat. A stone was kicked ahead of him. They shared the path. So bloody near to the tent camp, and they shared the track. Crane was reaching for his belt, hand moving at glacier speed.

They shared the bloody path. All the tracks in south Lebanon, all the trails running on the hill slopes of the west side of the Beqa'a, and they, by God, shared it. Holt breathed out, tried to control himself, tried not to pant.

He heard the voices, clear, as if they were beside him.

Words that he did not understand, a foreign language, but a message of anger.

He could see nothing, but the voices carried in the night quiet.

A guttural accent, speaking English, seeking communication.

"I cannot see, I cannot know what I hit."

"More careful."

"But I cannot see . . ."

Holt heard the impact of a kick. He heard the gasp, muffled, then the sob.

"I cannot see to walk."

A noise ahead as if a weight were dragged, and new voices, Arabic, urging greater pace. Holt did not understand the words, knew the meaning.

Crane had the pocket night sight to his eye. He rarely used it. Crane's bible said that reliance on a night sight was dangerous, hard to switch back and forth between a night sight and natural night vision. They were making as much noise ahead as Holt had conjured up on the first of the night march tests in the Occupied Territories – so bloody long ago, back in the time before history books.

Holt thought the man who complained, who could not see, might be German or Austrian or Swiss German. There was a stampede of stones away from the path, and the sound of another kicking, and the sound of another whimper. He thought they were moving faster, he thought the noises moved away.

Holt waited on Crane.

He heard the call of a hyena above. He heard the barking of a dog behind and below from among the village lights of Ain Zebde. He waited on Crane.

Methodically, as was his way, Crane replaced the pocket night sight in the pouch on his belt.

"It's a European," Crane whispered.

"What's a European doing . . . ?"

"God, didn't you learn adding at school? There are three hoods with a European prisoner on our track. A European, with a bag over his head, who cannot see where he's going, with Arabs, that adds to the movement of a hostage."

"A hostage . . ." Holt repeated the word, seemed to be in awe of the word.

"Moving a hostage on my bloody route." A savageness in Crane's whisper.

"What do we do?"

"Keep going, have to."

"Why, have to?"

"Because, youngster, we have a schedule. We have an appointment. We have to move behind them, and move at their pace. I don't have the time to lie up. And I'm better keeping them in sight, I'm better knowing where they are."

"A hostage?"

"That's what I said."

"Definitely a hostage?"

"He's tied to one of them. He's got a European accent. He's short of trousers, just a blanket over him. We're in an area of Syrian control, so they move him at night. They'll be from Islamic Jihad or Hezbollah, they don't trust the shit Syrians any more than I do . . . Don't kick any bloody stone, youngster."

470

Carefully, with so much care, Holt pushed himself upright. He stood. All the time he could hear the fading sounds of movement ahead. He let Crane move off, get the fifteen paces in front. He struggled to ease the pressure of the straps on his shoulder.

Best foot forward, on a shared path.

He could not help himself. He should have concentrated solely on each footfall. There should have been nothing else in his mind, no chaff, no clutter, nothing other than the weight of the ball of his foot testing for the loose stone, for the dried branch, for the crisped leaf.

The chaff and the clutter in his mind were the thoughts of love and vengeance.

He had told his girl, his Jane Canning who was the personal assistant to the military attaché, that he loved her. A long time ago, he had told his girl that he loved her. His girl was ashes, he did not even know where the parents of his girl had scattered her ashes. Too distant from them to know whether they had taken her ashes to a sea shore or taken them to a heathland of heather flowers or taken them to the serenity of a woodland. His girl was ashes, gone, dust, earth. So many things that he could remember of her. Meeting in the canteen at the School of East European and Slavonic Studies and thinking she was stunning. Waiting for her when she was late and the tryst was the pavement outside the Odeon cinema in Leicester Square and hoping to God that she hadn't stood him up. Coming to her own bachelor girl flat, with a bunch of freesias and a bottle of Beaujolais and wondering whether he would get back to his own place before the end of the weekend. Holding her and kissing her when she had told him that she had landed Moscow for a posting, and wasn't it marvellous because he was headed there in a few weeks' time, and cursing that for those few weeks he would be without her and she would be without him. Scowling at her because she had put him down for ever and ever, amen, in the corridor of the Oreanda Hotel in Yalta . . .

"Don't be childish, Holt."

He had told his minder, his Mr Martins who worked the Middle East Desk of the Secret Intelligence Service, that he wanted vengeance. Bloody light years ago. He would know the man that they called Abu Hamid the moment that he could focus the lenses of the binoculars upon him. No doubt. He had seen the man they called Abu Hamid for nine, ten seconds. He didn't believe he would ever forget the face and the crow's foot scar. Bloody light years ago he had wanted vengeance, he had told Martins that he wanted the eye and the tooth, both. He thought that his desire for vengeance was sapped, he thought that he had simply never had the guts to walk away from Mr Martins in England, to walk away from Mr Crane in Israel. He thought that he was on the west slopes of the Beqa'a because he had never had the guts to turn his back on something as primitive as vengeance. He thought that he would in no way benefit from the sniping of Abu Hamid. He knew that nothing would change for Jane, nor for her parents either, even if they would ever know. And would anything change for him?

"I'd want him killed."

They were at the seventh rally point of the night.

It was where Crane had told him they would spend the few minutes of rest. An exact man was Crane, each rally point reached on time, the perfect instrument of vengeance.

Holt huddled against Crane. The wind caught at the sweat running on his body and chilled him.

"Can I talk?"

"Whisper, youngster."

"Where are they?"

"Ahead, perhaps a quarter of a mile."

"And it's a hostage?"

"What I reckon."

Holt swallowed hard. He caught at the sleeve of Crane's tunic shirt.

"He's more valuable."

"Riddles, youngster."

"A hostage is more valuable than sniping Abu Hamid."

"You know what you're saying?"

"There is more value in bringing back a hostage alive than in leaving Abu Hamid dead behind us."

"I didn't hear that." Crane tugged his sleeve clear.

"To bring back a hostage alive, that is a genuine act of mercy."

"Then you're forgetting something, youngster."

"I am not forgetting a fellow human being in danger."

"Forgetting something big."

"What is bigger than rescuing a man from that sort of hell?"

"Your promise, that's what you're forgetting."

"A hostage is alive, a hostage is an innocent . . ."

Crane turned away, his voice was soft and cut the edge of the night wind. "I gave my word, youngster. I don't play skittles with a promise."

"A hostage is worth saving. Is Abu Hamid worth killing?"

"I gave my promise. Pity you don't see that that's important."

"They aren't worth it, the people who've got your promise."

"Time to move."

"A hostage's freedom is worth more than your promise."

"I said it was time to move."

Holt stood.

If I ever get out of this I'll hate you, Mr Crane, for abandoning a hostage."

"If you ever get out of this, youngster, it'll be because of my promise . . . Just stop pissing in the wind."

Crane searched the ground ahead with the pocket night sight. They moved off. The gap between them materialised. Holt could hear the distant sounds ahead of the progress of a hostage and his captors. To the east of them, below them, was the village town of Khirbet Qanafar. They went quiet, traversing the slope side of the valley wall. When they next stopped they would be at the lying up position overlooking the tent camp.

*

472

In the village town of Khirbet Qanafar the merchant lay on a rope bed and snored away the night hours.

Many years before, when he had first forsaken his lecture classes at Beer Sheba and moved into his clandestine life in Lebanon, he had found sleep hard to come by, he had felt the persistent fear of discovery. No longer; he slept well covered by a blanket that he fancied had come from the headman's own bed.

Beside the chair on which were laid his outer clothes, the merchant had spread out two plastic bags of the sort that were used to carry agricultural fertiliser. On these empty bags he had laid all the working parts of the pump engine that brought up water from one of Khirbet Qanafar's three irrigation wells. He had dismantled the pump engine during the late afternoon and early evening, then he had eaten with the headman and the headman's sons. In the morning, after he had woken and washed and fed, he would begin to reassemble the pump engine. He knew the reassembly would take him many hours, perhaps most of the day. He knew that in the dusk of the following day he would still be at Khirbet Qanafar. It was all as he had planned it. Crane would snipe at dusk. He slept easily, he was in position, as he had been told to be.

But how much longer, how many more years, could a university lecturer play the part of a merchant in spare parts for electrical engines and sleep in the bed of an enemy?

When he felt the softness of her body turn to cold, Abu Hamid rose to his feet.

The candle had gone, but the electricity supply was restored and light was thrown into the room from the alley way.

She lay at his feet. Only an awkwardness about the tilt of her throat and the lie of her head.

He went to the window. He edged the thin curtains aside. He saw the jeep parked at the end of the alley. There was the auburn glow of the driver's cigarette.

He had been briefed on the plan for the attack against the Defence Ministry on Kaplan. They asked him for his life, and for the lives of the men who would travel with him. Of course, they would watch over him.

He lay on her bed. He smelled the perfume of the sheets and the pillows. He remembered the small, groping hands of the boy child she had placed with gentleness on his shoulder.

Heinrich Gunter was pushed down onto his hands and his knees. As he propelled himself forward over the rough rock floor he sensed the damp mustiness of the cave.

*

All according to Crane's bible. They moved through the lying up position then doubled back to circle it.

They settled. Away below them were the lights of the camp, and the chugging drive of the generator carried up to their high ground.

18

Flooding it with gold light, the dawn slipped over the rim of the far valley wall.

It was as if the valley exploded in brilliance, with the low beams of the sun's thrust catching the lines and colours of the Beqa'a. At dawn, at a few minutes before six o'clock, the valley was a place of quiet beauty. The sun caught the clean geometric lines of the irrigation channels, it flowed over the delicate green shades of the early growth of barley and wheat, it bathed the rough strength of the grey yellow rock outcrops, it glinted on the red tile roofs of Khirbet Qanafar, it shone on the corrugated iron roofs of a commando camp. The sun laced onto the windscreen of a travelling car. The sun pushed down long shadows from the bodies of a flock of sheep driven by a child towards the uplands of the valley to the plateau where it would be cooler when the sun was high. The sun burnished the scrubbed whiteness of a flag that carried in its centre an outline of the Zionist state that was overpainted with crossed rifles with fixed bayonets.

And the sun, striking out, gave a shape to the conical tents of the camp.

The camp was no surprise, it was familiar from the aerial photographs.

There was the wire perimeter. There was the antitank ditch. There was the cluster of large sleeping tents. There was the latrine screen. There were the holes in the ground of the air raid pits, and of the armoury. There was the tent of the commander, set aside. There was the roof above the cooking area.

The generator had been switched off at the first surge of daylight, as if light were only needed as a protection against the dangers of the night. A complete silence at the tent camp. The only movement was the turn and wheel and casual stamp of the sentry at the entrance to the camp, and the hustling of the cook as he revived the fire after the night, and the drift towards the sun orb of the wavering smoke column, and the flag fluttering out the emblem of the Popular Front.

Above the camp, at a place where the steeper sides of the valley wall flattened out to offer a more gentle slope to the floor of the Beqa'a, the ancient ice age movements had left a gouged-out overhang of rock. The space under the lip of the protruding rock was shallow, not more than three feet deep, but the overhang ran some ten feet in length. The overhang was unremarkable. In the half mile or so to either side of this particular formation there were another nine similar devastations of the general line of the ground fall.

The overhang of rock was the place chosen by Crane for the final lying up position.

Crane asleep.

Holt on watch.

The sun lifted clear of the Jabal Aarbi on the east side of the Beqa'a. It was extraordinary for Holt how fast the cleanness of the light began to diffuse into haze. The sun was climbing. He tugged his watch out from under his tunic top, checked the time. Crane was sleeping well, like he needed to sleep. He would liked to have left Crane to sleep longer, to have the chance to rest the eye and to bring back strength into his muscles and calm into his mind. The watch was the taskmaster. He would be chewed out if he allowed Crane to sleep beyond his allotted time. He touched Crane's shoulder. Since they had reached the lying up position he had slept for an hour, and Crane had slept for an hour. But the sun was now up, and the camp was stirring. He could not think when they would next sleep.

Crane awoke.

God, and did he do it easily? For Holt it was a miracle of the world, Crane waking. A fast rub of the eye, half of a stifled yawn, a vicious scratch at the armpit, a scowl and a grin, and Crane was awake.

There were small figures moving from the tents, there was the first tinkle of a transistor radio playing music and travelling against the wind.

"Did you sleep all right?"

"I slept fine . . . what's moving?"

"Starting to be shit-shower-shave time down there. You know, Mr Crane, it's fantastic, us being here, them being there. I mean, it's what you said would happen, but until I was here perhaps I didn't ever quite believe it."

"You think too much, youngster, that's the problem of education."

"How's the eye?"

"Worry about yourself."

Holt heard the pitch of Crane's voice drop, he saw him turn away. Crane's tongue was rolling inside his cheeks, like he was cleaning his teeth with his tongue, like the action was a toothpaste substitute.

"What else is moving?"

"A boy over there with sheep, there . . ." Holt pointed to his right, through the scrim net that masked them. "Bit of traffic on the road. Nothing else. When do I start looking?"

The binoculars were in Crane's Bergen. Crane shook his head. "Think about it, youngster. Where's the sun? The sun's straight into us. You put the glasses up and you'll risk burning your eyes out, and you'll risk a lens flash. Neither's clever. You don't do any looking till the sun's a hell of a lot higher. Patience, youngster."

"Mr Crane . . ."

"Yeah."

"Mr Crane, what happened to the hostage?"

There was a tremor of annoyance across Crane's mouth. "What's it to you?"

"I just wanted to know."

"Are you going to make a thing about it, are you going to puke over me?"

"What happened to him?"

Crane whispered, "There's a cave a quarter of a mile back, that's where they went. We passed about a hundred yards higher. I'd say it's where they're going to hold him. Sometimes it's Beirut where they hold them, sometimes it's out in the Beqa'a . . . would be better in Beirut, won't be a hotel out here."

"Mr Crane . . ."

"Yeah."

"When we've sniped, when we're heading back . . ."

"No."

"Nothing we can do?"

"You want to get home, or you want to die? If you want to go home you walk right past the cave, if you want to die you call for tea and scones . . . Sorry, youngster."

Holt hung his head, his words were a murmur, the wind in the scrim netting. "Seems dreadful to leave him."

"Heh, Alexander the Great came through here, Nebuchadnezzar was here, the Romans had a go at it. There were the Crusaders and the Turks and the French and the Yanks and the Syrians, and my people had a try at it. Everyone's had a go at civilising this place, and Lebanon saw them all off. That's just fact, that's not education. And it's fact that you can't change things, Holt, not on your little educated own. You can't change a damned thing . . . forget him."

"It's rotten to turn our backs on him."

Crane looked for a moment keenly at Holt, didn't speak. He untied the laces of his boots, then pulled the laces tighter through the eyes and made a double bow. From a pouch in the Bergen he took a strip of chewing gum. He lifted the Armalite onto his lap. Holt watched him. Crane had his face against the netting and his eyes roved across the vista in front, down towards the camp. Crane's hand settled on Holt's shoulder.

"You'll be all right, youngster."

Holt gagged. "What are you doing?"

"Scouting, going to find myself a hide further down."

"You said that where we'd be lying up would be 1,000 yards."

"I want six hundred," Crane said.

"Is it the eye?"

"I just want six hundred."

"Can't you do it at a thousand?"

"Leave it, Holt." Close to a snarl.

Holt shook his head, didn't believe it. According to Crane's bible there should be no movement by daylight. According to Crane's text not even an idiot tried to move across open ground after dawn, before dusk. According to Crane's chapter the team never split. According to Crane's verse a thousand yards was best for the sniper. He couldn't argue. He stared at Crane. It was as if his fear, wide eyed, softened Crane.

"I'm not gone long, an hour, may be a little more. In an hour you start to use the glasses ... They're all shit down there, they can't see their assholes right now. On my own, just myself, a buzzard overhead won't see me. I find the place at 600 yards, and I'm back. You spot the bastard for me, we mark him, we follow him, we get to know him. Late afternoon, sun's going down, sun's behind us, sun's into them, that's when I move again. One shot at 600. I stay put, you stay put, till it's dark. I come back for you, and we move out ... Got it, youngster?"

"Got it, Mr Crane." There was a reed in Holt's voice, like he was a child, afraid to be alone.

The scrim netting was slowly lifted, and then Crane was gone.

There was a crag boulder to the right of the overhang, and Holt saw the shape of Crane, his outline broken by the camouflage tabs, reach the boulder.

He did not see him afterwards.

Holt screwed his eyes tight. He peered down onto the desolate and feature-less ground between himself and the tent camp and he could not find a movement. He could not credit that Noah Crane, on that landscape, had vanished.

Fawzi blinked in the sunlight. He stretched, he yawned, he pulled his trouser belt tighter.

He had slept well, heavily. The smile came to his face. He had much to be cheerful about. He was casting aside the sleep, he was basking in the sunlight and the memory of the previous evening. Last year's harvest, well stored and well dried leaves, and well packed. Much to smile about, because there were five packages in the locked rear of his jeep and each package weighed 10 kilos, and each kilo was top quality.

The posting in the valley as liaison officer to the recruits' camp had this one salvation, constant access to the old and new marijuana crop. He had done well in the weeks that he had spent setting up the camp and then introducing it to these boys of the Popular Front. His money was in dollars. Cash dollars, bank notes. For dollars an understanding could be negotiated with the customs officials at the airport. His dollars in cash, less the price of the understanding, could be carried in his hip pocket and in his wallet, to the cities of Rome and Paris and Athens. They were the holy cities he would make his pilgrimage to, when the creep Hamid had gone with the chosen ten to Damascus for the final preparation before the flight to Cyprus and the sea journey to the shoreline of Israel.

Much to be cheerful about, and the most cheering matter for Lieutenant Fawzi was that this would be his last day and his last night in the suffocating tedium of the Beqa'a.

There was a queue of recruits waiting to be served by the cook. He ordered an omelette, three eggs. He said that he wanted coffee. He went back to his tent, pulled out a chair from inside, waited for his food to be brought to him.

478

The smoke, pungent from the dew damp wood, played across his nostrils.

He held the binoculars as Crane had taught him. His thumb and his forefinger gripped the far end of each lens, and the outstretched palms of his hands shielded the polished glass from the sun.

Holt had stopped looking for Crane. He lay on his stomach, quite still, only allowing his head to move fractionally as he raked over the faces of the magnified figures moving lethargically between the tents.

He had covered the line in front of the cooking area, and the line in front of the latrine screen. He had followed the men as they emerged from their tents, until they ducked back into them.

He could not believe that he had looked with the power of the binoculars into the face of Abu Hamid and had not known him. He had seen no man with a crow's foot scar on his cheek. He had seen no man walk with the rolling gait of Abu Hamid crossing the street in front of the Oreanda Hotel. He could remember the long sitting wait on the hard bench in the corridor leading to the cell block of the police station in Tel Aviv. He could remember the beating given freely to the bomber. What if the man had lied . . . What if the man had lied to save his skin from the fists and the boots . . . The doubts crawled in him.

What if he had travelled to the Beqa'a and Abu Hamid was not at the camp? What if he had travelled to the Beqa'a and could not recognise Abu Hamid?

For the fourth time he started his search at the southern perimeter wire of the camp, and traversed north, searching for the face, and doubting.

He had laid her body on the bed.

He covered her body with the sheet and then the bed cover. He pulled the sheet high enough to obscure the bruising at her throat.

He had taken a flower from the vase by the window, a rose. He laid the flower on the bed cover across her breast.

He closed the door behind him. He walked down the steep steps and out into the noise and crush of the alley. He walked very straight, he walked with the purpose of a young commander who had accepted a mission of leading an assault squad against the Defence Ministry on Kaplan.

Abu Hamid climbed into the passenger seat of the jeep.

Holt set the binoculars down on the rock dirt beside his hands. The valley shimmered in the heat below him. The sun burned a whiteness from the tent tops, and flickered at those strands of the wire that were not rusted. Nothing wrong with the binoculars, he had seen the dart of the rats at the bottom of the wire. He was learning the life of the camp. The men were sitting in a half circle, swatting off the flies, watching a hugely fat young man demonstrate the stripping down and the reassembling of a machine gun. He could not see all of their faces, not at this moment, but he had checked each of the faces before they had sat down, and he had checked the face of the uniformed instructor. It had been a desperation to see if there was a crow's foot scar on the left upper cheek of the instructor, a last throw. The cook was on his knees blowing at the fire. Only the cook and a sentry at the entrance to the camp and a man asleep in a chair by his tent were not involved in the class session. He had come so far with Crane, three nights' march, a squashed-in lifetime, and Abu Hamid was not there. His head and his body ached and his whole heart sank in despair.

Major Zvi Dan went into the hushed badly-lit room that housed the communications centre.

He closed the door gently behind him.

It was a world where no voice was raised, where none of the men or women in uniform moved other than at a studied pace. The room was an empire of electronics. There was the purr of the teleprinters and the greenwash screens of the visual display units and the faint whisper of the recording equipment. Because of the nature of events, because Crane and Holt had walked into the Beqa'a, transmissions from the Syrian military that were intercepted by the antennae of Hermon would be relayed to the communications centre at Kiryat Shmona.

In a lowered voice he asked the communications captain if there was any information he should have. There was nothing.

Major Zvi Dan tore a sheet from the small notepad that he carried in his tunic breast pocket. On the paper was written the figures identifying an ultra high frequency radio channel. He asked that from the middle of the day that frequency should be continuously monitored.

Still he watched the camp. He played through in his mind what Crane would say to him, how he would reply. Definitely he's not there . . . Maybe he's a bit changed . . . If he was there I'd know him . . . If he had a beard . . . ? I'd know him . . .

Nothing further to look for at the camp. The men were at the machine gun still, three at a time, practising what they had learned. Mr Crane would have been disgusted. The fire in the cooking area was out, and the cook fellow was washing stainless steel dishes, and the sentry walked backwards and forwards across the road track to the camp looking as though he were asleep. The camp had nothing for him.

With the binoculars he tried to find Crane.

Couldn't find him, just as he could not find the man he'd come so far to see killed.

Holt was desolated, he had never been so alone.

*

480

"If there is no one else to whom you will communicate your information, then you have to wait."

The traveller settled deeper into the comfort of the armchair. The outer office was cool, pleasantly furnished. He had walnuts in a bag, their shells already cracked. "My information is only for Major Said Hazan."

The clerk did not trouble to hide his contempt. The man stank, was dressed like a peasant. His shoes had brought the street dirt onto the carpet.

"He has gone to a meeting, I do not have a time for his return."

"Then I shall wait."

The pieces of walnut shell flaked to the carpet. The traveller made no attempt to retrieve them. He chewed happily on the crisp interior.

Holt saw the dust plume spitting from behind the wheels of the jeep. He reached for the binoculars. He saw the markings above the jeep's engine, presumably Syrian army. He saw that a single passenger sat beside the driver.

His sight became a blur. Holt's head slashed sideways, away from the road view, away from the jeep. The magnified vision leaped from the roadway to the camp, from the tents to the camp entrance, from the sentry to the cook.

The cook had come out of the camp. He had skirted the wire. The cook now climbed the slope on the west side of the camp. Holt could see that he was scavenging. In the hugeness of the binoculars' tunnel vision the cook seemed about to step into the overhang of rock. Holt could see that he whistled to himself. He watched him smile, pleased, because he had found a length of dried wood. He watched him tuck the length of wood under his arm and climb again. He watched him, slowly and unhurried, hunting for more wood, and climbing the slope.

Holt did not know where Noah Crane hid.

At the entrance to the camp Abu Hamid jumped clear of the jeep and strode through the gap in the wire. The jeep reversed away.

He saw Fawzi's lesson. He thought that Fawzi would have messed his trousers if he had ever been called on to fire a heavy machine gun in combat. His throat was dry. He walked to the cooking area. He saw the dead fire. No coffee warming. High on the hill slope above the camp he saw the cook foraging for wood.

The vision of the binoculars roved.

The cook had an armful of wood, so much now that he had wavered twice as if uncertain whether more was needed.

The open falling ground was devoid of cover except for long-dead trees lying strewn and ossified. The sun had burnt the bark from them.

The deep clumsily-dug ditch.

Refuse bags and the sheets of discarded newspaper, trapped on the coiled wire. The men were all sitting, bored and listless, no longer attentive to the gesturing officer in front of his class.

The new arrival . . .

The new man in the camp walked to stand behind the sitting instructor, listened for a few moments, turned away.

The binoculars followed him.

Something in the stride, something in the bearing. The twin eyepieces were rammed against Holt's eyebrows and cheekbones. He had seen the right side of the face, he had seen the full of the face, he had seen the short curled hair at the back of the head.

The new man now seemed to walk aimlessly. A tent floated in front of him. Holt swore.

The man reappeared, doubling back, smoking. Left side of the face.

Holt could hardly hold the binoculars steady. Breath coming in pants, hands trembling. He gulped the air down into his lungs. He forced the air down into his throat, breathing as a sniper would, winning control of his body. Crane's bible, breathing critical.

He saw the man's left hand raised to his face. He saw the finger peck at a place on the left cheek. He saw the hand drop.

Holt saw the crow's foot scar.

The breath shuddered out of his chest.

The vision of the binoculars bounced. The tunnel of sight bounced, fell. He had seen the crow's foot scar. The shadow pit of the well of the scar, four lines of the scar spreading away from the dark centre.

The cook . . .

The cook still coming up the hill, bending here and there for a piece of wood, carefree.

Abu Hamid . . .

Seen beside the other men in the camp, Holt thought Abu Hamid was taller than he had remembered him, and thinner, and his hair was longer and falling to the olive green collar of his fatigue top. All doubt was gone. He felt a huge surge of exhilaration – and he recognised it, a sudden, sharper, stronger fright. But Noah Crane and young Holt had done it, they had walked into the bloody awful Beqa'a valley, and they had found him. They had him at close quarters, had traced him behind the lines, on the other side of the hill. And where the hell was Noah Crane?

The cook . . .

The cook had set down his gathered bundle, and come higher. He would collect another armful and then go back for the first. The cook meandered on the hill side, searching.

Abu Hamid . . .

Abu Hamid walked amongst the tents. To Holt he seemed a man without purpose. Sometimes he would insinuate himself close to the officer who lectured the young soldiers. Sometimes he would turn and walk away as if the lecture bored him. He flitted, he was aimless. Holt, in his mind, saw Jane and the ambassador. He saw the blood rivers on the steps of the hotel. He saw the white pallor of death on her face, on his face. He wondered if there was indeed a sweetness in revenge, or whether it would merely be a substitute, saccharine dose . . . He knew the excitement at the discovery of Abu Hamid, he could not imagine whether he would find pleasure, fruit, satisfaction in Abu Hamid dead. He had never hurt a human being in his life, not even at school, not even in a playground fight. No answers.

The cook . . .

As if struck by an electric shock, the cook jerked backwards, scattering the branches of wood behind him. Crane appearing, seeming to thrust himself up from under the feet of the cook. Holt saw everything. The tunnel of his binoculars was filled with the cook trying to heave himself backwards, with Crane rising and groping and grasping for him. The cook screamed, a shrill, carrying scream. The scream winnowed over the hillside. The scream was clear to Holt who was four hundred yards from the cook, to the tent camp that was six hundred yards from the cook. Holt heard the rising cadence of the scream. He saw the flash of the blade. He saw the body of Crane merge with the body of the cook. He heard the scream cut, snuffed out.

Fawzi's words had been lost. The recruits had first stiffened, swung, then jacknifed to their feet. They had seen the cook on the hillside, seen him try to twist away, break into flight. They had seen the assailant. They had heard the death of the scream. Abu Hamid charged from in front of his own tent towards the class, towards the DShKM heavy machine gun.

Holt lay on his stomach pressing his body as far as he could back into the recess of the rock overhang. He saw the brightness of the blade, and he saw the cook crumple to his knees, then slide to his face. He realised at once the enormity of it. Their cover was gone. He was hiding, but Crane had no hiding place. He thought the cook might even have stepped on Crane, he thought the cook had been close enough to Crane to have actually put his boot onto the back of Crane's camouflaged head or the back of Crane's camouflaged body.

Holt watched Crane. The hugeness of the tunnel vision seemed to give him an intimacy with Crane who was four hundred yards further down the hillside. He believed he could see the turmoil of decision in Crane's features. Crane looked back down the hillside, down the slope towards the tent camp. Holt followed his eye line, flashed the tunnel view of the binoculars towards the tent camp. The recruits were streaming towards the entrance between the coiled wire. Back to Crane. Holt saw the hands of Noah Crane fumbling at his waist, then he saw him crouch. Sharp movements now, decision taken, mind made. Crane back onto his feet. Holt saw that he no longer wore his belt. He peered again to be sure. Crane no longer carried his belt on his waist. According to Crane's bible the belt was never taken from the body, not to sleep, not to defecate. Crane no longer wore his belt. Crane had his back to Holt. He gazed up high onto the hillside as if his eyeline was a half a mile higher than the rock overhang, as if his eyeline was far to the south.

Holt heard Crane's shout. Crane's hands were at his mouth, cupped to amplify his shout. Crane bellowed towards a place on the hillside. Holt thought that Crane shouted in Hebrew, that he called a warning.

Crane started to run at an angle on the hillside.

More understanding, but then a child could have understood.

They were young, the pursuers. They were fast on the hillside. They were swarming amongst the rock outcrops, over the broken ground. He was taking them away. His warning was a deception, he was leading them away from Holt.

There was the first ranging burst from the machine gun. Three, four rounds. There was the first red light of a sighting tracer bullet.

Holt could not take his vision, his magnified gaze, away from Crane. The pursuers, teenagers, half the age of Crane, must gain, would gain, on the quarry. A second burst, a second flailing flight of tracer. Holt could no longer see Crane's face, could see only the heaving shake of his back as he ran, away from Holt, ran for his life. Holt saw the puff pecks of the bullets striking rock and scree and stone.

Crane sagged. He stumbled, he fell. He rose again.

Out aloud, Abu Hamid shouted his triumph.

Three, four round bursts of 12.7 mm ammunition. Aimed bursts from a tripod. Muzzle velocity nine hundred yards a second. He had seen his target go down, rise again, collapse, rise again. He had his hit.

Holt saw Crane go forward.

He seemed to hobble. He was ducking and weaving as he went, but slower, each step deeper into pain. He understood. The vixen's loyalty to her cub. A scarred, world weary, bitchy old vixen giving life to a wet-behind the-ears cub. The gunfire had stopped. No more shooting. Holt could see that the pursuers were now too close to Crane to make it either safe or necessary to fire again. The pursuers bounded over the diminishing ground, hunted down their man. He heard Crane shout again, make another pretence at a warning to phantom men in a position ahead of him.

Holt saw the cave mouth.

Holt saw the first head, shoulders, appear at the mouth of the cave. The mouth of the cave was a hundred yards ahead of Crane's line. It was the edge of Holt's vision. It was the place that was half masked from him. Four men came out of the cave's mouth. One man wore only the grey whiteness of underpants upon the pink whiteness of his body. Chaos on the hillside, chaos for Crane who was wounded, chaos for three men of the Hezbollah who were discovered and flushed out, chaos for a hostage prisoner. The three men ran. The hostage prisoner stood alone. The gap between Crane and his pursuers narrowed.

Holt watched. Crane was engulfed.

He let the binoculars fall from his eyes.

His head drooped, down into the dirt floor of the rock overhang.

The tears misted his eyes, ran bitter to his lips.

Crane was dragged down the hillside. The hostage prisoner was escorted after him.

A moment when the lights seemed to go out, when hope was lost.

The argument was ferocious.

"I wounded him, my shooting. My boys captured him. I should take him."

"You've work here."

Abu Hamid and Lieutenant Fawzi face to face.

"It was us who caught him . . ."

"Me who will take the Jew . . ."

"You want to take the credit from us."

"You have men to choose, you have a mission to perform. You will stay."

"So that you will take the credit."

"So that you can prepare your mission."

In the hand of Fawzi was the dog tag ripped from the neck of the prisoner, kept safe in Fawzi's hand just as the prisoner would be safe in Fawzi's possession.

"I should take him to Damascus."

"I order you to stay here. You will perform your duty."

Fawzi walked away. He went to the knot of recruits that had gathered round the prisoner. He shouldered aside the man kicking the prisoner. He thought that by now they would all have had their turn with the boot. He saw the blood seeping from the knee of the prisoner. He saw the mouth twisted to stifle an agony. He told the recruits that the prisoner should not again be kicked.

He went to his tent. He knew enough of the English language that was common between them to receive the garbled thanks of the hostage prisoner.

He sat at the table that was set between his bed and the bed used by Abu Hamid. He switched on the battery power for the radio. He waited. When the lights glowed, when he had transmission power, he broadcast his success to Damascus.

Holt watched.

The body of the cook was carried down the hillside on a stretcher made of rifle slings and the wood he had been collecting, and along with the body was the Armalite rifle that Crane had carried. A second search party had scoured the cave and brought down to the camp boxes of food and weapons and bedding.

Holt saw all that. He was undisturbed. The recruits of the Popular Front had no interest in that part of the hillside where Holt lay under the rock overhang and the screen of scrim netting.

Holt watched the camp. He could see Crane lying prone on the earth, he could see the blood on his legs. He could see the rifles that covered Crane's every pain spasm.

They had not found Crane's belt. The belt lay amongst the rocks, deep amongst them, at the place where Crane had begun his decoy flight. Holt tried to memorise the place, tried to recall each detail of Crane's movement so that he could remember that exact place where Crane had crouched to conceal his belt.

Major Said Hazan swivelled his chair so that his back was to the traveller, so that he faced the wall map. He studied the two red-headed pins that he had set into his map. It was Major Said Hazan's style to repeat each piece of information given him so that there should be no possible error, no missed inflection, no false interpretation.

"And the information came from an Englishman?"

"An Englishman of middle years, staying at the guest house of the Kibbutz Kfar Giladi, and he said, 'How did you know about the infiltration last night?' That is what he said."

"And that 'last night', that was the night that Olaffson said the Israelis had fired flares to blind the night equipment?"

"That is correct, Major."

He spoke to himself, he ignored the traveller. He stared at the red-headed pin that marked the unsubstantiated interception.

"Why are the British going into the Beqa'a?"

The traveller shrugged. Fragments of walnut tumbled from his clothes to the white pile of the carpet.

"A wretch such as I, Major, how could I know?"

He needed to think. He required moments of contemplation. Major Said Hazan was denied the moments.

A sharp tap at the door. A bustling entrance from his clerk, a sheet of paper handed to him. He studied it. He seemed no longer to see the traveller. He reached for a telephone. He demanded that the Jew prisoner be brought to Damascus by Air Force helicopter. He demanded that the Jew prisoner be brought to the custody of Air Force Intelligence. To win his demands he invoked the authority, and the fear of that authority, of that building in which he worked.

Major Zvi Dan rocked on his feet. He stood in the middle of the communications centre. He held loose in his hand the report of the intercepted traffic. For the third time he read the message, as if in the frequency of the reading he might find a straw. No comfort, nothing to cling to.

"INTERCEPT.

TRANSMISSION TIME:	10.47 HOURS LOCAL.
TRAFFIC ORIGINATED:	PFLP TRAINING CAMP, NR KHIRBET QAN-AFAR, BEQA'A.
TRAFFIC DESTINATION:	AFI HQ , DAMASCUS.
CODE:	2ND SERIES, AFI.
MESSAGE:	ISRAELI SERVICEMAN CARRYING IDENTIFICATION OF NOAH CRANE, REL: JEW, I/D NO: 478391, CAPTURED WHILE ON SURVEILLANCE OF CAMP, WOUNDED. IN SAME OPERATION, LINK UNCERTAIN, FRG NATIONAL HEINRICH GUNTER, HOSTAGE, FREED, UNHURT. SEARCH OF AREA INTO WHICH CRANE FLEEING FAILED TO FIND REMAINDER OF INFILTRATION PARTY. REQUEST EYE BRING TO DAMASCUS. SIGNED, FAWZI (LT)."

No comfort, no straw, each reading worse than the last. The communications officer came quietly to his side. He asked, "The frequency we are to monitor – we are still to monitor it?"

"Yes," Major Zvi Dan said.

He went outside. He went into the bright sunlight. Midday and the sun swirling off the dust of the parade area, and off the tin roofing of the huts, and off the armour plate of the personnel carriers. From the troops' quarters he heard the cheerful playing of music from the Forces' station. He passed beside the verandah outside the canteen. He knew that Rebecca watched him, but he could not bring himself to speak to her. His face would have told her.

He was familiar with disaster. His work often travelled in tandem with catastrophe. Many times he had known the pain and the catastrophe of losing a field agent. The hurt was never more manageable for being familiar.

He went into the building block. He walked to the sentry who lolled in his chair outside the door. He gestured for the door to be opened. Percy Martins sat on the bed. Major Zvi Dan saw the dulled scowl of Martins's welcome. He passed the sheet of paper to the Englishman. He let the Englishman hold the sheet of paper, as if for authenticity, then he translated line by line from the Hebrew.

"God . . ."

"You had the right to know."

"Holt, what about Holt?"

"He is alone."

"What can we do for him?"

"He is beyond our reach."

"He's just a boy."

"Then he should never have been sent."

"Can he not be helped?"

"If it were Crane who were free, if it were Holt who was taken, then there is perhaps something we could do for Crane, something; but he would have to do much for himself. I doubt if it works on the other side of the coin."

Percy Martins's hands covered his face. His voice was muffled through the thickness of his fingers.

"Is it because of what I did?"

"I have no means of knowing."

"What will they do to Crane?"

"Torture him."

"Will he talk?"

"How would you respond to torture, skilled torture, Mr Martins? Put on your shoes, please."

"Where are you taking me?"

There was a cold, rueful smile on Major Zvi Dan's face. "London will want to know what has happened. They will want to set in train whatever machinery they can to minimise the damage."

He took Martins to an office with a secure telephone. He dialled for him the number of the station officer at the embassy in Tel Aviv.

In a dust storm the helicopter of the Syrian Air Force took off from beside the camp. The power of the rotors, thrashing for lift, buffeted the tents, scattered the refuse that clung to the coiled wire on the perimeter.

Heinrich Gunter now wore the tunic and trousers of a recruit of the Popular Front. Clothes he had been given, explanations none. He could not comprehend how his escape from his captors had come about. He thought his freedom had been gained by the man who lay on the floor of the helicopter. The man was dressed in military clothes that were indented with camouflage tabs, and his leg was badly wounded and no-one had attempted to dress the wound, and he was handcuffed to the bulkhead and he was covered by the handgun of the Syrian officer who had boarded the helicopter at the camp. He saw that the man he believed had brought about his freedom bit hard at his bottom lip as though he were suffused in pain, as if he would not show his captor his pain, as if he refused to cry out, gasp.

Through the portholes of the Gazelle helicopter, Gunter saw laid out beneath him the bright and tranquil breadth of the Beqa'a valley.

They clapped, the men and the boys, and the women from behind their face scarves trilled their appreciation. There was the drone of the working generator, there was the splash of water lifted from great depths and now free to run in the dug channels.

The merchant grinned and bowed to receive the congratulations.

The merchant was asked by the headman of Khirbet Qanafar to take food at his table, to share the midday meal. He was pleased to accept. He fancied he could smell the cooking of partridge. He was pleased to accept because it suited him to stay at the village town of Khirbet Qanafar until last light.

The merchant had heard the shooting perhaps two miles north up the valley. News came that a Jew had been captured, that a hostage prisoner had been freed. Only one man captured . . . In his long years in Lebanon he was practised in deceit, he could guard his emotions.

He would be honoured to take food with the headman, and with the headman's sons.

He had done it as he thought Crane would have done it.

When the sun was behind him at last Holt crawled out of the fragile cover of the net and down the hillside. He thought that he had been moving for a little more than an hour. Flat on his stomach, stomach ground against the earth and sun-scorched rock, he had gone the four hundred yards from the lying up position to the place where Crane had killed the cook.

The blood was there. The blood reinforced the truth. The truth was the capture and the throwing through the hatch door of the military helicopter of Noah Crane.

He could hear the shouting and the triumph from the camp. Singing and the yelling of slogans, voices competing one with another. Then he found Crane's belt. It was wedged down between two small rocks and half buried by a trailing network of undergrowth.

Crane had left his belt on purpose. Crane's bible, do nothing without a reason.

Slowly, with great care, each movement weighed and considered, young Holt began the stomach crawl back towards the lying up position, and the heat shimmered over him, and the sun burned through the cotton of his tunic top.

As Crane himself would have done it.

19

It was two o'clock in the afternoon.

It was that part of the daytime during which the valley slept. Low on the Beqa'a, where the Litani river and the irrigation channels made the shades of green, only the butterflies moved, hovering between flowers. That part of the day when the men had slid off to their homes, and their women to the coolness of their houses, and the children had gathered under the shade-spreading trees. The soldiers in their nearby temporary barracks had taken to their sleeping cots. The shepherd boys dozed, their flocks had tucked in their legs and knelt and panted. A great sloth blanketed the valley.

At two o'clock in the afternoon Holt managed to reach his lying up position again.

He lay under the scrim net and he gasped down the warm air. He heaved to draw the strength down into his lungs. He felt the sweat running on his body. He drank water until his belly, his bladder, could take no more. He had no shortage of water. He had the water from Crane's pack. He had no shortage of food because he had Crane's food. As he dragged the air down into his chest, as he poured the water down his throat, he could lie outstretched under the rock overhang because he had also Crane's place. He had Crane's water, food and his place. He was alone.

When he had rested a little, when he had drunk heavily, he turned to Crane's belt. He opened each pouch in turn.

Two pouches holding litre water bottles.

One pouch holding a single day's emergency dehydrated rations.

One pouch holding two of the spare magazines for the Armalite rifle.

One pouch holding the survival kit. Matches, candle, flint, magnifying glass, needles and thread, fish hooks and line, compass, Beta light, flexi saw, capsules of sedative and antibiotic and antihistamine, surgical blades, plasters and butterfly sutures, and a condom.

One scabbard pouch. The knife was in the cook.

One small pouch holding five rounds for the Model PM. He took the pouch from the belt, clipped it to his own belt.

He anticipated that there was only one pouch that mattered to him. It was days ago, nights before, that he had identified the one pouch on Crane's belt that was not duplicated on his own. Perhaps he was nervous of intruding into a secrecy that was particular to Noah Crane. He did not doubt that it was this last pouch, the largest on Crane's belt, that Crane had meant for him. Holt opened the flap and drew out the rectangular green painted metal cased box. He saw the switches and the dials. There were signs, directions, printed on the box, in English.

He read. His lips moved. The words croaked in his throat.

"Property of the Armed Forces of the United States of America."

His eyes flitted.

"Search Air Rescue Beacon, Mark V."

He strained to read, in the dappled shadow of the scrim netting, the smaller printed information.

"Three second bleep pattern . . . Can guide to 100 metres . . . To last 14 days . . . Extend aerial for maximum effect . . . Power switch . . . Red Spot, Green Spot . . ."

Holt shivered. In the heat he trembled. He understood. The beacon device was the last ditch defence. It was for a cock-up, and because Crane didn't talk about cock-ups, then he didn't talk about it. The beacon had been left to him by Crane. He saw that the switch could go to the green spot or to the red spot, and he didn't know to which frequency they would be locked, and he didn't know what the range was, and he didn't know how the bleep transmission would be affected by the mountain and valley terrain, but it had been left for him by his mentor . . . Wait on, wait on, Holt. No bloody stupid ideas about crying in the sand and switching to green spot, or to red spot, and sitting on his backside offering up prayers. He was stuck between the training camp in the valley and the commando camp further up the valley and the armed men of the village town of Khirbet Qanafar, all that below him, and above him there were the troops guarding the surveillance installations on the Jabal el Barouk . . . Wait on, Holt . . . He wondered whether the leaving of the beacon was meant as a means of escape or whether it was meant as an encouragement.

He repacked the pouch. He found a space for it, just, on his own belt.

An encouragement.

He turned, heaved his body round. He lifted his binoculars. He had seen that Abu Hamid had not boarded the helicopter. He had watched Abu Hamid into his tent. The camp was now in siesta. Just the sentry at the entrance on the move and that rarely.

"He awaits you, Major."

"You are to be congratulated, Fawzi."

"For which, Major, I thank you."

"Tell me what happened."

Fawzi sat forward in the chair. He had the attention of Major Said Hazan, of the once-burned eyes and the once-scorched ears.

"I was taking a class through the detail of the assembly and stripping of a DShKM machine gun. The camp cook was on the hill above the camp collecting wood for the fire on which he cooks. I think he must have stumbled on this Crane. He shouted. He had a chance to shout before he was stabbed to death by the Jew. His shout alerted us. Immediately I took over the machine gun, and when the Jew started to flee I began firing. I have to confess, Major, that at first I was not successful, but in moments I had the range. I achieved a disabling hit. The moment I had done that, and seen that the Jew no longer had the capacity to run, I organised the capture party. I led a group of the Popular Front recruits onto the hillside, and we captured the Jew. He was not in a condition to resist."

"It was well done, Fawzi."

"I was carrying out my duty, Major."

"And the hostage, Heinrich Gunter?"

Fawzi shrugged. "I can only give you what is an opinion, Major. I think that our finding him was chance. I cannot see a connection between the Jew and a hostage. And the hostage has given no sign of any link between them. I believe that the flight of the Jew happened to take him towards a cave where the hostage was held. I believe that in fear the Hezbollah or the Islamic Jihad simply abandoned their hostage and much equipment besides. But it is good for us, regaining the hostage?"

"It is very good indeed. In the power play of diplomacy at the moment when our nation is confronted with the lies of the West European nations that we are a state which sponsors terrorism it is a beautiful thing that we are able to deliver this Heinrich Gunter to his ambassador, quite excellent. But it is the Jew that matters."

Fawzi warmed. "To me, in the direction of his flight, from his actions, he tried to warn the others in his infiltration group of danger . . ."

Major Said Hazan clapped together his mutilated hands. "Closer to the security zone we block them. The orders have been given. So, he awaits me."

So much to concern Major Said Hazan. He had the evidence of an infiltration. He had an unconfirmed interception. He had the report of the conversation of an Englishman at Kiryat Shmona. He had the detail of the capture of the Jew named Crane, on the hillside above the tent camp occupied by the recruits of the Popular Front.

Major Said Hazan stood in front of his mirror. He tugged down the jacket of his uniform, he straightened his tie, he smoothed back the few hairs left on his scalp.

"I have bad news, Prime Minister."

The Director General stood in the centre of the room. His pipe was in his pocket. The Prime Minister had been in a full meeting of the Cabinet. A note had been carried in, the discussion on the plight of the inner cities had been shelved, the Prime Minister had come out.

The Prime Minister was at the window, staring down at the spring bursting garden.

"Lebanon?" The voice was a murmur.

"You will remember that we sent two men in. We sent an expert in covert infiltration who was also an accomplished marksman, and we sent the young diplomat who was the eyewitness . . ."

"Of course I remember."

"We have lost the marksman. The marksman has been captured alive by the Syrians, and taken by helicopter to Damascus." It was the voice of a bell tolling.

"This is neither more nor less than I expected."

"The diplomat has not been held."

"And I wanted it called off."

"You said, Prime Minister, that the diplomat was fortunate to have the chance of real adventure. He has that chance now."

"Where did it happen?"

"In the target area."

"Holt, that's his name isn't it, the diplomat? Can he get out?"

"Frankly, no," the Director General said curtly.

"They were at the target and they had not fired?"

"If they had succeeded at the target we would have known of it. There is no information."

The Prime Minister twisted, venom in the eyes, a spit in the words. "You have made a fool of me. I will be ridiculed in the chancelleries of Europe, in Washington. This government will be badly damaged. You don't concern yourself, of course, with such matters."

"Prime Minister, my concern at present is for the safety of young Holt, and it is for the life of Noah Crane."

"And if your Mr Holt is captured or killed, as seems most probable, will you still blather to me about vengeance? Will you send another clandestine team to Lebanon? . . . It was utterly preposterous, indeed it was criminally stupid."

"Recriminations, Prime Minister, regrettably do not help them."

"And what does help them, pray?"

"Sadly, nothing that I know of. I will keep you informed, Prime Minister."

When he had gone, the room was silent. The Prime Minister paced. Beyond the closed window the wind whipped the dust on Horse Guards and bent the trees in the walled garden. The clouds scurried low, the lights were dull in the room, and the face of Holt was unknown. The Prime Minister's lips pursed in angry concentration, but no effort could conjure up the face of the boy in such danger, nor of the assassin Abu Hamid, nor of the far away terrain of the Beqa'a.

The Prime Minister lifted a telephone, asked for the Cabinet Secretary in his Downing Street office.

The Prime Minister said briskly, "A covert mission in Lebanon has failed. I want the Foreign Secretary here at two, I want his principal Middle East people with him . . ." The Prime Minister paused, "And I would like you to draw up a list of names, three, four if you prefer, for us to consider as replacements for the Director General . . . Casualties? What do you mean, are there casualties? My dear man, we are dealing with a diplomatic catastrophe, not a train derailment."

The Prime Minister went to lunch – soup and whole–meal bread and a glass of fresh orange juice. A working lunch with close advisers, and the agenda involved future government initiatives to encourage industrial investment in Scotland.

He ate his food cold. Holt did not dare light the hexamine tablets to heat the water. The packet told him that the dehydrated flakes were intended as a beef goulash. He poured cold water into the packet and stirred it to a dark porridge with his finger. He ate as much as he could, as much as he could without vomiting. He drank a pint of water. He checked his watch, he measured the passing of the afternoon. He tried not to think of Noah Crane.

When he had eaten and when he had drunk, when he had stifled the hunger pain, and the pain of isolation, Holt took the condom from the barrel of the Model PM. Meticulously, stage by stage he started to clean the rifle with the graphite grease.

From his vantage point, as he wiped the working parts of the rifle, he gazed down onto the tent camp. He reckoned the siesta would soon be finished, he reckoned they would emerge soon.

As Crane would have done it . . .

Holt couldn't help himself, couldn't wipe away the thoughts of Crane, tried and failed. In a dungeon, in a basement, in a cell. The interrogators howling at him, the blows raining on him.

He wondered if he would have the time, the time to wait until he was ready, until the sun started to slide in the late afternoon.

He said, "My name is Noah Crane. My IDF serial is 478391."

The kick heaved him across the tiled floor.

"My name is Noah Crane . . ."

The army boot again, into the kidney area at the small of his back.

"My IDF serial is 478391."

The army boot stamped onto the knuckle of his hand. His eyes were closed. They had gone with their gloved fists for his eyes first. His eyes were puffed shut. His leg, where the 12.7 mm round had taken away the flesh tissue and the bone at the knee, no longer hurt him. Too much hurt from the fresher wounds. He was not handcuffed and his legs were not tied, yet he was too weak, too exhausted, to protect himself. He lay on his side, he tried to curl himself forward into his sleeping position, but that was no protection because they could then kick the back of his head, the back of his neck, the small of his back, the base of his spine. He knew that there were four of them in the room. He knew they were high in the building because strong light filtered through the dropped venetian blinds. He knew that in the room were two men who wore the uniforms and arm markings of sergeants in the Air Force. He knew that also in the room was the lieutenant who had brought him from the Beqa'a. He knew that these three men were not the ones that mattered. The one who did matter wore the uniform of a major. The man sat on a hard wooden chair against the wall and ground his spent cigarettes on the tiles. The face of the man had been rebuilt. Before his eyes had closed he had seen the smooth baby skin of the major who asked the questions in quiet and cultured English.

"Mr Crane, you are being your own enemy."

"My name is Noah Crane."

"You need attention for your leg, the doctors and the nurses and the surgeons are waiting . . ."

"My IDF serial is 478391."

"You have to tell me what was the tasking of your mission into the Beqa'a . . ."

"My name is Noah Crane."

"You have to tell me what was the object of your mission."

"My IDF serial is 478391."

"Mr Crane, by your own hand, with your own knife, you murdered a poor cook boy. You are not a prisoner of war, Mr Crane. To us you are a common criminal. Do you know, Mr Crane, what is the fate of common criminals convicted of the murder of innocents . . . ?"

"My name is Noah Crane."

"We have in our criminal code, Mr Crane, an instrument of execution. In our native tongue we call that instrument the *khazuk*, sadly I do not have present with me such an instrument to show you. It is, Mr Crane, a sharp pointed staff that is driven down into the body of the condemned. To our judges the *khazuk* is a deterrent. It is the decision of the executioner into which part of the body he drives the *khazuk*. The result is the same, it is simply the timing of death that is at variance . . ."

"My IDF serial is 478391."

He heard the rustle of the cigarette packet. He heard the click of the lighter. He stiffened his muscles. He could not protect himself. It was the signal. When the major lit a cigarette and leaned back and inhaled, then the boots flew. The lieutenant kicked hardest. Crane gasped. The lieutenant kicked as if his promotion depended on it. He wanted to cry. Heavy toe caps belting at his shoulders and his back and his spine.

"Mr Crane, I think you are a racist. I think you believe that because you are a Jew and I am an Arab you are superior to me. I think you believe that I am foolish"

"My name is Noah Crane."

"Would you like me to demonstrate to you, Mr Crane, that I am not foolish?"

"My IDF serial is 478391."

The boots in again, the kicking and the stamping, and the hands going for his short cut hair and dragging up his head so that his face could be kicked. He thought he was falling, falling in a pit, dark sides, black bottom. He thought of Holt, white light on a hillside, white light of a bullet path over a hillside. Falling, tumbling, helpless. And he thought of the face of Holt, the face of the youngster. A thousand yards, and getting into five inches . . . God, the pain . . . God, the pain in the bone at the end of his spine. And the pain was blackness, darkness, the pain riddled through him, and he was falling, backwards, down.

He felt a calmness. He felt a peace through the battery of the boots. A hillside. Rose flowers and oleander bushes and watered cyclamen. He heard the singing of the rabbi's prayers. He heard the rattle crash of the volley. He heard the beauty of the bugle playing. He walked on the slope of Mount Herzl. He was a stranger amongst the men from Kiryat Shmona who had come south to the cemetery, and the rabbi in army fatigues, and the chief of staff in starched uniform. It was the bottom of the pit, it was the end of the darkness, the blackness. It was sunlight on the slopes of Mount Herzl.

"Mr Crane, because I have to demonstrate to you that I am not foolish, answer me . . . When you were infiltrated through the NORBAT sector there was an Englishman staying at the guest house of the Kibbutz Kfar Giladi. Why was the infiltration the concern of the Englishman?"

He forced open his eyes. His vision was narrowed by the swelling at his cheeks, his eyebrows.

He hesitated. "My name is Noah Crane."

"When you were infiltrated you travelled with an Englishman. Mr Crane, who is the Englishman? Why is an Englishman involved in the infiltration?"

He stared at the constructed face, at the pink underskin. There was no challenge in his voice. "My IDF serial is 478391."

He pushed himself up, the pain flooded inside him. He knelt in front of the major. He gazed into the face. He was losing, he had reacted. He thought of Holt, the clean young face of Holt. He thought he loved the boy. He thought he should have been the father of the boy. And he asked the boy for a thousand yards, and he asked the boy to shoot into five inches diameter. He felt the wash of despair.

"Mr Crane, in me rests a decision; the decision that is mine is whether you go from here to a military prison to await some exchange, or whether you go from here to the El Masr gaol to await the convenience of the executioner and the *khazuk* . . . Mr Crane, why is an Englishman concerned in an infiltration? Why were you on surveillance on the hillside above the camp of the Popular Front recruits?"

He whispered hoarsely, "My name is Noah Crane."

As if they were the only men in the room. As though the tormentors had evaporated. The major with his surgeon's face, the marksman with his slashed, puffed, bleeding face.

"Why are the English concerned with this camp? Help me, Mr Crane, because I am trying to understand. What is particular, what is important about this camp?"

The major shook his head. His laugh tinkled. He used his hands – how could he have been so blind. The major beamed his pleasure at Crane. A low voice, as if he confided in the wretch who knelt in front of him.

"Abu Hamid?"

"My IDF serial is 478391."

He saw the pleasure in the peculiar wide-apart eyes of Major Said Hazan. He saw the satisfaction curl the mouth that was lipless.

"You know the name of Abu Hamid, Mr Crane?"

"My name is Noah Crane."

"Abu Hamid is the commander of the camp where the Popular Front recruits are undergoing training . . . Abu Hamid is the slayer of a British official . . . Abu Hamid is like a toy to me . . ."

Again the major laughed.

"You thought me a fool. You mistook me, Mr Crane."

"My IDF serial is 478391."

"You are boring me, Mr Crane. I have what I require. I have the target for your infiltration. You may take it, Mr Crane, that from this moment the target is taken out of the reach of your English plan."

He seemed to see Holt. He seemed to see the jutting barrel of Model PM.

Noah Crane lurched to his feet. The weight gave at his wounded knee. He fell forward. He cannoned down onto the sitting major. He saw the throat, he saw the grafted skin above the knotted tie, below the stubbed smooth chin. His hands found the throat. His hands locked on the throat.

He seemed to see the corridor aperture of the telescopic sight, and the wavering of the cross-hairs on the chest of a sallow skinned, dark haired man who was marked by a crow's foot scar on his left upper cheek.

He clung to the throat. He felt the blows of the lieutenant. He felt the scrabbling fingers of the sergeants. He heard the shortening gasps of breath.

He seemed to know the gentle two stage squeeze on the trigger of the Model PM. There was the sunlight shafting between the water green trees on Mt Herzl. There was the ripple of the singing, there was the floating of the flowers, there was the love of his people, and there was Holt's love.

He squeezed. They could not pull him back. He could hear their shouts, he could feel their hammered blows. He clung to the throat. The man no longer fought him. He saw the pinkness of the face dissolve, washed to pale grey blue. He saw the pistol in the hand of the lieutenant.

Noah Crane seemed to hear the youngster, Holt, fire.

The Foreign Secretary slammed down his hand onto the mahogany polished table top.

It was a theatrical gesture, but he was not ashamed of it. One of his aides took a shorthand note, for posterity. His two senior advisers on the Middle

Eastern Desk at FCO shuffled their hands. He knew they were having an affair... An affair, albeit adulterous, between an Assistant Secretary and a Deputy Assistant Secretary, between two 70-hours-a-week aides, was a regrettable but supportable nuisance.

Lebanon, the Beqa'a, was totally unsupportable. It was the end of the world.

"I do not understand how this could have happened."

The Prime Minister drew doodle faces on a pad and kept silent.

The Foreign Secretary warmed, "Only at this moment of failure am I for the first time informed of a clandestine adventure into Lebanon. At no stage was I consulted, but for the record I'll tell you what my advice would have been: forget it, that's what you'd have been told. My opinion was not asked for, and where do we find ourselves? We sent in two operatives. One is now captured and presumably pouring his heart out in Damascus. The other, untrained, will be blundering around in the Beqa'a, a headless chicken with capture inevitable. Prime Minister, have you any remote idea of the damage that will be done to British interests in the Middle East and in the Gulf when Crane and Holt are paraded in open court in Damascus? Years of hard economic endeavour, years of patient diplomacy, will have been undone by this folly. It goes without saying that I shall be forced to consider my position as a member of Her Majesty's Government."

"It stood a good chance of success," the Prime Minister said bleakly.

"Ah, success ... success is different, success is all important, but we do not have success. We have instead a mission so ill-prepared that even the basement of the White House would have blinked at it."

"If the brute had been killed ..."

"If, Prime Minister, if ... but one is captured and the other is certain of capture. It is a disaster, and a perfectly avoidable disaster, had you chosen to confide in your colleagues."

"We had to show our strength, the strength of the free world against terrorism."

"Your concept of strength is different to mine. I cannot see that I can be of further help to you."

The Foreign Secretary pushed back his chair. He swept his papers, and his map of Lebanon, into the mouth of his attache case. He stood.

"Then get out," the Prime Minister said. "If all you can offer is the threat of your resignation, just go."

The aide who took the record wrote furiously then slapped shut his notepad, buried it in an inner pocket. The Foreign Secretary led out his team.

For a long time the Prime Minister sat bent at the table, digesting the loneliness of the room.

And no comforting face. Only the prayer that the young man, Holt, was running, running hard, from that Godforsaken place that was the Beqa'a.

As Crane would have done it ...

498

Everything that Holt could remember.

The light was going down. Below him the shadows of the tents lengthened. He saw the first figures emerging from the tents, as if in the coming coolness their rest time was complete.

He shared the rock overhang with a small lizard. The reptile showed no fear of him. He thought there was a cheerfulness about the lizard, as he would have said there was a cheerfulness about the chaffinches and the robins that came to the lichen-covered bird table on the lawn of his parents' home.

He had cleaned the rifle. He had pulled the 4 × 2 cloth through the barrel, pulling from the bolt end, according to Crane's bible, because to pull from the muzzle end was to risk damaging to a fractional extent the precision of the rifling. He had pulled back the bipod legs and adjusted them so that each was calibrated to the same length. He edged the anti-flash extension to the barrel out through the scrim netting. He took from Crane's Bergen a plastic water bottle and pushed the bottle out under the netting, and then tipped its mouth so that the water ran onto the rock and dirt that was below the muzzle. He saw the dribble of the water, and the colouring of the ground. According to Crane's bible, wet ground under a muzzle reduced the chance of a dust puff at the moment of firing when the bullet and the gases burst from the barrel. A dust puff, youngster, can give away the firing position.

As Crane would have done it . . .

He had a degree in Modern History, and his special subject was 1653–58, when Oliver Cromwell was Lord Protector of the Commonwealth. He was an entry into the Foreign and Commonwealth Office through the diplomatic service "fast stream". He was a Third Secretary with particular interest in the political development and sociological movements inside the Union of Soviet Socialist Republics. He was on his belly and watched by a lizard and under a rock overhang on the other side of the hill. He was considering whether he could put a 7 mm Remington Mag bullet into a five inch diameter target at a thousand yards.

Holt saw the tent flap move. He reached for his binoculars. Holt saw Abu Hamid step clear of the dark opening of the tent. He watched Abu Hamid yawn and stretch and spit.

He looked for the length of the shadows. He tugged his watch up from under his shirt. Holt thought that the sun was still too high, that he must wait for a minimum of another half an hour.

Zvi Dan said, "From what we've picked up on the monitoring they've lifted Crane to Damascus."

Martins asked, "Will you get him back? In an exchange?"

"Alive? If he is alive? Not for months, years, and then only if we have a jewel to trade. We don't have such a jewel. Dead? If they have killed him? They extract a high price. The last time we sent them back a swarm of prisoners, we had in return three coffins, in one was the wrong body, the other two were filled with stones. Does that answer your question?"

From the bed Martins looked up at Major Zvi Dan. "Nothing on Holt?"

"They haven't caught him, we would have heard. They know Crane was not alone, they have set blocks further south, nearer to the border."

"Thank you, I appreciate your telling me."

"It is too late to be angry," Major Zvi Dan said.

Abu Hamid had not slept. He had lain on the camp bed and had watched the radio. The radio would tell him what fate awaited him.

He thought that the radio would have told if they had found the body of Margarethe Schultz. He could see her in his mind, and he could see on her breast the crimson flash of the flower that he had laid there. He felt no guilt. He thought that what he had done was justified. He thought that what they would do to him would also be justified. Of course, he would not be arrested. Of course, he would not go to the El Masr gaol. Of course, he would not be driven to a small square at dawn and be dropped from a gallows beam. What they would do to him, what would be justified, was that they would send him ashore on the beaches of Israel.

In his spider handwriting on a food carton he had written the names of the ten. He walked through the camp. He sought out each of the ten. They were those who would stand at his side. They were those who would protect him.

He would never be taken.

He heard the first bickering argument flare behind him. One had not been chosen, one had been chosen. The imbeciles did not even know for what they were or were not chosen. But already the argument. When he had spoken to the ten men, he drifted towards the cooking area, and gave encouragement to the pressed volunteer who would prepare their food, and he kicked more wood onto the fire and spluttered in the surge of smoke.

It was a bargain.

Jane was no part of the bargain. Nor was his country, the United Kingdom of Great Britain and Northern Ireland. The bargain was with Crane, for his being taken and for the freeing of the hostage prisoner. That he would fire a sniper rifle for the first time in his life, try to get into five inches diameter at a thousand yards, no longer had anything to do with vengeance or patriotism. He would fire for Noah Crane, miserable old goat. He would use the rifle for Crane who had a disease in the retina of his shooting eye. He would not walk away from Noah Crane.

He saw the smoke surge up from the fire. He watched the smoke climb and then curve where the wind took it. With the compass from his belt he could estimate that he would be firing on a line east south east. He followed the smoke trail, he matched the trail to his compass. This was the crucial calculation. If he made the wrong calculation then he would betray the memory of Noah

Crane. He reckoned that the trail of the smoke was moving east north east. Burrowing down into his recollection of figures that he had once been told, he dragged out the figures showing a bullet's deviation with wind blowing at ten miles an hour at a deflection of 45 degrees. At 1,000 yards the wind deflection would push the bullet a matter of five feet and two and a half inches off course. But at 900 yards the wind deflection would be four feet and a quarter of an inch. And at 1,100 yards the wind deflection would be six feet and seven inches.

Crane had said that the lying up position was a thousand yards from the centre of the camp. If Crane had it wrong, was 100 yards too long, then Holt would shoot 14 inches wide. If Crane had it wrong, was 100 yards too short, then Holt would shoot 16 inches wide. It was the difference between a killing shot and a wounding shot, and a shot that missed altogether.

The target had to be still, and not about to move. To cover one thousand yards the bullet would need two seconds of time. If the target took one step in that two seconds . . . God . . . miss.

The distance of a thousand yards had to be exact, because that was what the sights would be set to. If in reality the distance was 900 yards then the bullet would reach its target 18 inches too high. If in reality it was 1,100 yards then the bullet would drop to a target point 20 inches too low.

All of these minute calculations had to be correct. If any were wrong, he would be breaking his bargain.

Holt grinned at the lizard. The lizard was his only friend.

He checked that his Safety was on. He eased back the greased bolt. He gazed for a moment at the bullet that lay in the palm of his hand. He thrust the bullet into the breach of the Model PM, then drove the bolt handle forward.

He had seen two of the recruits fighting, teeth and boots and fists. He could remember the queues that he used to see outside the GUM store in Simferopol. Men and women queued outside the GUM in Simferopol without knowing what they were queuing for. Two of his recruits were fighting, and more were arguing, and they could not know for what the ten had been chosen.

They sidled around him, those ten that he had selected. Inside the ten were four to whom he had assigned responsibility as squad leaders at the camp. Two of the other six were considered to be proficient soldiers on an all round evaluation. There was one who had scored five consecutive hits in training with the RPG-7. There was one who played with wires and the forces of electricity and who understood the workings of a radio. There was one whose twin brother had been killed by the Israelis in 1982, he would fight hard. There was one who would make Abu Hamid laugh, and who could write in Hebrew and in English, and speak the Jewish tongue.

Perhaps they thought they were going to be sent to Simferopol . . .

He waved for them to sit.

It was the centre of the camp. It was between the cooking area and the first line of the bell tents. He had prepared what he was going to say. In Simferopol the Russian instructors had always said that a commander should prepare his statement of orders and tactics.

The low sun was warm on his shoulders, on the back of his neck, the sun that was soon to dip into dusk behind the great escarpment of the Jabal el Barouk.

He was a changeling.

No longer the graduate and the diplomat, Holt was the technician.

He had no love in his heart, he had no hate in his mind.

The fine cross hairs of the Schmidt and Bender PM 12 x 42 telescopic sight did not flicker over the back of a sitting, living, breathing human being. The cross hairs lay upon a target.

He had no thought of his girl, no thought of his dead ambassador. His thoughts were on the time of a bullet in flight, and the angle of wind deflection, and the distance between the lying up position and the centre of the tent camp as measured by Crane from his aerial photographs.

With his thumb, Holt drew back the Safety.

None who had known him before would have recognised the changeling at that moment. Not his parents, not the men and women at FCO, not the staffers who had been his colleagues in Moscow . . . not Jane, certainly not Jane Canning.

He held the stock forward, just behind the bipod, with his left hand. The butt was pulled hard into his shoulder. His right eye was locked against the circle of the sight. His index finger searched for the trigger guard, and inside the guard to the trigger.

He took a long singing breath, forced the air into his lungs.

As Noah Crane would have done it . . .

"It will be a mission that will bring anguish to our enemy. It will bring pride to our people. Each one of you, of us, has known the cruelty of our enemy. We are honoured to have the chance to strike a blow at that enemy . . ."

He saw the glow in their eyes, he saw the fervour in their faces. He felt the swelling pleasure that he was their leader.

Half the breath heaved out.

Trigger squeeze to first stage.

"Wish me luck, as you wave me goodbye,

Cheerio, here I go, on my way,

Wish me luck as you wave me goodbye . . ."

He hummed. The breath was pressing for release in his throat. The cross hairs were steady.

502

He squeezed.
Holt fired.

The path of a bullet in the Beqa'a.

"Our target is Tel Aviv . . ."

He seemed to rise up. He seemed to be lifted from his haunches and then punched forward. There was a force that drove him.

Abu Hamid fell, bursting blood, against the body of the recruit who had scored five consecutive hits with the RPG-7 and against the recruit who understood the workings of a radio.

Abu Hamid fell and he did not move.

20

The economic sub–committee of the Cabinet had ended.

It was a full fifteen minutes since the secretary had slipped silently into the room and laid the message form beside the Prime Minister's papers.

The chairman of the sub–committee, the Chancellor, was neatly packing away his papers at the far end of the table.

"You'll forgive the presumption, Prime Minister, but you are displaying a certain cheerfulness that I can hardly put down to our business of the last two hours."

"That obvious, Harry?"

"Very obvious, Prime Minister."

The Prime Minister leaned back, there was a comfortable smile. The meeting hushed.

The Prime Minister said, "One of the hardest features of my office is to exercise real power, to exercise real influence. I try often enough, and I rarely succeed."

"But this time you have succeeded?" The Chancellor was adept at the unsubtle prompt. "Can you say?"

The Prime Minister glanced down at the cryptic handwritten message. "Not yours, not mine, but Abu Hamid's, on the salver."

"You'll keep this to yourselves of course ... When Ben Armitage was shot dead in Yalta, and an aide also died, we let a lie be known, that the murderer was a local criminal. We knew in fact that the killer was a member of the Palestinian Popular Front. I put in hand an Intelligence operation that located the killer in the Beqa'a valley of east Lebanon. I took the decision, not lightly, to send a covert team into the Beqa'a valley so that a precisely calculated vengeance should be wrought upon this murderer. It would be the clearest indication to his Syrian masters that we will never be attacked with impunity ... Last night, gentlemen, at dusk, that vengeance was exacted."

"That's first class, Prime Minister."

"I'll not deny that I agonised over the decision, over the consequences of failure, for which of course I would have taken the blame, but if you venture nothing then you win nothing. This government, our government, has shown that we are in the forefront of the war against international terrorism."

"You are to be most warmly congratulated, Prime Minister."

"Thank you, I accept your congratulations with pleasure, and later, when I telephone him I anticipate receiving the congratulations of the President of the United States. We are not a nation of boasters, gentlemen, I like to think we are a nation of quiet achievers . . . it's been a good meeting. Thank you, Harry."

Major Said Hazan was buried with full military honours in that section of the military cemetery reserved for Air Force officers who had died in the service of the Syrian Arab Republic. There was a large turnout of dignitaries and senior ranking officers. The cause of death, as announced in the Damascus morning newspapers, was given as heart failure brought on by the ravages of an old war wound, bravely borne. Amongst those who carried the coffin to the deep cut grave was Fawzi. He wore a new uniform for the occasion, and the uniform carried the insignia of a captain, and the brigadier who headed Air Force Intelligence and who was the pallbearer immediately ahead of Fawzi, had told the young man that in the circumstances he was right to have shot the Jew. And no doubt the brave major had been so severely injured in his throat that the Jew's very first assault was fatal.

After the service, after the mourners had dispersed, after the band and the honour guard had been bussed away, the brigadier walked with Captain Fawzi to a distant part of the cemetery where the cypress trees shaded the closely-mown lawns. The brigadier offered Fawzi a job in his department, and offered him also the task of finding a replacement leader for a seaborne mission against the Defence Ministry on Kaplan. When they had finished, they walked back towards the cars, and the brigadier linked his arm to Fawzi's elbow.

"Tell me, who shot Hazan's boy?"

"In shame I do not know."

The name of Holt was not known. The secret of Holt had died with the locking of Crane's fingers on the windpipe of Major Said Hazan, with the blasting away of Crane's life by the Makharov pistol fired at point blank range.

"Come in, Percy. . . . For God's sake, man, you look dead beat."

"Didn't get to bed last night, sir, and had to be at the airport at five."

"It's been a first class show." The Director General beamed, and waved Martins to a chair, and he shouted through to his outer office for coffee, and he lifted a half bottle of cognac from his desk leg drawer.

"Thank you, sir."

"I tell you this, when I heard that the sniper chap had been caught, I thought it was all over for us."

Martins eased back in the chair. The personal assistant handed him coffee, in cup and saucer, and the Director General topped up the coffee with cognac. He seemed not to feel his age, nor his tiredness.

"Well, a fair amount of work had gone into preparing young Holt. I thought from the start, from the time I had him down in the country that this couldn't be a man and boy operation, that they had to go in as equals. I put Holt through a pretty tough induction, toned him up so that he would be just about as able to operate on his own as in tandem, and it paid off."

"And you had damn all help at the far end – more cognac?"

Martins reached forward with his cup. He was a good deal surprised: there was no shake in his hand. He drank. He felt the glow beneath his stubble-covered cheeks. It had been a conscious decision not to shave. He was straight in from the front line.

"Couldn't put it better, sir, damn all help. I had to insist, lay down the law, that we should have a hot extraction programme after the snipe. Didn't win me any friends, but I had my way. I arranged for them to carry in a Sarbie beacon, and I cudgelled the locals into putting a receiver into the transport of an agent they had operating in the Beqa'a. That was the first thing I made them do, when they got windy about the chopper back-up in the first place. So, Holt fired, knew enough to have avoided detection, then he laid up until darkness, then he moved off. I had predicted that such a long range shooting would create total confusion in Hamid's camp, not much of an idea where the shot had come from. Holt moved off after dark and when he was well clear he activated the bleep. The car driven by this Mossad fellow, their agent, picked him up. I'm the last one not to give credit where credit is due, the agent did his part well, used his lights and his horn to attract Holt, took him on board and drove like hell for the border . . ."

The cognac was coursing. He felt the dampness in the socks he should have changed on the aircraft. The Director General sat on his desk, hunched forward, an eager audience.

". . . So far so good, but of course the Syrians had picked up the bleep and were reacting, and they had road blocks between Holt and the safety of the UNIFIL sector and the security zone. I really lost my rag, sir. I was in their communications area, and I just demanded that a helicopter be sent. Made the air quite blue, sir. They were jabbering about missile umbrellas, all that sort of rubbish, but I won the day. Well, in the end they sent up a helicopter, they located the car about three miles short of the road blocks, quite a short run thing, they lifted out Holt and the agent. I've no complaints about the way they managed that. That's the short of it, sir."

"Remarkable, Percy."

"Thank you, sir."

From the leather box on the table, the Director General passed Martins a cigar, and lit one himself. The smoke fogged the room.

"You'll take the weekend off. Go and get yourself an ugly big pike. You'll be back here on Monday morning. Your ears only, for the time being. For your information, Mr Anstruther informs me he is seeking fame and fortune in the commodities market in the City. Mr Fenner is returning to Cambridge, an academic future. As from Monday morning, Percy, you will head the Middle East Desk."

"That's very good of you, sir."

The Director General swung his legs down to the carpet.

"And Holt, Percy?"

"Peculiar young man, sir. Not the easiest to handle. Of course, he's been under strain, haven't we all? He was pretty insistent that I drop him at Paddington station on my way in from the airport. I've got the number where he'll be for the next few days. He's gone home . . . I've got something for you, sir, something of a souvenir."

Martins led the Director General through to the outer office. Behind the coat stand, in the corner next to the door, was the Model PM Long Range. "He wanted the sling. That would be enough to remind him of Crane, he said. That was the sniper, sir." Martins laid the gun, immaculately clean, on the table in the corner of the Director General's office.

"Good of you, Percy. The Department will be proud of the trophy."

After Percy Martins had gone, probably in search of bait from a fishmonger, the Director General stood at the window of his high office and he traversed the sky line, and his eye was hard against the sight circle, and he aimed at the flags that flew from the corporation tower blocks across the river, and he followed the flight of a gull. He thought the boy was, as the Prime Minister had said, lucky to have had the opportunity. He thought he would have given an eye tooth to have had the opportunity to fire that rifle in the service of his country. He would take it to Downing Street in the early evening, just the thing to cap a damn good show. He asked his personal assistant to warn the Cabinet Secretary to alert security that he would be coming over at six o'clock and would have a rifle with him.

Together, Major Zvi Dan and Rebecca cleared the barracks room at Kiryat Shmona that had been the home of Noah Crane.

They needed only one black plastic dustbin bag. Into the bag went the second pair of boots, the two sets of old uniforms, the underwear and the socks and the pyjamas, the few items of civilian clothing. There was a letter from a clinic in Houston, there were a few old newspapers. All went into the bag until it bulged. The intercepts from Hermon had told Major Zvi Dan that Crane would never again use the contents of the bag.

He knotted the top of the bag.

Rebecca said, "Did we win anything?"

Major Zvi Dan muttered, "We lost a man who was without price."

"Not anything?"

"We lost an agent. Menny can never go back. Perhaps he, also, was beyond price."

"The British won."

"They won only vanity. Only conceit."

"Didn't Holt, at least, win?"

"If you had asked him I doubt he would have told you that he had won anything that was of value to him."

Rebecca carried the bag and Major Zvi Dan hobbled behind her. She took the bag to the corner of the camp where the rubbish of the troops was burned. With his finger Major Zvi Dan made a hole in the bag, exposed the paper, and with his lighter set fire to the bag.

A team of army engineers was set to work to dismantle the bell tents. They worked, stripped to the waist, in the midday heat. The recruits were not there to help them, they had in the morning been taken by bus to the Yarmouq camp outside Damascus.

High on the hillside above the work party was a small and unnoticed rock overhang. Under the overhang, hidden in shadow, undiscovered, lay two Bergens, and on top of one pack was a carefully folded square of scrim netting, and on top of the other pack was a single, used cartridge case.

Beyond the camp perimeter wire was a cairn of sun-bleached stones. The cairn marked the grave of a young man who had given himself the name of Abu Hamid, who had been a fighter for a refugee people, who had been a foreign cadet at the military academy at Simferopol, who had once been frightened of death, who had a crow's foot scar on his cheek.

The depth of the grave, the weight of the stones, were reckoned to be proof against the hyenas who would come to scavenge the camp site once the army engineers had lifted the tents onto their lorries and driven away.

21

In the darkness he walked on the moor.

Away below him, distant and separated from him by the black void, were the lights of cars moving on the roads between Dulverton and Exford, and Hawkridge and Withypool, and Liscombe and Winsford.

The moor was his, as the Beqa'a had been his and Crane's. He walked silently in this wilderness, each footfall tested, and for company he had the deer herds, and the hunting foxes, and the rooting badgers, and the sheep that had been freed from the pens in the valley and allowed to wander in search of the new summer grass of the higher ground.

He walked until the dawn light seeped onto the royal purple expanse of the moor, and when it was time for him to settle into his lying up position then he came down from the moor and took the road to the stone house that was the home of his mother and father.

In the early morning he packed a bag, and he told his mother that he was going back to work, and he asked his father to drive him to the railway station at Tiverton Junction.

His father gazed into the secret and unexplaining eyes of his son.

"Are you all right, Holt?"

"I'm all right, it's the others who have been hurt."

Home Run

to William and Rosalin – with love

Prologue

[June 25, 1982]

She was led down the iron steps and across the hallway and out into the chill of the morning. She would have gone on her toes to protect the rawness of the wounded flesh on the soles of her feet, but the guards on either side of her held her firmly above her elbows and she was hurried across a chipstone yard. She did not cry out. She did not flinch from the pain that burst into her body from her feet.

There was a jeep parked on the far side of the yard. Beyond it four posts in front of a sandbagged wall. There were two groups of soldiers lounging on the ice wet grass between the jeep and the stakes and some were cleaning their rifles. She saw the ropes that were knotted to the posts. They were waiting to do their work, but she was not a part of that work.

At the back of the jeep she was handcuffed, then lifted roughly inside under the loose canvas. Her escorts climbed in after her. She was pushed to the floor where the fuel fumes merged with the sweat stench of the black and hooded *chador*. The jeep lurched forward. She heard the exchange between the driver and the sentries at the gate, and then she heard the early morning choking whine of the street traffic. She closed her eyes. There was nothing to see. She had learned when she was taken to the gaol, three months before, that her ears were to be her eyes.

It was an hour's journey to the airfield.

The canvas at the back of the jeep was raised, the tail dropped. She was levered out of the jeep. For a moment she was slumped on the tarmac, before the guards hoisted her to her feet. She saw no pity in their faces, she thought that they hated her as their enemy. She knew where she was. As a child she had many times been brought here by her mother to welcome home her father from field exercises away from the capital. She could remember soldiers and junior officers, all polished and creased and snapping to attention to salute her father as he passed them. She could remember the disciplined laughter all around her as she had broken free from her mother's hand and raced forward to jump at her father's chest. Precious memories now. She was shepherded by her guards up the rear ramp of the aircraft.

As she was taken forward in the closed cave of the aircraft the light of the morning died and the soldiers tucked in their boots and shifted their rucksacks and their weapons to allow her and her escorts to pass. They took her to the front of the aircraft to where some seats had been curtained off with sacking. The guard who fastened the seatbelt across her waist leered into her face, and his breath was heavy with chillis. The engine pitch rose, the aircraft stumbled forward.

The flight from Tehran to Tabriz, a distance of 350 miles, took 75 minutes. She did not turn her head. She did not try to look out of the small porthole window behind her left ear. She did not need to see the gold sun streaming from behind the great mountain of Damavand. She sat still, unmoving, unspeaking. She found a place on the cabin floor in front of her, a place amongst the ammunition boxes and the ration crates. She stared down at the place.

It was an old aircraft. She heard the rumble of the engines and sometimes the cough of a missed stroke, she heard these sounds above and dominating the reading of the Qur'an from beyond the sacking screen. Her guards talked quietly and kept their eyes from her, as if contact with her could contaminate them, taint their souls. She tried not to think. Was her short life an achievement, was it wasted? Better to shut her mind to thoughts.

The pitch of the aircraft changed. She closed her eyes. She had no God, she willed courage into her body.

The transporter rattled down onto the long strip of the Tabriz field and the interior was flooded with light and the squeal of the tail ramp going down. After the pilot had braked and the aircraft had stopped, she was kept in her seat until the last of the soldiers on the far side of the sacking screen had gone with their kit and weapons and ammunition and food. Their voices trailed away from her. She wanted so much to be brave. She wanted so much to be worthy of her father. The guards unfastened the safety belt. They made her stand. From a plastic bag one of the guards took a loose white robe, with open seams and tapes under the armpits. The white robe was lifted over her head, and the tapes were tied at the sides. She was alone. In four days she would have been eighteen. She had been brought to the second city of her native country for public execution.

They led her down the echoing interior of the aircraft, out into the bold crisp sunlight of the morning. She was a small, waif figure amongst the men. She wanted to think of her father, and she could not because the pain of her body had crept through to her mind. She wondered if her father, at his same moment, at the moment when he was lashed to the post in the garden of the Evin gaol, had thought of her, his daughter. A short and hazed thought, and then gone. The lorry waiting a few feet from the aircraft ramp spilled out its exhaust fumes over them. A guard on each elbow, half walking her, half carrying her to the back of the lorry, and a small knot of men waiting there for her arrival. The young Mullah was there. She had stood in front of him in the courtroom high in Block One of the Evin gaol in the late afternoon, only yesterday. Perhaps he had travelled from Tehran to Tabriz last night, after he had heard the case against her, weighed it, passed judgment, announced sentence. Perhaps he had boarded the aircraft after her and sat away from her and amongst the soldiers. It was of little matter. The Mullah stared into her face. She tried to stare back at him, but her guards pulled her forward to the back of the lorry and lifted her bodily up and inside. The Mullah had taken a very few minutes to hear her case. She had not spoken in her defence.

She wanted it over. She did not know how long she could stay brave.

The lorry drove into Tabriz. She was not innocent of the crime of which she had been convicted. Yes, she had thrown the grenade. And yes, her regret was very keen that it had not killed more of the pigs. She knew why she had been brought to Tabriz, she knew it was the custom of the regime to exact retribution and punishment at the scene of the crime.

Sometimes the lorry was held up in traffic that not even the bellow of a siren could clear. Slow, jerking progress. She pictured in her mind the road they were taking. It was the same route that she had travelled with the two boys into the city, the heart of the city and the offices of the *pasdaran*. To her mind, the *pasdaran* were the symbol of slavery, repression, bigotry. The Islamic Revolutionary Guards were the embodiment of an evil that had consumed her nation . . .

The lorry stopped. The hands of the guards rested on her arms. She saw that they watched her, eager to see how she would be, in the last minutes. They lifted her from the wooden seat of the lorry, propelled her towards the open end of the lorry. Numbness in her mind, a quivering weakness at her knees. She heard the bellowing of a tannoy, and realised that it was the same voice, hushed and musical then, that had sentenced her to death late yesterday. She stood at the edge of the lorry's floor. There were people as far as she could see. A roar greeted the sight of her. The sound of the voices came at her as waves across shingle, repeated and again. Impossible to make out what was shouted because her ears were still confused by the pressure drop of the aircraft. The faces told her. The faces were shouting their hatred, their pleasure at what was to happen to her. As far as she could see, faces of hate and faces of pleasure. She could not see the Mullah but she heard the excitement in the shrillness of his voice.

Hands reached up for her. She was lifted down from the lorry. No pain in the soles of her feet now. Her guards dragged her forward, and men in uniform forced a passage clear ahead of them.

She saw the crane.

The crane was on a platform behind the cab of a truck. The truck was outside the front gate of the offices of the *pasdaran*. The truck was parked where she had thrown the grenade, where the two boys who had been with her were shot down, where she had been captured. There was a table of heavy wood under the lowered arm of the crane. There was a noosed rope hanging from the crane, and beside it a man in the combat uniform of the *pasdaran*. He was stout, heavily bearded. At the side of his leg he held a long strip of leather.

The guards lifted her very easily onto the table. She gazed around her. She was aware that the executioner now crouched beside her and she felt the tightness of the leather strip at her ankles. So ridiculous. So ridiculous that so many had come to watch the putting to death of so small a person, so young a person. So ridiculous, all of those people in front of her, below her. So ridiculous that she smiled. Her face broke into a smile. The smile of

517

her youth. The smile of her puzzlement. She heard the Mullah's voice above all the thousand other voices in unison. And then suddenly the shouting had gone.

A great booming quiet around them as the executioner draped round her neck the string that carried the white cardboard sheet on which was spelled out in large characters her crime. His fingers fumbled with the noose of the rope. He pulled the noose over her head, tightened it under her chin.

He had never known such quiet.

They would all remember her, all of those who watched the handcuffed girl in the white robe, standing alone on the table as the executioner jumped down.

The arm of the crane surged upwards.

She died painfully, struggling, but quickly.

For two hours, high above the street, her body hung from the arm of the crane.

The old man made his way along the corridor.

He was an institution in the building, a throwback really to the days before the Service had been equipped with consoles, software and instant communications. In his own way the messenger was something of a celebrity at Century House because of the time he had been with the Service. He, almost alone, had known intimately the warren of the former offices that spanned Queen Anne's Gate and Broadway; he had been on the payroll under seven Director Generals, and it had become difficult for any of the older people at Century to imagine being able to cope without him. His approach was slow. He had never quite mastered the artificial limb fitted below the right knee cap. He had been a young man when he had lost his leg, a corporal of infantry on garrison duty in Palestine when he had stepped on a crude anti-personnel mine. He was paid for a 38-hour week, and not a week went by when he was inside Century for less than 60 hours.

Across the Thames, muffled by the sealed windows of the tower block, Big Ben struck nine thirty. The steel toe and heel caps of the messenger's shoes scraped along the composite tiles. There was silence around him. Office doors locked, rooms darkened. But he could see the light at the distant finishing post of the corridor. This evening, every weekday evening, the messenger performed a personal service for Mr Matthew Furniss. He carried by hand the transcript of the main evening news bulletin on the Home Service of Tehran Radio, monitored and translated at the BBC premises at Caversham, relayed by telex to Foreign and Commonwealth Office, and thence to Century.

He paused at the door. The transcript was gripped between his thumb and a nicotined finger. He looked through the dusk of the open plan area and towards the light shaft that was the door into the inner office of Mr Furniss. He knocked.

518

"Come."

The messenger thought that Mr Furniss had a lovely voice, the sort of voice that would have sounded lovely on the wireless. He thought Mr Furniss with his lovely voice was also a lovely man. He thought Mr Matthew Furniss was the best of the Old Guard at Century, and a proper gentleman.

"You're so kind, Harry . . . Bless you, and you should have been home hours ago."

It was a sort of a ritual, because the messenger brought the transcript every weekday evening, and every weekday evening Mr Furniss seemed so pleasantly surprised and grateful, and he thought that evening that Mr Furniss looked rotten, like the world was on top of him. The messenger knew enough about the man, plenty, as much as anybody at Century, because the messenger's wife in the years gone by had baby-sat, minded the girls, for Mr and Mrs Furniss. The room stank of pipe tobacco and the ash bowl was brimming. That was not usual, nor was the bottle of Grants that was on the desk and had taken a beating.

"No problem, sir . . ." The messenger handed over the transcript.

Twenty-four hours earlier, to the minute, the messenger had delivered the previous monitored and translated news bulletin from the Home Service of Tehran radio. It was all very clear in the messenger's memory. Mr Matthew Furniss had given him his chirpy and conspiratorial smile and eased back in his chair to gut the resumé, and the chair had snapped forward, and the paperwork had flaked down from his hands onto the desk top, and he'd looked as if he'd been hit. That had been last night . . . The messenger watched. He peered through the smoke haze. The evening's transcript was on the desk and Mr Matthew Furniss was scanning it, taking it line by line. He stopped, he looked as if he was unwilling to believe what he read.

The messenger stood by the door. He saw the fist over the transcript clench, saw the knuckles whiten.

"The bastards . . . the filthy, vicious bastards . . ."

"That's not like you, Mr Furniss."

"The wicked, fucking bastards."

"Not at all like you, sir."

"They hanged her."

"Hanged who, sir?"

The messenger had seen the moment of weakness, but it was gone. Furniss poured a generous measure of the whisky into a fresh glass and offered it to the messenger, and the small glass already on the desk was filled, splashed to the top. The position of the messenger at Century was indeed unique, no other uniformed servant of the Service would have been offered hospitality in the office of a senior Desk man. The messenger bent and scratched at his knee where the strapping chafed.

"The daughter of a friend of mine, Harry . . . What you brought me last night told me that it was on their radio that she'd been tried, found guilty, sentenced, probably a short ten minutes of play acting at justice. And tonight it says that she's been executed. Same age as our girls, roughly . . . a sweet kid."

"If anyone harmed your girls, Mr Furniss, I'd want to kill them."

"Yes, Harry . . . I'll drive you home. Be a good chap, find yourself a chair outside, just one phone."

The messenger sat himself down in the outer office. He could not help but hear. Carrying papers, post, internal memoranda around the corridors of Century he knew so much, eavesdropped so often. He heard Mr Furniss place, through the operator, a call to California. He heard the calm voice the far side of the partition wall. "Kate, that's you, Kate? It's Mattie. I'm very sorry, Kate, but I've awful news. It's Juliette, she died this morning in Tabriz. Put to death. I'm terribly, terribly sorry, Kate, and our love to you and Charlie . . . You're still going to send him? Of course, we'll look after Charlie, whenever you think he's ready to come . . . Kate, our very sincere sympathy." He heard the telephone placed down gently. That was awful, hanging a girl, that was diabolical. There was no call for hanging seventeen-year-old girls, not in Harry's book. Mr Furniss was in the doorway, coat over his arm.

"Time we were going home, Harry."

1

Mahmood Shabro always invited Charlie Eshraq when he threw a thrash in his office. Shabro had known his father, and his sister and his uncle. The wide windows looked out onto the busy east end of Kensington High Street. There was a teak veneer desk and shelves and cabinets. There was a computer console in the corner, a pile carpet on the floor with a centre-piece of a good rug brought many years before from home. The easy chairs were pushed against the walls that were covered with photographs of a far away country – mosques, landscapes, a bazaar scene, a portrait of an officer in full dress uniform and two rows of medals. Mahmood Shabro was somewhat rare among the London exile community, he had done well. And when he did better, when he had clinched a deal, he celebrated, and he asked the less fortunate of his community to push out the boat with him.

Mahmood Shabro was a conduit for electrical goods going down to the Gulf. Not your low life stuff from Taiwan and Korea, but high quality from Finland and West Germany and Italy. He didn't do badly. He liked to say that the oil rich buggers down in the Emirates were putty to him.

Charlie could put up with the cant and boasting of the Shabro husband and wife, and he could put up with the caviare and the canapes, and the champagne. A thousand top of the range Zanussi washing machines were going down to Dubai, and some cretin who was happier on a camel was paying the earth for the privilege of doing business with Mahmood Shabro. Good enough reason for a party. He stood by the window. He watched, he was amused. He was not a part of the cheerful talk that was fake, the tinkling laughter that was fraud. He knew them all, except for the new secretary. One man had been a minister in the penultimate government appointed by Shah Reza Pahlavi as the roof was caving in over the Peacock Throne. One was once a paratroop major who now drove a mini-cab, nights, and he was on orange juice which meant he couldn't afford one evening off to get pissed. One was a former judge from Esfahan who now collected Social Security payments and who went to the Oxfam shop for shoes. One had been a policeman and now went every two weeks to the offices of the Anti-Terrorist branch at New Scotland Yard to complain that he was not given adequate protection for someone so obviously at risk.

They had all run away. They weren't the ones who had ripped off the system and come out with their dollars folded in their wife's underwear, if they weren't far sighted enough to collect them from banks in Switzerland. They were all pleased to be asked to Mahmood Shabro's parties, and they would eat everything within reach, they would drain every bottle.

Charlie always had a good laugh out of Mahmood Shabro. Mahmood Shabro was a rogue and proud of it. Charlie liked that. The rest of them were pretence, talking of home as if they were off to Heathrow next week for the flight back, talking about the regime as if it were a brief aberration, talking about their new world as if they had conquered it. They had conquered nothing, the regime was in place, and they weren't going home next week, next year. Mahmood Shabro had put the old world behind him, and that was what Charlie Eshraq liked. He liked people who faced facts.

Charlie was good on facts. Good enough on facts last month to have killed two men and made it clear away.

The talk flowed around him. It was all talk of home. They had exhausted their congratulation of Mahmood Shabro. Home talk, all of it. The economy in chaos, unemployment rising, the Mullahs and Ayatollahs at each other's throats, the war weariness growing. They would have gagged if they had known that Charlie Eshraq had been home last month, and killed two men. Their contact with home was long range, a drink in a hotel bar with the captain of an Iran Air Jumbo who was overnighting in London and who was prepared to gossip out of earshot of his minders. A talk on the direct dial phone with a relative who had stayed inside, petty talk because if politics were debated then the line would be cut. A meeting with a businessman who had travelled out with foreign currency bankers' orders to purchase items of importance to the war effort. Charlie thought they knew nothing.

He reckoned Mahmood Shabro's new secretary looked good. Charlie and the girl were younger by 25 years than anyone else at the party. He thought she looked bored out of her mind.

"I rang you a few weeks back – good party, isn't it? I rang you twice but you weren't there." Mahmood Shabro at his shoulder.

He had been watching the girl's backside, when her skirt was tight as she had bent down to pick up a vol-au-vent that had been dropped on the carpet and that was steadily being stamped in. The carpet, he supposed, was worth fifteen thousand.

"I was away."

"You travelling much, Charlie?"

"Yes, I'm travelling."

"Still the . . . ?"

"Travel courier," Charlie said easily. He looked across at the secretary. "That's a pretty girl. Can she type?"

"Who knows what talent is concealed?"

Charlie saw the watchful eyes of Mrs Shabro across the room.

"You alright, Charlie?"

"Never better."

"Anything you want?"

"If there's anything I can't get by myself, I'll come to you."

Mahmood Shabro let go of Charlie's arm. "Save me the taxi fare, take her home."

He liked Mahmood Shabro. Since cutting loose from his mother and pitching up in London without a family, Mahmood Shabro had been a friend, a sort of uncle. He knew why he was Mahmood Shabro's friend. He never asked the man for anything.

The secretary had come to his corner of the room, taking her boss's place. She had a bottle of champagne in her hand. He thought it must have been the last bottle, and she had come to him first to fill his glass almost to the lip before moving on and pouring out a few drops for everyone else. She came back, bearing the empty bottle. She said that Mahmood Shabro had told her to put a bottle aside for herself. She said with those eyes that had been worked with such care that she would not object to sharing the bottle. She told him that she would have to clear up. He told her his address and gave her a key and a note to cover the cab, and he said that he had to meet a man on his way home, that she was please to wait for him.

He went out into the early summer night. It was already dark. The headlights of the traffic flow scratched across his features. He walked briskly. He preferred to walk. He could check for a tail. He just did the usual things, nothing flash. Round the corner and waiting. Stopping on a pavement, spinning, walking back, checking the faces. Just being sensible.

He went to his meeting. He had put out of his mind the gathering of no-hopers, losers, dreamers, in Mahmood Shabro's office.

She was nineteen.

She was a mainliner.

The middle of the evening, and the darkness spreading. She stood in shadow at the side of the toilets in the small park area off the main shopping street. She was a mainliner because dragon chasing and mouth organ playing were no longer sufficient to her.

Lucy Barnes was a tiny elf girl. She felt the cold. She had been waiting for two hours, and when she had left the squat the sun was still hovering amongst the chimneys of the small terraced homes. The sleeves of her blouse were fastened at her wrists. The light above the toilet block had been smashed and she was in a black hidden space, but she wore a pair of wide dark glasses.

Two weeks ago she had sold the remote control colour 16-channel portable television set that had been her parents' birthday present to her. She had spent the money, she had used up the grammes of scag the sale had bought. There was more money in her pocket, more notes crumpled into the hip pocket of her trousers. That afternoon she had sold a teapot from home. Georgian silver, good price. She needed a good price.

The bastard was bloody late, and her legs ached in cramp, and she was cold and she was sweating. Her eyes were watering, as if she was crying for him to come.

Mattie Furniss would not have shared the conviction with even his closest colleagues, but the last fourteen weeks had convinced him that the Director

General was just not up to the mark. And here they were again. The meeting of Heads of Desks, Middle East/West Asia, had kicked off an hour behind schedule, it had dragged on for close to three hours, and they were bogged down a third of the way down the agenda. Nothing personal, of course, simply the gut feeling that the Director General should have been left to vegetate in main stream diplomacy at Foreign and Commonwealth, and not been inflicted on the Service in the first place. Mattie Furniss was a professional, and the new Director General was most certainly not. And it was equally certain that the Secret Intelligence Service of Century House could not be run as if it were merely an offshoot of FCO.

Worst of all was the inescapable conclusion that the Director General, wet behind the ears in intelligence tradition, was gunning for Iran Desk. Israel Desk, Mid East Desk, Gulf Desk and Sub-Continent (Pakistan) Desk, were all in his sights, but Iran Desk was taking the bulk of the flak.

"That's the long and the short of it, gentlemen, we are simply not producing top quality intelligence material. I go to JIC each week, and they say to me, 'What is actually *happening* in Iran?' Perfectly fair question for Joint Intelligence Committee to be asking me. I tell them what you gentlemen have provided me with. You know what they say? They say to me, and I cannot disagree, that what they are getting from us is in no way different from what is served up by the usual channels along the Gulf . . ."

"Director General, if I may . . ."

"Allow me, please, to finish. I'd appreciate that . . ."

Mattie sagged back in his chair. He was the only smoker round the mahogany table that the Director General had imported upon arrival. He had his matches out. Every other DG he had worked for had stuck to one on one meetings where a bit of concentration could be applied, where speeches would seem inelegant. He smoke screened himself.

"I won't be able to defend my budget proposals for the coming year if the Service is producing, in such a critical international theatre, the sort of analysis that is going into FCO day in and day out. That's the crux of it, Mattie."

It was the fourth time Mattie had listened to this monologue. The three previous sessions he had stood his corner and justified his position. He sensed the others round the table praying he wouldn't bite. On three previous occasions he had delivered his answer. No embassy in Tehran as cover for a resident Station Officer. Not a hope in hell of recruiting anyone close to the real power bases inside Iran. Less and less chance of persuading British technicians to do any more than decently keep their eyes open while setting up a refinery or whatever. Three times he had come up with the more significant data that his agents in place had been able to provide . . . all water off a duck's backside . . . including the best stuff he had had last time from the boy, and unless they finished soon he would be too late to pay for it.

"I hear you, Director General."

The Director General hacked a cough through the wreaths of smoke drifting past him. "What are you going to do about it?"

524

"Endeavour to provide material that will give greater satisfaction than the hard won information my Desk is currently supplying."

The Director General flapped in front of his face with his agenda paper. "You should go out there, Mattie."

"Tehran, Director General. First class idea," Mattie said. Israel Desk was the youngest in the room, high-flier and still irreverent, too long in the field, and having to bite on the heel of his hand to stop himself laughing out loud.

"I cannot abide facetiousness."

"Where would you suggest I travel to, Director General?"

"The fringes."

Mattie asked quietly, "To what purpose?"

"Pretty obvious, surely. To brief your people on what is now required of them. To take the opportunity to get your agents in place out from inside so that they can be advised, in exact terms, of our needs."

He bit at his pipe stem. "You are forgetting, Director General, that Desk Heads do not travel."

"Who says so?"

"Since ever, Desk Heads do not travel because of the security implications."

"Do not travel, wrong. Do not usually travel, right."

If he bit through the stem of his pipe he would at the same time break his teeth. "Is that final?"

"Yes it is. And I think we'll pause there."

There was a rapid gathering of papers. Israel Desk was already out of the door when the Director General said, "Goodnight, gentlemen, and thank you for your patience. What's worth doing is worth doing right."

Mattie Furniss didn't wait for the lift to get up to the 19th floor. He ducked away from his colleagues for the fire escape stairway. He went down nine flights at two steps at a time, praying that the boy would still be waiting for him and for his present.

It had been a short road for Lucy Barnes from home in a mews house in London's Belgravia to the attic of a terraced house in the West Country town. On this cool and early summer evening she was at the end of her financial resources. She had gone to London that week, she had broken into the family home through a kitchen window, she had taken the teapot. They would change the locks after that. Probably they had already changed the locks. She couldn't remember now why she had only taken the teapot. She had no idea where she would go for more money, for more scag, after the doses that were on the floor beside her were exhausted.

A short road. Cannabis smoking behind the school's sports pavilion, an act of adolescent defiance and experimentation. She had been through dragon chasing, heating the scag powder through tinfoil and inhaling the fumes through a soft drinks tube. She had tried mouth organ playing, dragging the same heated fumes into her lungs through the cover of a matchbox. One and a half years after her expulsion – and pretty goddam embarrassing that had been because darling Daddy was already signed up to hand over the prizes at next term's Speech Day – she was a mainliner and needing a grand a month to stay with it.

The pusher had said this was new stuff, purer than he had ever had through his hands before, the best stuff he had ever been sold. None of the usual dilution shit in the cut, no talcum or chalk dust or fine sugar. Real stuff, like it had been before the dealers got to be so bloody greedy.

She loaded the hypodermic. She could estimate the dose, didn't use fragile weighing scales. She sat cross-legged on a square of threadbare carpet. The attic was lit by the beam from a street light that pierced the dirty glass of the skylight window. She could see what she was doing. The arm veins were no longer any good to her, the leg veins were failing on her. She kicked off her shoes. She wore no tights, nor socks. Her feet were dark stained, she had not had a bath in more than a month, but she knew where the veins ran on the underside of her feet.

She gritted her teeth as she inserted the needle behind the ball of her right foot. She drew back the arm of the hypodermic, sucking blood into the container, allowing the blood to mix inside the syringe with the scag powder. Slowly, trying to control the trembling of her thumb, she pressed down on the syringe.

She lay back on the bare mattress. She anticipated the peace and the dream.

The boy was where he had said he would be.

Old habits would die hard for Mattie Furniss. The old way of doing things was to meet in a park's open spaces where it was comparatively easy to guard against surveillance and eavesdropping. The boy was a shadow under a sycamore tree close to the lake. He was almost trotting, and the supermarket bag flapped against his trouser leg. Out in the road that fringed the park a van did a U-turn, and its headlights played across the open ground with the manoeuvre and the boy was lit. Tall, bearded, a fine looking boy. Mattie had known young Eshraq so long that he would always regard him as a boy. But Charlie did not seem to Mattie like any other 22-year-old that he knew, not in build and stature, not in temperament or attitude. A hell of a fine young man, but then so had his father been . . . He reached the tree. He drew at his breath. He had run all the way from Century on the other side of the river, over the Bridge and across Whitehall to the park. He would have to put in some extra training if he were to finish the half marathon this summer.

"Tied up, dear boy. Apologies."

"No problem, sir."

Mattie liked the way that Charlie addressed him. That was his father's stamp on the young man, and his mother's too, in fairness to her.

"Long time, dear boy."

"It's a new skill for me, learning to write reports, sir. I hope it will be of use to you." Charlie reached into his blazer pocket, took out a thick envelope, handed it to Mattie. Mattie didn't examine it, just slid it down into an inner pocket of his suit then drew across a zip fastener at the top of the pocket, another old habit. Wouldn't do for a Desk Head to get his pocket picked in the Underground.

"I'm looking forward to it . . . Heard from your mother?"

"No." Charlie said it as if it didn't matter to him that his mother never wrote nor telephoned from California. As if it was nothing to him that the golf course and the bridge club and the riding school filled his mother's days and evenings, that she regarded him as a relic of a former life in Iran that was best forgotten, that was painful to remember.

"I read about your escapade, the good old *Tehran Times*. Carried on the radio as well."

A slow smile on Charlie's face.

". . . You weren't compromised?"

"There was a search afterwards, plenty of roadblocks. No, they didn't know what they were looking for. They put it down to the 'hypocrites'. It went quite well."

Mattie could almost have recited the text of the IRNA communique reproduced in the *Tehran Times*. In separate incidents in south Tehran two Islamic Revolutionary Guards martyred in broad daylight by MKO (*Mojahedin-e Khalq* Organisation) counter-revolutionary *mustafaqin* (hypocrites) working in conjunction with American mercenary agents. Now that Harry had retired, gone more than four years, the IRNA communiques reached him ahead of the BBC's transcripts. He missed the messenger's service.

"We came up with a nice one for the next run," Mattie said. He offered the supermarket bag that was taut from the weight of its contents. "Instructions inside."

"Thank you."

"I'll want another report."

"Of course, sir. Mrs Furniss is well?"

"Grand form, and the girls. You'll come down to the country when you're back? We'll round up the girls. Make a weekend of it."

"I'd like that."

"You alright for money? I could scrape the bucket a bit for you."

A present in a plastic bag he could manage with ease. Money was harder. Money had to go through Audit. The present in the plastic bag was by his own arrangement with Resources/Equipment, on the ninth floor.

"I'm fine for money, sir."

"Glad to hear that."

He saw the boy hesitate. The boy looked as though he were framing his request and not certain as to the best face to put on it. He felt the first drops of rain, and he was sweating now from his run.

"Cough it out."

"The target that I want most has an escort and his car is armoured."

"Meaning?"

"It would be difficult to get close enough."

"And . . ." Mattie wasn't going to help.

"I need what they call stand-off capability. Do you understand that, sir?"

"I understand." Mattie gazed into the boy's eyes. The hesitation was gone, the request had been made. There was cool and attractive certainty in the boy's eyes. "You would have to go for longer, your reports would have to be regular."

"Why not," Charlie said, as if it was a small matter.

Mattie thought of the boy's father, a generous host, a true friend. He thought of the boy's uncle, a mountain of a man, a superb stalker of boar and a brilliant shot. He thought of the boy's sister, delicate and winning her arguments with the brilliance of her smile, and kissing him when he brought gifts to the villa. He thought of Charlie's mother, brittle because she was uncertain, brave because she had tried to blend and assimilate her foreignness into that society of the wide and prosperous avenues of North Tehran. It was a family that had been dismembered.

"That would be very expensive indeed." A sharpness in Mattie's voice. Yes, he was a stickler for protocol and procedure. No, he should never have allowed his Service life to meld with the crusade that was the boy's.

"I could pay for it."

Mattie Furniss was off on his travels, and that was no business of the boy's. And he didn't know his schedule yet. He did not know when he would return, when they could next meet. So much to talk about. They should have been talking in comfort of gentler matters, relaxed, they should have been gossiping – not prattling around the subject of stand-off capability and armour-piercing weapons under a tree in St James's Park for God's sake, with the rain beginning to come down in earnest. He took out his pen and a sheet of paper from a leather backed pad. He wrote briefly on it. A name, an address.

"Thank you, sir," Charlie said.

The keen statement. "In for longer, the reports more regular."

"Please give my best regards to Mrs Furniss, and to the girls."

"Of course I will. They'll be glad to know I've seen you." He wondered whether the boy had been more than a friend to his daughters, either of them. They'd been very close, down in the country, and when his brood were all in London and the boy was their guest. It had been in London, three years before, in their little drawing room, the boy on his first trip from California and away from his mother, that Mattie had told Charlie Eshraq, as straight and as baldly as he could, what had happened to his sister and his father and his uncle. He had never seen the boy cry since then. Bottled it all up, of course.

"When do you go, dear boy?"

"Pretty soon."

"You'll telephone me, at home, before you go?"

"Yes."

"You'll go steadily?"

"Yes."

The rain dribbled over Mattie's face, and caught at his trimmed and silver moustache and darkened the front of his shirt. The boy's face was a blur in front of him and masked by the fullness of his beard.

"If anything happened to you, while you're away, Harriet and I, and the girls, we'd be . . ." Mattie squeezed the boy's shoulders.

"Why should it, sir?"

They parted.

He walked home. Mattie felt dirtied because he encouraged the folly of the boy, and yet he did not know how he could have dissuaded him. And he had the thick bulk of the envelope in his pocket, and the boy had said that he would be going in for longer, and that the reports would be more regular. He thought that in a decent world Matthew Cedric Furniss would deserve to be flailed alive.

He fervently hoped that Harriet would still be up and waiting for him. He needed to talk to her, play a record, and be warmed and wanted. He had never in three years seen the boy cry, and the boy had murdered two Revolutionary Guards and planned to go back in again with his present in a plastic bag. The boy was talking about stand-off and armour-piercing. He was talking about war, dammit, and the boy was no less than a son to him.

Mattie said an abbreviated prayer for Charlie Eshraq as he crossed at the traffic lights outside his London flat. And if the boy had bedded his daughters then good luck to him.

He was soaked. His face ran with water. His sodden trousers were clinging to his shins and his shoes squelched. When he looked up he saw the light behind the curtain welcoming him.

There could be as many as 50,000 persons addicted to heroin inside the United Kingdom.

On that night one of them, Lucy Barnes, had failed to compensate for the increased purity of the dose with which she injected herself. Alone, in a coma and on a stinking mattress, she choked to death on her own vomit.

2

The detective had led the way up to the attic. During that day he had become familiar enough, as familiar as he wanted to be, with the cramped space under the slope of the roof. He eased back against a wall, brushing against the peeling paper. Below him the stairway protested at the weight of the two that followed him. The local detective thought it understandable that the Secretary of State would have his own man from Protection with him. The bodyguard would have lived long enough in the Secretary of State's pocket to have become a part of the retinue, almost family. He understood that the Secretary of State needed a face to trust. The Secretary of State emerged into the attic, white dust and cobwebs on the collar of his black overcoat. The detective had taken to the furthest corner, he left the centre ground to the Secretary of State and his bodyguard. He had seen them all. The ones on the breadline, and the most powerful in the land. They all came bowed and subdued to witness the place, the stinking corner, where their child had died. Usually the mothers came too. He knew that some would be aggressive, some would be broken, some crippled with shame. Their child, their future, blown away by a hypodermic syringe. The room was pitifully bare, and even more confused than when the police had first been alerted by the ambulance team because his squad had turned the place over and ransacked every inch of it. The mattress had been taken apart. The girl's clothes had been put into a black plastic sack after examination. Her papers were collected into a cellophane bag which would go to his office for further examination.

The bodyguard stood at the top of the stairway. He gave the sign with his eyes, he told the local man to get on with his talk. The Secretary of State was known to the policeman only through the television in his living room and the photographs in the newspapers that he never seemed to find time to read but which were kept for lighting the fire before he went to work. The Secretary of State was not a pretty sight, looked like a man who had been kicked hard in the testicles an hour before. He could stand, but the colour was gone from his face. He'd done well, the local man, he had had the name, alerted the Metropolitan, and now had the parent where the parent wanted to be, and all this before the rat-pack had wind of the excitement. Drily he thought to himself, if nothing else went right on this one then getting the Secretary of State into and out of this crap heap before the photographers pitched up was good going. He took the lead from the bodyguard.

"Lucy had been living here for several weeks, sir, at least she was here for a month. Only known means of support, the Social Security. Preliminary post mortem indicates that she was a serious victim of addiction – we don't regard users as criminals, sir, we tend to refer to them as victims. Her wrist veins have been used, no good anymore, and her thigh and shin veins have also been used. She had taken to using the smaller veins in her feet as an injection route. I am assuming that you were aware that she was addicted, sir – I mean, it must have been pretty obvious, obvious that is if you were still in touch with your daughter . . ."

The Secretary of State had his head down, made no response. Just like all the rest of them, feeling it a duty to get some feel of where their child had died. Christ, the room stank.

". . . We cannot yet be certain of the cause of death, not in exact terms, that will come later when Pathology have had their full whack, but the first indicators are, sir, that she took a rather pure dose. What she took was just too much for her system. That causes a coma, and then vomiting. Blocked windpipe does the rest – I'm sorry, sir."

The Secretary of State's voice was a flat monotone. "I've an old chum, medic in London. I talked to him right at the beginning. I said, 'Whose child becomes an addict?' He said, 'Your kid.' He said, 'No one worries when the addict is that nice kiddie from next door, but by Heavens they worry when it's the nice kiddie upstairs.' We thought that we had done everything for her. She went to the best schools, when she went onto heroin we sent her to the best withdrawal clinic. Just a waste of money. We cut her allowance, so she sold everything we'd ever given her. She moved out, then came back and stole from us. Can you imagine that, officer, stealing from her own parents . . . of course, you can imagine it, you are accustomed to the misery caused by this addiction. The last thing we did was have the Ministry's own security system in our own house changed. I mean that's coming to something, isn't it, when the Secretary of State for Defence has to have his own alarm system changed because his own daughter might want to break in . . . Her mother will want to know, can't hide much from her mother, would she have been in pain?"

"Coma first, sir. No pain." The detective was past shock, past sympathy, and way past apportioning blame. He could be matter of fact. "She had the stuff. It's if she hadn't had the stuff that she would have been in pain."

"How much would it have been costing her?"

"From what we've seen, anything between a hundred and two hundred a week – when it's got that bad."

The local detective wondered how the politician would survive it. He wondered whether he would shut himself away from public life once the storm blew, the headlines tomorrow and the Coroner's Court reporting. Whether he would carry on as if his public and private lives were separate compartments. He wondered if the pursuit of his public life could have so damaged a private life that a lone, lost child took to a syringe for companionship, for love.

The Secretary of State had a good grip on himself, his voice was clear. Nothing staccato, nothing choked. "A colleague of mine said recently, 'This abuse brings hardened criminals and indulgent users together in a combination that is potentially lethal for good order and civilised values – the price of ultimate failure is unthinkable.' That was before Lucy had her problem, I didn't take much notice of it then. What are you doing about it, officer, this lethal combination?"

The local detective swallowed his first thoughts. Not the moment to spit out his gripes about resources and priorities, and bans on overtime payment which meant that most of his squad clocked off on the dot of office hours. He said, "Gather what evidence we can, sir, try and move our investigation on from there."

"Do you have children, officer?"

"Yes, sir."

"What age?"

"About half your Lucy's age, sir."

"Could it happen to them, what happened to her?"

"As long as the stuff's coming in, sir, flooding in like it is – yes, sir."

"What would you want done, officer, if she had been yours?"

"I'd want to get to the fuckers . . . excuse me, sir . . . to the people who made the stuff available to your Lucy."

"You'll do what you can?"

"Bluntly, sir, that's not a lot. Yes, we will."

The bodyguard had flicked his fingers, a small gesture close to the seam of his trousers. The local man had the message. He moved around and behind the Secretary of State, to the head of the staircase. The bodyguard was already warily descending. There was music playing on a lower floor. The detective had had one session with the other residents of this terraced house, and he would have another later that afternoon when he had got himself shot of the big man. He hadn't been heavy with them, the others in the squat, not once he had discovered who Lucy Barnes' father was. Counter productive, he would have said, to have leaned too hard on them right now. He wanted their help, he needed all they could give him. From the top of the staircase he looked back. The Secretary of State was staring down at the mattress, and the bag of clothes, and the junk litter that might the previous week have been important to a nineteen-year-old girl.

He paused at the bottom of the stairs.

"What does he think I'm going to do about it?"

The bodyguard shrugged.

Two, three minutes later, they heard the creaking of the stairs. The detective thought he saw a redness at the eyes that were distorted by the Secretary of State's rimless spectacles.

On the pavement the Secretary of State paused beside his car. The chauffeur was holding open the back door. "Thank you again, officer. I am not a complete fool, by the way. I understand the very real difficulties that you face in your work. I can promise you one thing. I will, quite shamelessly, use every vestige of my authority and influence to ensure the apprehension and prosecution of those responsible for Lucy's death. Good day to you."

He ducked down into the car. The bodyguard closed the door on him, and slipped into the front passenger seat. The detective saw the Secretary of State lift from a briefcase a portable telephone, and the car was gone, heading away fast.

He went back upstairs. In a confined space he preferred to work alone. Half an hour later, under newspapers, under a loosened floor board, a long way back in a cavity, he found Lucy's diary.

"This is a great deal better, Mattie. Much more what I've been looking for."

"I'm gratified."

"I'll explain to you my assessment of Iran theatre . . ."

Mattie studied the ceiling light. It was not so much an impertinence, more an attempt to avert his eyes so that the impatience could be better disguised.

". . . We are talking about the region's principal geopolitical and military power, sitting astride the most important petroleum trade routes in the world. We are talking about the country with the potential for regaining its position as thirteenth in Gross National Product, with the largest army in Western Asia, with no foreign debt, with the capacity to blow over every other regime in the area . . ."

"I have specialised, Director General, in Iranian matters since 1968 – I have actually lived there."

"Yes, yes, Mattie. I know you are close to Iran. Short service commission in the Coldstream liaising with the Imperial army, '65 to '67; Station Officer '75 to '78; Bahrain and Ankara after the Revolution. Give me the credit, Mattie, for being able to read a personal file. I know you were familiar with Iran before your entry to the Service, and that since entry you have specialised in that country. I know your file backwards and I'll tell you what I think: you're probably too close to your subject. My training is as a Kremlinologist, I'm a Cold War freak, and I should think you have a clearer view of how we should be targetting the Soviet Union and its satellites than I have. Just as I believe I have a clear idea of what's required from Iran. It's time we understood each other, Mattie . . ."

Mattie no longer stared at the ceiling. He looked straight ahead of him. He hadn't his pipe out of his pocket, he hadn't his matches on the mahogany table. He had his fists clenched. He could not remember when he had last felt such anger.

"You're in a rut. That's why I've been brought in to run Century. There are too many of you in a rut, going through the motions, never questioning the value of material. I won't accept paper pushing . . . This is the best material you have supplied me with."

Mattie squinted his gaze across the table, across to his rewrite of Charlie Eshraq's report. Good, but not that good. A useful start for something that would get better.

". . . It's crude, but it's factual. In short it is the sort of material that crosses my desk all too infrequently. There are five valuable pieces of information.

One, the movement of the 8th and 120th Battalions of the IRG 28th Sanandaj Division from Ahvaz to Saqqez, movement by night indicating that this was not simply a tactical readjustment, but more the reinforcing of a particular sector prior to using those Guards in a new push. The Iraqis would like to know that . . ."

"You'd pass that on to the Iraqis?" A hiss of surprise.

"I might. Good material earns favours . . . Two, the German engineer on his way to Hamadan, and at Hamadan is a missile development factory. Good stuff, stuff we can confront our friends in Bonn with, make them quite uncomfortable . . . I've marked up all of what I consider to be relevant, five points in all. The training camp at Saleh-Abad north of Qom, that's useful. Fine stuff."

The Director General had carefully placed his pencil on the table. He upturned a glass and filled it with water from a crystal jug.

"And who is going to emerge as the power among the clerics, and how long the war is going on, and what is the state of disaffection amongst the population, am I to presume that is unimportant?"

"No, Mattie. Not unimportant, simply outside your brief. Analysis is for diplomatic missions, and they're good at it. I trust there will be more of this."

"Yes."

"Who is the source?"

"I think I've got your drift, Director General."

"I asked you, who is the source?"

"I will make sure that a greater flow of similar material reaches you."

The Director General smiled. The first time that Mattie had seen the flicker of the lines at the side of his mouth.

"Please yourself, Mattie, and have a good trip."

Charlie Eshraq was personal to Mattie, and would not be shared with anyone. He stood, turned and left the room.

Going down in the lift he wondered what the boy was making of his present. It was personal and private to Mattie that on his last journey inside Charlie had killed two men, and equally personal and private that on this journey he would kill another.

They had been colleagues since University, since the youth section of the Party, since sharing an office in the Research Division headquarters in Smith Square. They had entered parliament at the same election, and the Cabinet in the same reshuffle. When their leader finally determined on retirement they would probably compete in the same dogfight for the top job. That time had not yet come, they were close friends.

"I'm dreadfully sorry, George."

Once the Home Secretary's assistant had brought in the coffee, placed it on the desk and left, they were alone. It was rare for two such men to meet without a phalanx of notetakers and agenda minders and appointment keepers. The Secretary of State sat exhausted in an easy chair, the plaster dust and the cobwebs still on his overcoat. "I want something done about this stinking trade." "Of course you do, George."

The Secretary of State looked hard into the Home Secretary's face. "I know what you are up against, but I want them found and tried and I shall pray you get them convicted and sentenced to very long terms, every last one of the bastards that killed Lucy."

"Very understandable."

"My detective told me that we are stopping one kilo out of ten that comes in . . ."

"We have stepped up recruitment of both police drugs officers and Customs. We've put a huge resource at the disposal . . ."

The Secretary of State shook his head. "Please, not a Party Political, not between us. I've got to go back to Libby tonight, I've to tell her where her – our – daughter died, and then I shall have to leave her and put on a cheerful face for dinner, ironically enough with some bigwigs from Pakistan, from the heart of what I expect you know is the Golden Crescent. I don't think, and I mean this, I don't think Libby will survive tonight if I cannot give her your solemn promise that Lucy's killers will be found and brought to book."

"I'll do what I can, George."

"She was a lovely girl, Lucy, before all this . . ."

"Everything we can do, that is a promise. You'll give my love to Libby. I'm so very sorry."

"Oh, you'd by God be sorry if you had seen how Lucy died, how she was – dead – and where she died. Libby will need the strength of twenty to survive this. In my heart of hearts I have known, for almost a year, how it might end but I couldn't imagine the depths of it. You must see it day in and day out, but this time the minuscule statistic on your desk is my dead daughter and I am going to hold you to your promise."

The detective worked his way steadily through the diary. He found an asterisk in red biro on every third or fourth day of the last few weeks, the last against the date on which the girl had taken her overdose. There were also telephone numbers. There was a string of seven-figure numbers, almost certainly London numbers, which for the moment he discarded. He had wrung from the others in the squat that Lucy Barnes had not been away from the town in the last days of her life. The local numbers were five-figure numbers. There was one number underlined in the same red biro. The local detective worked to a formula. He would work into the early evening, and then lock away the papers on his desk, put on his coat and drive home. What other way? If he and his two juniors worked 25 hours in the 24 they would still make no noticeable dent on the narcotics problems that had spread even to this country town. Where did the bloody stuff stop? The detective went to the area seminars, he had heard endlessly of the big city problems. And their problems, the problems of the major city forces, were his. If he hadn't shut it away, locked it into the drawer of his desk each evening, then the scag and coke would do for him too.

Before he put the key back into his pocket, he told the better of the two juniors to get onto the telephone exchange and cut all incoming and outgoing calls from the underlined number.

He wished them well, bade them a "Good evening", and left for home.

"The gloves off, is that what you're asking for?"

He was a former Chief Constable. He had seen it all and heard it all. He wanted the guidelines crystal clear, and from the horse's mouth. He headed the National Drugs Intelligence Unit, based on New Scotland Yard, with responsibility for co-ordinating efforts to stem the flow of narcotics into the country.

"Yes, I suppose that's it. Yes, that is what I am asking for." The Home Secretary shifted in his seat. His own Private Secretary was busy at his notepad, and at the back of the room the policeman's aide was scribbling fast, then looking up to see whether there was more. The Home Secretary wondered how similar their two notes would be.

"What I could say to you, Home Secretary, is that I might be just a little concerned at hard-pressed and limited resources being diverted on to one case, however tragic, merely because the victim happened to be well connected. You would understand that I could say that, would be entitled to say that."

"It's no doubt a straightforward case. It's nothing that hasn't been success-fully dealt with countless times. I just want it solved, and fast," the Home Secretary said.

"Then I'll tell you, sir, what's landed on our desks over the last few days . . . Four Blacks bullock their way into a house and shoot the mother and her schoolboy son, the boy's dead. That's drugs related. A blind widow is beaten up in the West Country, for a hundred pounds in her pension book. That's to pay for drugs. Twenty-eight policemen injured in two months in West London in one street, in 150 yards of one street, because we're trying to put a stop to trafficking in that street. What we call designer drugs, cocktail amphetamines, there are at least two new laboratories in East London which we haven't found. A six-year-old kiddie who's hooked on reefers, and his Mum's come in to tell us that he pinched £150 out of her handbag to pay for them . . . That's what's hitting our desks at the moment. Now do I hear you rightly, sir? Do I correctly hear you say that that type of investigation, pretty important to the men and women involved, goes on the back burner?"

"Yes."

". . . because the daughter of a Cabinet Minister is dumb enough to squirt herself an overdose?"

"Don't let's play silly buggers."

"Thank you, sir, I'll attend to it."

"And be damn certain you get a result."

There was a wintry smile on the policeman's face, a smile that sliced the Home Secretary's defences. He looked away, he didn't want to see the man's eyes, the message of contempt that a man in his position could break the civilized order of priorities because he had given his word to a colleague.

"You'll keep me informed," the Home Secretary told his Private Secretary. "And you can ring down for my car."

"Charlie Eshraq rang," Harriet Furniss said.

Mattie was heaving out of his overcoat. "Did he now?" Reaching to hook it tidily behind the front door. "And what did he have to say for himself?"

It was Mattie's way that he did not bring his office home. He had told his wife nothing of his dealings with the boy, nor that Charlie, whom Harriet Furniss treated as a son, had killed two men on his last journey home. They had been married for 28 years, and he had spent 21 of them as a member of the Secret Intelligence Service and he had stuck to his rule book, and the rule book said that wives were no part of the Service.

"He said that he was sorry that he had missed you. He was off tonight . . ."

"Was he now?" Mattie made a poor fist of unconcern.

Harriet would have noticed, but she would not have commented. Harriet never attempted to draw him out.

"He said that he had a rather good job for a few weeks, something about playing courier to tourists in the Aegean."

"That'll be nice for him."

"He said thank you for the present."

"Ah, yes. Just a little something that I saw, and posted to him," he said, too fast. He could lie with the best of them at Century, and was a miserable failure at home.

"He said it would be very useful."

"That's excellent. The country this weekend, I think, Harriet. Some reading to be done."

He kissed her on the cheek, like it was something that he should have done earlier. In all his married life Mattie had never looked at another woman. Perhaps he was old fashioned. He thought a little more each day of his advancing years – his next birthday would be his 53rd – and happily acknowledged that he was just damned lucky to have met and married Harriet (née Owens) Furniss.

He opened his briefcase, took out the black cloth-bound book that was all of its contents. He went to work each morning with a briefcase, as if it were a part of his uniform, but he never brought it home filled with office papers. He showed her the elegant lettering on the spine, *The Urartian Civilization of Near Asia – an Appraisal*. She grimaced. He opened the book and showed her the receipt from the antiquarian bookseller.

"It had better be your birthday present."

His birthday was not for another nine weeks. She would pay for the book as she paid for most of the extras in their lives, as she had paid the girls' school fees, as she had paid the airfare for Charlie Eshraq to come over from California to London years before. Mattie had no money, no inherited wealth, only his salary from Century, which looked after essentials – rates, mortgage, housekeeping. Their way of life would have been a good deal less comfortable without Harriet's contributions.

"How did Charlie sound?"

"Sounded pretty good. Very buoyant, actually. Supper'll be frizzled."

They went down the hallway towards the kitchen. He was holding his wife's hand. He did it more often now that the girls had left home.

"You'll have something to get your teeth into for the weekend?"

"Indeed I will . . . That wretched man who's bought the Manor Farm, he's ploughed up the footpath across Ten Acre. I'll have plenty to keep me busy."

God help the poor bastard, Mattie thought, the newcomer from the big city if he had come down to the countryside and ploughed up a right-of-way and made an enemy of Harriet Furniss.

She looked into his face. "The Urartians, aren't they Eastern Turkey?" She saw him nod. "Is that where you're going?"

"Gulf first, but I might get up there." There were times when he wanted nothing more than to talk through his days, to share the frustrations and to celebrate the triumphs. But he had never done it and he never would.

In the kitchen he made himself a weak gin and tonic, and gave Harriet her schooner of Cyprus dry sherry. Supermarket gin and cheap imported sherry, because drinks came out of the housekeeping. He was quiet that evening. While she washed up the pots and loaded the dishwasher, Mattie sat in a chair by the window, and saw nothing through the opened curtains, and wondered how far on his journey Charlie Eshraq had travelled.

"Come on, Keeper, for Christ's sake . . . get a wiggle on."

The pub was full, getting near to closing time, and the swill underway before "Time" was called.

David Park was away from the bar, outside the group. He stared back at them.

"Bloody hell, Keeper, are you in this round or are you not?" There were six of them up at the bar, and some had shed their jackets, and all had loosened their ties, and their faces were flushed. A hell of a good evening for all concerned, except for David Park. He hadn't made his excuses and gone home to Ann, but he hadn't played much of a part in the piss-up that had been inevitable after Mr Justice Kennedy's remarks following the sentencing.

"Keeper, it is your round."

True, it was David Park's round. He drained his bitter lemon. He made his way to the bar. In a quiet voice, and the barmaid had to heave most of her bosom onto the beer mats to hear him, he ordered six pints of Yorkshire bitter, and a bitter lemon with ice. He passed the beers from the bar to the eager waiting hands.

"Bloody good, Keeper . . . Cheers, old mate . . . 'Bout bloody time too . . . Keeper, my old love, you are something of a wet towel tonight . . ."

He grinned, fast, as if that were a weakness. He did not like to acknowledge weakness.

"I'm driving," he said calmly. He slid away from the heart of the group, back to the fringe. His radio call sign was Keeper, had been ever since he had been accepted into the Investigation Division. He was Park, and so some bright creature had labelled him Keeper. Mucking in, getting pissed-up, falling around, they weren't Park's talents. He had other talents, and Mr Justice Kennedy had remarked on them and commended the April team's dedicated work, and to everyone else in April that was reason enough to be on their seventh pint with a cab home at the end of it. Mr Justice Kennedy had handed down, late that afternoon, a Fourteen, two Twelves, and a Nine. Mr Justice Kennedy had called for Bill Parrish, Senior Investigating Officer and in charge of April team, to step up into the witness box so that the thanks of "a society under threat from these hellish traffickers who deal in wickedness" could be expressed. Bill Parrish in a clean white shirt then had looked decently embarrassed at the fulsome praise set out by the old cove. Parrish earned, basic, £16,000 a year. David Park earned, basic, £12,500 a year. The bastards who had gone down, for Fourteen and Twelve and Nine, were looking at a couple of million hidden away in the Caymans, and not touchable. It would take Park 40 years to earn what the bastards had waiting for them after their time, less remission, and by then he would be retired with his index-linked pension to cuddle. He liked the chase, cared little about the kill, couldn't care less once the 'cuffs went on. Parrish would get a great welcome from his wife when he made it home after closing, and she'd pour him another jug full and sit him down on the settee and roll the video so that he could belch his way through the recordings of the two main news bulletins of the evening and hear the message to the nation that Customs and Excise was super bloody marvellous, and keeping the nation safe, etc, etc. Park hoped Ann would be asleep.

April team was Iranian heroin. Park had been four years with April and had an encyclopaedic knowledge of Iranian heroin. He had been the front man in this investigation, deep inside the guts of the organisation that was doing the running of the scag, he had even driven for them. Ann knew sweet nothing about what he had been at. Best if she were asleep when he reached home.

He watched the group. He thought they looked stupid and very drunk. He couldn't remember when he had last been the worse for wear in public. One of the reasons he had been selected, that he could be relied upon invariably to stay the right side of the bottle. To be less than 1000 per cent clear-headed on a covert operation would be real bad news, like a shotgun barrel in the back of the neck. He didn't tell Ann what he did. He told her the generalities, never the details. He couldn't have told her that he was insinuated into a gang, that if his cover were blown he'd be face down in the Thames with the back of his skull a bloody remnant. He thought one of the guys was going to fall over.

Bill Parrish had detached himself from the group at the bar session, made his way stiffly to Park. An arm looped around his shoulders. He took the weight.

"Mind if I say it . . . ? When you want, you can be awesomely priggish, David."

"You can say it."

"April's a team, a shit hot team. A shit hot team stands or falls on being together. Being together doesn't match with one bugger on the edge and looking down his nose."

Park disentangled the arm, propped it onto the mantelpiece of the bar's fireplace. "Meaning what?"

"Meaning that this has been a great scene, worth celebrating."

Park dragged the breath down into his lungs. Parrish had asked for it. He'd get it.

"Did you see them in there? Did you see them when they were being sent down? They were laughing at us, Bill. One Fourteen, two Twelves and a Nine, and they were looking across at us like it was some sort of crack. Did you see their women in the gallery? Deep tans from the Costa. And that wasn't paste on their fingers, ears, throats . . . Hear me, Bill. What we are at is a confidence trick. We aren't even scratching at these pigs, and here we are pretending we're winning. It's a confidence trick the Judge plays too, and that way the British masses go to their beds tonight thinking everything is hunky-dory. We're kidding ourselves, Bill. We're not winning, we're not even doing well. We're drowning in the bloody stuff . . ."

"That's daft talk, David."

"How's this for daft talk? Heroin's an explosion, cocaine's gone through the roof, 'phets are up, with cannabis we're talking tonnage not kilos. We're deluding ourselves if we pretend we're on top of it. We're down on the floor, Bill. Yes or no, Bill?"

"I've drink taken, I'm not answering."

"Sorry, out of order. You know what I think . . . ?"

He saw Parrish roll his eyes. Wouldn't be the first time that Keeper had spouted his view of salvation.

"Give it me."

"We're too defensive, Bill. We should be a more aggressive force. We should be abroad more, we should be ferreting down the source. We shouldn't just be a line of last resort with our backs against the wall. We should be out there and after them."

Parrish gazed into the young face in front of him, into the coolness of the eyes that were not misted with drink, at the determined set of the youngster's chin. He swayed. "And where's out there? 'Out there' is the arse end of

Afghanistan, it's the happy little villages of Iran. My darling, you go there on your own. You don't go there with your old Uncle Bill."

"Then we might just as well give up – legalise the stuff."

"For a joker who's going to get a Commendation, who's just had the Judge's praises sung up his bum, you are mightily hard to please, Keeper . . . You should go home. In the morning, a good shit and a good shower and a good shave and you'll feel no end better."

Parrish had given up on him, headed back for the group.

He stood a few more minutes on his own. The rest had now forgotten him. He could not help himself. He could not turn it off, like they could. He was right, he knew he was right, but none of them came over to join him, to hear how right he was. He called across to say that he was on his way. None of them turned, none of them heard him.

He drove home. He observed the speed limit. He was stone cold sober. It meant nothing to him that the Judge had singled him out for praise. It only mattered that there was a war, and it was not being won.

Home was a two-bedroom flat in the south-west suburbs of the city. He could afford to live in the flat because of his overtime and Ann's work in a local architect's office. He garaged his Escort at the back of the block. He felt half dead with tiredness. He was a long time selecting the right key. What made him tired, what made him want to throw up, had been their looks from the dock as they had heard sentence. The bastards had laughed at April's best effort.

Inside there was a note on the narrow hall table.

"D. I've gone to Mum's for the night. Might see you tomorrow if you've the time, A."

The detective, bright and early, thanked the supervisor at the exchange. A small country town, of course there were easy and unofficially good relations between the exchange and the police. The number that had been disconnected last evening had been reported out of order three times during the night. One caller had left his name and telephone number. And not a name that surprised him. Young Darren was quite well known to the local detective. He suggested to the supervisor that it would be quite in order for the telephone to be reconnected.

In his office he told his subordinates when they came in not to take their coats off, and he handed them the address, and told them to bring in Darren Cole for a chat.

He was whistling to himself, Gilbert and Sullivan. He would enjoy talking old times to young Master Cole, and talking about Lucy Barnes' purchases. A fine start to the day until his clerical assistant informed him that he was required in the Chief Superintendent's office, and that two big shots were down from Constabulary Headquarters.

3

He was dressed as a *pasdar* in the loose-fitting dun khaki uniform of the Revolutionary Guards, and he walked with a limp that would be noticed but which was not ostentatious.

He had left his motorcycle a hundred yards behind where the man that he followed had parked his paint scraped Hillman Hunter. He had trailed the man through the alleyways of the closed bazaar, past the steel shuttered doors, and towards the Masjid-i-Jomeh. He walked on, ignoring the pain of the pebble taped under the ball of his right foot. He watched as the man passed the guards at the outer doorway of the mosque, entering the dark shadow beneath the linked domes. When the man was lost to him, Charlie veered away, and crossed between the sparse traffic to the far side of the street. For years now there had been heightened security at Friday prayers, all across the country, ever since the bomb hidden beneath a prayer mat had exploded at Friday prayers at Tehran University. Charlie watched and waited. The Guards at the entrance to the mosque had seen the young man who now sat on the cracked pavement across the street from them. They had seen his limp, and they waved to him, and smiled a comrade's greeting. A veteran, they would have supposed, of the great marshland battles on the perimeter of Basra far to the south, maybe a casualty of the fierce fighting around Halabja on the mountain road to Baghdad. Charlie knew that men in uniform, and with guns in their hands, and who were stationed far behind the lines, always had respect for a wounded veteran. He would cross the street and listen to the Mullah's words from the loudspeakers high on the domes of the Masjid-i-Jomeh, and he would talk to the Guards.

Charlie had not been brought up to respect the faith of modern Iran. It had been his father's concession to his American-born wife. His mother had had no religion, Charlie had been raised without the teachings of the Ayatollahs, and without the teachings of the Christian priests who had served the expatriate community in Iran. The children he had played with, been taught with before he went to the American school, they had taught Charlie enough of the Moslem faith for him to be able to pass as a believer. He would want to talk with the Guards. Talking was what Charlie did well, and he was better at listening.

He listened to the Guards. He let them talk. Duty rosters, "hypocrite" outrages, troop movements. To questions about himself he was modestly reticent, his wound was a small thing, he hoped that soon he would be fit to return to the service of the Imam.

Charlie saw the man come out of the mosque. At one moment he was

542

listening attentively to their talk, at the next he had made his farewells, pleading weariness, he must rest, and he had drifted away.

He had known the name of the man for two years, and he had known his address for seven weeks, since he was last home. He knew the age of the man and the name of his wife, and the number of his children, and he knew the man's work. He knew by heart the case histories of at least a dozen of those executed by this man since the Revolution. He knew that, depending upon the order of the Islamic Revolutionary Courts, sometimes the man made his executions by hanging and sometimes by shooting.

The man was at peace, safe after communication with his God, safe in his home city, safe in the service of his Imam. The man had hanged a teenager of the Baha'i faith who had refused after torture to recant his heresy. He had shot the 94-year-old former Captain Iraj Matbu'i, who had been helped to the execution post, sentenced for leading the Gendarmes against the Mullahs in the Mashad revolt of 1935. In public, he had hanged Juliette Eshraq.

Charlie had known the man's name for two years, since he had first returned to Iran, since he had scraped away at the story of his sister's death. It had taken longer to find the names of the two Guards who had lifted her on to the table, beneath the crane, in front of the Guards' barracks in Tabriz. These two he had now hunted and killed. He knew the name of the investigator who had tortured his sister. He knew the name of the Mullah who had tried and sentenced his sister.

He saw the man climb into his old car. He rode behind him across the bridge, over the broad river that was swollen by the melting mountain snows from the north, along the straight road beside the cemetery and the gardens that once had been the city's pride. The midday heat, trapped in the valley, blistered the squat concrete buildings. Charlie felt the warmth of the air on his face as he rattled in the wake of the Hillman Hunter, bouncing over the coarse paving of the old road.

The car ahead of him pulled off the road, no signal, wound up a dry dust lane. Charlie braked, cut his engine, dismounted and seemed to be adjusting his chain. He watched the children stream out of the house, and the man laugh with them, reach for them, and lift them.

He had seen enough. Charlie remounted and powered the motorcycle away.

Young Darren had been left to sit in an Interview Room, watched over by an expressionless policewoman, and sweat.

His two juniors reported to the local detective, and in the Chief Superintendent's office, sitting back easily, feigning the indifference of rank, were the big shots from Constabulary Headquarters. The local detective liked what he heard. Young Darren had been lifted outside his address, taken on the pavement as his hands were busy with the keys and door handle of his car. Two arresting officers approaching from different directions, and the suspect taken unawares, and without the chance to dispose of the evidence.

The detective heard them out, then muttered a lukewarm congratulation. He could play politics with the best of them. Nothing too fulsome, because that way he gave the impression that it wasn't a miracle that they had done it right. When they had finished, and bowed their way out of the presence, the detective addressed himself to his seniors. He had the file. He glossed through the prime detail. Cole, Darren Victor. Age, 24 years. Address . . . Previous: Possession (fined), Possession (fined), Possession (6 months). Common–law wife, two babies. Income: No visible means. Upsum: Hick, second–rate villain, pusher and user . . . Young Cole was what would be expected in a country town. Small time, small beer, not the sort of chummy who would ever expect to be confronted in the interview room by big shots from headquarters.

They left the local detective with no doubts. He was working to them, they were in charge, they had taken over. He would do as he was told and be thankful for it. He didn't complain, had never in his police career tried to buck the system. He was to go back to Darren Cole's address with his two juniors and a dog, relieve the uniformed constable who had been left to watch over the woman and her brats, and take the place apart. He would not be required for the interview with chummy, and God help him if he came out of that house with at least one evidence bag not filled.

In the interview room they dismissed the policewoman. They introduced themselves, a Superintendent and a Chief Inspector. They sat and tilted their chairs back as if that were more comfortable. They looked at Darren Cole like he was filth, like they'd want a good wash after being in the same room with him. Their chummy's eyes flickered, hovered from one to the other. They let him soak it in, they wanted him soft.

"It's Darren, right? Darren Cole, is that right?" The Chief Inspector said softly.

Their chummy pursed his lips, stayed quiet.

The Superintendent said, "I am going to assume, Darren, that you are not wholly retarded. I'm going to give you the benefit that you are not completely dumb. Now it's not every day that the likes of my colleague and I miss our breakfast to get down here to talk with a shit bag such as yourself, Darren. Have you got me?"

Young Darren nodded, nervous and showing it.

"Can we start again, Darren?" The Chief Inspector passed his pack of cigarettes across the table, and Darren Cole fished one clear and his hand was shaking as he held the cigarette to his mouth. It was lit for him. Neither of the big shots took a cigarette. "You are Darren Cole, is that right?"

A feeble reed reply. "Yes."

"Good boy, Darren . . . I said to my colleague that Darren Cole was cute enough to know what's good for him. I said that Darren Cole would know how to behave. You push scag, chummy."

"Might have done . . ."

"You push it regular."

"Maybe."

The Chief Inspector's voice hardened. "Regular."

"So, I do."

"You pushed to Lucy Barnes."

"I don't know the names."

"To Lucy Barnes."

"Perhaps."

"Getting silly again, Darren . . . To Lucy Barnes."

"Yes."

"You gave Lucy Barnes her scag."

Darren shrugged.

The Superintendent said, "Lucy Barnes is dead, chummy. On the slab. Don't tell me that you didn't know. Christ, is this bloody cow town so bloody slow . . . ?"

There was a quiet knock at the door. A uniformed policeman came in and handed the Superintendent a folded message sheet. He read it slowly, he smiled slowly, then he handed the message sheet to the Chief Inspector. Another smile and then the fast look of satisfaction between the two of them. Darren Cole saw the signs. He was shrivelling in his chair.

"The dog's been down at your place, Darren. I tell you what, when you get through this, when you've done whatever's coming your way, then I'd learn to hide things a little better. I mean that approximately 400 grammes of what we are presuming to be a prohibited substance, namely heroin, could be better hidden than under the bloody mattress. That's making it easy for the dog, Darren, oh dear, oh dear me . . ."

"That's not very clever, chummy," the Superintendent shook his head.

They had the well oiled routine, they had been working in tandem for more than a decade. Straightforward, this one, a roll over.

"You are looking at a bad scene, Darren," the Chief Inspector said it as if it hurt him.

"I didn't know she was dead."

"You've only done an open prison, Darren. Closed prison isn't the same. The Scrubs, Pentonville, Winson Green, Long Larton, Parkhurst, they're not the same as where you were. They are nasty news, Darren. Do you know what you're looking at, Darren?"

Cole did not reply. His head was sinking.

"You could be looking at a tenner, Darren, because of who and what Miss Lucy Barnes was. God's truth, Darren, a tenner. A very hard time in those places, Darren, if we weren't speaking up for you."

The voice was muffled through the hands, pathetic. "What do you want?"

"We don't want you, chummy, that's for sure, we want up the chain from you. We'd speak up for you, if you gave us the name of the dealer."

A long silence in the Interview Room.

The Superintendent said easily, "Just the name of your dealer, chummy."

Cole's head burst upwards. He was actually laughing. His shoulders and upper body were convulsed, like it was the funniest thing he'd ever heard. His mouth was frothing.

"You trying to get me blown away? I don't get less than a tenner if I grass,

I get stiffed. You get a name and they don't ever forget. Shove it, mister."

For the next hour Darren Cole stared fixedly ahead of him. His mouth never opened.

The big shots from Constabulary Headquarters seethed, shouted, bribed, and won nothing. The local detective had a quiet chuckle around lunchtime when he heard how well they had done.

In cumbersome longhand, using a thick-nibbed pen, in handwriting that only Miss Duggan could decipher, Mattie wrote out the signals. There were those to the Station Chiefs around the Iranian frontiers and sea boundaries, where the watchers of events inside that closed country operated, and there were those that would be received inside Iran. The Station Chiefs in Dubai, Bahrain and Ankara were informed by coded teleprinter messages beamed by the aerials on the roof of Century House to a radio farm in Shropshire and then on to a booster clinging to the summit point of the Troodos mountains in Cyprus, that Codeword Dolphin was coming. Signals to inside Iran were drafted for transmission on the evening Farsi language commentary as broadcast by the World Service of the BBC from Bush House. Those signals would be received by a man who worked in the Harbourmaster's Office at the newly developed port of Bandar Abbas, by a man who had a carpet business in the close and covered alleyways of Tehran's bazaar, and by a man who repaired heavy goods vehicles in a yard behind the old railway station at Tabriz.

When she had sent down the messages and signals to the basement, his PA reverted to form. She began to fuss him with detail. Were Mr Furniss' inoculations up to date? When could he manage an appointment with the medical staff for malaria pills, stomach pills, sleeping pills for the aircraft? She would go to the third floor for his travellers' cheques, but would he sign this authorization? And for his tickets. Please sign here, here and here. And would he be wanting the car to collect him for the airport directly from home, or from Century? Should a final appointment be arranged with the Director General? And inside the passport was a folded slip of paper as a reminder not to forget the girls, nor Mrs Furniss, of course. "I don't suppose she was taken in for one moment by that cardigan I found in the Strand last time you came back."

The routine of travel was no longer second nature to him. He gave way before the organizational blizzard that was Miss Duggan. He sat on the two-seater sofa in the partitioned office, he had the ripple of her keyboard in his ears. Quietly he read his book. He was stocking his mind with detail. Wonderful people, the Urartians, an extraordinary and flourishing civilization of three hundred years, and then gone. A thousand years before Christ's birth, this stocky people had made their mark across the wedge that was now divided between Turkey, Iraq and north-eastern Iran. He was already an authority of some stature concerning their artefacts, their belts and earrings and bracelets, their cuneiform script that he had seen gouged out on the walls of ruins and caves. Most certainly he would get to the Van Kalesi. The Urartian fortress at Van, safely inside Turkey, was earmarked as the next stop after Tabriz. Very much indeed he would look forward to being there. He summoned up the memory of Van Kalesi, built of dressed stone blocks that weighed up to 25 tons apiece, the canal that brought water to Van from 40 miles away. A civilization reduced by the Assyrians to bronze trifles and pottery shards, and amusement for men such as Mattie Furniss. The book he now read described the excavation in 1936 of a Urartian fortress town in present day Soviet Armenia, the first time that he had come across a readable and unabridged translation of the report. The purpose of his reading was cover. Whenever Mattie travelled in the Gulf and Near Asia it was as an archaeologist. One day he would write his own book on the Urartians. Damned if he knew how he would get it published commercially, but if all else failed Harriet would probably pay for a private printing of his view of Urartian culture.

Miss Duggan was locking her papers into the wall safe. Time for lunch. Time for the canteen queue. He seldom took lunch in his office, he enjoyed the chance to spend the time with colleagues at the formica topped tables of the canteen. The food was edible, the view across the river was always interesting. He put a marker in his book and followed her out.

Mattie was a popular figure at Century. Not just because of the long time that he had been with the Service, but because no man, young or old, senior or junior, could remember the least discourtesy or pomposity from the Head of Iran Desk. He had not reached his rank by treading on the prospects of anyone else on the staff. He was generous to any colleague in difficulty, or who sought his advice. Many did. He would never have claimed to be popular, was not even aware of it.

He went down in the lift with Israel Desk.

"Sorry about what happened the other day up there, Mattie. The DG's no right to speak like that in front of colleagues, nor privately. I didn't reckon at the time it would have helped you had I stood your corner, if it happens again I will. Chin up, eh, Mattie . . ."

Mattie could summon his fluent smile, as if little things like that didn't annoy him.

At the counter he took a full lunch on to his tray because Harriet was out that night, a committee on something or other, and at home he'd be doing for himself. Percy Martins was behind him. Percy Martins ran Jordan, Syria and Iraq. He had done something worthwhile, and quite insane, a couple of years back and had himself promoted a light year beyond his ability, and the new DG hadn't yet got round to sorting it out.

"Thanks for that about the Sanandaj units, Mattie. We slid it down to the Baghdad chappies, by now it'll be into the Iraqi system. Very grateful . . . Sorry about your run in with the bossman. My own view is that he's no background and shouldn't have been let past the front desk. If there's any time you need speaking for then I'm your man . . ."

A tiny, warm smile, which said, "wouldn't be necessary, old fellow, but thanks all the same".

He found himself a table. He needed to be alone. He had his knife into the liver when the seat opposite was taken. Old Henry Carter . . . Good God, thought he'd gone in the first reshuffle. Henry Carter, bachelor, prissy old thing, but sharp, had been in place when Mattie was joining. He couldn't imagine what Henry Carter did round the place these days. Used to be something about safe houses and de-briefs, never quite certain, and it was the way of the Service now that work was specialised that officers were not encouraged to gossip with men and women from unrelated sections. Such a hell of a quiet voice, and it was rude not to listen, but so damned hard to hear what the man was trying to say.

"I can see it in your face, you thought I'd gone. Should have done, I was supposed to have been pensioned off last year, but I managed twelve months' extension. They all think I'm a lunatic, still being here, but what does a retired spookie get up to? I dread retirement, it's the only thing in my life I'm actually frightened of, handing my I/D in and walking out of Century for the last time. Sorry about your problems, that man needs a brain scan . . ."

It must be all round the building, Mattie concluded, and that was extremely unprofessional . . . Two others came over and muttered at him, as if to a bereaved husband, before he had finished his treacle tart and custard. He felt that he was being set up as a faction leader. He would not tolerate that. He would refuse most categorically to become a centre of resentment against new management.

Carter asked, "What are you going to do, Mattie, when you retire?"

"Write a book. The tale of a lost civilization."

"That's very good. Sub-title, A History of the Secret Intelligence Service."

The news from the National Drugs Intelligence Unit was spring water clear.

"Listen, my friend, I have a powerful breath on my collar. If you can't get a dealer's name off a pusher in the backwoods, just let me know, one hour from now, and I'll send down one of my graduate trainees. Do I make myself plain, old friend? The name of the dealer or you're off the case."

The telephone purred into the ear of the Superintendent. He was flushed. His Chief Inspector was head down into his notes and not wishing to witness the discomfort.

"Our local hero, where is he?"

"Still down at the Cole residence."

"Get him here."

The Chief Inspector gagged. "You're not going to hand it over to him?"

"Right now, if it would concentrate that little bastard's mind, I'd hand it over to the dog."

The radio transmitters and the teleprinters were in the guts of the building, and that was where the decipher clerks worked, in a constant air-conditioned breeze. The signal from London was passed to the junior spook.

The junior spook had now to walk up two flights of stairs, and down a corridor that was shared with the Military Attaché's office before getting to the secure area from which the Service worked. The original Embassy planners had made no allowances for the fall of the Shah of Iran and the consequent upgrading of the mission. That Bahrain would become a listening post, a base for watchers and analysts of events in the country across the Gulf waters, had not been foreseen. To rebuild the Embassy to satisfy the needs of the Service was out of the question. To have moved the Service personnel out of the Embassy and into quarters of their own would have increased their running costs, and denied them the Embassy security umbrella.

The tea boy had carried cups of tea and soft drinks up the Embassy stairs, down the Embassy corridors for 25 years. He had access to any part of the building with his thirst quenching tray except the secure upper corridor beyond the Military Attaché's office. The tea boy saw the Station Officer going down the second flight of concrete stairs, his lightweight jacket slung on his shoulders, making for the golf course before the light went. He recognised the voice of the junior spook. He heard him say, half way down the first flight of stairs, "Just through, 'Dolphin' is on his way. Here next week."

"What the hell for?"

"Something about reassessment of aims and means."

"That's bloody inconvenient . . ."

The junior spook hurried on up, past the first floor corridor and towards the secure upper storey.

An hour later, his cups, saucers, and glasses washed and laid out on a draining board with a tea towel covering them from flies, the tea boy left his place of work, and walked out into the dry glare heat of the late afternoon.

The local detective lit a cigarette. As an after-thought he tossed one to Darren across the width of the cell. They were alone. The smoke curled between them. There was the smell of damp and vomit from last night's drunks.

"Let's understand each other, Darren, so that no mistakes are made which might later be regretted. We've got you for a tenner because you have volunteered the information that you pushed to Lucy Barnes. That and possession of 428 grammes of scag. That's all wrapped up. Trouble is that it's gone beyond that. You see, Darren, and you have to look at these things from our point of view, we find 428 grammes of scag under the mattress of the bed that you share with your lady love. I don't think I'd find it difficult to persuade any dozen good men and true, women would be easier, mind you, that your lady knew the stuff was there. I'm marching on, Darren, and you must stop me if you're not following me: so now we have an accomplice in your trading. That's not going to be nice for her, Darren. I'll put it another way: that's going to be very unpleasant for her. I reckon we do her for a fiver . . . See it from our point of view, Darren – you haven't helped us, and we're getting you a tenner. You haven't helped us, and we're getting your lady a fiver. So, what happens to your kids, Darren? They get Care. They get Care orders. They get to be scooped up into council care. By the time your lady comes out they'll be fostered off, nice couple of kids, and God knows, it's not always a disaster, fostering. But she won't get them back, you won't get them back. That's looking at it from the bad side, Darren. Look at it from the good side. You know me, you trust me. You know I'm straight. What I say I'll do, I bloody well do. Straight swap, as far as I'm concerned. I get the dealer's name and detail. You get a great write up from us for the judge and no charge against your lady, and no council care order for the kids. I'm leaving you a piece of paper, Darren, and a pencil, that's the brown item here with the lead in it, and I want you to write that name down, and every last thing you know about that man. Don't think you'll be helping me, Darren, think that you'll be helping yourself . . ."

Half an hour later the detective carried upstairs four sheets of paper covered by a sprawling hard worked handwriting, and a name.

"Bloody well done," the Chief Inspector said hoarsely.

"Won't be forgotten," the Superintendent said.

"If you don't mind, sir, I'll be off. Bit past the time I usually get home."

He started out of his sleep.

He heard the latch door close. He was awake, but there was a long moment when he could not gather where he was, when his own sitting room seemed a stranger. He heard the footfall beyond the door. It was all there in front of him, there was the vase on the mantelpiece that his parents had given them for Christmas two years back, there on the sideboard was the photograph of himself and Ann, marrying. There was her sewing basket beside the fire grate . . .

Park called out, "Is that you?"

He could hear her shrugging off her coat. He heard her voice. "Who else would it be?"

He had his mind clear. The wall clock told him it was seven. Seven what? Which seven? He shook his head. Christ, and he had been so tired. The plate on which he had taken his lunch was on the arm of the chair, bucking as he moved. It must be evening. He must have been asleep six hours. All of April had a day off, courtesy of William Parrish, and none of the hours lost going through the Civil Service time sheets. He hadn't changed two bulbs, he hadn't fixed the washer on the kitchen sink tap, he hadn't tacked down the carpet in the hall, he hadn't even made their bed.

She came into the sitting room.

"What are you doing here?" As if she were astonished. "I didn't think you'd be here . . ."

"We were given a day off." He stood, he felt ashamed that she should see the plate on the arm of the new chair. She had bought the chair. He had said they couldn't afford it, she had said that she refused to live in a slum and that while she was working she would bloody well spend her money how she pleased.

"Why, why did you have a day off?"

"There was a trial finished yesterday. We had a good result. We were given a day off."

She picked up the plate. There was no mark on the chair's arm but she flicked it with her fingers anyway. "There was a trial yesterday that ended at early afternoon, I know that because I heard it on the car radio coming home. I sat here until past nine . . . I am a dim little thing, aren't I, but I didn't understand how it would take you more than five hours to get from the Old Bailey, Central London, to here."

"We had a celebration."

"Nice for you." She headed for the kitchen. He followed. She spat over her shoulder, "A pity about the tap."

"I'm sorry."

"David, if there is a choice between April, the Lane, or your home, me, I know where the apple falls. Please, don't tell me you're sorry."

She was a great looking girl. She had been a great looker when they had first met, when he was on uniform duty at Heathrow, and a great looking girl in white at their wedding day, and a great looking girl when he had come home to tell her, all excitement, that he had been accepted into the Investigation Division. She was still a great looking girl, shovelling his dirty plate into the dishwasher. Ann had bought the dishwasher. David had said they didn't need a dishwasher, Ann had just gone out and bought it in the sales. She was as tall as him in her heels, and she had flaxen blond hair that she drew up into a pony, and she had fine bones at her cheeks and a mouth that he thought was perfect. She worked in the outer office of a prosperous architect, and she dressed to impress the clients.

"So, you all went off to the pub, where there was, of course, no telephone . . . and I presume you took the opportunity to tell them how they were getting it all wrong."

"I told Bill what I thought we should be doing . . ."

"Great way to celebrate."

He flared, "I said that I thought we weren't winning. I said that we should be more aggressive, work overseas more, I said that the men we put away yesterday were laughing at us when they were sent down . . ."

"God, they must think you're a bore."

"Do you know that last year our cocaine seizures were up by 350%? Do you know that means that three and a half times as much stuff came in last year as the year before . . ."

"What I care about is that my husband works 70 hours a week, that he's paid what a probationer constable in the Met gets. I care, used to care, that my husband is never at home when I want him, and when I am privileged to see him all he wants to talk about is filthy, sleazy, nasty drugs."

His breakfast plate, and his breakfast mug followed his lunch plate into the dishwasher.

"It's a disease that'll kill this country – AIDS, that's nothing in comparison. Ann, there's a billion pounds spent on drugs in this country each year. It's the principal reason for mugging, burglary, assault, fraud . . ."

"I don't know anyone, David, who is a junkie. No one in our block is, that I know of. No one in my office. I don't see junkies when I'm shopping. Drug addiction is not a part of my life, except when you bring it into our home."

"It's not something you can just turn your back on," he said flatly. "Whether it's me you're married to or anyone else."

She turned. She came towards him. She put out her arms and looped them around his neck. Her mother had told her to come back, and not just to collect her suitcases, her mother had told her to try again. One last bloody time, she had told her mother, she would try again. "Are they all like you, in April?"

"Yes."

"All on 70 hours a week, seven days a week?"

"When it's hot, yes."

"Do all their wives bitch?"

"Those that have stayed, yes."

"I bought some steak, and a bottle."

She kissed him. He couldn't remember when she had last kissed him. He held on to her, and the telephone rang. He picked the telephone off the wall bracket.

"Yes, it is, hello Bill . . ."

He felt her arms coming away from his neck. He saw the sadness flood her face. He was listening. He saw her grab inside her bag, and slap the meat down on to the kitchen table.

"The Lane tomorrow. Eight sharp. Look forward to it . . . Ann, she's great, she's in great form. Thanks, Bill, see you in the morning."

He could see that she was crying. Park did not know how to stop his wife's tears. He did not know how to tell her of his excitement because the April leader had called him for a meeting, eight o'clock in the morning, at Investigation Bureau's offices on New Fetter Lane, and promised a good one.

The teaboy's message was carried by a passenger from Bahrain to Abu Dhabi on the Gulf, and then flown on, having been passed to a member of an IranAir cabin crew, to Tehran.

The message reached the desk of a counter-subversion investigator in an office on the fourth floor of a small office block, close to Bobby Sands Street, once Homayoun Street. The block was not identified in any way, but was a part of the Ministry of Information and Intelligence. To the investigator the transcript of a briefly heard conversation was a source of amazement.

The investigator had read the message several times. He knew "Dolphin".

There would have been a dozen men in the section who knew the codename of Matthew Cedric Furniss. He had known the codename from far back, from times that were not referred to when he had worked for a different master, before the Revolution. He was astonished that the same codename was still maintained over so many years. In the Islamic Republic of Iran the British Secret Intelligence Service was hated with a loathing second only to that reserved for the Central Intelligence Agency, the Spies for the Great Satan. The investigator was not a man to initiate action, too great a survivor for that. To have survived a career with the *Sazman-e Amniyat Va Ettelaat Keshvar*, the Organisation of National Security and Intelligence, to have found a safe haven in an organisation dedicated to rooting out all traces of SAVAK, that was survival indeed. His way was to assemble information and present it to those few people in the regime who had the power to act. To many, the investigator was a valued tool.

On his computer, IBM state-of-the-art, he punched up the entry on Matthew Cedric Furniss, and composed a brief note on the information that the British head of Iran Desk was travelling in the region to pass on a reassessment of intelligence aims and means.

The investigator always worked late in his office. He liked the cool and calm of the evening, the silent shadows in the corridors. He made his decision, he lifted his telephone. When he talked it was against the distant thunder of an air raid striking the west of the city.

He travelled on a false passport in his wife's maiden name, and with the occupation of "Academic".

Harriet had seen him off, which was unusual, but then it was wholly unusual for a Desk Head to journey abroad. They had had their little nuzzles at each other's cheeks, and he had told her to get back to the Bibury cottage and keep on giving that city farmer hell, double-time, over the rape of the footpath.

Actually Mattie was rather pleased to be airborne, in harness again, but he hadn't said that to Harriet. Good to be on the road, not pushing paper.

4

The car had coughed to life, and thick fumes poured from the exhaust. He let the engine run while he thanked his neighbour for the loan of the charged battery that had been attached to the leads. He could ask any small favour of his neighbour and it would be granted. His neighbour knew his work. Most men, in fact, who knew his work, treated him with respect. No man in his company offered him offence or cursed him. Perhaps no man in Tabriz could feel with certainty that he would never look across the space of a cell at the deep brown eyes that would peep from the slits of the tight-fitting black mask that he had taken to wearing when he performed his work. The highest in the land, and the lowest, would all walk in the fear that they might, one day, feel the grip of his thick fingered fist upon their arm. It had not been done by himself, but he knew the man who had carried out the sentence of the Special Court of the Clergy on Mehdi Hashemi, and Hashemi had been the protege of the man named by the Imam as his successor. Likewise, he knew the man who had put Sadeq Ghotbzadeh to death, and Ghotbzadeh had been the Foreign Minister of the nation and the favourite of the Imam. No man in Tabriz trifled with the executioner. He was adept in hanging and shooting and lashing and organising the casting of stones at women taken in adultery, and in the handling of the newly arrived machine that was powered by electricity and that could slice with a guillotine knife through the fingers of a thief. He would use it this day: a thief who had stolen from a vegetable grower. And three executions, all in the city: a trafficker in narcotics, a Kurd who had aided the "hypocrites", a rapist of small children.

His wife was scrubbing shirts in the yard behind the house. She hardly acknowledged his shouted farewell from the back door. His children, all four of them, were playing with a deflated ball around their mother's legs, too intent on their game to hear him. Inside the house, from a cupboard beside the bed in the room he shared with his wife, he took a 9 mm Browning pistol – old, well cared for, accurate. He heard the car engine running sweetly beyond the open door.

He walked out into the morning. He tiptoed between the rain puddles because he had earlier shined his shoes. He climbed into his car, and laid the Browning, that was loaded but not cocked, on the seat beside him, and he covered the pistol with yesterday's *Ettelaat*.

As he drove away he hooted his horn. He smiled briefly, he did not think that the sound of the horn would interrupt the game of football.

He tacked up the lane, avoiding the deeper holes, going slowly so as not to damage the suspension of the old Hillman Hunter. He rolled to a halt at the junction with the main road. There was a flow of lorry traffic heading towards the centre of the city. He waited for the gap.

He saw a young man a little down the far side of the main road, facing towards the city centre, astride his motorcycle. The young man was stopped at the side of the road. The young man wore a blue tracksuit, and was well bearded and bare headed, and he carried a satchel bag slung around his neck.

He saw the gap open for him, a small space, and he lurched the Hillman Hunter forward, seized his opportunity. He heard the high long blast of a horn behind him, but the Hillman Hunter had little acceleration and the lorry's brakes seemed to punch the air as the huge grille closed on his rear view mirror. Another howling blast on the lorry's horn and then he was under way. It was always a difficult manoeuvre, getting out of the lane in which he lived, and joining the highway into Tabriz.

He was boxed in. There was a central reservation to his left. There was a Dodge pick-up to his right, filled with construction labourers. There was a cattle lorry to his front, there was a lorry with refrigerated cargo behind him. He could not go slower, he could not go faster. No matter that he could not pass the livestock lorry. He was not late for his work.

When he looked into his rear view mirror, he saw the motorcyclist. That was an excellent way to travel. The motorcycle was exactly the right transport for going into the city in the early morning's heavy traffic.

It was the motorcycle that had been parked on the side of the highway. The executioner looked ahead, then checked in his side mirror, and he saw that the motorcyclist had pulled out from behind him, and was now poised to come alongside him, and to pass him, coming through the narrow gap between the Hillman Hunter and the Dodge pick-up. That was freedom, to be able to weave in and out of the heavy trucks . . . He saw that the young man on the motorcycle had reached inside his bag that hung across his chest, that he steered the motorcycle only with his right hand.

He was aware of the shape beside him, looming close to his wound down window.

He saw that the motorcycle was virtually against the side of his car.

He saw the grin on the face of the rider, the rider grinning at him, and the rider's arm was outstretched above the roof of his car.

He heard the thump of an impact on the roof of his car.

His window was filled by the grinning face of the rider.

Cold sweat, sweat racing on his chest, in his groin. He could not stop. He could not pull over. If he braked hard he would be swept away by the refrigeration lorry behind him, 60 kilometres an hour and constant.

It never crossed the executioner's mind that he might be the victim of an innocent joke. He was reaching for his pistol, and he was watching the motorcycle power away ahead of him, he flicked off the safety, but what could he do? He couldn't fire through the windscreen. There was a moment when the motorcycle rider, the young man in the blue tracksuit seemed to swivel in his seat, and wave back at the old Hillman Hunter, and then was gone. He no longer saw the motorcyclist, only the lorry tail. He did not know what to do . . . Where to turn to.

He was staring into the mirror above him, and he saw the image of his own eyes. So many times he had seen staring, jolted, fear filled eyes.

Charlie had had to turn one last time to wave, and to see that the box was held to the roof of the low-slung yellow car. The metal box contained two pounds weight of commercial explosive, a detonator, and a stop-watch athletics clock wired to explode the detonator and the polar-amon gelignite 45 seconds after the control switch had been pulled. A nine-pound strain magnet locked the tool box to the roof of the Hillman Hunter.

He waved, he saw the tool box stuck like a carbuncle on the car's roof.

He twisted the accelerator handle, then stamped up through the gears. Great thrust from the motorcycle, taking him speeding past a cattle lorry.

Charlie, in those stampeding moments, could imagine the stench of fear inside the car, the same fear smell as the man would have known when he took the arms of those who had been brought to him. He swerved in front of the cattle lorry.

The explosion blew in from behind him, buffeted him.

The thunder was in his ears.

The hot wind rushing over his back.

And the motorcycle speeding forward.

He took a right turning, he was off the main highway. He accelerated along a lane and scattered some grazing goats that were feeding on the verge. He took another right. He careered forward, full throttle. He was on a track parallel to the main highway, two hundred yards from it. He glanced to his right and could see above the low flat-roofed homes the climbing pall of smoke.

He went fast, and he was whistling at the wind on his face, and he was blessing the present that had been given him by Mr Matthew Furniss, who was his friend.

"So why hasn't it been given straight to us, why are the 'plods' involved?"

There was a sort of democracy inside the Investigation Division. A military type of rank structure had never been part of the Lane's style.

The Assistant Chief Investigating Officer showed his patience. He did not object to the directness of the challenge, that was the way of the ID. "The police are involved, David, because at this stage of the investigation the death of Lucy Barnes is still a police matter."

"They'll cock it up," Park said. There was quiet laughter in the room, even a wisp of a smile from Parrish who sat beside the ACIO. The whole of April team was in the room, and they didn't mind the interruptions from Keeper. When he wasn't hanging round the edges in the pub, when he was at work, Keeper could be good value, and he was good at his job.

The ACIO rolled his eyes. "Then we will have to sort out what you regard as an inevitable cock up, if and when we gain control of our friend."

It was one of the working assumptions of the Investigation Division that its members were superior creatures to policemen. The senior officers did little to suppress the boast. Morale was critical to the *esprit de corps* for the war against the fat cats and the traffickers and the money bags. Most men in the ID would have put their hands on their hearts and sworn that a policeman just wasn't good enough to be recruited into one of their teams. Unspoken, but at the depths of the resentment of policemen, was the pay differential. The guys on April and the other teams were civil servants, and paid at civil servant rates. True, there were allowances to boost their take-home, but they were poor relations. There were plenty of stories of the bungling of the plods. Customs had targeted the Czech-born importer and overseen his arrest following a £9 million seizure, the plods had been guarding him when he had escaped out of a police cell. Customs sitting at Heathrow and waiting for a courier to come through with all the surveillance teams ready and poised to follow the trail to lead to the real nasties, except that the plods had flown over to Paris and picked up the creep there and blown all chances of the arrests that mattered. Near open warfare. The police had suggested they should form an élite squad to tackle drugs; Customs said the élite squad was already in place, the Investigation Division, a squad in which no man had a price, which is more than you could say of . . . and so on and so on.

"For us to gain control, what has to happen?"

They were on the upper floor of the building. No self-respecting policemen would have tolerated such premises. There were cracks in the plaster of the walls, there were no decorations other than annual leave charts and duty rosters. The lukewarm green carpet was scarred from where it had been heaved up for the new wiring, and from the latest shift round of the desk complexes. They were all on top of each other, the desks, and half large enough once the terminals and keyboards had been shoved on to them. It was home for the April team, and at the end tucked away behind a plywood and glass screen was Parrish's corner. The ACIO and Parrish sat on a table and shared it with a coffee percolator, and dangled their legs.

"Right, if the whining's over . . . Lucy Barnes was supplied by Darren Cole, same town, small time. Darren Cole names as his dealer a Mr Leroy Winston Manvers, about whom the courts have not yet been told, about whom CEDRIC is a mine of happy information . . ."

For effect, that wasn't needed, he held up the print-out from the Customs and Excise Reference and Information Computer. A good deep shaft of a mine with a quarter of a million names, and room for half a million more, CEDRIC was their pride. They didn't reckon the plods could hold a prayer to it, and bitched every time Central Drugs Intelligence Unit at the Yard wanted a peep at their material.

". . . Leroy Winston Manvers, aged 37, Afro-Caribbean origin, no legit means of support, Notting Hill Gate address, a real bad bastard. I am not

557

going to read the form to you, try and manage that for yourselves . . . What has been agreed by CDIU is that we shall mount a surveillance on the address we hold for Manvers, while our colleagues of the police will be investigating all background leads, associates, etc. It is, however, important, gentlemen, that one point remains high in your minds. We will be happy to put Manvers inside, happier still if we can get a conviction which permits seizure of assets, but the principal reason for our involvement at this early stage of an investigation is to move beyond Manvers, the dealer, and into the area of the distributor. The identity of the distributor is our headache. We want the body who is providing heroin to Leroy Winston Manvers. Do not doubt that this investigation has a high priority . . . Questions?"

"Why?" Park asked.

"Goddammit, Keeper, wash your head out." Parrish snapped.

"Facts of life, young man," the ACIO said sharply. "And don't give me shit about it. The facts of life are that the only child of the Secretary of State for Defence dies from a heroin overdose. That Secretary of State has a good cry on the Home Secretary's shoulder. That Home Secretary pulls a load of rank and calls the shots. That's why . . . More questions? No? Bill will give you all the details . . . Last point, I have laid down for you the priority, adhere to that priority. Thank you, gentlemen."

After the ACIO had left, Parrish sorted out the initial details of the surveillance that would be mounted from late that morning on a third floor council flat in Notting Hill Gate.

Because he had opened his mouth, because he had had too much to say, and because he never seemed to care what hours he worked, it was pretty well inevitable that Park would start the surveillance duty. He wasn't complaining. And he didn't ring Ann to tell her that he didn't know when he'd be home.

He did not ring her because he was not thinking of her. He was studying a photograph, covertly taken, and recent, of Leroy Winston Manvers. Just staring at the photograph and absorbing the features.

". . . Our entire land is now engulfed with the bereavement, separation, death, destruction, homelessness, corruption and despair brought about by the clerics' anti-human rule and catastrophic war. The clerics have brought ruination on our people. Do you know, ladies, gentlemen, that because of the chronic economic situation more than 8,000 factories in Iran have had to shut. Our oil revenues were the envy of the world, but we now find that production is down by more than one half, because of the war . . . Perhaps you are less interested in the cold figures of economics, perhaps you are more interested in the fate of human beings. I tell you, nevertheless, that economics have brought poverty, unemployment and starvation to millions of our people. But I will tell you about the effect on human beings of this cruel war, fought with the cynicism of those clerics while they themselves are safe behind the lines. Do you know that to continue this thirst for blood the clerics now send children to that front line? Don't take my word, take the word of a newspaper. A newspaper wrote: 'Sometimes the children wrapped themselves in blankets, rolling themselves across the minefield, so that fragments of their bodies would not scatter so they could be gathered and taken behind the lines, to be raised over heads in coffins.' Ladies and gentlemen, have you ever heard anything more obscene? That is the regime of the clerics, a regime of bankruptcy, a regime of blood, a regime of callousness . . ."

When he paused, when he mopped perspiration from his forehead, he was loudly applauded. It surprised him that so many had come to listen to him during a lunchtime in the City of London. It saddened him that he did not see his brother in that audience. He had urged his brother at least marginally to involve himself in the political world of the exiles. He could not see his brother, he accepted that failure.

He sipped at a beaker of water.

At the back of the hall was an Iranian student, enrolled at a Bayswater college, and taking a detailed note of all that Jamil Shabro said in his vilification of the reign of clerics.

Jamil Shabro spoke on for twenty minutes. When finally he sat down he was warmly applauded, and his hand was pumped by well-wishers, and he was congratulated for his courage for speaking out against tyranny.

And that afternoon the student in the English language took his written notes to a mosque in West London in which hung a photograph portrait of the Imam, and upon production of his Islamic Republic of Iran passport was admitted to an inner office.

In the outer corridor to the Cabinet room, after the meeting had broken up, the Secretary of State for Defence made the opportunity for a private word in the Home Secretary's ear.

"I'm in Washington for a week, won't be back until the day before the funeral. I'm going home now, pick up my bag, then the airport . . . what can I tell Libby? I have to tell her something."

"It is a police investigation, George. They've got it going."

"What do I tell Libby?"

The Home Secretary said softly, "You can tell her that we have the pusher, that we have a good line into the dealer. You can tell her that the Yard, the National Drugs Intelligence Unit, and Regional Crime Squads are all involved. You may also tell her that one of Customs and Excise's rather useful heroin teams is watching developments in the hope that the dealer will lead us on towards the distributor. If one word of this got out, George, one word, I would be severely embarrassed . . ."

"That will be a great comfort to her . . . we cannot shake it off, the guilt. Why didn't we notice things at the start? It's as if the disintegration of a happy child just passed us by, Libby's taken it all fearfully . . ."

"I hope to have more positive news by the time you come back."

The conversation was ended. The Chancellor and Energy and Education were spilling from the Cabinet room, full of good humour at the latest Opinion Poll which gave government a six point lead, and in mid-term.

Another meeting finishing, another conference table in Whitehall left with empty cups and filled ashtrays, the weekly session of the Joint Intelligence Committee had broken. There had been no politicians present. The Committee was the purlieu of civil servants and permanent officials. Had a politician been present then the meeting would have been severely constrained. Amongst these men there was a feeling that those who were reliant on the voters' whim were not altogether to be trusted with the nation's fortunes. Present had been the Directors General of the Secret Intelligence Service, the Security Service, Military Intelligence and Government Communications Headquarters, Foreign and Commonwealth officials, and in the chair had been a Deputy Under Secretary with the formal title of Co-ordinator of Intelligence and Security. This Committee decided what the politicians should see, what they should not.

The Co-ordinator had waved back into his chair the Director General from Century, a barely observable gesture to indicate that he should stay behind after the others had gone to their cars and their bodyguards.

"Between ourselves, and I didn't want to express this thought in front of the others, I had no wish to embarrass you, I think you've done rather well," the Co-ordinator beamed. "You were put in to do a job of work at Century, and I'd like to say that I reckon you're at grips with the problems there. From the Prime Minister downwards, we wanted that place shaken out of its complacency, and you are achieving that."

"It would be easier to manipulate a brick wall, but we're getting there," the Director General said grimly.

"It was time for fundamental changes in attitude and direction. We have agreed to get away from the dinosaur belief that the Cold War is still the focus. Agreed?"

"I'm shifting resources from the East European Desks and into all Mid-east areas. There's a measure of resistance . . . Do you know Furniss?"

"Doesn't everybody know Mattie Furniss, good fellow."

The Director General was hunched over the table. "He's a very good man, and he's seeing the light."

"Iran is critical to our interests."

"That's why I've packed Mattie off down to the Gulf. I've told him what I want."

"Have you now . . ." The Co-ordinator rolled back in his chair. "You brought some good stuff to the meeting. Is that Mattie's stuff?"

"He's running a new agent. Keeping the fellow tight under his wing." The Director General chuckled. "Typical of Mattie. I tell you what, I gave him a good kick up the arse, and he's been good as gold since. He's running a new agent, and he's gone down to the Gulf to sort out those that he has in place inside, and to breathe some fire into our watchers on the perimeter."

"Excellent. The Iranians believe, quite literally, they can get away with murder these days. I think the Pentagon taught the Libyans a lesson, and we have done the same to the Syrians. They're both better mannered now. In my opinion, it's time the Iranians were given a short sharp shock of their own . . . Why don't you stay and have a bite of lunch here?"

In Bahrain, Mattie had met the carpet merchant from Tehran. The man brought in foreign exchange, and his family were left behind, and he had two sons conscripted, so he could usually get a · visa to fly out and back. And in Bahrain he had talked with his Station Officer. And he had picked up a tail.

Mattie had flown from Bahrain to Dubai to see the junior in place there, and he had been watched on to the aircraft and watched off it. He had dealt with the junior in a bit over four hours, given him the pep talk, told him to chuck out his University essay style, and to get himself down to the docks more often, to ingratiate himself more with the shipping fraternity.

Had he taken the road from Dubai to Abu Dhabi, had he been driven the hundred miles from Dubai to Abu Dhabi, past the cars left to rust in the desert because the oil rich could not be bothered to fix another starter motor or whatever, then he might have noticed the tail. Travelling by air, watched through an airport, watched out of an airport, he did not see the tails.

And little opportunity here in the Gulf for him to lay a trail as an archaeologist. He found these communities with their air-conditioned Hiltons, their chilled ice rinks that were proofed against the 100 degree outside temperature, their communities of tax-avoiding British engineers, rather tedious. Van would be different, the Urartian ruins would be blissful.

He lost the tail that he did not know he had picked up in Abu Dhabi. He employed his standard procedures. He had checked into the hotel, been given a room on the 20th floor of an architectural monstrosity, and then slipped down the fire escape service staircase and out through the work force entrance. He had entered the hotel wearing his dun-coloured linen suit, left it in jeans and a sweatshirt. And he sweated hugely as he walked the few hundred paces through the city to the small office that was nominally base for a firm of international marine surveyors. In a first floor room, the venetian blinds down, he met the man who worked in the Harbourmaster's office in the Iranian port of Bandar Abbas.

Mattie had to hug the man. That, also, was standard procedure. He was not fond of overt displays of affection, but it was the way of these things that a man who had come secretly by dhow across the waters of the Gulf must be hugged like a prodigal returned. The man kissed him on both cheeks, and Mattie could smell the man's last meal. It must not concern Mattie Furniss, Head of the Iran Desk, that the man had perspired his fear of discovery while lying amongst the nets and hawsers of a dhow that had ferried him from

Bandar Abbas to the wharfs of Abu Dhabi. If the dhow had been boarded, if the man had been discovered by the Guards, if the man had been taken before a Revolutionary Court, then the man would have been tortured, would have screamed for the release of execution. And yet Mattie must, as a professional, keep himself emotionally aloof.

They sat down. They sipped tea. The man listened, and Mattie gave him the prepared lecture.

"It is detail that we want. Hard facts . . . I don't just want to know that a Portugese or Swedish or Cypriot registered ship is coming in to Bandar Abbas with containers on the deck, I can get all that from satellite photography. I want the contents of the containers. I want the markings on the containers . . ."

He watched the man, saw that his fingers were twitching at the string of beads that he held over his lap. If over the years he had become emotionally involved with the man then he would have found these demands well nigh impossible to make.

". . . There is an international arms embargo on Iran. No weapons of war are supposed to be shipped into Bandar Abbas or any other port of entry, yet we understand that the Iranians are spending 250 million dollars a month on hardware. We want your country, your regime, strangled of arms supplies. Without the arms supplies the war effort will fail, and if the war effort fails then the clerics are gone. That's the incentive for you."

Not, of course, for Mattie Furniss to share with an agent Century's exasperation at the government of the United States of America who had dispatched 2,086 tube-launched optically-tracked wire-guided missiles to the clerics along with a plane-load of spares for their old F-4 Phantoms. He could have reeled off the roll of honour of countries shipping arms to Iran: USSR, China, UK (anything from anti-aircraft radar to military explosives), Italy, Spain, Greece, North and South Korea, Taiwan, Pakistan, Syria, Libya, the Czechs, the East Germans, the Japanese, Brazil, Argentina, the Netherlands, Israel, Portugal, Belgium, even the Saudis . . . Where a buck was to be made.

". . . Fine, we know that they are steadily turning to home produced weaponry, but for the moment it is not sophisticated enough for modern warfare, and must be backed up by essential spares for items such as strike aircraft – that's what we have to know about. Don't shake your head, you can walk on water when you set your mind to it. Any arms shipment is going to be met with security, with military vehicles, it's going straight through the Customs checks, no formalities. Those are the ones that we have to know about . . ."

Those who knew Mattie Furniss down in the Cotswolds, the other weekenders in Bibury, the cocktail set of Saturday evenings, would have described him as a very straight sort of cove, a pretty gentle sort of fellow. Those who talked to him about footpaths, and milk yields, and the Stock Market, would have been upended to have known that he would drive a volunteer, a very brave spy, to suicidal risks, and seem to think nothing of it. He was a hard man. He was a Desk head in Century.

The following morning, while the official from the Harbourmaster's office was returning to Bandar Abbas, once more secreted in a dhow, Mattie was watched as he boarded the flight to Ankara, the capital city of Turkey.

He was missing four front teeth, and the rest were yellowed stumps. The old man's hair was tangled, uncared for. His lined face was the colour of a walnut. It was a tough life that he lived on the lower slopes of the mountain. He ran some hardy goats and some thick coated sheep on the side of the Iri Dagh mountain and in the shadow of the summit, always snow capped, that rose to 8,800 feet above the level of the distant sea. On a clear day, and in the early morning when the sun was rising behind the mountain, it was possible for the old man to look down on to the metropolis of Tabriz. His glance would be cursory. He had no interest in that city.

He was steeled by the roughness of the ground on which his livestock grazed, on which he grew vegetables close to his stone-walled, tin-roofed home, and he was tempered by the sadness of his old age.

Majid Nazeri closed the wooden plank door and walked towards the building where the animals wintered and where he stored their fodder. He walked like an old soldier. He had no part of the present world which was why he was happy to live in this isolation, alone with his dogs on the slopes of Iri Dagh, away from Tabriz which the regime had made their own.

He inserted into the padlock the key that hung from a leather thong around his neck. There was a cut of pain on his face, because the new shoes that he had been bought would take weeks to mould their soles around the misshapen outlines of his feet. He was not ungrateful for having been bought the shoes, but it would be the next winter before they were comfortable for him. The nearest habitation was the village of Elehred, away over the mountain to the north, towards the Soviet border. He had chosen to spend his last days in a wilderness that housed the free soaring eagles, and the ravaging wolf packs, and the leopard if he was lucky enough to see it and his body smell were not carried on the stiff winds that never forsook the slopes of Iri Dagh.

He had not always been a recluse. He had once known how to polish boots. He had known how to pour and serve a pink gin with the right measure of bitters, and he had been familiar with the formation of a platoon sized unit in attack, and he had once stood at attention an arm's length from the Shah of Shahs. Majid Nazeri had risen to sergeant in Charlie Eshraq's grandfather's regiment, and he had been batman to Charlie's father. The day that Charlie's father had been arrested, he had started the journey from Tehran to Tabriz, and then travelled on, northwards, in search of a place where he could shut out the abomination of what happened on the lower ground beneath him.

It was two years since the young Eshraq, the quiet man replacing his memory of a noisy boy, had reached his home on Iri Dagh, found him.

Always, when Charlie came to him and then left him, he wondered whether he would see the young man again. Always when Charlie left him, after they had exchanged their gruff farewells, there was a wet rheum in his old eyes. It was of small concern to him that his once keen sight was sliding from him. His dogs were his sight, and as his eyes faded so also disappeared the hazed outline of the city of Tabriz. Charlie had told him that it was in the city of Tabriz, in front of the headquarters of the Revolutionary Guards, that Miss Juliette had been hanged. He had no more wish to see the grey outline of the minaret towers of Tabriz.

To Majid Nazeri, his life winnowing away, Charlie was an angel of revenge. To the old soldier, loyal servant and batman, Charlie was the last of a line he had worshipped.

He pulled open the door of the shed. He had old rags in his hand, the remnant of an army shirt that had rotted on his back.

He spent all of that afternoon polishing the petrol tank, and the wheel spokes, and the engine work of the Japanese motorcycle that was Charlie's. The motorcycle did not need cleaning, and by the time that Charlie had next taken it down the stone track to the road running from Ahar into Tabriz then it would be filthy. And after he had cleaned the motorcycle he checked that the blocks on which it was raised to protect the tyres were firmly in position. He never knew, never asked, when Charlie would next be hammering at his door, shouting for admission, squeezing the breath out of his old body.

He picked up the discarded two parts of a blue tracksuit, and he took them to the stream beside his house for washing.

The dusk was closing in. He did not have to go to his bed of rugs and furs as soon as the darkness came. Charlie had brought him kerosene for the lamp hanging off the central beam of his main room. He could sit on his wooden chair, and long after the night had come to the slopes of Iri Dagh, and the dogs outside had started their chorus to keep away the wolves from the animals' stockade, he would gaze at his most prized possession. He would stare at the gilt framed photograph of the army officer and his foreign wife and their two children.

The joy of Majid Nazeri's life was Charlie Eshraq's coming, his despair was Charlie Eshraq's going.

He had reverted to the clothes of a *pasdar*.

He was sleeping towards the back of the Mercedes bus. Several times he was jolted awake by the man sitting next to him, because the Guards had stopped the bus at a block and were checking papers. His own papers were in order. Like every Iranian he carried with him at all times his Shenass-Nameh, his Recognition Papers. The Recognition Papers listed a false name, a false date of birth, a false record of military service in the Guards. The papers aroused no suspicion. He was unarmed, he had nothing to fear from a search of his one small bag. He had been wounded in the service of his country, he had been home on convalescent leave to the home of his parents in the line city of Tabriz, he was returning to Tehran where his unit was to be re-formed. He was greeted with friendship by the Guards who searched the bus.

The bus stopped at a café. Charlie dozed on. He had no wish to queue for food. He had eaten well at the home of Majid Nazeri early in the morning. To be hungry was to be alert, and it was sensible of him to sleep because in the morning the bus would arrive in Tehran.

He had the signature of the Mullah on his proposals for action. The investigator only proposed. The Mullah, whose signature and office stamp were on the document, had been chosen with care by the investigator. He knew his man, he knew which cleric could be trusted to rise, a trout in a waterway in the Elborz hills.

It was late in the night. The room in which the investigator worked was without decoration, save for the portrait of the Imam. So different from the office he had occupied when he had been the trusted servant of a plucked Peacock. No carpet now, no drinks cabinet, no easy chairs, no colour television. In the struggles waged amongst the Ayatollahs and the Mullahs in the twilight months of the Imam's life the investigator did not believe the dice would fall for those who were described as the Pragmatists, the Realists, the Moderates. He believed that the victors would be men such as the Mullah, whose signature he had on the two proposals.

The city was quiet below him. He telephoned to the Manzarieh camp on the northern outskirts of the capital. He waited for the telephone to be answered in the building that was once the hostel of the Empress Farah University of Girls and was now the Revolutionary Centre of the Volunteers for Martyrdom.

5

She was different, but she was the only girl amongst them. He had been given short shrift by the boys. She wore no make-up, and her dark hair was combed away from a centre parting, and she had discarded the headscarf that would have been obligatory out on the street, and she wore the jeans and the blouse that would have to be covered by a *chador*.

"I might have been away, OK, I've been away, but that wasn't my decision. I was taken away. Now I am able to make my own choice, and that choice is to come back and live my life inside Iran."

They had all been his friends, the boys and the girl, at the American School. The name of the girl was La'ayya. Charlie sat on a straight-backed chair and the girl lounged on the wide sofa. This was the reception room of the villa of her parents. Before the Revolution there would have been framed photographs of La'ayya's father, about his official business, and with minor members of the First Family. The images of the other life were gone, along with the servants and gardeners. Her parents were taking the last of the snow on the ski slopes above the Caspian Sea. The girl was alone in the villa that was set back from the wide street, where the cherry blossom was starting to bloom, and she was amused, and not frightened as the boys had been.

"I went with my mother to California. I loathed it. I was sent to London, where we have friends. I live there, but I hate that city too. I am Iranian and I want to make my life in the country that is my home."

He had said the same to the boys. None of them had wanted to hear him out. He had been given little chance to talk in any one of the boys' homes before being shown the door, but the girl was in no hurry to expel him. She had always had more guts than any of the boys in his class. Now she smiled frankly at him.

"You don't believe me?"

"I'm not a fanatic, Charlie. I don't pray for the eternal life of Khomeini. I just exist here. If anyone tells me that they want to live here when they have the chance to live in California or London then I think that either they are addled in the head, or they are lying."

"But you haven't thrown me out, the madman or the liar. The others were fast enough."

"Your father was killed, and your sister, and you talk about coming back as if it were the matter of crossing a street . . . Let me tell you why the boys are frightened of you. When you left there were 22 of us in the fourth grade. The boys that you have been to see and me, we are the only ones still living in Tehran. There are eight in exile, and eight have been killed."

"A war doesn't last for ever, not for ever, a war finishes. The Imam finishes. There is a new country to be built. There will be a new Iran, and that will be my country . . ."

Her eyebrows flickered. "You believe that?"

"It is why I am coming home."

And then the keenness of the girl. "And what part in your new order would I play, or the boys who rejected you?"

He was thinking that he needed a place to store the weapons that he would carry back on his next journey which would be the last journey, that he might need a driver or a minder at his back.

He said, "I would want someone who will share my vision."

She laughed. She sounded as though she mocked him. "You know nothing of Iran . . ."

"I know that I want to live out my life in my own country."

She stood. She played the hostess. She walked towards the door. "I am in love with life, Charlie. I too have friends, relations, who were taken to the Evin gaol, and to the Qezel Hesar gaol and to the Gohar Dasht gaol, and I don't wish to follow them. Nor, Charlie, do I believe a single word, not one, that you have told me."

She had been leggy and spindly when he had last seen her. He thought that now she was beautiful.

"When I come back I will come here, to see you, to show you my truth."

She grimaced. "And we could go for a drink in the cocktail lounge of the Hilton . . . Trouble is, Charlie, that the Hilton is now the Independence Hotel, Oppressed Area Base Three of the Mobilisation Volunteers of Beitolmoqaddas, it is now the property of the Deprived People's Organisation. Goodbye, Charlie. It was amusing to see you, but not sensible."

"I did not believe you would be afraid."

There was the first moment of bitterness in her tongue. Her voice was sharp. "That's California talk, or London talk. You insult me. You know nothing of my Iran, you know nothing of my life. You come here and you tease me, you laugh at me, and for whatever reason you also lie to me."

"What would you like me to bring you?"

"If you contact me then you put me at risk."

"Just tell me what you would like."

"Soap," she said simply.

She let him out of the house.

He thought she was very pretty, very sad. She closed the door before he had reached the pavement. He walked away down the street, and his feet trampled the early fall of the cherry blossom.

The first time he had come to the Manzarieh camp in Niavaran the statue of Lord Baden Powell, Chief Scout, had been at the gate and he had been employed in the secret police of the former monarchy. He had been sent to the Empress Farah University for Girls to arrest a student who was believed to be a member of a Tudeh cell. The hostel for the College girls was now sealed from the outside by heavy coils of barbed wire, guarded by troops of the Mobilisation of the Deprived Volunteers, separated from the main expanse of open ground by electrified fences. And much that was different in the appearance of the investigator and his transport. The dark grey suit and the BMW coupé had given way to plain grey trousers, and sandals on his feet, and a long shirt outside his waist band; his cheeks were laced in stubble, and he drove a humble Renault 4. It was not quite necessary for him to have renounced all of his previous life, the SAVAK trappings, but the investigator was a cautious man.

In what had once been the Dean of Studies' office, the investigator was made welcome and given tea. Each time that he came to this room it was to seek advice on the suitability of a candidate for operations overseas. It was the responsibility of the Director of the Revolutionary Centre to consider the target, the location, the method of attack, and then to recommend a volunteer. The investigator had been many times to Manzarieh because the regime was often anxious to exercise the long arm of its discipline against traitors in exile.

The students at Manzarieh were trained in the teachings of the Qur'an, the ideology of the Imam, and close quarters killing. Prayers at dawn, noon and dusk, learning the trade of killing for the rest of the day. To brief the Director he took from his attaché case his notebook. The Imam glowered down from the wall at him. He tried never to think about it, but he had been at the meeting where the assassination of the Imam in exile had been discussed. If the investigator had a nightmare in his life it was that a minute of that meeting should have survived, a minute with a list of those attending.

His voice was a forgettable monotone.

"The exile is Jamil Shabro. In spite of warnings telephoned to his home in London he has continued to vilify the Imam and the Islamic government of Iran. I will leave with you a resumé of his most recent speech. It is our suggestion that explosives be used. One restive tongue is cut out, but a hundred others are silenced by fear."

The Director gazed down at the photograph of Jamil Shabro. "London . . . London is so very open to us."

"There is another matter . . ."

The investigator reached again into his attaché case. He produced a second file. On the outside, written large in the investigator's hand in the Farsi language, was a single word which if translated back to the English would have been written as Dolphin.

He saw the high steel gates open, and he saw the car's bonnet pushing into the narrow space, and he saw the Guard who had opened the gate duck his head in respect.

The width of the street was 40 paces. The traffic was solid. The Mercedes could not nudge into the flow. It was as it had been the last time that he had stood on that pavement. The building behind him was abandoned, its garden was overgrown and the oleander bushes had been allowed to grow wild and provide a screen of evergreen cover. He had been in the garden, and he had seen the place where he could stand on the wall of the old and demolished conservatory and see over the outer wall of the derelict building. The driver of the Mercedes hammered at his horn, and made space.

He saw the Mullah. He saw a man who was still young. The face of an academic. Charlie saw the thin glasses, and the sallow face, the clean turban, and the shoulders of his camel hair cape. The Mullah sat alone in the back of the long Mercedes, and Charlie noted once more that the car windows distorted the width of the face inside. He noted also that the carriage of the Mercedes was low over its tyres. The Mercedes was armour-plated along its sides and its windows were of reinforced glass.

The gates creaked shut. The Guard was again positioned outside them, his rifle slung on his shoulder. The Mercedes had moved on.

Charlie drifted away.

He walked for a long time. He liked to walk because when he walked he could rehearse what he had learned in the previous hours.

He had that morning found the investigator. He had not seen him, but he had discovered his place of work.

Charlie was staying in a small hotel. In London it would have been a guest house behind Paddington Station. In Tehran it was down an alleyway crowded from dawn and beyond dusk with food stalls and metal craftsmen. A well scrubbed little establishment, and cheap. There was a telephone in the hallway of the hotel. All morning he had telephoned different numbers at the Ministry of Information and Intelligence. He had been passed from one number to another. Fifteen calls, and always the same question. He had asked to be put through to the man. Fourteen times he had been denied. The fifteenth time, he had been told to hold. He had heard the extension ringing out. He had been told that the man was not in his office . . . and he had rung off. An hour later, more depth disguising his voice, he rang again. He had said that he had an appointment at the building, but had lost the address. Now he knew.

The procession passed him.

Students marching, goosestepping.

Boy children striding and overstepping, uniforms too large.

Women shuffling their feet under the full flow of their *chadors*, the widows of the war.

Men carrying buckets, and money being thrown from the pavement into the buckets, screwed up bank notes.

Portraits of the Imam carried high, the streets filled with the shouting of the slogans.

Charlie put some notes into the bucket when it reached him. Not to have contributed would have attracted attention.

He found a taxi.

An age it took, to wind through the clogged streets, through the drab and smog-blanketed mass of the city. He would never be at ease in the south of Tehran. It was the shrine of the Imam, the working class ghetto of those who shouted loudest for the war, for the death of their enemies. South Tehran was the bedrock of the Revolution. He kept his peace in the taxi until he was dropped.

He stood outside the main entrance to the Behesht-i-Zahra cemetery. It was a pilgrimage for Charlie Eshraq. Each time he came to Tehran he came to the cemetery. He had to wait at the gate as a line of taxis drove through. There was a coffin on the roof of each taxi, martyrs were being brought back from the front line, with a horde of family mourners alongside them for an escort. He followed. For hundreds of yards Charlie walked amongst the graves. A rippling sea of flags. Small wooden and glass-fronted box shapes, on stilts, in which were placed photographs of the dead. He saw a bulldozer excavating the yellow earth from a pit the size of a swimming pool, waiting for the dead from the next battle. He saw the raven women and old men and small children threading between the death markers.

He hurried on. His country's youth was laid to rest here amidst the keening cries of women, the drone of the bulldozer, and the coughing of old taxi engines. The Gateway to Heaven Cemetery, and there was a queue to get there. Deep inside the Gateway was the Fountain of Blood. The water spouting from the fountain ran red. Charlie thought that was sick. He thought it was as sick to colour the cemetery fountain water as it was to issue young soldiers going to the front with plastic keys, made in Taiwan, so that if they were killed in battle they could get through the Gates, make it to Paradise. On his first journey here he had given a bribe to a clerk in the Administration Office. A hundred dollars in small notes, and that had produced the burial charts, the names against the numbers.

He could not forget the way to this outer plot . . . far beyond the flags and the stilted boxes and their photographs, were the bare concrete slabs on which, while they were still wet, a number had been scratched. He would not forget the number of his father's grave.

His father had said that a professional soldier, a soldier who foreswore politics, had nothing to fear from the Revolution and his father lay in a grave marked only by a scratched number.

He had no idea where his sister was buried, or his uncle who had been clubbed, butchered, shot on the roof of the Refah school where the Imam had made his first headquarters after his return from exile. This was the only grave that he knew of, and each time in Tehran he was drawn to it.

Mattie Furniss could not abide sloppiness. It bred complacency, and complacency was fatal to field operatives.

He was not good at delivering an old-fashioned dressing down, but he felt it time to let the Ankara Station Officer know that he was quite dissatisfied with what he had seen.

The Ankara station was not located in the Embassy building. The Service had several years before taken a long lease on the third floor of an office building in the government sector of the Turkish capital, where the high-rise blocks seem to stretch without end. The cover of the office was that the Service staff working there were employees of a British firm of structural engineers.

They had an hour before an appointment at the Turkish National Intelligence Agency, the only occasion on this trip when Mattie went official. An hour, and he intended to use it well.

"Don't interrupt me, Terence, that's a good fellow, and do not imagine for a single moment that I get pleasure from what I am about to tell you . . . It's the oldest scenario in the book. A chap gets abroad, and all that he's absorbed when he was on courses at home goes out of the window. We'll start at the beginning, the car that picked me up and brought me here. The driver, he was not alert. We were cut up by a car full of men, and your driver just sat there, never considered the prospect of kidnapping, of having to take evasive action, your driver was dead from the neck up. It is the third time I have been to this office, and each time your driver has taken the same route. Your car is not fitted with a rear-seat passenger mirror as it should be. Your driver came into the hotel this morning to wait at Reception for me, and when he had met me, taken me out to the vehicle he made no effort to check for an IED . . ."

"Mr Furniss, this is Turkey, not Beirut. We don't have Improvised Explosive Devices on every street corner."

"Hear me out, Terence . . . Your car is not armour-plated, your tyres are not run flats, and I would hazard a guess that the petrol tank is not self-sealing . . ."

The Station Officer said, "Run flat tyres cost three thousand pounds each, Mr Furniss. I don't have a budget for that sort of carry on."

"I will take it up with London . . . this room has been furnished by someone who has ignored every precaution in the book. Windows without the blinds drawn, anyone from that building, that one over there, can see you inside, could shoot you. That painting, is that shatter-proof glass? An elegant cocktail cabinet, but glass-fronted. Has no one told you that glass splinters and flies when explosives are detonated?"

"This is not a High-Risk posting, Mr Furniss."

"Neither is Athens, nor is Brussels. We were scraping chaps off the walls there who a few moments before would have happily said those cities were not High-Risk."

"I'll get them fixed, sir."

"Very wise . . . Now I'd like to turn to matters Iranian . . ."

Mattie Furniss set out in detail the kind of information he would be requiring in future from the Station Officer on the Iranian theatre. He painted a picture that filled the young and fast-promoted Terence Snow with bleak despair. He required minutely recorded and frequent de-briefs of Iranian refugees who had successfully legged it through the mountains and the river gorges, past the patrols, and into north-east Turkey. He had no use for the opiate dreaming of the exiles in Istanbul, he wanted fresh, raw intelligence.

They walked down the staircase together. Mattie said that the next morning he planned to head off towards the World War One battlefield at Gallipoli. He said that his father had been there, a gunner, never talked much about it. And then his voice lit up, and he said that they would follow that visit with a couple of days pottering amongst the excavated ruins of Troy. Did Terence know that all of the finest examples of Trojan jewellery had been lodged in the Berlin museum, and then pillaged by the Soviets in 1945? No, he did not.

"And then I think we'll go up to Van together."

Good grief. Three days non-stop tutorial. Terence's spirits sank. "I'll enjoy that, Mr Furniss."

The council flat was home to Leroy Winston Manvers and his wife and his four children. The door was sledge-hammered, off its hinges, and the wind brought the rain in from the walkway outside. It was three in the morning and the dog had failed.

The dog was a decent enough looking spaniel, and the handler was quite a good-looking girl, a bit butch in her dark slacks and the tightness of her navy regulation sweater. Park hadn't noticed her. Great while the dog was still searching, the dog had kept the adrenalin moving for them all. But the dog had failed and was sitting quietly at the feet of the handler, and all the rest of the team were looking at Park, because he was the Case Officer, and the decisions were his. Couldn't talk in the living room. Leroy had the sofa with the children in blankets beside him, and his wife hugging her knees in the only other easy chair. Park was in the corridor, standing over the dog and the team were milling around him, still hanging on to the pick-axe handles and the sledge-hammers that had taken the door off, what they called the keys. Pretty calm Leroy looked to Park. Vest and underpants, hair dread-locked, and the composure that Keeper could best have wiped with a pick-axe handle.

Parrish was there, but out on the walkway. April's team leader was taking a side seat, leaving the tactics to the Case Officer.

Keeper did not believe that the stuff was not there.

The flat had been under 24-hour surveillance for a full week. The flat had had the works – check on all movements and photographic record. Each pusher visit logged. Each movement out by Leroy tailed. Each meeting listed. Eighteen hours a bloody day, Keeper had done in one or other of the surveillance vans. He could have kicked the tail off the dog, because the stuff had to be there.

"Are you *sure?*" A venom when he spoke to the handler, like it was her fault.

"Not me, dearie, *I'm* not sure," the handler said. "And she's not saying there's nothing there, she's just saying she can't find anything. That's different to being sure it's clean."

The straight search had already been done. Leroy and family in the main bedroom while the living room and the kitchen and the kids' rooms were gone over. Leroy and family in the living room while the bathroom and the main bedroom were gone over. All the beds stripped, drawers out, cupboards opened, everything gone through, but that shouldn't have been necessary because the dog should have led them to it.

What to do? To start again? To begin from the front door again?

The two constables were watching him. Customs had their own Search Warrants, and their Writs of Assistance that meant they could do just about anything short of shoving a broom handle up Leroy's backside, but they were obliged to take the constables with them. Supercilious creatures, both of them. They were armed, the April team were not. The constables were there to see there was no Breach of the Peace, that April didn't get shot up.

He could pack it in. He could take Parrish into the kitchen, and he could tell him that in his humble opinion Leroy Winston Manvers just happened to be clean, and they could all go home to bed. It didn't cross David's mind that he should do any such thing.

Back at the Lane they had a photographic record of the nine known small-time pushers visiting Manvers within the last seven days. No way the place was clean.

"Take the place apart," he said.

He showed them how. Down on his hands and knees in the hall, both hands on the carpet, and the carpet ripping off the holding tacks. Crowbar between the floor boards, and the scream of the nails being prised up and the boards splintering. Parrish in the doorway looked away, like he was contemplating a cash register of claims for compensation if the search didn't turn something up. Plus Racial Harassment, and the rest of the book, all coming his way. But he didn't intervene.

The sounds of a demolition job inside the flat. One of the team watched Leroy every moment, watched his face, tried to read apprehension, tried to find a clue from his face as to whether the search was warming, and not just lifting boards.

There was the shout, a coarse whoop of celebration, and Duggie Williams, codename Harlech, was lifting out from under the kitchen floor an insulated picnic box. The top came off. There were at least a dozen cold bags, and there were the packets at the bottom.

The dog handler said, "It's not her fault, dearie, don't go blaming her. I've always told you that she can't cope with frozen stuff."

By the time they had finished, and sealed the flat, and taken Leroy off down to the Lane, and dumped his wife and kids on the Council's night duty Housing Officer, going home didn't seem worth it to Park. The last two nights she'd left the spare bed made up for him.

Not worth going home anyway, because he wanted to be up early and talking with Leroy Winston Manvers.

6

Bill Parrish always went home. Whatever time he finished, whatever time he had to start again, he went home for a snuggle with his wife, a clean shirt, and a cooked breakfast. Park reckoned he couldn't have been in his house above an hour. He would have taken the early train from Charing Cross down into Kent, walked from the station to his modern estate semi-detached, had his snuggle and his shirt change and his shave and his breakfast, and walked back to the station to be amongst the first of the morning's commuters back to Charing Cross.

David had changed his shirt in the Gents, and he had shaved, he had gone without breakfast, and he hadn't thought about Ann, and he hadn't slept. He lolled back in his chair, he didn't stand when Parrish came in reeking of aftershave lotion. The clerical assistants wouldn't be in for another half an hour, and the rest of April would come straggling back to the Lane over the next two hours. Parrish wasn't fussed that his Keeper didn't stand for him. Customs and Excise had their own *esprit de corps* and it wasn't based on a military or a police force discipline.

He saw that the coffee percolator was bubbling gently, and he rinsed out his own mug that was still on the tray beside the coffee machine, tide-lined, from the briefing before they had gone out to bust Leroy Winston Manvers.

"Been to see Leroy?"

"No."

"What's in the other cells?"

"Nothing, empty."

"Better not let him sleep too long."

Wouldn't have been worth coming in early if he had not been able to guarantee that Keeper would be sitting back in his chair at his desk in the April office.

"You've told the ACIO we've got him?"

"Certainly. He's impatient."

"A result is what matters?"

"Very much David, a result matters. He's got the CIO on his back. The CIO has CDIU standing over his shoulder. The CDIU is under pressure from the politician. They want to hear what Leroy has to say and they want it in a hurry."

"And I'm covered?" Keeper asked.

"Like it never happened."

It went against Parrish's grain. To Parrish, 30 years in Customs and Excise, 26 years in the Investigation Division, it was out of order for an investigation to take priority because of connections. But he was a part of a system, he was a cog, he didn't argue.

"Then we'd better get on with it."

Keeper led him down the stairs, didn't use the lift, because the lift would be getting busy with the early risers coming to work. All the squeamish ones would be in early – the secretaries and the accountants, and those from the Value Added Tax sinecures, and the computer boffins. Didn't want to see them. Down the stairs to the basement of the New Fetter Lane building.

They came to the reinforced door of the Lane's cell block. Park pressed the bell, and stood aside for Parrish to come forward.

A short chat. Parrish would be taking charge of the prisoner. The guard could go and take a cup of tea and some pieces of toast in the canteen, and have a cigarette, and chat up the girls there, and not hurry himself. The guard looked from Parrish to Park, and saw the expression on Park's face, and said that he would be pretty happy to have a cup of tea and some toast.

Park went inside the cell. Parrish leaned against the wall in the corridor, and thought that he might throw up his cooked breakfast.

The dealer wasn't that often on his feet before midday and he had made the mistake of sleeping naked. He came warily off the cell bed when Park tore the blankets away from him.

"My lawyer . . ." the man said.

"We'll deal with him next. You first."

With a short left arm punch, Park hit Leroy Winston Manvers in the pit of his stomach. The man's body bent, and as it uncoiled, the man gasping for breath, Park's knee jerked into Leroy Winston Manvers' groin. The man collapsed, folding himself into and over the pain. Park pulled him upright by his hair. One violent heave. And then, very calmly punched him. Again and again.

All the blows were to the body, those parts of the body that were hard to bruise, except for the testicles.

The punches belted into the flabby body of the big man. When he was on the tiled cell floor, when he was whimpering, when he thought his body would break in the pain, then the questions came.

Through the running pain, Leroy Winston Manvers could hear the question.

"Who is the chummie?"

He could hear the question, but before he could focus on it he was once more flung upright, crashed into the corner, bent, protecting his groin.

"You supplied Darren Cole, what is the name of the chummie who supplied you?"

And his eyes were filled with streaming tears and he could hardly breathe and he thought that if he didn't kill this fucker then he was going to be dead, and he threw a flailing blind hook with his right fist, and a huge explosion of pain landed and blossomed in his guts and his head struck the floor, and the voice came to him again, the same as before, "The chummie that supplies you, who is he?"

"He's Charlie . . ."

Park stood back. He was sweating. He stared down at the demolished man on the cell floor.

"I'm listening, Leroy."

The voice was whispered, wheezed. "I know him as Charlie . . . Charlie Persia. The stuff is from Iran . . ."

"Keep rolling, Leroy."

"He's from London, Charlie Persia, but he goes to get it himself."

"And he is Iranian?"

"But he lives here."

"What age?"

"Your age . . . less maybe . . . ah Jesus, man."

It was a minute since he had been hit. Another fear winnowing in the mind of Leroy Winston Manvers. "You get me killed."

"That's OK, Leroy. You're quite safe here. Charlie'll be dead long before you get out of here."

"Don't you tell that I grassed."

The dealer crawled to the bunk against the cell wall, and he lifted himself on to it, and his back was to Park. He said nothing more.

The guard was hovering by the door to the cell block corridor. Park told him that the prisoner was tired and should be allowed a good sleep.

Park took the lift up to the April office with Parrish white-faced beside him, his fist locked on the notebook.

The lights were on. The girls were at the keyboards and answering telephones, and Harlech, in his shirtsleeves, was massaging the shoulders of the redhead as she worked.

"Go home now, Keeper, just go off home." Parrish said.

His *pasdar* uniform was folded into Charlie's rucksack.

He had travelled by bus from Tehran to Qazvin. From Qazvin, after a long wait under the plane trees of the Sabz-i-Meidan, he had joined another bus heading for Resht on the Caspian Sea. He got off by the river near Manjil, and had hitched his way along the track beside the fiercely running water. He had no fear. His papers were good, as they ought to have been at the price he had paid for them in Istanbul. He had a ride from a local official on the pillion of an ancient BSA for fifteen painful miles, and he had been thankful to have been able to spend two hours mostly asleep in a donkey cart.

He had reached the village shortly before noon.

The stone dwellings, too few, too insignificant to be marked on any map of the region, nestled at the base of hills and alongside the river. Once every decade on average, when the spring came following a particularly heavy snowfall in the mountains, the river would overspill and leave a deposit of loam soil across the washed down fields. The plain beside the village was an excellent area for all crops.

Because of its isolation, and because of the quality of the fields beside it, the village was a place of quite startling prosperity. There was no outward sign of that wealth. The American dollars and the Iranian *rials* that the headman had accumulated he kept buried. It was his persistent fear that the village would one day attract attention, that the wealth of his community would be discovered and that he would be taken by the Guards to Qazvin and put to death in the yard of the Ali Qapu. Charlie had never been able to prise from the headman how he planned to use the cash that he risked his life to amass.

He had eaten with the headman, and the headman's sons and brothers. They had slaughtered and roasted a goat in his honour. He sat now on the carpet that covered the dirt floor of the principal room of the headman's house. They would be good Shi'a Moslems in the village, they would follow the teaching of the Qur'an. He looked for the fault in the pattern, the mistake of the craftsman weaver. There was always a mistake in even the most precious carpet. Only God could make what was perfect. For a human creature to attempt perfection, to try to imitate God, was heresy. He could see no flaw . . . He had eaten too much, he had allowed the rich meat of the goat to blunt his wits. In the evening he would need to be at his sharpest. He would negotiate with the headman then.

The village was condemned to sleep for the afternoon. The sun belted into the tin roofs of the houses, and scorched the alleys between. There was a corner of the room where he had been told to leave his rucksack and where blankets had been laid out.

He stood in the doorway of the headman's house and gazed out towards the grey brown of the flowing river, across the rich fields, over the shimmering scarlet of the poppies in flower.

The packets taken from the picnic cold box in Leroy Winston Manvers council flat had been sent to the Scotland Yard forensic laboratory in Lambeth for analysis. And with the packets had gone the instruction of the ACIO that absolute priority was to be attached to the first, if superficial, study. There were only 24 scientists at Lambeth who specialized in drugs-related investigations, and their backlog was soaring. A cocaine possession charge had just a month earlier been thrown out by an inner city magistrate after he had been told at five remand hearings that forensic had not yet come through with its results. Simple analysis was now subject to a nine week delay. So the ACIO had demanded that all else be dropped, this was a matter for the best and the brightest. He could do that once in a while, heaven help him if he made a habit of it. When he was bawling down a phone line, when he was trying to extract blood from men and women already drained dry, it was inevitable that the ACIO would ask himself whether they were all, all of them at the Lane, wasting their bloody time. Was government, parliament, authority, really serious, when they confronted the drugs epidemic with just 24 scientists? Buggered if he knew whether they were serious, buggered if he cared. He was long enough in Customs and Excise to realise the absurdity of getting steamed under the collar about resources. In the last week he had been up before the National Audit Office to justify the way he ran the drugs teams, and the week before that he had had to defend a paper to the Staff Inspection and Evaluation Board. He had talked to Bill Parrish. He knew what had happened in the cell early in the morning after the door had closed behind his Case Officer. Typical of Parrish, that he had gone straight into the ACIO's office and shared the dirt, spread the load up the ladder, so that if the shit was flying then it would be the ACIO fielding it and not dear old Bill.

When he was alone in his office, when he was not spitting about the delays in forensic analysis and the scrutiny of the National Audit Office and the nit-pick ways of the Staff Inspection and Evaluation Board, the ACIO could understand the way the system worked. The system was pretty bloody rotten. The system said that if a Cabinet Minister's daughter took an overdose because she didn't know that the heroin was of a purer quality than she was used to, then her disgusting self-inflicted death took priority over the very similar deaths of the ordinary and the humble. It was a surprise to him that young men like Park ever chose to get themselves involved or stay involved, and he thanked the good Lord that they did.

The ACIO had his preliminary report brought over the river by courier just as his secretary was bringing him his afternoon pot of tea and a buttered scone.

He read.

Initial study showed that the probable origin of the 34 packets, total weight at 2 kilos and 742 grammes, was Northern Iran. Attention was drawn to a stencilled marking on each plastic packet, a small symbol of a dagger. The symbol had been observed on other hauls over the past six years. The quality of heroin in packets stamped with the symbol of the curved blade dagger was invariably high.

He rang Parrish's office on the floor below.

"Don't you worry, love . . . Just leave him to me."

Park pushed himself up from his chair. The front door was already open, Ann was putting the key back into her handbag, her head was down, and his father was standing behind her. He was all puffed up, chest out, back straight, as if he was going on duty. Maybe he was, because he wore his navy blue trousers, and a white shirt and black tie, and his old anorak in which he was always dressed when he was either on his way to the station or when he had just clocked off. His father was a big man, and Park reckoned that because he sat all day either in a Panda or in the station canteen, he had a gut on him. Since his father was a policeman David had gone into Customs and Excise, a sort of bloody-mindedness, and he had had a bellyful as a kid of hearing his father moaning about the force.

He led them into the living room and closed the file that he had been reading.

Inside the room he could see clearly into Ann's face. She was red-eyed. His lip pursed. She had no business taking their marriage into his parents' home, and crying in front of them.

"Very nice to see you, Dad . . . Mum well, is she? . . . I was catching up on a bit of reading. We had a late night up in town and they sent us all back with a day off . . ."

"It's freezing in here . . ." Ann strode forward, snapped on both bars of the electric fire.

He paid the electricity bill. The last bill had been £148.74. He remembered that. He had had to pay the electricity in the same week as the telephone that had been £74.98, and the car service that had been £101.22. He had gone overdrawn.

He looked steadily at his father. "As I said, I was catching up on a bit of reading. I'm doing a paper for the ACIO. What I really want is to get out of heroin and join a team who do cocaine. This paper is to persuade the ACIO to put a man into Bogota . . ."

He wondered if his father knew where Bogota was.

". . . Bogota is the capital of Colombia, Dad. We've got a Drugs Liaison Officer in Caracas, which is the capital of Venezuela . . . but I reckon that Caracas is too far from the action. We need much more hard intelligence on the ground. Colombia exports 80% of the world's cocaine. I rate heroin as peaked, but cocaine is really growing up. I mean, last year's heroin figures were just about the same as the previous year, but cocaine was going through the roof. There could have been half a billion pounds' worth going through the UK system last year. Do you know, there's a place called Medellin in Colombia where the big traffickers live quite openly. We've got to get in there after them. Having a DLO in Caracas means that too much of our intelligence is secondhand. Do you know, Dad, that last year the Drugs Enforcement Agency made a seizure in Florida of ten tons of coke? That's worth fifty million dollars on the street. That's where the action is. What do you think, Dad?"

"What I think is that you're getting to be the biggest bore I've ever met."

"That's not called for."

"And the biggest prick."

"Then get out of my house."

"I'm here at Ann's invitation and I'm staying until I've done some talking." A flush was in his father's face, big veins leaping in his neck and his forehead. "Is that all you do when you get home, bore on about drugs?"

"It matters."

"Do you think Ann cares two pins about drugs?"

"She's made her feelings plain."

"There's nothing else in your life, it's getting to be an obsession."

"What do you want me to do, chat up bloody geraniums in a bloody greenhouse?"

"Look after your wife – try that for a change."

"Don't lecture me on how to look after Ann."

"If someone doesn't have a go at you, you won't have a marriage to worry about. You don't deserve Ann."

"You're out of order."

"Not as out of order as the way you treat your wife."

He exploded. "Something you never learned, Dad, but if you don't do a job with commitment then it's not worth doing at all. In ID we don't just clock watch, we're in the front line. We're not just handing out parking tickets and checking shotgun licences, and taking down the details of people's bloody cats that have got lost – we're in the front fucking line. If we all go home when the bell rings then there's no line left, and all that filth is swimming in here. Got me? Have you the wit to comprehend that? You know what I did this morning when you were watering your bloody geraniums before another second rate day, what I did while she was painting her face before getting into her posh little office, you know what I did . . . ? I beat shit out of a man. I hit Leroy Winston Manvers every place where the bruises don't show. I kicked him, punched him, till I was fucking tired . . . until he gave me a name. Isn't that what you 'old fashioned coppers' used to do? Hand out a bit of a belting, in the good old days. I smashed up Leroy Winston Manvers because he's a heroin dealer, and he fixed up the pusher, and the pusher sold to some government crap artist's daughter. I hit shit out of Leroy Winston Manvers because I hated him. I hated him as much as I wanted the name of his distributor . . . That's what it does to you, that's the fucking filth you get into when you're hunting the distributors. You don't have an idea, do you? Not a fucking idea. I could go to gaol for five years for what I did this morning . . . I tell you, I enjoyed hitting the black bastard. I loved hitting him. You know what? He gave me the name. He was such filth. He's a pig. He makes more money in one month, probably, than I can make in ten years. He's a rat from a sewer . . . They don't ask you to do that, do they, Dad? They don't ask an old fashioned constable to be Case Officer when we're talking heroin, do they, Dad?"

"Like you said, David, out of order." His father stood.

Ann said, "I'm sorry, Pop, for asking you."

"I can't walk away from it," David said. "You can follow me if you want to. If you don't want to then I go on by myself. That's fair warning. You do what you like, I'm not quitting."

"Do you want to come with me, love?"

David saw his wife shake her head. She was muttering on about getting some supper, and she was gone out of the room and heading for the kitchen.

"We love that girl, David, your mother and I. We love her like she's ours."

"I don't hold that against you, Dad. I'm glad of it. But don't turn her against me. There's enough to contend with without that. It's a war we're in, do you see that, goddammit, a war."

But his father's face was set, astonishment, fear, disgust. And then he was gone.

It was a game to them. He thought at the end he would get what he wanted and they would concede. He played the game. He even rose off the carpet and walked out of the house and into the dirt street, stood in the moonlight and listened to the dogs yelping and the distant wolf howl. All part of a game because they were all tired and looking for sleep, then they would give him the whole of the seventh kilo.

They could have taken Charlie's money and put him down an old well or dug him into a field.

The thought was in Charlie's mind, but not uppermost. He reckoned on their greed. He believed the squirrel mentality of the headman preserved him. They would want him back. It was his protection that the headman had no notion that this was Charlie's last shipment.

Late in the evening the headman's hand snaked out, grasped Charlie's hand. Charlie reckoned that the headman was tired, or that he wanted his wife and bed. The strong dry hand caught Charlie's, held it, shook it, sealed the bargain. A game was at an end.

The cash was in wads of fifty notes, fastened with elastic bands. Charlie fetched the rucksack and put the ten bundles carefully on to the carpet in front of him. He sat cross legged. That was awkward to him, and his back ached from the stretching of muscles that were unused. When his hand was shaken then he knew that his safety was guaranteed. Never in much doubt, but that was certainty.

Charlie left the village before dawn. In his rucksack were seven kilos' weight of pure heroin powder in sealed plastic bags, and on the bags was the stamp of the drugs' pedigree. He had watched them stencil on to the plastic the symbol of the curved dagger. That early in the morning there was no cart to carry him alongside the river. He strode out on the dirt trail.

This was the currency that would buy him armour-piercing missiles. He was in a hell of a good humour, and whistling to himself, and he was alone in the mountains of his homeland.

Keeper, restless, fretting, pacing the ragged and worn carpet in April's office. He was a bloody pain, and even Parrish didn't have the spirit to tell him that to his face, and Harlech, who was the nearest that Park had to a friend, just cursed him and stayed quiet.

Charlie Persia. The great silent stomach of the computer had no entry on Charlie Persia. Nothing under the name, and nothing like it from the scores, hundreds, of cross referenced Suspicious Movements Reports that were daily fed into CEDRIC's system.

It was Keeper's opinion that Leroy Winston Manvers had come clean in his pain, had told all. Charlie Persia was the name that the distributor traded under. He believed that. The face and the gasping admissions of Leroy Winston Manvers had a truth about them. He knew from forensic's analysis that the packets found in the Notting Hill council flat were of Iranian origin. He took as his base position that Charlie Persia was Iranian, had carried the good, hard stuff to London. He waited on a phone call to take him forward now that the computer had come up blank. He needed a break. He needed luck. And he was pacing because his phone call had not been returned, and because he did not know where else the break would come from.

It had been luck that had heaved Park out of uniform at Heathrow Airport and into the ID on the Lane. He would never have argued with that. He had spotted the girl coming off the Varig from Rio, and she looked like a towrope, and her accent was an East London slur, and her clothes weren't good enough for a return ticket to Rio, and she had been the only passenger he had stopped all that morning off the overnight intercontinentals. She had had an airline ticket and £500 for couriering a kilo of cocaine, fastened in a sanitary towel between her legs. That was a break, that was noticed. Luck was different, luck could only be taken advantage of. A slack half hour between the clearing of the Customs hall and the arrival of the next jumbo and he had gone out into the concourse to get himself an afternoon paper, and he had seen the man waiting at the barrier, in position to meet a passenger off the incoming flight. At Heathrow they had the police mug-shots of all convicted pushers and dealers. Not everyone looked at them, but the young David Park had made a point of studying them every week. He recognised the face, eighteen months at Isleworth Court and he could only have been out a few weeks. That was luck, recognising the chummie. He had tipped off the local ID based at the airport. The "greeter" had been watched, the meeting had been observed, the passenger had been challenged and asked to return to the Customs area . . . a few grammes more than a kilo stuffed into the cavities in a pair of platform shoes, and back to Isleworth Court for the "greeter", and seven years for the courier. Luck, but there were those in the ID command who said that a man earned his luck, and his luck had been noticed, noticed enough for his application to join the Investigation Division to be processed at speed.

When the telephone on his desk rang out Park was at the far end of the room and he charged for it. God, and he needed the break and the luck when CEDRIC had gone down on him.

Ann . . . would he be in for supper? He didn't know . . . Should she cook for two? Probably best not . . . Did he know what time he would be home? Could she clear the line, he was waiting on a call.

He pounded on over the carpet. The carpet was a disgrace, and so were the blinds that sagged unevenly across the windows, and so was the crack on the upper wall behind his desk that had been there for a year and not repaired. Without luck he was going to stay grounded.

The telephone call, when it came, left him flattened. The Anti-Terrorist branch at Scotland Yard had the most complete records on Iranians living in London. A Chief Inspector told him that they had no record of any exile who went under the name of Charlie Persia . . . sorry not to be of help.

The folder on his desk contained a single typed sheet which was the preliminary report from forensic. Another sheet was his own hand-written record of the interview with Leroy Winston Manvers. He was certain that his man took the name of Charlie. He thought the man was most probably an Iranian. He had written TANGO One on the outside of the folder. Tango was ID's word for a targeted suspect.

For the moment, he was damned if he knew how he would put a face into the Tango One folder.

The investigator worked late into the evening. He had no family, he had no call to go back to the cramped one-bedroomed flat that had been his home since his former life. Beneath his window the Tehran streets had emptied. The recruit from Manzarieh Park would be flying out in the morning, that part was simple, but the arrangement of the detail of the collections that he would make upon his arrival, and the back-up that he would receive on the ground, all of that required care. It was, of course, his intention that no "smoking pistol" would remain behind. He was working at long range, and great distances always posed problems. When he had finished with the matter of Jamil Shabro, traitor and collaborationist, he switched his attention to the business of the British intelligence officer, Dolphin/Matthew Furniss, in the city of Van.

He had on his desk all the sightings marking Furniss' progress across Turkey, just as he had them for his journey around the Gulf. The man came like a lamb to him, to within reach.

As the crow flies, the ebony scavenging crow, the city of Van was sixty miles from the nearest crossing point into Iranian territory.

The watch on Furniss had been kept to a bare minimum. He had been shadowed from airport to hotel, from hotel to airport. Away from his hotel, in between his flights, he had been free of his tail. That was of no matter to the investigator, not at this moment.

He worked late because, early in the morning, he would fly to Tabriz to put in place the final pieces of a mosaic of which he was proud.

7

"The fascinating thing about this region, Terence, is that it was never touched by the European civilizations. Here what you have are the unadulterated remnants of the Hittites and the Urartians and the Armenians."

As far as the Station Officer from Ankara was concerned, Van was one of the most forgettable cities it had been his misfortune to visit. His eyes streamed and he had an aggravating catarrh from the street dust thrown up by the traffic. To Terence Snow, Van was quite stunningly ordinary.

"It's all lying around here to be picked up. Get a spade, dig in the right place, and you'll find the artefacts of old Sarduri, king here in ninth century BC. Fascinating . . ."

The Station Officer's chief preoccupation was how to attract the attention of a taxi that would stop where they stood a hundred yards down the street from the hotel where the orderly tourists waited in line, and his second anxiety was how he was going to extricate himself altogether from this cultural excursion and get back to Ankara.

"Do you know, Terence, that within half an hour's drive of here there are cave paintings made 15,000 years ago? I cherish that sort of knowledge. I believe it gives a man a sense of his own mortality, which is absolutely healthy."

"Yes, sir . . ."

The morale of the Station Officer had been on the wane almost since their flight out of Ankara had been airborne. They had flown over the huge, bleak wilderness of the interior. Never mind the history, he reckoned that Van was a quarter of an hour beyond the outside rim of civilization, ancient or modern. No car at the airport, though it had been booked from Ankara. No rooms for them at the Akdamar hotel, booked and confirmed by telephone. True, he had the car now, and he had two singles in the Akdamar, but they had taken sweat and fury and the last iota of his patience. When he was back in Ankara he'd dine out on the baroque excrescence where they had laid their heads in their first night in the city. Warmly commended by the hall porter in the Akdamar but unlisted by any of the guide books. No hot water, no breakfast, no toilet paper . . . And these people thought they were ready to sign on for the European Economic Community.

What really pissed him off was the certainty that his Desk Head was completely at ease in this godforsaken town.

He was angry just being there. He was frustrated by his inability to wave down a taxi. He was careless. He was playing host to the man from London and he was not running his checks. He had not seen the man who had followed them from the hotel steps, and who now lounged against a wall behind them.

"Have you ever bought jet here, Terence? It's really quite excellent. You can alter the stones, make a very pleasant necklace with the local stuff."

The Station Officer's wife might well have thrown him out of their flat if he had come home to her with a peace offering of Van jet. He smiled. He couldn't help liking Mattie, everyone in the Service liked the man, but, Christ, you had to wonder whether he wasn't just a wee bit soft in the head.

"No, sir, I never have."

They had spent two days talking to refugees from Iran. The Station Officer would have had to hand it to Mattie, that the old blighter was ever so casual, ever so easy in his approaches, and he had them eating from his hand as he milked them. The Station Officer appreciated that the talk was for his benefit, that he was being shown what was expected of him in the future. The Desk Head had been talking about him coming up to Van or Hakkari or Dogubeyezit at least once a month henceforward, to where the refugees crossed. The Station Officer wasn't good with the refugees. Frankly, they embarrassed him. They were young, they were still in shock, they were exhausted from their hike across the mountains and from the long nights of fear from the Iranian and the Turkish military patrols. Bloody unpleasant as it was, the Station Officer would have to admit that the Turkish authorities had no choice but to police their frontier and turn back those trying to cross out of Iran. They had three quarters of a million Iranians, draft dodgers and riff-raff, settled in their country. They had problems of gang crime and heroin trafficking from the refugees. They had every right to turn the refugees round and send them back whence they came. Bit bloody stark though, when he thought of the young, exhausted faces he had seen these past two days.

"That's our boy, Mattie."

The taxi had swerved over to them. From afar there was a chorus of protest reaching out from in front of the hotel. Mattie didn't seem to hear.

They went fast.

The Station Officer damn near cracked his head open on the taxi's roof when they flew over the potholes. They skirted the huge inland sea of Lake Van, azure blue, with a ferry boat on it making a postcard, and they rattled north. Through Caldiran and on to the Dogubeyezit road, and the surface worse, and the driver not attempting evasive action. The Station Officer was rubbing his forehead, and saw that Mattie had his eyes closed, as if he were catnapping. He lit a cigarette. He thought he understood why Mattie Furniss was a Desk Head, and why he had no enemies in Century. They were on their way to meet a field agent, a man from inside, a guy who was taking one hell of a risk to travel outside, and Mattie had his eyes closed and was beginning to snore. The Station Officer reckoned that was true class. He had been fussing about a taxi, and Mattie hadn't given a damn, because he would have believed that a field agent who had crossed out of Iran wasn't going to be going home when his contact was a quarter of an hour late. He was being given a lesson in how to soak up the punishment of getting to the sharp end and meeting up with agents whose necks were on the line. Sit back and let it happen, and don't bother if you start to snore, well done, Mattie . . . He checked behind. No tail. Should have done it earlier, should have checked when he was still hot from not being able to find a taxi. He could see a long way back down the road, and the road was clear. After two days with his Desk Head he could have drafted a tourist pamphlet on Van's history. He knew that Xenophon had led his Ten Thousand in battle at Van, that Alexander had been there, and Pompey, and the Mongols of Tamerlane; that Van had not come into the Ottoman empire until Sultan Selim the Grim had done the necessary butchering in AD 1514. He wondered if, in 25 years' time, he would be able to sleep in the back of a taxi on the way to brief a field agent, and seem as antediluvian to a young Station Officer.

When Mattie started awake, and looked around him and had his bearings, and had apologised with a shrug as if it were rude to sleep, then the Station Officer invented an important meeting in Ankara the next day and asked whether it would be alright for him to catch the morning flight. No problem. He hadn't the spunk to tell Mattie outright that it was his wife's birthday, and that they were throwing a thrash for her at his flat.

They stopped the taxi at the front of the coffee shop. There was a repair yard at the back, and a shed of rusted corrugated iron. The yard was a cemetery for disabled vehicles, some cannibalised, all defunct. The Station Officer saw the lorry with Iranian registration plates.

It was a good place for a meeting. Any long-distance Iranian driver might have cause to stop at the yard.

He thought the agent must be an old friend of Mattie's. The Station Officer stood back and watched the beaming welcome of the man who pumped Mattie's hand, and then held his arm. The Station Officer had joined the Service straight from Cambridge, he was well thought of and young for the Ankara post, but by now he thought that he knew nothing . . . He saw a field man take hold of a Desk Head's arm and cling to it as if Mattie's arm were a talisman of safety. He saw the controlled affection in the way Mattie tapped with the palm of his hand at the knuckle of his agent, the close gesture of warmth. He could not have told his wife, but the Station Officer fancied that if he ever faced a crisis of his own, then he could be certain of Mattie Furniss' support. He had no agents of his own behind lines, he was an analyst. He had men in place, inherited of course, in the Ministry of the Interior and the Army and the Jandarma and the Ministry of Foreign Affairs, but that was in Ankara, not behind the lines and in Iran. Mattie had his arm around the agent's shoulder and he was walking him round the lorry, out of sight from the road, and from the mechanics who laboured in the shed with their oxyacetylene cutters . . . He knew nothing . . . He would not have known of the perpetual, grey fog fear that blanketed a field agent, and he would not have known of the kind strength that was given the field agent by his controller.

He was not included. He was left for an hour to kick his heels.

He was sitting on an old upturned oil drum when Mattie came back to him.

"Did you get all you wanted, sir?"

"Stiffened his backbone, told him what we need. Usual carrot and stick job . . . Your meeting in Ankara tomorrow, won't go on too long I hope."

"Shouldn't think so, sir."

"Don't want it to interfere with your party."

Mattie was walking away, and the Station Officer had seen the dry vestige of the smile.

The bus churned through the miles as the road climbed towards Zanjan. Through the dusted window Charlie could see the small oases, surrounded by poplar trees, and the mud brick villages on either side of the route. It had been night when he had travelled from Tabriz to Tehran, but high sunshine now and he could see into the spreading distance. There was no heat haze, the altitude of the road was too great for mists. He was looking south of the road, he wanted to see the ruins that when he was still a child Mr Furniss had first told him about. The Mausoleum of Sultan Oljaitu-Khodabandeh in the sprawl of ruins near Soltanieh. Charlie, eight years old, and meeting the friend of his father at their villa. Mr Furniss always had good stories to tell the boy. The Mausoleum of Sultan Oljaitu-Khodabandeh had stayed in Charlie's mind. A man, a Sultan of the Mongols, had died 550 years before, and he had sought immortality, and his resting place was a monument that reached 170 feet above the ground. That was the ultimate folly. There would be no photographs of Charlie Eshraq ever raised on a wall. None of his sayings ever daubed on high banners. When he died . . . whenever . . . Charlie wanted a grave like his father's. A corner of a cemetery with a number scratched into the wet cement slab, and weeds at the edge. He thought that made him his own man.

When they passed it, the Mausoleum was clear from the windows of the coach, and Charlie wiped hard at the window although most of the dirt was on the outside of the tinted glass. He saw the great octagon shape of the building and the cupola dome. He saw the goats grazing at its base.

The sight of the Mausoleum was only of a few seconds. No other passenger on the bus bothered to look at it. He thought that he hated men who built mausoleums to their memory, and who had their photographs overlooking public squares, and who demanded that their sayings be scrawled on banners. The hate was active in his heart, but did not show on his face. He appeared relaxed, dozing. He was leaning on his rucksack on the seat next to him. He had no fear that the rucksack of a *pasdar* would be searched at a road block. He had the correct papers. The Guards would be friendly to a *pasdar* returning to Tabriz, they would not search him.

He hated the men who built mausoleums, and despised them.

He remembered what Mr Furniss had said to him, when he was eight years old.

"A man who is afraid of death, dear boy, does not have the courage to live."

In the car taking him from the airport to the Guards Corps headquarters in Tabriz, the investigator listened to the radio. The *pasdaran* operating from speedboats had rocketed a Singapore flagged tanker en route to Kuwait, and crippled it. Many soldiers had been martyred after the Iraqi enemy had once again dropped mustard gas on their trenches, and of course there had been no condemnation from the United Nations Security Council that was in the pocket of the Great Satan. Spies, belonging to the Zionist regime of Baghdad, had been arrested in Tehran. *Mojahedin-e Khalq* counter-revolutionaries had been captured at the western borders carrying 250 kilos of explosive. The Islamic Revolution Committees' Guards had carried out exercises in Zahedan and displayed their ever-increasing readiness to destroy outlaws and smugglers. A bomb had exploded in Tehran's Safariyeh Bazaar, no casualties reported. A grenade and machine-gun attack on the Guards Corps Headquarters in Ressaalat Square in Tehran had been repulsed. The Speaker of the Majlis had spoken at a military meeting of the success of the Republic's home-produced ground-to-air missile in bringing down an enemy MIG-25 over Esfahan. Thirteen foreign cargo ships inspected at sea, and allowed to continue . . .

The war was endless. He had been at war all of his adult life, he had worked ten years for the SAVAK, and ten years for the Ministry of Information and Intelligence. All his time at the SAVAK, reading the files, assessing the statistics of opposition, he had known the certainty of ultimate defeat, so he had built the bridges, covertly prepared for the transfer of power, avoided the firing squads that had been the fate of most of his colleagues. He had changed sides, and he could not now predict the shape of things after this next defeat. Military defeat seemed to him most probable, but would it alter the power structure in Tehran and if so, how? The investigator could read between the lines of a news bulletin. Ever increasing references to battles, losses, insurrections, threats from outside the country, they were all to prepare a crushed people for even greater sacrifices. To himself, he would wonder how many more sacrifices the people, however willing, could sustain . . . There had been a time when he had believed in the ultimate victory. When the MKO had shown their naïvety and attacked in force, and been thwarted, beetles under hobnails, then he had thought that victory was close. But the war went on, and the bombs went on.

He had chosen the radicals. He had banked on their success over the moderates.

The man from Manzarieh Park who flew to London that morning, IranAir, he would strengthen the hand of the radicals, and the matter of the Englishman, Furniss, if that were successfully accomplished, that would be muscle in their arm.

Coming into the city of Tabriz, the driver had slapped a police light on the roof of the car, and had hammered the vehicle's siren.

They came to the square outside the Guards Corps Headquarters. There was heavy security at the gate, even the investigator travelling in an official car was asked to produce identification. There had always been security at this building, since a bitch girl had thrown a grenade at the gate and the Guards. An office had been prepared for the investigator, direct telephone lines had been installed, and a telex link with Tehran. He at once examined again the arrangements for the movement of the transport, and he summoned the men who would travel for their final briefing. Later he would oversee the preparations at the villa.

"You'll be alright, sir?"

"Of course I'll be alright, Terence, and do stop nannying me. I will not drink the water, I will eat only in the restaurant, I forswear salads, and yes thank you, before you ask, I do have ample loo paper. All in all, even without you as nanny, guardian or devoted student, I shall be in bliss. I will be pottering on the battlements of the Van Kalesi. I will be climbing the stone steps on which the feet of Sardur the Second stood. I will stand in the rooms that were his home 750 years before the birth of Christ. I don't know when I shall have that chance again. Not now that you are trained to undreamed of heights, Terence. I fancy I am redundant here. What do you say?"

The Station Officer smiled wanly and slapped the inside pocket of his jacket. "I'll get your report off as soon as I'm in the office."

"Yes. It will give them something to chew on. It is a perpetual source of amazement to me how much a field man can provide if he is directed in the right way. I mean, you might not suppose that running a repair depot in Tabriz gives you the chance to observe much that is important to us, and you would be wrong. They'll be pleased with that."

They would be pleased with what they had because they were now beggars searching for crumbs. Sad but true, that the Desk Head, Iran, had been able to sprint round the Gulf and up to north-eastern Turkey and brief his three field men without the anxiety of knowing that he had missed an opportunity of meeting other operatives working inside. Iran Desk had access to the reports of only three agents in place. Not the sort of thing he would have discussed with Master Snow, of course, and the young man was left, most probably, in cheerful ignorance of the poverty of information from Iran. Mattie knew. He knew that Iran Desk was damn near dead. Eight years after the Revolution, eight years after the purges had started, Mattie Furniss was wafer thin on the ground. No question, not in the land of the Mullahs, of volunteers queueing up to offer their services to the Secret Intelligence Service of the United Kingdom. Looked at logically, he was rather lucky to have had a single agent remaining. The Americans never told him much about their operations inside Iran, and what they did tell him he took with a fistful of scepticism.

For all the money they had to spend, which he did not himself have, he doubted they had many more agents than he. The wear and tear of terror, of arrests, firing squads, had left him short handed. He was down to three agents . . . and to Charlie Eshraq. Thank the good Lord for Charlie Eshraq.

"I'll meet you off your plane, sir."

"That's kind of you, Terence. Run along now, and give your lovely wife the excellent evening she deserves."

Mattie watched the Station Officer slip away into his taxi. He thought Terence Snow had much to learn, but at least he was capable of learning it. More than could be said for the buffoons in Bahrain . . . His report was gone, a weight off his mind. He would write a fuller report when he was back at Century. He had sat up half the night writing it, and sipping sweetened yoghurt, alternately with water, bottled, and the substance of the report pleased him. In Mattie's experience the preliminary report was the one that would do the business. His longer paper would circulate wonderfully swiftly and be back in the files within 48 hours.

At the reception desk he ordered a hire car.

In the lounge he introduced himself to a group of tourists, and chatted easily with them to pass the time before the car arrived. Americans, of course. Such stamina for travel, it always impressed him. From Milwaukee and Boise, Idaho, and Nashville. They were going to Lake Van in the afternoon in the hope of seeing pelican and flamingo and they told Mattie that if they were lucky, and if their tour literature was to be believed, then they might also see Greater Reed Warblers and Redshanks and Potchards. He was mightily impressed with the power of their field glasses and camera lenses, and humbly suggested that it would be prudent not to point these implements at anything military. In the morning they would be heading on for Ararat. They gave Mattie a catalogue of their expectations and he did not disabuse them. It seemed only too possible that they would indeed light upon Noah's Ark. Such very pleasant people. It was the pity of Mattie's life that he so rarely mixed with the likes of them. And it was an immediate pity that they would be off to capture Mount Ararat first thing in the morning, and would not be able to share with Mattie the glory of the Van Kalesi, fortress of Sardur the Second.

In good humour, and thinking well of Terence, Mattie Furniss bought a card to post home.

George's wife was out of earshot, being wonderfully brave as they would afterwards say, a thoroughbred performance, shaking hands and thanking other mourners for coming.

Four of the Secretary of State's staff had come to the service, showed support, and a pretty impressive turnout altogether. The photographers and reporters were kept back from the porch of the building by police and a crash barrier. George walked away with the Home Secretary at his side.

"Are you backing off?"

"Most certainly not."

"I expected results by now."

"We're working very hard."

The Secretary of State snorted. "There have been no charges."

"There will be, very soon."

"She was just a child, destroyed by scum . . ."

Typical of the man, the Home Secretary thought, that he should pick a fight outside the chapel in which his only child had just been cremated. The Home Secretary would not tell him what he deserved to be told, not at this moment. Nobody had made little Lucy take the damn stuff, she was a volunteer, she hadn't had to be press-ganged. If that pompous sod had spent less of his time working the constituencies, burnishing his image, if he had spent a little more time at home. If that poor suffering mother hadn't been so mountainously self-obsessed they certainly wouldn't be here now.

"I can tell you, George, that in addition to the pusher of the heroin your daughter used, we now also have in custody the dealer, that's the next step up in the chain, and we have the beginnings of a line to the distributor. The distributor . . ."

"I know what a distributor is, for heaven's sake."

"No, I'll tell you, George, what the distributor is. The distributor is bringing into the United Kingdom anything upwards of half a million sterling, street value, of heroin. He is a practised criminal with too much to lose to make the sort of mistakes that enable us to pick him up the instant you flick your fingers and call for action. Are you with me, George?"

"But you're going to get to him? If you wouldn't do it, make it happen as a simple duty, you will by God surely do it, whatever it costs your vast empire, as an act of friendship."

"It will be done."

"I will hold you to that."

The Secretary of State turned and stalked back to his wife's side, seeming impatient now to be away. The Home Secretary was breathing hard. God, and he'd been very close to losing his temper. He thought that if that man ever became Prime Minister then he might just as well pack up the black car and return to his farm. He thought that mucking with pigs would be preferable to sitting in Cabinet with an elevated Secretary of State for Defence. He watched them go, sitting back in the limousine with their faces lit by flashbulbs.

The border was a small stream, knee deep and a body's length across and cutting through a gully of smoothed rocks. The water was ice cold, biting at his feet, sloshing in his boots. The crossing point was at the apex of a salient of Iran territory to the west of the village of Lura Shirin. Each time he had taken this route he had travelled alone. He was north of the sector through which the refugees usually tried to escape, with the help of Kurdish villagers who would lead them to the frontier if the money were right. With his life, Charlie Eshraq trusted no other person. He had heard from the exile community in Istanbul many stories about the crossing of the frontier. In the cafés, in the bars, he had spoken with those who had come through, stripped of their money by the guides, their nerves shredded by the patrols on either side. He knew that the Guards Corps regularly patrolled the Iranian side and were committed to hunting down those that they hated most, the draft dodgers. He knew that Turkish paratroopers were set out in strength on the west of the border with night vision equipment and with helicopter gunships. He knew that a boy, running from conscription, running from a place in the trenches outside Basra, could evade the Guards Corps patrols only to be caught by the Turks and handed back. The first time he had crossed he had chosen a route that was well away from the paths used by the Kurdish guides.

When he had forded the stream, he felt a small sense of sadness. He remembered the wetness in Majid Nazeri's eyes, and he thought of him polishing the motorcycle. He thought of the girl. He knew he would not be happy until he was back.

He moved forward as quickly as he dared. It was a steep rock climb up a feeder gully, the rucksack was heavy on his back. His hands were cold and slippery and he worked hard to get away, up out of the stream bed. He wanted to be over the line of the ridge before the sun had risen behind him, before he could be silhouetted on its back.

Araqi flew to London on a jumbo of IranAir. During the flight and on disembarkation he wore the blue livery of a cabin steward. By chance he was known to one of the Guard Corps who travelled the route as a sky marshal. They silently acknowledged each other and made no occasion to exchange greeting. Araqi knew the sky marshal, one of four on the aircraft, because they had been together at Manzarieh Park.

He would not see the sky marshal after the crew had left the aircraft because it was the job of the guards to stay with their charge at all times. The sky marshal would sleep on board, while Araqi travelled with the incoming and outgoing crews to the hotel in West London where there was a permanent block booking for IranAir personnel.

Araqi rode in the airline bus to the hotel. Whereas many of the crew, excepting the Captain and Second Officer, would double up, he had been allocated a room to himself. It was a small point, but it should have been noted by the Anti-Terrorist squad personnel that watched over matters Iranian in the British capital. A number of factors led to this oversight: there was intelligence on the movement of an Active Service Unit from West Belfast; there had been a diversion of manpower following the planting of incendiary devices in two Oxford Street department stores by the Animal Liberation

Front; the squad's guard was perhaps a degree down since there had been no Iranian terrorist action in the United Kingdom for eleven months; and to cap it there were casualties from the virulent influenza sweeping the city. Later there would be an inquiry as to how that small point had been missed, but that would be the familiar if painstaking slamming of the stable door.

The materials would be delivered to Araqi; he would manufacture the bomb, he would put it in the killing place, and then he would get himself back to the hotel and leave the country in the same way as he had arrived. Those were his concerns. The provision of the explosives and the reconnaissance of the target would be handled by others, they were not his concern.

Araqi was a dedicated man. He had brought with him the map of the world from the aircraft's inflight magazine, and he had in his case a small compass. So when he knelt in prayer he could be certain that he faced the shrine of the black Kaaba building at Mecca.

After his prayers, behind his locked door, waiting to be contacted, he read verses from the Qur'an.

He recognised the wide sweep of the shoulders, and the wisping hair that ranged over the collar of the old linen jacket. And the voice was unmistakable. Ancient Britons nearly always shouted when they spoke to a person whose native tongue was other than English. The whole of the reception area was aware that Mr Furniss was visiting one more fortress, would be handing over the car at noon the next day, and would then be checking out.

To Charlie Eshraq, tired and dirty himself, it was quite wonderful to have walked into the Akdamar, in search of a hot bath, and found Mr Furniss.

He stood back. There were mud stains on the trousers of Mr Matthew Furniss, as if he had been kneeling in the earth, and his shoes were mud-caked. He waited until Mr Furniss had finished at his desk, and slung his camera bag on his shoulder, and had headed for the staircase. He thought that he knew which camera would be in the bag. It would be the old Pentax, everything manual, that had photographed him on the grass lawn behind the cottage. His mother, in California, had a picture of her son taken on the lawn at Bibury with that camera. He followed his father's friend up the stairs and on to the first floor.

When Mr Furniss had stopped outside a door, when he was scrabbling in his pocket for his room key, Charlie spoke.

"Hello, Mr Furniss."

He saw the man swivel. "I'm Dr Owens," he said. Charlie saw the astonishment and the recognition. "Good God . . ."

"It is a real surprise."

"Fantastic, dear boy. Quite amazing. What on earth are you doing here?"

"Looking for a bath, Mr Furniss."

"You'll be extraordinarily lucky to find some hot water, but you're very welcome to the bath."

"And you, Mr Furniss, what are you doing here?"

He should not have asked that question. The question was cheek. He saw the fun streak in Mr Furniss' eyes. Mr Furniss had long ago told Charlie that he could make an old man feel young.

"Turning over some old stones, what else?"

So natural . . . the door was opened. Charlie was hugged, like a son, and his back was slapped as if he were a large dog. The room was chaos. The only patch of order was the bed which had been made. No one had tidied the clothes, clean or dirty, and the guide books, and the handwritten notes, and the drawings of sections of the Van Kalesi lay scattered on and about the dressing table.

"An extreme form of liberation, dear boy, a man staying in a hotel on his own . . . Good heavens, Charlie, you've just walked out today? Forgive me meandering on. You must be done in. Can I send for something for you to eat and drink? Meantime, run a bath. What would you like most?"

After a stone-cold bath and a trolley of food, Charlie set out to tell Mr Furniss all that he was clearly impatient to hear. Charlie told him first of his crossing of the frontier. The bus ride from Tabriz around the shores of Lake Urmia to Rezaiyeh. Moving at night, on foot, into the hills and then on into the mountains. Crossing . . . Slipping the Turkish army patrols, getting to the main road. Hitching to Van.

And then he talked of unit movements between Tehran and Tabriz. He talked of a meeting on the bus with a sergeant in artillery who complained that on the front line Dezful sector the 105 mm howitzers were restricted to seven shells a day. He talked of the Mullah that he had shadowed, and how the bazaar gossip had told him that the Mullah was climbing high in the faction that was radical. He talked of a mechanic in the Engineers who had told him in a café that an armoured regiment positioned at Susangerd was about to be mothballed because every one of the 72 British-built Chieftain tanks had a mechanical failure and the unit was without spare parts. He talked of the feelings that had been expressed to him about the *Mojahedin-e Khalq* and their operations into Iran from behind the shelter of the enemy Iraqi army. ". . . they're dead. They cannot exist inside the country. They do nothing outside the border areas, believe me. There is no resistance inside the country. The resistance has been crushed . . ."

For two and a half hours Charlie talked and Mr Furniss covered every sheet of the hotel notepaper that was left in the room. The interruptions were few. When they came they were nudgings of Charlie's memory, prompting him to recall further what he had seen, what he had heard.

"First class, dear boy . . ."

"What are your own movements now, Mr Furniss?"

"Tragic but true, business has overtaken recreation. I've fixed myself a military pass into the Toprakkale army zone. Quite pleased about that. It's a closed area, but there's a fort inside the perimeter. I meant to go this afternoon, but it'll have to wait until tomorrow. Always work first, eh?"

"Is that why you are in Van, to visit ruins?"

Charlie smiled at Mr Furniss' frown. Then the grin, as if the mischief were shared. He believed he could see a glow of happiness in the older man's face.

"Did you use my little cracker?"

"I did it just as the instructions told me."

"Tell me, Charlie."

"The motorcycle, the drawing up alongside, slamming it on the roof. I saw his face before I drew away from him. He didn't know what it was, but he had fear. There was nothing he could do because he was boxed around by lorries. He couldn't stop, he couldn't get out. He had nowhere to go."

"I will never forget what a fine child was your sister."

"When I go back again, inside, I have to have armour-piercing."

"One step at a time, dear boy."

"What else, sir?"

"Well, just remember what a fine girl Juliette was. Put the rest of it out of your mind. You've done enough."

"With armour-piercing weapons I can take out the Mullah who sentenced her, and I think that I can get also to the investigator who tortured her. I have identified both of them."

He saw that Mr Furniss was staring out of the window. He thought he understood why Mr Furniss had turned his head away. The view from the hotel room window was nothing more than a mass of different, improvised roof tops. It had been Mr Furniss who had told him the detail of his father's execution and the hanging of his sister. Each time, then, Mr Furniss had turned away his face.

"But if I don't have the armour-piercing it would be much harder. In fact, I don't know how it could be done."

"I think it would be better, Charlie, if you didn't come down to Bibury again . . . more professional that way."

"Is that going to be a problem, that sort of weapon?"

"Dear boy, I've told you where to go. You can buy anything if you have the money. Do you have the money?"

"The money is no problem, Mr Furniss."

Parrish wasn't surprised to find that Keeper had beaten him into the Lane.

He poured himself coffee from the percolator.

"Nothing . . . ?"

Park shook his head.

". . . What have we got?"

"Surveillance on Manvers' place. The name and type at ports, airports . . . nothing's showing."

"Something'll show, it always does."

"Well, not yet it hasn't."

"What I always say . . . Fortune favours the patient."

"It's bloody hard," Park snapped. "I don't think I was cut out for Fortune."

Mattie was tired. He had slept badly because the young man with a blanket bed on the floor had tossed, rolled, right through the night, and then been gone at first light.

He was elated. This visit to the ruins in Toprakkale military was the zenith of his whole journey. But he was running late. That was inevitable, given the fascination of the ruins, and he had to get the car back to Van, pack up his bags, settle his hotel bill, and catch the flight to Ankara.

Because he was exhausted, excited and in a hurry, he was not aware of the Dodge pick-up closing on him from behind. He had not thought twice about the tractor hauling a trailer from a sheep pen by the roadside ahead of him. He had not planned his route from Van to Toprakkale, merely followed the map. He did not react well . . . The tutors at Portsmouth would have been disgusted. All those hours teaching him AOPR: Awareness, Observation, Planning, Reaction. If it had been Mattie's class and a youngster had let himself into that mess at the training centre, Mattie would have roasted him in front of all the others.

A straight stretch of road was all he saw. The road ahead empty except for the tractor and its long trailer stacked high with bales of fodder. It was empty behind him, and he wasn't checking, except for the pick-up.

Mattie should have been in a performance car. He should have been using a professional driver. He should have seen the block ahead, and the block behind.

The tractor stopped.

And that should have triggered the alarm bell for Mattie. He should have gone off the road, risked a soft verge. He should have tried the "bootlegger turn", hand brake on and wheel spin to throw him round.

He was like a lamb to the slaughter. He pumped the brake gently, he brought the Fiat 127 to a stop. He pressed the horn, once, politely.

There was a violent shuddering crash as the Dodge pick-up smashed against the boot of the Fiat. Mattie was flung back, skull against the head rest. He twisted, heart-racing, sickening fright welling into him, to look behind.

Men running from the pick-up towards him, one from either side, and a man coming at him in front, charging towards the car. He saw the handguns and the machine pistol. Three men coming at him, all armed. His engine had cut when he had been rammed.

The door beside him surged open. Christ, and he hadn't even locked his door . . .

He shouted loudly, in English, "I haven't got much money, I'll give you . . ."

He was pulled out, thrown onto the road surface, a boot went into his face, his wrists were heaved to the small of his back and he felt plastic ties going sharply into his flesh. He was dragged towards the rear door of the pick-up.

Mattie understood. He would have been a bloody fool not to have understood.

He was lifted and thrown hard into the back of the truck. The doors slammed. Light died.

The Immigration Officer gazed from the young man standing in front of his desk back down to the Travel Document.

"Stateless Person . . . ?"

"The government of Iran does not recognize my old passport. I hope soon to have British citizenship, and a British passport."

The Immigration Officer squinted down at the writing. "And you are . . ."

"Charles Eshraq."

The eyeline, at measured speed, moved again from the Travel Document to the young man who wore a smart navy blazer with a travel company's logo over the breast pocket.

"Sorry . . ."

"I am Charles E...S..H..R..A..Q."

When he worked fast at the desk top that was out of sight of the man standing in front of him, the Immigration Officer could still maintain an air of impenetrable boredom. His fingers were flicking at the pages of the book with the print-out of entries. It was sharp in his mind. He and the rest of his shift had had the briefing when they had come on duty in the late afternoon. The queue was stretching out behind the man. That was alright, too, they could all wait. He had the Iranian, he had Charles/Charlie, born August 5, 1965, and he had a Customs ID call. The name in the Suspects' Index was Charlie Persia, probably a nickname, followed by the reference letter "0". "0" was Customs referral. The Immigration Officer pressed the hidden button on his desk top.

The Supervisor hovered behind him. The Immigration Officer pointed to the travel document, Charles Eshraq. Place of Birth: Tehran. His finger slid across to the Suspects' Index, Charlie Persia, assumed Iranian. Date of Birth: early, middle 1960s.

"Would you mind stepping this way, sir?" The Supervisor asked, and his hand rested easily on Charlie's sleeve.

"Is there a problem?"

"Shouldn't think so, sir. Just routine. This way, please, sir."

598

8

"We put the dog onto his bag – hung on like it was marrowbone."

The room was crowded.

There were men from the Immigration Control, and from the uniformed Customs strength, and Park stood dead centre. Parrish and Harlech were hanging back by the door. Park listened carefully. He had learned long before that the initial brief was the important one, and he would make his Case Officer decisions from that first information.

"We've him sat in a room now. He thinks there's something wrong with his documentation. I tell you what, he doesn't look fussed, not like I'd be if I had the sort of quantity in my case to make the dog go clean off its whistle. OK, your airport dog will get a good sniff every so often, so they're not as you might say blasé, but, Jesus, I've seen nothing like it."

Parrish had not yet recovered his sanity from the style of the journey down from the Lane to Heathrow. He still looked like a man clutching a spar in a high sea. Harlech was pale from sitting in the passenger seat where he could not escape from the swerving and the overtaking and the raw speed; Harlech would tell the rest of them later that Keeper's drive down was the worst experience in his life. Harlech had been the late duty, Parrish had been clearing his desk and checking the overtime sheets, and Keeper had just been using up time, polishing his shoes for the third time that day, when the telephone call had come through from the airport.

"We got his ticket off him, and the baggage tag was stapled. We collected the bag off the trailer and let the dog close. Damn near pulled the handler off his feet." The senior uniformed officer had been Park's guv'nor at the airport. He didn't like the boy, but he'd seen his quality and he had written a fulsome recommendation for transfer to ID. ". . . The bag is a rucksack, the ticket is from Istanbul. Listen, the dog tells you a fair amount when it gets going. The way that dog went then, our chummie is carrying one hell of a load. We haven't opened anything up, we haven't touched anything. So, it's your baby."

Parrish wasn't saying anything, still shaking his head like he were trying to get rid of the bad dream of the Escort's wheel caps touching the wheel caps of a taxi. Park would not have been able to remember when he had last been so elated at the contact with a suspect. He was the Case Officer. Like the man said, his baby.

"I'd let him run." He knew that there were two other cars on the way to Heathrow, April team members summoned without apology from home. "Just as soon as we've the back-up."

The lift of Bill Parrish's eyebrows told him of the concern. Normal practice would have been to bust the chummie, and if the chummie wasn't to be busted, then the second most obvious procedure would have been to open the rucksack, empty the contents and substitute dross for the real thing. Parrish's raised eyebrows were a warning to him.

"Sorry, Bill, but what I'm saying is to let him run."

It was Parrish's style to trust to the flair of the young men in the ID. If he had a deep disliking inside the civil service office where he worked it was for those of his contemporaries, the old lags, who believed that only age and experience counted when decisions were taken. Parrish backed his youngsters, he gave them their heads, and he sweated blood over it. He went to a telephone. He leafed through his diary. He dialled the home number of the ACIO. He was brief. He didn't tell the ACIO that the dog had gone berserk when confronted with the rucksack, that they were sitting on a major haul. He reported that there were thought to be traces of narcotics in the suspect's baggage. He said that a man of Iranian birth, and travelling on a UK-issued Stateless Person's document, the right sort of age, would now be carrying the April team's tag of Tango One. He said that Tango One would be released from the airport as soon as he was satisfied that a sufficient number of personnel had gathered for effective surveillance. Perspiration on his forehead, not blood . . . by Christ, there would be blood if Keeper fouled up. Nothing in this world surprised him, not since an archbishop had been stopped by his Customs colleagues at Rome and waved his arms about in protest and thereby dislodged three packets of heroin that had been stuck in his belt under his cassock. Nothing surprised him, not even that a young man should try to walk through Heathrow with a heavy load of stuff in a rucksack. Most of them tried the clever way. Most of them used carefully hollowed out Samsonite cases, or chess pieces fashioned from solidified cocaine, or they stuffed it up their backsides, or they swallowed it in cellophane packets. They'd try any bloody thing. It did not surprise Parrish that Tango One had it loaded in a rucksack where even the most casual search would have found it. And yet, what did they stop? They stopped one PAX in a hundred, or one in two hundred. A fair risk, a chance worth taking . . .

"It's okayed, David. You can let him run . . ."

He took Keeper out into the corridor, out of range of the men in the room.

Only Harlech heard the ferocity of his whisper into Park's ear. "If you screw up, David, I'm gone, and the ACIO who has backed you will be gone with me, and we'll bloody well hang on to your legs to make sure, damned sure, that you go down with us."

"I hear you, Bill."

"Too right, you'd better hear me."

The telephone rang, and it was passed to Parrish, and he listened and then told Park that the two other April cars had arrived, were outside Terminal 3, waiting for instructions.

They set off down the corridor. The man from Immigration, and Parrish and Keeper and Harlech, and a uniformed Customs man caught them up carrying a khaki rucksack. Parrish would have sworn that he could see flecks of the dog's saliva on the rucksack's flap. The rucksack was grimed with dried mud. They didn't open it. That sort of bag was much harder to unpack and repack than a suitcase. No need, really, because the dog had told them what they would find. They transferred from Customs and Excise territory to Immigration. A new set of corridors, another set of duty rosters pinned to notice boards.

In the door of the room where Tango One had been sat, and where he was watched, there was a one way window. Keeper went close to it, nose against it, stared through the glass. There was the slightest quickening of his breath. He had the break and he had the luck, and he had not really believed in either. He looked through the window at Charlie Persia. Charles Eshraq, now Tango One. He saw a well-built young man with a strong head of dark hair, and a beard of a couple of months, and he saw that the man sat quietly and flicked ash from his cigarette into the tinfoil ashtray. He saw that the man was calm. He wouldn't go in himself. He motioned Harlech to the window. Wrong for either of them to show their faces. He gave a wry smile to Parrish.

"Better we hang together than hang separately, Bill."

Parrish wasn't in the mood for banter. He shouldered past Harlech, opened the door.

Park stood close to the door. He could hear everything. Something massively reassuring about old Parrish's competence when it came to keeping the suspect at ease.

"I am really sorry about the delay, Mr Eshraq."

"What was the difficulty?"

"No real difficulty other than you happened to hit a desk man who was less than knowledgeable about Stateless Persons documentation."

"Is that all?"

"They're changing the form of the documentation and that young fellow had it in his head that the change had already taken place . . . You know what it is, late at night, no one to set him right until they called me."

"It's taken a long time."

"I'm very sorry if you've been inconvenienced . . . can I just have the details, Mr Eshraq? Everything that happens in Civil Service work, there has to be a report. Name . . . ?"

"Charles Eshraq."

"Date of birth, and place of birth . . . ?"

"August 5, 1965, Tehran. It is in the document."

"Never mind . . . Address in the UK . . . ?"

"Flat 6, 24, Beaufort Street, SW3."

"Very nice, too . . . Occupation, Mr Eshraq?"

"Freelance travel courier."

"Get all the sunshine, do you?"

"Eastern Mediterranean mostly, yes."

"We've delayed you horribly, were you being met?"

"No, I have my wheels in Long Stay parking."

"Christ, I wouldn't leave anything decent in there, I hope it's alright."

"It's only a little Suzuki jeep."

"Can we give you a lift over?"

"Thanks, but I'll take the bus. I'm not in a hurry."

"Well, it's quite a fine night. Again, my apologies. I suppose you've some luggage?"

"Just a rucksack."

"Let's go back to baggage reclaim then, Mr Eshraq."

Harlech and Park ducked away and into an empty office. Through the door he saw Parrish leading the Tango One out into the corridor. He told Harlech for Christ's sake not to let himself be seen but to watch chummie on to the bus and then wait to be collected by Corinthian by the bus stop. Then he sprinted to get to the Escort in the Customs parking lot. Keeper found the others, detailed Corinthian to collect Harlech and then join Statesman at the gates of the Long Stay parking lot, one a hundred yards to the west and the other a hundred yards to the east. "Target in a Suzuki jeep, Keeper's Escort not far behind. Take nothing for granted. He says he lives in Beaufort Street in Chelsea, but he's so fucking cool this one he may just fancy his chances at Windsor Castle. As soon as the line of flight is established, usual procedures to apply."

Then he hammered under the tunnel to get to Long Stay parking to give himself time to locate the Suzuki before his Tango One.

He had been held up at Immigration before, but never for so long.

It was not a surprise to him. The Immigration men always took a hard look at stateless persons' documentation. He had learned in Britain that foreigners were always given a hard time at the airport, almost part of an immigration policy. What had been a surprise was the courtesy of the senior man who cleared the matter up. That man was one in a thousand, and not a well man by the look of him. Wouldn't last, that was certain. He checked his mirror and saw that a dark coloured Ford, possibly a new Escort, was immediately behind him.

He had lived in London for four years, but it had never felt like home to him. He did not think that any of the exiles who had come first to London would have thought of the city as anything other than a temporary refuge. But it had effectively swallowed them all. They would still all dream of going home. They would dream, but Charlie was going, and he realized that this was his last journey back from the airport. "Get all the sunshine, do you?" Oh yes, he would be getting all the sunshine. He was off the motorway, and heading past the old Lucozade building. Temperature 5. He looked up into his mirror and saw that he was followed by a Vauxhall, almost certainly a Vauxhall.

There was no tension in his driving. He was controlled, at ease. It had not crossed his mind that he could be busted at Heathrow. He was Charles Eshraq, Stateless Person, but he would not be stateless for long . . . Charlie Eshraq had taken out two Guards with a handgun. He had blown away the executioner of Tabriz. He was the friend of Mr Matthew Furniss. He was going home with just two more items of business to deal with. And then . . . then he would be Charles Eshraq, Iranian citizen. Probably no longer the friend of Mr Furniss, certainly no longer the very close friend of the Misses Furniss. He thought of La'ayya and he patted the rucksack and made a wild calculation of what in perfumes and soap seven kilos of first grade heroin would buy. After the small matter of the armour-piercing missiles, of course. He was on the King's Road. He looked up into the mirror as he changed through his gears, as his foot eased on the brake. There was a Maestro behind him.

If he was quick with a shower, he would be in time to get to the pub before closing. Charlie Eshraq would get a great welcome before "last orders". He would tell some good stories about dumb tourists losing passports or knickers in the Turkish resorts, and he'd get a good laugh and a good welcome.

He parked.

He didn't look at the car on the other side of the road. He didn't see the couple clinching. He didn't hear Amanda, codename Token and the only woman of April's team, bitching that codename Corinthian, who this year had failed to complete the eighth mile of the London Marathon, could keep his bloody hand out from under her blouse. And he didn't hear Token issue a violent warning when Corinthian whispered that was just play acting in a good cause.

Charlie humped his rucksack up the stairs to his flat. He threw, street value, more than a million pounds sterling of heroin down on to the floor.

He went to the window and looked out on to the street below. A girl got out of a car opposite, slammed the door furiously and then got into the back seat. Charlie smiled to himself. He thought that La'ayya would have liked the King's Road, and he didn't suppose she'd ever see it.

He ran his shower.

Mattie was trussed tight.

He had lost the feeling below the ankles, and the pain was cutting at his wrists.

He was very alert now. Old training was surfacing, things that he had been taught ten years before, and twenty years. For Christ's sake, he had even lectured on it, back at the Fort at Portsmouth. He had been a student more than once on the Escape and Evasion courses, and he had been the instructor. He knew it all. He was lying on the hard and hurting steel ribbing floor of the pick-up. His captors had put a gag of thick leather in his mouth and lashed the thongs at the ends of the gag behind his neck.

The training had told him that the optimum escape moment was at the very moment of capture. That's what he had told his students. Right, he had been looking for the optimum moment, been looking at it from the start, right into the barrel of an automatic pistol. The optimum moment was also the time of the maximum danger – that, also, he had told his students. The time of the lift was the time that the hit squad were most highly stressed, most irrational. He had looked up the barrel of the automatic pistol and been kicked in the head. His ear had bled, was now congealed. He rationalised that his bleeding ear would have been shot off, with half his head, if he had struggled at the roadside. He was an old man, and there were four of them and none of them looked half his age.

Two of them were in the back section with him, and both now wore cotton hoods with eye slits, and both kept handguns trained on him, and neither had spoken.

He was aware that, at first, the truck had travelled several miles, and that then the engine had been stopped for what might have been three hours. He knew that when they had stopped they had been in a garage or a farm shed because he had heard the doors being shut, and he had heard the echo as the engine was cut, and later restarted, which told him that the vehicle was in a confined space. He lay alone. The pain had come and gone and reached point after point that he thought would be unendurable. He weighed pain against anxiety. He worked to restore the circulation in his hands and feet, told himself over and over that another opportunity to escape would present itself.

The truck doors opened, his bonds were examined by torchlight, and then the outer doors were opened and the truck headed off again, a long drive, over those awful bloody roads. It was part of his training to remember everything possible about his journey after capture, basic stuff that. Easy enough in the New Forest, or the back terrace streets of Portsmouth, damn sight harder after the shock of capture, after being kicked in the head, and when there were two handguns a couple of feet from his ear. A weekly game of squash did not leave a 52-year-old in ideal shape for kidnapping, but he understood that they had driven a good distance.

He had been aware first that the pace of the truck had slowed, and he could hear other vehicle engines around him. He heard voices, Turkish spoken, and then the truck was accelerating. He thought they were back on a decent road surface. The truck lurched to a stop, Mattie slid forward and into the bulkhead and scraped his scalp.

He heard the driver shout, *"Asalaam Aleikum."*

He heard a voice outside, *"Aleikum Asalaam."*

The truck gathered speed. The words were revolving in his mind.

"Peace be on you."

"On you be peace."

Mattie had lived in Iran as a military liaison officer, and he had lived there as the Station Officer. Second nature to Mattie to recognise the greeting and the response.

604

He was sagged on the floor of the truck. He was inside Iran, beyond the reach of help.

From the Customs post a telephone call was routed through the office that had been made available in Tabriz to the investigator. The message was terse. The investigator was told that a Dodge pick-up had just passed through the frontier and had begun the 150-mile journey to Tabriz.

In his former life, the news would have been cause enough to break out a bottle of French champagne . . . much that was missed from the former life. The investigator instead, in his turn, made a telephone call, to the Tehran office of the Mullah who was his protector, to the man who had authorised the kidnapping. Unable to celebrate with champagne, the investigator curled up on his camp bed, tried to catch a few hours of sleep.

No, Dr Owens had not checked out, and that was an embarrassment to reception because they had been promised he was going and they had a client for the room, and it was still occupied with Dr Owens' possessions.

No, Dr Owens had not brought back his car, and the hall porter had twice been phoned by the rental company.

From the airport, after the Van flight arrived without Mr Furniss, it had taken the Station Officer a full hour to get through on a payphone from Ankara to Van. It took him another hour to reach the Embassy's Air Attaché.

No, of course he had confirmed there were no flights to Van that night.

No, for crying out loud, this was not a trivial matter. He wanted a light aircraft, and he wanted the Air Attaché to pilot it, soon as possible, like an hour ago.

"I was half into bed, Terence. This is on the level?"

"Sadly, yes . . . right on the level."

It had been a ghastly flight in a light Cessna across a great expanse of raw countryside, buffeted by gale force winds. The Station Officer was a poor air traveller at the best of times, but now he noticed not at all the yawing progress of the aircraft. The Air Attaché didn't speak to him, had his hands full. He took his cue from the furrowed anxiety of the young man strapped in beside him.

When they'd landed, the Station Officer asked the Air Attaché to go directly to the Akdamar, to make sure that the room in the name of Dr Owens stayed sealed.

He went to the local offices of the *jandarma*. He said that he was from the British Embassy. He knew the registration number of the hired Fiat. It was close to dawn when the report came in, car discovered abandoned, indications of an accident. He was taken to the scene. He said that Dr Owens, the driver of the damaged car, was a distinguished archaeologist and the guest of the Ambassador. He tried to minimize the concern that had brought him at night across the country, and a poor job he made of it. The headlights of the jeep had picked out the Fiat's rear reflectors. It was on the verge, off balance, it seemed, both right hand wheels sunk into the soft mud. They gave him a flashlight and let him make his own examination. To them it was a small matter. No big deal, death on the roads, not in eastern Turkey, and this wasn't death, this was just a missing person. True, there was nothing inside the car to suggest that Mr Furniss was hurt, no blood stain that he could see, no broken glass. But outside he saw the Fiat's skid tracks on the tarmacadam and he saw the dirt trail across what would have been the path of the Fiat. He saw the broken shields of the brake lights and the indicators and the stoved-in bumper. Pretty straightforward . . . A vehicle coming off the open fields in front – wide tracks, probably a tractor or farm lorry – a vehicle ramming from behind . . . and the unaccompanied Desk Head in between.

The *jandarma* officer said, "It is possible that he has been concussed, that he has wandered off the road . . ."

No chance.

". . . There is no other explanation."

The officer drove him to the Akdamar.

He gutted the room. Clothes everywhere, books and papers too, and many pages of scribbled notes, not in English certainly, must be some sort of code. He looked carefully at the disorder and decided that it was as Mr Furniss had left it, that it had not been searched. He packed everything into Mr Furniss' suitcase.

The Station Officer paid Dr Owens bill. He woke the Air Attaché from a deep sleep in an unlit corner of the lobby.

"Sorted out your little problem, Terence? Knickers all untwisted, eh?"

"No, I am afraid the news is all bad."

"Anything I can do?"

"Just fly us home. No jokes. No japes. No funny faces. Just don't say anything at all. Please."

Standing on the hotel steps, waiting once more for a taxi, the Station Officer felt an aching anxiety. Whatever else, Mattie Furniss was not gone walkabout in eastern Turkey nursing a concussion. He had been thinking, how would it have been if he had been there too? Would he be alive now? Where would he be? Come what may, he'd be crucified, he knew that, for leaving a Desk Head alone. Probably finished altogether.

They took off, with the dawn rising behind them.

A blustering wet early summer morning in London. The traffic clogged the Thames bridges. The commuters below the high windows of Century House swarmed in ant columns along the pavements.

The first report from the Ankara Station Officer was deciphered then passed, marked URGENT, to the desk of the Night Duty Officer. The Night Duty Officer was ready to clock off, and he was enjoying his last cup of coffee when the message reached him. He signed for it, he read it, and he spluttered coffee over the morning newspapers. There was a procedure for catastrophe. Telephone the Director General's PA. The PA would alert the Director General wherever he was. The Night Duty Officer would then ring the Director General on a scrambled line.

The Night Duty Officer read over the message in a clear and firm voice. That was a sham. His throat had dried, his fingers drummed on his desk. He knew Mattie, everyone at Century knew Mattie Furniss. He listened to the silence at the other end of the distorted connection.

"Did you get that, sir?"

A clipped voice. "Yes, I did."

"What can I do, sir?"

A longer silence. What could anyone do? And what the hell was old Mattie, a Desk Head, doing in Turkey? Last he'd heard of him he was in Bahrain and God knows what he was doing there. Not the Night Duty Officer's place to question . . . The Night Duty Officer had cause to think well of Mattie Furniss. His son had had pretty serious problems with his teeth, came up one day at lunch in the canteen, and Mattie had taken a note, and a week later he had the name of a specialist in Wimpole Street, and the specialist had sorted out the problem over the following nine months, and the bills hadn't been bad. The Night Duty Officer's wife always spoke well of Mr Furniss, and when the Night Duty Officer went home that morning he would not be able to tell her that Mattie Furniss was posted missing, and in a country he'd no business being in.

The voice jolted him.

"All the West Asia Desk Heads, and the DDG, in my office at nine – inform Downing Street that I'll be there in half an hour. I shall require to see the PM."

The telephone clicked, went dead.

The truck had slowed, and there were the sounds of a city's traffic flow around him. He thought that they were close to a commercial area. He could hear the hawkers' shouts, and whenever the truck stopped he could smell the pavement food stalls. They had come down a fast road for two or more hours, that could only be the Tehran road from the border. If they were now in a city then they had reached Tabriz. A lifetime ago since he had been in Tabriz. That was wrong . . . A lifetime ago was being trapped and kidnapped on the road from Toprakkale. That was more than a lifetime ago.

In the hours that he had lain in the truck no word had been spoken to him. His head, where he had been kicked, was not hurting any longer. His gag was constantly painful. His mouth was parched. His feet were dead, below the binding.

The truck stopped, lurched forward and then swung to the right, revving in low gears, stopped again. The engine was cut. He heard everything. The click of the door, the squeaking of the driver's seat as the driver left it, and then it slammed shut. The same at the passenger side. He heard a low conversation beside the driver's cab, but too quiet for him to understand what was said. He saw his captors in the back of the truck move towards him. He didn't flinch. He was not afraid, not yet. Their hands came at his face. He could smell their breath through the masks they wore. He did not try to wriggle away from them, because he thought that would have invited a beating. They fastened a strip of cloth around his eyes.

Mattie was lifted down from the truck. He felt a warm wind on his cheeks. The binding on his ankles was freed. The blood was pounding at the base of his shins, and squeezing down again into his feet. Hands held him upright. He could not have walked by himself, and he was half carried, half dragged up some steps and then manoeuvred into a doorway. They went up a full flight of stairs, and they crossed a small landing, and a door was opened. The strip of cloth was removed from his eyes.

He stood in the centre of the room.

The gag was taken from his mouth. The strap was released from his wrists. The door closed behind him. He heard a key turn.

He stared around him.

The window was barred on the inside, had no glass, and beyond the bars the space had been boarded up with plywood. There was an iron bed frame, like the ones used by the junior boys in the dormitories of his old school. There was a flush lavatory in one corner and beside it a table on which was a plain ceramic water pitcher and a steel bowl. There was no other furniture in the room. He turned. The door was heavy wood, there was a spy hole at eye level. The walls were freshly whitewashed over plaster. The floor was tiled.

If he had been planning a custody cell for a prisoner such as himself he would have created a very similar room. The kidnapping, the lack of any form of communication, the cell, they were all much as he would have planned them himself. Mattie Furniss, Desk Head at Century, long time officer of the Service, was a professional, and he could recognise the professionalism of his captors.

He sat on the bed. He massaged his ankles and his wrists. He forced his mind to work at the detail of his cover. His cover was his only protection.

The Prime Minister sat rigid at the edge of the sitting room chair. The coffee was untouched, the toast had cooled.

"And he's just disappeared off the face of the earth?"

"Not disappeared, Prime Minister. The signs all point to his having been kidnapped."

"But to have been there at all, that tells me he's not very important . . ."

"In that theatre of operations, Furniss is of the utmost importance."

"Then you had better tell me what he was doing all by himself – I suppose he was all by himself? You haven't lost a whole department, have you? – in such an obviously risky enterprise?"

"In my opinion, Prime Minister, the performance of the Service on Iran had been second rate. Upon taking up my position at Century I determined to get that Desk back on course. I told Mattie Furniss, who is incidentally a quite outstanding servant of his country, what I wanted. Obviously affairs inside Iran are at a crucial point. We need to know, very precisely, who is going to come out as top dog in the new Iran. We are talking about a sophisticated and very capable regional super-power, one that controls huge resources of oil inside its own borders and one which has the capacity to destabilize every smaller state on its frontiers, possibly excepting Iraq. We earn very considerable sums of monies from the Gulf states, from the Kuwaitis, from the Saudis. All of those earnings are potentially at risk in the barely disguised warfare between moderate and radical factions for ultimate power in Tehran. The American government has wished to put its markers down in that battle, we more prudently want only to have a better perspective on the end result. For the time being at any rate. Obviously if the radical faction wins out we may have to kiss goodbye to billions invested in that region, billions of future sales. We are talking about the possible perversion of one of the great economic markets currently open to us, along with the loss of great numbers of jobs, if the radicals win and continue to export revolution and Islamic fundamentalism."

"I don't need a Foreign Office tract, Director General. I just want to know what the devil this obviously senior man is doing all by himself in a very dangerous part of the world."

"It was I who made the decision that Furniss should travel to the Gulf and Turkey . . ."

"*You* made that decision?"

". . . to the Gulf and Turkey to visit our watchers and also to hold meetings with some of our principal operatives inside Iran."

"I suppose this decision flies in the face of long established practice at Century. This is symptomatic of your new broom, is it, Director General?"

". . . in order that those with day–to–day responsibility for Iranian intelligence should know more fully what was required of them."

"Day-to-day Iranian intelligence. Yes, well, you haven't said so in so many words but I take it we may assume that Iranian intelligence will be exactly what Mr Furniss will be dealing with, even now."

"It hardly bears thinking about, Prime Minister."

"You sent him, you'd better think about it. You're running a tight ship, Director General. Do all your people go overseas with a Union Jack sewn on the breast pocket? Does his passport say 'Iran Desk, Century'?"

The Director General said, and his eyes gazed back into the Prime Minister's sarcasm, "Naturally he is travelling under a well–established alias. He is an archaeologist, rather a distinguished one, I gather. A specialist on an early Turkish civilization, I believe."

"I dare say he is, but archaeologists do not ordinarily disappear an hour's driving time from the Iranian border. Or do they, Director General? I have very little information on archaeologists. It sounds to me as though Furniss' cover was blown, as I think you put it, long before he got anywhere near Turkey. You wouldn't have to be terribly bright to wonder what a specialist in an early Turkish civilization was doing hopping round the Gulf in his Olympic blazer. And if he is inside Iran, if he is identified, then he is going to have a difficult time?"

"Yes, Prime Minister."

"Well, thank you, Director General. I think that's enough excitement for this morning. Keep me posted, please, and kindly resist the temptation to send in a team of Israeli snipers to see if they can find him. I think you have enough of a mess on your hands as it is."

He let himself out of the room. He took the small lift to the ground floor. On the pavement between the front door and the car, he gulped for air. Furniss must be an imbecile. And now, by God, he'd be paying for it. And so would a great many others.

The car drove away down the lane. Harriet Furniss watched it go. The wind was up, and a gale was forecast, and she thought that the blossom would not be much longer on the trees. He had been very nice to her, the young man, and he had emphasized at least three times that it was the Director General who had personally sent him. Not that it mattered, whether the young man was pleasant or unpleasant, the message would have been the same.

Mattie was missing. It was believed that Mattie had been kidnapped. Mattie was an archaeologist . . . so pathetic. A woman could have run Century better, and still had time for the housework. She was very deliberate in her movements, she bent down to her garden kneeler and went on with the weeding of the border that she had been at when the young man had arrived. There was a surprising amount of groundsel in the border this year . . . She was numbed. Cleaning the groundsel out of the bed was her safety . . . She was crying softly. She loved that man. She loved the calmness and the kindness and the patience of Mattie, and she loved his gentleness. No, he was not as clever as she was. No, he could not paint as she could. He did not enjoy the theatre or music as she and the girls did, but she loved that massive and reassuring strength. He was the man she had depended on throughout her adult life. She could not remember the last time that he had raised his voice to her . . . Those fools in London, fools for what they had done to her Mattie.

She spent the whole morning on the border. She filled a wheelbarrow with weeds. She cried her heart out for the whole morning.

Khalil Araqi walked 200 yards from the hotel's rank, flagged down a taxi and asked for the McDonalds in the Strand. He then walked back up the Haymarket, and all along the length of Regent Street, and to any casual observer he would have been seen to spend a long time looking in shop windows. The stops in the windows and doorways of the stores enabled him to check frequently that he was not tailed. He followed exactly the instructions that he had been given in Tehran. He did not expect to be followed, and he could detect no one following him. On the corner of Brook Street and Bond Street, after he had waited at the kerb side for three, four, minutes he was picked up by car. He was taken by the student of the English language south and west across the city. Araqi had been to London before, but that was many years earlier. He gazed around him. He was at ease. His confidence in the planning behind his mission was complete.

They parked 500 yards beyond the mews.

The student followed Araqi back up the road, well behind him. There was a narrow entrance to the mews cul-de-sac, and Araqi's eyes roved to find the lighting above so that he could estimate the fall of shadows at night inside the cobbled entry. Briskly, Araqi walked the length of the cul-de-sac, keeping to the right hand side, keeping away from the 5 series BMW. There were cars parked outside each of the brightly painted front doors.

He was satisfied.

When he had driven back to within ten minutes' walk of the hotel, the student gave Araqi a brown paper package. The student did not know what was in the package, nor that it had been brought by a courier from West Germany, passing the previous evening through the port of Felixstowe.

The student was told at what time, outside the garage on Park Lane, he should collect Araqi that night. For the rest of the day, Araqi worked on the assembly of an explosive device by which a mercury tilt system would detonate one kilo weight of military explosive.

The PA stood in front of the desk.

"You won't shoot the messenger, sir?"

The Director General winced, his head dropped.

"Tell me."

"We've got Mr Furniss' bag back from Turkey. All his kit that the Station Officer, Ankara, collected from his hotel. There's a report which I couldn't make head or tail of but which Miss Duggan has typed up for you. You'd better read it . . . sadly, it gets worse. Mr Furniss' passport was with his things. That's the passport in his wife's maiden name. What it would appear is that Mr Furniss does not have supporting documentation of his cover."

"That just about caps it."

The Director General had served half a lifetime in the Foreign and Commonwealth with Benjamin Houghton's father. He and Houghton's father were golfing partners of old and they had once courted the same girl, she'd turned them both down. He had made certain when he came to Century that young Benjamin would be his Personal Assistant. The boy was cheeky and casual and very good. He would go a long way, if he cared to stay the course.

"Just thought you should know, sir."

And Houghton was gone, almost indecent haste. Just the same at the meeting with the Deputy Director General and the Desk Heads. They'd all been exasperatingly aloof, distinctly themselves. Bastards.

The Director General began to read Furniss' report, apparently based on the observations of an agent travelling quite widely inside Iran. Very recently, too. Not world shaking, but good, incisive stuff. His PA came through on the internal phone. A meeting with the Permanent Under Secretary, Foreign and Commonwealth, at two. A meeting with the Joint Intelligence Committee at three. A meeting of the Service's Crisis Management Committee at four, with the possibility of a teleprinter link to Ankara. The Prime Minister at six.

"Would you like me to raffle the ballet tickets, sir?"

"No, dammit. Call Angela and ask her to take one of the children. And you can, too, cancel anything you had planned for this evening."

He didn't notice the builders' van parked opposite the block of flats, across the playground from the concrete entrance way. He stared up at the side windows of the flat. There were no lights on, and it was a damp clouded morning. There should have been lights on in the flat. He knew the children did not go to a pre-school, and he knew that the flat should have been occupied at that time in the morning.

He did not hear the click of the camera shutter, and he did not hear the suppressed whisper of Harlech as he reported Tango One's arrival into a lip microphone. To have heard the camera noise and the voice whisper Charlie would have to have been hard up against the grubby side of the builders' van. Charlie stood in the centre of the playground. Kids played on the swings and larked in the sand pit, their mothers sitting and nudging their pushchairs and pulling on their cigarettes, huddled in conversation. There was a Corporation cleaner out with a broom and a bin on wheels rounding up the swirl of crisp packets and fag wrappers and coke tins. There was a soccer kick-about and the goal posts were snapped off young trees.

He climbed three flights of concrete stairs. Charlie saw the plywood hammered across the door of the flat. He ran down the stairs, fighting a fierce anxiety. All around him was the normality of the estate. The young mothers heaving their lung smoke into their kiddies' faces, the cleaner whose work would never be completed, the kids who played their eternal soccer. The flat of Leroy Winston Manvers seemed to Charlie as dead as the broken goal post trees. He was irresolute. Inside Iran, inside his own country, closing with the silenced pistol on two Guards, riding behind the executioner of Tabriz he would not have known the feeling of sudden apprehension. That was his own ground, the estate in Notting Hill in West London was a foreign country to him.

He looked around him. There were the parked cars, and the builders' van, and the people . . . there was a stunning ordinariness about the estate on a grey morning.

He snapped his back straight. He walked forward. He went to a group of young mothers. He pointed up to the flat with no lights.

A snort of rich laughter. They were the women who would have been at the front for a public hanging in Tabriz, they would have thought that a good show. Bright laughter, enough to make them choke on their fags. A cigarette was thrown down, not stamped out.

"Got busted, didn't he. Old Bill took away plenty. He won't be back."

Charlie felt winded, the control ripped from him. He took off, and he had the hoots of their mirth behind him.

Half an hour later, when the mothers had retrieved their young and scattered, the builders' van pulled lethargically away from the estate.

"What he is not going to do is dig a hole in the ground and bury his stuff. He is going to find another dealer. He's sitting on a pile. He's got to find somewhere else to drop it."

Parrish thought he agreed. He thought Keeper had taken a good attitude.

"Where is he now?" he asked quietly.

"Top end of Kensington High Street, his motor's on double yellows. Harlech says he's looking pretty pissed off. The sign on the door where he's gone says it's an Import-Export company. Haven't any more yet."

"Tally ho, Keeper."

Park grinned. "For the moment it's fine, but it's just a beginning."

"Home Office files, a stateless person has to have a guarantor."

"Nice one, Bill."

"What would not be nice would be for you to lose track of a load of stuff. Got me? That would not be nice."

The load of stuff was still in the flat in Beaufort Street, Park would have sworn to that. The Suzuki had the canvas back off, and the stuff wasn't in the cab. There was a watch on the front and back of the flat, 24 hours, and the tail was solid on the jeep when it went out, just as it had been solid when Tango One had come out earlier in the morning and gone down to the delicatessen for a pastry and a coffee.

Park would be going down to the Home Office. Parrish would be linking the radios. That was the way Parrish liked it best, left in the Lane with just the typists and clerical assistants to spoil him and share their lunches with him, and keep him fuelled up with coffee. The youngsters all out, raring to go and gone. It took a fair amount to wind up old Parrish, it took the whole of his team out and hunting to wind him right up.

He was in one hell of a great mood that morning, and thumping out on two fingers his progress report for the ACIO. Of course he was excited, of course it had been one hell of a risk to let Eshraq and the stuff loose.

"You're very kind. I thank you."

"For nothing."

Mahmood Shabro walked through the outer office with Charlie. He was no fool, he saw the way his new secretary glanced up from her desk at the boy. He saw the trace of the smile at Charlie's lips. He took Charlie to the outer door.

"You pass to Jamil my best wishes."

"I will, Mr Shabro. I will see him tomorrow, if he can manage that."

He had not asked why Charlie should wish an introduction to his brother, the renegade and the fly one from whom he kept a secure distance.

"Look after yourself, my boy."

The outer door closed on Charlie's back. He stood in the centre of the outer office for a moment.

"I think Charlie has disappointed you, my dear."

She shrugged. "He might have rung."

"He should have rung."

"I mean . . . I don't just go, go out, with anyone. I'm not that type . . ."

She was efficient, she had his outer office organised, she was starting to learn the detail of his work. He wanted to keep Polly Venables. It was a peculiar request that Charlie had made to him that morning for an introduction to his brother. His brother was involved in politics, and his brother had no visible means of financial support. Nevertheless, he had arranged the meeting.

"It would not be wise for you, Polly, to concern yourself too greatly with Charlie."

Park strode out of the Home Office building.

It had taken only an hour. He had in his briefcase a photocopy of the paperwork completed at the time of issue of a stateless person's travel document to Charles Eshraq, refugee from Iran.

The name of the guarantor was Matthew Furniss, Foreign and Commonwealth Office.

9

"Good morning, Mr Furniss." The voice was a wind whisper in trees.

Mattie started up from the tiled floor. He had been doing his press-ups.

"It is excellent to stay in good health, Mr Furniss."

His jacket and his shirt were on the bed, his shoes were placed neatly under the bed. He was sweating under his vest and his hair was dishevelled. Of course they had watched him through the spyhole in the door. They would have waited until he was stripped down for his exercises before making the entry. The fitting of the plywood screen on the window had tiny gaps in it, and he had known hours before that it was daylight. He did not know how many hours because his watch had been taken from his wrist when he was still semi-concussed in the truck. He had sat for what he reckoned had been hours on his bed, sometimes he lay and tried to sleep, waiting for them to come, and when the hours had drifted away he had decided to do his exercises. Of course they had watched him.

"It is my great pleasure to meet you, Mr Furniss."

Mattie spoke fluent Farsi, but the man spoke almost unaccented English. It was another tiny shaft into the shell of his spirit.

He was stumbling to his feet, and breathing hard. He would have liked to have stood his ground in the centre of the room, but his muscles were blood alive and his lungs heaved. He sat down heavily on the bed, and he started to pull his shirt over his shoulders.

"You are . . . ?"

"I am the investigator in your case, Mr Furniss."

"Do you have a name? A name would be a small courtesy. And let me tell you my name. I am not your Mr Furniss. I don't need an investigator, thank you. I am Dr Owens, University of London, and I insist on being released immediately and on transport, at once, to my hotel. This has gone on long enough."

"Excuse me."

The man glided across the room and bent down close to Mattie and with sure movements he threaded the laces from Mattie's shoes and pocketed them, and then his hands came to Mattie's waist and he unbuckled the belt from the trousers and pulled it clear. There was a small expression of regret in the hazel eyes. Mattie read him. Not regret that he had to take away his prisoner's laces and belt, but irritation that it had not already been done.

It was the first time that he had been spoken to since his capture. The tray on which food had been brought to his room was on the floor beside his shoes. Neither of the men had spoken when the food was bought. The door unlocked, the tray put down just inside the door, a second man standing behind the one who had carried the tray.

It was as Mattie would have done it himself.

He had his shirt buttoned. He had his shoes loose over his socks. He smoothed down his hair.

He supposed that he was surprised that the investigator was not wearing a suit and tie. He noted the American jeans, faded, and the long tailed shirt, out of the trouser waist, and the sandals, no socks. He saw the harsh, short cut of the man's hair. He thought the man was a little younger than himself, he had spotted the grey pepper pot flecks over the temples of his head, and care lines below his eyes. Pretty horrible eyes. Eyes without life.

"I should explain. You are in the Islamic Republic of Iran, Mr Furniss. You are of interest to the struggling masses of our people in their fight to rid themselves of American and Zionist and British domination. That is why you are here."

He straightened his back, he drew the deep breath down. "I am an archaeologist, I am not very interesting to anybody and I am no part of what you call British domination."

The words hung, fell. Mattie saw the smile curl at the mouth of the investigator, but no humour in those awful eyes. He said nothing.

"I can only suggest that you have made, whoever employs you, has made a mistake of which I am the victim. If a scholar cannot go about his work then the world has come to a pretty pass. I have devoted my adult life to the study of the Urartians, to their culture, to their architecture, to their disappearance. You have people in London, I presume. You can check what I say with the Curator of Near Eastern Antiquities at the British Museum."

"No doubt, Mr Furniss."

The smile had gone from the investigator's face.

"I would be most grateful if you could make such checks as speedily as possible so that this ridiculous business can be concluded. I have no quarrel with the people of Iran, with their Revolution. I am not a politician, I am a scholar. I am engaged on work that is purely historical in its nature, and before I lose my patience will you kindly get it into your head that my name is O.W.E.N.S., Owens. I am not, quite obviously, who you think I am."

"Mr Furniss, I came this morning to see you to establish that you were well, that you had not been injured. I did not come to discuss the cover story that you have manufactured for yourself."

"Cover . . . this is preposterous. Go away, now. I have had enough of this. Go away and check before you get yourself into serious trouble."

"Mr Furniss, later today you will be brought some sheets of paper and a pencil. You may begin to write down your reasons for travelling to that area of Turkey which has a common border with our country. You should write of your activities most fully."

"I will, most gladly. You'll have a full account, and by the time I am finished I shall expect you back with a handsome apology. But I must warn you, I shall take this matter up at the British Embassy in Ankara, apology or no apology."

The hazel eyes hovered over Mattie's body, seemed to weigh him, explore him. The voice was softer than before.

"Mr Furniss, let me remind you: between 1975 and 1978 you were the Station Officer in Tehran representing the British Secret Intelligence Service. There was a day in February, 1976, a morning, as I remember, when you came to the headquarters of the SAVAK. I remember it clearly because it was I who brought in the coffee for you and the officers with whom you met. Myself, Mr Furniss, I handed you the coffee . . . I do not recall a discussion of Urartian fortifications."

Like a punch to the stomach. "I'm afraid you have a case of mistaken identity."

"When the paper comes, Mr Furniss, it is advisable that you fill it."

Mattie's head dropped. He heard the shuffle of the sandals on the tiles, and the door opening on oiled hinges, and the turning of a key.

A pale body, sinew under the skin. Park never wore a vest. In his chest of drawers at home he had vests that Ann had bought him the first January Sales after they were married, and they had never been worn. The girls in the April office didn't look up because none of them was that interested in Park, a cold creature, and anyway they were pretty used to seeing men with their shirts off, strapping on the canvas harnesses for radio transmitter/receivers. It was a harness that could support a Smith and Wesson .38, but the ID never carried "pumps". If the guns were thought necessary, then the marksmen were supplied by the police. Park had the microphone on a cord around his neck, and he shrugged back into his shirt, and put the clear plastic earpiece in place.

There would be two cars and a van in place that morning. They could follow Tango One wherever he cared to lead them. The van had a miserable clutch and wouldn't be able to keep up with the cars, but it would get there eventually. Corinthian would be on the Pentax with the 500 mm lens, Keeper would be telling him what was wanted on the celluloid, what wasn't worth it.

Parrish had wandered out of his office.

"Still in his pit, is he?"

"He came out for his bun and coffee, went back in . . . we'll be there in half an hour."

"Anything on his phone?"

"He hasn't used it."

"What about the profile?"

"I'm going to do half day in the van, then have Harlech take over. Then I'm going down to shake up the FCO chappies a bit."

"Ah yes, the best and the brightest," said Parrish.

Park grinned. The military and the Foreign Office were the officers, the police and the ID were the poor bloody infantry, that was Parrish's unchangeable view. Parrish would never take a six-bedroom farmhouse in Tuscany for his holidays, he was in a caravan at Salcombe . . . for that matter Park didn't take any holidays at all.

"I was actually quite polite last night. I asked for their personnel officer, I explained that I needed to talk to a Mr Matthew Furniss, and the guy went off, bloody supercilious but perfectly nice, and came back twenty minutes later and just shut a real heavy door in my face. Didn't say he was abroad, nor on holiday, just that he wasn't available. I sprang about a bit, got absolutely nowhere. He looked at me like I'd come in with the cat. Upshot is, I'm back there at four. I promise you, Bill, I'll have an answer then."

"I'll come down with you," Parrish said.

"Frightened I might thump someone?"

"To hold your delicate hand, Keeper – now get yourself moving."

Parrish thought his squad were the pick of the world, and he was buggered if he was going to have them messed around by some creep in the Foreign and Commonwealth. He'd be an interesting fellow, Mr Matthew Furniss, guarantor of a big-time heroin distributor.

The Director General showed himself that morning. He saw himself as the captain of a storm-shaken ship, not that he would have cared to voice that feeling. He believed passionately in the responsibilities of leadership, and so he wandered the corridors and rode the lifts, he even took his coffee in the canteen. He took Houghton with him, the only fairly anonymous courtier, to whisper the name of any officer he didn't know and his job in the Service.

Century was compartmentalized. The North American Desk was not supposed to know of the day-to-day successes or failures of East European Desk. East European Desk was supposed to be insulated from Far East Desk. No other Desk would know of the abduction of Mattie Furniss. That was the system, and it was bust wide open. The Director General found his whole building riddled with rumour and anxiety. He was asked to his face if there was any news of Mattie Furniss, whether it was true about Mattie Furniss. He sought to deflect all but the most persistent, to reassure them, and to switch talk whenever possible to other matters – the new computer, the cricket match against the Security Service on Gordon Street's ground, the rewiring of the building that was scheduled to begin in the autumn. He decided to call it a day long before he reached Iran Desk's office.

Back in his office he sent for his Deputy Director General. The man was just back from three weeks in Bermuda and paid for, no doubt, with family money. The sun had tanned the Deputy's face, darkened it to the roots of his full head of blond hair and accentuated his youth. The Director General would finish his career in public service when he left Century, and it was assumed throughout the nineteen floors that the Deputy would follow him into the DG's job. Their relationship, twenty years apart as they were, had been at best strained since the arrival of the Director General from Foreign and Commonwealth, because the Deputy had narrowly missed the nod for the job himself, said to be too young and to have time in the bank. The DDG regarded himself as the expert and the DG as the amateur. They worked best when they had clearly distinct spheres within which to operate. But on that morning the Director General was not in any way combative. He needed movement, he would have to suffer a third meeting in two days with the Prime Minister in the late afternoon.

It was agreed that field agents inside Iran should be warned of a possible compromising of their security, but not at this moment advised to flee the country. It was agreed that the World Service of the BBC, English Language, should report, and without comment, that a Dr Matthew Owens, an English archaeologist, was reported missing while on an expedition to north-eastern Turkey. Little thing, but could be a boost to Mattie's cover. It was agreed the Turkish authorities should not for the time being be informed of Mattie's true identity; they might, in limited circles, know from his meetings in Ankara, but it would not go at a government to government level; Station Officer, Ankara, to hack that into place. It was agreed that Central Intelligence Agency should not be informed at this stage. It was agreed that the Crisis Management Committee should be kept in session for the duration. Iran Desk to report directly to the DDG until further notice. The DDG to select a senior officer to go to Ankara and work with the Station Officer to prepare a minutely detailed report on Furniss' time in Turkey. Precious little to take to the Prime Minister, but until they had some indication of who had abducted Furniss – and God alone knew where that was going to come from – there was nothing else that could sensibly be done.

The Director General ticked off the points agreed.

"Did you know that Furniss was running a new agent? Some very useful material. I had Library run through a check on him this morning. Nothing there. No case history, no biography. That is most peculiar. I mean, Furniss is steeped in procedure . . ."

"Furniss can't even type." The Deputy Director General said coldly. "That woman, his PA, is like a mother hen to him. Flossie Duggan. She types everything for him, she'll have the Case and Biography on the floppies. She'll have them in Mattie's safe. DG, you'll have to fight your way past her. But that's hardly top concern now. That's just one agent that's now vulnerable, one of several."

The Director General cut in. He was hunched forward over his table.

"What's the scuttle-butt downstairs, I mean, on this news? It's clearly not a secret."

"You want to know?"

"Of course I want to know."

"They're saying that Mattie warned against it, that he was pressured into going. That the security of a senior member of the Service was put in jeopardy."

"Perhaps that's the black side."

An explosion across the table. "For Christ's sake, with what he knows, they're going to torture it out of him. They may already have started. And we stand to lose the whole of our Iran network, because it's all in Mattie's head. They'll torture him for those names. Do you know about torture, DG?"

The DG leaned back and swivelled his chair to face the grey morning beyond the windows. "Is he a brave man?"

"It's nothing to do with being brave. Don't you understand that? It's about torture."

There was a light knock at the door. The Director General swung to face it. Bloody little Houghton, and not waiting to be called in.

"I don't know why you bother to knock, Ben. What the hell is it?"

"Sorry to interrupt, sir. Something rather puzzling has come up. Personnel are asking for guidance. FCO's been on. They've had a little cretin from the Customs round, asking to see Matthew Furniss."

"*Customs?* I don't believe it . . . What in heaven's name for?"

"It's someone from the Investigation Division, sir. Quite a serious outfit, I gather. They have established that Mattie was guarantor to a young Iranian exile now resident in the UK . . ."

"So, what is he, out of date with his renewal?"

There was a blandness about Benjamin Houghton that could infuriate the most high and the most mighty. "Not as serious as that, sir. Just that he's been trafficking in heroin, quite a lot of heroin by the sound of it."

Parrish's voice crackled into Park's ear.

"April One for April Five, April One for April Five."

"April Five to April One, come in. April Five to April One, come in."

"What's moving, April Five?"

"April Five to April One, be busier in Highgate bone yard. Tango One is still inside the location. We've done well. We're just inside the mews entry. We've got a great lens view on the front door. Harlech is in the street, he's squared the meter maid. There's a back entrance to the house, just an alley, Token's on that. Tango One's jeep is in the alley."

"Sounds fine. You ready for the goodies?"

"Ready, April One."

"OK, April Five . . . The 5 series is registered in the name of Jamil Shabro, Iranian born, age 57, address as per your location. But he's choice. Vehicle Registration has a cut out on that number. We had to go through the Met. Got the bum's rush from the plods, referred to Anti-Terrorist. Tango Four is on their list for security guidance."

"What does that mean?"

"It means that Tango Four has got up the Ayatollah's nose. Getting interesting, eh? Tango Four has security briefings from the Anti-Terrorist mob, varying his routes, that sort of chat. They say Tango Four is a devious crap artist, but he's got guts because he stands up at the drop of a hat and pitches the old aggro back at the Ayatollah."

"So we just sit tight."

"You just sit tight, April Five."

It took more than one hour for the news to seep from Heathrow Airport to the offices of the Anti-Terrorist squad on the fifth floor of New Scotland Yard.

The IranAir flight, non-stop from London to Tehran, had taken off more than 40 minutes ahead of schedule, at 20 minutes before noon. The news came via the British Airports Authority to the armed police officers stationed at the airport and who watched over all incoming and outgoing flights of that airline. From them, the information was passed to the Special Branch officers on duty at Heathrow, and they in turn filed their report which was, after processing, sent on the internal fax to the Anti-Terrorist squad.

The fax finally landed on the desk of a Detective Sergeant. It was bald, factual, related to nothing else. He thought of an aircraft taking to the skies, leaving behind more than a handful, he supposed, of furious passengers. Still, they'd mostly be Iranians. No one else would be fool enough to fly IranAir. That made him smile. But he was a thorough man. He rang through to the Authority and asked if they had been given a reason for the new flight plan.

Operational reasons . . . what else? He asked if the plane were now actually airborne.

The Detective Sergeant hurried down the corridor to the office of his superior.

"The bloody thing's in French airspace now. I'd have ordered it held if it were still on the ground. If they're going early for 'operational reasons' then that says to me that they're carrying someone out, someone who's got to get clear. We're sitting on a bang, sir."

There were the usual photographs, silver-framed, of the old soldiers with their Shah of Shahs. There were gold embossed invitation cards to functions, all exile binges, most of them on which the hosts requiring the pleasure listed all their decorations and titles. There were volumes of Persian poetry, bound in calves' leather on a walnut side table. The interior could have been lifted straight from North Tehran, save for the picture window from knee height to the ceiling looking down on to the mews.

The daughter was upstairs and Charlie could hear the rattle of her cassette music from the floor above, and the wife was out shopping. Charlie was alone in the living room with Jamil Shabro.

"What's it for, Charlie?"

"Does it matter?"

"Too double damned right. You ask for a contact, you tell me why."

"Pretty obvious. I have stuff, I want to dump it."

"Don't be insolent, boy. Why?"

"What anyone trades for, money."

"What do you want the money for?"

"I think that's my business, Mr Shabro."

"Wrong. My business. You come to me, you want me involved, and I am involved if I send you to a dealer. I don't fuck about, Charlie. You give me some answers, or you go away empty."

"I hear you."

"Charlie . . . You're a nice boy, and I knew your father. I would have bet good money that you would not have begun to think about running heroin, and you end up at an old fucker like me. This old fucker wants to know why you want the money."

Charlie said, "I want the money to buy armour-piercing missiles . . ."

He saw Jamil Shabro's jaw fall.

"That way I can destroy those who murdered my family."

He saw the widening of the man's eyes.

"When I was in Iran last week and the week before, I killed the executioner of Tabriz. On my previous visit 1 killed two Guards. There is still unfinished business."

He saw the blood run from Jamil Shabro's face.

"When I have the money, when I have the armour-piercing missiles, I will go back inside Iran, and I will dedicate my life to the future of our country."

"Charlie, you must be in love with death."

"I love my country, Mr Shabro."

Jamil Shabro's hands flexed together. There was the sweet smile of reason. "I know about your family, Charlie, your father and your sister and your uncle, we all know about that. We understand your outrage . . . but you are talking like a fool . . ."

"It's you who talk, Mr Shabro, and it's you who left. The Communists and the Democrats and the Monarchy Party, they all fucked up. They don't have the right to demand another chance. I do, my generation does."

"I risk my life for what I believe, I have been told that by the police."

"While I am inside Iran, Mr Shabro."

Jamil Shabro walked the length of his living room. He disliked the boy for his arrogance, he admired the boy for his guts. For the first time in many years Jamil Shabro felt a small sense of humility, humility before the courage of Charlie Eshraq.

"I help you, you have my name, you go back inside, you are taken. When they interrogate you they will have my name. What happens to me?"

"You're in London, Mr Shabro. And I have many names that are more precious to the Mullahs than yours."

He went to his desk. He flipped open the notepad beside the telephone.

622

He wrote a name and a London telephone number. He tore the sheet of paper from the pad. He held it, tantalisingly, in front of him.

"I get ten per cent."

"That's fair."

There was no handshake, just the passing of the paper, and the sound below of the front door opening.

Jamil Shabro went to the doorway, and he shouted into the music upstairs that he was going out, and that her mother was home. She had struggled up the stairs, cloaked in a fur coat and weighed down by two plastic Harrods bags and a third from Harvey Nichols. Perfunctorily, as if he did it because there was a stranger watching, he kissed his wife.

"This is Colonel Eshraq's boy, Charlie, dear. He needs a drink . . . Charlie, my wife."

"Very pleased to meet you, Mrs Shabro."

"I don't know when I'll be back."

The bags were dumped on to the carpet, the fur coat draped over them.

"What would you like, Mr Eshraq?"

"Scotch would be excellent, a weak one, please."

He heard the front door shut. He thought that Jamil Shabro hadn't been able to get out of the house fast enough, not once his wife had returned. It amused Charlie, the way she punished him, spending his money. She brought him the drink in a crystal tumbler, and there wasn't much water, and then she was back to the sideboard, lacing vodka with tonic. He sipped his whisky. From the window he could see Jamil Shabro bending to unlock the door of his car. The door was pulled open and he saw the man's glance flash up to the window, and his wife waved vaguely to him.

"Cheers."

"Cheers, Mrs Shabro."

She stood beside him. He wondered how much money she spent on clothes each month.

"I'm exhausted – shopping is so tiring in London."

Charlie watched the three-point turn. He heard the scratch of the gears. He saw a battered van parked at the top end of the mews. The turn was complete.

"I'm sorry, she's rather a noisy child, my daughter."

The car burst forward.

He saw the light.

The light came first.

The light was orange fire.

The 5 series BMW was moving, lifting. The passenger door separating from the body, and the boot hatch rising.

The windscreen blowing out. The van alongside rocking.

The body emerging, a rising puppet, through the windscreen hole.

He felt the blast. Charlie cringing away, and trying to shelter Mrs Shabro.

The full length window cracking, slowly splintering into the half drawn curtains, and the hot air blast on his face, on his chest. The same hot air blast as had hammered his back on the wide road leading into Tabriz.

He heard the thunder. The thrashing of an empty oil drum. The dead hammer blow of military explosive detonating.

He was on the carpet. There were the first small blood dribbles on his face, in his beard, and his hands were resting on glass shards, and the woman was behind him.

Charlie crawled on his knees to the open window, to beside the ripped curtain shrouds. The sound had gone. The 5 series BMW no longer moved. There was the first mushroom of the smoke pall. The body of Jamil Shabro was on the cobbles of the mews, his right leg was severed above the knee and the front of his face was gone. His trousers seemed scissored at his groin. Charlie saw the back doors of the van opening.

A man spilling out, with a camera and a long lens hanging from his neck, and the man was reeling drunk. A second man coming. The second man clutched, like it was for his life, a pair of binoculars. Two drunks, neither able to stand without the other, holding each other up, pulling each other down. Two men, and they had a camera with a long lens and binoculars.

Charlie heard the shout.

The shouting was above the screaming of the woman on the carpet behind him. The woman was nothing to Charlie, the shout was everything.

"April Five to April One, April Five to April One . . . for fuck's sake come in . . . This is April Five, Police, Fire, Ambulance, immediately to April Five location . . . Bill, there's a bloody bomb gone off."

Charlie understood.

"There are casualties, Bill. Tango Four's been taken out by an explosion . . . Just get the fuckers here, Bill."

There was a girl running into the mews. Running for dear life towards the two men, and she had a personal radio in her hand.

Surveillance. His meeting with Jamil Shabro had been under surveillance.

He went fast.

He went down the stairs. He went out through the garage door at the back into a small garden, and he went over the high trellis wood fence at the back because he could see that the gate was bolted. He sprinted the length of the alleyway to the jeep.

The body had not been moved, but it was covered now with a groundsheet. The leg was in a plastic bag, holding down a corner of the groundsheet. Harlech's traffic warden, hardly a stitch of clothing left on her, had been tenderly loaded into the first ambulance and driven slowly out of the mews. Too slowly, Park thought, for survival. The scene of crime photographer went about his work. The mews was sealed off but there was a great mêlée of men round the car. There were men from the local force, uniformed and plain clothes, there were

Special Branch, there were Anti-Terrorist squad, and two who stood right back and didn't seem to Park to know quite what they were doing there. He had those two as Security Service. There were a couple of WPCs in the house, and all of them out in the street could hear the crying. There were ambulance crews still in four other houses in the mews. Two cars close to the blast had been wrecked.

Corinthian had gone to hospital. He'd been taking a photograph of Tango Four as the BMW had driven towards them, he'd had the body of the camera heaved into his nose, cheekbone and eyebrow. He'd have some stitches and a technicolour eye.

He had seen quite a deal in his time, but he had never seen anything remotely like the havoc in the mews. He was on the outside, so was Token. They were the ID and they had strayed into police territory. Of course, the local force had not been informed that April were on their patch. Of course, the Anti-Terrorist squad had not been informed that an Iranian exile, on their files as "at risk", was being targetted. So naturally Keeper and Token were getting the cold shoulder. They'd be caught up with, later. They'd be interviewed when the mess was cleared. Park was still dazed. He had the noise in his ears. He had the ache in his shoulder from when he had been pitched across the dark interior of the van. He was lucky to be alive.

Parrish arrived. He strode past the constable who held out an ineffectual hand to stop him and into the mews. He walked straight to Park.

No rubbernecking, no preamble.

"Where did he go, Tango One?"

"He's not in the house now," Park said.

"You were round the back, Amanda. Did he come out of the back?"

She was looking at the cobbles. She had her handkerchief tight in her hand. "I heard the bang, I came running. They could have been killed."

Parrish snarled. "Next time you want to play Lady with the Lamp, for Christ's sake get a relief first."

Parrish had his personal radio in his hand. There was a tight anger in his snapped words. "Alpha Control, this is April One. If any of April team are not doing good works could they be got soonest, if it does not interfere with visiting hours, to Tango One's home location, and report back on whether Tango One is in residence. Out."

They walked out of the mews. Park thought half the plods were looking at him like it was his fault, like it had happened because the ID had nosed in. The muzzy haze in his ears was clearing. He hadn't done it before, but he took Amanda's hand in his and gave it a squeeze.

The message came back into Parrish's earphone when they were close to the Lane. He heard it. He didn't take his eyes away from the traffic in front. He turned to Park, all phlegmatic.

"Tango One's done a bunk. He went off in a hell of a hurry, didn't even close his front door. Well done, Florence Nightingale, we've lost the bastard. That hurts. It hurts rather more that we've lost a heap of scag."

"Leave off it, Bill. She did what anyone would have done. That wasn't a firework. Another thirty paces and we'd have been gone."

"Rotten old world, Keeper, you can quote me . . . You going to be fit for the Foreign Office?"

"Yes," Park said.

When the body had been moved, when the widow had left with her daughter to go to the home of the dead man's brother, a team of detectives went inside the mews house. There was no point at that time in trying to interview the widow and her daughter, both hysterical and about to be tranquillized.

"I regret, Mr Parrish, that Mr Furniss will simply not be able to contribute to your investigation."

"We would like to establish that for ourselves."

"You misunderstand me . . . there is no question of Mr Furniss being able to talk to you."

Park thought that if he had been a yobbo and lost his passport in Benidorm, then they'd have treated him better. He and Parrish were in iron framed chairs in a Foreign and Commonwealth Office interview room. There were two men on the other side of the polished table, one of whom didn't speak. The one who spoke wore a three-piece suit, a stiff collar in this day and age, would you believe it, and a Brigade of Guards tie puffed out, and his voice was a drawl as if it were almost as much as he could manage, having to speak to the likes of Park and Parrish. Park felt a pillock anyway, because at the Lane the duty nurse had put an Elastoplast over a dressing soaked in witch hazel across a ridge of bruise on his forehead.

"We usually find that we are the best judges of who can, and who cannot, help us with our inquiries."

"Let me try it out on you, Mr Parrish, with words of one syllable . . . You will not see him."

"I am a Senior Investigation Officer in the Investigation Division of Customs and Excise. I am working on a case involving the importation from Iran of several hundred thousand pounds' worth, street value, of heroin. My principal suspect, the importer, was issued with a Stateless Person's travel papers naming Matthew Furniss as a guarantor . . . I hope I haven't gone too fast for you . . . that makes Mr Furniss necessary to my investigation as I build up a profile of a resourceful and dangerous criminal."

"You should exclude Mr Furniss from your investigations, Mr Parrish."

"We are getting dangerously close, I must warn you, to obstruction. Obstruction is a criminal offence."

"I doubt it, in this case."

"In some quarters the importation of heroin is regarded as a very serious matter."

626

"Quite rightly, but Mr Furniss will not be able to help you."

"I'll go over your head."

"That's your privilege, but you will be wasting your time. My advice would be to stay with the essentials."

"You'll eat those words."

"We'll see. Good luck with your investigation, gentlemen."

They drove back to the Lane. Marooned in traffic, Parrish turned on Park.

"You were a lot of help."

"Stood out a mile."

"Tell me, clever clogs, what stood out a mile?"

"He's a spook."

"Enlighten me."

"Secret Intelligence Service, the jokers over the Thames in the tower block. He was telling you to piss off, Bill. If a spook is sent over to tell us to go away, then it stands to reason that Matthew Furniss is an intelligence wallah, presumably pretty big. Otherwise they wouldn't try that sort of high and mighty shit."

"Sickening, but you're probably right."

"I want a promise, Bill."

"Shoot."

"They're going to try and block us, I bet you. Right now the phones are purring. We've got Iranian heroin, Iranian exiles, we've got car bombs, and we've got a big boy spook. They don't want grubby little Customs sniffing into that."

"What's the promise?"

"That we don't back off, Bill, just because a stiff white collar tells us to."

"Promise."

"Screw them, Bill."

"Too right, young Keeper, screw them."

He started to sing "Jerusalem". Parrish was in full flood by the time they made it back to the Lane.

In the evening, when his food was brought to the door, Mattie gave his guard three sheets of paper filled with his handwriting. The text detailed his study over many years of the Urartian civilization that had been based around the present day Turkish city of Van.

10

There was a good term he used when he gave the lectures. It was one that he had heard himself when he had first attended a kidnap briefing: "emotional rape". It was a good enough description for Mattie to be going on with. He was without his watch and the belt for his trousers and the laces for his shoes. He was without contact. The breakfast tray had been brought to his room, left inside the door, taken away an hour later, nothing said, no eye contact.

His father had been a regular soldier. His father had been a hard and austere man with no gift for conversation, living his life to high standards. Mattie had followed him into the army. Mattie had been the young officer in the Brigade of Guards, and brought up to the same standards. Perhaps he had rebelled against those standards, his father's rigid code, perhaps that was why he had left the military and gone to Century, and yet the standards and the code remained his bed-rock. The pure soldiering had appealed to him less and less. He had spent too much time as a young officer as liaison in Iran, wearing his own clothes and mixing with civilians, but the deep base of disciplines had stayed with him. He had been lectured, and he had himself lectured, on personal standards as a weapon against the despair that came after the shame of the "emotional rape".

Had it been possible to speak with his guards, then he would have spoken with courtesy, but hard to be courteous to a pair of sods who never caught his eye, never acknowledged his thanks. He had already done his exercises, and that was important, always important to stay mentally and physically fit. He went to the wash basin beside the lavatory. There was no brush to clean the pan of the lavatory, and that was a small wound to him because he thought he would have benefitted from being able to set a standard of a clean lavatory. He went to the wash basin. There was no cloth to wipe clean the basin, but he could make something of that with his fingers. Only one tap. He was denied hot water. Well, Mattie Furniss could live without hot water. He turned the tap. A few moments of pressure and then the spurt was reduced to a dribble. The water ran ochre brown. God alone knew what filth was in the water, but the rules demanded that he wash. His hands were cupped to take the soiled water, and he closed his eyes tight, and splashed the water on his face. He took off his shirt, cupped his hands again, and washed underneath his arms. He could not shave, of course, and the growth on his cheeks was an irritation. When he had finished washing he began to wipe the basin clean, to peel away the grime.

Tomorrow, if there was a tomorrow, he would wash his shirt. Today he rinsed his socks. He could wear his shoes without socks. Christ, Harriet, how do I dry my bloody socks? . . . Harriet . . . who would have been to see her? He had once been to visit a Century wife in crisis. Just her own crisis, not the Service's crisis, just that the lady's husband had piled in with his car on a road out of Sharjah. He hadn't made much of a job of telling her the news, but he and Harriet still received a Christmas card from her every year. He wondered how they would be with Harriet . . . Harriet always washed his socks at home, and she knew how to dry them, even when it was too wet for them to go outside, and in the days before they had a proper heating system in the cottage at Bibury. The poor darling who washed his socks, and knew how to dry them, he had never, ever, talked to her about the risk . . . never. Not when he was Station Officer in Tehran, not when he was running the show down in the Gulf, not when he was packing the clothes as she passed them to him from the wardrobe for this trip. If Harriet had ever said to him that, God's truth, old boy, this life really pisses me off, this life is for kiddies, this life is not for us, old boy, then Mattie would have been shaken to the roots, but he would have packed it in. He hoped they would have sent a good man to see her.

After he had hung his socks on the bedframe, he had cleaned the basin again. Good lord, made in the UK. He could see the manufacturer's emblem, and the symbol of the Queen's award to industry. Must have been a good little export order. Purveyors of bathroom ceramics to His Magnificence.

"Christ, Harriet . . . I am so afraid . . ." His lips mouthed the words. "These charming domestic scenes will surely end, my darling."

"Survive, old boy." That's what she would say and that was the name of the game, survival. Survival was going back to Harriet, one day, going home. And the price of going home, at any rate going home in a skin she would recognize, well, that price was unthinkable. "Don't think it, old boy. You can't afford to think it because you know so much. So many lives depend on your silence."

"You'll tell the girls, won't you? Get them to come and take care of you until this is all over. Oh yes, it will be over. Sooner or later, most probably later, it will be over. I rather fancy there'll be a debriefing of sorts and then they'll drive me to Bibury and you will be at the door. It will be summer still, oh yes." He wiped the underside of the basin with his hands and saw the beetles. Small black beetles on the floor. They had an entry point where the tiles were poorly fitted against the wall.

He started to count the beetles. They were difficult to count, because the little blighters were meandering all over the floor under the basin.

He had not heard the footfall, nor the bolt being drawn back, nor the key being turned.

He was counting beetles, and there were three men in the room. There was a moment of annoyance when he lost his place among the beetles. The men came fast. He was dragged upright. His arms were twisted behind his back. One of the men buried a fist in Mattie's hair and pulled him across the room. Pain on his scalp, and pain at his shoulders from his bent back arms, and his

629

shoes flapping loose and his trousers dribbling down over his hips.

He was trying to remember the rules. At all times courtesy and good manners. Bloody important. Bad mouth them back and he'd get a kicking. Fight them and he'd get a beating. That's what he used to tell his students at the Fort. "No future in getting a good hammering if the only witnesses to your pride are a gang of low-life thugs."

The one who had hold of Mattie's hair kept his head bowed.

He could only see the floor. He could only see the steps down. He was propelled forward.

They were going fast down the stairs and then across the entrance hall of the building, and towards the back of the hall, and into a narrow doorway. Down a flight of breeze block steps, into the cellar.

A room of white, bright light. He saw the zinc bathtub. He saw the hose pipe that was attached to a wall tap. He saw the heavy hooks protruding at different heights from the wall. He saw the plank bed with the leather thongs fastened at each end. He saw the lengths of insulated cable lying casually on the floor.

He saw the table and the two chairs, and the white, bright light was facing one of the chairs. That chair was empty. In the other, his back to the light, was the investigator.

He was put down on to the empty chair. He wriggled on the hard seat to get the waist of his trousers back up from his hips. The men who had brought him down the two flights of steps were all behind him. He could hear their breathing, but he could not see them. He could only see the face of the investigator, and if he looked past the face of the investigator then there was only the ferocity of the white, bright light. He could feel the tremble in his thighs, and in his fingers. He could feel the sinking of his stomach and the looseness.

He heard the creaking turn of a tape-recorder's spools. He thought the machine was on the floor beside the feet of the investigator. He could not see the microphone. The investigator put a small attaché case on the table and opened it. He took out the sheets of paper Mattie had written, and a single cardboard file holder. He closed the attaché case, put it back on the floor.

The investigator pushed the file halfway across the table. The light fell on it. The title of the file was "DOLPHIN". The investigator took the handwritten sheets of paper and held them in front of Mattie's face and tore them into small pieces.

He saw them flake to the floor.

"I am not stupid, Mr Furniss, and I had not expected that you would be stupid either."

As soon as he was out from under the railway bridge, the rain streamed down over his face.

He turned, but no one stirred or watched him go.

Because Charlie had brought a bottle of sherry he was good news amongst the dossers who used the pavement under the bridge. He hadn't had more than one swig himself. The bottle had passed from hand to hand, and he had even been lent a sheet of cardboard packing to use as a blanket. Good guys. Didn't bother with questions. Guys who had accepted him because he'd passed round the bottle.

The rain was dribbling off his nose. He might be back, and he might not. He was another of the city's flotsam, footloose for the day and congregating for the night where there was shelter from the rain. He could have gone to a hotel, or to a boarding house, but Charlie had reckoned that was risk. He had felt safer in the dossers' sleeping place. He had been aware of the light of a policeman's torch on his face, past three in the morning. They wouldn't be looking for him amongst the dossers, no way.

At the Underground entrance he ducked out of the rain. He bought a newspaper; scanned it fast. He saw the photograph of the burned out, blown up car, and he saw a picture of Jamil Shabro, and the caption "dedicated monarchist". Three dead. Shabro, the traffic warden, DOA, and an old lady who lived right above the blast. Five seriously injured, the old lady's sister among them, blinded in both eyes. No mention of a surveillance operation. He had not dreamed it, and he had no means, even now, of gauging what was the scale of the hunt. They'd pick him up, sure as hell, because they'd mounted surveillance on his meeting, they'd have him held at the airport whenever he flew back.

And then the jigsaw pieces started tumbling. They had spotted him at Heathrow on the way in. That was what the performance at the airport was all about. He'd been under surveillance ever since. They could have lifted him and the rucksack at any time. Why had they not? What were they waiting for? Maybe they would think Jamil Shabro was his dealer. If so, that gave him a tiny breathing space. One less hand at his throat.

Inside the ticket hall he dialled the number that Mr Furniss had given him in St James's Park.

He was answered by a secretary. He asked for Mr Stone. He said he wouldn't give his own name.

"Yes?"

"Who is speaking?"

"I am a friend of Mr Matthew Furniss."

"Of Mattie's?"

"He said I should call you."

"Did he now – in what connection?"

"To discuss business with you."

He heard the hesitation. "Mattie said that?"

"He told me to come to you."

"What's the name? No name, no meeting."

"Charlie."

"Hang on. Shan't be a second."

Flossie Duggan responded to the winking light, lifted her telephone. Neither of her telephones had a bell. Mr Furniss did not like telephones ringing all day around him. She was still red-eyed and her waste paper basket was a quarter filled with screwed up Kleenex.

"He's not here at the moment, Mr Stone. . . . Yes, he knows Charlie. Old friend of Mr Furniss' family. Is there anything else, Mr Stone? . . . And best wishes to you, too."

He fed more coins into the machine. He wrote down the address and the time of his appointment, then rang off.

Inside the station he paid for a key to a left luggage box, and at the box, and masked by its open door, he lifted a Sainsbury's bag from his rucksack, before squeezing it into the locker. He wound the top of the plastic bag round his wrist. He went back to the telephones.

Another call, another meeting set up.

Charlie carried away from the Underground station one packet containing a full kilo of pure and uncut heroin.

"Good God . . . What are you doing here?"

Park didn't think, too tired to think, just opened his mouth. "Bill told me to get home."

She had a super mouth, except when it was twisted, when she was bloody furious.

"Marvellous, you came home because the philanthropic Mr Parrish said it was alright, remind me to grovel to him . . . What's that on your head?"

His hand went up. He felt the Elastoplast, and it was curling at the edges. "There was a car bomb . . ."

"The Iranian?"

She must have just come back from work. She had an apron over her work dress, and the vacuum cleaner was out of the cupboard and plugged in.

He said, "We were on a surveillance, the car went up about 30 yards away. We got chucked about a bit."

"It's today, afternoon. That was yesterday, morning."

He hadn't kissed her yet. He was still in the doorway. And so hellishly tired, and it was an old script.

"We had a panic on."

"All the telephones down, were they?"

He didn't know whether she was picking an argument, or whether she was concerned that he had been close to a car bomb. Her cheeks were flushed.

He reckoned she wanted the fight. He could remember holding Token's hand the previous day – never understood why Token didn't have a steady fellow – he just wanted cocoa hot in his throat, and his head cool on the pillow.

"I said a panic. We picked up a target the other night at the airport. I don't know how much, but he's got a substantial amount of stuff. Yesterday morning he visited Shabro, the Iranian who died. The target got away. We don't know where he's gone. It was my decision to let him run, and we've lost him, plus a hell of a load . . . That's what I mean by a panic. That's why I didn't think of ringing you . . ."

"David, what the hell is happening to us?"

"I'm just pretty tired."

"When are we going to talk about it, when?"

"Right now, I want to go to sleep."

She flounced aside, made a way for him. She snapped the switch on the vacuum cleaner and he had to step over the cable to get to the bedroom. At least the suitcase was back on top of the wardrobe.

He didn't register that the vacuum cleaner had gone off.

She came into the room. She sat on the bed beside him.

"Is it really bad for you?"

"If I foul up? Yes."

"How bad?"

"Kiss goodbye to a Liaison Officer posting . . ."

"In Bogota?"

"Yes."

"Well, that's the best news I've had all week. It sounds like hell on earth, does Bogota."

"It just seems important to me."

"More important than *anything?*"

"I'm very tired, Ann . . . I'm sorry I didn't ring."

She went to the dressing table. She took off it an opened envelope, and picked an invitation card out from the envelope.

"What is it?" His eyes were hardly open.

"Invitation . . ." She laughed, a brittle ring. "The ID Mid-Summer Ball . . . are we going, David?"

"It'll be awful."

"I want to meet all of those wonderful people who are so important to your life. I am going to talk to all those fantastic people who have the power to send us to Bogota . . ."

"We'll go."

"You stand me up . . ."

"I said that we'll go."

". . . and we're dead."

"I'm just so tired . . . Ann, I don't want us to be dead."

"Then do something about it."

She had the apron off and her shoes and her dress, was half undressed, when she saw that he was asleep.

At the airport he had worn a blazer with the badge of a travel company sewn on to his breast pocket. The travel company knew nothing of a Charlie Eshraq, had employed no courier in Turkey during the period of Charlie's last trip out of the United Kingdom.

In his flat they found a receipt from a bucket shop – followed up, blood out of a stone and the threat of a VAT inquiry before the blood started to trickle. Three return tickets to Istanbul.

No address book. No cheque stubs. The place was eerily clean. Fingerprints, yes they had all that. But that wasn't going anywhere. Not a single photograph to build on. Nothing to say whether Eshraq was his real name. The coffee shop and the laundromat knew him, had never seen him *with* anyone, if you know what I mean. The owner of the flat had never met him and an estate agent, who blushed rather prettily Statesman thought, said he paid always in cash, always on the nail. There were three possible leads. Manvers, who may have known nothing about him at all. The man in the Import-Export business in Kensington, who turned out to be the brother, wouldn't you just have guessed it, of the Iranian in the car, so his office was shut very tight and the family scarpered and the Anti-Terrorist people were taking the line that if the ID were going into the film business and if Mr Park thought he was Mr David Puttnam that was all very well, thanks for the tip-off, and do us a favour, son, don't ask us to tell you where Mr Shabro's brother is, because you people are bad news and anyway you're so clever that you can surely find him without assistance from Anti-Terrorist Branch. Mr Corinthian's film? No, it was still being examined. No, the Met would probably want it for a couple of days. Expect it in a week or so.

And there was Furniss of the FCO, as Harlech called him.

The ACIO said that Leroy Winston Manvers was now on remand at Brixton prison and out of reach, and that they'd had their chance with him, and no way were they going back there now that the dealer was in the hands of a Legal Aid solicitor.

So Parrish had said to the ACIO that this Matthew Furniss was the key, and the ACIO had not been able to contradict him.

Three of them went to the Home Office. The ACIO had roped in the head of the National Drugs Intelligence Unit, they'd gone round to New Scotland Yard and picked him up. They'd leaned on him, so that he couldn't excuse himself.

Into the Home Secretary's office.

The ACIO did the talking. Bill Parrish did the prompting. The head of the NDIU was the weight behind them.

"What it comes down to, Home Secretary, is that we are being denied access to this Matthew Furniss. Now, we've played this very straight. We have not,

I repeat not, chased this man and sought him out. We accept that he may be a sensitively placed government servant, and we have gone through the correct channels, and we've been blown off . . . Let's not beat about the bush. We were instructed to carry out an investigation into the supply of the heroin that ultimately killed Lucy Barnes. Quite disproportionate resources have been deployed . . . and we're being blocked. It's right that we should be frank with each other, Home Secretary. You wanted a priority made of this case."

"You've lost this man Eshraq, and you've lost his heroin?"

"Correct, Home Secretary. We lost him in freak circumstances, you will agree. If we are to get him back, and get his stuff back, without wasting an immense amount of time then we have to have Matthew Furniss."

"I'll look into it."

"Either that or the investigation has to go into the trash-can, sir."

"I said that I would look into it, Mr Parrish. Thank you, gentlemen. Good day to you."

Parrish, not a vindictive man, thought that the Home Secretary looked like a cornered rabbit. Not his to reason why, but he didn't mind taking a small jolt of consolation from the man's discomfiture.

It was a well arranged meeting. No chances taken. Charlie liked that. He had been under surveillance, and he was pretty sure that he had busted the surveillance, but he liked the style of the Greek and the meeting. He had been picked up in Chiswick in West London by an anonymous little bastard with a sallow face and bad eyes. That had been arranged on the telephone. He was pretty sure that the rendezvous was checked out, that they were watched by the Greek's payroll. He was told to take the Underground to the end of the District line in Wimbledon. His description must have been telephoned on, because after he had kicked his heels and had a couple of coffees at the station cafeteria, he was met again. They put him in the back of a van and they drove him round for an hour and a half, and when the van stopped, and he hadn't an idea where he was, then the back doors had opened, and the Greek had climbed in beside him.

The Greek was thorough. He had Charlie stripped down in the van to his underpants. No way he was going to be stung, that Charlie was going to get away with a microphone in his clothes. That was the preamble, then there was the business. A quarter of a kilo of pure heroin on display. The Greek was no baby in the game, and the Greek knew the stamp on the wrapping. Enough of the stuff to have covered a teaspoon was taken out of the packet, and was passed in a small see-through sachet through the slightly opened back of the van. Going for analysis, running a fast check. Good style, Charlie liked it, more thorough than Manvers had ever been. The check came back. The sachet was passed again into the interior of the van, there was an anonymous raised thumb. They'd talked business while the analysis was being done.

"Cash is hard."

"Cash, or no deal."

"You brought it in yourself?"

"From the Qazvin district. I collected it myself."

"And there's going to be more?"

Charlie lied. "Yes, it'll be regular, and top grade."

"And you're looking for . . . ?"

"A quarter of a million, for seven kilos."

"Two hundred."

"Two fifty."

"If it's tomorrow, in cash, two hundred thousand is top whack for seven kilos."

"I'll call tomorrow for a meeting."

They shook hands. There was a clinging oiled sweat on the Greek's hands. Charlie thought it was a good deal. The Greek would get double what he was paying Charlie, but Charlie didn't cough at that.

"What's it for?"

"What the hell does that mean?"

The Greek smiled. A twisted smile. He had a deep scar at the side of his chin from far back, from a school playground fight with Stanley knives. "Just that this isn't your scene – so, what's it for?"

"Something you won't ever hear about."

"What on earth does he want?"

Benjamin Houghton could see the nervousness in Miss Duggan's face. The likes of Flossie Duggan were never called to the nineteenth floor. She was a few years short of retirement, less than Mr Furniss had left to him, but she had had his promise that he would get an extension for her, she would go when he went. It was her whole life, being the Personal Assistant to Mr Furniss. More than anything else she dreaded the day when she must hand in her polaroid cards and try and pick up old age away from Century. She had joined the Service in 1950 after she had read an advertisement in a smart magazine in an optician's waiting room that called for applications from "Girls of good education for position in London with good prospects and possibility of service abroad – aged 18 to 30". She would be going, when she handed in her polaroid card, to Weston-super-Mare where her sister kept a guest house, open only in the summer season. She would have her debrief, a day or two of counselling, and she would be out on her neck with her memories. To Flossie Duggan, genteel and poor and loyal, Mr Furniss was the finest gentleman that it had been her privilege to work for.

"He just wants a little talk with you."

"He's already stolen Mr Furniss' floppies."

"That's not fair, Flossie . . ."

"Miss Duggan." The boy would never have been so impertinent if Mr Furniss had been there.

"The Director General is entitled to see the computer records of a Desk

636

Head even when those records are stored in the Desk Head's personal safe and not where they belong, in Library. So can we go, please."

He saw the neatness of Mattie's desk, his ashtray had been cleaned ready for his return. His pencils were in a holder, sharpened. His In tray and Out tray were empty. He thought that the photograph on the shelf behind the desk, Mrs Furniss, had been polished. There were some late daffodils in a vase beside the photograph. She was registering her defiance, taking her time to cover up her keyboard with its plastic shroud, and then she was rifling in her handbag for her lipstick. Again, he could see her nervousness, because the effect of the vivid lipstick against her pale and puffed skin was appalling.

"I hold him responsible."

"Tell the Director General that, Miss Duggan, and he might just chuck you down the lift shaft." He held the door open for her.

She gripped the hand rail in the lift.

He led her down the corridor, and made way for her so that she could go first into the outer office. He knocked.

"Miss Duggan, sir."

She walked in. She hesitated. She heard the door shut behind her.

She hated the tall and thin-boned man who rose from his chair, a leather backed chair, and beamed at her, and waved her to a sofa. He was certainly responsible.

"Good of you to call by, Miss Duggan . . . distressing times for all of us. Would you like sherry?"

She shook her head.

"I am sure that even with Mr Furniss away you are extremely busy, Miss Duggan. I'll come straight to the point."

The Director General had come in front of his desk and he perched himself on the edge of it.

"Presumably, Miss Duggan, you are pretty well up in Mr Furniss' activities for the Service?"

She nodded her head emphatically. That was one of Mr Furniss' little jokes. The worst time of the year was when she took her holiday at Weston-super-Mare, just one week, and she wasn't there to run his office.

"First of all, Miss Duggan, we are all, every one of us, doing our best to get Mr Furniss back, that goes without saying . . ."

She glowered at him. He should never have been sent. Desk Heads were never sent abroad.

". . . All of the very considerable resources of the Service are engaged in that. Now . . ."

She blurted, "It was a folly sending him in the first place."

"This is not a kindergarten, Miss Duggan. The Service is an active arm in the defence of this country. If the risks are too great for individuals then they are at all times entitled to transfer wherever they wish."

She might have slapped his face. There was a haggardness at his eyes. There was a thinness at his lips.

"We have been through the discs from Mr Furniss' personal computer, and we can find no record of an individual with whom we believe Mr Furniss to be associated. To maintain private files is in breach of all standing instructions. It is a sufficient misdemeanour to have you summarily dismissed. Do you hear me, Miss Duggan?"

She nodded.

"Miss Duggan, who is Charlie Eshraq?"

She told him.

It is the age of light speed communications, but the tit pushers and the button thumpers still rule.

The information was first gathered by the Anti-Terrorist squad. They in their turn fed the information into the central computer of Criminal Records. A lead from Criminal Records, and that same information was passed to the National Drugs Intelligence Unit. For further detail the National Drugs Intelligence Unit punched into the jointly operated CEDRIC computer.

What followed started the sprint down the corridors, the raw excitement.

She was jolted out of her sleep by the ringing of the telephone.

He wasn't going to wake. An earthquake wouldn't have moved him. The curtains were still open, but the darkness had come down outside, and she could see the rain pelting the window panes. The telephone was on his side, but he wasn't going to pick it up. Ann leaned across him. Her breast, out of her slip, was crushed into his face, and he didn't stir. She wriggled, she kissed her man. He looked ten years younger, at peace. She reached for the telephone.

Softly, "Yes?"

"David?"

"This is Ann Park."

"Bill Parrish – could I speak to him?"

She looked down. She saw the calm in his sleep, and she saw the livid bruise on his forehead.

"He came home injured . . . Why wasn't I told?"

"Because I'm not a nanny, Mrs Park. Please get him to the phone."

"Damn you, he's asleep."

"Tickle his toes, whatever you do. Wake him up."

"Mr Parrish, have you any idea what life is like for me because you can't manage your bloody office for ten minutes without my David?"

"I went to your wedding, and I'm not daft . . . just wake him up."

"He's exhausted and he's hurt, and he needs the rest."

"Don't accuse me, young lady, of not caring. Have you forgotten Aberystwyth . . . ?"

She would never forget Aberystwyth. They hadn't been married then. A stake-out on the Welsh coast, waiting for a yacht to come in from the Mediterranean and drop a load off on a beach. A ruined cottage had been the base camp for the April team, and David was the new boy, just selected, and the wedding had been postponed until after the knock. Bill Parrish had broken every rule in the C & E's book. Parrish had told his Keeper to get his fiancée up to a camp site four miles from the cottage, and he'd made damned sure that David slipped away to the tent where his Ann was every single night. She had cooked their supper over a calor gas burner, cuddled him and the rest in her sleeping bag, and sent him back to the stake-out each dawn. It had been heaven for her, and Bill Parrish had fixed it, and it had never happened again.

"He wouldn't do it now," she said. "Why can't you get someone else?"

"We're all in the same boat, and it's the way we work, and if we don't work like that then the job doesn't get done."

"Oh boy, have I heard that before."

"Do me a favour, wake him up."

Her voice was breaking. She was across David and she could hear the constant rhythm of his breathing. "You're destroying us, you're breaking us apart."

"He'll be collected in half an hour. Tell him there's movement on the target."

She put the phone down. She woke him. She saw the flare in his eyes when she told him what Parrish had said. She watched him dress fast. She fed him some scrambled egg and toast in the kitchen, and all the time he was looking out of the window, waiting for a car's headlamps. When she saw the lights she could have cried. She cleared away the plate. She heard the doorbell. He grabbed for his anorak, shrugged into it, opened the door.

Ann still wore her slip. She stood in the kitchen, and she could see through to the front door. There was a girl standing there. A boyish, stocky girl, with her hair cut short, and a windcheater like a sleeping bag. She saw her husband go out.

They walked across to the car. She could see them. When the tail lights had gone, then Ann Park cried.

Token talked, Keeper listened.

"It's the oldest one I know. There was a notepad beside the telephone in Shabro's flat. The Anti-Terrorist people had a look at it, and there was an indent. A name and a number. They checked, there's quite a bit on the name at Criminal Records, all drugs-related, so they fed it over to CEDRIC. He's hot. He's been busted for possession and went inside, but that was years back. More important, just a couple of years ago he was in the slammer and went to the Bailey. He should have got a Fifteen for dealing, but the bastard had a nobble. Four of the jurors came out for him. The trial had cost nearly a million, had run for four months. Public Prosecutions didn't go back for another bite. His name was written on the notepad in Shabro's house. It's Shabro's writing. The top note wasn't in Shabro's pockets. If that doesn't add up to Tango One finding himself a dealer in lieu of Manvers, I'll do a streak round the Lane.

Cheer up, David, it's going to work out. We've got taps on him, and we've got surveillance on him . . . Your Missus, David, what was up with her?"

Two guards carried Mattie back up the two flights from the cellar.

He was not unconscious – that had been before, many times. He was conscious and the water dripped from his head. To himself, he was now detached from the pain in his feet, and he was aware of what went on around him. He could hear no traffic in the street outside. He thought that it must be very late in the night. He had no sense of how many hours he had been in the basement, nor could he remember how many times he had lost consciousness, and how many times he had been dunked in the zinc bathtub.

He thought that he was still in control of himself. He could understand that there was no longer any more point in them beating him because the pain had begun to cancel itself out. He was carried because he could not stand on his feet. His head was sagging, and he could see his feet. His shoes were gone. His feet were grotesque, bloody and swollen. He could not count how many times in that long day they had thrashed the soles of his feet with the heavy electrical flex, and how many times he had lapsed, thank the Good Lord, into unconsciousness.

They took him into his room, and they let him fall from their arms and on to his bed. He lay on his bed, and the pain came out of the numbness of his feet. The pain came like maggots tunnelling from rotting meat. The pain spread from the soft ripped flesh at the soles of his feet and into his ankles, and into his shins and calves, and into his thighs, and into his guts.

It was just their beginning.

Through the long day, into the long night, the investigator had not asked Mattie a single question. Softening him. Beating him and hurting him. Just the start, unless he would scream for the pain to stop. The questions would follow when they thought it opportune, when they judged it best to peel from his mind the names held there.

The pain throbbed in him, welled in him. He lay on the bed and he writhed to escape from the pain, and with his eyes clenched tight he could see all the time the sweat forehead, the exertion, of the man who swung the electrical flex back over his shoulder and then whipped it back on to the soles of his feet.

They had given him nothing. Not even the dignity of refusing their questions.

11

"How are we this morning, Mr Furniss?"

Nothing to say. Mattie took in the greater heat in the airless cellar.

"The doctor came, yes?"

Nothing to say. It was a ritual. Of course the investigator knew that the doctor had been to examine him, because he had sent the doctor. The doctor had been sent to make certain that no serious damage had been done to the prisoner. A slob of a man, the doctor, and his eyes had never met Mattie's because the bastard had betrayed his oath. The doctor had glanced at the feet, taken the pulse, above all checked that his heart would last, stretched up the eyelids to see the pupils, and checked with a stethoscope for Mattie's breathing pattern.

"How are your feet, Mr Furniss?"

Nothing to say. He could stand, just. He had leaned on the shoulders of the guards who had brought him down, but his feet could take some weight.

"Please, Mr Furniss, sit down."

He sat, and the pain sang into his legs as the weight came off the feet.

"Mr Furniss, it has been broadcast on the World Service of the BBC that Dr Matthew Owens, an archaeologist, is missing in Turkey . . ." The smile was winter water. The voice was powder snow soft. "They are trying to protect you, and they cannot. Do you understand that, Mr Furniss?"

Nothing to say.

"They cannot protect you."

Stating the bloody obvious, dear sir. Tell me something I don't know . . . Through all his mind was the memory of the pain, and the memory of the dying that seemed to come each time he had lapsed towards unconsciousness. That was yesterday. The art of resistance to interrogation, as taught by Professor Furniss, was to take it one day at a time, one step at a time. Yesterday had been endured, survived . . . but they had not questioned him. Yesterday was gone, so forget yesterday's pain. Yesterday's pain was what they wanted Mattie to remember. The "old school" had been put through the full works on the Resistance to Interrogation courses at the Fort – the old school in the Service reckoned that they were a tougher breed than the new intake – resist at all costs, never crack, hang on to the bitter bloody end, and some fearful disasters there had been on simulated interrogation sessions. Queen and Country, that's what the old school believed in.

If he cut the pain from his memory, then the mind was voided, then filled with other matter. The other matter was the names. He tried to find the guards beyond the brilliance of the light in his eyes.

"What were you doing in Van, Mr Furniss?"

"I've told you, repeatedly, I was visiting the fortress of Sardur the Second."

"That is particularly idiotic, Mr Furniss."

"I cannot help the truth."

"It is idiotic, Mr Furniss, because you deny reality. Reality is this cellar, reality is the power at my disposal. Yesterday was amusement, Mr Furniss, today is the beginning of reality. If you go on with this fabrication, then it will go badly for you, Mr Furniss."

Stick to the cover, cling to the cover at all costs.

"A long time ago, yes, it is possible that you saw me in Tehran. I've been out of that sort of thing for years. I am an academic now. I am an authority on the Urartian civilization."

"That is your sole interest."

"The Urartians, yes."

"In Turkey?"

"The Urartian civilization was based in north-eastern Turkey and across the frontier of modern Iran as far as the western shore of Lake Urmia. That was the scope . . ."

"Did the Urartians, Mr Furniss, travel to Dubai, Abu Dhabi, Bahrain? Is it necessary for an academic, an authority in this rather limited field, to be escorted around the Gulf by the various Station Officers of the Secret Intelligence Service?"

The light was in his face. The guards were behind him. He could just make out the rhythm of their breathing. They would have been told to be still, to offer to the prisoner no distraction from the questions of the investigator.

"I am an academic."

"I think not, Mr Furniss. I think you are Dolphin. Desk Head for Iran at Century House in London. You were a regular soldier and posted to Iran to liaise over arms sales to the former regime. You were the Station Officer in Tehran from 1975 to 1978. In 1982 and 1983 you were the senior Station Officer in Bahrain with responsibility only for Iranian affairs. In 1986 you spent four months in Ankara. You were promoted to Desk Head on January 1st, 1986. You are a senior intelligence officer, Mr Furniss. Understand me, I do not want to hear any more about your hobby. One day, perhaps, I shall have the pleasure of reading your published work. For today we shall put away hobbies, Mr Furniss, and just talk about what you were doing on this journey around our borders."

The names were in his head, swirling. He was a man under water and trying to hold his breath, and his breath was the names. In time, as night follows day, the lungs would force out the breath, the pain would spit out the names. Even the old school knew that. It was a question, simply, of how many nights. How many days. The agents should have been warned by now . . . But was it known who held him? Would Century flush out its best men before they had confirmation that Mattie was in Iran?

What would he have done himself, in their place? He thought of the complications of the structure for getting the necessary signals inside Iran. He knew how complicated it was, he had set the system up. Far more complex than bringing the agents out to the prearranged rendezvous meetings that he had just had. Oh, a lifetime of complications if the agents were to be aborted, and no going back. London would not be hurrying to destroy its network. He swept the names from his mind. He lifted his head. There was escape from the white bright light only in the face of the investigator.

"It is quite scandalous that an innocent scholar . . ."

The investigator gestured with his arm. The guards came forward, ripped Mattie up from his chair.

Charlie made his call. The same telephone box, after the same night's sleep under a cardboard blanket.

After the call, after he had helped the dossers pile away the packing cases, he went to the left luggage inside the ticket hall of the Underground station, and he took out his rucksack.

They had a fine view of the Greek's house.

Parrish had smoothed it. Keeper reckoned that Parrish was gold-plated when it came down to sweet talking for window space. It was a great window. The early summer foliage was not yet thick enough on the trees to obstruct the vision across the garden and across the road and across the Greek's garden and on to the front porch of his house.

It was an old Victorian house that Parrish had fixed, weathered brick three stories high with an ivy creeper thick enough to have held the walls together. They had chosen the top floor for the camera position and from there their sight line went well clear of the high paling fence opposite. Keeper and Token knew her life history by now. She came upstairs on the hour, every hour, with a pot of tea and biscuits. She was a widow. Her late husband had been a brigadier general. She had lived alone in the house for nineteen years, and every year she resisted another try by the developers to put a cheque in her hand – this year it was for three quarters of a million pounds – so that they could bulldoze her property and replace it with a block of flats. She didn't think her cats would want to move. She had no love for her neighbour across the road. His dogs were a threat to her cats. Anything that threatened the owner of the dogs was fine by this lady. From the upper window they could see the dogs. Dobermans, lean and restless, wandering, and cocking their legs against the wheels of the midnight blue Jaguar outside the front porch. She was an artful old girl, the general's widow. Keeper had seen her giving them both the coy look, and checking the ring on his finger, and observing that Token's finger was bare.

He was comfortable with Token. She let him talk about Colombia, about targetting the problem at its source. There had been other cars come and go at the house across the road. They had photographed all the movements, but they hadn't seen the Greek. They had the mug shots done by the plods of when he was last in custody. It was a hell of a house that the bastard lived in. Half an acre, heated swimming pool, hard tennis court, five, maybe six bedrooms.

The general's widow was telling them that when her husband had first purchased The Briars they had been able to look across fields, real countryside.

The radio crackled to life.

"April One to April Five, April One to April Five . . ."

"April Five, come in April One . . ."

"Tango One has been on the telephone to your location. Text of call coming . . . Tango One: It's Charlie here. Your location: Same place as yesterday, same pick-up. Bring it all . . . Tango One: Right . . . Did you get that, April Five?"

"April Five to April One. Received, understood, out."

His head shook, and his knees.

Token said, "Keeper is back from the dead."

"What's Keeper mean?" the general's widow asked.

"It's a very solid person, Ma'am, and very vulnerable." Token smiled.

"Those brutes got out once, they killed one of my cats. They tore Disraeli to shreds."

"George, a word in your ear."

The Secretary of State for Defence paused in the corridor outside the Cabinet room.

"The distributor. A strange thing has happened and I may need your help."

"What on earth do you mean?"

"Customs and Excise have a suspect. He has a vague profile. They are trying to get into that profile, and they reckon that a chap called Matthew Furniss, listed as FCO but in reality SIS, could help them. The spooks won't wear it. Mr Furniss is being kept under wraps. The Customs investigation officers can't get at him." The look of pure rage on George's face was worth all the humiliations of the past weeks. As he slipped into the doorway, he said, "Just thought you'd like to know."

Parrish sat hunched forward at the console on the top floor of the Lane, co-ordinating a raft of radio signals competing for attention. This was big enough for the investigation of which Harlech was Case Officer to be sidelined, and for Corinthian's to be relegated out of sight. Big enough to soak up all of April's resources.

Parrish to Keeper: "April Five, just keep remembering that your single responsibility is Tango One. Our brothers look after every other Tango but Tango One."

Harlech to Corinthian: "April Seven to April Eleven ... Heh, ugly nose, this is just fantastic, this is just brilliant. What they're doing is this. They've Tango One in the white van and there's another van about 50 yards behind, that's the green one. They're taking Tango One's stuff from the white to the green, that must be where they're running the spot checks. You got me? They're doing it all on site. The Jag's parked between the two, the Jag Tango is in the white van with Tango One. This has to be Christmas. It's the best I've ever seen."

Keeper to Token: "April Five to April Nine. Try another walk past. You got the canvassing board. Do another run down, those houses you missed out the first time. I want to know if the Tango One van has the engine running. I have to know when those wheels are about to go."

Corinthian to Keeper: "April Eleven to April Five. Just to keep your knickers dry, Keeper, this is the layout. Tango One is in the white van, plus the Greek. The stuff is taken from the white van to the green van, probably running the checks on it. The guy who takes it to the green van then comes back empty and reports through the rear doors. Dangerous looking creep in blue overalls. So, the stuff is in the green van. The green van is for the plods. Are you clear, April Five?"

Parrish talking to all April call signs: "Keep it going, very cool, very calm. Any bugger shows out, he's in uniform for the rest of his natural. Tango One is to run ... That is confirmed. Tango One will run. We are only concerned with Tango One."

A quiet road running beside the brick perimeter wall of Richmond Park. Two vans parked in the road, and a Jaguar car separating them, and a girl calling at the houses on the park side and asking questions on the doorsteps about which washing powder the occupants used. A 500 mm lens in an upper room 175 yards north of the green van. Three more cars parked in the road, two of them facing the direction that the white van would come if it didn't do a three point.

"This is great stuff ..."

"I watched it packed myself."

"And there's more ... ?" The Greek could not hide the greed.

"I'll be coming back with more, a couple of months," Charlie said.

The hand of the Greek rested lightly on Charlie's arm. "You get lifted and you talk and you get the knife, wherever. You won't know how to hide."

Charlie said, "My friend, you get lifted and you talk and you get the bullet, your head blown. Take it as a promise, I'll find you." Charlie flicked his fingers through the wads of £20 notes. They went into his rucksack.

There was a handshake, of sorts.

"You be careful there, when you go back."

"Watch yourself across the road," Charlie said.

There was a flash of light as the van door opened. The Greek gave him his mirthless, twisted smile and stooped out.

As the van pulled away Charlie heard the big thunder cough of the Jaguar's engine.

In a side street in Hammersmith, near the river, a police Landrover rammed the white van, front off-side wing, crashed it and jammed the driver's door tight.

In Shepherds Bush, detectives of the Drugs Squad boxed the green van.

An hour later, across the city in the Essex suburb of Chigwell, the Greek had been back in his house three minutes. A police marksman put down his cup of tea in the house opposite, asked the general's widow please to stand well back, and shot both Dobermans clean through the heart, four seconds between shots. The marksman spoke briefly into his radio and shut the window, and was very much surprised to be kissed, just under his ear, by the old lady. They were still at the window when a Landrover with a ramming guard attached drove fast into the high wooden gates, smashing them. A few seconds later the pseudo-Georgian front door splintered open at the second massive blow of a policeman's sledgehammer.

On the Underground, starting at Wimbledon station, Keeper and Token and Harlech tracked their Tango One, and above them, through the traffic, Corinthian drove as if his life depended on it to stay in touch.

He was dropped with his bodyguard, as always, at the door of the Cabinet Office, and he walked through that building and down steps, and then through the deep corridor linking the Cabinet Office to Downing Street. At the final door, the security check, before entry to Downing Street, he was greeted like an old friend by the armed policeman. He had known that policeman since forever. God alone knew how the man had wangled the posting, but he seemed never to have been more than 100 yards from Whitehall all his working life. Always the sort of greeting that put him in a better mind frame.

His bodyguard peeled away from him. He'd be in the Waiting Room, and he'd be brought a cup of coffee by one of those haughty, leggy kids who hit the word processors down the corridor. A good life his bodyguard had, nearly as cushy as the policeman's on the tunnel door. The Director General was shown into the Prime Minister's office.

For a moment he wondered whether a previous meeting had overrun. He nodded coolly to the Secretary of State for Defence. They'd met a few times, but the Secretary of State was too flashy by half for his taste.

"Thank you for coming so promptly, Director General."

As if he had the choice.

"It is much appreciated. You know each other? Yes. I am sorry to say that a most serious complaint has been brought to me by my colleague."

646

He couldn't help but notice the unease of the Prime Minister, nor the hostility of the Secretary of State.

"I'm sorry to hear that, Prime Minister."

"George's daughter, Lucy, died a short time ago following a narcotics accident . . ."

The Director General stared back. He read the newspapers. The girl was an addict.

". . . An investigation is in process by the police and Customs and Excise to try to identify the importer of the narcotics concerned . . ."

And then he saw what was coming.

". . . Their very strenuous work, as I gather, leads them to a foreign national currently holding a Stateless Person's document which was issued on the guarantee of good character provided by a member of the Service. Customs and Excise quite properly wish to interview that member of the Service, but the Service have pulled down the shutters."

Had the Prime Minister been told who it was? Couldn't have been. Would surely have made the connection.

"It's outrageous," the Secretary of State chimed.

"I think we can get this sorted out quite quickly, don't you, Director General? Before it gets out of hand."

No, obviously hadn't a clue. "In front of a third party, Prime Minister, I am not free to discuss this matter."

"You damn well will." The Secretary of State's voice rose and his jowls were purple.

The Director General looked the man up and down. He'd learned that from his Classics master at Marlborough, a cutting stare from ankle to Adam's apple. "I am answerable to the Prime Minister, sir, and to the Foreign Secretary. Matters affecting the Service are beyond the remit of Defence."

"Just let's have this crystal clear. You are saying that the importing of heroin is a matter which affects the Service. Is that it? What the devil is the Service coming to, I should like to know. Are you importing heroin, Director General? Is that it? Is it your Secret Service that I must hold responsible for the death of my only child?"

"George, I believe that's enough."

"No, Prime Minister, it most assuredly is not enough. I demand that the Director General produce this Matthew Furniss, and straight away, and stop wasting valuable police time, Customs people's time, or tell us without all this waffle about matters affecting the Service why he won't."

"We all know how precious is police time, George. I don't think you, of anyone, need labour that, but did you say Matthew Furniss? Was that the name?"

"Yes, Prime Minister. That is the Service man's name. The Home Secretary tells me that the importer is an Iranian called Charles Eshraq."

"Well, Director General, what will you say to all this?" And there seemed to have evaporated from the Prime Minister the anxiety he had detected earlier.

"I would say this, Prime Minister. I might in different circumstances simply explain to you in what way the Service is affected and in what million-to-one chance lies its connection to the death through narcotics addiction of the Secretary of State's daughter. But I have just observed the hysterical speculations and accusations of a man with whom, unless ordered to do so, I shall share not one iota of information relating to this case or any other. Furthermore it is quite outrageous that a dedicated public servant should be vilified when, as the Prime Minister well knows, he is in no position to defend his good name."

"I'll see you broken."

"Your privilege, sir, to try,"

"Prime Minister, are you going to tolerate that impertinence?"

"I hope, Prime Minister, that I may count upon your support."

A reeded and hesitant voice. "I am going to think about it."

There were many thoughts cavorting through the Director General's mind as he marched back through the tunnel. He thought of Mattie Furniss, prisoner, facing torture. He thought of three quarters of an hour with Miss Duggan, a woman whose loyalty he could only admire, and two glasses of barley water to keep her talking, and the story of Charlie Eshraq. He thought of a girl hanged from a crane. And he thought of the value that Eshraq could be to the Service. So long as he wasn't named by Furniss under torture. So long as he wasn't caught by Customs and Excise first.

"April Five to April One, April Five to April One."

"April One, come in April Five."

"Just a sitrep, Bill. He's in the pub, apparently killing time. He's had one half pint in front of him for an hour, not had anything since we last called you. What did the boss say?"

"Had his arm twisted half out of its socket, that's what ACIO said. Sold him my line, a good line and I say it myself, we want to see where Tango One leads us, clean up the whole network. Bossman'd be happier if he was in cuffs, but he can stand it because we've the stuff."

"How much was it?"

"Around seven kilos, that's one hell of a load, Keeper. You know what? It's the same markings on the packets as Manvers' load. That sweetened the boss' pill."

"That's the bastard, isn't it, not knowing."

The Deputy Director General sat in the easy chair. "The more noise we make, then the worse it can be for him. I mean, we can hardly ask the Swedes to trot round to the Foreign Ministry and ask the night duty chappie if they're interrogating a British Desk Head who we have reason to believe they've kidnapped across an international frontier . . . No, we've got to sweat on it, and you've to make a decision."

"Aborting the agents? I'll decide in the morning."

"You owe it to them, to give them time to abort. Field agents are brave people. If they're lifted they will be lucky to be hanged."

The Director General seemed to miss his stride. His eyes closed as if he was in pain.

"Didn't you know that, when you took the job?"

"I'll decide in the morning."

"We may have hours, hours, Director General. Mattie is going to be having their names tortured out of him, he's going to be hung up by the fingernails until the names come tumbling out, willy nilly. It is only a question of when, not a question of if or if not."

"In the morning, I'll make that decision . . . Poor old Mattie."

All day he had been suspended from the wall hook. He had read about it often enough. Everyone who studied the affairs of Iran knew of this method of extracting confessions. He thought it must be a day, but he had gone insensible three times. He had no track of time. The pain in his back, his shoulders, his ribs, was more sharp than had been the pain in the soles of his feet. It was a pain as if he were snapping, as if he were the dry kindling that he put across his thigh at Bibury. His left arm was above his left shoulder and then twisted down towards the small of his back. His right arm was below the shoulder and then turned up to meet his left arm. His wrists were tied with leather thongs, knotted tight. The thongs were on the wall hook, looped over the carcase hook. Only the toes of his feet were able to touch the floor. When the strength of his toes collapsed and he sagged down, then the pain was excruciating in his shoulders and his ribs burst. It had been better at first. His feet, swollen, bruised, had been able to take most of his weight. Through the day, however long the day had been, the strength had seeped from his feet. The pressure had built upon the contortion of his arms. He had gone three times, sunk into the foul-smelling heat, unconscious. They hadn't taken him down. They had just thrown water into his face. No respite from the hook on the wall. Ever increasing pain that hacked into his back and his shoulders and his ribs . . . God . . . God . . . couldn't know how his muscles, how his body, survived the weight, or his mind the pain.

"Mr Furniss, what is the point of your obstinacy? For what?"

Answer in not less than 750 words. Bloody good question.

"Mr Furniss, the most resolute of the fighters amongst the 'hypocrites', the MKO, they appear on television and they denounce to the world all of their former comrades, all of their former activities. How does that happen, Mr Furniss?"

"I haven't the least idea . . . It's not the sort of thing an archaeologist would . . . know about." He heard the scratchy hoarseness of his voice.

"The bravest of the 'hypocrites' betray their comrades and their ideals because of pain, Mr Furniss."

He had seen the photographs. He knew what they did to their enemies. He had seen videotapes of the confessions. Raven-robed women, track-suited men, sitting on a dais and lit by the cameras in a gymnasium at the Evin gaol, and competing with each other to slag off their comrades and their cause, and still not escaping the firing squad or the hangman. It hurt him to talk. Getting air down into his lungs so that he could speak brought more pain stabs in his back and shoulders and ribs.

He mouthed the words. No voice in his throat, only the twist of his lips. He was an academic, and his research was concerned with the Turkish city of Van.

He remembered one lecturer at the Fort. He had been an elderly man and his back was bent as though he suffered from curvature of the spine, and the fingernails had never grown back over the sheer pink pastel skin. He had talked in a thick, proud, Central European accent, guttural. There had been brave pride in the speaker's eyes, and above a faded and shined suit he wore the collar of a Lutheran pastor. They had been told that the speaker had spent the last two years of the Second World War in Dachau. He talked faith, he talked about his God, he talked about prayer and of the strength that his religion had been to him. Mattie was not a regular church-goer, not in the way that Harriet was. When he was in church he bent his knee with the rest of the congregation, and he sang in a good voice, but he would not have called himself close to his God. What a wonderful arm faith had given that speaker in the dreadfulness of Dachau. Mattie was alone, as the speaker had been alone in his Dachau cell, as the disciples had been alone in the face of persecution. Mattie would have said that his religion was based on a knowledge of what was right, what was wrong, and he would have said that he was afraid of death because he did not believe himself yet ready to face his Maker. He wished that he could pray. He could not pray because the pain diverted his mind. He wondered how that speaker had prayed while the fingernails were ripped off, while his spine was damaged.

"Mr Furniss, you are a gentleman. This should not be happening to you, Mr Furniss. This is the treatment that is proper for the 'hypocrite' scum. It does not have to happen for you, Mr Furniss. Help me, help yourself. Why were you travelling? Who were you meeting? So very simple, Mr Furniss."

In truth, Mattie did not think that at that moment he could have spoken the names. The names were gone. There was only pain in his mind. The light was in his face. The pain soared when he tried to turn his head away from the light and away from the face of the investigator. The investigator sat on a stool not more than four feet from Mattie's cracked, dry lips. He thought the pain was good. He thought that the pain squeezed out of his mind the names of his agents. He could smell the cigarettes of the guards. They seemed to smoke continuously.

Abruptly the investigator flicked his fingers. He slid off his stool, and went to the table and began to push his notepads into his case.

To Mattie, the expression of the investigator was neither that of annoyance nor was it of pleasure. A job of work done.

"Mr Furniss, there is tomorrow, and after tomorrow there is another day, and after that day there is another. Each day is worse for you. For obstinacy you will pay a high price."

"No, Mother, there is no crisis, it's just that Mattie is a little overdue . . . I am not prepared to discuss Mattie's work with you, Mother . . . There is no need for you to come, Mother. You cannot come anyway because you would be missing your bridge on Friday. I am perfectly alright, Mother . . . I'm sorry, but I really am much too busy to have you come here. If there was something wrong then I would have the girls here. The girls are not here . . . Mother, I really do not want to have you come to stay . . . Will you listen to me, I don't want you here, I don't want anyone here . . . I am not crying, Mother, I am just trying to get on with my life."

She put the telephone down.

She thought that she had been miserably rude. She turned back to the minutes of the previous evening's meeting of the Conservation Society.

She tried not to think where he was, how he was, her Mattie.

At Century they would not be expecting a fuss from Harriet Furniss. It would have been, she thought, in Mattie's file that his wife was psychologically sound. It would have been noted that her two children had been born in Tehran because she hadn't thought it necessary to come home for the births, and there had never been trouble from her when they were in the Gulf, nor when they were in Ankara on short stay. It would have been entered in the file that she was a good sort, and did well on the Embassy circuit, the right stuff to be a Desk Head's consort.

Even so, to go these last days without a call from anyone at Century was very, very hard.

"April One to April Five, April One to April Five . . ."

"April Five to April One . . ."

"OK, Keeper, your location . . . The occupier is listed as Mr Brian Venables, Christ knows what Tango One is there for . . . Venables works, middle rank, for Thames Water."

"Understood."

"When do you want relief?"

"Bill, I'm going nowhere . . . don't argue, Bill, you'll have to burn me off him . . . In my locker, Bill, there's a battery razor and some socks, I wouldn't mind them."

"What about the others?"

"We'll want back-up at dawn. We're all staying . . . Bill, Token says that in her locker she has a change of kit in a green plastic bag."

"Sweet dreams, champions. April One to April Five, out."

12

The gale from the rotor blades flattened the robes of the Mullah against his chest, buried the material into the crotch valley between his legs. With one hand he clung to the brilliant white onion shape of his turban, with the other he steadied the spectacles on his nose. There was a full load for the helicopter. There was a Divisional Commander and two staff officers, there were casualties, and there was the Mullah and his bodyguards. The light was up on the landing zone, harsh and clear, and it would be several hours later and when the sun had climbed that the pastel haze would settle over the battlefield. By then the sentences would have been carried out.

They lifted off. It was a French helicopter, and new, and mounts had been welded on at the open doorways to take heavy machine guns. To avoid ground-to-air missiles from their enemy the helicopter pilot flew low over the rear area of the battlefield. It was a killing zone to the east of the Iraqi town of Basra, much fought over. The Mullah, strapped in his canvas seat, his back against the hull, was a young man in anguish. There had been that morning, as the red sun had slipped above the flat horizon, an artillery barrage. Some of the worst of the casualties were on the deck of the helicopter, their stretchers against his feet, and medical orderlies holding drips, but the casualties were only those who had been hit close to the landing zone, the fortunate few. When he twisted his head the Mullah could see through the dust-smeared portholes of the helicopter, and when he looked straight ahead he could see past the torso of the machine-gunner in the open doorway. They hugged the flat and featureless ground. He saw the old trench lines that had been disputed four, five, six years before, where that dawn's shells had burst. He saw the angular dead, and he saw the stricken faces of the wounded and he saw the stretcher parties running towards them. He could see the tanks hull down, sheltered in revetments, that would stay hull down until there were spare parts.

Nothing grew upon this battlefield. Where there had been fields there were now just the patterns of the armour tracks. Where there had been trees there were now only the shell-broken stumps. Where there had been marsh weed there was now only a yellow mat because the weed had been sprayed with herbicides to kill potential cover for an enemy. The helicopter scurried over a rear camp, tents and bomb-proof bunkers, and it flew sufficiently low for the Mullah to see the faces of the troops who squatted on the ground and stared up. They were the same faces that he had seen further forward at the front the night before. The sullen gaze that had greeted his speech of exhortation. Pressed troops, afraid to ask with their voices, bold enough to demand with their eyes: where is the air support, where are the tank parts, where is the victory, when is the end?

That same morning he had sat in judgment of fifteen recruits who had held back in the last assault on enemy lines. Young men, eyes downcast, denounced in monotone by their officers and sentenced by the Mullah to field execution. There could be no tolerating cowardice.

The Mullah had won his spurs in the service of the Imam as one of the investigators of the coup attempted by air force officers of the Nouzeh barracks at Hamadan. He had seen the tears and the pleading of the pilots, and he had not been diverted.

He had achieved good results, satisfactory enough results for him to be chosen above many to unravel the plot woven around the Great Satan's attempt to fly a commando force into the country for the release of prisoners from the Nest of Spies. So many traitors to be found, and he had found so many. He had found those who would have driven the lorries, and those who would have made the airbase available, and those who had switched off the defensive radar. For himself, he thought the plan of the Great Satan was an absurd plan, bound to fail.

The Mullah was a devotee of the Revolution, a child of the ferocity of the Revolution. He knew no other way.

When they were out of range of the Iraqi ground-to-air missiles, the helicopter climbed. It would fly first to a field hospital. After that, with two further stops for refuelling, the helicopter would fly on to Tabriz. At the front, close to the artillery exchanges, he had slept badly. On the way to Tabriz he dozed fitfully, and the straggling thoughts in his mind were of a man known as Dolphin.

Brian Venables was late leaving home. He was late because the guest had been in the bathroom when it should have been clear for him, and he was late because his wife had forgotten his breakfast. Too busy scrambling eggs for the guest. And to top it all, the look on his Polly's face across the kitchen table had been shameless, damn near brazen.

Brian Venables had not brought up his daughter to have her bring home a foreigner and then have that foreigner creep in the small hours across the landing into his Polly's room. That was clean out of court, and they would talk it out this evening. Oh yes.

He went down his neat front path to the newly-painted wrought-iron gate. The last of the blossom was still on the trees in the road. Once Wellington Street had been a quiet and respectable street, but the riff-raff were closing in. He slammed the gate shut behind him.

He walked down the pavement.

He saw the two scruffs inside the car. Brian Venables was a founder member of Neighbourhood Watch in his road. Two scruffs sitting in a car and watching the houses. He had listened to every word that the WPC had told them when the Neighbourhood Watch had been introduced. They wait for the man to go to work, for the children to go to school, for the wife to go shopping. Well, those two youngsters were in for a shock. He swung on his heel.

They were watching the house. They had seen the man come out on to the pavement, with his raincoat and his briefcase, then stop, turn to go back inside. Corinthian had said that he had probably forgotten his sandwich box. The patrol car came up fast alongside them, from behind.

Park swore softly. There was the rap on the driver's window.

"Driving licence . . ."

"Piss off," Corinthian mouthed.

"OK, laddie, out."

Corinthian just reached inside his anorak and lifted clear his Customs and Excise I/D card. He held it up to the uniformed constable's face. "Do get lost."

The constable stiffened, full height, full authority of his uniform. "Down at our Division, have they been informed you are on our patch?"

"Please, just go back to your canteen," Corinthian said.

The constable tried for a long, hard stare, didn't find it easy, but he went back to his patrol car.

Park had his radio against his mouth. His voice was terse. "April Five to April Nine and April Seven . . . 1 don't know how bad it is, we may have shown out, may not. On your bloody toes for Christ's sake. Out."

"What do you reckon?" Corinthian asked.

Keeper was thinking what Bill Parrish would have to say to his little Keeper if they were blown by the plods. He wasn't liking what he was thinking.

Charlie came down the stairs.

He had heard the telephone ring while he was packing the rucksack. He felt pretty good. Not having slept too well, that didn't matter. She was a great girl, and her Mum was good, and the breakfast had been brilliant. Not as brilliant as Polly. Polly was marvellous, and her father was a pig. He hesitated at the bottom of the stairs because he'd thought Polly's father had left, and now he could hear his voice on the telephone, ending a conversation.

He heard Polly's mother querying Polly's father. He put down the rucksack and listened.

Polly's father said, "No, the police were not complaining, and they had no cause to complain. That's what they're there for, that's what crime prevention is all about. Two men sitting in a car watching our street, that certainly entitles me to know what is going on. They have our street under surveillance, that's what the police said, the Health and Social Security have our street under surveillance, looking for those loafers who work on the black, cleaning windows and such, and then draw unemployment. That's what the police said. I'm off,

654

then. And I trust that your gentleman friend will be gone by this evening."

Charlie beamed at Polly's father as they passed in the hall. He thought the man was pretty shaken when he knew he'd been overheard. The door banged. Polly's mother, starting to wash up, said, "That's quite ridiculous. You can't get a window cleaner round here for love nor money."

The smile was gone from Charlie's face. Polly's father had said surveillance. He felt he had been kicked in the stomach.

She came into the hall and she had a happy light in her face. He felt the shiver in his legs and the sweat on his stomach. Surveillance. He heard the clatter of the dishes.

"What's at the back?"

"The garden and the garage."

"And there's another road?"

"Has to be another road, dumb head, or there wouldn't be a garage – why do you want to know?"

She was owed it and she wouldn't get it, an explanation. He carried the rucksack into the kitchen. Formally, because that was the way he had been taught as a child, he thanked Polly's mother for her hospitality. He opened the kitchen door and walked through into the garden.

She followed him.

She caught him down by the small vegetable patch, her father's joy.

"Are they watching for you, Charlie?"

"It doesn't help you to know."

"It is for you. Why, Charlie?"

"It's a long story, and there isn't enough time."

He should have been gone. If they were watching the front, then they might have the back covered.

She had hold of his hand. "What have you done wrong?"

"Nothing, everything."

"Mr Shabro told me what had been done to your family. He said that you weren't capable of friendship."

Gently, he took away his hand from her. "Perhaps one night we'll go dancing, dance till it's morning. You have to believe that I'd like that."

"Is that a lie, Charlie?"

"No, it's not . . . sweet Polly, the more you tell someone the more you involve someone, the more you involve them then the more you open them to hurt . . . it's best left unsaid."

"Will I see you again?"

Charlie caressed her cheek. "We'll dance all night. Promised."

"Am I not old enough to know? Is that it?" A bitterness, a choke, in her voice.

"It would hurt you to know."

He kissed her.

He felt the sweetness of her.

Perhaps one night they would go dancing . . .

He ran out of the back of the garden.

There was a grim satisfaction in it for Keeper. They'd all sweated, each of them on the track that had lost the Tango, then found him again. Token had done well when he'd come out of the garage and gone fast to the right and then turned in mid-stride. Token had done well to keep walking and go straight past him. Token said she'd been close enough to rub the sleepy dust out of the Tango's eye and she'd said that she found him quite dishy. Harlech had done well, because the Tango had climbed on a bus, and then hopped off at the lights and doubled back. Harlech had done a terrific job because he'd been fast enough on the radio for the car to pick the Tango up. Corinthian had tracked the Tango down on to the Underground, and stayed with him for the train jump, predictable but tricky. Then Token's turn again, in her reversible anorak with headscarf and the glasses with no power in the lenses. Between them they'd held on to him, all the way to King's Cross main line station.

It was Keeper's opinion that the Tango was trying what he thought were good evasion tactics, and Keeper reckoned he was a rank amateur, good instinct and poor training, but he wasn't complaining.

He sat on the InterCity. He could see the back of the Tango's head. Harlech was way down the carriage and he would be able to see the top of the Tango's forehead, and Token was in the carriage behind Keeper, and Corinthian was in the carriage ahead. Going very smooth, hammering at a hundred miles an hour plus on the rails heading north.

David reckoned that the Tango might have nodded off, his pillow the rucksack which had to hold the best part of a quarter of a million pounds in cash. Unless Mr Venables had it, and that didn't seem likely, not if he was tipping off the constabulary. Better get Statesman in to give the gnomes the once over after dark.

Mattie Furniss knew it was late at night.

It seemed an age since they had carried away the tray on which his supper plate had been, and the glass of water.

They came for him when he was lying on his bed, when he had taken off his trousers, and he had pulled the blanket over his body to hide his nakedness from the peephole. His underpants were hanging over the bottom of the bedframe to dry.

It had been a hideous day. He had been waiting for the rattle of the door, and the sight of the men come to take him down to the cellar. There had only been the tray with his food in the early morning, and the tray for his food in the early evening. He had heard a car come in what he had judged to be the middle of the day, and he had heard voices outside, and he thought that he had heard the voice of the investigator, but they had not come for him.

He could walk, just about, on his own. The soles of his feet were heavily swollen, but he had learned a rolling gait that would take him over a short distance. He was hunched from the strain that had been put on his shoulders.

When at last they came, they had not allowed him time to put on his trousers, nor the pants, nor his socks. Between his guards, Mattie Furniss went down the stairs. He wore only his shirt. He was hobbling and bent. He was beyond reach of help, he was going towards pain.

Down the stairs and into the hallway, and his instinctive turn was to the left, towards the doorway to the cellar. He was pulled to the right.

He stumbled and fell. They let him go down, and his knees felt the coolness of the tiled floor. They jerked him up and on to his feet and the pain shivered through him.

They took him through a kitchen. There were moths arcing around the light bulb that had no shade. There were two large metal pots on an electric cooker and on the table there were plates laid out with salads at the side. He saw the food that was unlike anything that was brought on the trays to his prison room. He was frog-marched through the kitchen and out into the glare of the lights in what he thought must be the yard at the back of the house.

The light came from the headlamps of a Mercedes car. The lights threw a bright wash across the yard and against the wall of concrete blocks. He thought the height of the wall was a foot or so above the height of his own head had he been standing erect and not been bent by the pain in his shoulders and ribs. That, too, was instinctive, that he checked the height of the wall. Many scenes now, all fast in his mind. He saw the pockmarks where bullets had struck the wall, and the holes were in a group that was only three, four, feet across. He saw the guard who cradled a rifle, probably a Soviet AK–74, across his elbow. He saw the investigator standing with his hands deep in the pockets of his trousers. He saw a young cleric with the turban of brilliant white and the camel hair cape and the thin-rimmed spectacles.

It was done as if it were a routine in which the only character who didn't know his part was Mattie. And he was learning, so fast. No talk. The sounds of the engine of the Mercedes idling and of the scrape of Mattie's feet across the hard earth yard. The feet scraped because he was losing the power to walk, going jelly in the legs. Across the yard to the place in the wall with the bullet holes.

They had to drag him.

The use was gone from his legs. Thinking of Harriet who was his wife. Thinking of the cottage that was his home. Wanting to plead, and wanting to cry, and the voices strangled in his throat. Against the wall the guards loosed his arms. He collapsed. The dirt was on his knees, and on his arms and on his chest. Death was grovelling in the dirt yard of a villa on the outskirts of Tabriz. Death was choking in the night air, beyond the reach of help. Death was feeling the slackening of the gut muscles . . . Death was the metallic crack as a Soviet rifle was cocked. There was a hand in his hair and his head was wrenched upwards and his body weight was taken so that he was left in a kneeling position and the cold damp dirt of the yard cloyed on his privates. Too frightened to pray, like that Lutheran pastor would have prayed. Thinking of all those who were too far from him to help him, but closer than the God he hadn't troubled to know. Thinking of the men at Century and Flossie Duggan. Thinking of Harriet alone in the cottage at Bibury where the spring was over and the summer was coming, and of Will, who would be coming soon to cut the grass around the apple trees. Thinking of the agents in Tehran and Tabriz and the Harbourmaster's office in Bandar Abbas. Thinking of Charlie who should have been his son. They would all see the morning, they would all know the freshness of another day. The morning, and another day, they were beyond his reach.

Against the back of his neck, where his hair thinned out, was the pressure of the barrel of the rifle. There was a pain prick from the fore-sight.

No questions.

No demand for names.

He opened his eyes. He saw the face of the investigator and the face of the cleric, expressionless.

He was shaking, and as his neck rolled so the muzzle of the weapon followed. There was the firing click.

His ears exploded. His stomach failed.

He rolled, fell, collapsed.

He was on the dirt in the yard, and his mouth gaped and bit at the filth.

Mattie heard the low chuckle of the investigator. His eyes opened. He gazed into the cleric's face. He saw a silently mirthless smile.

He was pulled to his feet. His urine had run down the length of his thighs and had stained the dirt. He couldn't speak, couldn't help himself up. He made no attempt to cover himself as they took him back into the kitchen and past the cooker where a meal was in preparation, and up the stairs, and back to his prison room.

He was their toy.

On his bed he wept. The names were in his mind. In his mind were the names of the agents and the name of Charlie Eshraq.

Mattie could recognise it all, the shredding of his will to fight.

From his room he could see the west face of the clock. Big Ben showing a couple of minutes past midnight. He had slept on the decision, and he had killed a whole day on the decision. He had taken advice, but the decision was his. He could keep his options open no longer.

He went down to the thirteenth floor.

He didn't knock, he went straight into the room. A very strange noise in the room stopped him in his tracks. Past midnight in Central London and the sounds were of the countryside at dawn. They'd put old Henry Carter on night duty. Finding a job for Henry in the twilight of his service at Century was putting him on night duty in the room used by the Crisis Management

Committee. There was a camp bed over by the window. The man wore long combination underpants and a woollen vest with short sleeves and buttons at the throat. Typical of Whitehall, typical of government service, that a Crisis Management Committee should wind up once it was past midnight as a solitary individual, past retirement if he wasn't mistaken, sitting in ancient underclothes, and listening to God knew what . . . The man was quick off the bed, and was straight into his suit trousers, and was hooking on the braces over his vest. Didn't bother with his shirt. There was an expensive radio on the floor and a cassette was playing through it. A sharp note on the track amongst what, to the Director General, was a clatter of noise, and he saw the attention of Henry Carter waver, then disappear. A moment of bliss on his face. He switched off the machine.

"Sorry, sir, bless you for your patience . . . *phylloscopus inornatus*, that's the Yellow–Browed Warbler, a little beauty. I did the tape in Norfolk last weekend. I thought I had her, never can be sure. Very intense, very penetrating call. Did you hear it, sir? Just off to Siberia for the summer, remarkable little lady . . . Apologies, you didn't come in here to listen to a Yellow–Browed Warbler."

The Director General handed over a single sheet of paper, in his own hand, his own signature. Carter read it. He hadn't his close work glasses on and he had to hold his spectacles away from his face to get a clear focus.

"You'll not mind me saying it, sir, but it's a wee bit late."

"You don't have a drink in here, do you?"

Henry took a bottle of Scotch from a cupboard, and two glasses, and he poured two liberal scoops.

The Director General drank deep.

"I know we've warned them, sir, but we've taken an awful time to tell them to run."

"Big step, Carter, dismantling a network. A bigger step when that network is down to three agents and will take years to rebuild."

"I just pray to God they've got time."

"Furniss, he's trained to withstand pressure."

"Interesting usage, pressure . . . sir."

"For Christ's sake, we are talking about the dismantling of a network."

"No, sir, if you'll excuse me, we are talking about pressure."

"He's been trained . . . Please, I'll have the other half."

The glass was taken, filled, handed back.

"Oh yes, sir, he's been trained. He was very good at the Fort. One of the best lecturers they've had there. But my experience is that training and the real thing are wholly different."

The Director General shuddered. His hands were tight on the glass.

"How long can he hold out, that's what I need to be sure of."

"He's a man I've been proud to know for more than twenty years, but if he's in Iran it's asking rather a lot of him that he hold out this long."

The Director General headed for the lift and his car home. He left Henry

Carter to the business of sending the messages that would instruct the three agents to take flight.

13

"I am Matthew ... Furniss. I am ... the Iran Desk ... Head at Century House."

It was said ... It was as if they were all exhausted, as if a birth had taken place and Mattie was the mother and the investigator was the midwife and the confession was the child.

He could see into the investigator's face, and there was running sweat on the man's face and red blotches from his exertion, and the breath came hard to the investigator. Mattie lay strapped on the bed. He could see into the face of the investigator as the man reeled away, as if he'd run more distance than he could cope with, and the heavy duty flex sagged from the man's hand. He could not take any more of the heavy duty flex on the soles of his feet. The pain ran up from his feet and into his knees and into his thighs and up into his stomach, in his stomach the pain spread out and burst into every particle of him. The pain was in his mind, and his mind could take nothing more.

It was done.

"Matthew Furniss."

It was as if they had all been on a great journey together. There was Mattie who had endured, he no longer knew how many days, there were the guards who had started the day playing football with him, blindfolded, punching and kicking him from one to the other and heaving him against the damp scrape of the cellar walls, there was the investigator who sweated because of the force he had used to beat the soles of Mattie's feet. All on a great journey together, and the guards and the investigator had broken Mattie, and Mattie was strapped to the bed and needing to talk to save himself from the pain.

The investigator gripped the side of his table for support, then steadied himself and breathed in a gulp of the cellar's foul, hot air. All the body smells were trapped in the cellar. He levered himself along the side of the table and threw the switch on the tape recorder.

That morning had been different, as if everything else that had gone before had been child's play. No breakfast brought down to the cellar while it was still dark outside, a long age hanging from the wall hook until the pain in his shoulders had given way to agony, then the football, then the beating with the heavy duty flex. As if they were now bored with him, as if they had other business to be about and could spare Mattie no more time.

So simple to speak the words. The hammering of new pain had ceased, and the tape-recorder was turning, and the investigator was sitting at the table, and the guards had pulled back to the wall and there was the rank sweet smoke of their cigarettes.

At that moment there was no thought in the mind of Mattie Furniss other than the killing of the rising pain. The pain stayed where it was. The guards came from behind and they unstrapped the thongs that held down his legs and his wrists. They let him lie free on the bed.

He must be a pitiful sight. Not Mattie Furniss at all. He had not washed, not after having been brought back from the yard the previous evening. His hair was unkempt and filthy, his lips were parched grey and cracked, his eyes were big and staring and racing. They had broken him. He curled his knees to his chest and tried to control the pain that was all over his body. Broken, but free from the beating.

"Well done, Mr Furniss. That was the hardest, Mr Furniss, and the worst is now past."

Mattie talked about Century.

He could see from the eyes of the man that little that he said was not previously known. He spoke in a slow wheezing monotone. There was no character, no wit, he was a tour guide at the end of a long season. The investigator had pulled up his chair close to Mattie, and he was hunched forward so that his face dominated Mattie. Sometimes the investigator repeated what Mattie had said as if that way he ensured that the microphone picked up the words with greater clarity. The investigator took no notes, to have written on a notepad would have deflected the concentration that now settled over Mattie. He talked about the budget that was given to Iran Desk, and he talked about the resources that could be made available to Iran Desk from the Station Officers in Ankara and Baghdad and Dubai and Abu Dhabi and Bahrain.

All the old loyalties, all he stood for, beaten from him.

He heard the drone of his own voice . . . he'd done them well. He'd stayed silent longer than they could have counted on. There was nothing that he should be ashamed of. He'd given them time to save the field men.

He was given a glass of water. He held it in his two hands, and the water slopped down his shirt front when he tried to drink, and his lips were rigid like plastic sheeting . . . he'd won them time. They should be thankful for what that precious time had cost him.

Mattie gave the name. ". . . His business is on Bazar e Abbas Abad."

He could see him clearly. He was hugely fat, sat on a reinforced chair in the back office behind a cave of merchandise and held court over cigars and coffee. He was a connoisseur of carpets and a collector of gossip, and he was a field agent of Century from far back. Mattie had known the merchant for twenty years, and it was Mattie's joke each time they met that he couldn't get his arms round his old friend when they hugged a greeting. There was gossip to be had from the merchant about the rivalries of the army colonels, about the inter-factional fighting amongst the Mullahs, about the industrialists squabbling for foreign exchange with which to buy overseas plant. Every time they met then Mattie laughed, and sometimes the choicest of the gossip, if it were of matters sexual, could even bring a smile to those witheringly dull fellows from the Agency across the ocean. He had known the merchant since he had been a liaison officer in Tehran, and there was a rug in front of the fire in the cottage at Bibury that had cost him an arm and a leg, and the last time he had been seriously angry with Harriet had been when she had put a wet pine log on that fire that had spat a knot on to the rug. Mattie named the merchant, and they brought a damp towel to put across the soles of his feet to quieten the anger of the pain.

Another name. ". . . he works in the Harbourmaster's office at Bandar Abbas."

When he was Station Officer in Tehran he had once made the long road journey south, and he had been sure that he had thrown off the tail of the SEVAK agents that was supposed to be with him, and he had gone to the home of the official from the Harbourmaster's office. The man had been recruited by a previous Station Officer, and until the Revolution had been of minimal importance, and maintained only because he did not want money. He was pure gold now, a field agent in the office which observed the comings and goings of merchant shipping in and out of the country's chief port. He had gone to the man's small brick house, he had sweated and sat on a floor rug and wondered why the ventilation chimney seemed so inadequate in the blasting Gulf heat. On that occasion, after the wife had scurried in with a tray and glasses holding diluted lime juice and scurried out, the official had told Mattie that he was a democrat, and therefore opposed to the regime of the Shah of Shahs. The Revolution had come, the official had found no democracy from the clerics, he had stayed on the list of active agents and he had begun to grow in importance. A small, frightened man, who believed that the work he carried out for Mattie was a short step in the long road to bring parliamentary rule to his country. A sandwich with sweet cheese was brought for the prisoner.

Another name given. ". . . he runs a repair workshop in Tabriz for lorries, and he also has contracts to keep the Revolutionary Guards' vehicles on the road."

A basic and human individual, a man who might have been in Mattie's eyes almost a European. The engineer was the sort of fellow who was always popular, perpetually in demand, and he worked all the hours that his God gave him. The engineer had been recruited in Turkey. A good and active Station Officer, long before this academic boy in the job now, had sought him out in a café and talked to him when he was over for the collection of a broken-down lorry that would need a new gear box. That Station Officer had been lucky. The son of the engineer's close friend had been shot in the old gaol in Tabriz after a cursory trial by the Komiteh. The engineer had been ready for recruitment. The engineer's pay went into an account at the Etibank in Van, and it was Mattie's business to know that the credit mounted and was never reduced. Perhaps there was a day on some far horizon in his mind when the engineer would drive out his truck, with his family hidden amongst a cargo. It was useful, the information provided by the engineer. In any time that approached normality it would have been second grade, but they were not normal times, and Iran Desk were pretty damn thankful to have anything coming out of Iran. Mattie had been given a glass of water and a damp towel again soothed the soles of his feet.

It was a good hotel. Charlie could sleep on the pavements with the dossers when he had to, not for the sake of it. The room was £66.50 a night and the best that Leeds could provide. He locked the door behind him. He went along the landing, he was carrying his rucksack by the straps, the two straps twisted around his wrist. He wore his cleanest slacks, a clean shirt and a navy blazer.

There was a man at the end of the corridor, in jeans and a sweatshirt, polishing hard at the muzzle of a fire hose. He didn't look at Charlie and went on with his polishing. Pretty damn obvious ... Charlie understood ... What could be so compelling about getting a shine on to a fire hose nozzle? A lift was waiting for him.

He came out into the hotel lobby. Too crowded for him to spot the watchers, and he wasn't hanging around to search them out. He knew what he was at. He strode across the lobby, not looking right and not looking left, went as though he belonged and hadn't a care in the world. He pushed his way through the revolving doors, then hesitated. It was colder up in the north than in London. There were taxis waiting in line, engines off. He paused on the pavement.

He moved sharply. He ducked back through the swing doors and across the lobby to the staircase.

He went up the stairs three at a time. Six flights to climb. He went up the stairs like there was no tomorrow, and took the last flight that was to the roof, and he put his shoulder against the stiffness of the fire escape door.

He stepped out on to the flat roof. He skirted the air conditioning machinery. He had no interest in a fine view over factories or the brick terraces or the munificence of the Victorian civic buildings and churches.

He went to the edge of the roof. He looked down on to the street below. He could see the line of parked taxis. His eyes roved. He saw a green saloon that was behind the taxis. He could see that there were two people in the front seats, and there was the exhaust showing that the engine was idling. He saw that the man who had been polishing the nozzle of the fire hose was now across the street, and his lips were moving and there was no one close enough to hear him.

In his bath, Charlie had remembered that he was a friend of Mr Furniss.

He was going to piss on them.

"Where the hell is he?"

"Went back up the fire stairs."

664

"I know he went up the bloody stairs – where did he go?"

"He was coming out and he just turned round."

"I've got eyes myself – where is he now?"

Harlech was across the road from the front of the hotel. Corinthian was stranded in the hotel lobby.

Token was round the back. "Not a whistle of him here."

There was the local joker, in the Sierra, to drive. Keeper thought he was going to be a disaster because he was VAT, and VAT investigators were the pits. When the Head Office came up from the big city they had to put up with whatever they could get, and they needed a local man for the driving. The VAT man said, "Not a bad start to the day."

The repartee insult was rising in Keeper. The interruption, the insult never spoken.

Corinthian into Keeper's earpiece: "April Eleven to April Five, our Tango One is in the lobby, heading for the front door . . . going through the front door, you should be picking him up."

"Your lucky day," the VAT man said.

Keeper saw Charlie come through the swing doors. He felt the relief jar through him. He saw the target walk towards the first taxi on the rank holding the rucksack. It had been Keeper's opinion that Tango One was a rank amateur, but he didn't know why the target had gone back into the hotel, and he didn't know what he had done there, and he didn't know whether they had all shown out, and he was no longer sure how amateur the target was.

They followed the taxi out of the rank. He told the VAT man that he didn't need a running commentary on the splendours of Leeds, thank you, and he had to shout at the joker to let Token through with the back-up car, and neither Token nor Harlech acknowledged them as they went by and took up prime station behind the taxi. They had the message too.

Perhaps the target was not such a rank amateur after all.

Herbert Stone was used to dealing with middle trade businessmen and government representatives. The boy fitted no pattern that he was used to. Middle trade businessmen came to him from Hamburg or Rotterdam or Barcelona because he had earned a reputation for discretion and efficiency, for putting paperwork into place with speed. Government representatives arrived at his office, once a vicarage, because they depended on his discretion in placing hardware in the hands of people they could not acknowledge.

He dealt with corporations and institutions, not with bearded young men who wore yellow socks, and who sauntered in with rucksacks, for heaven's sake. And the kid seemed relaxed, as if it were the most normal thing in life to take an InterCity north and then come and chat about taking delivery of armour-piercing hardware.

Herbert Stone followed the principles of the Shavian Andrew Undershaft – he would do business with anyone, offer a realistic price, not trouble himself with principles or politics . . . and the young man had given Mattie Furniss' name, and Furniss' office had confirmed the connection. Century put quite a bit of business his way, matters too delicate for public knowledge. There had not been as many Belfast produced Blowpipe shoulder-fired ground-to-air missiles in the mountain valleys of Afghanistan as there had been Californian built Stingers, but the British had been there, their warheads had joined the fireworks, and Stone had been the conduit used by Century to get the missiles into the hands of the Mujahidin, never mind that they generally made a hash of them.

He would be wary, cautious, but never dismissive.

In a neat hand, in pencil, he wrote down the detail of Charlie Eshraq's order. It was a pleasant, airy office. There was no illustration of any matter military on the walls, just watercolour originals of the Yorkshire Dales. He might have been noting the necessary information prior to the issuing of a personal accident policy.

"If I'm to help you, and I'm not at this stage saying that I can, if I'm to help you then there has to be a degree of frankness between us . . ."

"Yes."

"If you lie to me then I might just lie to you. Your problem, you have to trust me . . ."

"But I am recommended by Mr Furniss, that's your guarantee . . ."

True, that was on the youngster's side, and a surety for him too. "What country do you mean to operate in – where will the weaponry be used?"

"Iran."

No whistle in the teeth, no pursing of the lips. "And the delivery point?"

"Past Turkish Customs, I collect in Turkey."

"What targets for armour-piercing?"

"First target is an armoured Mercedes, 600 series. After that I do not at the moment know."

"Not all to be fired in one engagement?"

Charlie paused, considered. "Each one different. Perhaps more vehicles, not tanks, perhaps buildings."

The scratching of Stone's pencil. "I see."

"So, what should I have?"

For the first time Stone was shaken. A small, puzzled frown escaped him. "You don't know what you want?"

"I'm not a soldier, what should I have?"

Everyone who came and sat in Stone's office knew what they wanted, problem was could they get it. They wanted howitzers, or 81 mm mortars, they wanted white phosphorus shells, or ground-to-air, they wanted attack helicopters, or a Claymore system of ground defence. None of them, his clients, ever asked his advice on what they should have.

"Do you have *any* military experience, Mr Eshraq?"

"None."

The pencil stopped, hovered . . . but it was none of his business. "Light

Anti-Tank Weapon. It's called LAW 80. How many are we talking about?"

Charlie said, "Three, maybe four."

Stone looked up from his notes. "I see. We are talking about a relatively, ah, small order."

"Yes."

There was a crocodile of barges going down the Thames, and seagulls hovering in chaos over the cargo.

The Deputy Director General was concise. "You won't know this man, this Stone, but he's used by us. He's an arms dealer, reliable sort of fellow. Right now Charlie Eshraq is sitting in his office and trying to place an order for a handful of LAW 80 missiles."

"I was never in the forces, what do they do?"

"They bust tanks . . . Stone rang through two or three days ago to check on Furniss' reference. Miss Duggan told me this and I asked Stone to ring me as soon as Eshraq appeared. He's trying to buy these missiles to take back with him into Iran. Does he get them, or not?"

The seagulls swirled in aerial combat over the barges. "It would be an illegal exportation, no doubt."

"Yes, but we're not squeamish. Presumably he brought back heroin in order to pay for these weapons, as soon as he has the weapons he'll be going back inside."

"Shows extraordinary courage." The Director General had a son at university, studying philosophy, and allergic to the lawn mower. "I like young people with purpose and guts."

"That's Eshraq – in full."

"Give them to him. Give him this anti-tank whatever . . ."

The Deputy Director General grimaced. "Quite, but it ignores the problem."

"What problem?"

"The problem of Mattie Furniss. The problem of Mattie talking, spilling under torture what he knows about his agents and about his young protegé. Got me?"

The Director General swung away from the window, swivelled his chair.

"I tell you what I think . . . I think Mattie is a very experienced and dedicated officer. I think he's of the old school. I think he'd go to his grave rather than betray his network."

The Deputy Director General murmured, "That's just not realistic, sir. I am afraid all we know today about interrogation techniques tells us that he will, inevitably, brave as he unquestionably is, talk. Would it help you to meet with our own interrogators, have them to tell you what, exactly, is being done to Mattie?"

"It would not . . . It is simply that I have a greater faith in the resilience of an old dog. And furthermore, you stand there lecturing me as though you know for certain that Furniss is in an Iranian torture chamber. Well, you don't. We don't. We haven't the least idea where he is. He may have been kidnapped by Turkish thugs who haven't the slightest notion who he is. He may be with some freelance outfit who simply want to ransom him. Tell me, if you would, how long it has generally taken for any of the extremist sects in Beirut to announce the capture of hostages. They're on to a telephone to Reuter before you can count to ten, or there is no word for months. There is no pattern about which we can be definite. So we'll just play it my way, if you don't mind."

"So, what is your instruction?"

The Director General said, "Eshraq is to have his missiles. He is to be encouraged to return to Iran. Give him any help he needs, without tripping over the Customs people, if you can."

The Deputy Director General, swearing silently, flushed at the cheeks, went back to his office and spoke to Herbert Stone.

Parrish pounded down the fifth floor corridor of the Lane. Those who saw him, through open office doors, and those who flattened themselves against the corridor walls to give him room, wondered whether he'd got the trots or whether he'd heard the Four Minute Warning. He charged into the ACIO's office, and the ACIO had an Audit team with him, and none of the Audit team complained, just packed their briefcases and left. The door closed behind Bill Parrish. He didn't wait to collect his thoughts, gather in his breath.

"Just had Park on, from Leeds, right? Park is with Eshraq, right? Eshraq is currently sitting in the office of one Herbert Stone. Mr Stone sells weapons. Eshraq is buying weapons. That's the strength of it. He's using heroin money to buy weapons . . . This is going too far. Eshraq's run enough, it's time to knock the bugger over."

The ACIO rang through to the CIO and while he was talking Parrish loosened his tie and thought he was too old for this sort of caper, far too bloody old.

The voice was in her ear.

"I'm terribly sorry, Mrs Furniss, I really am sorry, but I just cannot talk about it on the telephone. It's an open line, you see. They haven't been in touch with you? It's a scandal. I know I shouldn't say this, Mrs Furniss, but the day of the gentleman is past here . . . Mrs Furniss, please don't ever say to anyone that I spoke to you . . . They don't know what to do. They know that Mr Furniss was kidnapped in Turkey, they believe that he was then taken into Iran. After that they don't know anything. They've set up a Committee to watch developments, but they've staffed it with fools, people like that old idiot Carter. I mean, Mrs Furniss, those sort of people are not competent enough. I was taken up to see the Director General. He had me in his office.

He is not a gentleman, Mrs Furniss, I hold him responsible. What he was interested in was all I knew about Charlie. You see, Mr Furniss kept all his files on Charlie in his personal safe, didn't let them go down to Library, and didn't let me put them on any computer roll which anyone else could plug into. They were very concerned about Charlie. To tell you the truth, Mrs Furniss, they seemed more concerned about Charlie than they were about Mr Furniss. Mrs Furniss, I don't know what it is, his trouble, but Charlie is in some sort of trouble, very deep, I'd swear on that. It's disgraceful, Mrs Furniss, them not being in touch with you every day, should be in touch with you two or three times a day. I have to ring off, goodbye, Mrs Furniss. Mr Furniss has a great many friends here and they are all thinking of you. Goodbye."

She was grateful to kind Miss Duggan. When she was a child, before she had been sent away to school, her parents had employed a Flossie Duggan as a nanny, a nice, soft woman with a big bosom and a well of loyalty. Mattie used to say that, at Century, life would not be worth living if he didn't have Flossie Duggan to take care of him.

Harriet Furniss would not have called herself a Service wife, rather described herself as a Service widow. The Service had no room for wives. In more than twenty years, since Mattie had come out of the Coldstreams and joined the Service, she had never set foot inside Century. How could she have done? She had never even been allowed to drive to the corner on the Embankment and wait to collect him after work. She had never been to a social function that involved Century people. The only person that she knew at Century was Flossie Duggan, because Flossie would once or twice a year come down to Bibury and type up a report over a weekend if it had to be on the DG's desk or the DDG's desk first thing on a Monday morning. The life of the Service was a closed book to her. Little boys playing secretive games. But dangerous games. So hideously dangerous that Mattie was a prisoner in Iran . . . and she had good memories of Iran. She remembered when they had been young and together there, when she had been the young mother of two small girls, the swimming trips to the Caspian in the summer and the skiing trips to the Elborz in the winter, when the future was stable and set to last for a millennium. It had been a lovely country, kind and welcoming and comfortable. Infuriating, too, because it had aped Europe and of course she couldn't get a plumber or an electrician, never for love and rarely for money. Endless dinners by candlelight, because as night followed day it was inevitable her social calendar would be dogged by power failures.

She looked out into her garden. It was time to strip the wallflowers from the beds, but the rain was beating on the windowpanes. She loved her garden in summer . . . She could picture Mattie pacing the lawn and then coming inside to tell her, bluff and stiff because he could never handle matters that were emotional, that Juliette Eshraq had been hanged from a crane in a square in Tabriz. She would never forget that, how he had walked backwards and forwards past the lupins and pinks and stocks before he had come inside to tell her of the execution of the girl she had known as a cheeky and darling child perched on her knee.

And what could Miss Duggan have meant about Charlie being in trouble and why did the Service know anything about Charlie? He was bound to call when he came back from his trip overseas. She would get him down to the cottage and ask him. Straight out. She wasn't going to let Charlie get himself mixed up with Century. That would be unbearable.

She thought of her man. Darling Mattie, everybody's friend, her husband.

Later, she would go down to the Post Office for some stamps, and if she were asked then she would put on a smile and say that Mattie was fine, just abroad for a few days, and before she went to the Post Office there were more circulars to send about the footpath.

She was a Service widow, and she would be good at it. Mattie would expect that.

Herbert Stone had the brochure on the desk in front of him.

"It's just what you want, Mr Eshraq, and it's the best of British technology. Very much up to date, only been in service with our own forces for a few months. 'Provides an exceptional hit and kill capability for its size and weight . . . outstanding accuracy against both fixed and moving targets is achieved using a built-in spotting rifle . . . high technology warhead provides excellent kill probabilities from all angles of attack . . . not complicated to teach . . . zero maintenance.' Sounds pretty good, and it is. It'll get through 650 mm of armour, it has an effective range of 500 metres, and the whole thing weighs only ten kilos. The beauty of LAW 80, Mr Eshraq, is in the spotting rifle, you fire a tracer round, you get a hit, you depress the main firing button and away you go. If this is designed to take out a main battle tank then it goes without saying, Mr Eshraq, that it will make a frightful mess of an armoured Mercedes."

"What is it going to cost me?"

"Let's have a drink . . . you'd like a drink, Mr Eshraq?"

"What will it cost?"

"Expensive."

"How much?"

"Right, Mr Eshraq, no drink, just the figures. We're talking about a round half dozen, correct?"

"No, four."

Herbert Stone's voice did not waver. There was no apology. "I'm quoting you £50,000 for four . . ."

"What does that include?"

Herbert Stone had seen that the young man hadn't blinked, hadn't gagged. "Each missile would cost the army £2000, that's for ordinary bulk dealing. You are not ordinary and you are not bulk, and if I had not just spoken to a colleague of Mr Furniss you and I would not be dealing at all. You have a good friend, young man, but even with friends there are complications. You don't want all the seamy details, do you? You just want delivery through Customs at Istanbul. For that money you get four missiles. Don't worry yourself with the details, Mr Eshraq."

"Four missiles at £50,000?"

"Right," said Stone and made a swift note.

Charlie bent over, and he lifted his rucksack on to his knee. He delved into it. He laid on the edge of the desk a dirty shirt, and two pairs of dirty socks, and then his washing bag. From the bottom of the rucksack he drew out a plastic bag. He pushed the washing bag and the socks and the dirty shirt to one side, and from the plastic bag he took the first wad of notes, wrapped by an elastic band. Other wads followed. A less experienced businessman might have showed surprise, but Stone had the first wad in his hand and was counting. Twenty-pound notes, one hundred notes in each wad. The heaps of notes moved from the side of the desk where Charlie sat with his laundry, across to Stone's side. Twenty-five wads of notes on the desk top, and Charlie lifted the bag back into the bottom of his rucksack, and covered it with his clothes and his washing bag.

"That's it, thank you." The money was shovelled, fast, into Stone's safe.

"Mr Stone, what are the complications that cost so much extra, please?"

It was a reasonable question, and that was how Stone treated it. "You're better off without details, Mr Eshraq, details tend to get messy in the wrong hands . . . I have to have a cut. They have to come off the tail of a truck, and someone has to put them on a truck, and someone has to make the paperwork right, and someone has to find a bit of room on a lorry, one or two palms to be crossed at frontiers on the way to Turkey, and someone has to make sure Istanbul doesn't look that closely at what's coming through. There are quite a lot of people who would go to prison for quite a long time, that adds up to the difference, as you think of it, above £2000 per weapon."

Charlie said, "In that price, in the load, I'd like there to be included three wholesale cartons of bath soap, the best there is, whatever Mrs Stone would recommend. Can you manage that?"

"Yes, I believe we can manage that."

"I'll give you my number in London. You'll call as soon as you are ready?" Charlie's eyes narrowed. "If they were tampered with, if they didn't work . . ."

"I think we can let Mr Furniss be our mutual surety, don't you, Mr Eshraq?"

Park said, "If we don't get into Colombia and start to hit the bastards in their own backyard, then we're going to lose. It's the Americans who are at the sharp end at the moment, but our turn's coming. We won't avoid the really big cocaine traffic if we don't act much more positively. The demand's here, for the lunch time snort, and that demand'll grow in London just as it's grown in New York. Do you know that there's a guy in Medellin, that's in Colombia, who has a fortune estimated at two billion dollars? That's cocaine money. We have to go in, get stuck in on the ground. We can't just be sitting at Southampton and Dover and Heathrow."

The VAT investigator chewed gum and said, "Myself, I never reckoned to change the world between nine and five, five days a week."

"We have to beat the power of these bastards. Did you know that there was a Justice Minister of Colombia, and when he quit he was given the job of Ambassador to Hungary – and he was shot there, in Hungary. That's the power of the bastards, that's what's got to be beaten."

"Good luck," the VAT investigator took the gum from his mouth, put it in the ashtray. "So, you're off to Bogota?"

"If I can get there."

"Me, I'm looking forward to staying in Leeds and sorting out the fiddles of Mr Gupta and the corner shop."

Park said, "Haven't you ever wanted to do anything that mattered?"

"Smart talk. Makes a change. We don't get much smart talk up here."

"Terrorism, that's crap compared with the drugs threat, and that's not recognised . . ."

"Are you married?"

"What of it?"

The VAT man settled comfortably in his seat and peeled another strip of gum. He said airily, "Your good lady, is she going to Bogota?"

He didn't answer. Park had the camera at the window. He photographed Charlie leaving through the front door, and when he had the photographs then he was on the radio and alerting his team. Corinthian passed them, on foot, and in the mirror he saw Harlech and Token in the back-up motor.

Tango One was walking back towards the centre of the city, and the rucksack was trailing from his hand, and the tail was on him.

David Park had them all keyed.

They couldn't let the target run much more, not now that he was into weaponry, and too damn right he was going to get himself to Bogota when this target was knocked. Been right to let him run up to now, but all changed once he'd started talking hardware. Too damn right he didn't know if Ann would be with him.

"You asked to be kept informed," the ACIO said. "So I am informing you that it is our intention to arrest Eshraq."

"When will this be?"

"Tomorrow at four a.m."

The Home Secretary lowered his eyes. "You could do me a favour."

"What sort of favour, sir?"

"You could allow me to consult."

"*Consult*, Home Secretary? The case is 2000 per cent rock solid."

"No, no, I don't mean on a point of law. You've run a splendid show. I've nothing but admiration for the way it's been handled. No, it's not that. It's . . . it's, well, frankly, it's odd, but it's turned political and I need to consult upwards."

"There's nothing odd about that, sir. It started out political. 'Turn the country upside down, chaps, bring in the pusher, bring in the dealer, spare no expense, bring the distributor to book, scrap every other investigation' – and we did – and I rather think my job was on the line if we didn't. Well, Home Secretary, we did. We've got him, this heroin importer, this degenerate killer, the man who carried in the stuff which Miss Lucy Barnes killed herself with – or are the political fortunes of Mr Barnes so wonderfully on the wane that heroin has been struck from the political agenda?"

"Commissioner, I am totally sympathetic to your point of view, believe me."

"I'll believe you, Home Secretary, if, and only if, you fight our corner. You've got, well, I am in danger of revising that, because you are a politician and *you* have nothing – the country you are elected to serve has got a dedicated, a passionately dedicated Investigation Division. They earn peanuts, they work twice as hard as you do. They get no perks, hardly any holidays, and they deliver. They deliver and you want to consult."

"I take in what you say."

The ACIO took out his small notepad. He wrote down his home telephone number. "Four a.m., sir. You can reach me at home this evening. But we'll be rooting for you, sir. Don't let us down."

It was a slow process, getting the messages to the field agents. Some messages could be sent over coded inserts into broadcasts of the BBC's World Service, but an order to close shop, abandon ship, must be delivered by hand. Terence Snow was to send a low level but reliable man to Tabriz. The Station Officer in Bahrain had to find someone to fly to Tehran. The Station Officer in Abu Dhabi had to find a dhow owner to ferry the message across the treacherous Gulf waters to Bandar Abbas. Of course, it would have been quicker to have enlisted the help of the Agency, but then it would also have had to be explained that Mr Matthew Furniss, Desk Head (Iran), had been lost. And that was news that Century were unwilling to share with the Americans, a matter of dirty linen made public.

Charlie slept in his hotel, the plastic bag under his pillow.

The green Ford Sierra was outside the hotel. The VAT investigator had gone home, and Keeper was asleep across the back seat with the Vodaphone cradled in his arms. Harlech and Corinthian and Token had the room across the corridor from the target, and would be on two-hour shifts watching the door.

Keeper was well asleep when the Vodaphone warbled in his ear.

"That you, Keeper?"

"Bill? Yes, it's me."

"Are you sitting comfortably? No knock tomorrow . . . Got that? No lift in the morning . . ."

"For Christ's sake, Bill . . ."

"I said, no knock tomorrow."

"Why not?"

"David, the tablets just come flying off the mountain, and I pass on the messages."

"I don't fucking believe it. What more do they want?"

"What they do not want is for the target to be lifted."

"I hear you."

"You cuddled up with Token?"

"I am bloody not."

"Good thing . . . do us all a favour, give your missus a bell, will you? I gave her my promise that you'd be back for the dance. Sweet dreams, Keeper . . . just ring your missus in the morning, and you do not lift the target."

The boot went in, and the fist.

There was a hand snaking into Mattie's hair in order to pull up his head, so that it was easier to punch him, kick him, so that it was harder for him to protect himself.

He was trying to tell them the name, but his lungs were emptied by the beatings into his stomach pit, and he had not the breath to shout the name. His throat was too raw to speak the name. If he told them the name then the beating and the kicking would stop.

The man was too good to have been fobbed off with three names. Mattie had known why the beating had started again. He had shown the flicker of success. He thought he had won small victories with three names. The investigator had read him. Buying off the pain of a beating with three names. But three names was the sliding slope. It was what Mattie would have taught at the Fort – once the names start then the walls come tumbling in. He had no more defence. He had used all the tricks that he knew of. The last trick had been the feigning of unconsciousness, and the cigarette end, lit, on the skin under his armpit, tender, had blown away the deceit in a scream of pain.

He knelt on the floor. His arms hung at his side. There was the taste of his blood in his mouth, and there was a tooth socket for his tongue to rest in. He hated the men that he had named. The pain and the shame had been brought down on him because he had known their names. The fist in his hair held his head upright, and they punched and slapped his face, and they buffeted the bridge of his nose so that there were tears in his eyes, and they kicked his stomach and his groin. For Mattie, the only way of ending the pain was to surrender the name. He had thought he could satisfy them with three names, and he had failed.

His arms flailed around him, as if he tried to drive them back. If he did

674

not drive them back, away from him, then he could not draw the breath into his lungs and the saliva down into his throat, and he could not name the name. He did not see the flick finger gesture of the investigator. He was not aware that the hand was no longer in his hair, and that his body had buckled. He saw only the investigator's face.

His chest heaved. The breath flooded into his body.

"You killed his sister."

"Did I, Mr Furniss?"

"You tortured her, you killed her."

"Who did I torture, who did I kill?"

"His sister . . . he's going to get you for his sister."

"Where is he going to come from, to get to me?"

"Coming from UK, coming through Turkey, coming through the Dogubeye-zit frontier post."

"How is he going to get to me, for what I did to his sister?"

"Armour-piercing missile, for you and the Mullah who sentenced his sister."

"Who is the Mullah who sentenced his sister?"

"I don't know."

"How will he come here, to get to me?"

"Papers, papers of the *pasdaran*."

"Where do the papers come from?"

"Istanbul."

"Where in Istanbul?"

"From a hairdressing shop, in the Aksaray district, it is just to the right of the Mirelaon church. It is the only hairdresser there."

"When is he coming, with his papers from the hairdressing shop?"

"Very soon."

"Would he be known to me, my hopeful assassin?"

"You knew his sister, you tortured her. There were two Guards that took her to the execution, he shot them in Tehran. The executioner of Tabriz, he blew him up, bomb on a car roof. You'll know him."

"Mr Furniss, what is his name?"

He knelt at the feet of the investigator. His head was bowed down to his knees. From his clothes there was the smell of vomit, in his nose was the smell.

"God forgive me . . ."

"What is his name?"

"Harriet . . . Please, Harriet, forgive me."

"His name, Mr Furniss?"

"Charlie, you can't know what they've done to me . . . the pain, Charlie."

"The name?"

"He's coming to get to you, for what you did to his sister. He's Charlie. His name is Charlie Eshraq."

"We'll get the doctor to you . . . Thank you, Mr Furniss."

14

It was morning. There was enough of a knife line of light at the edge of the plywood over the window to tell Mattie that it was morning, another day. He rolled a little on the bed and his knees were hunched against his stomach as if he still needed to protect himself from the boots and the fists. He could feel the tightness of the bandages around his feet, and there was the irritation of the stitch that the doctor had put into his lower lip. At first he was too frightened to move, because he believed that any movement, any slight movement, would hurt him. With the movements of his muscles and his limbs he was like a man walking in a darkened room, hesitating and testing. He went from his side to his back, and he lay on his back and looked at the ceiling light. The ceiling light was always brilliant, bright enough for him to have to sleep with the blanket pulled over his head. From his back he manoeuvred himself across to his other side. All of his concentration, his determination, had gone into those movements. He had managed the movements . . . He rolled back until his spine was against the mattress. He gazed at the light bulb that was recessed into the ceiling, and that threw a trellis of faint shadows through the mesh that protected it. He closed his eyes. Not bloody much to show for it, a couple of bandages and a single stitch and aches all over his body . . . not bloody much for cracking, for talking. His eyes were squeezed shut. He tried to shut out all that was around him.

Pretty damn easily he'd talked.

More easily than he'd have believed.

Less hurt than he'd have thought possible.

He could move from his side to his back and to his other side and on to his stomach. The pain was . . . to have cracked and not been hurt, that was agony. What had he said? A hazed memory. The memory was of the face of the investigator, and with the eyes of the investigator seeming to plead with him for the telling of it. The memory was of the hair-covered hands of one guard, and the nicotine stains of another guard's fingers, and of the stale sweat smell of their fatigues, and of the rough dirt of their bootcaps. What had he said? There were sounds in his mind. The sounds were of his own voice speaking names. Good names, the names of old friends . . . God, the shame of it . . . God, the bloody disgrace of it . . . It was faint, he could not be sure that he heard the voice. The voice seemed to say the name of Charlie Eshraq. Couldn't be certain, but the voice amongst the confusion seemed to be the voice of Mattie Furniss.

"His name is Charlie Eshraq."

No, no, couldn't be certain, and the memory was misted.

"His name is Charlie Eshraq."

For years in the Service he had used them. They were almost friends to him, almost family, and he'd named them . . . and they hadn't even hurt him so that it lasted. He had his fingernails, and a back he could straighten. He had not been hurt as the Gestapo gaolers had hurt that Lutheran pastor who had come to the Fort and talked of his faith. Shame and disgrace and failure . . . He rolled off the bed. Gently, as if he were frightened, he lowered his feet to the tile floor. He put the weight of his body on his feet. It was as if he wanted to feel pain, as if the pain in his feet would justify his having talked. Of course there was pain, but not enough pain. The pain was sustainable when he put his weight on to the soles of his feet. They wouldn't understand in Century. They had a routine in Century for those who came back – if he ever came back – those who'd talked under interrogation. A debrief and a goodbye. No one wanted to know about a man who had talked. All the successes forgotten. And the irony was that it had been Mattie who had contradicted the Embassy's reports in the late '70s, Mattie who had said the Peacock throne was on shifting sand and would sink. Good reporting, and all for nothing. A debrief for damage limitation and then a goodbye that was cold and without emotion.

He heard an engine revving outside. He struggled to get up from the bed and he pressed his ear against the plywood at the window. The engine dulled the voices, but he recognised the voice of the investigator. There was a place in hell for that man. Mattie Furniss would never forget the voice of the investigator. Then the scrape of the tyres on chip stones and the squealing of a gate. Mattie understood. The investigator would be setting up the surveillance on the field agents. He would return. Mattie tried to calculate how long it would have taken to abort the field agents. He knew the system because he had drawn it up himself. He couldn't keep track of the days any more, should have done, should have scratched a marking for each day on the wall beside his bed. He didn't know whether he'd given them enough time. What he'd been through, that would be a suite at the Ritz compared with what the field agents would suffer in the interrogation rooms at Evin.

Mattie would have whetted the appetite of the investigator, he knew that. He'd be back. They would strip him and gut him of all he knew, and then they would kill him. Stood to reason, they would take their fill of him, and they would dispose of him. They would take him through the kitchen and across the yard, and they would put him against the concrete block wall where the other poor bastards had been put.

In his life he had never known such agony of failure.

If he didn't make it back . . . in time, they'd hear at Century that their man had cracked. Just as the Agency had heard that Bill Buckley, good guy and brave guy, had cracked. The bastards had tortured Buckley and then they sent the tapes of Buckley screaming to Langley. The shit pigs had made sport with Bill Buckley's pain.

He went to the wash basin and he ran the tap, and when the water came it did not matter to Mattie that it was foul-tasting and ditchwater brown.

While the water still dripped from his beard growth he sat on his bed. He waited for them to bring him his breakfast. He would watch each movement of the guards when they brought him his breakfast.

Past six, and Charlie sang in his shower. He felt good. He knew what was the source of his soaring spirits. It was his meeting with Mr Stone, gun runner By Appointment. Stone had taken Charlie's money, and would deliver, because Charlie was the friend of Mr Furniss. He began to realize that the friendship of Mr Furniss was a protective shield to him.

He dressed and packed his rucksack.

He came out of his room quickly. He walked on the corridor carpet on the balls of his feet, and he went quietly, and he could hear the scramble of movement behind the door across the corridor, and he heard the static and the squeal of a radio hurriedly activated. He ran down the fire stairs.

In the lobby he went briskly to the swing doors. He drifted into the street.

Charlie turned, and he went past the line of taxis. At the end of the line was the green Sierra.

The call on the radio, fed into his earpiece, had battered Keeper awake.

Still in the back of the car. He was wrenching the sleep out of his eyes and shaking his head clear. Harlech telling him that Tango One had come out of his room. Corinthian telling him that Tango One had crossed the lobby.

He sat upright. He saw Tango One coming down the line of taxis, and behind Tango One was Corinthian spilling out through the swing doors, and then behind Corinthian was Token, fumbling to get her blouse into her jeans. Why the hell was Token tucking her blouse in? Why the hell did it ever get untucked when she was mounting night surveillance in a hotel room with Harlech? Harlech would be at the back, in the car park, getting the back-up on to the street. Of course Token had to sleep, like he'd slept, silly thought, and fast because the target was closing on his car, striding up past the taxis. It happened, it wasn't desirable, but it sometimes happened, that a target would walk right past the surveillance position, within spitting distance. The routine was to look away, get your face out of his field of vision. Make it look like there was nothing there out of the ordinary.

This was just about the closest that he had been to Tango One, just closer than the one-way window at Heathrow. He turned away. He had yesterday's newspaper in his hands, and his head was away from the pavement, and his body was low in the back seat. All standard procedure.

The car lurched.

The front of the car bucked down.

His eyes opened. Keeper's eyes coming half out of his head. He gazed through the front windscreen at the back of Tango One.

Tango One sat on the bonnet of the green Sierra, and his feet swung close to the nearside front wheel and he was grinning as he looked down and through the windscreen. The fucking Tango was sitting on the bonnet of Keeper's car . . . no standard procedure for that one. Keeper looked into the amused face. Past Tango One he could see Token stop dead in her tracks, and Corinthian behind her.

"Excuse me. He wound down the rear window. "Would you mind getting off my car."

He heard the voice that mimicked his accent. "Excuse me . . . excuse me, would you mind getting off my back."

All the training said that in a show-out then the surveillance team backed off, and fast. Keeper couldn't back off. He was half lying in the back of his car, and the target was comfortable on the bonnet.

Token was twenty yards from the car, and hesitating, and not knowing what was expected of her, and Harlech had stalled his engine and there was a frustrated horn hammering behind him, and Corinthian was cutting through the traffic to get to the far side of the road, which was right. A bitter, raw anger in Keeper.

"Would you mind getting off my car, please."

Again the mimicking of his voice, but this time shouted, "April Five to April One, April Five to April One . . . for fuck's sake come in, please. What a funny little name, April Five."

"Get off."

"Get off my back."

The words were clear in Keeper's memory. There was room for discretion when there had not been an order. But there had been an order. "You do not, repeat not, pull in Tango One." Bill had not said, "You do not, repeat not, put your fist in the target's grin." He climbed out of the car. He felt awkward, stiff, from sleeping in the back seat, and out with him came an empty soft drink can that clattered into the gutter beside him.

"Get the hell off my car, Eshraq."

"Didn't you hear me, April Five? Get off my back."

"I'm going to stay on your back until they close the door on you."

"I don't think so, April Five."

"I'll put you off my car."

"Try."

"Don't think, Eshraq, that Furniss can protect you."

And Charlie Eshraq laughed at him, the flash of wide white teeth.

"Out of your depth, April Five. Heh, April Five, can you swim?"

And he was left. He stood beside the car, and he had to put his hand on the roof of the car to steady himself, and it was not the tiredness that had weakened his legs. He was trembling with rage.

They went through the routine. They watched the target in his seat throughout the journey, as if they hadn't shown out, as if he hadn't sat on the bonnet of the Case Officer's car, as if they knew what they were doing, as if it hadn't been the biggest foul-up any of them could remember.

No one actually asked Keeper what had been said at the green Sierra saloon, because none of them dared. The April team went back to London and half a dozen rows in front of them Charlie Eshraq slept.

Keeper went forward, matching the motion of the train. He caught at the seat heads to balance himself.

His hand brushed the ear of Charlie Eshraq when he went past that seat, and he saw the annoyance curl on the man's face. Didn't give a damn. He was whistling, cheerful.

He went to the buffet. Twelve cans of Newcastle Brown, four whisky minatures, eight packets of crisps, eight packets of roasted peanuts.

He spilled them down on to the table. Harlech looked like he couldn't remember when Keeper had last volunteered his shout, Corinthian looked like it was Christmas morning, Token was grinning.

He sang. Big voice, might have had a trace of baritone, but he didn't know about such things.

> *Eshraq has only got one ball,*
> *His Dad had two but they were very small,*
> *Khomeini has something similar,*
> *But the Shah had no balls at all.*

Heads turned. Business men dropping their pocket calculators and their financial reports, and Eshraq twisting his head to look back at them. "One more time," Keeper shouted.

> *Charlie has only got one ball,*
> *His Dad had two but they were very small,*
> *Khomeini has something similar,*
> *But the Shah had no balls at all.*

And into the decibel joke competition. Loudest laughter wins. Token's was filthy, Harlech's was rugby, Corinthian's was subtle, which meant he couldn't win, Keeper's was Irish. Filth rules. A miniature emptied into Token's second can. They were all laughing, all rating it a hell of a good morning, and Token had her arm looped up and over David's shoulder and she tousled the hair at the back of his neck.

"Well done, big boy."

He looked forward to what he could see of the shoulder six rows in front of him. He looked past the dark suits and the starched shirts and the disapproval.

"Just to let him know that I'll take his legs off at the knees."

"Go home, David."

"I will go home when I know what is happening."

"What makes you think that I know what's happening?"

"That's not an answer, Bill, and you know it."

"It's the answer you'll have to make do with."

"We could have knocked him and you blocked it."

"I told you, David, it was up the mountain from me."

The frustration showed. Park thwacked his right fist into the palm of his left hand. Parrish didn't look as though he were impressed. It was the first time that Park had ever shouted at Bill Parrish, because Parrish was a cuddly old sponge, and shouting at him was blowing bubbles out of the window. Too nice a man to shout at.

"For fuck's sake, Bill, we are talking about a heroin trafficker. We are talking about a heroin distributor. We are talking about a joker who is walking away from major dealing. Since when did that sort of track get a block on it?"

"The instructions to me, the instructions that I passed on to you, were that Eshraq should not be lifted."

"It's criminal, Bill, and you know it."

"Me, I know nothing, and I do what I am told. You should do what you're told and go home."

David Park went to the door. He turned, he spat, "And I thought this was supposed to be a serious outfit, not a comic strip . . ."

"Don't give me that shit, Keeper."

"And I'd have thought you'd have honoured your promise."

"Listen . . . don't pull the old holy number with me . . . listen. The ACIO went to see the Home Secretary last night, said we were ready for a lift. The Home Secretary called him in his beauty sleep. I shouldn't be telling you, but the Home Secretary gave the instruction, that's how high it came from. You want to know what's happening, I want to know what's happening. What I know is that on the top floor the ACIO and the CIO are not available to me. I will be told what is happening when they are ready to tell me, and you will be told when I am ready to tell you . . . So do me that favour and bugger off home . . . Did you ring your missus?"

"He's just a filthy little trafficker . . ."

"I hear he saw you off."

"What the hell . . . ?"

"Merely making an observation . . . Did you ring your missus?"

"He's a cocky little swine."

"And you showed out to him – so go home and take your missus out and buy her a pretty dancing frock."

"Are you going to let them walk right over you?"

"That's a slogan, and that's not worthy of you . . . just go home."

A few minutes later, from his window, Bill Parrish saw David Park on the street below, walking through the traffic like it wasn't there. He thought that he might have destroyed one of his best young men, and he hadn't known how to stem the rot. He called up on the radio. He was told that Tango One was back at his flat. He had two of the April team on the flat, but the soul had gone out of the surveillance and the investigation, and the bugger of it was that no one had felt it necessary to tell Parrish why the block had gone down. Why take it seriously . . . it was only heroin, it was only kids' lives being chucked on the garbage heap, it was only evil bastards getting rich off misery. Why worry? Only bloody fools would worry. Bloody old fools like Parrish, and bloody young fools like Park. He knew that Park hadn't taken any leave for two years, and he hadn't put in for holiday time for the coming summer. He might just book a couple of weeks for the two of them on the Algarve, and handcuff Keeper to his Ann and kick him on to the plane. Could be sentimental, Bill Parrish when he wanted to be. It was a crying shame, that couple was. Another day . . . of course, there would be another day.

One step at a time, sweet Jesus. It was the favourite hymn of Bill Parrish who was a rare Christian once a year, late at night and Christmas Eve. One step at a time, sweet Jesus, the hymn that he liked to hear on the radio when he was in his car. One step at a time . . . and he ought to teach the words to Park, if the youngster hadn't gotten himself run over crossing Holborn and not looking. He rang the ACIO's extension, and was told he was in a meeting. He rang the Bossman's extension, and was told he was in conference. One step at a time, sweet Jesus . . . it was only heroin.

He sat on the floor of his prison room beside the door. He had worked out the angles of vision from the peephole in the door, and he believed that where he sat he was hidden if his guards checked at the peephole before entering. He sat on the floor in his underpants and his vest and his socks. He had used the pillow on his bed and his rolled up shirt and his bunched together trousers to make a shape under the blanket. He always slept with the blanket over his head, to shut out the ceiling light. He had put his shoes at the end of the bed and half covered them with the blanket. A long time he had listened at the door before making the preparations, long enough to satisfy himself that he was not watched.

They had shamed Mattie Furniss, humiliated him. To break that shame he would kill. He would try, damned hard, to kill.

Eventually the Mullah remembered Juliette Eshraq. Not well, of course, but he remembered her.

He had to remember her. If he had not remembered her then he would have been the only living being amongst close to two thousand present at the hanging who had forgotten Juliette Eshraq. The investigator thought it a great spur to memory, his information that the brother of Juliette Eshraq was coming to Iran with an armour-piercing missile on his shoulder, and revenge in his mind.

682

"But you are assured, Excellency, of my best endeavours. It is in my interests, also, that the brother of Juliette Eshraq be found. If he is not found then it is me that he will come for, after he has gone to you."

When he left the Mullah, now very clear in his recollection of Juliette Eshraq who had smiled at the crowd who had come to see her lifted high on the crane's arm, he went to his own office in the capital and there he made the arrangements for the watching of an official in the Harbourmaster's office at Bandar Abbas, and of a merchant in carpets, and of an engineer who repaired broken lorries.

It would be late in the evening before he could catch a military flight back from Tehran to Tabriz.

Go for it, that was the Major's oft-repeated injunction at the Fort. Go for it.

"You go for it, gentlemen, because if you're going to be all namby-pamby then you'll fail, and after you've failed then you'll wish to Christ that you'd never tried. If you like living then you go for it, because if you don't go for it then you won't be living."

Mattie sat on the floor behind the door and he gazed at his made up bed, and he listened for the footfall of the guards bringing him his evening food.

The Major was from Hereford. The Major had grown tired of lying on his belly in ditches in Northern Ireland and branched into consultancy, which paid better and which was safer. It was said of the Major that he had once spent two clear weeks living rough on the fringe of the Creggan Estate in Derry, and that was not a friendly place. The Major advised multi-national companies in the security of their overseas executives, and he came down to the Fort to let the Service know the current thinking on Escape and Evasion. He said that a prisoner must look for the opportunity of escape from the moment of capture. He said that it didn't matter how often the circumstances of imprisonment changed, the captive must be prepared to rip up his plan and start again. And there was another story about the Major. A new high-security gaol in Worcestershire, and the first convicts due to arrive on a Monday morning. The Friday before there had been an escape prevention drill. The Major had been the guinea pig, and he'd been out by the evening; problem was, the Major said he'd been paid to get out, not to tell how he'd done it. Never did tell them . . . Mattie thought of the Major and scratched his memory for every last nugget of what he had been told.

There were low voices on the stairs, and the soft shuffle of sandals.

The bolt was withdrawn, the key was in the door.

15

There was the numbing shock spreading from the heel of his hand. And the body was at his feet.

There was his food tray on the table.

Go for it . . .

Mattie went. Fast and cold, just as the Major had told them. He went out through the heavy door. He went straight at the second guard standing back from the doorway. He saw the surprise wheeling across the face of the second guard, and Mattie's hands were at his throat and his knee rose sharply with all the force Mattie had into the man's groin. No going back because the body of the guard who had carried the food tray was on the tiled floor behind him. The second guard crumpled to his knees. Mattie let go of his throat and brought his knee swinging back into the man's face. His head flew back, struck the wall. One more jerk with the knee to the head now slumped against the wall, and he was almost gone. Mattie dragged him into the prison room and then his hands were closing on the man's throat. The guard picked feebly at Mattie's wrists, and his eyes bulged, and his tongue arced, and his voice choked, and his breath died. The Major had always said it would be easy, if they went for it. Nothing easier than chopping the heel of the hand on to the nape of a man's neck. Nothing simpler than locking the fingers around a man's throat, and taking the pressure on to his windpipe, so that it sealed. His fingers were a tourniquet, and the voice and the breath and the life of the second guard were dying. He felt no fear. He felt only a determination to carry out all that he had been told. The second guard was sinking to the tiled floor, and all the time he looked up and into the face of his killer. Wrong place, dear boy, to come looking for mercy. It had been the second guard who had always smoked and seemed so casual and so indifferent when the real pain was being worked into Mattie's body down in the cellar. Never any mercy in the cellar from you, dear boy. The second guard had his hands on Mattie's wrists, and the stupid, pathetic creature had not had the wit to let go of the hands and to go for the pistol in the holster at his belt. Bad mistake, dear boy. Mattie heard the last choke shudder, and his fingers on the second guard's throat had the weight of the man's corpse.

He dragged the body of the second guard across the tiles and towards the bed.

A hell of a weight, and the tiredness was flooding into Mattie. With his foot he pushed them both under the iron framed bed.

He took the tunic and plimsoll shoes off the bigger of the two guards. The man was taller than Mattie and had the bigger feet, and his plimsolls went on to Mattie's feet over the bandages, and he took the holster belt, and when he had retrieved his own trousers from under the blanket, then he threaded the belt through the loops and put on the tunic. He had the pistol. He checked the breech and the magazine. It was East bloc manufacture and it was a hell of a time since he had last seen a pistol made in Czechoslovakia. He took bread from the food tray, forced it into his trouser pocket along with a chicken piece and a fistful of rice.

Mattie stepped out on to the landing.

He listened. There was a radio playing. He recognized a news bulletin on the radio, the Tehran Home Service, and he could hear low voices. There was no other way. The way out was down the stairs. The pistol stayed in his holster. If he had taken it out then he would have had to spend time learning its mechanisms, he had not that time. The Major had always said that the initial movement was what gave you the chance of escape. He went down the stairs. He stopped at the bottom of the stairs. It was a good house for him. The house had concrete floors under the tiles, and a concrete staircase. No sound as he came down the stairs. The hallway ran the length of the villa, from the front door, and into the kitchen at the back. He paused again, he kept himself flat against the hall wall. Ridiculous, but he was actually listening to the news broadcast, something about the price of long-grained rice. Come on, Mattie, get on with it. He saw the poster of Khomeini in front of him, across the width of the hallway, sellotaped to the wall . . . Up yours, dear boy . . .

The voices that he heard were low, relaxed, and came with the radio from behind a nearly closed door that was opposite to him. The Major had said that the guards who most mattered were the guards that had never been seen by the prisoner. There could be guards outside. Mattie had to accept that there might be guards outside the villa and that he had no idea of their positioning. He was listening, but his ears were filled with the radio broadcast, and the words of the men inside the room. He pushed himself away from the wall and walked past the door, trying to make himself upright. He should have brought the tray, either as disguise or something to throw. He undid the catch on the holster, put one hand on the butt of the pistol and went into the kitchen. No one there. They had already eaten. His own food would have been the last to be prepared. The sink was stacked with plates and with cooking dishes. They'd come soon, perhaps when the radio broadcast was over. They'd wash the dishes and then they'd wonder where were the two guards who had taken the food tray to the prisoner.

Mattie told himself that he was going for the wall in the back yard, he was going and he wasn't stopping. If they were going to stop him then they were going to have to shoot him.

The kitchen was behind him. He had passed through the door and he would have been silhouetted in the doorway. He didn't know a way of going through a doorway, from a lit room and out into darkness, without throwing shadows.

The back yard, beyond the kitchen, was the only area outside the villa that he had seen, and he knew there was a high wall. If there was one guard outside then the likelihood was that he would be at the front, by the gate, but that was the area of chance.

He went on tiptoe across the yard. He had never heard a dog, and he didn't think there was a dog there. The Major had said that dogs were the nightmare of the escaper, but he hadn't heard a dog, not a guard dog nor a pet dog. He went for the wall. He went for the wall where there were the bullet marks in the concrete blocks. If they caught him, if they brought him back, then it would be at the wall that his life would end. He reached up. The palms of his hands and his fingers could just reach the top of the wall.

A terrible pain when he pulled himself up. In his shoulders and his upper back and down to the cage of his ribs. The hurt was from the times that he had been on the hook in the cellar. He struggled to get his feet off the ground, and he scrambled with his knees to give him purchase up the wall. There was a moment when he had his head and his shoulders above the summit of the wall, and then he was balancing on his chest and the pain was excruciating. He could see into a street, and he could see low bungalows.

There were the headlights of an approaching car. The lights played on the centre of the road and lit up the walls of the buildings, and the lights were rushing closer to the wall of the villa, surging towards Mattie who was high on the wall and working to swing his legs on to the top of the concrete blocks.

Behind him, through the open kitchen door, came the signature music of the end of the news broadcast. He knew the music because most days at Century he listened to the recording picked up at Caversham. He thought that if he fell back from the wall then he would never find the strength again that had carried him to the top of the wall, and the music at the end of the broadcast told him there would in a few moments be guards in the kitchen. He had his elbows over the top of the wall, and he ducked his head as low as was possible, and his legs dangled, and the blood and the pain roared in his feet. He waited for the lights to pass, and it seemed to him impossible that the lights would not search him out for the driver. So bloody long. He seemed to hear the shouting in the kitchen, and the stampeding of feet, and he seemed to feel the hands grabbing at his knees and at his ankles and dragging him down.

The lights passed.

Quiet behind him, grey shadow ahead of him.

He heaved himself up and on to the wall. He levered one leg across. He rolled, he slid and fell.

Mattie tumbled eight feet from the top of the wall and down on to the weed verge at the side of the road, and he was winded.

Go for it. It would have taken more than the breath being knocked from his lungs to hold him. He was up and he ran.

He did not know where he was running. Distance was the name of the game. He hobbled down the street, away from the prison gate. Mattie ran for survival and running was risk. He did not know whether there was a curfew in Tabriz, and if there was a curfew then at what time it started. He didn't know where in the city he had been held. He only thought he was in Tabriz.

He ran until the stitch cut into his belly lining. When he saw a café, benches outside, chairs and plastic topped tables inside, he had slowed and crossed to the far side of the road. Where there was a shadow he tried to find it, and he had to skin his eyes to peer ahead of him, hard because his head was shaking from the exertion of running, because it would be fatal to be running and not looking and to barge into a patrol of the Revolutionary Guards.

He ran for a full five minutes. He was 52 years old, and he thought that he had run a mile. He had run on back streets, and he had heard laughter and shouting from inside small homes, and he had heard the voice of a radio announcer reciting verses from the Qur'an.

When he rested, when his legs and his wind had died, he crouched in a concrete storm drain.

Grab any luck that begs to be taken, the Major had said at the Fort. Luck is earned. Luck doesn't show itself that often, and if it's not grabbed then it's gone. He thought of Harriet, and he thought of his girls. The first time this day that he thought of his women tribe at home. They would have expected it of him, and it's for you, my darlings, that I run. No other beacon for Mattie.

A car pulled up in the street, ten paces from him. The driver took a parcel from the back seat of the car and carried it into a house. The engine was left running.

The driver made a gift of a car to Mattie.

Out of the storm drain, into the car. At first very gently away, hardly changing the beat of the motor. And once round the first corner, then he really went at it. He had not driven so fast since the year before he was married, since he had owned the Austin Healey Sprite. No sports car, this, but the bloody thing went, and he drove like there was no tomorrow, and probably there wasn't. He drove away out of the town, until he was surrounded by darkness, and then he stopped and axed the lights. He found a map in the glove compartment.

He was, by his best calculation, between 150 and 200 miles from the Turkish frontier, and by the grace of God, the stars were clear and bright and he was on the north-west edge of the town that he thought must be Tabriz.

The three guards who had been in the house placed the blame in entirety on those two men who had taken no precautions to defend themselves . . . The investigator would have done the same in their position, in his position he would do the same.

The investigator was told that there had been a period of fifteen minutes between the time that the food had been carried upstairs, and the discovery of two comrades, dead in the prisoner's cell.

Furniss had a start. More important was the fear of the guards who had survived. While they had searched the villa a full hour had passed, and only then had they summoned an ambulance. The police had not yet been informed, neither had the army, neither had the head quarters of the Islamic Revolutionary Guards. They had waited for the investigator to return.

It crossed his mind that he could do worse himself than make tracks for the Turkish frontier. But there was too much blood on his hands for him to be welcomed into asylum by the western agencies.

It was like a wound to him, the escape of Matthew Furniss. He had the names of three agents, and the name of an infiltrator, nothing more. He had no detail yet on the running of Century's Iran Desk, on the collaboration between Century and Langley, on the gathering of intelligence from the British listening posts on the frontiers and the American satellites. He should have had hard information on the passing of information from the Americans and the British to Baghdad, and on the battle engagement instructions to Royal Navy warships on the Armilla patrol. He had taken so little, and he had promised so much to the Mullah, and the Mullah would, no doubt, have repeated these promises to his own patrons. Well, he would start again when Furniss was recaptured, as he must be. No one would shelter an English spy in Tabriz. Deep in his gut was the tremor of insecurity, the ripple of the sensation of his own vulnerability.

When he had pieced together the story, he had himself driven to the IRG headquarters in the centre of the city. He gave the commander photographs of Matthew Furniss. He described what he knew him to be wearing when he escaped from the gaol, warned him that Furniss was armed with a pistol.

He wrote out the messages to be sent by radio.

He sent a terse report to the Mullah in Tehran.

He sent a description of Matthew Furniss to the Army Command of the north-west region.

There was no choice but to broadcast his failure over the airwaves.

Mattie had driven out on the Marand road. He had the map, and he reckoned the petrol tank had a minimum of a hundred miles, perhaps more. He would draw attention to himself if he speeded, and if he dawdled then he faced the greater risk of being trapped inside the gun net when the alarm was raised. He took the wide bridge across the Meydan Chay. He rattled past factories that had been idle for years now that the war had soaked the resources of the nation; huge unlit ghost buildings. Just after the road crossed the old railway track that had once carried passengers and exports into the Soviet Union, he swung left off the main road. Any time on the main road had been risk, and he was sure that at Marand, the high oasis town, and at Khvoy, that was a centre of agricultural production, there would be road blocks. The road blocks would not necessarily be for him, but he could not afford to be stopped when he had no papers for the car, and no papers for himself.

The road that he chose was metalled for a dozen miles, then petered out into dirt and stone. The car took a hammering but he would not have need of it for long.

When he was high above the northern shore of Lake Urmia, when he could see the lights of the villages where before the Revolution a good wine had been produced, he saw the road block ahead.

Mattie recognized the block because on the road in front there was a line of tail lights, red, queueing, and he could see a torch being waved. There was a queue. It must be half a mile ahead of him. He was slowing, going down through his gears. He killed his lights . . . he pulled up to a halt. He had used his luck to make good ground away from Tabriz . . . No choice now. It was time to walk. No way of knowing whether this was a block in position to halt him, or just there for routine. He swung the wheel hard to turn in the road.

He hadn't reckoned they would have read the manuals. He hadn't rated that there would be a guard stumbling up from the tree thicket at the side of the road, probably been dozing, probably awakened by the scrape of the tyres on the gravel hard shoulder of the tarmac road. He switched his headlights back on and saw the guard lumbering into the centre of the road. The lights blinded the guard. The guard was old, and under his forage cap there were locks of silvered hair and his beard was down to his throat, he seemed to wave at Mattie while the car was twenty yards from him, only realized at the last moment, in time to raise his rifle, aim the barrel into the heart of the light. Mattie drove straight at the guard.

He felt the shudder blow of the impact. He felt the heave of the bouncing wheels. For what felt many seconds Mattie's heart stopped. He drove, every second expecting a machine gun to sweep his life away. No, that was absurd. Not on this back road. And the odds were that the old man was alone. Should have stayed where he was, fired first, no questions. Perhaps the old man had children or grandchildren who had run from the guards. Past the next corner he saw a track into the trees. He turned on to it and followed it far enough to be hidden from the road and pulled the wheel hard to the left and sank the car into scrub. Out, Mattie, out. He was drained. He would gladly rest in this wood. *Out*, Mattie, the guard's in the road. Right, Major, be right with you.

Mattie took the pistol and the map and got out. He let the dark flood into his eyes. He searched in the car and then in the boot, but there was nothing he could use. He thought of Harriet's boot, first aid kit, blanket, shovel . . . Mattie, get on with it. Coming, Major, just checking.

There was no sign of lights approaching. He walked cautiously towards the dark shadow in the road. The body was still. He suppressed a little jolt of regret for the old man who had not stayed in hiding and shot him as he turned. It's alright, Major, Mattie's not going soft on you. This was a good guard. He may be a dead guard, but he did me a favour. Costly favour, oh yes. And he hauled the body into the trees. Five yards in, rest a minute, ten yards in. Fifteen will do.

He found the rifle. The bolt mechanism was crushed. And there were no rounds in the magazine, and not one in the spout. He carried the rifle to where the guard lay. Poor defenceless old man. If he'd had a round, you stupid cunt, Furniss, you'd be dead. Now, get the hell out of here.

His stomach was empty, he had not yet touched the bread and the chicken and the rice squashed into his pocket, damp on his thigh. On his feet were plimsoll shoes. The mountains were ahead of him, dark against the night sky. He reckoned he had four or five hours of darkness left to him. He walked out of the treeline, took his bearings from the stars and began to climb.

She had had the family row, and forgotten it.

Her case was at the foot of the bed, and her dress was on the floor. Polly didn't care that she had stormed out of the house with her father shouting and her mother crying, and she didn't care that the dress that had cost her £199.95 was crumpled on the floor.

His head was across her stomach, and his beard tickled at her skin, and her fingers played patterns across his shoulders. He had loved her and he'd slept, and he had given her the best evening she had ever had before he took her to his flat. He was a dream when he danced. Polly had never learned to dance, not properly, not until that night when she had been shown the magic of the tango and the rumba. She knew a bit of quick-step and she could waltz if she wasn't watched too closely. She hadn't known that she could dance as she had danced with Charlie. And the meal had been amazing, and the drink had only been champagne, and his attention had been total.

She had forgotten the family row. She had forgotten what Mr Shabro had told her. Must have been jealous, the old goat.

"Have you traced it?" Corinthian asked of his radio.

The reply was in his ear. "As far as we can go . . . but there's a problem. Vehicle Registration say they are not permitted to give out any details on ownership of that registration . . . That's all."

"So, what do we do?"

"Try pretending it isn't there."

"That's daft."

"And that's the best you're getting."

He shivered. He hadn't the engine running so there was no heating. In the passenger seat Token was asleep, and she'd forgotten herself, or she was so hellish tired, because she had let her head slide down on to his shoulder. But he didn't rate his chances. He didn't rate them because all the skirt seemed to want to talk about was goddam almighty Keeper. In the considered view of Peter Foster, codename Corinthian, Keeper was not long of their world, stood to reason. He could not be long with them because the guy was too intense, too tied down by all the shit about winning the narcowar in Bogota, in the Golden Crescent, that sort of shit. Keeper might be the best they had,

690

but it couldn't last. The guy ran too hard. Himself, he paced himself, he wasn't in a hurry, he did his job and he clocked up the overtime, and he thought that he might, just, grow old in Customs and Excise. Keeper wouldn't . . . Keeper was a shooting star, bloody brilliant, and then gone.

It didn't bother Corinthian that the light was going out of the investigation, had been on the slide ever since the order had come through from the Lane that Tango One was not to be knocked. No one from Parrish downwards seemed to know what the fuck was going on, and the target was cocky enough to have gone back to his address like there had never been a problem, like importing heroin and being under ID surveillance didn't spoil his day one bit. Great looking fanny he'd with him, and a great looking bill he'd have run up at the swish joint he'd taken her. The light had gone so far down the hill, over the other side, that Keeper had gone home, been sent home, and they weren't told when he'd be back . . .

She started. She awoke, and then she realized where her head was, and he gave her the evil eye, and she gave him the daggers. She straightened in her seat.

"Bugger . . . I was just about to rape you," he said.

"Oh, do piss off."

"Quite the lady."

"Is it still there?" She turned to look back down the street at the other car. "What's the news on it?"

"No news is permitted on that registration."

She shook her head, tried to get the sleep out of her eyes. "What does that mean when it's at home?"

"It's what they tell you when the vehicle is used by either the Security Service or the Secret Intelligence Service. What confuses me is, are they watching the target, or are they watching us?"

The radio messages, relayed from Tehran, went to military and IRG bases on the western side of Lake Urmia, and to the north. But this was wild and mountain country, an area through which a fugitive could with luck pass undetected and over which no security screen could guarantee success. The lake lies as a huge natural barrier between the Iranian hinterland and the mountain ranges that peak at the Turkish frontier.

The messages were in simple codes. It was not possible to send complicated enciphering to outposts such as Mahabad and Oshnoviyeh and Reza'iyeh and Dilman and Khvoy.

The messages were plucked from the airwaves by antennae at the Government Communications Headquarters outpost at Dhekelia on the island of Cyprus.

He was south of Dilman, too far south to see the lights of the town. Ahead of him were the mountains. His sights were set on Mer Dag, immediately across the border, his 12,600 ft beacon. He had long ago wolfed down the food that he had taken from the prison. Now he was famished. His shoes were disintegrating. He had torn off the sleeves of his shirt, and the sleeves were now bound around the plimsoll shoes to hold them together. He had walked through two complete nights, and when the sun was high, when the lake shore was at siesta, he had walked in the haze heat. All through the daylight hours he could see the summit point of Mer Dag. It was his target . . . There was the ache of hunger in his stomach, there was a numbed death in the muscles of his legs, there was throbbing pain behind his forehead. Stick to the goat tracks, Mattie, and find water. Very well, Major. He would find water. The mountain summit floated in the moonlight ahead of him. He thought that it was too late now to fail.

The Director General was taking breakfast at his desk, his appetite sharpened by the brisk walk over Hungerford bridge.

The door flew open. The coffee slurped over the rim of his cup.

To the Director General, Henry Carter was a most incredible sight. He wore no tie or jacket, no shoes even. Henry Carter had barged into his office, practically brought the door in with him, and now stood panting, obviously unshaven, in front of the desk. The Director General could see the top of the man's vest at his open shirt front.

"He's on the run, sir . . . splendid, isn't it? . . . Dolphin's running."

It was the third consecutive day that Park had been at home, and all of them weekdays. Ann was dressing for work, and late. She hadn't an idea why he had stayed at home, and since he was as tight as a soup tin, she didn't dare ask. He had begun redecorating their spare bedroom – God alone knew why, they weren't awash with overnight visitors. They hardly had any visitors. She thought it was a peace move on his part, and in the evenings she had cooked his meals and tried to remember what he liked, and she'd ironed his shirts, and she'd hidden her feelings in concentration on one television programme after the other.

She had known there was a target, and he had told her that the target was not to be arrested. She didn't know any more than that. And, small mercies, not a squeak about Colombia.

He was still in bed.

They had a sort of routine in bed. She went to bed earlier than him, and she'd pretend that she was asleep when he came in. And he pretended that he acknowledged that she was asleep. The pretence worked until he was asleep, and he wasn't ever long going. She thought that she had never seen him so deeply exhausted. When he was asleep she'd lie half the night on her back with her eyes open, and she could have screamed . . .

He was still in bed and she was dressing in front of the wardrobe. She hadn't shown it to him yet. The dress had cost her what she earned in a week. It was black, full skirt, bare back, a halter at the neck. The dress was as bold as anything she had bought since they had been married.

It was an impulse.

She took the dress from the wardrobe. She held it against her body. She saw that he was watching her.

"For the dance, David . . . Is it OK?"

He said, "It's super."

"You mean that, really mean it?"

A quiet voice, as if the strength had been taken from him. "It's a terrific dress, I really mean that."

"I hoped you'd like it."

"You'll look wonderful."

"We are going, aren't we?"

"Sure, we're going."

"You want to go, don't you?"

"I want to go, I've joined their club."

"David, I'm trying, no riddles, what club?"

He struggled to sit upright in the bed. "The club all the others are in. The club that's worrying about the pension scheme. The club that's ratty about annual leave and days in lieu of Bank Holidays. The club that's serving out time. The club that's given up. I've joined their club, Ann. Entry to the club is when you don't fucking care that a heroin trafficker is running round Central London like he owns the fucking place . . . Yes, we're going. We're going to have a hell of an evening . . . Ann, that dress, it's really brilliant."

She went on with her dressing. "Things will get better. You'll see." And she blew him a kiss as she hurried to be at work.

Mattie had walked until he could not put one leg in front of the other.

He had crawled until he no longer knew where he was going, where he was. The sun beat down on him. He had no food and he had no water. The track was of hot, sharp rock, and he had no more strength and he could not walk on rock and the plimsolls were ripped from his feet. He lay on the path.

Don't panic, Major, just getting the old head down. Just leave me in peace. I'll be better when it's cooler.

For a moment Harriet had forgotten her husband. She put down the telephone. He was a sweet man who lived out on the Cirencester road from Bibury, and one of the few people that she knew who lived in the community for seven days in each week, didn't just commute down at weekends. He had some pull, and he could get things done. He had rung to say that the farmer was bending, and was going to agree to roll a strip across the middle of the ploughed field so that the right of way was intact. It was a little triumph for all of them who had contested the ploughing up of the track. Actually there was no good reason why the old route should not have been re-drawn round the outside of the field, but that would have surrendered the principle. The principle said that the footpath ran across the middle of the field, and it had run there for more than a century, and the principle said that if only one person wanted to walk that path a year then the route should stay unploughed. She revelled in her small triumph. Mattie would have enjoyed . . .

If Mattie had been there, then he would have enjoyed her moment.

So many times they had been separated, and she had never felt such loneliness.

She seemed to shake herself. It was a gesture that was all her own, as if she were shrugging away dust from her shoulders, as if she were hardening her resolve.

She hadn't even told the girls.

The phone rang. The bell was in the hall, recessed into a rafter, and the ringing burst throughout the whole cottage. It was a loud bell so that it could be heard if she and Mattie were out in the garden.

Each time the telephone rang, she expected the worst. There was a couple in Bibury who had lost an only son, a paratrooper, at Goose Green five years ago and in the final push on the Argentine machine-gun nests. They'd sent an officer down from the depot to break the news. She didn't think they'd send anyone down from Century immediately, but she had supposed that the Director General would at least speak to her on the telephone.

She had shaken herself. She was prepared.

"Mrs Furniss?"

She recognized the voice. "It is . . ."

"Flossie Duggan, Mrs Furniss, from Mr Furniss' office . . . I've only a moment. Have you heard anything?"

"I have not."

"Dreadful, they are . . . Mrs Furniss, there's some wonderful news. Well, it's nearly wonderful. Old Carter, that idiot, he told me. He's escaped. Mr Furniss, I mean. He'd been night watch in the Committee's room, and he was so up in the air that he went into the DG's office without his shoes on. Apparently he doesn't wear his shoes at night when he's on duty . . ."

"How extraordinary."

"Indeed, that's rather the tenor of things here nowadays. Oh dear . . . sorry, sorry . . . what'll you be thinking of me. What I meant to say was, yes, that he's escaped, Mrs Furniss. He's on the run, that's what Carter went to tell the DG. It's been picked up by the monitoring people abroad, they listen to everything, they've heard the messages on the radios inside Iran. Mr Furniss has escaped. They're all searching for him of course but the main thing is, he's free."

"But he's still inside?"

"But he's not in his prison, Mrs Furniss. That's wonderful news, isn't it?"

694

"Miss Duggan, you are very kind to call. I am so grateful. What would we do without you?"

Harriet put down the telephone.

She closed the front door behind her. She didn't remember to lock the front door, nor to take with her a raincoat. She walked down to the church, old and lichen-coated stone.

He came out of his stupor because a boot was in his rib cage and was pushing him over from his stomach to his back. The boot was in his ribs as if he were a dog, dead in the road. Mattie saw the gallery of faces above him. They were all young faces, except for one. The one face was cold, without sympathy. A tribesman's face, heavily bearded, and the man wore the loose shirt and the all embracing leather waistcoat and the baggy trousers of the Kurdish mountain people. There was an ancient Lee Enfield on his shoulder. The look on his face seemed to say that if the body had not been on the path, in the way, it would have been ignored. Eight young faces. They were all boys, early twenties, late teenagers. They gazed down on him. They carried packs on their back, or there were sports bags in their hands. He lay on his back, then struggled to push himself upright. He understood. Mattie knew who had found him. A young smooth hand ducked down and pulled the pistol from his waist. He did not try to stop it. Because he knew who had found him he had no fear of them, not even of the tribesman who would have been their guide on the last stage towards the frontier.

Mattie spoke in Farsi.

Would they have the kindness, in the name of humanity, to take him with them?

Would they help him because he had no footwear?

Would they share food with him, because it was more than two days since he had last eaten?

They were nice enough, the boys, they were tense as if it were an adventure, but they welcomed Mattie amongst them, and the guide just spat and grunted in the Kurdish patois that Mattie had never mastered. The guide now had the pistol.

Mattie was given bread and sweet cheese, and he was allowed to sip from a water bottle before the impatience of the guide overwhelmed the anxious care of the boys. Two of them helped him to his feet and supported him, his arm across their shoulders. Damn good kids. And heavy going for the kids, with Mattie as their burden, and the track was wild, difficult, damn bloody awful. He saw butterflies, beautiful and vivid, beside the path, on flowers that he did not know from England. He saw high above them the winter snow that was still not melted. They passed through thick forest that had taken root where there seemed to be only rock and no soil. They went down into gullies and waded through ice cold torrents, and they climbed razor rocks out of the gullies. Mattie was no skeleton. They were struggling, all of them, and particularly those two who supported Mattie. The guide didn't help them. The guide was always ahead, scouting the route, sometimes whistling for them to come forward faster. Without them he would have been finished. Probably would have frozen to death, carrion for beasts of the mountain.

They wanted to know who he was, of course, and at first he had made a joke of it and told them that he was in Iran to sell tickets for the World Cup finals, and then he had said quietly and between the spurts of pain when his feet hit the rocks on the track, that he was like them, that he was a refugee from the regime. Some of them spoke English, some came from the sort of household in Tehran where English could be taught with discretion. They were dodging the draft. He knew that long before they told him. They were the kids from rich families who couldn't bear to give their offspring up to the butchery in the trenches outside Basra. They'd have paid through the nose for the guide, and some would have more money in belts around their waists for after they had an entry visa to California or Paris from Turkey. They'd learn, Mattie thought. They'd join the wretched flotsam in the refugee camps, and they'd learn the hard way that Turkey didn't want them, that America and France didn't want them. One thing was pretty damn certain in Mattie's mind. The two boys who had manhandled him up the rock slope, levered him down the track, carried him across the fast streams – he'd do his uttermost to get them visas into the United Kingdom. They told him, those who carried him, that they were going to make for Hakkari, that they had heard there was a refugee centre at Hakkari administered by the United Nations. They said that once they had reached the camp there they could send telegrams to relatives who were already living in the United States. They thought that their relatives would be able to fix the visas. Had their friend ever been to America?

They came to a ridge. The snow-peaked summit of Mer Dag was away to their right. The guide had stopped, was crouched down. They struggled the last paces to reach him, and Mattie had swung his arms off the shoulders of the two boys.

The sun was crisp in an azure sky above them.

The bandages, mud brown, trailed from Mattie's feet. No pain now in his feet.

The guide pointed below.

There was a path snaking down from the ridge and in the far distance was the sprawl of a small town, and running further away from the town was a twisting road. It was Turkey.

And the guide was gone. He gave them no farewells. There was no hugging, no slapping of hands on the back of the guide. He was just gone, loping away down the path that they had just climbed. Mattie felt the moistness in his eyes. He had taken his luck, and he was within sight of home. The tears came, rolled on his bearded cheeks. And around him the elation bubbled.

"Wait, wait . . . wait . . ." His arms were around the shoulders of two of the boys and they had his weight between them. He spoke slowly, so that he could be translated by those who understood him. Too important, he didn't trust himself in Farsi. "How are you going from here?"

"We are going down the hill."

"We are going to the refugee centre."

Mattie said, "You must, you must absolutely go down the hill by night."

"We have nothing to be worried of, Mister."

Mattie said, "You must wait until nightfall." He tried to summon his authority.

"And you?"

"Different, I'll get down on my own . . . now be good lads." Mattie said.

"Mister, you cannot even walk."

"I'll roll down if I have to, but you should go by night. Let me go ahead and prepare the people on the other side to expect you – their army patrols."

They were all giggling at him, and they were no longer listening to him. They were the children that he knew so well from his own house, and from the homes of every one of his contemporaries, children who thought their parents were half-witted. He was hoisted up.

"I really do urge you . . ." But they had no patience for him. They were too happy. They went down the slope. The wind cut at their clothes, deadened their ears. The pain welled in his legs, but he shrugged away the hands that offered to help him. He had started on his own and he would damn well finish on his own. There you are, Major, we made it and we will have a long night's carousing over this adventure, you and I. They were coming down the slope fast. Darling, he thought he heard Harriet cry out. Darling. They were strung out in a line.

"*Dur . . .*"

The shout in the clear air.

Mattie saw them.

"*Dur . . .*"

He thought they were paratroops. Toughened, hard men. Weapons that were aimed as if their use was second nature. He saw five at first, blocking the track down the slope. He knew a little Turkish, and the word to halt would have been clear enough if he had known nothing. He didn't have to be a linguist. There were more of the patrol at the flanks now. Guns covering them. Mattie raised his hands. His hands were high above his head. His mind was clear. There might be officials of the United Nations at Hakkari, but there would be no officials of the United Nations High Commission for Refugees on the upper slopes of Mer Dag. He looked for the officer.

He pushed his way past a rifle barrel. He had the authority now. He was filthy and he could barely hobble without support, but he had been commissioned in the Coldstream Guards, and for a few weeks in his life he had been a junior commander of the Sovereign's guard at Buckingham Palace. He knew how to deal with soldiers.

He saw the tabs on the officer's shoulder, the American-style bars. He would understand English if it were spoken slowly and loudly.

"Good afternoon, Lieutenant. My name is Furniss. I am an official of the government of Great Britain. I am in flight from Iran, and I ask for your help. Should you wish to confirm my identity then you should radio back to your headquarters and tell them to contact my Embassy in Ankara, Mr Snow . . ."

He was waved forward. He was trying to walk upright, with dignity. He thought the officer had a good bearing, might have been on a NATO exchange course. He passed each of the young men, the draft dodgers, the refugees, the flotsam.

"Now, most important, any help that you can afford these boys, Lieutenant, my government will be grateful for it. Without their assistance I would not have been able to cross your frontier. I ask you to treat them with compassion."

The officer looked through him. He gave orders, sharp and clear commands. A corporal was at Mattie's arm, and leading him further down the slope. When he looked back he saw that the boys had been corralled by rifle barrels and were sitting hunched on the track. Mattie was taken forward, whether he wanted to go or not. At the edge of the track, Mattie stopped. He resisted the tug of the corporal's hand on his sleeve.

"What are you going to do with them?"

The officer gestured, in annoyance, to his corporal. Mattie was forced off the track and into thorn scrub. He had been taken from sight. He sat on the earth, and his head was buried between his knees.

He saw the officer take from his belt a Very pistol. He saw the burst of colour high above him. Afterwards he heard the officer shouting on the radio.

It might have been fifteen minutes later, it might have been half an hour, it might have been his lifetime, and between the foliage and sprigs of the thorn Mattie saw the patrol of Revolutionary Guards approach carefully down the slope. The refugees were prisoners, they were given into the custody of their own people. They didn't struggle, no one broke away and ran. They went meekly.

"They are scum," the Lieutenant said. "And they bring into my country drugs and crime."

"They saved my life, goddammit," Mattie said.

"You could have gone back with them."

He had not argued. He had not jeopardized his own safety. He thought that it would be a long time before he forgot the laughter of the boys at the warnings of an old man, and he thought that the Major would have wondered what all the fuss was about.

An hour later the radio crackled to life. Orders from headquarters. The biggest man in the patrol, a giant of a man, lifted Mattie on to his shoulders and tucked Mattie's thighs over his arms, and carried him like a child under the sinking sun, away down the slopes of the Mer Dag.

16

Houghton did the opening, not that successfully, and the first cork careered into the ceiling of the Director General's office and chipped the plasterwork.

Champagne, and a good vintage, the PA had been sent out with a wad of notes from the Director General's wallet. Must have run all the way back with it.

The occasion called for the best.

"I said he'd surprise us all . . . not quite true, I said he'd surprise a lot of people. I had faith in him. Always the way, yes? Just when life seems darkest the sun blesses us. I tell you what – Furniss is a real hero. You can have your soldiers doing daft things and getting medals for what they've achieved in the heat of battle, no harm in that, but Furniss has done it on his own. Can you just imagine how the chaps are going to be feeling back in Tehran, all of those unshaven baskets? They'll be slitting each other's throats . . . A toast to Mattie Furniss . . . I'll bet he feels like a million dollars right now."

The Deputy Director General muttered, "He hasn't been on a Fun Run, Director General."

Ben Houghton said, "I can't get a link through to him. We expect that the Turkish military will have taken him down to Yuksekova, they've a base there. Crisis Management have been trying to patch through a line, but they can't make it through. Pretty soon now he'll be airlifted to Ankara."

The Director General beamed, "There's a hand that I am much looking forward to shaking."

"The debrief comes first," the Deputy Director General said. "He'll be sanitized until his debrief is complete, that's the way things are done."

"So when do I get to congratulate him?"

"When he's debriefed, and after the debrief there'll be the Inquest."

"You are one hell of a killjoy, you know that. You're a real damp rag."

"It's no more or less than Mattie would expect. We debrief him on what's happened, who held him, and then we hold the Inquest as to how he was in a position that left him so vulnerable. Mattie'll know the form. My view, he's likely to be scarred for rather a long time, that's just my personal opinion."

"He's done bloody well."

"Of course he has."

"And I'll not have him harassed."

"No question of him being harassed, Director General, just debriefed."

The Deputy Director General proffered his glass to young Houghton. He refilled his own glass, and then the Director General's and the DDG had the last of the bottle. If the Director General ever stumbled under a Number

Nineteen Omnibus, and the Deputy Director General moved into this office, that young man would be out on his neck, damn fast.

The DDG knew the answer, but he still asked the question. "Have we spoken to Mrs Furniss?"

Ben Houghton said, "She's been out ever since the news came through, no answer on either of her phones. She hasn't been forgotten."

"Well done, Furniss. This calls for a second bottle, I think, Ben. Damned shame that we aborted the network, but at least we can move Eshraq."

The Deputy Director General frowned, then the smile caught his face. "Forgive me, I may have sounded churlish . . . Good old Mattie . . . he's been terrific. I don't think it would be out of order for you to meet him off the plane if that's what you'd like . . . Director General. Again, forgive me, but I want you to understand that labelling Furniss a hero may well, will almost certainly, be somewhat misplaced. He will have talked, and this whole expedition has cost us a network. Realistically it all adds up to Dunkirk, not to the Normandy landings."

"I'm wagering that he'll have surprised you."

"Also, we may not have aborted our people in time. I can show you the photographs from Kermanshah when the MKO moved out and the Mullahs came back in, if you would like to see them. The hangings were photographed. Mattie getting himself captured was only one inevitable step away from a death sentence for our field agents, even, you may console yourself, if the signals to bring them out had been sent without delay."

"They may well come out, and Mattie may well not have talked, in which case perhaps, who knows, they can go back in again."

"We're not talking about Bond or Biggles, Director General, we are talking about one man against a very sophisticated team of torturers. We are talking about a regime that will do unspeakable things to their own people, and who won't have cared a toss what is done to a foreigner."

The Director General said, "I am at a loss to know what you want."

"I would want to know whether Eshraq is compromised before we let him go back."

"My money is on Mattie, and I'll drink to him."

And between the three of them they killed the second bottle.

It might have been the sense of guilt that had dogged the Station Officer ever since he had left Mattie Furniss unprotected in Van, but he most certainly made wheels turn now. From the moment that the Military Attaché at the Embassy had passed on the news of the refugee Furniss falling into the hands of a patrol near the border in Hakkari province, Terence Snow had wheedled facilities from his contacts. An official in the National Intelligence Agency had earned a handsome gift.

Mattie sat beside the road.

He had a paratrooper's smock draped over his shoulders, and a medic had cleaned his feet and then bandaged them, and a colonel had loaned him a stick to help himself along.

The road was the airstrip. It ran along a shallow valley between Yuksekova and Semdinli. The road was widened and reinforced and provided a facility for fixed wing to land in all weathers, night and day, and had been built to further military operations against guerillas of the Kurdish Workers' Party.

There were lights laid out, fired by portable generators, and the area where Mattie sat was illuminated by the headlights of military jeeps and trucks. He sat on an old ammunition box. He was a source of interest to the soldiers, they were crowded behind his back, silent and watchful. They gazed at him with a fascination because they knew that he was an Englishman, and they knew that he had walked out of Iran, and they knew from the medic that the soles of his feet were cut and horribly swollen from beatings. He had lost that sense of exhilaration that had gripped him when he had stood on the ridge looking down into Turkey. He was overcome with exhaustion. Of course he was. He could still see in his mind the picture, cruelly sharp, of the Revolutionary Guards coming down the slope and the boys being escorted at gunpoint up the slope. And there was Charlie, and there were his agents. He wanted only to sleep, and he declined food. The last food he had eaten, before the ridge, had been the boys' food freely shared with him.

The Hercules C–130 came down on to the road, a noisy and jolting landing, and the reverse thrust was on from the moment the wheels touched. The aircraft taxied towards the knot of soldiers, and when it turned Mattie had to shield his face from the flying grit thrown up from the hard shoulder by the four sets of propellors. The pilot kept the engines idling while Mattie was helped up the rear loading ramp. It was only when the aircrew had fastened his seatbelt for him that he realized that he had forgotten to thank the paratroop officers for their hospitality. He waved as the loading ramp was raised, but he couldn't tell whether they would have seen. On full power the Hercules lifted off, then banked heavily to avoid a shoulder of the Samdi Dag, then climbed for cruising altitude. They were three hours in the air. He was offered orange juice from a paper carton and a boiled sweet to help his ears during the descent to Ankara, otherwise the aircrew ignored him. They were taking him back from a nightmare, returning him to the world that he knew.

They were on a military airfield. They were parked beside an executive eight seat jet. On the jet were the roundels of red and white and blue.

The Station Officer made no secret of his emotion. He hugged Mattie.

"God, Mr Furniss, you've done magnificently well. and the Director General said for me to tell you . . ." He recited, " 'Warmest personal congratulations on your epic triumph.' "

"Very decent of him."

"You came through, Mr Furniss, I can't tell you how pleased I am, how proud I am to know you."

"Steady, Terence."

"You're a hero, Mr Furniss."

"Is that what they think?"

"Of course. They had the whole army out trying to catch you and you got clean through them. You beat the bastards."

"Yes . . . What about my agents?"

"All I know is that the abort signals were sent."

"But are they out?"

"That I don't know. I'm very sorry, Mr Furniss, but I've been ordered not to attempt any sort of debrief on you. That's the usual form, I suppose."

Snow took Mattie's arm and led him to the steps of the executive jet, and a nurse came down them and took over and grabbed firmly at his arm and hoisted him on board, and when he ducked into the interior there was an RAF corporal to salute him, and through the open door of the cockpit he saw the pilot leaning sideways so that he could wink at Mattie, and give him the thumbs-up. He was strapped into a seat, back to the driver, always the way of RAF flights, and Snow was opposite him, and the nurse was peeling off the bandages from his feet, even before they took off, and there was a look on her face that suggested that no one could be trusted with medical hygiene but herself. The plane had come from Cyprus, from the Sovereign Base at Akrotiri. They roared away into the night, lifted sharply, as if the pilot would have preferred to be at the controls of a Tornado strike plane.

Terence Snow kept his silence. That was the way of things when a Service man came back from captivity. Nothing should interfere with the debrief, standard operating procedure. When the nurse had unwound the bandages of the Turkish army medic, when she had examined the puffed, welted soles of Mattie's feet, then he saw the frown settle on her already stern forehead, and he saw the Station Officer wince. The nurse took off his shirt, tugged it off him, and her lips pursed when she saw the bruising at the base of his shoulders. The swollen feet and the bruised shoulders brought a gentleness to the nurse's fingers, and a gaze of youthful worship from the boy. He could have wiped the gentleness out of her fingers, and the adulation from his eyes. He could have told them that he was a fraud. He could have shouted inside that small aircraft cabin, going home at 550 surface miles per hour, that the Service's hero had cracked and talked.

They put down at the Royal Air Force base at Brize Norton in the small hours of the morning.

He was helped down from the aircraft and into a waiting ambulance, a lone vehicle on the huge airfield. He was driven to the Base hospital.

The Director General was waiting for him, and his hand was pumped.

"Bloody good show, Furniss. Welcome home. It's a Red Letter day for all of us."

They ran an electrocardiogram test. They asked him for a urine sample and then put him in the lavatory where there was a bag under the seat because they required his stool to check for typhoid or dysentery. They X-rayed his feet and his chest and his shoulders. They did blood tests on him for signs of vitamin deficiency. They were brisk and methodical and quick, and Mattie saw that the form they filled in with the results of the examination and the tests was blank at the top, at the space provided for the patient's name. Over the new bandages on his feet they gently fitted plastic slippers, and they told him he should see his dentist within the next week.

The Director General was waiting for him in the reception area. He beamed at him. Mattie grinned back, ruefully, like a man embarrassed by all the attention.

"Well, Furniss, I don't know what the devil you've been up to since we last saw you. I expect it will make a superlative story and one which the Prime Minister will not want to see published, dear me, no, but you'll dine with us when you're up to snuff, I do look forward to that. Messages of deep esteem from Downing Street. Should have said so at once. And Mrs Furniss. I expect you'd like to put through a call before you leave here. Snow, arrange that will you? Then you'll be off to Albury for a day or so, Furniss, just to get it all off your chest, but you know all about that."

"My field agents . . . ?"

"Steady down, old chap. You worry about yourself, leave the others to us. Carter's coming down, he'll tell you what you need to know about your agents. It's been a wonderful show, Furniss. I said you would surprise us all. But I mustn't keep you from the telephone . . . Well done, Furniss, first class. The Service is very proud."

From the road outside they could hear the telephone ringing.

The telephone had rung three times while Parrish and Park had sat in the car.

It was ringing again as the woman drove past them and then swung sharply to pull into the drive at the side of the cottage.

And as soon as she had her door open she was hearing the telephone ringing, because she was out of her car like a rabbit, and she hadn't bothered to close the car door, and she'd left her keys in the front door.

Park started to move, but Parrish's hand rested lightly on his arm.

"Give her a moment."

It had been Parrish's initiative, the drive to Bibury. No warning, just pitching up at Park's address, waiting for Ann to leave, then coming to the door. Park had already started on the spare bedroom ceiling, and he hadn't been given time to clean the paint off his fingers.

"We'll just give her time to answer. I'm out of line, but I might just be past caring. It's all too ambiguous for a simple soul like me. I have a direct order that Tango One is not to be lifted, and yet I am ordered to maintain a low level surveillance on him – I don't know what that adds to . . . I am told that we will get no help in locating Mr Matthew Furniss but the ACIO is not telling me that I cannot approach Furniss. If it adds up to anything it is that on the top floor of the Lane they haven't a clue what we're supposed to be doing. I'm pushing my luck, David, because I don't appreciate being pissed on. So, if I get my wrist slapped, and you get your butt kicked, then it's all in a good cause . . . Come on."

They stepped from the car.

"I'll do the talking," Parrish said. "You can give her the keys."

He smiled, a real hangman's smile. He reached for his wallet in his inside pocket. When he knocked on the door he had the wallet open so that his identification card was visible.

She came to the door.

She was radiant.

Park handed her the keys, and Parrish showed the ID and she grinned at the keys, like a small girl.

"Mrs Furniss?"

"Thrilling, isn't it? Do come in. It's quite wonderful. I suppose they sent you down when I wasn't answering the phone. I've been at my elder daughter's . . . You've come all the way from Century, a wasted journey? You'll have a cup of coffee before you go, of course you will. I suppose really I should be opening the champagne, the DG said that he opened champagne last night. He said the whole Service was proud of Mattie, that's a splendid thing to have said of your husband . . ."

"When will Mr Furniss be home?"

"You will have coffee, I'm so excited, do come inside . . ." She had stepped aside, then stopped, spun. "You should know when he's coming home."

Parrish asked calmly, "Did you look at my ID?"

"You're from Century, yes?"

"Customs and Excise, ma'am, Investigation Division."

Her voice whispered, "Not Century?"

"My name is William Parrish, and I am investigating heroin trafficking from Iran. My colleague here is Mr Park."

Her hand was across her mouth. "I thought you were from my husband's office." She stiffened. "What did you say you want?"

"I'd like to know when I can interview your husband."

"What about?"

"In connection with a guarantee given by your husband to a man now under investigation."

She barred their path. "We don't know anyone like that."

"Your husband knows a Charles Eshraq, Mrs Furniss. It's about Eshraq, and your husband standing guarantee to him that we've called."

She stared up from her eyeline that was level with the knot of Parrish's tie. "Have you been through Century?"

"I don't have to go through anyone, Mrs Furniss."

"Do you know who my husband is?"

Park could have smiled. Parrish wasn't smiling. He would be later, right now he had his undertaker's calm.

"Your husband is the guarantor of a heroin trafficker, Mrs Furniss."

"My husband is a senior civil servant."

"And I serve my country too, Mrs Furniss, by fighting the importers of heroin. I don't know what threat your husband safeguards us from, but where I work the threat of heroin coming into the UK is taken pretty seriously."

She was shrill. "You come here, you barge into my house, you make preposterous allegations about a boy who is virtually a son to us, on the morning that my husband has just returned home after breaking out of an Iranian torture gaol."

"So he's not here at present?"

"No, he isn't here. I should think he will be in hospital for a long time. But if he were here, Mr Parrish, you would be terribly sorry you had had the disgraceful manners to break into this house . . ."

Parrish said, "Maybe it's not the best time . . ."

She went to the hall table. She picked up the telephone. She dialled fast.

Her voice was clear, brittle. "This is Harriet Furniss, Matthew Furniss' wife. I want to speak to the Director General . . ."

Park said, "Come on, you disgraceful person, time we barged out."

They left her. When they were at the gate they heard her voice rise in anguished complaint. They reached the car.

"Shall I serve my country and drive?"

"I tell you what, Keeper, that wasn't one of my happiest initiatives, but we did shake the nest."

He had spoken to the Prime Minister, and the Prime Minister had asked after Mattie Furniss and said he must be a quite remarkable man, and the DG bathed in reflected glory. He looked forward rather keenly to the first of the debrief papers that would be coming through in a couple of days, and he would certainly send a digest across to Downing Street. Now he was making a tour, being seen, as he put it to Houghton.

They were in that section of the third floor occupied by Assistance (Photographic) when he was passed a telephone by Ben Houghton. For a moment he was puzzled. He had spoken to the woman at breakfast time.

He listened.

"No, no, Mrs Furniss, you were quite right to reach me . . . intolerable behaviour. Rest assured, Mrs Furniss, you won't be troubled again."

The four wooden packing cases and the two cardboard boxes were the first items to be loaded into the container. The lorry had backed into Herbert Stone's driveway. He gave the driver a manifest for the packing cases that listed Machine Parts for Agricultural Equipment. Later the container would be filled with more machine parts for tractors and refrigeration units. The haulage company was a regular carrier of machine parts to Turkey.

When the lorry had left he went inside his house, and into the quiet of his work room. He telephoned the number Charlie Eshraq had left him and told him that the soap was on its way, and he gave him the name of a contact, and where he should go and when.

"I tell you, Bill, it wasn't sensible behaviour."

"If you want London to become like Amsterdam, Chief, then sensible behaviour would be the order of the day."

"And I don't want a press office handout."

"My guys have worked their balls off, we just don't like to see it go down the plug hole."

Parrish had been at the Lane for one and a half years longer than the Chief Investigation Officer, and for two and a half years longer than the ACIO. He rarely spoke his mind. When he did he could get away with murder.

The ACIO said, "If you'd come to us first, Bill, cleared it with us . . ."

"You wouldn't have let me go."

The CIO was hunched forward in his chair, elbows on his desk. "There's another way of looking at it, Bill. We are stretched so damn thin that in effect we are a fraud. We intercept a minute proportion of what's brought in. I know that, you know that . . . When you are losing the battle, as we are, then we need friends where friends matter . . ."

"You have to go for the throats of the bastards and hang on."

"It's a great world that you live in, Bill, and it's not a world I see much of across this desk."

"So, who are the friends we need?"

"They're the high and the mighty . . . and right now they're peeved with you."

"I just gave the nest a little shake."

"Very self-indulgent of you, Bill, and no help to me, because I am summoned to a meeting this afternoon with the faceless wonders at Century House. What do I tell them, Bill?"

"To get fucked."

"But my world isn't your world, more's the pity, and I'm looking for friends . . . I have one man in Karachi, one DLO on his ownsome, and when he goes up to the North-West Frontier, who escorts him? The spook escorts him, and drives the Landrover. Why does my DLO ride in the spook's Landrover? He rides in it because I don't have the funds to provide a Landrover of our own. I have one DLO in Cyprus, and how does one man get to know what's coming out of Jounieh, how does he know what's sailing from any Lebanese port? Cyprus is awash with spooks . . . I am trying to cultivate friends, Bill, not shake the nest and telling them to get fucked."

"I promised Park, and he's the best I have, that I wouldn't let your friends the faceless wonders stand in our way."

"Then you opened your big mouth too wide. Tell us about your Keeper,

Bill. We begin to hear quite a lot about Master Park. Is he ready for a move upwards, do you think?"

"We're going to have a celebrity on our hands," the Director General mused.

"How so?"

"I anticipate great mileage out of Furniss. They'll want him at Langley. The Germans'll want him, and I dare say even the French will recognize that they could learn a thing or two."

The Deputy Director General said coolly, "I'd put that out of your mind for a start. If I were in this office, I would make double damn certain that no one outside this building gets to know that we allowed a Desk Head to plod about on a hostile frontier without a semblance of security. It'll get out sooner or later, of course. As like as not Tehran will be drafting a press release even as we sit here: Why We Let British Spy Go, and, by the way, not a few people will be wondering already."

The Director General scowled. "I don't mind telling you that I told Furniss that the whole Service was proud of him."

"Not clever . . . I'm going to run a fine toothcomb over Terence Snow. The report on how Mattie came to get himself kidnapped is pretty conclusive. Indeed, I doubt that he has any sort of future here. He'll have to go back to Ankara in the short term. There may just be a way he can be useful to us in the short term."

"You're a hard man."

"I am what the job requires."

The snort of the Director General, "And Furniss, has he a future?"

"Very probably not, I am afraid."

The Deputy Director General reported that a man had been sent down to Bibury with the instruction to break the bones of any Customs Investigation creature who came within a hundred yards of the Furniss cottage, and he said that he would be at the Director General's side at the meeting with the Customs hierarchy.

"What sort of people will they be?"

"I expect you'll be able to charm them, Director General. Think of them as glorified traffic wardens."

He had no doubt that his life depended upon the success with which he stood his ground against the inquisition of the clerics.

Ranged on the far side of the table to him were four of them. They were the power and the glory of the Revolution of today, and once he would have called them fanatics and bigots. They were the ones who had been to *maktab* where the Mullahs taught the Qur'an to boys aged four, and then they had become the *talabeh* who were the seekers after truth as handed down from the wisdom of the Ayatollahs. They had taken child brides because it stated in the book that a girl should not experience her first bleeding at her parents' home. They had spent time in the holy city of Qom. It was the failure of the SAVAK that these creatures still existed. They were his masters. He claimed that he had already bled the British spymaster dry before his escape. He told them of the young Eshraq, and they were quiet as he explained the mission of Eshraq, heading back towards Iran, and they heard of the precautions that were in hand to prevent the traitor crossing over the frontier with armour-piercing missiles. He said that Eshraq's first target was the Mullah who sat immediately in front of him. He saw the way that the others turned sharply to the one amongst them who had been singled for attack, and he told them that he, himself, was the target that would follow.

For more than an hour and a half he defended himself, and at the end he told them of his arrangements to prevent Eshraq crossing the border.

It was implicit in his argument that if he were removed, if he were sent to Evin, then the shield in front of his masters would have been dismantled.

The life of Charlie Eshraq would safeguard the investigator's life. Nothing more, nothing less.

He had flown back to Tehran from the Gulf that morning to resume work at the new power station to the west of the city.

He browsed in the bazaar. He was on the Bazar e Abbas Abad, amongst the carpet shops.

He paused. He could not linger for more than a few seconds. In front of him were the heavy steel shutters, and fastening them to the concrete paving was a powerful padlock. His eye caught that of the man who stood in front of the next cavern of carpets, open – and the man ducked back into his shop. There was no sign, no explanation of why this one business should be shut. If there had been illness, if there had been bereavement, then he would have expected an explanation from the merchant's neighbour.

He walked on. He walked into the warmth of the sunlight beyond the bazaar's alleys. He took a taxi back to his hotel, and in his basin he burned the message that he had been paid to carry.

Henry was late getting down to Albury.

Everyone who knew Henry Carter, which wasn't many, had told him that he should dump the Morris 1000 Estate on the nearest Corporation tip and failing that at the side of any road, and buy something reliable. Trouble again with the carburettor.

He was late getting down to Albury, and Mattie had already arrived, and the men who had brought him from Brize Norton were fretting to be on their way. He ignored the show of annoyance as he struggled through the front door with his bag and his Wellington boots and two weatherproof coats, binoculars, camera with a long lens, and tape-recorder. Typical of the sort of youngster they recruited into the Service now, neither of them offered to help, and they scarcely bothered to report that Mattie was in one piece, sound asleep now, before they were off.

There weren't many of them, the old brigade, left at Century these days, and it was obvious that the Director General would have wanted one of the long servers to be down at Albury to take Mattie's debrief. He would not have called himself a friend of Mattie Furniss, rather a colleague.

He looked back through the front door. He had heard the call. He was festooned with his gear. He saw the bird. *Picus Viridis*. The Green Woodpecker was halfway up a dead elm across the lawn. There would be gaps in the debrief for him to set his camera on a tripod, and to rig his microphone. He went inside. It would be something of a reunion for him, coming back to the country house in the woodland of the Surrey hills. Mrs Ferguson greeted him. She was rather a dear woman, the housekeeper, and there had been a time when he had actually thought of making a proposal of marriage to her, but that was quite a long time ago and he had been at the house for weeks on end. It was her cooking that had settled it. It was awful. She pecked his cheek. He saw George behind her, hovering at the kitchen door. George touched his cap. He wore a cap always now, since the baldness had set in, wore it even in the house. A loyal fellow, George, but lazy, and why not, with so little to do. Through the kitchen he could see that the outside door was closed, and the door shook and there was ferocious scratching from the far side of it.

"Am I not to be greeted by old 'Rotten'?"

George grinned. "Your gentleman doesn't like dogs, and he certainly doesn't like Rottweilers."

Not many did. Henry had a fear of some men, and of most women, but of no animal, not even an animal that weighed more than a hundred pounds and was famously unpredictable.

"Then make sure the brute's kept clear of him."

He had to smile . . . Wouldn't do for Mattie Furniss to have fought his way out of an Iranian prison only to find himself savaged by the safe house Rottweiler. He looked around him. He could see the glimmer of fresh paint on the woodwork and the carpet in the hall had been cleaned. Things were looking up.

"Where is he?"

"He's just come down. Been asleep ever since he got here. He's in the library."

He left George to carry the bag and his kit upstairs. He hoped that he would have his usual room, the one that overlooked the vegetable garden where the songbirds gathered to feed off the groundsel and dandelion seeds.

He walked through to the library. His feet echoed on the bare board floor. It had been a bare board floor since the pipes had burst in the freeze of three winters before and the carpets had been ruined and not replaced. He opened the door. He was almost obsequious. He went on tiptoe into the room. To call the room the library was somewhat overstating the case. Of course, there were books on the shelves, but not many, and few of them would have held anyone's interest. The books had been a job lot when a local house had been cleared out on the death of a maiden lady without surviving relations.

Mattie was in a chair by the empty hearth.

"Please, don't get up, Mattie."

"Must have just nodded off."

"You deserve a very long rest . . . I mean, what a change . . . where were you, Mattie, 24 hours ago?"

"Walking out of Iran, I suppose. It's pretty strange."

"You've spoken to Mrs Furniss?"

"Had a few words with her, thank you. Woke her up at first light, poor thing, but she was in good form . . . Flapping a bit, but don't they all?"

"There's grand news through from the medics. A very good bill of health, no bugs."

"I just feel a bit shaken."

Henry looked into Mattie's face. The man was completely shattered.

"I'll tell you something for nothing, Mattie. . . . In twenty years' time, when the DG's been forgotten, when no one at Century will know my name, they'll still talk about 'Dolphin's Run'. Dolphin's run out of Iran is going to go into the history of the Service."

"That's very decent of you, Henry."

"Don't thank me, you did it. The fact is that the Service is buzzing with collective pride. You have given us all, down to the tea ladies, one hell of a lift."

He saw Mattie drop his eyes. Perhaps, he had been over the top, but he knew the psychology of the debrief, and the psychology said that an agent back from abroad, where he'd had a rough time, needed praise, reassurance. A colleague of Henry's, with a brood of children, had once likened the trauma of return to a woman's post-natal depression. Henry couldn't comment on that, but he thought he knew what the colleague had meant. He had told the Deputy Director General when he had been given his marching orders, before finding that his carburettor was playing up, that he would take it gently. It would have been scandalous to have taken it otherwise, after a man had been tortured and broken . . . oh yes, the DDG had been most sure that Mattie would have been broken.

"Thanks, Henry."

"Well, you know the form. We'll hammer through this over the next few days, and then we'll get you back home. What you've been through is going to be the basis of study and teaching, no doubt, at the Fort for the next decade . . . Shall we get down to things some time this evening? Mattie, we're all very, very excited by what you achieved."

"I think I'd like to be outside for a bit. Can't walk too comfortably just yet, perhaps I'll sit in the garden. Can you keep that ghastly dog at bay?"

"By all means. I'll ask George to put him in the kennel. And I'll see if Mrs Ferguson can find us something rather special to drink this evening. I don't think we can hold out much hope for the meal itself."

17

A good early start, because Henry Carter thought that Mattie would feel stronger at the beginning of the day. They ate breakfast of tepid scrambled eggs and cold toast. They discussed the possible make-up of the team for the first Test. They had a chuckle over the new switch in the Socialists' defence policy. Henry told Mattie about Stephen Dugdale from Library who had been laid low last week with thrombosis. It was a good room, the old dining room, fine sideboards, and a glasses cabinet, and a carving table, and the main table could have seated twelve in comfort. The worst thing about eating in the dining room and at the big table, in Carter's opinion, was that Mrs Ferguson having polished the table then insisted that it be covered with a sea of clear polythene.

"Shall we make a start then, Mattie?"

"Why not?"

He settled in the chair by the fireplace. Across the hearth rug from him Carter was fiddling with a cassette player. It was the sort of cassette player that Harriet had bought the girls when they were teenagers. He saw the spools begin to move on the cassette player. He could see the investigator, he could see the cellar walls, he could see the bed and the leather thongs, he could see the hook on the wall, he could see the length of electrical flex wire . . .

"How long is this going to take?"

"Hard to say, Mattie. Depends on what you've got to tell me. My immediate target is to get home."

"Goes without saying. . . . Where shall we begin? Shall we start in Van?"

Mattie told the tape-recorder everything about the way the attack on his car had been carried out. He felt uncomfortable describing his carelessness. Henry looked rather schoolmarmish but didn't interrupt. Mattie's account was perfectly lucid. He seemed to Henry to take pleasure in the clarity of the narrative, in the orderly compilation of details that would one day be of value at the Fort. At eleven Mrs Ferguson knocked and came in with coffee and a packet of chocolate digestives. Mattie stood at the window until Henry said, "This house they drove you to?"

"I was blindfolded when we got there, I didn't see it. When I went out of it then, it was dark."

"Tell me what you can about the house."

"They didn't take me on a tour, they weren't trying to sell it me."

He saw the puzzle at Henry's forehead. Stupid thing to have said . . .

"Is there a problem, Mattie?"

"I'm sorry – of course, there's a problem. You are asking me to recall a house where I was tortured, where others have been put to death."

"We'll just take it slowly, that way it won't be so painful. You've nothing to be ashamed of, Mattie."

"Ashamed?" He spoke in Henry's soft voice. He rolled the word. "Ashamed?" Mattie spat the word back at him.

The conciliatory raising of the hands. "Don't misunderstand me, Mattie."

"Why should I be ashamed?"

"Well, we've been working on the assumption . . ."

"What assumption?"

"We had to assume that you had been taken by agents of the Iranian regime, and that of course you would be interrogated, and in due course that you would be, well, broken or killed . . . That was a reasonable assumption, Mattie."

"Reasonable?"

"You'd have made the same assumption, Mattie, of course you would."

"And at what stage did you decide that Mattie Furniss would have been broken?"

Henry squirmed. "I don't know anything about pain."

"How could you?"

"Myself, I wouldn't have lasted a day, perhaps not even a morning. I think just the knowledge of what was going to be done to me would have been enough to tip me into the confessional. You shouldn't feel bad about it, Mattie."

"So, I was written off?"

"Not by the Director General. I am afraid almost everyone else did."

"Most touching faith you had in me. And did you shake the dust off my obituary? Had you booked St Martin's for a Memorial? Tell me, Henry, who was going to give the Address?"

"Come on, Mattie, this isn't like you. You've been on this side of the fence. You know what the form is."

"It's just abominable, Henry, to realize that Century believes a senior officer of the Service will cave in at the end of the first day, like some damn Girl Guide – I'm flattered . . ."

"We made our assumption, we aborted the field agents."

A sharpness in Mattie's voice, "They're out?"

"We aborted them, they're not out yet."

Mattie sat upright in his chair, his chest heaved. There were still the pain pangs deep in his chest. "You assumed that I would be broken within 24 hours, can I assume that you aborted as soon as I went missing? How can it be that two weeks later the agents are not out?"

"It was felt, I believe, that aborting a very precious network was a big step, takes years to rebuild. It took them a little time to get to the sticking point. Part of it was that the DG convinced himself that you would never talk. All sorts of waffle about Furniss of the old school. Frankly, I don't think he knows the first thing about interrogation. Anyway, wiser heads prevailed, as they say, and the messages were sent, but the agents are not yet out."

"Christ."

Mattie stood. Dreadful pain in his face. Pain from his feet that were bandaged and inside bedroom slippers that would otherwise have been three sizes too large.

"It wasn't easy, knowing nothing, hearing nothing."

A cold whip in Mattie's voice. "I clung on, I went through hell – yes, hell, Henry, and at Century you couldn't get your fucking act together . . . it makes me sick to think of it."

"I have the impression that there was more interest, more interest even than in the safety of the field agents, in whether Eshraq was compromised."

Mattie swung his shoulders. His eyes fixed on Henry. "What do you know about Eshraq?"

"That he is of very considerable importance."

"While I was away my safe was rifled, yes?"

"Rifled? No, Mattie, that is unreasonable. Of course we went through your safe. We had to know about Eshraq . . ." Henry paused. The silence weighed. He looked up at Mattie. There was the attempt at kindness, and understanding, and friendship. "I gather that Charlie Eshraq is not just important for his potential in the field, but also that he is very close to your family."

"So my safe was gutted."

"Mattie, please . . . we had to know everything about the boy, and now we have to know whether he is compromised."

"So you burrow about in my private files and you find that he is close to my family, is that it?"

"That's right."

"Here you assumed that I would talk to my torturers about a young man who is like a son to me?"

"I'm sorry, Mattie, that has been our assumption."

"Your assumption, but not the Director General's?"

"Correct."

"But all the rest of you?"

"The Director General said he thought that you would go to the grave before you named names."

"You, Henry, what do you think?"

"I've seen the medical reports. I know the extent of your injuries. I have an idea of what was done to you. To have escaped after all that argues a phenomenal constitution, phenomenal courage."

"I killed three men getting away. I broke the neck of one, I strangled one, I drove one down."

"If there were doubters, Mattie, they will obviously keep their doubts to themselves. I didn't know that, of course, and I am horrified to hear it. One has no idea what one may be capable of *in extremis*."

"Am I capable of betraying Charlie, that's what you are asking yourself."

"To me, Mattie, God's truth, you are one of the finest men that I have known in my lifetime with the Service, but no one, no one in the world, is capable of withstanding torture indefinitely. You know that and nobody in the Service is holding it against you. Everyone thinks it was wrong to send you – my God, I hope the DG doesn't listen to this tape – and, well, to tell you the truth, quite a few people think you were a fair old chump to be gallivanting about on your own near the border. That's what comes of being an archaeologist, I suppose."

Mattie smiled at the irony. He walked to the window. He did not need to hold on to the chair backs. He walked as if there were no pain in his feet, as if he could straighten his back and there was no pain in his chest. He stared out. There was a brisk sunshine lighting the lawn.

"I may have named the field agents, I can't be certain. There were times that I was unconscious, I might have been delirious. There were times when I thought I was dead and certainly prayed I would be. But that was, oh Christ, after days of agony. If the agents were not aborted immediately then I won't accept the blame for that . . ."

"And Eshraq, did you name Eshraq?"

The dog was barking in the kitchen, frustrated at being denied the run of the house. Mattie turned, stared levelly across the hearth rug at Henry.

"No, Henry, I couldn't have done that. I'd much sooner be dead than have done that."

"Mattie, truly, I take my hat off to you."

The lorry began the journey from the north of England to the port of Dover. Midday Saturday, and the lorry observed strictly the speed limits set for it. The driver would not approach the Customs checks at Dover until the evening of the following day. Lorry movement through the port of Dover was always heaviest on a Sunday night, when the drivers were jockeying to get a good start on the Monday morning on the through routes across Europe. The volume of traffic on the Sunday night sailings dictated that the Customs checks on outgoing cargo were lightest. And the early summer was a good time, also, for the sale of machine parts. The ferries' vehicle decks would be jammed with both commercial and holiday traffic. The chances of the lorry's cargo being searched, of the containers being stripped out right down to the four wooden packing cases, were very slight. The haulage company also took care to check whether there was any form of tail on the consignment. The lorry had been followed away from the warehouse at the loading depot by a car that checked to see whether it was under surveillance. The car varied the distance between itself and the lorry; at times it was a mile back, and then it would speed up and catch the lorry. The purpose of this was to pass the cars travelling in the wake of the lorry, and to look for the tell-tale evidence of men using radios in the cars, or vehicles that were too long in the slow lanes.

It was a wasted exercise.

The Investigation Division had no tail on the lorry.

Not yet six o'clock and she had already had her bath. She was at her dressing table. She could hear him in the next room, working at the final touches. It was the trip out with Bill Parrish that had set him behind. He hadn't told her where they had gone, and she hadn't asked. He might not have told her where he'd been, what he'd done, with Bill Parrish, but at least when he had returned he had peeled out of his work clothes and put on the old jeans and the sweatshirt and headed back to his decorating. He was pretty quiet, had been ever since he'd come back from the north of England, and she was almost sorry for him. More vulnerable than she'd ever known him. She thought he must have been wanting to please her, because he had set out to decorate the spare bedroom. Not that David would ever have admitted to a living soul, let alone his wife, that his case was up the river and no punt. She didn't care what he said. She'd liked coming home from work and finding the flat smelling of paint and wallpaper paste. It was a big change in her experience, that her husband had gone down to the DIY and had managed the best part of a week without referring to Bogota or the Medellin cartel.

"Who am I going to meet there?" she called out.

"A gang of complete morons."

She yelled, and she was laughing, "Will it all be shop talk?"

"Absolutely. Blokes all up at the bar, wives sitting down by the band."

"You'll dance with me?"

"Then you'd better wear boots."

He came into the bedroom. She could scent the paint on his hands that were on her shoulders. Christ, and she wanted them to be happy. Why couldn't they be happy? In the mirror, his face looked as though the light had gone from him. Her David, the Lane's Keeper, so crushed. It was a fast thought, she wondered if she didn't prefer him when he was bloody minded and confident and putting the world into its proper order.

He bent and he kissed her neck, and he was hesitant. She took his hands from her shoulders and she put them inside her dressing gown, and she held them tight against her.

"I love you, and I'm just going to dance with you."

She felt his body shaking against her back and the trembling of his hands.

Past six o'clock, and a Saturday evening, and the magistrate sat at his Bench in a yellow pullover, and his check trousers were hidden under the desk top.

The convening of the court on that day of the week, and at that time of day, guaranteed that the public gallery and the press seats would be empty.

Parrish, in his work suit, stood in the witness box.

"I understand you correctly, Mr Parrish? You have no objection to bail?"

Boot-faced, boot-voiced. "No objection, sir."

"In spite of the nature of the charges?"

"I have no objections to bail, sir."

"And the application for the return of the passport?"

"I have no objection to the passport being returned, sir."

"You have no fear of the defendant going abroad and not surrendering his bail?"

"No fears, sir."

"What sort of figure of bail are you suggesting, Mr Parrish?"

"Two sureties, sir. Two thousand pounds each would be my suggestion, sir."

The magistrate shook his head. It was as though he had now seen everything, heard everything. Day in and day out the police sniped at the magistrates for their willingness to grant bail. There could be many reasons and he was not going to waste time speculating on them. If that's what the Investigation Division wanted, that's what they wanted. What he wanted was to get back to the golf club. He granted bail on two sureties of £2000.

The flight had been delayed, technical problems. The problems were resolved a few minutes after Leroy Winston Manvers and his common-law wife and children boarded the British Airways 747 to Jamaica.

When he'd seen the bird up then Bill Parrish drove home to change for the dance.

The detective thought that Darren Cole was very pale, and his fingers were nicotine stained because that was the only fix he was getting on remand.

He resented being pulled from home on a Saturday evening and told to drive halfway across the county. He wasn't in the mood for hanging about.

"You're coming out, Darren. Tomorrow morning, eight o'clock, you're walking out. The charges against you will not be pressed, but they will be held in reserve. The charges can be reactivated if you should be so silly as to open your dumb little mouth to any scribbler, anyone else for that matter. I wouldn't come home if I were you. You should stay away from my patch. There are people who know that you grassed and if they know where to find you then they will most certainly come looking. Take the wife and the kids and take a very long bus ride, Darren, and stay safe. Have you got me, young 'un?"

The detective left the necessary paperwork with the Assistant Governor. He could be phlegmatic. He reckoned that letting out young Darren Cole would save three, four, days of court time. He was not concerned with the morality of letting out a proven narcotics pusher. If his Chief Constable could cope with the morality then there was no way that a detective was going to get out his worry beads.

He would have liked to know why Cole was being given the heave, but he doubted if he ever would.

*

"Who was it, George?"

Libby Barnes called from her dressing room. She sat in front of the mirror in her underclothes and housecoat, and she worked with the brush at applying the eye shadow.

"It was Piper Mother."

"On a Saturday evening? Is it something serious?"

"Called about Lucy . . . I'm not supposed to tell you this, but you've the right to know. I've lost, dear. I wouldn't want you to think that I lost without a fight, but I've lost, and that's the long and the short of it."

The photograph was in front of his wife, at the right side of the dressing table mirror. A photograph of when Lucy was sixteen, and sweet. A happy teenager in a Corfu café. The photograph had been taken the last time they had been together as a family, before Lucy had started her problem.

"What do you mean, you lost?"

"The boy who pushed to Lucy has been freed from remand in prison. He will not go to trial. The man who supplied the pusher will also not face charges and has been allowed to leave the country. The importer of those drugs, who has been under intense Customs and Excise investigation, will not be arrested . . ."

"And you've swallowed that?"

"Not lying down . . . It's for the best, Libby. A trial would have been awful, three trials would have been quite hideous . . . all those bloody journalists at the front door . . . perhaps it's best to forget."

Libby Barnes whispered, "And best for your career."

She held the photograph tight against her chest and her tears made a mockery of the work at her eyes.

"Piper Mother did say that, yes."

Charlie watched her go, and he was left on the pavement where the streets merged into Piccadilly. He watched her through the traffic and he saw the hips swing, and he saw that her shoulders were well back, and once he saw her shake the long hair free of her collar and the hair tossed and caught in the last of the sun.

First he lost her behind a bus that was caught at the lights, and then she was gone. She had been carrying her bag loosely against her knee. She was going home with her new dress, because Polly Venables and Charlie Eshraq were going nowhere. She'd go back to Mahmood Shabro on Monday morning, and she'd try to forget Charlie Eshraq because he had told her that he was going back to Iran.

He turned. The other girl was still close to him. She was leaning against the shop doorway, and she wasn't even bothering to pretend. The car was behind her. All the time that he had been walking with Polly, the girl had been close to him, and the car had been hugging the kerb. She was a dumpy little thing, and he thought they must have cut her hair with garden clippers, and he didn't understand why she wore an anorak when it was almost summer.

He walked up to her.

"I'm going to have a drink, April lady. Would you join me?"

Token snarled back at him. "Piss off."

The truck driver was Turkish and he drove his Daf vehicle with the choke out so that the engine seemed to race, as if on its last legs. He manoeuvred into the narrow cul-de-sac and then killed the engine in front of the battered sheet metal gates. When the engine was off, when he could look around him, there came to him the curious quiet of the repair yard. From his cab he could see over the wall and into the yard. No work there, no activity. He had been told they worked late into the evening.

There was a child watching him from against the wall, chewing at an apple.

The Turk called to the child. He asked where was the engineer.

The child scowled at him. The child shouted back the one word.

"*Pasdaran.*"

Choke in, the engine running smoothly, the driver backed his truck out of the cul-de-sac. He drove at speed out of Tabriz, chewing and chewing and eventually swallowing the message that had been taped against the skin of his belly.

She had heard of all of them, heard their names, but she had never before been able to put faces to the names.

She knew them by their actual names and by their codenames too, because sometimes David referred to them at home by one and sometimes by the other.

If she had been honest, and she might be honest later when they were home, and that depended on how much she had drunk, then she might have said that she didn't think that much of them. There wasn't much that was special about any of them. On Ann's table were some of the names she knew best. There was dear old Bill, unusually quiet, and his wife who had not yet closed her mouth. There was Peter Foster, whose collar was too tight, and whose wife hadn't stopped talking about the standard of teaching at Infant and Primary school level since they sat down. There was Duggie Williams, who was Harlech, and he was in a foul mood because, according to David, he had been stood up. Mrs Parrish was talking about the holiday they were going to take in Lanzarote. Bill wasn't saying much, and looked as though he had had a death in the family, and Foster seemed as if he might choke. But she rather liked Harlech. She thought that Harlech might just be the pick of them, and she thought that the girl who had stood him up must be just a bit dumb. The music had started, the band had begun, but the floor was still empty, and there was no way she would get David on to his feet before there was quite a throng. The glasses were filling the table. The raffle tickets had been round, and they would be drawn, and then there would be the buffet supper, and after that she might get David on to the floor.

Duggie Williams brought her a drink and changed places with Maureen Foster to sit next to her.

"You must be half bored out of your knickers."

"I beg your pardon."

"How did Keeper get you to come along?"

"It was I that said we were coming."

"You must be off your pretty head."

"Perhaps I just wanted to have a look at you all."

"Then it's a bloody miracle you haven't run away already . . . I'm Harlech."

"I know. I'm Ann."

Bill had started talking. Ann couldn't hear what he was saying, but David was leaning away from her to listen.

"We're not in the best of form."

She said drily, "I gathered."

"We've lost a nice juicy one."

"He told me a bit."

"We got fucked up – excuse me – your man, trouble with him is that he cares."

"Don't you?"

He had strong eyes. When she looked at Harlech then it was into his eyes. She had nowhere else to look. It was only from the side of her eye that she saw Bill's empty chair.

"Not a lot bothers me, that's because of where I used to work. I used to be at Heathrow . . ."

"So was David."

". . . He was front of house . . . me, I was back stage. I was on the stuffers and swallowers drill. You know what that is? Course, you don't. Nobody tells a nice girl about swallowers and stuffers . . . I used to be on the duty that checks the daily in from Lagos – I never found anything else that the Nigerians were good at, but, Christ, they can stuff and swallow. Do you want to know all this? You do? Well, the women stuff the scag up their fannies, and the men stuff it up their arses, and they both swallow it. Are you with me? They put it in condoms and they stuff it up and they swallow it down. We have a special block for the suspects, and that's where I used to work before I came to ID. We shove them in a cell, and we sit and watch them, and we feed them on good old baked beans, and we wait. God, do we wait . . . Has to go through, law of nature. Everything has to come out except from where the women stuff theirs, but that's a job for the ladies. You have to be like a hawk, watching them, and every time they go in then it's out with the plastic bag and on with the rubber gloves and time for a good old search around. They train by swallowing grapes, and they dip the condoms in syrup so they travel more comfortably, and they use something called Lomotil, because that's a binder.

You know, once we had a flight in from Lagos and we pulled in thirteen, and we had every bog in action that we could lay our hands on. We were swamped, and just as well, because half of them were positive. When you've sat, hours and hours, watching guys crap, after that not a lot seems to bother you. Got me?"

"He doesn't tell me things like that."

"Complaining?"

She didn't answer. Bill was back, talking urgently into David's ear. She heard her man swear, quiet, then he turned to her.

"I'm sorry, I've got to go with Bill. It may take an hour or two. Duggie, will you look after Ann? Will you get her home?"

"You're joking." She didn't believe it.

Bill shrugged. He was standing at David's shoulder.

"I'm sorry, love, I'll see you when I do."

He was gone, and Bill was trailing after him. No, she didn't believe it.

"Do you like dancing?" Harlech asked.

The investigator reported to the Mullah.

A veteran in survival, the investigator had determined the necessity of reporting in person twice every day to the Mullah. Twice every day he drove through the traffic jams to the expropriated villa where the Mullah held court. He held the cards in his hand, not as high cards as he had hoped, but cards of value. He had in those cells at Evin that were reserved for political prisoners of great sensitivity an engineer from Tabriz and a carpet merchant from Tehran.

He had a tail on an official of the Harbourmaster's office in Bandar Abbas, to see where the man would run, what else could be trawled.

He had the plan in his mind of the show trial at which confessions would be made. Confessions, their extraction and their presentation in court, were the great pride of the investigator. A confession was the closing of a book, it was the finishing of the weaving of a carpet, it was orderliness. The confessions of the engineer and the carpet merchant were near to being in place, and that of the official in the Harbourmaster's office would follow when he was ready to receive it.

On that evening, late, in the office of the Mullah, he reported on all these matters, and he received permission to continue the surveillance in Bandar Abbas. Later, sipping freshly pressed fruit juice, he talked of Charlie Eshraq. He was very frank, he kept back nothing.

"Mattie, I don't want to go on about this, not all night, but you are quite sure?"

"I'm getting very tired, Henry."

"The investigator was a professional, yes?"

"Old SAVAK man, knew what he was at."

"And it went on being pretty violent?"

"Henry, if you knew how ridiculous you sounded . . . 'pretty violent' for Christ's sake. If you've got any heavy duty flex in the garage here we'll see, if you like, if we can elaborate the distinctions. Violent, pretty violent, or we'll try twelve hours of continuous violence and see what that becomes. Or haven't we been through this all before . . ."

"Yes, Mattie, yes, we have . . . It's so important that we are absolutely clear on this. Your investigator is a SAVAK man, the worst of the breed, and violence was used against you, quite horrifying violence, on and on . . ."

"How many times do you have to be told, Henry? I did not name Charlie Eshraq."

"Easy, old chap."

"It is not easy to break out of Iran and then to come home to an inquisition."

"Quite right, point taken. Mattie, there were times that you fainted, other times when you were semi-conscious. When you were really groggy, could you have named him then?"

The room was shadowed and dingy. The light came from a ceiling triple, but one of the bulbs had popped early in the evening and George had stated that he had no replacements and would not be able to buy more bulbs until Monday. The furniture was old but lacking in quality, a Sotheby's man wouldn't have given the room a second glance, not as good a room as the dining room.

"When you're in a place like that, Henry, you cling to anything that's sacred. You hold on to your family, to your Service, your country, your God if you have one. Any damned thing that is important in your life you hold on to. When the pain's so bloody awful, the only things you can hold to are the kernels of your life. You have that feeling that if you broke, you would be giving them all that is sacred to you."

"I just have to be sure, that I understand you."

And it was such a damn shame . . . He thought that old Henry, tatty old Henry Carter who wouldn't have known a thumb screw from a bottle opener, might just be a better interrogator than the investigator in Tabriz.

Park drove, and Parrish was beside him with the directions written on a sheet of paper. He'd asked where they were going, and Bill had said that the building was called Century House. He'd asked why they were going there, and Bill said it was because the Chief had told him to present himself with Keeper in tow. No point in any more questions, because Bill hadn't any more answers.

They came down the Albert Embankment, and the tower blocks loomed against the night skyline. There was only one block alive with light.

Parrish waved for Park to pull into the forecourt. The Chief Investigation Officer was on the steps, and looking at his watch, and the ACIO was beside him, and then coming forward to organize the parking space. They climbed from the car, and Park locked the doors. They walked towards the main entrance. He saw a small brass plate for Century House.

The Chief Investigation Officer nodded curtly at Parrish then moved to stand in front of Park.

"Inside, your opinion isn't wanted, you just listen."

They were offered drinks, and on behalf of all of them the Chief declined.

Not an evening for social pleasantries, Park thought, just an evening for learning the realities of power.

He stood in front of the desk and the Chief Investigation Officer was beside him, and the ACIO was on the other side and a half pace behind, and Parrish was out in the secretary's office with a young twerp watching over him. Parrish hadn't even made it inside. The lesson was delivered by two men. One sat in an armchair, and did the talking, and was called DDG, and the other sat on the front of the desk. The one in the armchair drawled and the one on the desk, with his socks held up by suspenders, had a voice that was silk and honey. He heard it from the armchair.

"You don't have a right to the detail, Park, but I will tell you what I can, and you should understand that everything I propose has been considered and approved by your immediate superiors ... In your work for Customs and Excise Investigation Division, you are a signatory to the Official Secrets Act. That signature of yours is an obligation to life-long confidentiality, whatever recent events may have suggested to the contrary. What you hear in this room is covered by the Act. Between your superiors and ourselves, Park, there is a deal. You are being volunteered."

"That's nice. What have I done to deserve this?"

"Just button it, Park," the Chief said, side of mouth.

"Charlie Eshraq runs heroin. He is also a field agent of some value to the Service. Mr Matthew Furniss is one of the finest professional officers to have been reared by this Service in the last two decades. That's all fact. Eshraq, for reasons that are not your business, is about to return to Iran and he will be taking across the frontier a certain amount of hardware, purchased, as I am sure you will have deduced, with the proceeds of the sale of his last load of heroin. He is going back into Iran, and he will be staying there. He will be told tomorrow that should he renege on an agreement with us, should he ever return to the United Kingdom, then he will face prosecution on the basis of the evidence that you and your colleagues have collected against him.

"You will join Eshraq on Monday, you will accompany him to Turkey, and you will satisfy yourself and your superiors that he has indeed travelled back into Iran. Following your return to the UK, it has been decided by your superiors that you will then be posted as DLO to Bogota in Colombia. I can assure you that it will be my intention to make certain that you have there the full cooperation of Service personnel in that region. That's the deal."

"All neatly wrapped up between you, no loose ends. And if I tell you that it stinks, that I don't believe it? He doesn't belong to your outfit and if he does I'd like to know what's the point of my going to Bogota if you lot are running the stuff in the back door from Iran?"

"Watch it, Park."

"No, Chief, I won't . . . Just to get Mr Furniss' young friend off the hook and just to get me out of the way. That's it, isn't it?"

"Quite right, Park, we may just have to get you out of the way. Do you remember a Leroy Winston Manvers. An early morning interrogation, unsupervised, quite outside the book . . . ? You do? I gather the file isn't closed yet, some ugly first shots across the Division's bows from his solicitor. Isn't that so, Chief?"

"I think you're shit, sir."

"Five years' imprisonment, minimum. You could bet money that we'd know the judge. For the beating of a helpless black prisoner, it could be a bit more than five. Goodnight, Park. You'll enjoy Bogota. It's full of your type. Goodnight, gentlemen."

Park went for the door.

If he had looked into the face of the Chief Investigation Officer then he might just have put his fist into the man's teeth, and if he had looked at the ACIO then he might just have kneed the bugger.

"By the by, Park, a little note of warning . . ." The voice drawled behind him, an incoming tide over shingle. "Don't play any clever games with Eshraq, I think he'd give you more of a run for your money than Manvers did."

The dog slept in a wicker basket beside the Aga in the kitchen, on its back with its legs in the air, and wheezed like a drayman. The sound of snoring filled the night quiet of the house. He thought that a burglar would have to have kicked over the kitchen table to have woken the brute. But it was not the Rottweiler's growled breathing that kept Henry Carter awake. He would have been asleep by now, well asleep because it had been a hard enough day and rounded off with a good malt, if it had not been for the nagging worry.

The descriptions of the torture had been so wretchedly vivid. The telling of the brutality had been so cruelly sharp. Never, not ever, would Henry have accused Mattie of telling "war stories". Nothing was volunteered, everything had to be chiselled for, but in his own laconic way Mattie had transported Henry into a world that was deeply, desperately, frightening.

He understood why he had been chosen for the debrief.

Quite impossible that the Director General would have permitted any of those aggressive youngsters that now seemed to fill the building to be let loose on a man of Mattie's stature. Perhaps the Director General had been wrong. Perhaps one of the young men, brash and cocksure, would have been better able to understand how Mattie had survived the pain, had survived and kept Eshraq's name safe.

God forbid that he should be selling Mattie short, but Henry, coward that he was and without shame of it, could not understand it.

18

Sunday morning, and the light catching the east side of the Lane. Empty streets around the building, no rubbish wagons, no commuters, no office workers. The buses were few and far between, there were taxis cruising without hope.

The bin beside Park's desk was half filled with cardboard drinking beakers. He had long before exhausted the dispenser, which would not be filled again until early on the Monday, and he had been reduced to making his own coffee, no milk left over the weekend. Stiff black coffee to sustain him.

Some of it he had read before, but through the night he had punched up on to his console screen everything that the ID's computer had to offer on Turkey and Iran. That was his way. And a hell of an amount there was . . . And he read again what little had been fed into CEDRIC on Charlie Eshraq. It was his way to arm himself with information, and it was also his way to dig himself a pit when circumstances seemed about to crush him. He couldn't have gone home, not after the visit to Century. Better to get himself back to the Lane, and to get his head in front of the screen. He'd been alone until dawn, until Token had shown. She'd shown, and then she'd gone heaven knew where and come back with bacon rolls.

She sat at the desk opposite him. He was latching the plastic sheet over the console.

"I spoke to Bill last night, when he'd got home."

"Did you now?"

"He said you'd had a pretty rotten evening."

"And he was right."

"He said that Duggie took your wife home."

"I asked him to."

"He said that you might be in need of looking after."

She didn't wear make-up, and she hadn't combed her short hair, and her anorak was slung on the hook on the wall between the windows that looked down on to New Fetter Lane. She wore a sweatshirt that was tight over her radio transmitter. He thought that he knew what she was saying, what Parrish had said to her.

"Have you finished?"

"I've finished with the computer, I don't know what else I've finished with."

"Another day, another dime, David."

"You know what . . . ? Last night they walked all over us. We were the little chappies who had stepped out of their depth, and we were being told how to behave, and the Chief took it . . . I still feel sick."

"Like I said, another day. Do you want to come home with me?"

"What for?"

"Don't be a cretin."

"I'm going home, got to change."

"Might be best to give home a miss."

She was the girl he ought to have married, that's what he thought. He knew why she offered her place, her bed. He knew why she was on offer, if she had spoken to Bill Parrish on the phone.

"Thanks," he said.

He came round the desk and when she stood he put his arms around her shoulders and he kissed her forehead. It was a soft kiss, as if she was his sister, as if she could only ever be a friend.

"Don't let the bastards hurt you, David."

He slung his suit jacket over his shoulder. Still in the buttonhole was the red rose that Ann had said he should wear for the dance. He walked out on Token, who would have taken him home to her bed. He started up the car. It was a fast drive through the desert that was the city and it took him little more than an hour to reach home, and he'd bought flowers at a railway station stall.

She'd left the lights on.

The lights were on in the hall and in the bedroom and in the bathroom.

She had left the wardrobe door open, and inside the wardrobe there was a chasm, her dresses gone. The bed wasn't made, and the envelope was on the pillow, the pillow, for God's sake.

He went into the bathroom because he thought that he was going to throw up, and her dressing gown was on the bathmat and her bath towel, and beside her bath towel was his.

Perhaps that was the way it always was, that a marriage ended. The flowers were in the kitchen sink and he didn't know how to make a display of them.

There was a light knock at the door. Mrs Ferguson, beckoning Carter out. He went, and smiled an apology at Mattie.

If there was a way back then Mattie did not know it. He paced in the room. He faced the alternatives, and his future. There was no going back. To go back, to admit the lie, that was resignation. He was a member of the Service, and if the lie were admitted then he would be out of the Service.

"Sorry, Mattie, so sorry to have abandoned you. The telephone is one of the great tyrannies of modern life. Things are a little more confused. Our message to our man in Tehran, the message for him to abort, it didn't get through."

"Why not?"

"Seems that our man had disappeared, couldn't be traced. That's a shame."

A long sad silence in the room. And Henry's eyes never left Mattie's face. He walked across the carpet and he stood in front of Mattie.

"What I've always heard, and you know that I've no personal experience, when you start talking under pressure then you cannot ration yourself. If you start then you have to finish," he said.

The explosion. "Damn you, how many times do I have to tell you?"

"I think we'll have a walk down to the pub, you'd like that, wouldn't you, Mattie? I'll ask George to tether the hound."

The message was very faint.

The message from the short wave transmitter, that was in itself hardly larger than a cornflakes packet, was carried the 90 miles from Bandar Abbas, across the shipping lanes of the Straits of Hormuz to the listening antennae on the summit of the Jebal Harim in Oman.

Only the height of the Jebal Harim, 6,867 feet above sea level, enabled the message to be monitored. It was known by the Service that the transmitter could reach the antennae with short messages, and it had been given to the official who worked in the Harbourmaster's office for use only in emergency.

He knew his situation was critical, he knew he was being watched.

He sent the one short message.

He was a man filled with fear that spilled towards terror. And that afternoon he prayed to his God that he would have the protection of Mr Matthew Furniss, and the colleagues of Mr Furniss.

Park was waved forward by the Military Police corporal. There was no salute. A Ford Escort didn't warrant a salute from a corporal who was losing Sunday at home. Park drove forward, bumping over the rutted dirt track, and he parked beside the Suzuki jeep. On the far side of the jeep was a black Rover, newly registered and the driver was quietly polishing the paintwork and minding his own business. Park had changed at home. After he had tidied the bathroom and made the bed that Harlech had been in, then he had stripped off his suit and put the rose from his buttonhole in water, and put on jeans and a sweater.

He walked towards Charlie Eshraq. Eshraq stood with the man, the supercilious and drawling creep, who had lectured Park at Century.

He walked towards them, and their conversation didn't hesitate.

". . . So, that's it?"

"That is it, Mr Eshraq. Mr Park will accompany you to the border. You will not attempt to impede his job. You don't fool with him and he has been told not to play silly buggers with you. Got it?"

"And I get the weapons?"

"Mr Eshraq, if you were not getting the weapons then this afternoon's exercise would be somewhat pointless."

"I don't get to see Mr Furniss?"

"You will be handled from Ankara, good chap there."

"Why do I not see Mr Furniss?"

"Because from inside Iran you will need to deal with someone else. All that will be explained to you once you are in Turkey. Good luck, we'll be rooting for you."

The driver had finished his polishing, and had started up the Rover. There were no farewells. The car drove away.

In the cause of duty . . . Park walked to Charlie Eshraq.

"I'm David Park."

"No, you're not, you're April Five, but you may call me Charlie."

"I'll call you any name I want to . . . Probably, like me, you reckon this set-up stinks."

Eshraq was Tango One, trafficker in heroin, always would be. There was no handshake. Charlie turned his back on him and walked away towards the army Landrover. Park followed, and behind him the Military Police corporal reckoned that it was safe to light a cigarette. There was an officer standing beside the Landrover, and squatting on the low seats in the back were two sergeants. David saw the olive-painted case lying on the floor between their feet.

The officer said, "Which of you is it? I was told the instruction was for one."

"For me," Charlie said.

The officer looked him up, down. "The LAW 80 is pretty straightforward."

"Oh, that's good, you'll be able to manage the tutorial."

Park thought the officer might have cracked Charlie. He heard the sergeants laugh aloud.

They went out on to the range. The officer led. They'd given Charlie a tube to carry, and the sergeants each carried one. They seemed to walk a hell of a distance, past red flags, past warning signs, until they came to a place where the heather ground sloped away. There were tank tracks, and ahead of them was the burned, black hull of an armoured personnel carrier.

"Where are you going to use this, young man?"

"Is that your business?"

"Don't fuck me about, Mr Eshraq . . . On where you are going to use it depends my briefing. Are you going to use it in a battlefield condition? Are you going to use it over open ground? Are you going to use it in an urban environment? You don't have to tell me, but if you don't then you are wasting my time and you are wasting your time. Got me?" The officer smiled. He reckoned he had the upper hand.

"The first one will be fired on a street in Tehran. That's in Iran."

And the smile died on the officer's face.

"All I can say is that I am not totally confident at the moment," Henry said. It was the scrambled phone. "He's peculiarly aggressive when I attempt to pin down detail . . . Yes, it bothers me very much that I may be selling him short . . . I suppose we just have to soldier on. Thank you."

It was quiet in the house. They had indeed been to the pub, but that had not been a good idea, because the two pints of ale and Mrs Ferguson's lunch had given Mattie the excuse to retire to his room for a siesta. And it was Sunday afternoon, and the Director General was in the country, and the Duty Desk weren't quite sure where the Deputy Director General was, and the man who had taken the call from Carter was only a minion and Carter was a tedious fusser, and Mattie Furniss was a hero. Nothing would happen, not until Monday morning.

He crouched. His left knee was bent forward, his right knee was on the ground.

There were the steel gates ahead of him.

There was the derelict house behind him.

The oleanders were in flower and gave him cover, and he had elevation from the ruined and overgrown gardens and he could see over the wall that fronted the derelict house and he could see across the road and to the high sheeting of the security gates. There was a cramp settling in his legs, but he did not respond to it, and he struggled to hold the tube steady on his shoulder. The tube was well balanced and its weight of 18 lbs kept it firmly in place on his collar bone. His left hand gripped tight at the cradle under the tube, holding it, and the index finger of his right hand was on the smooth plastic of the trigger and the thumb of his right hand was against the switch that would change the firing mechanism from the spotting round to the main projectile. His right eye was locked on to the sight and in the centre of his vision were the steel gates to the Mullah's home. He knew that the Mullah was coming because he had heard the revving of the engine of the big Mercedes. The traffic in the road was continuous and the Mercedes would have to stop before it could nose out.

So hard to be still, because the adrenalin flowed, and the thrill of revenge stampeded in him. The gates opened. He saw two guards running forward and across the pavement, and they were gesturing for the traffic to stop, and the whistles in their mouths were raucous. The snout of the Mercedes poked through the gates. He had a clear view of the radiator grille and the front windscreen. The head-on target was not the best, side shot was better, but the side shot would be against an accelerating target . . . even better would have been the magnet bomb that Mr Furniss had given him, and the motorcycle, and the chance to see the face of the Mullah as he pulled away, as the pig knew that he rode underneath death – not possible, not with the escort car behind . . . He could not see the Mullah, he would be in the back, and through the sight he could only see the radiator and the windscreen and the face of the driver and the face of the guard who sat beside the driver. A boy pedalled past on his bicycle, and was not intimidated by the whistles and the shouts and the flailed hand weapons of the guards who were on the road, and the driver waited for the boy on the bicycle to clear the path ahead. The spotter rifle first. The flash of the red tracer round running flat, and the impact against the join of the bonnet of the Mercedes and the windscreen, and the windscreen had a clouded mark at the base, nearly dead centre. Thumb to the switch, push the switch. The finger back to the trigger. Holding the tube steady, ducking it back into the line of sight because the kick of the tracer round had lifted the aim fractionally. Squeezing a second time on the trigger . . . and the blast, and the recoil, and the white heat flash roaring behind him, behind his crouched shoulder. A shudder of light that moved from the muzzle of the tube at a speed of 235 metres in a second, and the range was less than forty metres. The explosion on the front of the Mercedes, the copper slug of the warhead driven into the body of the car, and the debris scabs following it, and the car rocked back, and lifted, and the first flicker of fire . . . What he had waited for. The car burned, and the road was in confusion.

"Move yourself, Eshraq."

The shout in his ear, and his hands still clasped the tube, and the voice was faint because his ears thundered from the firing.

"Get yourself bloody moving."

And the officer was dragging at his collar, and snatching the tube from his grip.

"You don't stand around to watch, you move as if all the demons in hell are on your tail, and about half of them will be."

The officer had flung the tube aside, and Charlie was on his feet. He saw for one last time that the smoke billowed from the armoured personnel carrier target. He ran. He was bent low, and he ran for more than 100 yards up the shallow slope of the hill and away from the officer and the sergeants and the three discarded tubes and the target. He ran until he reached Park.

At his own pace the officer walked to him.

"That wasn't bad, Eshraq."

He was panting. The excitement throbbed in him. "Thank you."

"Don't thank me, it's your skin that's on offer. You have to move faster in the moment after firing. You do not hang about to congratulate yourself on being a clever kid. You fire, you drop the tube, you move out. You were wearing ear protectors, no one else in the target zone will be and they will be disorientated for a few seconds. You have to make use of those seconds."

"Yes, understood."

"You won't have realised it, time goes pretty fast, but you were four seconds and the rest between the rifle aiming round and the missile discharge. Too long. The target today was stationary, that's kids' play."

"Inside an armoured Mercedes . . . ?"

"I'd rather not be the passenger. The LAW 80 is designed to take out main battle tanks up to 500 metres. No car, whatever the small arms protection, has a chance. Don't lose any sleep over that. Are you happy?"

"I will remember your kindness."

"Just give my love to the Ayatollah . . ."

Charlie laughed, and he waved. He walked away and Park followed him. He thought Park was like the labrador dog that Mrs Furniss had owned when the girls were still at school, and which had been detested by Mr Furniss. He thought the officer was great, because there was no bullshit about the man and he had given him the depth of his experience, and freely. He reached the jeep.

"I am going back to London, are you coming with me?"

"Those are my instructions, that I stay with you, but I've my own car."

He heard the tang of dislike in the brittle voice. "Then you can follow me."

"I'll do that."

"I'm going to my flat."

"I know where your flat is."

"I'm going to my flat and I am going to take a shower, and then I am going out to dinner. I am going to have a very good meal. Perhaps, you would care to join me?"

He saw the snarl on Park's face, his face was almost amusing. "I'll eat with you because I have to be with you, and I'll pay my own share. So we understand each other – I don't want to be with you, but those are my orders. I'll tell you where I'd like to be with you. I would like to be sitting alongside the dock in Number Two, Central Criminal Court, and I'd like to be there when a judge puts you away for fifteen years."

Charlie grinned. "Perhaps you'll win some other ones."

He had stayed in his room all afternoon, and when Henry had come to the door and knocked and told him that supper was ready he had said that he had no appetite and that he would skip the meal. It had been late when he had come down. He had been driven downstairs by his growing loneliness that had become keener as the light fell over the trees in the garden.

They were in the drawing room. For that time of year it was unusual for it to have been so cold, and Mattie stayed close to the fireplace, which was idiotic since there was no fire, but he felt the chill of his loneliness and he could not shrug the warmth back to his mind. Henry wasn't communicative. It was as though he was watching the clock, had decided that Sunday evening was his free time and that the debrief would continue in the morning. Henry had brought him a whisky, sat him in a chair with back editions of the *Illustrated London News* and *Country Life*, and returned to the study of a brochure advertising holidays for ornithologists. He craved to ask the question, but Henry was far from him, lost in the Danube's marshes. He held the drink. He hadn't spoken to Harriet, not since the phone call that was their reunion, three quick minutes, and stiff lips, and both too gushing because they were too old and too regimented to have cried down the lines, and he wouldn't speak to her again, not until this was over. Harriet would have known what he should do. And equally certainly Henry would turn down any request that he call her. Oh yes, he'd do it politely, but he'd do it. Carter had a calculator out, and must have been adding up the damage because just after he had made the final punch a frown ploughed his high forehead. Mattie saw that Henry did nothing by accident. He also realized that for all his seniority at Century, here he was subordinate. Old Henry Carter, Century's vacuum cleaner for gathering up the odds and sods of administration, was running the show, and had determined that Mattie Furniss would be left through that evening to sweat.

Henry smiled. Melting butter. A wrinkled choirboy's smile, such innocence.

"Too damned expensive for me. It'll be the Fens again."

Mattie blurted, "Eshraq, Charlie Eshraq . . . he was due to go back inside. Did he go?"

Henry's eyebrow lifted. Deliberately he put down the calculator and closed the brochure. "Any day now, going in the next few days . . . I must say, it sounds as if he's taken on more than he can possibly chew."

Mattie thought a knife could have been sharpened on Henry's voice.

"He's a fine young man."

"They're all fine young men, Mattie, our field agents. But that'll keep till the morning."

The Director of the Revolutionary Centre for Volunteers for Martyrdom was still in his office because on many evenings the office doubled as his bedroom. He was in an easy chair and reading a manual of the US Marine Corps on base security procedures, and he was happy in the discovery that they had learned nothing, the authors of this study.

They took coffee, thick and bitter, and with it was served orange juice. They were two men of cultures that were chasms apart. The Director had spent six years in the Qezel-Hesar gaol in the times of the Shah of Shahs, and he had spent six years in exile in Iraq and France. If a young Mullah who was a rising star had not offered the investigator his protection, then, in great probability, the Director would have used the pistol, holstered and hanging from a hook behind his door, on the back of the neck of the one time SAVAK man.

The investigator spoke of a watch that was now maintained on a barber's shop in the Aksaray district of Istanbul. He told of a man who would come to the shop. At the back of the shop, Charlie Eshraq, the son of the late Colonel Hassan Eshraq, would collect forged papers that he would use when he came back into Iran. He asked a great favour of the Director. He said that he would have this Eshraq under surveillance from the moment that he left the shop. His request was for a small force of men who would be in position on the frontier to intercept Eshraq at whatever crossing point he used. Would he come over at a crossing point? Of course – and the investigator had researched the matter – because of the weight of the armour-piercing missiles he was known to be bringing and their packaging he would have to come by road. He asked for the service as if he were a humble creature at the feet of a great man.

732

He asked for nothing. The Director would be most pleased to make such a squad available, in the name of the Imam.

The Director said, "Consider the words of the martyred Ayatollah Sadeq Khalkhali: 'Those who are against killing have no place in Islam. Faith requires the shedding of blood, we are there to perform our duty . . .' He was a great man."

And a great butcher, and a hanging judge without equal. His patron, the Mullah that he served, was but a boy in comparison with Khalkhali, the unlamented protector of the Revolution.

"A great man, who spoke words of great wisdom," the investigator said. And he asked the second favour. He asked that after Charlie Eshraq had collected his papers from the barber's shop, that the shop be destroyed by explosives. Profusely, he thanked the Director for his cooperation.

It was necessary for him, business completed, to stay another hour in the company of the Director. The Director was pleased to report the details of the killing in London of Jamil Shabro, traitor to the Imam, traitor to his faith, and guilty of waging war against Allah.

When they parted, in the quiet of the dark, on the steps outside the old University, their cheeks brushed each other's lips.

If the restaurant had been half empty, and not full, then Park would have sat at a separate table. There was only their reserved table, so he had to sit with Eshraq if he wanted to eat. And he did want to eat.

Eshraq made conversation, as if they were strangers who had crossed paths in a strange city and needed company. And he ate like he was starting a hunger strike in the morning. He ate *fettucine* for starters, main course bowl, and he followed with the *fegato*, and took the lion's share of the vegetables they should have shared, and he finished with strawberries and then coffee and a large Armagnac to rinse down the valpolicella of which he had drunk two-thirds of the bottle. Park hadn't talked much, and the first real exchange was when he had insisted on halving the bill when it came. He took his time, Eshraq, but he pocketed the money, and he paid the whole bill with an American Express card.

Park said, "But you won't be here, not when they bill you."

"Present from America."

"That's dishonest."

"Why don't you call the head waiter?" The mocking in the eyes.

"And you eat like a pig."

Eshraq leaned forward and he looked into Park's face. "Do you think where I am going that I will be eating a meal like this, do you think so? And you know what is the penalty for drinking wine and for drinking brandy, do you know?"

"I don't know, and I don't care."

"I could be flogged."

"Best thing for you."

"You are a generous member of the human race."

There was a hesitation, and Park asked, "When you get there, what do you do?"

"I build a life for myself."

"Where do you live?"

"Sometimes rough and sometimes in safe houses, at first."

"How long does it last?"

"How long is a piece of string, April Five?"

"I don't care, it's nothing to me, but it's suicide."

"What did your man offer you, many years ago? He offered you blood and sweat and tears, and he offered you victory."

He couldn't find the words. The words seemed to mean nothing. The face loomed ahead of him, and there was the chatter and the life of the restaurant around them, and the flapping of the kitchen doors, and laughter. "And you're not coming back. There's no coming back, is there? It's all one way, isn't it? You're going back, and you're staying there. Is that right?"

"You said that you didn't care, that it was nothing to you, but I have no intention of dying."

The bill came back, with his plastic. He put his tip on the table, between his coffee cup and the brandy glass, everything that Park had given him.

At the door, Eshraq kissed the waitress on the mouth, and he bowed to the applause of the other customers. Park followed him out. Eshraq was on the pavement and flexing himself, as if he was breathing in the London street air, as if he was trying to keep a part of it for himself, for always.

Park walked alongside him, back towards Eshraq's place. He followed the big bounding strides. There was an excitement about the man. Everything before was wind-up, tomorrow was real. They reached the entrance to the flats.

"Eshraq, I just want to tell you something."

"What?" Charlie turned. "What do you want to tell me, April Five?"

It had been going through Park's mind most of the time at the restaurant. He waited while an old lady walked her dog between them, waited until the dog had cocked its leg against a railing and was then dragged away.

"I just want you to know that we will follow you anywhere you go, except Iran. If you come out of Iran then we'll know, and that goes for the rest of your life. We'll circulate you, Eshraq, they'll hear about you in Paris, Bonn, Rome, Washington, they'll know you're a trafficker in drugs. If you come out of Iran, if you pitch up at any airport, then I'll hear, I'll get the call. You want to play games with us, just try us. That's the truth, Eshraq, and don't ever forget it."

Charlie smiled. He fished his keys from his pocket. "You're welcome to sleep on the floor."

"I prefer my car."

"Are you married?"

"What's that to you?"

"Just assumed you hadn't a home to go to."

"My instructions are to stay close to you until you go over the border."

"I asked if you were married."

"I was."

"What broke it?"

"If it's any of your business . . . you broke it."

The Director General was at the Joint Intelligence Committee, the Deputy Director General was on his way back from the country. Of all the many hundreds who worked on the nineteen floors and the basement at Century they were the only two who had an overall picture of Furniss' case. Both would be at their desks by the late morning of Monday, neither was available for the fast reaction that was needed to co-ordinate a jumble of information originating from differing sources. There was Carter's call from Albury on Sunday that had been logged by the Duty Officer. There was the monitoring of a short wave radio message in Oman that required immediate response. There was a report, brought by a Turkish lorry driver to Dogubeyezit, and from there telephoned to Ankara. Related matters, but early on that Monday morning, as the building strove without enthusiasm to throw off lethargy, those matters remained unrelated. The transcript of Henry Carter's message was passed to the Director General's PA. The short wave radio message ended on the desk of a man with the title of Special Services (Armed Forces) Liaison. The communication from Ankara lay in the In tray of the Desk Head (Near East).

Later, a sub-committee would be set up to examine means of ensuring that all crucial intelligence was distributed at once to the desks that were available to deal with it. There had been sub-committees with that brief as long as the old hands could remember.

Faced with the absence of the Director General and his deputy, the SS(AF)L officer took a car across the Thames to the Ministry of Defence, to ask a rare favour of old Navy chums.

They went on the morning flight.

Charlie's ticket was one way, Park's a return. They flew Tourist class. They didn't have to talk on the flight because Charlie slept. Park couldn't sleep, not with the stiffness settling in after a cramped night in the back of the Escort. He was grateful that Eshraq slept, because he'd had his bellyful of small talk.

It had started with a police phone tap on a dealer, but Parrish didn't tell them that, nor did he tell April team that there had been all but blood on the carpet when the NDIU had passed it from police control to ID. His style was matter of fact. He showed no signs of having had about the worst weekend he could remember since joining Customs and Excise. It would have been a passable weekend if his wife hadn't pitched in with her opinions, and her report . . . He told it as he knew it. The dealer's supplier was a Turk who operated out of the port of Izmir. The scag would be Iranian and across the land border and into Turkey, and then overland to Izmir. He had the name of the ship out of Izmir, and its route was via Naples. It was known that Naples, information provided by the Drugs Enforcement Agency, was a pick-up point for a consignment of Italian pinewood furniture. The assumption was that the scag would be coming into Southampton Docks all tucked up with the table legs. April would be there in force. He would be there himself, along with Harlech and Corinthian and Token and the new kid from Felixstowe who had joined them that day and who hadn't yet a codename which meant that they'd call him Extra, and there would be back-up from Southampton ID. Parrish said that it was good they had the dealer spoken for, and the supplier, but that they wanted the distributor. He reckoned the distributor would show at Southampton. They'd be going down that morning, and he didn't know when they'd be back, so they'd better have their clean socks with them. There were the jokes about the cars from the depot being clapped out, and the Vodaphones not working, all the usual crap . . . He was pretty pleased that they'd another investigation to latch on to so soon, and better still to get them out of London. Those of April who were not going to Southampton would be for the delights of Bethnal Green, chez the dealer, and for the banks where he had his accounts. The ship was coming in that night, was already down the Channel with a Brixham pilot on board, so could they get their backsides off their seats, please.

He'd finished. His finger snaked out, pointed to Duggie Williams. He gestured towards the inner office, and headed there.

He sat at the desk. He let Harlech stand. He'd get it off his chest. He thought April was the best team in the Lane, and he was damned if he'd see it broken.

"Saturday night, Duggie, that was insufferable."

"She asked for it."

"You only had to take her home, drop her."

"How did you know?"

"I know, but if I hadn't known, I'd have read it all over your face."

"She was ready for it."

"She was the wife of your colleague."

"I didn't start the dumping."

"He's your brother-in-arms, for heaven's sake."

"He's a prig and a bore and he doesn't keep his missus happy. Sorry, Bill, no apologies."

"If I catch you round there again . . ."

"You going to sit on the doorstep?"

". . . you're back in uniform."

"She was the unhappiest woman I've ever poked, and she's a good kid. And where is our brother-in-arms?"

"Don't know. Don't know where he is, what he's got himself into. . . . Lose yourself."

"The DG rang, Mattie, he's just back from the Joint Intelligence session. He wanted you to know that your praises were sung to the roof."

"Thank you, much appreciated."

"And I'm to tell you that you're being put up for a gong."

"I thought those sort of things were supposed to be a surprise."

"Be the Order of the British Empire, Mattie. I expect the DG wanted to cheer you a bit."

"Why, Henry, do I need cheering?"

"Your agent in Tabriz . . . Revolutionary Guards beat us to him."

"And what exactly are you implying?"

"Which comes on top of your man in Tehran, also not reached, also gone absent, although we don't know for certain that he was arrested. We do know it of the man in Tabriz."

"I'll tell you what I think. I think that I was compromised from the time that I landed in the Gulf. I think that I was trailed right the way across the Gulf, right the way to Ankara and on to Van. I think I was set up from the start . . . What's happened to my man in Bandar Abbas?"

"Making a run for it tonight. Navy are going to try and pick him up at sea. I think that's rather dodgy. He knows they are watching him."

"I told you. I gave their names. Looking back on it, on the moment that I knew, knew absolutely that my cover was a farce, was when the investigator asked me what I had been doing all round the Gulf. He practically gave me the addresses I had been at, starting in Bahrain. I wish you'd get someone on to this at once, see just who is in and out of that Service wing. But yes, what must have been two weeks later, I did give their names. But what I can't get over is the utter uselessness – it makes me sick to think of it – of day upon day of torture while the Service twiddles its thumbs and now you come moping in here and say alas, we've lost another agent. Lost, for God's sake, Henry, not lost, thrown away."

Henry said, "I'm on your side, Mattie, and was from the very start. No professional would have let it happen. I've told you that. But I'd like to leave the gaol now, come back to it later, and we'll certainly do as you say about the Bahrain station. I want to talk this afternoon about the actual escape . . ."

They sat either side of the unlit fire, and Henry was mother and poured the tea.

19

Carter wriggled in his shirt. He had not brought enough shirts to last him and he had had to entrust his dirty ones to Mrs Ferguson, and the woman used too much starch. The shirt was uncomfortable against his skin. Worse, the summer had come at last and even with the lounge curtains half drawn the room still sweltered, and Henry boiled unhappily in his three-piece suit and stiff shirt.

"Your investigator, Mattie, your torturer, what was he looking for in general?"

"They wanted to know why I was in the region, what was my brief."

"And what did you tell them?"

"I told them that I was an archaeologist."

"Of course."

"You stick to your cover story, it's all you have to hang onto."

"And you're not believed?"

"Right, I'm not believed, but you have to stick to your cover, whatever the holes are in it. And I was never going to be believed. The interrogator was an old SAVAK hand and he had met me years ago in Tehran. He knew exactly who I was. Called me Furniss the first time I was sat down in front of him. They caught a BBC bulletin saying that Dr Owens was missing. He made fun of that."

"On that day you still hadn't abandoned your cover?"

"Do you understand anything? You are alone, you are beyond help. If you give up your cover story then you are finished."

"They wanted to know your mission in the region, and what else were they fishing for?"

"Names of agents."

"They knew you were in the region, and they knew your identity . . . What did they know of the identity of the agents?"

"They didn't have the names."

"Did they have anything on them?"

"If they did they didn't give me any hint of it."

Henry said quietly, "You gave them what they wanted, but not the name of Charlie Eshraq."

He saw the head go down. He did not know how long it would take. It might take the rest of the day, and it might take the rest of the week. But Mattie had dropped his head.

"How many sessions, Mattie?"

"Plenty."

"Torture sessions, Mattie, how many?"

"Six, seven — they were whole days."

"Whole days of torture, and in essence the questions were the same?"

"What I was doing in the region, and the names of the agents."

"I'm very admiring of you, Mattie, that you were tortured day after day, that the questions were over such a small area range, and that you held the cover story so long, very admiring. Did you consider, Mattie, telling them a little about Charlie Eshraq?"

"Of course you consider it."

"Because the pain is so great?"

"I hoped the names of the field agents would be enough."

"You'll have to talk me through this . . . You are in great pain. You are the subject of the most vicious and degrading treatment. The questions are asked again and again because they don't believe you have named all the agents . . . What do you say?"

"You stay with your story."

"Damn difficult, Mattie."

"You have no choice."

"Through the kickings, beatings, faintings — through a mock execution?"

Henry made a note on the pad that rested on his knee. He saw that Mattie watched him. He saw the trickle of relief on the man's face. Of course he was relieved. He saw his inquisitor make a note on his pad and he would have assumed that Carter made the note because he was satisfied with the answer. And the assumption was incorrect. Henry noted on his pad that he must ring Century for more clothes for Mattie. There was always a stock of clothes held there for visitors. There was a wardrobe full of slacks and jackets and jerseys and shirts and underwear and socks, assorted styles and shapes. Even shoes. Mattie would need more clothes because he was trapped in a lie, and the debrief would go on until the lie was disowned.

"I think you are a very gentle man, Mattie."

"What does that mean?"

"I think that you care about people over whom you exercise control."

"I hope I do."

There was a sad smile on Carter's face. He would have been deeply and sincerely upset to have had Mattie believe that he took pleasure from his work.

"Mattie, when you left the kids on the mountain, the kids who lifted you up when you were finished, shared their food with you, and so on, that must have hurt."

"Obviously."

"Super kids, weren't they? Great kids, and they helped you when you were at your weakest."

Mattie shouted, "What did you want me to do?"

"You didn't argue their case. You told me that. You walked away from them and you sorted yourself out with the officer."

"I did try. But it's true I didn't upset the applecart as far as to get pushed back up the hill myself. My first priority, my duty as I saw it, was to get myself back to London."

"That's a heavy cross, that sort of duty . . ."

"You weren't there, Henry bloody Carter . . . you weren't there, you can never know."

The sun played on the windows and the distortions of the old glass were highlighted, and the brilliance of the rare sunshine showed up the dirt dust on the panes. If George, if the handyman, were to hold his job, then it was about time the idle wretch started to get round the windows with a bucket of warm water and a pocket full of rags. Carter said, "My assessment, Mattie, and this is not meant as a criticism, is that you were looking to save yourself . . . Hear me out . . . Saving yourself was pretty important to you. Saving yourself was more important to you than speaking up for those kids who had carried you to the border."

The hoarse rasp in Mattie's voice. "One minute you want me to hang on long enough in the victim's chair and get every bone in my body broken, fingernails tugged out, all that, and the next minute you want me to have got myself booted back across the border."

"I want to know what you would have done to save yourself from the pain of torture."

"Why don't you refresh your memory with a glance at my medical report? Or would you like me to take my socks off?"

"I need to know if you named Eshraq to save yourself from the pain of torture."

"I might have named them all the minute the interrogation began."

"No call for that, Mattie . . ." There was a grimace from Carter, as if he had been personally wounded. ". . . When I was down here, must have been a couple of years back, there was an old croquet set in the cellar. I've told that lazy blighter to mow a bit of the lawn. Would you fancy a game of croquet, Mattie, after we've had our lunch? . . . To save yourself, your own admission, you let those kids be herded to a firing party. What would you have done to save yourself from the pain of torture?"

"I've told you."

"Of course . . . Eshraq's going back over, very soon."

They went to their lunch, and through the open windows there was the coughing drone of the old cylinder mower out on the lawn, and the pandemonium of the dog at George's heels.

The route of the lorry had been through Calais, Munich, Salzburg, Belgrade, and then the poor roads of Bulgaria. Nineteen hundred miles in all, and a run of 90 hours. Sometimes the driver worried about the tachograph, sometimes his employer took care of his lorries and paid him extra money for hammering across Europe. There was the potential that the tachograph would be examined at a border post, but that potential was slight, and the driver, with extra funding, could live with that slight potential. The driver was skilled at negotiating the overland Customs point at Aziziye. It had been his habit for years to telephone ahead from Bulgaria to his friend at the Customs at Aziziye, to warn of his arrival. The driver called the Customs officer his friend, to his face, but in fact had similar friends at most of the entry points to European countries where he might be ending his journey and requiring Customs clearance. The bribe that was given to the Customs officer at Aziziye was not so much to prevent search of the containers on the lorry and its trailer, more to ensure a smooth passage for the cargo. A present, a gift, for the Customs officer was an essential part of any swift movement of goods. His vehicle was well known at the Aziziye crossing point. There was no reason for him to attract attention, and with the gift to his friend he ensured speed. It was a healthy arrangement, and paid for on this occasion by a carton of Marlboro cigarettes, a Seiko watch, and an envelope of US dollar bills.

The lorry travelled through. The seals of the containers had been legally broken. He had his manifest list signed, stamped.

The driver was free to drop off at an assembly of addresses the contents of his containers. He had brought into Turkey, quite illicitly and quite easily, four LAW 80 armour-piercing missiles, and he carried in his wallet a passport-sized photograph of the man to whom he would deliver four wooden crates, and he'd get a holiday with the wife and the kids in Majorca on the bonus he was promised for the successful shipment of the particular cargo that was stowed at the bulkhead of the container that was immediately behind the driver's cab.

A piece of cake, the Customs point at Aziziye.

The lorry headed for Istanbul.

The envelope contained a dog-eared and well-scuffed Shenass-Nameh Recognition Paper, and a Certificate of Military Discharge following injury, and a Driver's Licence for a commercial vehicle. Included also in the envelope was a letter of authentication from a factory in Yazd that produced precision ball-bearings and would therefore be classified as important to the war effort. And there were bank notes, *rials*.

As he took each item out of the envelope, Charlie held it against the light that hung down from the ceiling of the room at the back of the barber's shop. He looked for the signs of overwriting and over-stamping. It was right that he should check carefully. His life depended on them. He paid cash, he paid in sterling, £20 notes. He thought that the forger could have bought a half of the Aksaray district with what he made in documentation provided for the refugee exiles. He thought that he was a case of interest to the forger, because the forger had told him, not the time before, but the time before that, had confided in Charlie, that he was the only customer who looked for documentation to go back inside Iran. The barber's shop was in the centre of the

Aksaray district that was the Little Iran of Istanbul. To the room at the back of the shop there came, by appointment, a stream of men and women seeking the precious papers which were required for them if a new life were to be born out of exile. And he charged . . . He charged what he thought he could get, and those from whom he could get nothing received nothing from him. For a Turkish passport he charged $500, and this was the bottom of his range and full of risk to the bearer because the number would not tally with any of the records maintained on the Interior Ministry computer. For a British or a Federal German passport, with entry visa, he would expect to relieve his customer of $10,000. Most expensive, top of his range, was the American passport, with multiple entry visa, and there were very few customers who had managed to secrete that sort of cash, $25,000 in used notes. Sometimes, but only occasionally, the forger took diamonds in lieu of cash, but he was loth to do that because he had no knowledge of precious stones and then he must go and put himself at the mercy of the young Jew in the Covered Bazaar that was a thousand metres away down Yeniceriler Caddesi – and he might be cheated. With fast and busy fingers he counted the cash. When they shook hands, when Charlie had pocketed the brown envelope, when the forger had locked away the money, then Charlie noticed the tic flicker on the right upper eyelid of the forger. Charlie did not consider that the tic flicker might have been caused by fear, apprehension; he thought the twitching came from an over indulgence in close and painstaking work.

Charlie Eshraq walked out into the sunshine.

He looked up the street for his shadow. He saw Park. He was at least 150 yards up the street. Charlie was about to wave a curt acknowledgement when he saw the shadow turn away from him.

He had first seen the tail in the Aksaray district, where the walls were covered with posters that rubbished Khomeini, where the kids gathered to plot crimes that would bring them the money to get out of Turkey and onwards into Europe. He had first seen the tail when Eshraq had come out of the doorway of the barber's shop and started to walk towards him. He wasn't sure whether there were two cars, but he was certain that there was one car. There were three men, on the hoof. There was the man in the forecourt of the café who stood and then came after Eshraq as soon as he emerged into the sunshine; he was a tail because he left three-quarters of a glass of cola undrunk. There was a man who had been leaning against a telephone pole and who had been busy cleaning his nails, and his nails didn't seem to matter once Eshraq was out. There was a third man, and when the car had pulled level with him then he had spoken quickly into the lowered front passenger window.

He knew a tail when it was in front of him.

He'd thought that the tail was good in Istanbul. He'd thought the tail was better in Ankara. He didn't doubt that the tail had been in place from the time they had walked out of the terminal of the Esenboga airport, but he hadn't picked it up until Eshraq had gone park walking with the young man who called himself Terence. In the park, the Genclik Park, with the lakes and the artificial islands and the café's, he had kept himself back and he had watched Eshraq and his contact from more than a quarter of a mile. Three men again, but different from those who had done the footslog in Istanbul.

He could have rung Bill Parrish, and he didn't. He could have called up the ACIO, and he didn't. They had passed him on from the Lane. They would be into the priority of Harlech's case, and sifting everything else that had taken back seat to the Eshraq investigation. They wouldn't have wanted to have known that there was a tail on Eshraq.

He acknowledged that the tails were in place. He allowed them to stay in place.

A man who wore a new black leather jacket, and who had a trimmed goat's beard, he saw him in the Genclik Park and he saw him at the airport when he and Eshraq boarded for Van.

There was no communication between them. There was no bond in formation. Eshraq was moving to the frontier and Park was his shadow. They hardly spoke. When they spoke it was commonplace and factual. They spoke about where Eshraq was going, how long he would be there, where he would be going afterwards. That didn't bother Park, and it seemed to him that it didn't concern Eshraq. No need for it to have concerned either of them. They were the subjects of a deal.

And if Eshraq had a tail on him, had had a tail ever since he had walked clear of the barber's shop in the Aksaray district of Istanbul then that was his worry, not Park's.

49841/TL/7 6 87.
To: TURKDESK, CENTURY   CC IRANDESK, DDG.
From: ANKARASTATION
MESSAGE: CE Vanwards, in company of Park. Transhipment from UK complete, no hitch, and now in transit Vanwards. Have fully briefed up, beefed up, CE on communications procedures, and agreed that most epistles will be hand carried out by courier. CE in good humour, good morale. Eye stressed need for detail in material rather than frequency. My opinion, eye think they have major handful tripping over their frontier. Eye didn't meet Park. CE ignores him, says he is harmless. In answer your query — TURKDESK CENTURY 6 6 87 — CE says Park is no problem, but frightened of being away from home without him Mum, exclaimer . . . CE will cross 9 6 87, using Dogubeyezit checkpoint. CE has necessary papers to drive commercial vehicle inside, will be carrying hardware via commercial van, and supply of electrical flex as per your suggestion. Upsummer: No problems, looks good, more follows.
MESSAGE ENDS.

"You off then, Henry? That'll be a break."
"I'll be in London, Mattie, reporting back."

"I won't be sorry, Henry, if they slap your wrist."

"Probably will, won't be for the first time . . . What I was saying, it's not quite a matter of bolting the stable door after the horse has gone. There's still one horse in the stable. Eshraq is in the stable, not for much longer, but he's there right now. Are you quite sure there is nothing you wish to add to what you have already told me?"

"Quite sure."

"When I get back, if there's still enough light, we might get the mallets out again, very soothing is croquet. Do you think we should have a nightcap, one for the stairs?"

Boghammer Bill was a blip, lime-shaded, on the emerald wash of the screen.

The operator, the egghead of the radar room crew, had identified the blip, and called over the 2 i/c to watch its progress.

The crew of the Type 22 guided missile frigate were on Defence Watch. They were dripping sweat, those in the radar room, those on the bridge, those manning the 20 mm rapid fire close engagement guns. The middle of the night, and the temperature close to 95 Fahrenheit, and all crew members swaddled in the white gown action suits and hooded.

The technician knew that it was Boghammer Bill from the speed of the blip on the screen. It was a Swedish built patrol boat and the fastest craft in the Gulf.

The Type 22 would not hang about, not in the waters where it was now cruising, maintaining radio silence and blacked out, just outside the Iranian twelve mile limit, for any more minutes than were essential. The 2 i/c thought the world was getting dangerously daft. There was a bright moon, high in a clear sky, and there was no wind. It was a ridiculous night to be stooging just off the limit without identification or prior warning. They were east of the Iranian island of Larak and west of the small fishing harbour of Minab, far too bloody many sea miles from their regular station, on escort duty in the Straits of Hormuz. The 2 i/c knew the mission, but he didn't know his skipper's Rules of Engagement orders if they came under Iranian fire. They had been watching the dhow on the screen for more than half an hour, and they could picture the fishing craft chugging on a small engine away from Minab. The 2 i/c knew it was the dhow they were to rendezvous with because its course was directly towards the longitude/latitude reference that he had been given, and there were no other crawling blips on the screen. It was now seven minutes since the patrol boat had speared on to the screen, going fast out of Bandar Abbas, powered by engines that could attain in excess of 50 knots. Staccato reports from the 2 i/c to the bridge, gestures that were self evident from the technician to the 2 i/c. The dhow was on course for the rendezvous, and Boghammer Bill was on course to intercept the dhow some four miles short of the rendezvous. No hiding place, not on a clear night.

When he was home, on leave, when he was in Plymouth, the 2 i/c's idea of relaxation was to get himself up to one of the Devon water supply reservoirs and to put a small roach on to a damn great treble hook and let it flutter underneath a big bobbing float until it attracted the attention of a pike. Of course, the 2 i/c never saw the pike actually close on the tethered roach, couldn't see under the murk of the reservoir surface, but he imagined it. He told himself that the pike didn't stalk its dinner, it charged it. He thought of Boghammer Bill as the pike, he thought that some poor creature on the dhow was the roach bait. He watched the blips closing, he watched the racing speed of the blip that was Boghammer Bill. The blips closed, merged.

He had waited in his office at the Ministry building.

He had waited for the final message to be telexed to the Communications rooms in the basement.

In place were the arrest at sea of the official who worked in the Harbourmaster's office at Bandar Abbas. In place were three teams of men from the Revolutionary Centre for Volunteers for Martyrdom, settled into a Guards Corps barracks at Maku that was close to the main overland crossing point from Turkey. In place were three men who had tracked Eshraq from the airfield at Van to Dogubeyezit.

There was one aspect of the situation that still puzzled the investigator as he cleared his desk, shovelled the maps and the briefing notes into his case. Furniss had named Charlie Eshraq, and yet Eshraq was in Dogubeyezit. Eshraq was in the Ararat Hotel in Dogubeyezit. Why was he not warned off?

At this time, he did not concern himself with the man who had accompanied Eshraq from Istanbul to Ankara to Van to Dogubeyezit. Time enough for that, but later.

His car waited. At the military airfield, an aircraft waited.

He was a coming man. When he had Eshraq at the border he would be a man who had arrived . . . If Eshraq came to the border. Very confusing.

He had started early, certainly before Mattie Furniss was on the move. He had gone to his flat, one bedroom and a large living room and all the usuals, which was plenty for him, fixed rent, too, and they couldn't get him out, to collect his post.

He sat on the bench in front of the spinning soapy window. He had raised a few eyebrows. There weren't many who came to the launderette and stuffed into the cavern an armful of clean, ironed shirts. He'd paid for a double rinse, which he thought would be sufficient to sort out the starch once and for all. He gazed at the maelstrom in front of him. He was a regular and sometimes there were people there who knew him and talked to him. Quite a little social club on a Thursday evening.

He doubted there was a man or woman in the building who would want to hear what he had to say. Certainly not the Director General, who was giving him fifteen minutes. And it was bad news for him that the DDG was on his way that morning to Washington.

When his shirts were washed, rinsed and dried, he folded them carefully and carried them back to his flat and gave them a quick iron.

His car was on a good parking place, too good to lose, and so he took a bus from Putney Bridge along the river route to Century.

No one loved the bearer of evil tidings. But what choice did he have? He believed that Mattie was lying.

The dog was chained to the leg of the one solid garden seat. Mattie strode behind the mower. He had George at the wheelbarrow for the cuttings. He made neat lines.

He knew where Henry Carter had gone. Poor old Henry, and not half as clever as he'd thought, he had seen to it that the telephone in the hall was removed, but he had forgotten the telephone in Mrs Ferguson's bedroom.

He did the croquet lawn, close cut. He assumed that George was prepared to be outside with him, ferrying the cuttings to the compost heap, because George had been instructed to mind him.

His name is Charlie Eshraq . . .

Mattie mowed, pure straight stripes, and he scrubbed from his mind the echo of his own words.

". . . But he has told you nothing . . ."

"That is quite correct, sir, he has admitted absolutely nothing."

The Director General's smile was withering, "But you don't believe him."

"I wish I could, sir, and I cannot."

"But you have no evidence to substantiate your distrust?"

"I have the conviction that a man who is driven by days of torture to name his field agents is not going to be allowed to stop there."

"But why do you think he didn't make his escape before giving Eshraq's name?"

"Ah, yes. That, sir, is a hunch."

"And you are prepared to damn a man because of your hunch."

"On the basis of what I might rephrase as a lifetime of listening to debriefs, sir, I would simply avoid sending this young man into Iran until we are certain. No one has explained to me the reason for the haste."

"There are all sorts of things that you don't know, Carter."

There was a light knock. Houghton walked in like a man who has been told that his banker has defaulted. He didn't seem to notice Henry Carter. He laid a single sheet of paper on the Director General's desk. There was the moment of quiet while the Director General ferreted in his breast pocket for his reading glasses.

"From our naval friends in the Gulf. You'd better hear what it says, Carter.

It's timed at 0700. Message: No, repeat no, rendezvous. Subject craft intercepted by Iran Navy Boghammer missile boat. Believed all crew of subject craft taken on board before subject craft sunk. Boghammer returned to base, Bandar Abbas. We resuming escort duty . . . Message ends."

The Director General placed the sheet of paper back on to his desk. He removed his reading glasses.

"What would Furniss say?"

"Mattie would say that he had been through a hell that neither you nor I can comprehend in order that we would have had the time to get those three men clear. Mattie would say that our lack of resolution condemned our network to death."

"He admits the names came from him?"

"Yes, but only after withstanding what I reckon to be anywhere between five and seven days of torture."

"If he admits that, why then can he not admit to naming Eshraq?"

"Pride," Carter spoke the word as if it were an obscenity, as if he should now go and wash out his mouth with soap.

"What in God's name has pride got to do with it?"

"Eshraq is more or less part of his family. He cannot bring himself to admit that to save himself from pain he would betray his family."

"Are you really telling me, Carter, that Furniss would sacrifice Eshraq for his pride?"

"Just my opinion, yes."

The Director General went to his safe. He obscured the combination from Henry Carter's view. He played the numbers, he opened the safe. He took out a file. The file was old, worn. The writing on the outer flap was faint, faded. "Since he was taken I've been looking into Furniss' history. I've come across nothing that indicated any vestige of vanity. I have found only a man of outstanding loyalty and steadiness. Did you know that he was in Cyprus during the Emergency, in the Guards with a platoon, very young? Did you know that? I'm not surprised, because I gather that period is not on his general biography. He was on a search mission on the Troodos slopes. Some idiot decided that the brushwood should be fired so that an EOKA gang would be smoked out and driven towards the positions where Furniss' unit were waiting for them. The wind got up. The fire ran out of control. Furniss' platoon was surrounded by a wall of fire. The report I've read is from his Company Commander, who watched it all through field glasses. Furniss held his men together, kept them calm, waited until their clothes were damn near burned off their bodies. He waited until he saw a break in the fire wall, and he led his guardsmen through it. And all this time the platoon was under enemy fire, they lost six men. I haven't come across anyone in Century who knows that story. Obviously Furniss has never mentioned it. Does that strike you, Carter, as symptomatic of a vain or proud man?"

Carter smiled, tired, wearied. "That was about winning, sir, this is about losing."

"Well, tell me. What do you want?"

"I need some help with Furniss, sir. If you will be good enough to authorize it."

He had the number of the lorry and he had photographed the driver – that would wait, that was other business. Park looked down from the hotel room into the back yard. He saw the driver and Eshraq transfer the crates, one at a time, and heavy, from the lorry to the tail doors of the Transit.

The evening was closing on Dogubeyezit.

20

The car crunched on the drive, scattered the gravel.

Mattie heard it and he saw Henry's flickering eyebrow register the arrival of the car. Mattie coughed, as if he tried to draw attention to himself and away from the car that arrived at the country house at past ten in the evening, and Carter wasn't having it, Carter was listening for the car, and for the slammed door, and for the suburban chime on the bell in the porch. Mattie did not know what was to happen, only that something was to happen. He knew that something was to happen because Henry had been back four hours from London, and had not said what had happened in London, and had said precious little about anything else. Mattie understood. Henry's silence through the evening was because he was waiting, and now the waiting was over.

To Mattie it was absurd, the pallid smile of apology as Henry let himself out of the drawing room. He thought that it was possibly the end of the road for them both and he reckoned that he had Henry's measure. Another night, another day, survived, and he would be on his way to Bibury, and back to his desk at Century.

Of course, Mattie had not asked what Henry had been up to in London. To have asked would have been weakness. Weakness was no longer a part of Mattie's world. Weakness was the villa at Tabriz and the hook on the wall and the electrical flex and the firearm that was not loaded, and that was all behind him. Weakness was scrubbed away by the trek across the mountains to the slopes of Mer Dag. On that evening, after the long silences over supper, there was a part of Mattie's mind that could no longer remember with any clarity much of the days and nights in the villa. If he had tried, and there was no damn way that he was going to try, then he might have been able to recall fragments, moments. No damn way that he was going to try . . . *His name is Charlie Eshraq* . . . No damn way at all.

The door opened.

Henry stood aside, made room.

The man was sturdy. The hair on his head was close cut, barely tolerating a parting. He wore a suit that was perhaps slightly too small and which therefore highlighted the muscle growth of the shoulders. His face was clean shaven bar the stub brush moustache.

Mattie couldn't help himself. "Good God, Major, this is a surprise. Grand to see you . . ."

"I hear we've a little problem, Mr Furniss," the man said.

*

The moonlight was silver on the snow peak of Ararat. When he tilted his head, dropped his gaze, then he could see the outline shadow of the Transit. The heavy gates of the hotel's yard were padlocked for the night. The lorry and its driver were long gone, they would be in Erzerum tonight, he'd heard that said when he had watched from the window and seen Eshraq pay the driver off, seen him pay him off with the money that had once belonged to a Greek. Christ, and that was simple, watching the house of a Greek, with Token in tow, and doing the things that came easy to him. Nothing came easy for Park in a shared hotel room in Dogubeyezit.

Eshraq was sitting behind him, on the bed that he had chosen.

Eshraq had taken the bed further from the door.

Eshraq ignored Park. He had laid out on the bed a series of large scale maps of northern Iran.

Eshraq hadn't spoken for more than an hour, and Park had stood by the window for all of that time, and stared over the unmoving, unchanging vista that ran towards the distant summit of Ararat.

"Get up."

The voice rattled in Mattie's ears. There was no place of safety.

"Get up, Mr Furniss."

But there had never been a place of safety. No safety here, no safety in the cellar of the villa in Tabriz. They merged. There was the carpet of the lounge, and the tiled floor of the cellar. There were the pictures on the wall of the lounge, and there was the hook on the wall of the cellar. There were the armchairs with the faded floral covers, and there was the iron bed frame with the straps and the stinking blanket. There was the rasp of the Major's voice, and there was the hushed clip of the investigator's voice.

The hands reached down for him.

"I said, Mr Furniss, to get up."

The hands were at the collar of Mattie's jacket, and grasping at the shoulders of his shirt, and the jacket was too loose and did not make a good fit and was climbing up his arms and over the back of his head, and the shirt was too tight and could not be fastened at the collar and was ripping. He didn't help. He lay as lead weight.

He was pulled upright, but when the grip weakened, because his jacket was coming off him and the shirt was too torn to hold, then Mattie collapsed back on to the carpet.

He was lifted again, and the Major was panting, just as they had panted in the cellar. He was lifted to his feet, and he was held, and he was shaken, as if he were a rug. He was thrown backwards. His arms were flailing and found nothing to catch, and he cracked down on to the carpet, and the back of his head hammered the floor. He gazed up. Henry stood in front of the fireplace, looking away, as if he wanted no part of this.

Mattie no longer knew how long it had been since the Major had first slapped his face. Out of the blue. A question, a deflecting answer, and the slap homing on to his cheek. The smarting at his eyes, the reddening of his cheek. But the slap across the face had been only the start.

He had been slapped, he had been kicked, he had been punched. It was not vicious, the pain was not inflicted on him for the sake of it. The pain was a humiliation and a progression. They did not want to inflict pain on him, they only wanted him to talk. The blows were harder, the kicks fiercer. They wanted to do it with the minimum . . . The bastards.

He lay on the carpet.

Mattie let his head roll to the side.

Oh, yes, Mattie had learned from the cellar in Tabriz. Kids' play this, after the cellar and the hook on the wall and the electrical flex and the unloaded weapon. He looked at Henry, and Henry had his hand over his face. Mattie let his head sag. He lay still.

He heard Carter's voice, the whinny of apprehension. "They said that he wasn't to be abused."

"He's only faking. Do you want an answer or do you not want an answer?"

"For Christ's sake, it's Mattie Furniss . . . I want the answer, of course I want the answer, but I'll be minced if he's hurt."

"So, what's at stake, Mr Carter?"

"A mission – God, what a mess – the life of an agent is at stake."

He was splayed out on the carpet, and he was trying to control his breathing, as a man would breathe when he was unconscious, slow and steady. The blow came between his legs. He had no warning of the kick. He cried out, and he heaved his knees into his stomach, and he rolled on the carpet, and his hands were over his groin. His eyes were squeezed shut, watering.

"Good God, Major . . ." The tremor in Carter's voice.

"He was faking, told you." And the Major had dropped down beside Mattie. Mattie felt his head lifted. He opened his eyes. He saw the Major's face a few inches from his own.

His name is Charlie Eshraq.

"Mr Furniss, don't be a silly chap. What did you tell them?"

The merging of the face of the Major and the face of the investigator. Christ, they must think he was pretty piss poor. They were the same face, they were the same voice. Mattie Furniss did not talk, Mattie Furniss was Desk Head (Iran). And he had the second chance. He had lost the first chance, talked, cracked, broken. But he had the second chance. The pain was through his stomach, and the retching was writhing in his throat. He had the second chance.

"My name is Owens. I am an academic. A scholar of the Urartian civilization."

And he was sliding, slipping, and the blackness was closing around him.

Charlie lay on his bed. The light was off. He was close to the window and the moon silver filtered the cotton curtains. He knew that Park was awake. Park's breathing told him that he was still awake. He was packed, he was ready. He was going at the dawn. At the foot of the bed, beside the soap box, his rucksack was filled, and in the yard outside the Transit was loaded with drums of electrical flex for industrial use, and under the drums were three wooden packing crates. He was going in the morning, and Park hadn't spoken since the light in the hotel room had been turned off. There was the bleat of animals in the night air, the call of the goats and the cry of the sheep, there was once the wail of a *jandarma* siren, there was the drone of the hotel's generator, there was the whirring flight of a mosquito. He was Charlie Eshraq. He was 22 years old. He was the man with the mission and with the target. He was not afraid of death, not his own and not the death of his enemies . . . And why couldn't the bastard talk to him? Why in hell's name not? In the moon darkness, in the hotel room, he wanted to talk. If he had been with the dossers under the arches of Charing Cross station then he would have had someone to talk to. He was going back inside. He knew how to fire the weapon, and he knew the faces of his targets, and he knew the routes that he would use, and he was going back inside alone, and he wanted to talk.

"David, I want to talk."

"I want to sleep."

"David, is that why your wife went?"

"Why?"

"Because you have no love."

"I have no love for heroin traffickers."

"The heroin was for money, the money was for weapons, the weapons were for the killing of evil people."

"In my book, the evil people traffic in heroin."

"There was no other way."

"That's an excuse, Eshraq, and excuses don't make rights out of wrongs."

"David, who do you love?"

"None of your business."

"Anyone, anyone in the world?"

"I want to sleep, and I want to get out of this shit hole in the morning."

"Do you love your wife?"

"That's my business."

"My sister, David, she was my business . . ."

"I don't care."

"I will tell you what they did to my sister. They took her from the gaol at Evin, they flew her to Tabriz. They drove her to the centre of the town. They had brought a crane into the centre of the town. They stood my sister on a table and they put a rope around her neck. There were many hundreds of people there to watch her die, David. I am told by people who were there that when my sister stood upon the table and looked down on to the people who had come to watch her die that she smiled at them. She made the smile of a girl who was not yet a woman. It was talked about for many weeks afterwards, the way that my sister smiled ... They kicked her off the table and they hoisted the crane up. That was how she died. They tell me that he died in great pain, that she did not die easily. There were two men who held her on the table as the executioner put the rope around her neck, I killed them as I killed the executioner. If it had been your wife, David, and not my sister, would you not have wanted money for weapons?"

"Running heroin is wrong, for me that's the beginning and the middle and the end of it."

"Because you have no love?"

"Because I have no love for people who run heroin."

"Your father is alive?"

"My father is alive."

"Do you love your father?"

"I want to go to sleep."

"Is it shaming to say that you love your father?"

"My feelings for my father, that's not your concern."

"My father was in the gaol at Evin. He was a soldier. He was not a policeman, he was not in the SAVAK, he never commanded troops who were used to put down the revolt of the masses. He was an enemy of no man, and he was my father. I know about my sister, David, her last hours, and I know also something of the last hours of my father. I know that he was taken from his cell at dawn one morning out into the killing yard at Evin. He was tied to a stake in the yard, and shot there. When that has happened to your father, and your uncle has been butchered, is it wrong to want weapons?"

"You can talk all night, Eshraq. Me, I'll be sleeping."

He heard the heaving of the bed. He saw the shadow of Park's body toss as the back was turned to him.

He thought that by the next nightfall he would be far inside. He thought that at the next dusk he would be approaching the stone hovel of Majid Nazeri on the frost cold slopes of Iri Dagh. He would be where there were eagles, and where there were wolf packs, and where as the light came or as the light went there was the chance of seeing the fleeting passage of a leopard. Perhaps that was his world. Perhaps he did not belong, never had belonged, in the world of David Park.

"David, may I ask a favour?"

"I doubt you'll get it, what?"

"That you take back a letter for me."

"Just a letter?"

"To a very fine man, a very kind man, a man who knew about love."

There was the grated concession. "I'll take it."

Charlie crawled from his bed, and he went to his rucksack and took out the envelope. The envelope had been bent while it had been lying amongst his clothes and his map charts in the rucksack. He laid the envelope on the table beside Park's bed.

He stood at the window. Carefully, slowly, he edged aside the curtain. He looked down at the Transit. He saw the jutting nose of a Mercedes car, and he saw the white light flash. He felt the thunder roar in his ears, and he felt the hot heat back draught of the LAW 80.

"You should try to find love, David. Without love then life is empty."

He had waited all evening for a call to be routed through to the nineteenth floor.

His chauffeur was in the car park below. Houghton was yawning.

The Director General dialled the number, and they were a long time answering.

"Carter – is that you, Carter? Have you any idea of the time? It is past midnight, I have been waiting for two and a quarter hours for your call. What has Furniss said?"

The voice was faint, tinny. The scrambler connection had that effect. And the scrambler could not disguise the hesitancy of the far away metallic voice.

"He hasn't said anything."

"Then you've a problem, Carter, by Christ you have."

"I'm aware of the problem, sir."

"My advice to you, Carter, is that you have one hour . . . I want to speak to Furniss."

He heard the telephone put down, clumsily. He heard the tramp of departing footsteps. He waited. What was the bloody man at? He didn't know how he would ever again face Furniss. He heard the footsteps returning.

"Not possible at the moment, sir, to speak to Mattie."

"Carter, understand me . . . understand your position. I'll see you gutted if harm has come to Furniss, if you turn out to be wrong. I'll have you skinned. You have one hour."

He thought that he had betrayed Furniss. He felt deep shame. He strode out of his office, and he had no word for his Personal Assistant who padded behind him. He thought that he had betrayed a very good man.

The Station Officer could no longer stay awake.

On a pad beside the telephone in the bedroom was written the code of Dogubeyezit and the number of the Ararat hotel. The call from London, if it came, would be in clear. There was no difficulty in that. The codeword for a halt, a postponement, had been agreed via the teleprinter in his office before he had shut up shop for the evening. In an ideal world he should not have been snuggling against his wife's back, in his own bed, he should have been close to that wretched frontier, up in north-eastern Anatolia. He should have been hugging the Iranian border, not his wife's slim back. No question of him being there. The frontier was out of bounds, the border was closed territory after the lifting of the Desk Head (Iran). He had not been told the reason that there might, possibly but not probably, be a hold put on Eshraq's movement. He had no need to know why there might conceivably be a hold . . . If there were a hold then he would communicate it. He drifted towards sleep. He had rather enjoyed the company of the young man who had come to the park in Ankara. A bit wild, of course. Any man going inside Iran with LAW 80s was entitled to be a bit bloody-minded. But they had thrashed out their lines of communication. Not that he would last. Not possible that he would survive.

"Terence, is that 'phone going to ring tonight? There'll be murder if it does."

"Don't know, love, I really don't know."

They had not slept. They had lain on sleeping bags on the concrete floor inside the inner hall of the Guards' barracks at Maku. The investigator was amongst the last to push himself back up to his feet. There were some amongst them who prayed, and some who worked with clean cloths at the firing mechanisms of their automatic rifles. The investigator wandered out of the inner hall in search of the latrine, and after the latrine he would be in search of the Communications room and news from the men who watched a hotel across the border. It was sensible of him to leave the inner hallway for the latrine and the Communications room. If he had stayed then it would have been remarked that he had not prayed. It was hard for him to pray because the words of the Qur'an held no place in his mind. He had no time that early morning because his mind was filled with the vision of armour-piercing missiles and a Transit van and the man who had been named by Matthew Furniss.

He would enjoy his meetings with Mr Eshraq. He thought that he might enjoy conversing with Charlie Eshraq more than he had enjoyed talking to Matthew Furniss.

The clock was striking in the hall.

And the dog was restless, and sometimes there was the heavy scratching at the kitchen door, and sometimes there was the clamour of the animal shaking the big link chain on its throat. The dog wouldn't sleep, not while there were still people moving in the house and voices.

Mattie heard the clock.

The light was in his eyes. He was on the sofa and they had stripped his shoes off and they had heaved his feet, too, on to the sofa. His tie was off, and the shirt buttons were undone down to his navel. He could see nothing but the light. The light was directed from a few feet so that it shone directly into his face.

It was a long time since they had hit him, kicked him, but the light was in his face and the Major was behind him and holding his head so that he could not look away from the light, and the bastard Henry fucking Carter was behind the light.

Questions ... the soft and gentle drip of questions. Always the questions, and so bloody tired . . . so hellishly tired. And the hands were on his head, and the light was in his eyes, and the questions dripped at his mind.

"Past all our bedtimes, Mattie. Just what you told them . . . ?"

"A young man's life, Mattie, that's what we're talking about. So, what did you tell them . . . ?"

"Nobody's going to blame you, Mattie, not if you come clean. What did you tell them . . . ?"

"All that barbarian stuff, that's over, Mattie, no more call for that, and you're with friends now. What did you tell them . . . ?"

Too tired to think, and too tired to speak, and his eyes burned in the light.

"I don't remember. I really don't remember."

"Got to remember, Mattie, because there is a life hanging on you remembering what you told them."

Park watched the peace of Charlie Eshraq's sleep.

He wondered how it would be, to live with love. He was alone and he was without love. He was without Parrish, and Token, and Harlech, and Corinthian. He was without Ann. He was away from what he knew. What he knew was behind him, back at the Lane. What he knew had been stripped from him on the nineteenth floor of Century House.

He did not know how to find love.

He thought that going to Bogota was a journey to escape from love.

There was the sharp bleep of the alarm on Eshraq's wrist. He watched as Eshraq stirred, then shook himself. Eshraq was rubbing hard at his eyes, and then sliding from his bed and going to the window. The curtain was dragged back.

There was a grey wash of early light in the room. Eshraq stretched.

"Pretty good morning to be starting a journey."

There was a glass of Scotch and water beside him. The Major sat on the sofa beside him. Henry was at the window. He had his ear cocked and he stared outside, and probably he was listening to the first shouted songs of the blackbirds.

It was the third Scotch that had been given to Mattie, and each had less water than before.

The Major had his arm, shirt-sleeved, loosely around Mattie's shoulder.

The Major smiled into Mattie's face.

"You know where you're going, Mattie, in a few hours? You know where you'll be by lunch time? Do you know, Mattie?"

The slurred response. "I want to see a doctor, I want to go to bed and sleep, and then I want to go home."

"A magistrate's court, Mattie."

"Bollocks."

"The charge will be conspiracy to import heroin."

"Don't be so fucking silly, Major. It's too late at night for games."

"Charlie ran heroin. Heroin subsidized him. You ran Charlie. You're going down, old boy, going down for a long time."

And the arm was round his shoulder, and Mattie was trying to push himself up from the sofa and away from the calm of the voice in his ear, and he hadn't a prayer, hadn't the strength.

"Nothing to do with me."

"Fifteen years you'll get. Very hard years, Mattie."

"Not me."

"You'll be in with the queers and the con artists and the GBH lads, in with them for fifteen years. It's all sewn up, Mattie. How's Mrs Furniss going to cope with that? Is she going to traipse up to the Scrubs every first Tuesday in the month? And your daughters. I doubt they'll come more than once or twice."

"I don't know anything about heroin, nothing, not at all."

"Ask the magistrate to believe you, Mattie . . . Ask him to believe that you didn't know how Charlie Eshraq, more or less a son to you, funded himself . . . and ask Mrs Furniss to believe that you didn't know. It'll break her, Mattie, you being inside. Think on it."

"It's just not true."

"She won't have a friend in the world. Have to sell up at Bibury, of course. Couldn't face the neighbours, could she? Your neighbours'll be a bit foul, Mattie, the jokers in your cell, they have their pride and heroin they don't like."

"It's a lie, I know nothing about heroin."

"It's all been a lie, Mattie. It starts with the lie that you didn't name Charlie Eshraq . . . Did Eshraq fuck your daughters?"

The pause, the silence. Henry had turned. Henry looked at his watch, grimaced. The Major nodded, like he thought that he was nearly dry, close to home.

"Mattie, Charlie Eshraq was running heroin out of Iran when he was fucking your daughters. Do you reckon heroin came with the service, Mattie?"

"It's not, tell me that's not true."

There was the first shrill call of the birds.

"It's what I hear."

"God . . ."

"Pushed heroin to your daughters, Eshraq did."

"The truth . . . ?"

"It's you I want the truth from."

"Charlie gave that filthy stuff to my girls?"

"You've just had bad luck, Mattie, a long run of terrible luck."

There were tears running down Mattie's cheeks, and the hands that held the glass shook. The Major had raised his head and Henry could see his eyebrows aloft.

Carter said, from the window, "You named him, Mattie?"

"It wasn't my fault."

"No, Mattie, it wasn't. And nobody will hold it against you."

Henry came to the sofa. He had his notepad in his hand. He wrote a single sentence and he put a pencil in Mattie's hand, and he watched the scrawled signature made. He buffeted off the hall table on his way to the telephone and there was pandemonium in the kitchen.

The Major was at the door of the lounge, on his way out. It did not seem necessary for them to shake hands. Henry went back into the lounge. He went to Mattie. He took his arm and hoisted him, unsteady, to his feet.

"Can I go home?"

"I think that's a good idea . . . I'll drive you myself."

"Tell me that it wasn't true."

"Of course not, Mattie. It was an unforgivable trick. I am so very sorry."

Dawn was coming, and at first sight the day looked promising.

21

He was looking down from the window and into the yard.

There was a kid, ten or eleven years old, scrubbing at the windscreen, and Eshraq was hunched down by the front radiator screen and he already had the Turkish registration off and he was holding the Iranian plate in place while he screwed it tight. There were lights in the kitchens that backed on to the yard, and they threw shadows into the yard.

He was dressed and he was shaved when the telephone bell rang in the room. He was zipping shut his bag, and he had his passport and his wallet on the bed beside him, and the ticket for the flight back to Istanbul. The telephone in the room had not rung since they had arrived in Dogubeyezit.

Below him, Eshraq had the front plate secure, and was moving to the rear of the Transit. He was moving easily and casual in old jeans and trainer shoes and a service blue cotton shirt. And the telephone was still ringing.

He picked it up. He heard the clicking of big distance connections. He heard a small voice and far away.

"Is that room 12?"

"This is room 12."

"Is that David Park?"

"Park speaking."

"I want to speak to Charlie."

"He's not here."

"Bugger . . . I've been cut off twice on your switchboard. Can you get him?"

"Take me a bit of time."

"And we'll get cut again, God. Name's Terence, I met him in Ankara."

He remembered the Genclik park. He had been 400 yards back, and Eshraq and the man had walked, and there had been a tail. He remembered it very clearly. He could picture Terence. Terence was pale skin, almost anaemic, with fair hair and a missing chin, and he looked to have come from a good school.

"If you give me the message I'll pass it."

"You can reach him?"

"If you give me the message I can reach him."

"The telephones in this country are bloody awful. You guarantee he gets my message?"

"I'll pass it."

"This is an open line."

"That's stating the obvious."

"He's not to go . . . That is a categorical instruction from my people. He is not to approach the border. He is compromised, can't say more than that. He is to return to Ankara. Do you understand the message?"

"Understood."

"Most grateful to you."

"For nothing."

"I might see you in Ankara – and many thanks for your help."

He replaced the telephone. He went back to the window. The rear plate was in place and the kid was scrubbing dust off the Transit's headlights. There had been the tail in Istanbul, and the tail in Ankara. He assumed they had been better in Dogubeyezit, because he had not been certain of the men on the tail, not certain as he had been in Aksaray and the Genclik park. He was a long time at the window. There were many images in the mind of David Park. There was, in his mind, Leroy Winston Manvers back in the corner of the cell, and he was at safe haven in Jamaica. There was the wife of Matthew Furniss at the door of a cottage in the country, and her husband was the guarantor of a heroin trafficker, and he was on safe wicket back in the United Kingdom. There was Charlie Eshraq sitting on the bonnet of a Sierra saloon and mocking him, and he was on safe passage out. There were images of Ann and wet towels on the bathroom floor, and images of the supercilious creature who had done the big put down at Foreign and Commonwealth, and images of Bill Parrish stuck in an ante-room outside the office of the power and the glory at Century. He knew what was right and he knew what was wrong. He had to know. Right and wrong were the core of his life. He moved around the room. He checked each drawer of the chest and each shelf of the cupboard, and he frisked the bathroom. He made sure that they had left nothing behind. He slung on his jacket and put his passport and his airline ticket into the inner pocket with his wallet, and he threw his grip bag over his shoulder.

You will satisfy yourself that he has indeed travelled back in to Iran.

At the Reception he paid for the room. They had made out a joint bill, and he paid it. He folded the receipt carefully and put it into his wallet. He didn't give the porter a tip, because he couldn't claim on tips, and anyway he preferred to carry his own bag. He put his bag in the small hire car, locked it away from sight. He went back inside the hotel and took a side door beside the staircase, and then the corridor that led into the yard at the back. The tail doors of the Transit were open and David could see the drums of electrical flex piled to the roof and stacked tight.

"What kept you?"

He started. He hadn't seen Eshraq at the front of the Transit, he'd lost him. He was looking at the drums and he was wondering how successfully they hid the wooden crates.

"Just clearing up the room."

"Did I hear our phone go?"

"Front desk, confirming we were leaving today. Probably thought you were running out on them."

760

He saw the big smile on Eshraq's face. "I suppose you paid."

"Yes, I paid."

He saw the big smile and the big buoyancy of young Eshraq. Park didn't smile, himself, often, and it was rarer for him to know happiness. And Eshraq was smiling and he looked as though he had found true happiness.

And the big smile split.

"You hate me – yes?"

"Time you went for the border."

"Your problem, you're too serious."

"Because I've a plane to catch."

"And you'll do my letter?"

"It'll be posted."

"What I'm doing – don't you think it's worth doing?"

"Thinking about you makes me tired."

"Don't I get a goodbye and a kiss."

"Good luck, Charlie, brilliant luck."

He said that he would see Eshraq in front of the hotel. He walked back through, and out of the front doors. As he pushed them open he heard the farewell greeting from the Reception Clerk, and he didn't turn. He unlocked the car, and when he was inside he wound down the windows to dissipate the heat. Keys into the ignition. It was slow starting, he thought that the plugs needed cleaning. There was the blast of the horn behind him. The Transit came past him. He didn't think that he would see Eshraq's face again. He thought that the last that he would see of Charlie Eshraq was a grin and a wave.

He pulled out into the traffic. By the time that he had found a space there were two lorries between himself and the Transit. A wide and straight and pot-holed bone shaker of a road. Two lorries ahead of him he could see the Transit. He drove slowly. As far as he could see ahead there was the column of commercial vehicles heading for the Customs post.

Mattie stood in the hallway.

He could hear their voices. It was typical of Harriet that she should have walked back to the front gate with Henry Carter. She had that inbred politeness, it was a part of her.

Sweet scents in his nostrils. He could smell the polish on the walnut hall table. He could smell the cut chrysanthemums that were in the vase on the shelf of the window beside the front door. Sweet sounds in his ears. He could hear the passage of the honey searching bees in the foxgloves that lined the path between the house and the front gate, and he could hear the whine of the flies against the panes, and he could hear the purring of his cat as it brushed against his legs.

The car left.

She came back inside. She closed the front door. She latched the door and made him safe from all that had happened to him. She came to stand against him and her arms were loosely around his waist. She kissed his cheek.

"You need a jolly good shave, Mattie."

"I expect I do."

"What a dear man, that Carter."

"I suppose he is."

"He spoke so well of you, how you'd come through it all."

"Did he, darling?"

"And he said that you needed looking after. What would you like most, Mattie, most and first?"

"I'd like to sit outside in the garden, and I'd like *The Times*, and I'd like a mug of coffee with hot milk."

"He said it was pretty rotten where you'd been."

"We'll talk about it, but not yet."

"He said they're all talking about it at Century, your escape . . . Such a nice man, he said they were all talking about what they call 'Dolphin's Run'."

"I'll go and sit in the garden."

The sun was hardly up. There was still dew on the grass. He heard the first tractor of the day moving off to cut silage.

The road was quite straight and it ran bisecting a wide green valley. To his left was Ararat, magnificent in the sunlight. To his right was the lower summit of Tenduruk Dag. There were grazing sheep alongside the road, and when they were clear of the town they passed the folly palace of Ishak Pasha. He glanced at it. The building was above the road, dominating. He had read in the guide book that a Kurdish chieftain in the last century had wanted the finest palace in the wide world, and he had had an Armenian architect design it and build it. And when it was completed then the chieftain had had the Armenian architect's hands cut off, so that he could never design another that was as fine . . . Rough old world, Mr Armenian architect . . . Rough old world, Mr Charlie Eshraq.

Far ahead, where the haze of the shimmered heat had begun to settle, he could see the flat-roofed buildings of the Turkish Customs building, and he could just make out the blood red of the Turkish flag.

Amongst the fields stretching to the foothills of Ararat that was to his left and Tenduruk Dag that was to his right, he could see the brilliant scarlet oases of poppies. Where the poppy flowers were, that was a good place for the burying of Charlie Eshraq.

He eased down through the gears.

The Turkish Customs post was one old building of two stories and a sprawl of newer, more temporary, buildings. A wind lifted the flag. There were troops there, pretty lackadaisical bunch, too, and there was a Customs official in the centre of the road who seemed to stop, briefly, each lorry, speak to the driver, then wave it on. On the other side of the road was the queue of vehicles travelling the other way, coming out from Iran, stopped and waiting for clearance. No delays for the lorries going into Iran. The Transit was two lorry lengths ahead of him. And the going was slower. One hand on the wheel, and his thumb was inches from the horn. One hand on the gear stick, and his fingers were inches from the arm that could have flashed his lights.

The Transit was stationary.

The Customs official was walking down the length of a lorry and trailer, and heading for the cab of the Transit. Park watched. It was what they had sent him to do. He watched the Customs official peer into the driver's window, then nod his head, then step back, then cheerfully wave the Transit forward.

The lorries in front of him nudged forward. Park swung his wheel. He drove off the metalled surface and on to the stone grit of the hard shoulder.

He walked away from his car. He walked towards the buildings and the soldiers who were already seeking what shade was offered. His shirt stuck to his back, there was the shiver in his legs as he walked. He took as his place the flagpole. The wind pushed his hair across his face.

He estimated that the Iranian flag and the Iranian buildings were 500 metres down the road. He thought that the border was at a point that was halfway between the two where a small stream crossed under the road through culvert tunnels. The road fell on its way to the tunnels, then climbed on a gradual gradient towards the Iranian buildings and the Iranian flag.

The Transit was slipping away down the slope, going steadily for the dip where the culverts were set under the road. The wind in his hair, the sun in his eyes, the roar of the heavy engines in his ears.

A young officer, regular army, had strolled to stand beside him, would have seen a foreigner at the post, and wondered, been interested. There were binoculars hanging loosely at his neck. Park didn't ask. A fast, sharp smile, his finger pointing to the binoculars. He knew nothing of the Turkish, nothing of their generosity. His gesture was enough. He had the binoculars in his hand.

The Transit was climbing up the slope from the stream. His vision roved ahead.

He saw the buildings of the Customs post, and huge on the wall facing the oncoming road was the image of the Imam.

Past the buildings, uniformed and armed men held back a line of lorries from further movement towards Turkey. From a side door in the largest of the buildings he saw three men duck out and run, crouching and doubled, to take up positions behind parked cars. On the far side of the road, the far side to the buildings, was a heap of sandbags, inexpertly stacked and no more than waist height. With the glasses, through the power of the binoculars, he saw the sun flash on belted ammunition. There was a man standing beside the building closest to the roadway. He wore sandals and old jeans and his shirt tails weren't tucked in. He was not a young man. He was talking into a personal radio.

The Transit was into Iran, heading up the shallow slope of the road.

There was the crash of the gunfire.

He started up. He clasped his hands to halt the shaking.

"It's alright, dear, just the Pottinger boy . . . I don't mind him shooting pigeons, and I suppose I can't object at carrion crows, but I do think that killing rooks is the limit. I hope that you'll have a word with his father . . . Here's your coffee. Mattie, darling, you look frozen. I'll get you a warmer sweater, and when you've had your coffee, you're coming straight in."

The sun was sharp on his forehead. There was the distortion of the binoculars and from the heat on the ground, but he could see well enough.

The road was clear ahead and in front of the Transit, and a man in dun uniform had emerged from the ditch that ran alongside the road as soon as the Transit had passed him and he was waving down the following lorry. There was a moment, as the Transit came to an easy and unhurried stop beside the building, that it was the only vehicle within 100 yards in front or behind.

Quick, fast movements. The van surrounded. He saw the men who ran forward towards the back of the van, and he saw their weapons raised to their shoulders and aimed at the Transit. Carried on the wind, must have been a megaphone, he heard a shouted order. They were closing on the cab. He saw the door of the cab open. He saw the barrel shape, the tube shape, jutting out from the opened door.

There was the fire squirt.

There was the following thunder hammer of the recoil of the LAW 80.

Smoke and fire, and the building ravaged, and toy doll figures laid out in crazy posture under the galloping spread of black smoke and brilliant flames of the fire.

He saw the Transit burst forward. He wondered when in hell Charlie had taken the launcher from the crates in the back of the Transit . . . He had seen the flash of the brass cartridge cases. He knew where it would come from. He knew where the stopping fire would come from.

He thought the van might have made 25 yards. It was lurching forward, as if the driver was trying to hit the higher gears too fast. The Transit might have made 25 yards when the machine-gun behind the sandbags opened fire, belting the Transit. The van swerved, he saw that, he followed the swerve through the glasses. The van straightened. He was cold. He was not willing the escape of the van and nor was he cheering for the death of the van. He was the witness and he was watching. The Transit had swerved and it had straightened and it had swerved again. It was across the road. It was against the pole that carried the telephone line from the Customs post back into the interior. The hammer of the drum, the belt of the machine-gun, and the target was stationary, crippled. There was a shouting in his ear. It was the Turkish soldier, insistent but courteous. He held out his hand for his binoculars.

There was little more for him to see. There was the bright orange glow of the ultimate explosion. He watched a dream's destruction. He thanked the officer, who was lost in concentration on the scene unfolding across the valley, and he turned and walked back towards his car. He thought that if he hurried he would still be in time to catch the flight from Van. He turned only once. When he had opened the door of the hire car he looked behind him. The sun was a high white orb, its brilliance shed by the rising pillar of smoke. Park drove away. He drove back along the straight road to Dogubeyezit, and past the sheep flocks, and past the shrill patches of scarlet. A job done, a man going home.

22

She was first out of the Chapel and Belinda and Jane were close at her back. She had dressed rather boldly and that had been her decision and without the prompting of the girls. She wore a suit of navy and a matching straw hat with a crimson ribbon. Perhaps the girls would not have approved. She had worn the same suit and hat only once before, nearly two years ago, and then she had sat in the Gallery and looked down on to the Investiture Room. She had watched with pride as Mattie had gone forward to receive from his sovereign the medal of the Order of the British Empire. She thought it right, on this autumn morning, when the leaves cascaded across the road from the plane trees in the park, to wear the same clothes as on that day. Mattie would have approved, and he would have liked the way that she held herself.

She took her place a few yards from the doorway and there was a fine spit of rain at her back, and behind her the traffic streamed on Birdcage Walk. The girls were on either side of her. They were sentries positioned to protect their mother. Not that Harriet Furniss was in need of protection. There would be no choke in her voice, no smear on her cheek. She had been a Service wife, and now she was a Service widow. She understood very clearly what was expected of her.

She thought that the Director General had aged, that his retirement had not given him a new lease of life. His morning coat seemed too large and his throat had thinned.

"It was kind of you to come."

It was he who had insisted on Mattie's immediate retirement.

"To pay my respects to a very gallant gentleman, Mrs Furniss."

She knew that he had resigned from the Service on the day the report of the internal inquiry had reached Downing Street.

"You're looking well."

"Good of you to say so . . . I've a little to occupy me . . . I shall remember your husband with nothing but admiration."

It gave her strength to see his fumbling walk towards the parade ground, the man who had sent her Mattie to his doom.

She had made it clear that she had wanted none of them to make the journey from London for the funeral. The funeral, three weeks earlier, had been family and in Bibury, she had insisted on that. Two hard years they had been, from the time that he had come home to her to the time of death and release from his personal agony. Two wretchedly hard years they had been as the will to survive had ebbed from Mattie. The new Director General stood in front of her. His face was a little puffed as though he ate too much too often at lunchtime.

"Most fittingly done, Mrs Furniss."

"It was as Mattie would have wanted, I think."

"We miss him very much at Century."

"As he missed being there, desperately."

"They still talk about his run, it was a magnificent memory for us all. He's not forgotten."

"I expect that Iran Desk is substantially changed."

"Well, yes, very changed. Now that we have the Embassy back in Tehran we are much more efficient."

"I think Mattie understood."

"Should you have any problem . . . well, you wouldn't hesitate, I hope."

"Mattie would never have left us in difficulties."

The new Director General nodded. She thought that she would have gone on the streets, put her daughters into a workshop, before she would have gone back to Century to plead hardship. All so different now. In the last months of his life Mattie had fumed at the exchange of diplomats, the reopening of relations with the Islamic Republic of Iran. They had angered him, insulted him. She had seen those wounds on his body, she had forced herself to look at them when he was bathing and pretended that she saw nothing, and she had raged in her mind each time she saw our people and their people shaking hands on the television screen. She had no line into Century for gossip because Flossie Duggan had gone the same week that her Mattie had been brought back to her, nor did she want a line. The wind caught at her hair and she pushed it decisively back. There was a surge of men past her, faces that she did not know. She imagined them to be from the Century desks, and from the administrative departments, and few caught her eye, most avoided her gaze. Henry Carter stood in front of her, and he held a trilby across his chest. It was Henry Carter who had come down to Bibury a week after he had first brought Mattie home and who had gone out into the garden with him to report that Charlie had been killed on the Iranian border. And Mattie had never spoken the name of Charlie Eshraq, would never even let the girls refer to him, from that day to the day of his slipping, passing, going.

"So good to see you, Henry. Are you still . . . ?"

"Alas, Mrs Furniss, no longer. I have a part-time job with the Royal Society for the Protection of Birds, the mail-order section. I get the tea towels out, and the nesting boxes."

"Was anything achieved, Henry, that spring, by any of you?"

"Desperate question, Mrs Furniss. My opinion, it's better to believe that so much mayhem led to something positive, don't you think?"

And he was gone, before she could press him. He almost ran. They were almost all gone from the church now, and the music had stopped. There was a middle-aged man standing a few feet in front of her, making no move to come towards her. He wore an old raincoat that was too small for him and that was gathered in tight lines across his stomach, and the half moon of his hair blew untidily in the wind. He met her gaze, he stared back at her. He was an intruder, she was sure of that, but she could not place him. She straightened her back.

"Do I know you?"

"I'm Bill Parrish."

"Have we met?"

"I came once to your house, bit more than two years ago."

"You'll have to excuse me, I don't recall the occasion . . ."

"I'm fulfilling a promise to a friend, Mrs Furniss. He's abroad and can't be here. Me being here is closing a file, you might say that it's shutting up shop. A very nice service, Mrs Furniss."

She watched them all go. The old Director General was waving down a taxi, flourishing his umbrella at the driver. The new Director General was climbing into the black limousine. Henry Carter was arguing down the street with a traffic warden across the bonnet of an old car. Bill Parrish was striding purposefully towards Whitehall. She let the girls link their arms through her elbows. Had anything been achieved? Was there something positive? She hated them all, every last one of them who were now hurrying away to escape from the contact with the life and death of Mattie Furniss.